Retribution

Titles by Sherrilyn Kenyon

Retribution

SHERRILYN KENYON

St. Martin's Press
New York

RETRIBUTION. Copyright © 2011 by Sherrilyn Kenyon. All rights reserved. Printed in the United States of America. For information, address St. Martin's Press, 175 Fifth Avenue, New York, N.Y. 10010.

www.stmartins.com

ISBN 978-0-312-54659-5

First Edition: August 2011

10 9 8 7 6 5 4 3 2 1

For my husband, for too many reasons to count.
For my boys, who make me laugh and fill my life with joy.
For my friends, who keep me sane.
And for my readers, who have been begging for Sundown's book.
Thank you all for being part of my life and for filling my heart with love.

Don't let yesterday use up too much of today.

—CHEROKEE PROVERB

RETRIBUTION

William Jessup "Sundown" Brady
Man. Myth. Monster. 1873

WRITTEN BY

SOLACE WALTERS

They say the road to Hell is paved with good intentions. In the case of William Jessup Brady, it's been hand carved with a lever-action Henry rifle over his shoulder and a Smith & Wesson six-gun strapped to his hip.

At a time when the world is at its most violent, he's the meanest of all. Untamed. Uncivilized. A half breed mongrel dog spawned from the bowels of the Devil's lowest pit, he is the worst of the scourge that haunts our towns and kills indiscriminately. No one is safe or immune from his wrath. No one is safe from his aim. A gun for hire, he doesn't shirk from any target. Man, woman, or child.

If you have the cash, he has the bullet. A bullet he will deliver to his victim right between the eyes.

There are those who would make a romantic hero of this villain. Some who think of him like Robin Hood, but Sundown Brady takes from everyone and gives only to himself.

He is truly soulless.

The bounty on this man is $50,000—a fortune, to be sure—and still people are terrified even to try to bring him in. In fact, authorities continue to find the scattered remains of the poor, virtuous marshal who made the mistake of shooting at him in Oklahoma when Brady was robbing a bank. Not one shot hit its mark. Is there any doubt Brady sold his soul to Lucifer for immortality and invulnerability?

Though Brady takes pity on no one, this reporter wants to know if there is anyone out there with the temerity to end Brady's wickedness. Surely one of you fine, upstanding, decent men would like the fame and money that would come from ridding the world of the most sinister being ever to walk it. I pray you courage, good man. Straight aim.

Most of all, I wish you luck.

E*verything changes today.*" Unable to believe he'd lived long enough to see this undeserved dream, Jess Brady stood outside the church in his best, itchiest clothes. This was the last turn he'd ever expected for his miserable life.

He'd been robbing banks and staring down experienced men in a gunfight without flinching or breaking a sweat since he was thirteen years old. Yet here, right now, he was as nervous as a one-eyed buck in a barn fire. Every part of him was on edge. Every part of him fully alive, and for the first time since his birth, he was actually looking forward to the future.

His hand shaking, he pulled his old, banged-up gold pocket watch out to check the time. In five minutes, he'd leave his brutal past behind him forever and be reborn a new man. No longer William Jessup Brady, cardsharp, gunslinger, and hired killer, he was about to become William Parker, farmer. . . .

Family man.

Inside those bright white church doors was the most beautiful woman in the world, and she was waiting for him to come inside and make her his.

Dreams do come true. His precious mother had told

him that when he was a boy, but his harsh life and drunken father, who'd been consumed by jealousy of and hatred for the entire world, had kicked that out of him by the time he was twelve years old and standing over her pauper's grave. Nothing good had happened to him since the day she took sick, and the years of her suffering had left a deep-seated bitterness inside him. No one so pure of heart should ever hurt so much.

Not a single thing had ever given him pleasure or made him think for even a second that the world was anything but utter misery for the fools unfortunate enough to be born into it. Not until Matilda Aponi had smiled at him. She alone had made him believe that the world was a beautiful place and that the people in it weren't all vicious animals out to punish everyone around them. Made him want to be a better man. The man his mother had told him he could be.

One free of hatred and bitterness.

He heard the sound of a horse approaching. That would be his best man, Bart Wilkerson. The only other person in his life he'd ever trusted and the one who'd taken him in when he was a thirteen-year-old runaway. Bart had taught him how to survive in a cold, hostile world that seemed to begrudge him every breath he took. He'd taken bullets for Bart on three separate occasions, and the two of them had been through more turmoil together than two demons scaling hell's thorny walls.

Like Jess, Bart was dressed in a long dark coat suit with his graying hair freshly combed. No one would ever be able to tell, looking at them right now, that they were two notorious outlaws. They looked respectable, but Jess wanted more than that. He wanted to *be* respectable.

Bart slid from his horse and tied her up beside Jess's buggy, which he'd bought just for this day. Hell, he'd even decorated it with lilies—Matilda's favorite flower.

"You ready, kid?" Bart asked solemnly.

"Yeah." Scared though he was, there was nothing else in this world he wanted.

Nothing.

He'd already given all his ill-gotten gains away so that Matilda wouldn't find out about his past. For her, he'd do anything.

Even be honest.

Jess started for the doors with Bart one step behind him. He'd just reached the steps when a gunshot rang out.

He sucked his breath in sharply.

Sudden pain invaded every part of his body as the impact of the shot knocked his hat from his head and sent it flying. It landed a few feet away and tumbled until it got caught in a nearby bush. Jess tried to take a step forward, but more shots followed the first. And all of them hit various parts of his body.

Those shots made him do something he'd never done before.

He fell to his knees in the dirt.

His fury igniting, he wanted to return that fire, but Bart knew he'd sold his guns to buy Matilda's ring—that had been his final act of ridding himself of the old Jess Brady. He was completely unarmed. The one thing he'd sworn he'd never be.

How could I be so stupid? How could he have put someone at his back when he knew better?

Maybe this was his penance for the sins he'd committed. Maybe this was all a bastard like him deserved.

Gunned down on what should have been the happiest day of his life.

Bart kicked him to the ground.

Panting from the weight of the pain and tasting blood, Jess stared up at him. The one man he'd risked his life for countless times. "Why?"

Bart shrugged nonchalantly as he reloaded his gun. "It's all about the money, Jess. You know that. And right now, you're worth a fortune."

Yeah . . . how could he have forgotten their code? Having killed him, Bart would be the richest man in Gull Hollow. Not that he wasn't already.

Bart was the one Jess had given all his money to.

Jess coughed up blood as his vision dimmed. He was so cold now. Colder than he'd been even as a kid working in an early-spring field without shoes or a coat. His father had always told him he'd end up like this. *You're trash, boy. All you'll ever be, and you won't live long enough to be nothing else. Mark my words. You'll come to a bad end one day.*

And here he lay dying at age twenty-six. So evil, God wouldn't even let him reach the doors of Matilda's church.

But in the end, he was Sundown, and Sundown Brady didn't go quietly to his grave. *No damn man would kill him and live.* "I'll be back for you, Bart. Even if I have to sell my soul for it. So help me, God. I *will* kill you for this."

Bart laughed. "Give the devil my best regards."

"William!" Matilda's agonized scream hurt him more than the bullet wounds did.

He turned for one last look at her, but before he could take it, Bart coldly finished the job and denied him even the solace of seeing her face before he died.

Jess came awake with a curse. At least, he thought it was awake. Hard to tell, though, to be honest. It was darker here than the corner of his father's heart that had been reserved for any tender feelings the old bastard might have had for him. The silence was so loud, it rang in his ears.

He didn't even hear his own heartbeat.

'Cause I'm dead.

He remembered the pain of being shot, of trying to see Matilda in her wedding dress. . . .

So this is hell.

But to be honest, he'd expected flames and excruciating agony. Demons flying at him with pitchforks and smells akin to the stuff he'd mucked out of stables as a kid.

Instead, there was nothing inside the blackness.

"That's because you're on Olympus. At least your soul is."

He turned as a lonely light came up to show him the most beautiful woman he'd ever seen. Tall, lithe, and curvy, she had hair so red, it shimmered in the dim light. With glowing green eyes, she looked ethereal. More like an angel than like a demon, especially given the flowing white dress she wore that hugged her body. Something about its style reminded him of the white statues he'd seen in some of the fancier hotels he'd boarded in after they'd made a good haul over the years. "What's Olympus?"

She made a sound that reminded him of a filly about to buck off her rider for irritating her. "I grieve for the poor education of so-called modern man. How can you not know the name of the mountain where the Greek gods dwell?"

He rubbed his jaw and forced down his own irritation at her insult. Until he knew who she was, it probably wasn't wise to make her too mad. "Well, ma'am, no offense, but it probably has a lot to do with the fact I'm not Greek. I was born in Possum Town, Mississippi, and ain't been no further east than that."

She growled low in her throat, then spoke angrily in a

language he couldn't understand, which was probably for the best. No need in both of them being angry.

Clenching her fists, she settled down and pinned him with a killing glare. "I will try to speak so that you can understand me. I am the Greek goddess Artemis."

"I don't believe in gods and goddesses."

"Well, you should, because this one has a deal for you that I think will interest you."

Now, that made his ears perk up. "Deal how?"

She closed the distance between them so that she could whisper in his ear. "I heard what you said when you were dying at the feet of your best friend. Your soul screamed out for vengeance so loudly that it summoned me here to intercept you from your final destination."

He locked gazes with her. "You can send me back to kill Bart?"

"Yes, I can."

Rapid joy tore through him at the mere prospect. For that, she could insult him all day. "At what price?"

"You named it when you were dying."

"My soul."

She inclined her head to him before she patted him on the cheek. "That's the going rate for vengeance around here. But don't fret. There are other perks to being soulless. If you agree, I'll give you twenty-four hours to do whatever you wish to the one who betrayed you. No consequences for you whatsoever."

That he could sink his teeth into. His blackened soul had never been much use to him anyhow.

Artemis smiled. "You will have immortality and all the wealth you could ever imagine."

"I can imagine a lot."

"And still it won't fill even a corner of what you'll be given."

When something sounds too good . . .

He ran his thumb across his bottom lip as he eyed her suspiciously. "What's the mouseprint?"

She laughed evilly. "You are intelligent, after all. Good. It makes the job easier."

"Job?"

"Hmmm. You will serve in my army of Dark-Hunters."

He scowled. "Dark what?"

"Hunters," she repeated. "They are immortal warriors, foot-selected by me."

"Foot selected?" What was she talking about?

"Whatever the term is," she snapped irritably. "They are my soldiers who protect the humans against the Daimons who prey on them."

Technically, they were speaking the same language, but dang . . . Hard to follow a woman who used so many words he'd never heard before. "What's a Daimon?"

She set her hands on her hips as she paced in front of him. "In short, my brother Apollo's mess. Centuries ago, he created a race called Apollites." She paused to look at

Jess. "Arrogant of him, no? He thought man was weak and that he could do better." Then she returned to her pacing. "Anyway, he set them loose on mankind, and the Apollites turned on him and killed his favorite human concubine and *my* nephew. Not really wise. Why they thought Apollo wouldn't figure out who killed them is beyond me. So much for improvements, no?"

She rolled her eyes. "Apollites . . . ridiculous. At any rate, they are now cursed by him, and the only way they can live for more than twenty-seven years is to kill humans and steal their souls—we have an Atlantean whore goddess to thank for that little benediction to them." She flung her hand up in a gesture of supreme agitation. "Don't even get me started on how badly I'd like to kill her."

Artemis dropped her hand and faced him. "Anyway, that's where you come in, if you've been paying attention. You sell your soul to me, and you will spend eternity seeking and destroying the Daimons—the name given to the Apollites who feast on humanity. Are you out?"

"You mean in?"

"Whatever. Yes."

Jess considered it. Last time he'd made a bargain to go in with someone was Bart.

That hadn't worked out so well in the end.

"I don't know. I need to think about it."

Artemis splayed her hand out and waved it to her right. A shimmering light flickered there until images appeared.

Jess gasped at the sight. It was incredible. He saw everything as if looking through a glass window—so real, he
felt that he could reach out and touch it.

The images showed Bart kicking him to the ground
and then the final bullet that went straight into his skull.

This time, he saw not only Bart killing him from a distance, but also what Bart did after he stepped over his
body. Rage swelled up as Jess watched him kill Matilda's
father and the preacher, then drag his bride into a back
room.

"Enough!" he roared, unable to take any more. He'd
always known Bart was part animal, but that only proved
it. How dare he defile Matilda like that . . .

God damn him.

His fury raging, he glared at Artemis as he literally
shook from the weight of his need to bathe in Bart's blood.
"I'm in."

"There are a few more details you should know,
such as—"

"I don't care," he snarled, cutting her off. "So long as
it starts with me gutting that bastard, I'll do anything.
And I do mean *anything*."

"All right, then." A bright gold medallion appeared in
her palm. She grabbed his arm and pressed the medallion
to it.

Searing pain tore through him as he gasped in agony.
Still, she kept that medallion on his bicep, oblivious of the

smell of burning flesh, which was so foul, it made his stomach pitch. When she finally pulled it away, he felt completely drained and weak. And there was a strange double bow and arrow mark on his arm, where she'd pressed the medallion.

Just as he was about to ask her how he could fight anyone like this, a new warmth crawled up from his toes to the top of his head. Suddenly he felt stronger than he'd ever been before. More alert. He could hear things that made no sense. Things like Artemis's heartbeat and the whisper of voices from far away. He held more knowledge than he'd ever been taught.

It was like being a god, and yet he knew for all his newfound power, it was nothing compared to what Artemis had.

Cupping the medallion in her hand, she stepped away from him. "You have twenty-four hours, horseguy, to kill your betrayer any way you see fit and to take your revenge. Make them count. Oh, and know that you can't let daylight touch you. If you do . . . Well, you don't want to die without your soul. It's highly unpleasant. Sometime in the next few days, a man named Acheron Parthenopaeus will find you and teach you everything you need to know about being a Dark-Hunter. If you're smart, you'll listen to him." She gave him an evil smirk as she stepped back and raised her arms. "Welcome to the madness."

1

138 years later
Las Vegas, Nevada

"How are you doing?"

Abigail Yager barely understood those words as the male doctor stood over her bed, injecting her with a substance that could very well be lethal. But if it worked, it would be worth the risk. "What?"

"Abby? Can you hear me?"

She blinked slowly and tried to focus on Hannah's question. Everything was blurry. Even so, she could see the way the light played in Hannah's blond hair. The concern on her sister's beautiful face. "Um . . . yeah."

Hannah cursed. "You're killing her. Stop!"

The doctor didn't listen.

Hannah started for him, but before she could reach the far side of the bed, her older brother, Kurt, intercepted her. "Stop it, Hannah."

"We don't know what that will do to her. She's human!"

Kurt shook his head. "She needs it. If it strengthens us, it should do the same with her. Besides, it's too late. At this point, it'll either help her or she's dead. Plain and simple."

Could there be any less care in his tone?

Hannah shoved Kurt away. "I'm ashamed of you. After all she's done for us, you still see her as nothing but a human." She returned to Abigail's side and took her hand. "Stay with me, Abby. Don't leave me alone with an insensitive prick as the only member of my family."

"I'm not a prick!"

Hannah ignored him. "I need my big sis. C'mon, girl. Don't let me down."

Abigail couldn't really follow the angry exchange they were now engaged in. Honestly, all she heard was her heart pounding in her ears. She saw images of her past playing through her mind as if they were on a DVD. The old two-story house where the three of them had grown up. Of her and Hannah sneaking up past their bedtime to whisper and giggle about their latest celebrity crushes.

So many happy memories of that time . . .

Her thoughts turned to Kurt and Hannah's mother and father, who took her in after Abby's own parents had been slaughtered. They, too, had died years ago from their curse, and there was nothing she wouldn't do for her adoptive siblings.

And you just might be paying the ultimate price.

"Wait . . ."

Was that the doctor's voice?

The thrumming grew louder as she felt something shatter deep within her body. Arching her back, she screamed as every molecule in her body seemed to catch fire.

"What's happening to her?"

"Get your sister out of here."

Abigail heard Hannah protesting as Kurt jerked her from the room and slammed the door behind them. Tears streamed from the corners of her eyes. She could no longer see anything, and yet she saw everything. There was no way to describe it. It was as if she had a mirror to the world.

"Breathe," the doctor whispered. "Just breathe. I'm not about to let you die."

That was easier said than done. Pain lacerated her body. It was as if she was burning from the inside out.

Unable to stand it, she screamed until she could stand no more. This was it. In spite of what he said, she was dying. She had to be. Surely no one could withstand this much pain and live. There was no way she'd survive.

In fact, she felt the darkness coming for her. It was swallowing her whole. Piece by piece. Shredding her completely.

She turned her head from side to side, trying to breathe. Something had its hands on her throat, choking her.

Was it the doctor?

She couldn't focus. Couldn't see.

"Stop!" Her cry echoed in her ears.

Then as quickly as it'd come, the pain left her—like a bird that shot skyward for no reason. It was gone.

Her throat was so dry now. She tilted her head to meet the doctor's gaze. Concern etched his brow as he lowered the mask on his face.

"How do you feel?" There was only the smallest bit of his fangs showing as he spoke. Something else flashed. A memory of him that was gone so fast, she couldn't grasp it.

Was it important?

"I need water," she rasped.

"Do you crave anything else?"

"Yes," she breathed.

"What?"

Abigail licked her lips as the memory of her birth parents' deaths seared her. Even all these years later, that memory was perfectly intact, as if it'd happened only yesterday.

Barely four years old and dressed in her red Sesame Street pajamas, she'd hidden under the bed while the man her parents had called friend mercilessly slaughtered them with a shotgun. Those horrendously violent sounds were forever carved in her heart. From where she'd been, she saw the man's black cowboy boots, which caused the floorboards to squeak while he searched her room. Terrified, she'd watched him track blood all over her pink princess rug. She'd held her favorite teddy bear to her mouth and bit him hard to keep from crying out and betraying her location. He'd paused before her dresser, and there in the mirror she'd seen his face so clearly. So perfectly.

And as she heard those heavy footsteps leave her home, she'd sworn one thing.

To find that man and kill him as brutally as he'd killed her parents. To make him beg for a mercy she had no intention of giving him.

Retribution would be hers. . . .

"Abigail?" The doctor forced her to look at him. "What else do you crave?"

"The throat of Sundown Brady."

2

"Someone's killing Dark-Hunters."

Jess Brady scowled as his Squire, Andy, burst into the obscenely huge kitchen, huffing and puffing, with his dark hair sticking out all over his head as if the boy had been wringing at it—a habit Andy had whenever he was duly stressed.

Much less excited, especially since he'd been up only a few, Jess blew his breath across his steaming coffee. "Settle down, pup. I ain't had my caffeine yet." And he wasn't a morning person, even though his mornings were what most people called early evening.

Still the boy jumped about like a filly around a rattlesnake. Had *he* ever been that nervous about anything?

The answer hit him hard in the chest and did nothing to improve his irritability.

Jess quickly turned his thoughts away from that memory and focused on the boy he'd known since the day Andy was whelped.

Even though Andy was nearing thirty now, he was about as high-strung as anyone Jess had ever met. Times like this, he missed the old calmness of Andy's pa. Nothing had ever rattled that man.

Not even the time he'd landed in a nest of scorpions.

"Sundown . . . you don't understand. It's—"

He held his hand up to stop the boy midsentence. "I get it, kid. Case you haven't noticed, Dark-Hunters are on almost as many menus as humans are. Having something trying to kill us is about normal. Now, why you more flustered than a preacher in a whorehouse?"

"I'm trying to tell you." Andy gestured toward the door as if expecting the bogeyman to charge through it. "There's a human out there who is killing off Dark-Hunters, and someone needs to stop them."

Jess took a slow drink before he spoke. Ah yeah, that hit the spot. Little more, and he'd be as close to human as a deadman could come. "Well, that's just plain rude."

All that did was frustrate Andy more. "I really don't think you understand what I'm trying to tell you."

Jess scratched at the whiskers along his jaw. "And my mama drowned the dumb ones. I hear everything you're saying. There's a group of Buffys thinking we're the bad guys. Ain't my first rodeo, pup. It's been happening so long, they were called Helsings long before your daddy was a gleam in your granddaddy's eyes. Thank you, Hollywood and Stoker for that. Not like being undead didn't suck before. They just made it worse for us by cluing the rest of the world in that we exist. Now every goth with a thirst for immortality is cruising for us, begging us to bite them and turn them. Did I ever tell you about that time when—?"

"Sundown," Andy snapped. "I—"

"You need to check that tone, boy. Remember, I used to kill people for a living, and I ain't been up long enough to have much tolerance right about now. Knock it down a notch before I forget I'm supposed to actually like you."

Andy let out a long sigh. "Fine, but answer me this."

Dang, when had the kid turned into the Riddler? He should have curtailed all those *Batman* reruns when Andy was a boy.

"Did any of those others ever come after you guys in the past leading a Daimon entourage?"

Now, that got his attention. While it wasn't unusual for Daimons to use humans as servants or tools from time to time, it wasn't normal for them to follow one.

Jess set the coffee down on the stainless steel counter. "Come again?"

"Yeah . . . this one travels in a pack of Daimons, and has been slaying every Hunter they can find. She's taken out three here and four others in Arizona and Oklahoma."

Jess took a full minute to digest that. "How do you know about this?"

"I was contacted by Tawny, who got it from her mother." Now, to most, that'd sound bizarre. But like Andy, Tawny was a multigenerational Squire. A few thousand years back, the Squire network had been set up to provide a "normal" cover for the nocturnal Dark-Hunters during the daylight hours when they were sleeping. The Squires helped them to pass for humans, and most of all, the Squires shielded their existence from the rest of the world and took care of their day-to-day necessities so that they could focus on their job. Killing Daimons and freeing the human souls they'd stolen before those souls died and were forever lost.

But the best part about the Squires was that some of them were Oracles who could speak directly to the gods and get information from them that the Dark-Hunters could use to track and kill Daimons.

Tawny's mother happened to be one of those Oracles.

Deciphering what the gods said, however, was another matter.

Jess leaned against the kitchen counter and crossed his arms over his chest. "Tell me exactly what her mother said."

"She said that there's an ill wind coming and that you should guard your back. Lionel didn't fail to make it home before dawn. He was murdered and that his killer, a human leading a Daimon guard, was on the hunt for more of his kind."

Lionel was another Dark-Hunter who'd been assigned to Las Vegas. He died three nights ago, after he'd failed to make it to shelter before the sun rose—at least that was what they'd been told. Immortality had its price, and while the things that could kill them were few, those few were an ugly way to die.

Jess rubbed his thumb against his brow. "And the gods spoke that plainly?"

Andy hedged. "Well . . . not exactly. You know how they are."

Yeah, they always spoke in riddles that were tougher to unknot than a two-headed cobra. "So how—?"

"It's taken them days to decipher it, but she swears she's right and that you need to watch your back."

That, he'd been doing since the day the goddess Artemis resurrected him. Bart had tutored him well on guarding every angle of his body and staying alert no matter what or who. Jess wasn't about to ever be a victim again.

"Andy—"

"Don't *Andy* me. I believe her. She's one of the best Oracles we have."

He was right about that. But . . .

"We all make mistakes." And Jess had made more than his fair share.

A tic started in Andy's jaw. It was obvious he wanted to throttle Jess, but he knew better than to even try.

"Fine," he said, finally relenting on the matter. "Whatever. You're the one they're after, so it's none of my business. Plenty of other Dark-Hunters to work for. They're probably a lot less irritating, too." Then he changed the subject entirely. "I repaired your tracker and phone." He held Jess's iPhone out to him. "Try not to get it wet tonight."

"Not my fault the Daimon I was chasing decided to run through a water fountain." Damnedest part about living here in Vegas, there were huge fountains all over the place, and for some reason, Daimons seemed to think Dark-Hunters were allergic to water. Or maybe it was their way to piss them off before getting killed.

Andy ignored his comment. "Mom overnighted some of her oatmeal cookies for you. They're in the jar by the sink." He pointed to the container that looked like a Conestoga wagon, which was really out of place in the commercial-grade kitchen designed to feed a large army.

The thought of those cookies perked him up a lot. Cecilia made the best in the world. That was what he missed most about Andy's pa working for him. C used to have a fresh batch cooling on the stove every evening when he came upstairs for coffee.

Andy continued his report. "I picked up your laundry and hung it in the hall closet. I checked with the company, and your horses will be transported out here next week from your ranch, so you can quit pouting every time you pass the saddles."

Wow, he had no idea he'd done that. Huh . . . he'd have to keep an eye on his expressions. He hated to be that obvious to anyone.

Andy gestured toward the door. "The boots you ordered are in the box on the hall table, as are the throwing knives Kell sent to replace the ones you broke the other night. I couldn't get the black Stetson reblocked, so I have a new one on order. Your bike is fully gassed, and Sin has offered all of you free valet parking at his casino while you hunt. He'll have his staff leave the bike parked in front so that you can grab it and go when you're ready to head home, and if you get trapped in the city and can't make it back here before dawn, you can hole up in one of his rooms—they'll have a key at the concierge with your name on it. Is there anything else you need?"

That was the best part of Andy. Like his father, he was

as efficient as the devil's desk clerk. "Nope. Can't think of anything."

"All right. I'll have my cell phone if you need anything." The boy always said that.

Jess moved toward the cookies. "Have a good night."

Andy nodded before he went to the door. He paused as if he wanted to say something else—then he quickly took his exit to head to his apartment over the garage. For some reason, as the kid left, Jess had an image of Andy as a little boy chasing after his father. He could still see Andy's chubby cheeks, wide eyes, and freckled face. Hear him asking in that youthful tone if Jess would teach him how to ride, and then picking the boy up from the dirt the first time Andy was thrown by the Shetland pony Jess had bought for him. Little booger had gotten right back up, dusted himself off, and then climbed into the saddle like a trouper.

Now that little boy was a man strangers thought was older than Jess.

That was the hardest part of being immortal. Watching people he cared about be kids, grow old, and die while *he* never changed. And just like with Andy, he'd known the boy's father from the moment Ed was born. The Taylor family had been his Squires from the beginning of his Dark-Hunter life.

Even so, he'd kept a wall between him and them. Never letting them in too close. At least not until Andy.

He didn't know why, but that little shit had wormed his way past Jess's best defenses. In many ways, Andy was like his son.

There was only one other person in his long life that Jess had felt that way about.

He winced at another memory he wished he could purge.

Aching with remorse and grief, Jess pulled his watch out of his pocket to check the time. The moment he opened it, he paused to stare at Matilda's face in the worn-out sepia photograph that had been kept inside his watch since the day he was reborn. No matter how many years passed, he still ached over the loss of her.

That had been the only thing he truly hated about his rebirth. Knowing she was alive and not being able to see her. Dark-Hunters were forbidden from having families, and they were never to let anyone from their past know that they'd come back. It was part of what they swore to when Artemis created them.

Still he'd kept tabs on her while she lived and made sure that she never once wanted for anything. She'd gone on to marry and have six kids.

Without him.

To the day she died, she'd never known who her benefactor was. The Squires told her it was a trust fund set up by a distant uncle who'd died and left it to her. She never knew that money came from a pact he'd made with a goddess to even a score that no amount of violence could tally.

Sometimes dead wasn't dead enough.

His throat tightening, he closed his watch. There was no use thinking about what should have been. He'd done what he'd had to. Matilda had probably been better off without him, anyways. Sooner or later, his past would have caught up to them, and the result would have been the same.

At least that was the lie he told himself to make it all bearable. But inside, he knew the truth. No one could have loved her more than he had.

More than he did to this day.

"I miss you, Tilly." He always would. No one would ever again make him feel like she had.

Worthy.

Cursing, he curled his lip at his melancholy thoughts. "I'm turning into an old woman. Might as well start knitting and bitching about soap operas, gas prices, and rude drivers."

That wasn't what Sundown Brady did.

Nope. It was killing time, and he was in the mood to bathe in blood tonight.

3

Ren Waya coasted on the breeze as he heard the heartbeat of the earth thrumming in his ears. It sounded like a tribal drum, summoning the ancient spirits out of their slumber to make ready for war. And as he flew, Sister Wind carried a new scent to him. One he'd never smelled before, and given his extreme old age, that said a lot.

Something was here, and it didn't belong.

Unable to pinpoint it, he dipped down, then recognized a rider on the road far below. The motorcycle slowed from its feral speed as the rider came upon the Vegas traffic and lights. Ren let out a cry while he followed the sleek black motorcycle into town.

Swathed in a black duster, the rider was oblivious of being watched. Of course, the loud, thumping music inside the rider's helmet that was turned to a level that should be deafening might have something to do with that. Styx's "Renegade." The irony of that wasn't lost on Ren. If he could smile in his current form, he would.

The rider skimmed past traffic and turned into the brightly lit Ishtar Casino, which was styled after an ancient Sumerian temple. Ren lost sight of the rider as he drove under the parking pavilion. He banked to the right to miss the wall and circled back.

J*ess pulled his* helmet off before he gave his name to the valet.

The attendant snapped to attention. "Mr. Brady, sir, we were told to give you white-glove treatment. You may park your bike anywhere you want, and we'll make sure no one bothers it. If you have any problems or needs, have the concierge contact Damien Metaxas, and he'll take care of it for you."

A man could get used to this level of service—it was like being at Disney World. "Thanks," he said, then handed the valet a twenty.

Jess slid into a tight space at the front of the line of cars and limos, where his motorcycle should be out of the way, then parked his 2006 MV Agusta F4CC on the curb. At $120,000 a pop, his ride was a gold mine for any thief who had knowledge of motorcycles. Not that the money was that big a deal to him. Replacing it, however, was another matter, since they were as rare as a loyal friend, and he'd long grown attached to it.

Hate to gut a human for being greedy. But back in the day, he'd done worse for less.

He locked it down, put his helmet on the seat, then dropped the keys in his pocket. It was a little warm for his duster, but he preferred it, since it helped hide the weapons he needed for his trade. No need in scaring the civilians any more than was necessary.

Bad thing about Vegas, you couldn't spit without dropping germs on a Daimon. They practically owned this place. In fact, three of the valet drivers here were Apollites, including the one who'd spoken to him. And the casino manager, Damien Metaxas was, in fact, a full-blown Daimon that no Dark-Hunter was allowed to kill. They claimed Metaxas fed only on humans who deserved to die—rapists, murderers, pedophiles. But why would you take their word on it? Was anyone really checking?

Even when the casino owner, Sin, was a Dark-Hunter, he'd had them working for him.

"You're a sick SOB, Sin," Jess muttered as he pulled his sunglasses out and put them on.

Keep your enemies close, I guess. Still . . .

"You're late."

Jess grinned, making sure to keep his fangs from showing as he did so. He turned at the deep, accented voice that had come from behind him. "Didn't know Grandma was keeping tabs and setting curfew."

Two inches taller, Ren had his long, jet black hair pulled back into a single braid that trailed down his back. Even without that pissed-off expression, he was intimidating as all get out. At least to those who could be intimidated.

Jess definitely didn't fit into that category.

The only color on Ren's body was the bone and turquoise choker he wore as an homage to his Native American heritage—other than that, he was swathed all in black from head to toe. Jess asked him once what tribe he belonged to, but Ren had refused to answer. Since it didn't matter to Jess, he'd never asked again, even though they'd been friends for well over a hundred years.

Jess scratched at his whiskers, wishing he'd shaved a little closer. "I thought you were communing with Chocolate tonight."

Ren shook his head. "Choo Co La Tah."

"Isn't that what I said?"

Now, there was a pained expression for you. It was quite impressive. "For a man who was born speaking Cherokee, I don't understand why you can't pronounce things correctly."

"Ah, *potato, potahto*. Does it really matter in the grand scheme of things?"

"It does if you ever come into contact with him. Believe me, your mixed Cherokee blood won't buy you any tolerance where he's concerned."

Yeah, that was the thing about immortals. Many of them weren't exactly good natured. Many more were downright intolerant. And as for Choo Co La Tah, Jess was more than acquainted with him, but it was one of those things he *never* talked about. "Then I'll just make sure that I call him Exalted Being."

Ren laughed. "Wise choice."

Jess decided to change the topic to what had bothered him a few minutes ago. "So was that you flying above me as I rode in?"

"You saw me?"

Jess shrugged nonchalantly. "Don't you know, I sense everything around me." Even before Artemis had bestowed him with psychic powers, that was one ability he'd had from birth. No one had ever been able to sneak up on him.

Pulling a gun behind his back and shooting him was another story. Only someone as close to him as Bart had been could have killed him that way. Had Bart been a stranger, it would never have happened.

"And here I thought I was being stealthy."

Jess snorted. "With that girly caw you let out? Did a frog crawl down your throat and die, or what?"

Ren let out a short *heh* sound. "You better be glad I like you."

"I am indeed, for I have seen how you throw a knife, and it is truly awe inspiring. Now, if you don't mind . . ." Jess started away from him. If they stayed together too long, they'd deplete each other's strength. It was a fail-safe the gods used to keep Dark-Hunters from combining their powers and taking over mankind.

"Wait."

Jess paused.

"Choo Co La Tah wanted to warn me that something unnatural is coming from the west."

The direction of death for the Cherokee. He didn't know if Ren's people had the same beliefs as his mother's or not. "Yeah, okay. I'll watch for Daimons coming up the street."

"This is serious, Jess. We're nearing the Time Untime when everything resets. Of all men, you know what happens if things get misaligned."

Yes, he did. The Mayans weren't the only ancient Americans who had calendars. Many of the tribes had similar rotating cycles, including the Cherokee. "2012 ain't here yet."

"No, but the return of the Pale One has been sped up by whatever is coming. Be careful tonight."

Now, this was getting annoying, with everyone pecking at him like a bunch of hens. "Andy told me the same thing earlier."

"Two warnings. One night."

Time to listen. He understood. Too bad he hadn't had these warnings before he was gunned down as a human. That would have been a little more helpful than vague warnings to someone who was basically immortal and impervious now. But then, life was ever a study in a day late and a dollar short. "All right. I'll pay attention."

Ren inclined his head to him. "Good, 'cause you're the only reason I'm here, and I'd hate to think I uprooted myself needlessly." When Jess had been transferred out here a few weeks back, Ren asked to come, too. "Don't make me have to spirit-walk to cut your throat."

Jess snorted at the threat. "Got to say, dying would really wreck my best day. Been there, done that, and now that I think about it, Artemis forgot to give me the T-shirt."

Ren rolled his eyes. "You're psychotic."

"And we're down a Hunter, so we need to get patrolling before the Daimons start feeding."

Ren waved his hand in front of him and spoke a blessing in his native tongue.

Jess didn't understand it, but he appreciated the gesture. "Same to you, *di-na-da-nv-tli*." And with that, he started for the infamous strip, which was teeming with clueless tourists just waiting to become a walking Happy Meal for a Daimon.

Jess kept his pace leisurely as he used every sense he had to feel for any unnatural predator that was out and about. There was a strange vibe to the city, and it made him wonder about the depletion of the DH here.

The owner of the Ishtar Casino, Sin, he discounted from that list. Sin had fallen in love with one of Artemis's handmaidens and been redeemed from their service. So his was a happy exodus.

Lionel, Renee, and Pavel had all died over the last few months. Supposedly by bad luck. Lionel and Renee by not making it home before dawn. Pavel had been decapitated in a freak car wreck. At least, that was the official story.

After what Andy and Ren had said, Jess now wondered how accurate that was.

Two other Dark-Hunters had been moved in to replace those killed in action. Syra, who was better known as Yukon Jane, and Rogue, an Englishman whose proper speech belied his extremely psychotic ways. That boy definitely wasn't right.

Made him wonder who they'd move in to replace Lionel.

Guess I'll find out.

A pretty blonde walked past him on the street with a come-follow-me-cowboy look that grabbed his attention away from that line of thought. He let out a slow appreciative breath at the sass in her walk. He'd always been a sucker for a woman who knew how to handle herself and, more to the point, handle a man who was aching for her.

She smiled at him over her shoulder.

You got work to do, boy.

Yeah, but she was delectable.

Work, Jess. If Andy's right, there's a killer on the loose, and you need to find it and stop it.

He actually whimpered at the fact that he couldn't follow after the blonde. In Reno, doable. Here . . .

Too many Daimons.

Yet another reason they needed killing.

Sighing, he crossed Spring Mountain Road, heading north on Vegas Boulevard. He'd just passed the entrance to Neiman Marcus at the Fashion Show Mall and was nearing The Cloud when that familiar tingle went down his spine. One that was unmistakable.

There were Daimons nearby.

But where? People were all over the place. Hard to pinpoint a Daimon in a crowd this size. Not to mention the bright lights, even with his opaque sunglasses on, were hard on his light-sensitive Dark-Hunter eyes. Since Dark-Hunters were created long before the modern lightbulb, Artemis had given them incredible night vision that really hated anything bright. It was downright painful.

Closing his eyes, he focused his other senses. At first he was overwhelmed by everything he heard. But after a few seconds, it settled down so that he could pinpoint what he needed.

They were in the underground parking lot on his left.

Jess headed for it, making sure to keep himself away from any street cameras that the police might use for surveillance—that was one thing Rogue was the best at, since he'd come over from England, where their streets had more cameras than a fully stocked mega Best Buy store.

He ducked into the lot that was full of cars and vacant of people. At first he didn't hear anything more, and then . . .

To his right.

Pulling out his daggers, he kept them in his sleeves, just in case he happened upon someone who wouldn't understand why a tall, dark-haired man wearing really dark sunglasses and unseasonably warm clothing would be armed to his fangs. *Really, Officer, I was trying to protect humanity by killing these things that suck human souls out to live past their twenty-seventh birthday* just didn't cut it. Why no one would believe that, he couldn't imagine. Really, the audacity of modern courts and judges.

Jess came to an abrupt stop as he found something even more grisly than he'd expected.

There were four Daimons on the ground, literally feasting on what must be a demon of some kind. At first glance, it appeared human. But there was no missing the odd skin tone, slightly off from normal, and the smell of it.

That body wasn't human.

One of the Daimons looked up at him as if he'd sensed Jess's presence. "Dark-Hunter," he growled.

Now, normally, Daimons would do that and run away. That had been the standard operating procedure for the last 139 years.

These didn't run.

Well, not true. They ran *toward* him. Last time that had happened was his brief stint up in Fairbanks, Alaska, with Syra and a couple of others. And that hadn't gone so well for him. It was even worse for the other Dark-Hunters who had died there.

Jess caught the first one to reach him. He kicked the Daimon back and plunged his dagger straight into the Daimon's heart.

It didn't explode.

It just pissed the Daimon off.

Aw, now, wait a minute. . . .

"What the—?" His words ended as the Daimon picked him up and threw him against the far wall, where he slammed hard against the concrete. Pain exploded through his body. Been a while since he hurt this much. It brought back many an unhappy memory.

Still, he didn't take a lickin' and not give one back. No, sir. After flipping to his feet, he shrugged his coat off in one fluid movement and ran for his attacker.

Don't let them bite you."

Jess glanced over to where Sin had joined the fight. Almost a head taller, Sin wore his black hair cropped short. Dressed in black like Ren—something they all did, since it helped camouflage bloodstains they might collect in fights, and face it, it was a lot easier to look badass in black than in baby doll pink—Sin tossed him a new weapon, which was similar to a small scimitar.

He caught it just as the Daimon realized what was going on. The Daimon's eyes widened at the sight of the weapon. Now, that was what he was used to.

Respect.

Well, really fear, but he'd take it.

Sin flipped the Daimon nearest him flat onto his back and, in one swift stroke, beheaded him. He met Jess's gaze. "Now you know how to kill them."

Sure enough.

"Whatever you do, Jess, don't let even one of them escape."

Jess didn't. Of course, it took a little running, a near miss getting beheaded himself by a low-lying parking deck beam, couple of bruised ribs 'cause Daimons knew how to give a kick that counted, and more acrobatics than a man his age should be capable of, but he ran down the last one and made sure the Daimon took no more human lives.

Panting and sweating, he stood over the grisly body with a puzzled frown.

Sin grinned as he joined him. "That, I have to say, was highly impressive. You run like a jackrabbit. Too bad you were born before football. You, my friend, would have gone pro." He raked a hard stare over Jess's body. "They didn't bite you, did they?"

"Nothing not a willing female bites me, and definitely nothing without an explicit invitation." Jess indicated the body with a jerk of his chin. "Care to tell me why they're still here?" The one thing you could always count on with Daimons was the fact that they were self-cleaning. Kill one, and it exploded into dust. They didn't normally lie on the floor in a pool of blood, looking all grisly and nasty like that.

Sin kicked at the body. "Guess these haven't reached Reno yet."

"These?"

"Daimons who walk in daylight."

Ah, hell no . . .

This couldn't be good. "Come again?"

"We had a little bit of a problem here a couple of years ago. There was a hive of gallu demons who were preying on the tourists. I don't suppose you know what a gallu is."

"I'm a gunfighter, Jim, not a demonologist."

Sin moved past him so that he could burn the body on the ground. "Nice Bones impression. Roddenberry would be proud." He jerked his chin toward the burning body.

"Gallus are my pantheon's contribution to the nightmare list. Vicious and amoral, they don't care who they kill, and they are virtually indestructible."

"Nice."

"You have no idea. I had them contained here for a while. Unfortunately, they escaped."

That figured, and it was just like he feared. Suck City Limits was looming in the headlights. He should have known better than to take a detour from Normality. "So how many are running around now?"

"You miss the point, Dark-Hunter. They're not just here anymore, and they're spreading. Unlike a Daimon, one bite, and you become their slave. They can make more of themselves. That was bad enough. Then the Daimons realized they can feed on the gallu."

Jess shook his head. "Why do I have a feeling this is really about to piss me off?"

"Because it is. Once the Daimons feed on a gallu, they become immortal and absorb the demon's essence and powers into their bodies. As I said, Daimons can then walk in daylight, and the only way to kill them is to behead and burn them."

"And one bite, and I'm their slave?"

"Exactly."

Jess cursed. "And who thought this would be a good idea?"

Sin held his hand up. "Don't get me started. There are

idiots in all pantheons. Some days, I think the Sumerians had more than their fair share, and I only hope the idiocy is congenital and not something contracted later in life. Otherwise, I'm even more screwed." He accelerated the burning of the body. "But back to what needs to concern us most. So far the outbreaks have been containable."

That was one way of looking at it, he supposed.

Still . . .

"You know it might help if you'd actually told all of us about them before we run across them. Had you not shown up just now, I'd have been locked in a useless game of Whac-a-Mole, trying to kill them with a knife through the heart. I could have been gallu Daimon kibble. Really not cool, Sin."

"Hey, I just found out about these earlier today, and I was going to tell you about them."

"When? After they bit me and turned me into a Dark-Hunter gallu zombie?" Now, there was a horror movie in the making. He just didn't want to be the star of it.

Sin narrowed an angry gaze on him. "You left before I got down to you."

"I'm not that psychic, amigo. How was I supposed to know you wanted to talk to me?"

Sin scowled. "Didn't the valet tell you to wait?"

"Nope."

It was Sin's turn to curse.

Obviously the Apollite hadn't been as friendly as he

pretended. Jess tsked. "That's what you get for living with your enemies, Slim. Notice they don't flinch from stabbing you in the back."

"Neither do friends."

Jess grimaced at the touché. "Now, that's just cold, Sin. True," he admitted, "but cold."

"Yeah, well, I was trying to get your attention on the street. It's why I followed you down here. I wanted to warn you about them before you got into a fight with one."

That gave him pause. "You were following me?" And he didn't know it?

Impossible.

"Yeah."

Jess frowned at that. "Why didn't I sense you?"

"Maybe the blonde distracted you."

It didn't work that way. Never once had he failed to notice someone on his tail. Unless . . . "What are you?"

"Pardon?"

Jess raked a look over him, trying to find something to confirm his suspicion. "You can't be human, and I know you're not a Daimon or Apollite." Daimons, unless they partook of Clairol, were blond with lighter skin than Sin had. "You're no longer a Dark-Hunter, so . . ."

Sin gave a wicked half smile. "You're right. I'm none of those."

"What, then? Are you a god?"

Sin's smile went full blown. "Remember, Ray, whenever someone asks you if you're a god, the correct answer is always yes."

Jess snorted. "I saw that movie, and I think you misquoted it."

"The sentiment's the same."

Which meant Sin wouldn't answer. Fine. Jess wouldn't press the issue. He more than understood wanting to keep some things to oneself.

"Did you tell Ren about them?" Jess asked.

"Yeah. I caught him when I came down, then I went for you."

Thank God for that. He glanced at the scorched stain on the pavement that was the only thing left of the Daimons. He met Sin's gaze. "I appreciate the assist. And I have another question. Since I can't throw flames out of my hands like you did a minute ago, how do I dispose of these new Daimons we're fighting after I kill them?"

"We haven't worked out the kinks quite yet. But if you drop one, call me and I'll send out a cleanup team."

Jess shook his head. "Damn, you really can get anything in Vegas."

Sin laughed. "You have no idea."

No, but Jess was beginning to.

"Since you have so many of the enemy working in your casino . . . Have you heard of a human working with Daimons to kill Dark-Hunters?"

Sin's eyes widened. "What?"

That expression answered the question. "My Squire got word about it from the Oracles. I was just wondering if they might have misinterpreted whatever they got from the Powers That Be. I keep thinking if there was such a beast, Acheron would have called all of us with a warning." As their unofficial leader, Acheron tended to watch out for them, and he had powers that defied belief and understanding.

"Ash's powers don't necessarily work that way."

"What do you mean?"

"Think of it like having a fire hose turned on full blast," Sin said. "The water flows so fast, it's hard to control. He blocks his abilities unless he needs something, so that he doesn't get overwhelmed by it."

Jess wasn't so sure he believed Sin. Acheron was a walking contradiction who never spoke to anyone about himself. He couldn't imagine Acheron having a heart-to-heart chat with Sin, never mind explaining to the ancient Sumerian how his powers worked. "How do you know this?"

"Married to Artemis's handmaiden, remember? She knows a lot about Ash."

Now, that he believed. Be hard for Acheron to keep secrets from the goddess they all served. Sin was right. If anyone knew some of those secrets, it was probably his wife.

"So," Sin continued with his explanation, "if Ash isn't

focused on here, he won't know what's going on. You want me to call him about it?"

"Nah. I'll do it later." Jess never liked getting second-hand information. Too much room for people to forget something or get it misconstrued. He'd much rather have it straight from the horse's mouth.

Sin nodded. "Well, I won't keep you. I know you have a lot to do, and I have a casino to run and a wife and toddler to see to."

Yeah, but Jess envied him that last bit. A lot. However, he wouldn't begrudge Sin his good fortune. It was nice to know that life worked out for some people, and since Sin had been a Dark-Hunter, Jess knew the man must have suffered greatly in his first life. It did his heart good to see someone happy, even if it wasn't him. "Give the missus my best."

"Will do."

Jess went back for his coat while Sin took his leave. He glanced around at the remains Sin had burned and let out a tired breath.

New rules. New playing field. The gods must have gotten bored with them all. In the back of his mind, he could picture these new Daimons spreading like in a bad SF movie. Hell, he could even see the map with a superimposed image of a red horde spreading out like an epidemic.

And somewhere out there was a human playing vigilante on them.

Yeah, it was a good time to be in Vegas. He was so happy Acheron had reassigned him, and that was said with all due sarcasm.

He shrugged his coat on and returned to the street to continue his lonely patrol. As he walked among the crowd, he tried to imagine what it would be like to be one of them—an innocent person going about completely ignorant of the preternatural around him. A part of him had forgotten what it was like to be human.

Another part wondered if he'd ever really been human at all. His enemies and victims would definitely deny it. And he'd been nothing more than an animal.

Until Matilda.

"Gah, I'm maudlin again." Must be his lack of horses. Riding always made him feel better, and he'd been away from them for way too long.

Soon though, they'd be here and he'd be back to normal. At least as normal as an immortal could be.

Hours went by as he searched and found no target. It amazed him that the nightlife in Vegas didn't let up. The crowds did thin, but still . . .

Totally different world from what he was used to in Reno.

His phone buzzed in his pocket, letting him know it was time to head back so that he'd be home a few minutes before dawn. When it came to that, he never liked pushing his luck. No one wanted to spontaneously combust into flames, especially not in traffic. The thought of going Johnny Blaze just didn't appeal to him in the least.

He headed back for Sin's casino to collect his ride.

Jess hadn't gone far when a flash across the street caught his eye.

It was two Daimons pulling a woman into a storm drain. Jess sucked his breath in. Underneath the city was approximately a five hundred mile maze of drainage systems. It wouldn't take much for the Daimons to lose him down there.

He bolted across the street, hoping to catch them before they killed their prey or lost him.

The minute he was inside the drain, he all but let out a sigh of relief from the soothing darkness.

After removing his sunglasses, he slid them into his pocket and made his way through the smelly tunnel, which had about an inch of standing water in it. He curled his lip at the rotten garbage and other things he didn't want to think about. There were a number of homeless people who called these tunnels home. Some of them were every bit as dangerous to the average human as the Daimons he was after.

"Please let me go! Please! Please don't hurt me!"

He followed the sound of the woman's petrified cries. It didn't take long to find them.

Only it wasn't what he'd expected.

It was a trap, and he'd just barreled right into it.

4

Abigail had spent her entire life bracing for the moment when she'd see Sundown Brady again. Over the years, when she wasn't training to kill him, she'd played every imaginable scenario through her mind. Them meeting by accident. Her breaking into his house in the middle of the day to murder him in his sleep. A smoky, crowded bar where she walked up to him and then stabbed him in the heart and watched him fall to her feet as he died in utter agony. Even an abandoned movie theater where she trapped him inside and burned it to the ground. All to the tune of him begging her for mercy.

Yet none of those imaginings had prepared her for this.

For one thing, he was a lot larger than she remembered. Not just tall, which he was, but wide and extremely well muscled in a way very few men were. It was the kind of build that said he could snap her in two if he got close enough. His dark hair fell just past his ears and was a bit shaggy, as if he'd missed a haircut appointment. Two days' growth of whiskers shadowed a face that was so perfectly formed, he didn't look real. His eyes were black, and the intelligence there said nothing, absolutely nothing, escaped his notice.

Even with her new powers, she swallowed at the thought of fighting him. He wouldn't go down easy.

He'd probably take her with him.

But all she had to think of was her parents and the merciless way they'd died by his hands, and the fiery rage in her ignited to a level that wouldn't be intimidated or denied. It demanded his blood.

Sundown Brady was going to die tonight, and she was the harbinger who'd deliver it.

Jess froze as he saw the woman close up. Her black

hair was pulled back from her exotic features into a tight ponytail. Dressed in a pair of jeans and a dark purple shirt, she was armed from head to toe. But that wasn't what stopped him dead in his tracks.

For one instant, he could swear he was looking into Bart's face.

Time seemed to freeze as he took it all in. Her deep blue eyes that were shaped like a cat's. The dimple in her chin. The way she looked at him as if she could kill him.

It was like he was lying on the ground wounded again, looking up at Bart right before he pulled the trigger one last time.

"You bastard!" she snarled in a voice that was hauntingly familiar. One that brought back excruciating memories.

Before he could recover, she lunged at him.

Jess jumped back and twisted, sending her into the wall. He looked at the two Daimons, who were staying out of the fight for some reason. But he didn't have time to contemplate that as she came back at him, slashing at his body with a black KA-BAR.

He blocked her slash with his forearm across hers, then grabbed her hand. Dang, she was strong. Supernatural strong. Not to mention, she kept kicking at him. She fought like a well-trained wildcat.

"Let go of me!" she snarled, head-butting him.

That rattled his senses, but he refused to let go of her.

She was too quick and too close for that. If he released her, she'd get a shot in someplace that was going to hurt.

She looked past his shoulder to where the other two were sidelined. "Get him!"

Great. He slung her toward the Daimons. She collided with them, but it didn't slow them down.

His phone buzzed again, warning him he was running out of time. *I'm going to be a crispy critter if I don't do something quick.* While he could probably hole up here, he didn't want to chance it. Police and workers did occasionally venture down into the drains. All he needed was for one of them to find him loaded up with weapons.

Or worse, a flash flood could swoop down on him. Lionel had warned him on his first night here about seeking daytime shelter in the drains. Every year, there were a number of homeless who died from the flooding. While he couldn't drown, he could be swept into daylight, which would really suck for him.

He had to get out of here. Fast.

The really bad thing was he couldn't kill her. Dark-Hunters weren't supposed to kill humans, even when they were attacked by them. Stupid rule, granted. But it was one Acheron would have their ass over if they violated it.

And then there was the terrible suspicion he had about her identity. He wasn't sure if he wanted to be right or wrong. "Abigail?"

Anger darkened her blue eyes. "You do remember me."

How could he forget? "I thought you were dead."

She shrieked in rage before she attacked him with a fury that seemed to come from somewhere deep inside her. It was the same force that he'd had when he went for Bart.

Now that he knew who she was, there was no way he could hurt her. He choked on conflicting emotions. Relief, sorrow, and the deep need not to let her end his life. "I take it you're the one who's been killing Dark-Hunters?"

She lifted her chin proudly as she swung at him. "With relish. But you're the one I really want."

Why? All he'd ever done was protect her and her family.

He caught her arm and yanked her closer. "Ah, sugar, for that, all you had to do was get naked."

She curled her lip before she attacked even more viciously.

He staggered under a couple of well-placed blows. She was very well trained.

But then, so was he.

Jess twisted the knife from her hand and managed to finally catch her in a sleeper hold. She was harder to grip than a hungry greased pig. Luckily, he was used to pinning such ornery things. But if he'd been human, she'd have freed herself and been back on him.

He turned to the Daimons. "One step closer, and I snap her neck."

They exchanged a doubting frown.

"I mean it," he said as they looked like they were about

to pounce. He increased the pressure on her carotid and jugular. Within seconds, she was out. Still, he waited a few seconds more, in case she was faking. At this point, he wouldn't put anything past her.

Once he was sure she was unconscious, he slid her to a dry spot on the floor. "All right, punks. Bring it."

The moment he took a step forward, they ran deeper into the tunnel.

Well, at least they weren't the infected Daimons who could convert him.

Jess started to go after them, but rethought it. It was too close to dawn, and right now he had the prize of all time.

The woman who'd been hunting them.

A woman he'd once known . . .

"I can't believe you survived." But how? He had so many questions, they made him dizzy.

Best thing to do would be to interrogate her and find out what was going on and why she had such a hard-on for them. Hoping he didn't live to regret this decision, he picked her up and carried her back to the street. Now that she wasn't trying to kick his jewels into his throat, he realized just how tiny she was. Very well muscled, but short.

Like Matilda.

He squelched that comparison quick. She was nothing like his mild-mannered, soft-spoken bride-to-be. No one was. It was why he'd fallen in love with her and why all these decades later, he still ached from the loss of her friendship.

The woman in his arms was like everyone else he'd ever met. Treacherous. Lethal. Only out for herself. Whatever he did, he couldn't let himself forget that. She wanted him dead, and if he didn't stop her, she'd kill him and then move on to the rest of his colleagues.

No good deed goes unpunished. . . .

He'd protected her and her mother, and how did she pay him back? By trying to kill him.

How utterly typical.

Jess made it out as the sky was just starting to lighten. *I better hurry and be quick about it. . . .* It was getting a little too close at this point.

He hadn't gone far from the drain when he saw a police car driving by on the street.

Crap.

What were the odds that they'd not see him and keep going? Probably about as good as them believing he was carrying his wife back to their room after a heavy night of drinking.

Yeah . . .

He hadn't been *that* lucky in a long time. "I hope lockup doesn't have a window," he muttered under his breath.

The patrol car pulled up to the curb and stopped. "Hey, you there! Come over here."

Yeah, it was nice to know his bad luck was the only stable thing in his life.

Jess tightened his grip on Abigail as he debated his

options. None of them were good, especially since he was packing an arsenal under his coat. One they were sure to object to if they discovered it.

Making sure to act nonchalant, he moseyed over to the car. "Yes, sir?"

The officer glanced down at Abigail. "Is there a problem?"

Uh, yeah. You people are bugging the shit out of me when I need to be rocketing home. Jess forced himself not to betray his annoyance. "Little too much to drink. I was taking her back to the casino where we're staying."

The man narrowed his gaze suspiciously. "You need a doctor?"

No, he needed a break. "Nah, Officer. Thank you very much for the offer, though. She'll be all right. Well, the hangover will be pretty ferocious, I'm sure, but after a few hours, she'll be good as new."

"I don't know, George," the other officer said from the passenger seat. "I think we should call it in, just in case. Last thing we need is for him to be kidnapping her or something and we let him go. Think of the PR nightmare that'd be if he turns out to be a serial rapist or killer."

Jess had to bite back a curse at the paranoid asshole. Yeah, he *was* kidnapping her, but still . . .

She was the serial killer, not him.

"Hey, Jess."

He turned his head to see another police officer approaching from the sidewalk. At least this one he knew. "Kevin, how you doing?"

Kevin stepped between Jess and the car. "Is there a problem here?" he asked the other officers.

Was that drilled into them at the academy, or what?

"No," the officer in the car said quickly. "We saw him carrying the woman and just wanted to make sure nothing was wrong."

Thank God neither he nor Abigail had been bloodied or bruised during their fight and their clothes weren't torn. That would have been even harder to explain. As it was, her clothes were no more rumpled than if she had simply passed out from drink.

"Ah," Kevin said, dragging the word out. He indicated Jess with a jerk of his chin. "Don't worry. Jimmy and I'll take it from here."

Jimmy, Kevin's partner, came up behind Jess to wave at the officers in the car.

Both of them appeared relieved that they could pass this along to someone else. "All right. Thanks for sparing us the paperwork. See you guys later." The car pulled off.

Turning around, Kevin arched his brow at Jess and the woman he was holding. "Should I even ask?"

Jess shifted Abigail's weight. "Not if you want to keep your job, and I don't mean the one that doesn't afford you your million-dollar house." His phone started buzzing again with another warning about sunrise. Not that he needed it. The sky was turning a scary shade of light.

Kevin glanced up as if he were reading Jess's mind. "You're cutting it a little close to dawn, aren't you?"

"Closer than I meant to."

Jimmy gestured to their car, which was parked a few feet away. "C'mon, we can get you back in time."

"Thanks." Jess finally breathed easily. This would also keep him from having to wrangle her onto his bike and hold her there, especially since she'd be coming to any time now. He had to admit, having Squires who were cops came in handy. That was one thing Sin had set up well in this city. In Reno, they'd been light handed with a Squire network. But this place was hooked up to the extreme.

Jimmy held the door open for them. Jess got into the backseat and rested his package by his side and tried not to notice how amazingly pretty she was. It seriously messed with his head to see mixed in her features the person he'd once loved most and the only one he'd ever truly hated.

Life ain't fair.

And it was never simple.

Kevin and Jimmy got in and turned the siren on. They called in their break and sped him toward his house at warp speed.

"I appreciate y'all doing this."

"No problem," Kevin said with a grin. "It's nice to run through the streets when we're not really on a call. Makes me feel like Speed Racer."

Jess frowned as they passed the interstate ramp. "Wouldn't the freeway be faster?"

Jimmy laughed. "For you, civ. We don't have to stop for lights."

That made sense. It normally took Jess a little over twenty minutes to get from downtown to his eleven-acre compound on Tomiyasu Lane (depending on where he was when he started), but he did shoot out farther by taking the interstate. If they didn't stop for lights, they should be able to make it to his place in about the same time, maybe less.

With some luck, he might actually avoid combusting into flames in the backseat. *That* would be hard for the Squires to explain to their watch commander. Though it might be entertaining to see them try if *he* weren't the stain.

Kevin glanced at Jess in the rearview mirror. "So you want to tell us about the woman now?"

"Not really."

Jimmy scratched at the back of his neck. "Are we going to have to file a missing persons report on her later?"

"I doubt it. She's running with a group of Daimons. They're usually not the kind to call you guys." And he knew for a fact that she had no family.

Unless she'd married.

His breath caught as he realized he didn't know anything about her now. Hell, she could be married to a Daimon or Apollite. The very thought made him ill. But humans did occasionally fall in with them for one reason or another.

63

She could be someone's mother. . . .

Surely she wouldn't have been on the street hunting Dark-Hunters if she had dependents.

Would she?

Jimmy turned around in the seat with wide eyes to stare through the partition at him. "Is she the one the Oracles have been talking about? The human killing you guys off?"

I should have kept my mouth shut. Now all the social network sites used and run by the Squires would be lighting up like a Christmas tree. "I think so, but I'd appreciate it if you'd keep this between us until I have a chance to ask her some questions."

"Absolutely." Jimmy slapped Kevin on his arm. "Told you it was real. Hah! You owe me twenty bucks."

"Yeah, yeah, whatever," Kevin groused.

They didn't say anything else as they sped down South Las Vegas Boulevard. Jess felt that familiar tingle at the back of his neck. The sun was dawning. The sky turning brighter with every heartbeat. And they were still a couple of miles from his home. Worse? He had to knock her out again as she started coming to.

Jess rubbed his thumb and index finger together—a nervous twitch he'd developed as a gunfighter. It was the same feeling he had right now. One mistake. One delay.

He was history.

Only this time, he wasn't relying on his instincts and skills to survive. He was relying on theirs. . . .

The first rays were cresting just as they pulled up to the black wrought iron gates that protected his driveway. Jess slinked down in the seat as he used his iPhone app to open them. He also signaled for the garage doors.

Come on . . . let's go. . . .

His skin was already burning something fierce. It wouldn't be long before he'd be dead.

Kevin shot them through the gates before they'd finished opening and across his long driveway. Too long, he realized as Kevin hauled ass down it and they still weren't under cover. Why the hell had he bought a house with a two-mile driveway? Okay, slight exaggeration, but damn. It seemed like forever before they were inside the garage.

Jess breathed a long sigh of relief, and he leaned back in his seat. "That's about as close to bacon as I want to come for a while."

Without commenting on that, Jimmy came around to open his door and let him out. "You need any help with her?"

He shook his head. "Nah, I got it. Thanks, though."

Jess had just pulled her from the car and was heading to the back door when Kevin blocked his path. The Squire pulled out a pair of cuffs. "You need these?"

That actually made him laugh. "Think I can handle a little filly without them." Then again, given the whipping she'd put on him earlier, he might want to rethink that.

Pride goeth before a fall. . . .

Kevin returned them to the pouch on his belt. "All right. We'll see you later."

Jess inclined his head to them before he carried her into the house.

He hesitated inside the door. Now what to do with her? He hadn't thought this far ahead, and while he should have done it in the car, he'd been a little preoccupied with thoughts bursting into flames.

His best bet would be to take her into the basement with him. There was plenty of room down there to keep her locked up and away from anyone who might think about releasing her before he wanted her set loose.

Or worse, her hurting Andy while she was trying to escape.

That definitely wouldn't do.

All right. Back to the original plan. He'd hold her downstairs in his domain.

He carried her to the hidden elevator and into what Andy called his six-thousand-square-foot dungeon. It hadn't been all that easy to find a house in Vegas with a basement, especially one this size as well as a home that also had a stable for his horses. When Andy first told him about this place, Jess had thought he was joking.

Andy wasn't. The house was actually sixty-five thousand square feet. Seventy-two thousand under the roofline.

It was amazing what a man would do for his horses.

Hell, he'd lived in smaller towns. But all things said

and done, the house was perfect for him, since it allowed him to stay downstairs undisturbed. Down here, he wasn't locked in by the daylight. He could live an almost normal subterranean life.

The house had a total of eighteen bedroom suites, with three of them being in the basement. He took her to the one closest to his room and laid her down on the bed. He started to walk away, but something about her held him by her side. She looked so fragile like this. However, the painful throbbing in his jaw where she'd slugged him said she was anything but.

What had made a little thing like her hunt them so viciously?

The Daimons must have lied to her. They did that a lot. Countless humans had been used as their tools over the centuries. The Daimons promised them eternal life, and in the end, they murdered the humans when they were done with them.

But her anger had run deeper than that. She'd fought like she had a personal grudge.

He sighed as he thought about the last time he'd seen her parents. That had been one screwed-up night. To this day, he could still see the blood splatters that had covered the room. The blood that had covered him . . .

There had been no sign of Abby in the house, and he'd definitely looked for her. He'd always hoped she was at a friend's.

The most disturbing thought was that she'd been there.

That she'd seen them die. That thought made him sick to his stomach. No child should witness the horrors of that night. Just like he wished Artemis had spared him the sight of what happened after he'd been killed.

Some memories weren't worth keeping.

And when the police had been unable to locate her, they'd all assumed her dead.

Yet here she was . . .

Grown up and kicking ass.

Frowning, he ran his hand down the side of her cheek. She had the softest skin he'd ever felt. Smooth. Inviting. Warm. He'd always loved the way a woman's flesh felt under his fingers. There was nothing more succulent.

Her features were exotic and intriguing. So different from Laura's, and at the same time, he could see enough of Laura there that it tugged at his heart. Laura had been both a haven and a hell for him. Around her, he'd felt connected to the past, and that connection had stung as deep as it'd comforted. He'd tried to let her go, but he couldn't sever the tie.

Now he wished he had.

Maybe then Abigail would have had a normal life. A woman her age ought to be out with her friends, having fun and enjoying her youth. Not coming after Dark-Hunters. Definitely not killing them.

A smile tugged at the edges of his lips at her ponytail. He didn't know why, but that reminded him of her as a kid. She'd had a lot of spunk even then. And it was weird to be so attracted to her now, having been there when she was born. He tried not to think about that whenever he was with a woman. On a level he didn't want to acknowledge, it bothered him. He was old enough to be their great-great-great granddaddy.

But he wasn't altruistic enough to be celibate either. There was only so much a man could do. Especially since they didn't know how old he was. To them, he was another mid-twenty-year-old guy they met in a bar and took home.

However, Abigail knew.

And she hated him for it.

He turned her face toward him. Her eyes opened just a slit, and when he saw them . . .

He pulled back.

What the hell? His heart pounding, he gently lifted one lid. Sure enough, her eyes were red with yellow threads running through them.

She wasn't human after all.

At least not fully.

Oh yeah, this was bad. *Real* bad. Was she the enemy from the west that Ren had been talking about? Prophecy and Oracle warnings never made much sense to him. Trying to unravel them was enough to give even the stoutest mind a nine-day migraine.

And he was too tired right now to think it through. He needed some sleep before he dealt with this. Or at least a break . . .

He covered her with a blanket, then made sure that

she had no way out of this room until he was ready for her leave.

At the door, he lowered the lights so that she'd be able to see the room when she came to, but not so bright that they'd disturb her.

He glanced back at her, and his breath caught in his throat. With this light and with her head tilted, she looked so much like her mother that it temporarily stunned him and took him back in time.

He saw Matilda lying on the bank of the stream where she'd taken him for a picnic not long after their engagement. The sun had been so warm that she'd fallen asleep while he read one of her favorite dime novels out loud to her. Her serene beauty had enchanted him and he'd spent hours watching her, praying for that afternoon not to end.

I love you, William.

He could still hear her voice. See her beautiful smile. Clearing his throat of the sudden lump, he shook his head to clear it, too.

Abigail wasn't Matilda.

But as she lay there without the hatred shooting out of her eyes at him, she was every bit as beautiful, and it stirred emotions inside him that he'd sworn he buried.

Not wanting to think about that, he went to his room and pulled off his coat and weapons. While he undressed for bed, his thoughts sped around his head as he tried to figure out what had happened to her.

Where she'd been all this time.

I should have checked her for an ID. Yeah, no duh. That would have given him her address and let him know if she was still a Yager or if she'd married.

Feeling like a complete dolt, he went back to see if he could locate one.

He pushed open the door and froze.

The bed was completely empty, and she was nowhere in sight.

5

Abigail came awake with a jerk. The last thing she remembered was being strangled by her worst enemy. Pain hit her hard as she came to terms with what had happened.

I failed. . . .

After all these years, she'd finally found the man who'd ruined her life and killed her parents. And he'd overpowered her with an ease that sickened her. She'd risked everything and even allowed her body to be used as an experiment. Still, it hadn't been enough.

I hate you, Sundown Brady. You rotten bastard!

For a moment, she feared she might have died. But as she focused on the opulent room she was in, she realized she was alive.

And it was *o-p-u-l-e-n-t*.

The bed she lay on was an ornately carved California king with a dark blue silk duvet that was so light, it felt like moving air. The furniture was the kind of high-end quality that looked like an antique, but wasn't. There didn't appear to be any windows, yet the ten-foot ceiling seemed too high to be a basement. And the French tray above her had a beautiful mural painted inside it of a lush forest scene with gilded deer.

I've died and gone to a palace. . . .

That was what it seemed like. The room she was in was bigger than her entire house.

Biting her lip in trepidation, she slid off the bed and wandered around. Her first stop was the door that someone had locked. Not that she was surprised. Far from it. She'd have only been shocked had it opened.

Abigail closed her eyes and tried to use her newfound powers to feel what was around her.

Nothing showed. Which meant nothing. She was still too new to her powers to fully command them.

"You were right, Hannah," she whispered. "I should have honed them better before I took off after Brady." But from the moment Jonah told her he had the updated dossier that told them where Sundown was patrolling, she'd been impatient.

Now she was paying for that stupidity.

Where am I? She had no clue to anything. While the room was lush, it didn't have much in it other than the bed and a dresser and armoire along with two chairs and a coffee table. There was no phone, computer, or clock.

Had Sundown kidnapped her? It was the most likely scenario since she doubted she'd been abducted by a prince, and that made her heart rate speed up. Why would he do that and not kill her?

Unless he wanted to torture her . . .

Yeah, that would be more his speed. Dark-Hunters were said to be vicious killers who lived to hear their prey beg for mercy while they died. Though to be honest, this didn't look like a torture chamber. It looked like a palace. The kind of place Jonah would love . . .

And then she felt sick as her thoughts turned to Perry and Jonah, who'd been with her when she attacked Sundown. No doubt they were both dead. Tears choked her at the thought of their loss. They'd been good friends to her for many years. Better than she deserved some days. She could barely remember a time when they hadn't been part of her life.

Now they were dead because of Sundown, too. Damn him!

She cursed as she ran through their last few minutes together. Jonah was the one who'd first identified Sundown on the street. She'd wanted to go after him immediately, but Perry had come up with the idea to get him down to the drain so that they could ambush him and keep their actions out of sight of any passersby or police.

Why hadn't it worked? Her powers should have been enough to defeat him. It was like something else had shielded him from her attacks.

Frustration welled up inside her until she sensed someone approaching her room. She quickly returned to the door and glanced about for something she could use as a weapon. There really wasn't anything unless she yanked a picture off the wall, and those were so large and unwieldy, they wouldn't do her any good. Not to mention, they were actual paintings and didn't have a glass front for her to shatter and use. He didn't even have a lamp in here to bash him over the head with. The light came from overhead cans that were on a dimmer switch. She'd turn the light off completely, but that wouldn't help. His eyesight would be much better in the dark than hers.

It didn't matter. She'd beat him down by hand if she had to. He would not defeat her this time.

She pressed herself back against the wall as the door slowly opened.

. . .

Jess *paused as* he saw the empty bed. Having survived numerous ambushes in his human life, he knew she'd be nearby, waiting to jump him.

And not in a way a man wanted an attractive woman to jump him.

Since she wasn't in his line of sight, she must be behind the door. That thought had barely finished before she kicked it into him with everything she had, which was a lot for a little thing. The door hit him hard and slammed against his arm and face. Oh yeah, that was going to leave a mark.

Stunned, he staggered back.

That was a mistake. She came around the door with a feral growl and launched herself at him. Damn, it was like trying to fight off a mountain lion. Come to think of it, he'd rather fight a mountain lion.

Those, he could shoot.

"Stop!" he snarled, trying to get her off him as she pounded him with her fists.

"Not until you're dead!"

He hissed as she bit his hand. "Trust me, you don't want me to die."

She elbowed him hard in the stomach. "Why not?"

Jess tried to get a grip on her, but she twisted out of his hold and kicked him hard in the leg. He put some distance between them in the hallway. "You're locked in my soundproof basement, where no one will ever be able to hear you scream—and they won't dare come down here to check on me, since they're not allowed." Definitely not true—he always had a hard time keeping Andy out of his hair, but she didn't need to know that. "They'll just think I'm coming and going on my own. You got about a day's worth of food in the pantry down here. After that, hope you don't mind eating rotting Dark-Hunter carcass, 'cause, babe, that's all you're going to have."

Abigail paused at his words. She would call him a liar, but something in his eyes told her he was being honest. Besides, it made sense from what she knew about Dark-Hunters and their habits. She'd been told by her Apollite brethren that their Squires lived in fear of them and that the Squires interacted with the Dark-Hunters they served only when they had to. Some of them had even welcomed death at Apollite hands to be free of their Dark-Hunter masters. "I could break down the door."

He scoffed at her bravado. "This was designed as a fall-out shelter with ten-foot-thick steel walls. Unless you're packing some heavy artillery in your foundation garments, sweetie, it ain't gonna happen. Ain't no cell service down here or anything else. It's like a tomb, which it will be if you kill me. But that's up to you."

She wanted to tear his throat out. Unfortunately, even though she ached to kill him, her self-preservation kicked in. Last thing she wanted was to die . . . at least before he did. "Why did you bring me here?"

"Why are you killing Dark-Hunters?" he countered.

Stepping back, she raked a repugnant sneer over him. At least as much of one as she could, given his wardrobe change. Dressed in a pair of red flannel Psycho Bunny pajama bottoms that added a sense of humor and whimsy to his I'll-rip-your-throat-out tough guy aura, and a gray T-shirt, he looked . . .

Normal. The only thing lethal about him now was his giant size and those dark eyes that promised her death.

She swallowed before she answered. "Why do you think?"

"Other than the fact that you're as loco as a three-tailed cat in a rocking chair factory, I'm as clueless as a newborn colt."

Abigail's stomach churned at his words. "Oh I forgot. You think it's all right to kill innocent Apollites and humans and prey on them. Well, I have news for you, buster. We're not taking it anymore. Your days of killing us are over, and we're hunting *you* now."

Frowning, he snapped his head back with a baffled expression. "Come again?"

"Are you deaf?"

"No, ma'am. But I know you didn't just accuse *me* of killing the very things I protect."

His denial shot a fresh bomb of rage through her. Grinding her teeth, she lunged at him.

Jess caught her against his chest. She stomped his instep. Cursing, he bent over and stumbled back. Big mistake. She slammed her hands across his ears. Pain splintered his skull. She would have kneed him in the face had he not put a little more distance between them.

Sick of being beat on, he cursed himself for declining the handcuffs.

His only course of action was to wrap himself around her and brace her flat against the wall so that she couldn't continue to hurt him. "Stop fighting," he snarled in her ear.

"No! You took everything from me, and I'm going to kill you for it."

That only confused him more. "What are you talking about?"

"You murdered my parents. You bastard!"

For a few heartbeats, he couldn't breathe as he flashed back to his life as a human. Change out the word *parents* with *father* and make her a man, and he remembered the day when someone else had leveled that accusation. After it was said, the man drew his gun and shot him.

The bullet had gone into his shoulder. Acting on pure instinct honed by countless gunfights, Jess had pulled his own Colt out and returned the favor. Only his bullet went straight through the man's head. It wasn't until Jess checked him that he realized that man was a sixteen-year-old boy who'd stared up at him in agony while the light drained out of his eyes. The father he'd mentioned had been a card-sharp who'd tried to gun Jess down outside a saloon a few weeks before that. Stupid fool had pulled a derringer on him. Jess had disarmed him, and when the gambler went to stab him, he'd shot him at point-blank range.

Justified.

But the kid's death . . .

That was one of dozens of such memories he wished to God he could purge out of his mind.

"I haven't killed a human being in over a hundred and forty years, and I damned sure didn't kill your parents."

She shrieked at him, then thrashed about with enough force to free herself from his hold. "You don't even re-member? You worthless, rotten—"

He caught her hand before she slapped him. "Honey, I haven't shot a human since I was one. Only piece of loco around here would be you."

She shoved him back and tried to kick him. "I saw you with my own eyes. You gunned them down in cold blood."

That set fire to his temper. He might have been a lot of things, but that . . . that . . . "Oh, like hell. I have *never* in my life killed *anyone* in cold blood."

She curled her lip. "Right . . . You're a hired killer. It's all you've ever known. You've never cared who and what you put down so long as you got paid for it."

"*Was*"—he stressed the word—"and those I killed, I did so in a fair duel. They had as much a chance of living as I did." While he was the first to admit he'd been a cold-blooded criminal, unlike Bart, he'd had lines he wouldn't cross. Things no amount of money could make him do. "I swear to God that I did *not* kill your parents."

Abigail hesitated. He meant what he was saying. She could see it in his eyes and hear it in his indignant tone. "How could you forget that night? I heard you fighting with my father. You left and then came back and broke into our house."

He held his hands up to emphasize his point. "I have never broken into a house. A bank, most definitely. A train a time or two to rob payrolls, but *never* someone's home."

"You're lying."

He shook his head. "I don't lie. I've got no need to."

"Bullshit. I was there. I *saw* you."

"And I'm telling you right now that I wasn't. On the soul of my mother, I didn't kill them. And while I fought with your dad, I never once struck him or even insulted him." Then to her utmost shock, he went to a cabinet a little farther down the hallway and opened a drawer that had a safe with a hand scanner. He put his palm on top and opened the safe. Inside was a handgun and KA-BAR. He pulled the knife out.

Her heart pounded as she realized he was going to stab her. She braced herself for the fight.

It didn't come.

Instead, he flipped the KA-BAR around so that the blade faced his body and the hilt was toward her. "If you really, truly think I killed your parents, have your vengeance." He placed the knife in her hand.

Completely caught off guard, she stared at him with the weight of the knife heavy in her palm. *You've waited your whole life for this. Cut his throat.* So what if she died afterward? She'd have her vengeance.

She wanted his life with a passion that was undeniable. It was a primal need that screamed out for his blood. But something in her gut told her to wait.

And in that instant, she had another memory. Sundown sitting at her kitchen table, coloring with her. "Dang, Laura, you have a real artist here. I've never seen a better rendition of Scooby-Doo."

Abigail had beamed with happiness while her mother brought them both a cup of hot chocolate. When her mother turned her back, Jess had added his marshmallows to Abigail's cup because they were her favorite. He'd winked at her and then held his finger to his lips and cut his eyes to her mother's back to tell her to be quiet about it so that neither of them would get in trouble for it. She couldn't count the times he'd done something sweet like that for her.

Sundown had been their friend.

No, her rationale countered. He'd killed them. She'd seen his face in the mirror of her room. He didn't know how to be anyone's friend. He was treacherous to his core, and if he was offering her a knife . . .

"What kind of trick is this?"

He didn't back down or blink. He stood right in front of her, looking at her through his thick lashes. His presence was terrifying and overwhelming as a tic beat a fierce rhythm in his jaw. "No trick. Believe me, I understand that soul-deep need to kill the person who took what you loved away from you. I know for a fact that I'm innocent, but I won't fault you for your belief, wrong though it is." He dropped his arms to his sides. "You want to kill me, go for it. I won't stop you. But know that when you do, you'll be spilling innocent blood yourself. May God have mercy on your soul."

Growling in anger, she moved to slice his jugular, expecting him to catch her hand and use the knife on her.

He didn't.

"I *will* kill you," she said between clenched teeth. She *could* behead him. She had no doubts.

He continued to stare down at her. "Do it."

Determined, she pressed the blade so close to his throat that it drew a bead of blood onto the dark carbon steel. Still, he didn't budge. He merely stood patiently for her to end his life.

"What are you waiting for?" His words sounded like a taunt.

She ground her teeth in fury at herself. "I'm not you. I can't kill someone who's defenseless."

"Nice to know the other Dark-Hunters you murdered had a fighting chance."

She pulled the blade away from his throat. "Oh, spare me, you blood-sucking bastard. I know exactly how you prey on people and then blame the Apollites for it."

He scowled at her. "Wait, wait, wait. I'm confused. First I'm a murderer, and now I'm guilty of preying on all humanity. Woman, who have you been talking to? They done got your head screwed on backwards and then some. We're not the bad guys in all this. The Daimons are the ones killing humans, not us."

What in the world was he talking about now? "Daimons? What's a Daimon?"

He choked. "You work with Apollites and you've never heard the term?"

"No. Are they some kind of demon?"

Sundown folded his arms over his chest as he gave her a disbelieving grimace. "Daimons are the Apollites who live past their twenty-seventh birthdays."

Was he on something? Surely, he knew the history of her adoptive people even better than she did. "Apollites can't do that. It's impossible."

"Uh, yeah, they can. I know, 'cause they're what we hunt. Every night. Without fail."

She rolled her eyes at his lunacy. "You are such a liar."

"Why would I lie?"

"Because you're one of the ones who kills humans and then blames it on the Apollites," she repeated, stressing the words so that even he could understand them. "You use them as your scapegoats, and this must be the lie you tell to justify it."

"And that makes sense in what alternate universe? Really? Why would we blame something neither humanity nor Apollites know exists to cover up these supposed crimes we commit? Hell, it'd make more sense to blame little green men. Who told you this malarkey?"

Before she could answer, something bright flashed to her left.

Lifting her hand to shield her eyes, she cringed in pain. It was absolutely blinding.

When the light faded, there was another man in the hallway with them. One with an evil sneer, who looked like he'd been bred for no other purpose than to kill. Tall with jet black hair and icy blue eyes, he was gorgeous. Dressed in a blue shirt and jeans, he had a small goatee. He glanced at her, then locked gazes with Sundown, who seemed to know him. "Do I have to kill her for seeing me pop in?"

Sundown shook his head. "She already knows about us."

The unknown man tsked at him. "Risky, boy. Acheron finds out you've been spilling your guts to civs, he'll have your ass."

Sundown ran his thumb down the line of his jaw. He held an expression that said he was oddly amused. "It's not what you think, Z. Turn on those god powers and use them. I am not responsible for her knowledge of nothing."

Z scoffed. "Impressively screwed-up syntax there, Cowboy. Glad I could follow it . . . Sort of. As for the powers, don't really have time to scan her and I really don't give a shit. Rather kill her and save myself the expended energy for something I might actually enjoy . . . like picking my nose."

Ew. Someone was socially awkward. She wasn't sure at this point if she liked Z or not. He was rather off-putting.

"So why are you here?" Sundown asked.

"Got a huge problem."

Jess didn't like the sound of that at all. He slid his gaze to Abigail. "I already got one of those. Don't need another right now, little buddy."

Zarek laughed evilly at his term of endearment. Only Jess could call the Roman ex-slave that and live. The one thing about Zarek, it didn't take much to motivate him to murder. He hated all people and wanted nothing to do with the world at large. That being said, the two of them went way back, and but for Jess, Zarek would be dead now and not married to a Greek goddess.

It was a debt neither of them spoke about. Ever. However, Zarek wasn't the kind of man to forget it either. They had an unspoken bond of friendship that ran as deep as a blood tie.

Zarek sobered. "Well, that's just too bad, Hoss. 'Cause I'm here to drop this one right in your lap. Someone killed your buddy tonight."

His heart sank at the news. "Ren?"

"Other friend."

Jess scowled. Like Z, he tended to shy away from most folks. His past didn't exactly lend itself to trust. "I only have you and him. So I'm pulling a little blank here on who you might be referring to."

Zarek slapped him across the back. "Think, bud. Fierce immortal who likes to gamble in Sin's casino, wear tacky shirts and watch anime."

Jess sucked his breath in sharply as he understood. "Old Bear?"

"Give that boy a biscuit." Zarek's tone dripped with sarcasm. "He finally got it."

Jess couldn't believe what Z was saying. It wasn't possible. Old Bear was one of the four Guardians and powerful beyond belief. "How?"

"Some fool beheaded him around one A.M."

The woman frowned at them. "Are you talking about the Native American Dark-Hunter stationed here?"

A bad feeling went through Jess as he met her gaze. Surely she wouldn't have been so stupid as to . . .

"Say you didn't."

"Kill him?" she asked. "Fine. I didn't . . . but I did."

Oh yeah, this was bad. The kind of bad they made horror movies out of. In fact, he'd rather be naked in a zombie flick with no ammo or shelter, coated in brain matter and wearing a sign that said COME GET ME, than face what they were going to have to face now. "Honey, let me give you a quick lesson. Just 'cause someone's a few centuries old and fanged, doesn't make them a Dark-Hunter."

Zarek concurred. "And some of those fanged immortals we actually need. Old Bear happened to be one of them."

She rolled her eyes dismissively. "Pah-lease."

Jess ignored her. There was no need in arguing with her right now. They had much bigger problems than her pigheadedness. "How bad is it?" he asked Zarek.

"Well, he was the Guardian for the West Lands, where his people had banished some of the worst of their supernatural predators. Now that he's dead, the balance has shifted and those he guarded can be set free."

Jess hated to even ask the next question. But unfortunately, he had to. "And they are?"

When he answered, Z's tone was as dry as the desert. "Nothing too major. A couple of plagues. Some scary weather anomalies. . . . oh, and my personal fave—" He paused for effect, which told Jess how bad it was going to be. "—the Grizzly Spirit."

Oh yeah, that was quite a stellar lineup from hell. Literally. "You're kidding me, right?"

Zarek shook his head. "I don't have a sense of humor, you know that. The Dark Guardians will be moving after Choo Co La Tah now, since he's the North Guardian. If they can take him down, they can free the ones he guards, too."

And set loose an apocalyptic war that would make the Daimon leader, Stryker, look like a wuss. Yeah, that was just what they needed.

The woman set her arms on her hips in pique. "What are you people talking about?"

"Nothing important." Zarek raked a nasty glare over her. "Just the end of the world as we know it, and for the record, I don't feel fine. Neither will you when it all comes slamming down on your head."

Jess dragged Zarek's attention back to the more important matter. Saving the world from those who would put a major hurt on it. "Where's Choo Co La Tah now?"

"Ren was with him at the time Old Bear died. Now he's guarding him. When the sun goes down, Ren'll need help moving Choo Co La Tah to the Valley of Fire."

Now, that made no sense. "Why?"

Zarek shrugged. "You'll have to ask Ren yourself. I didn't inquire and no one elaborated. All I know is it's something to do with a prophecy from their pantheon, and for that reason, I can't go with you. Apparently the area you have to go into is protected from any god or demigod born outside their pantheon. I'm only here as a messenger. Ash would have come for this, but his wife's in labor."

"Why'd he call you?"

Zarek gave him a droll stare. "My charming personality."

Jess snorted in derision.

"Fine, asshole. I'm sure it had to do with the fact that he figured you wouldn't shoot me."

That was a good bet, and Ash had no doubt refrained from calling Andy because the boy was too high-strung to deal with news like this. Andy would still be in his room, freaking out over the end of the world and trying to get laid before it occurred. "Why didn't he call me himself?" For some reason, Ash's calls came through even down here. That man had the best cell service ever.

"He tried. You didn't answer your phone. And since he's a little busy with his wife threatening to castrate him over her labor pains, he sent me in."

Now, *that,* Jess would have paid money to hear. He couldn't imagine anyone threatening Ash.

He slid his gaze back to Abigail, who'd been nothing but trouble since the moment he followed her into the drain. The call must have come in when they'd been fighting.

Zarek walked over to her. "And thank you, Miss Priss, for making this easy on us." He snapped his fingers and a rope appeared on her hands, binding them together.

She shrieked in outrage until Zarek manifested a gag over her lips to stifle her insults.

"What are you doing?" Jess asked.

"Making it easy on *you.*"

Completely baffled, he frowned at Zarek's actions. "Making what easy on me?"

"Transporting her."

At this point, Z was starting to wear on his nerves. "Would you stop acting like a third-rate Oracle and spit everything out so that it makes sense." 'Cause right now, he had no idea why Zarek had her bound up like a Christmas goose, and he was too tired to keep chasing answers.

"Glad to. In order to set everything back to normal and stop the hell to come, Choo Co La Tah has to go to the Valley and offer up a sacrifice of the one who killed Old Bear." He passed a wry grin to the woman. "That'd be you, sweet cheeks."

6

Jess gaped while Abigail backed away at Zarek's dire words, but she couldn't go far. Zarek threw up his hand to hold her in the hallway next to them. Even before he'd married a goddess, Zarek had held some impressive telekinetic powers. Nowadays, they were downright sick.

He gave Zarek a disbelieving stare as he digested his orders to kill her. "You're telling me that Acheron, my boss, the really tall Atlantean pain in most of our asses, actually authorized the killing of a human?"

Zarek shrugged. "I can see your confusion. It is highly out of character for him. But since she's been killing off Hunters . . . I guess he figures it's tit for tat. Or maybe he's just having a really bad day."

"You're seriously not joking?"

Zarek let out an irritated growl. "Really? How many more times are you going to ask me that? I could be on a beach right now with my wife, son, and daughter, baking in the sun while they frolic and play. Am I? No. I'm here, and I want nothing more than to yank you around with bullshit 'cause this gets me off more than my wife running in a bikini."

Jess counted to ten before he let Z rile him. That was the thing about Zarek. The man had a short fuse, and Jess's wasn't all that far behind his. Not that he blamed Z for it. As bad as Jess's childhood had been, it was a picnic in paradise compared to what Z had suffered.

Still, those orders were so contrary to what they normally were that he couldn't wrap his head around it. Acheron profaned hurting humans in any way. Why would he be okay with it now?

That alone told him just how scary this whole thing was. Playtime was over.

Jess removed the gag from Abigail's lips. No need in making this worse on her. He expected her to shriek and curse. At the very least, head-butt him again and fight.

Instead, she was remarkably calm, given the fact she'd just heard Zarek call for her death. "You are not sacrificing me . . . to anything," she said between clenched teeth.

Zarek scoffed. "You started this, babe. The choice is simple. Either you die alone, nobly like a good sport, or the entire world dies with you, which I don't think they'd appreciate much. So put on your big-girl pants and own up to what you and your stupidity caused. It's *Joe Versus the Volcano* time."

He folded his arms over his chest. "But in the end, I don't give a shit what you do. With the exception of the cowboy there and my family, I hate people with a passion that makes your feelings for Jess look like a schoolgirl crush. Lovely thing about my current situation, I'm truly immortal. You annihilate humanity and the world . . . I'm still good. So whatever you decide, it won't affect me personally. I would say you're the one who'll have to live with the guilt. But either way, you're dead. Whatever. I delivered my message. My job here is done, and I need to get back to the one that I'm still not sure how I let them talk me into doing—which is even weirder and scarier than the Dark-Hunter gig." He turned his attention to Sundown. "Jess, call me if she wusses, and I'll make sure you survive the holocaust." He vanished.

"Thanks, Z," Jess called after him. "Always nice chatting with you."

Now what should he do? Really . . . it was the kind of thing that even *his* vast and varied experiences had never prepared him for. Yes, he'd dealt with Daimon outbreaks galore. A run-amok Daimon slayer up in Alaska who'd walked in daylight. But Daimons who were demons and could convert anyone they bit, and all-out death prophecy were a whole new territory for him.

Jess wasn't sure where to go with that.

Abigail's eyes were filled with a mixture of panic and suspicion. She did not appear happy. Not that he blamed her. He'd hate to be told he had to sacrifice himself to save the world. It would seriously muck up even a great day. And honestly, he wasn't sure he'd be any more inclined to do it than she was.

"He was lying." Her voice had a tiny tremble in it.

Wouldn't it be great if life were that easy? You got bad news, you called it a lie and everything was fixed. . . .

One could only hope.

Jess sighed in sympathy. "Unfortunately, Zarek doesn't lie. And as you saw, he doesn't pull punches either. He's as frank and tactless as the summer day is long." He cut the rope on her hands and let it fall to the floor. "You still going to fight me?"

She rubbed at her wrists. "Given what he said, I was thinking about running."

Well, at least she was honest. That, he could appreciate. He slid his knife into the back of his pants, waiting to see when she'd bolt.

Abigail stood there, unsure of what to think or do. Sundown watched her with a nonchalance she knew was misleading. His reflexes were as honed as any she'd ever encountered or fought. The fact that her demon-enhanced powers weren't enough to subdue him said it all. None of the others she'd killed, including Old Bear, had stood toe to toe with her for very long.

Never mind knocking her out and kidnapping her.

In fact, Old Bear had barely put up a fight. Why, if he was so important, hadn't he fought harder?

Why hadn't she double-checked his identity? How could Jonah have made such a bad mistake?

And before she could decide on an action, the ground beneath them shook. The force of it was so great that it knocked both of them off their feet.

Abigail hit the floor with enough impact to steal her breath and bruise her elbow. Gah, that hurt. She definitely could have done without that on top of all the other delights this day had held.

Pushing herself up, she met Sundown's gaze from across the hall. "Was that an earthquake?" While rare in Vegas, they did happen. But usually they were minor. This one had felt much, much larger.

"I don't know." He got up and went into a room across the hall.

You should run for it while he's distracted.

The only problem was, she didn't know where to run to. Since there were no obvious windows or stairs, she'd have to search for an exit. That would probably be obvious to Sundown, who'd then stop her.

And that thought died as he turned on the TV and she heard the news.

It wasn't an earthquake.

The ground outside the city was bubbling and opening up, and scorpions were flooding out of the crevices like some bad horror movie as they overran everything. Thousands and thousands of them.

How could there be so many? She'd never seen more than a handful in her entire life. Honestly, it looked like the earth was vomiting arthropods.

She shivered in revulsion.

Sundown let out an audible breath. "Now, there's something you never think about seeing, huh? Zarek definitely wasn't exaggerating about the plagues he mentioned. Why couldn't it be locusts like other people have? No. Leave it to Old Bear to do something different."

She shook her head in denial. "I didn't do this." It wasn't possible. There had to be another explanation as to why this was happening. One that didn't point the finger at her.

Maybe the scorpions were bored?

Or the Scorpion King was ticked off that no one had built a casino for him? At this point, she was willing to grasp any straw that didn't tell her to kill herself to save the world.

"Hon, you're the one who said you killed Old Bear. I tried to deny it, but you corrected me. And if you did cut his head off, you *did* do this. Accept it." He flipped the channel to another view of the scorpions swarming over a road downtown toward people who were screaming and running to get away from them. "Welcome to the apocalypse. Ain't she pretty?"

Abigail felt sick as more tremors shook the ground under them. She braced herself against the wall to keep from being thrown off her feet again. "He looked like a Dark-Hunter," she insisted. "He didn't correct me when I called him one."

Sundown arched a brow at her. "He had fangs. So what? Plenty of things not a Dark-Hunter have fangs, including Hollywood actors and kids playing vampire. You should have checked his membership card before you attacked. Good grief, what if you'd run across a Masquerade group? Would you have slaughtered a bunch of innocent kids?"

"Of course not. I'm telling you, Jonah did do recon on him. He did recon on all our targets. The man I killed tonight was a Dark-Hunter. Jonah would never have authorized hunting and terminating someone else."

Sundown gestured to the TV with the remote in his hand. "Obviously somebody had bogus information. Or he just plain lied."

She started to respond when all of a sudden, the floor near her buckled. She'd no more righted herself than dozens of scorpions swarmed out, scattering across the floor as they'd done in the desert. And worse, these were the deadliest ones. Bark scorpions. Whereas a sting from a single one *might* not kill her, to be stung by this many would without fail. The neurotoxins in their stinger were known to be fatal.

And she was allergic to them.

Shrieking, she tried to get away, but the floor shifted even more, pitching her toward them. Frozen in terror, she couldn't move as she watched them wide-eyed.

I'm going to die. . . .

She had no doubt. They were going to overrun her and sting her all at once.

Everything seemed to slow down as they advanced on her with a swiftness that was indescribable. Those little bodies twisted as they moved their legs faster and faster, their tails arched and thrusting for a strike. . . . She couldn't breathe as the sound of their scuttling feet and snapping pinchers echoed in her ears.

Her entire body cringed in expectation of the pain. They were on her.

Just as they swarmed her feet, she was yanked off the floor and shaken until the scorpions fell away. Once they were clear, she was thrown over a well-muscled shoulder and carried from the room as if she were a rag doll.

Sundown slammed the door shut behind him and set her back on her feet. Unable to speak, she flicked the one remaining scorpion on her boot to the ground and then stomped it until it stopped moving.

Every millimeter of skin on her body crawled in revulsion. It was like they were on her again.

But her relief was very short lived. The scorpions were now tearing through the door.

She gaped in disbelief of their power and persistence. What were they going to do? "How are they doing that?"

"I ain't gonna ask them right now. Don't really rate on my importance scale." Sundown sprinted to a locked cabinet. He entered a code on the electronic lock, then opened the doors. It was a gun case with enough weaponry inside to arm a small nation.

Sundown grabbed a pump-action shotgun and a bunch of shells, which he put into his pockets. She ran toward him as the scorpions began flooding into the bedroom from the space they'd made under the door.

He slammed the cabinet doors shut and then pulled her behind him before she could arm herself. With a feral gleam in his eyes that was more frightening than the scorpions, he opened fire on them.

They blew back in every direction like a clawing cloud.

But it didn't stop them. They kept coming, and in greater numbers.

Desperate, Abigail looked at the cabinet. "You have a flamethrower in there?"

"Yeah. Bad news, though—it'd burn down the house if we used it, and that wouldn't do us any good."

There was that. However, she'd rather be burned alive than stung by that number of scorpions. "What are we going to do now?"

"Find a steam roller?"

If only . . .

"You're not funny." Growling, Abigail tried to think of a real solution. The first thing she'd learned as a kid when they found a scorpion in her bed was that scorpions didn't react to insecticide, and even if they did, Sundown would have had to have gallons of it to stop them. The only way she knew to kill them was to squash them.

Yeah . . . her feet weren't big enough to even make a dent in that horde. She'd be overrun and dead in a matter of seconds.

"What we need here, folks, is a really big chicken."

She scowled at his bizarre comment and the fact that his drawl had actually gotten deeper as he spoke. "What are you? Hungry? Now?"

He laughed at her irritation. "Nah. They love to hunt and kill scorpions. Damn shame I don't have a flock or two million of them right about now. Who knew? I just hope those damn things aren't chowing down on my Squire."

Sundown pulled her through a doorway and into another bedroom. He held the gun in one hand as he slammed the door shut and locked it.

They could hear the scorpions on the other side, scurrying about. The sound made her cringe. It wouldn't take them long to breach this door, too.

"We're dead, aren't we?"

Jess wanted to deny it, but right now, he couldn't think of anything else to escape. They were out of rooms to run to, and the scorpions were chewing his door down. Not that it mattered in his case. He couldn't die from their stings.

But the woman could.

And even without death, those sons of bitches would hurt. Not exactly something he was craving.

He glanced around the room, then grinned as an idea hit him. "Get on the bed."

She stiffened indignantly. "Excuse me?"

Jess grinned at the direction her thoughts had gone. Normally he wouldn't mind, but right now, sex was the last thing either of them should think about. "We need height. Get on the bed." He didn't wait for her. He launched himself at it. He loaded more shells into his gun, then fired up at the ceiling.

"What are you doing?"

He didn't respond as he reversed the gun and used the stock to widen the hole by slamming it against the plaster and knocking it down. *Don't let the damn thing go off by accident.* If it did in this position, it'd take out a piece of his anatomy that he sure would miss.

Abigail let out a squeak before she sidled up against him. She actually wedged herself between him and the wall. Any other time, he'd appreciate having those curves pressed so close against his body.

But right now . . .

"They're swarming in."

He glanced over his shoulder to confirm her words. "All right. I think there's enough room that I can lift you up into the floor above."

Sundown was trying to save her? Abigail was stunned by his offer. Especially since she'd been trying to kill him just a short time ago. Before she could respond, he dropped the gun, then braced his hands on her hips and lifted her up with an ease that was startling. She reached for the hole he'd made and pulled herself up through it.

It wasn't easy, but she finally wiggled all the way through the tight opening.

Laughing in triumph, she started for the front door, which was only a few feet away. She'd barely gone a step when she heard Sundown firing at the scorpions again.

He was still trapped.

Leave him. He didn't deserve anything better than to be stung until his head exploded. Every part of her wanted to hear him screaming in pain.

He saved your life just now.

So what? That didn't undo her parents' deaths.

But what if he wasn't lying? What if someone else had

really killed them? If he died, she might not ever find out the truth.

The thought made her pause. If Sundown hadn't killed them, who did?

And why?

There's more to all of this. She could feel it with every heightened instinct she possessed.

I've never been an unreasonable person. She prided herself on that fact. When others panicked and freaked, she was always calm and rational. Methodical.

More gunshots sounded.

Unable to leave him to the scorpions until she knew more, she reversed course toward the hole in the floor. She knelt down so that she could see him below. Sure enough, the area around the bed was crawling with the arthropods. "Give me your hand."

Sundown looked up at her with a shocked expression that would have been comical if they weren't in such a bad situation.

She leaned down and held her hand out to him.

"Get back," he snapped.

"I can help you."

He grinned at her, flashing his fangs. "I'm a little wider than you are, sweetheart. I won't fit through that."

She started tearing at the floor to widen it.

Jess arched a brow as he realized what she was doing. Damned if she wasn't trying to help him. Who'd have thought? Amazed, he turned the gun around and started pounding at the ceiling on the other side with the stock again.

Within a few minutes, they had the hole bigger.

And the scorpions were already on the bed.

Jess kicked at them before he handed her the shotgun. "Back up and I'll jump."

She took the gun and vanished.

Cursing as a couple of the scorpions stung his leg, he launched himself at the ceiling. He caught it barely and hung above the bed that was now completely swimming in those nasty little buggers. He kicked his legs until he was sure they were free of scorpions. His arms bulged as he pulled himself up, through the hole and onto the wooden floor. He made it, but his skin was stinging from the scrapes of wedging himself through. Not to mention his leg that was on fire from the scorpions.

Abigail was crouched by a wall, aiming the gun at him.

Jess ignored her as he moved to the bookshelf against the wall and slammed it down to cover the hole. Hopefully, that would delay them a bit longer.

Abigail cocked the gun.

Now, that amused him. "You can't kill me with a bullet, darling. You'll just piss me off."

"Maybe, but shooting you might be fun." She lowered the barrel to his groin. "And while I might not be able to kill you, I sure could ruin your social life."

He laughed at her conviction. "There's only one problem with that."

"Yeah?"

He indicated the shotgun with a jerk of his chin. "The gun's not loaded. I used the last of the ammo downstairs."

She opened the gun and cursed as she realized he wasn't lying. "Figures."

Yes, it did. He wouldn't have handed it to her otherwise. He hadn't been *that* stupid in a very long time. Still, he admired her gumption.

Jess took the gun back and made a mental note of where the sun was shining in his house and where it wasn't. *Man, I hope Andy remembered to lock the house down.* If not, she'd stand a good chance of escaping, and there would be nothing he could do until dark.

Unless he wanted to shoot her. He did still have a couple of shells in his pocket . . .

Another quake shook the house.

She gasped in alarm. "You think that's more of them?"

"Our luck? Probably."

"How do we stop them?"

He had no idea. Not this many of them. If he were Talon, he might could drop the temperature here to freeze them to death. But unlike the Celt's, his Dark-Hunter powers didn't include weather control.

No sooner had that thought gone through his mind, than the house went completely dark. As dark as a midnight sky from the days when he'd been human and out on the range. He hadn't seen anything like this in decades. Not since modern lights had dimmed the night skies.

"What's going on?"

He ignored her question as he peeked around the wall, toward a window. Thunder rolled like an angry growl. A moment later, snow started falling.

Jess gaped at the last thing he'd expected to see. Now, that was more startling than the scorpion invasion.

"It's snowing." In April. In Las Vegas . . .

Yeah, the world was definitely coming to an end.

Abigail didn't believe his words until she stepped past him to look outside. Sure enough, large clumps of snow fell from the sky. The contrast of the white against the black was absolutely beautiful.

And yet . . .

"I really did start the apocalypse," she breathed. There was no other explanation. Things like this didn't happen except in movies and end-of-the-world prophecies. "What have I done?"

Sundown rested the gun on his shoulder in a manner that smacked of his past. He looked like a rogue cowboy, locked and loaded and ready for the next round. All he needed was a hat, and he'd be the perfect cliché. But what really bothered her about it was how sexy that pose made him even in Psycho Bunny pajama bottoms.

I have lost my mind.

Surely the stress of the last few minutes had driven her insane. It had to. There was no other way she could see him as anything but a monster.

She swallowed. Her adoptive father had always told her that evil was beautiful and seductive. Otherwise, no one would ever fall for it. That was why Artemis had made the Dark-Hunters so sexy. It was how they lured their victims in before they slaughtered them.

Whatever she did, she couldn't let herself forget that.

Sundown shrugged. "Well, it appears to me that you have opened a big old can of worms. And according to what Z said, you're the only one who can close it."

She pressed her fingers against her temple to help relieve the ache that was starting right behind her left eye. "All I was trying to do was protect my people and family from *you*."

"I was never your threat."

Abigail started to argue, but she'd barely parted her lips before the floor beneath her feet literally opened up and sucked her down.

Oh, dear Lord, she was going to die!

7

Jess dropped his gun and launched himself at Abigail as she slid through the floor. At first, he was sure she'd fallen to her death right before his eyes. That thought hit him a lot harder than it should have. The pain was indescribable.

But somehow, against all odds, he felt

warmth in his palm and a weight on his arm that made his spirits soar with relief.

He'd caught her. . . .

Looking over the side of the hole, he saw her panicked face staring up at him, and that was the most beautiful thing he'd seen in over a century.

She was alive.

Abigail's heart thumped wildly as she swung in a precarious arc. The only thing that kept her from crashing onto the marble floor ten feet below was one hand.

And it belonged to her enemy.

"I gotcha." Sundown's grip tightened on her hand in a silent promise that he wouldn't let go.

She locked both her hands around his and hoped he wasn't holding a grudge against her for anything. "Please don't drop me."

He actually winked at her. "Not on your life." He pulled her up slowly, taking care not to scrape her against the jagged edges of the floor where pieces of wood waited to impale her.

In that moment, she could kiss him for his fast reflexes that had saved her life, and for the care he was taking to pull her up and not hurt her.

But her relief didn't last long. As soon as her head popped through the hole, something grabbed her leg from below and yanked her hard enough to take her back through it.

Sundown's eyes widened.

I'm going to die. She was sure of it as the pressure on her legs increased with a determination that said it wouldn't relent until she was a stain on the floor below.

Yet somehow Sundown maintained his firm grip on her hands. He pulled her up again.

Again, something jerked her down. She kicked her legs and struck nothing. Yet there was no denying that some invisible force had her by her ankles.

If only she could look down to see what it was. "What's going on?"

"I don't know. I don't see anything. I just wish whatever it is that it'd let go." His face turned bright red as he held on to her with a determination that said he really did care whether she lived or died.

Abigail blinked back tears from the pain of being the rope in a tug-of-war that would mean her life if Sundown lost.

He growled as the muscles in his arms bulged from the strain. She stared into his eyes, which were dark with conviction, and used those as her lifeline.

"Thank you," she whispered to him.

Inclining his head to her, Jess felt his grip slipping. Whatever had her was increasing its pressure to the point he knew it was only a matter of time before she fell from his hands.

He'd failed to keep his promise to her mother. The

last thing he wanted was to see her die, too. *I can't let go. . . .*

What choice did he have?

The answer came from somewhere deep inside him. A forgotten prayer his mother had taught him from the cradle to use whenever things were too hard and he wanted to give up.

Aike aniya trumuli gerou sunari. . . . Those words whispered through his mind. *I am White Buffalo and I will not be stopped.* Yeah, okay, so it sounded better in her language than in English. Still, it echoed and he felt an inner strength rising with every syllable as he continued silently chanting it. *Our people never met an enemy they couldn't defeat. Their blood flows inside of you,* penyo. *You are my pride and my gift to the Elders who watch over us. Listen to them when you're weak and they will help you. Always.* He heard his mother's voice as clearly as if she sat beside him.

He saw the fear in Abigail's eyes as she realized her hands were slipping.

"Aike aniya trumuli gerou sunari!"

Abigail gasped at his angry words and the bright flash of red that shone through his pupils an instant before he jerked her up through the floor so fast, she barely realized she'd moved. He gathered her in his arms and hugged her close, as if he was as thankful she was alive as she was.

Even though she hated him, she was too grateful to

shove him away. Instead, she reveled in the sensation of his hard body pressing against hers. She clung to him while she shook from relief and tried to squelch the fear that the invisible force would grab her again and take her back into the hole. Her blood rushed thick through her veins as she buried her face in his neck and inhaled the warm scent of his skin.

He'd saved her. She was alive.

In that moment, with all the endorphins coursing through her, she felt as if she could fly.

Jess couldn't move with her cradled against him as she breathed raggedly in his ear, sending chills down his arm. Every inch of her body was pressed against his. And deep inside, he felt something in him stir. Something he hadn't felt in a long time. Before he could rethink his intentions, he nuzzled her neck. A low moan escaped her lips. He started to pull away, but she cupped his head, stopping him.

Then she did the most unexpected thing of all.

She kissed him.

For a full minute, he couldn't breathe as he tasted her. Her lips were incredibly soft as she swept her tongue against his, teasing and warming him. He couldn't remember the last time a woman had kissed him with this much passion.

Abigail knew she shouldn't be doing this. In the back of her mind was the voice that tried to remind her that she hated him. And yet he'd saved her life. More than that, he felt like heaven. Never had she experienced anything like this.

Like she belonged.

There was no explaining it. It was something deep within that welcomed him even while her mind called her all kinds of stupid.

But before she could examine that thought further, the floor started rumbling again.

They pushed themselves to their feet and then away from the hole as some unseen beast from below began a fierce howl. It sounded like a pack of hungry coyotes. . . .

Backing them up, Sundown put himself between her and the hole. He retrieved his gun from the floor.

An instant later, six men and one woman shot up from the opening. With dark hair and eyes, they curled their lips in a purely canine fashion as they stalked toward the two of them.

Jess braced himself for the attack he knew was coming. He'd never much cared for shape-shifters, and these were going to be brutal. "C'mon, punks," he goaded. "You want to fight or sniff each other's crotches?"

The leader ran at him. With a bright flash of yellow, he turned from a man into a coyote. Jess reversed his shotgun so that he was holding it by the barrel. Using the stock like a bat, he knocked the coyote into the wall, where it hit with a heavy thud.

The others changed form and came at him full force.

"Run!" he said over his shoulder to Abigail.

She didn't listen. Rather, she ripped the tacky antlers off the wall that Andy had put there as a sick joke—that boy had never been right in the head—and held them to defend against their attackers.

It was a bold move, and he seriously hoped those antlers broke during the fight so he'd never have to look at them again.

Even though Jess had a feeling he was wasting his time, he went ahead and loaded his gun with the shells in his pocket, then opened fire on the coyotes. The first one he shot yelped, skidded sideways, rebounded off the wall, then kept coming.

Yeah, all it did was piss the coyote off and give him some target practice. But what the hell? He kept shooting until he was empty again while he and Abigail backed down the hallway.

Until she stopped moving.

He slammed up against her.

"You're about to be in daylight."

He glanced over his shoulder to see the truth of that. Had she not stood her ground, he'd have been in some serious pain right about now. "Much obliged." With no choice and with their retreat cut off, he took a step forward to fight.

The coyotes launched themselves at the two of them.

Jess moved to hit one, but they never made contact.

The coyotes slammed into an invisible wall that magically appeared around him and Abigail. Yelping, the coyotes tried to attack again and again—they couldn't.

Yee-haw on that. He just hoped whoever was shielding them was a friend.

Abigail moved to stand beside him. She reached out to touch it, and apparently there was nothing there. She waved her hand around but it contacted nothing. Meanwhile, the coyotes couldn't touch them.

Interesting . . .

She frowned in confusion. "What is this?"

"Don't know. But given everything else that's happened so far, I'm not real sure it's a good thing." For all he knew, that magic wall might be protecting the coyotes from something ugly about to happen to the two of them.

As if on cue, an evil growl, low and deep, echoed around them.

The coyotes hesitated at the sound.

Abigail swallowed in fear. When the scariest of scary were wary, it was time to take note. She whipped out her mental notepad to wait on whatever evil was about to pounce.

She didn't have to wait long before a huge wolf launched out of the walls to attack the coyotes.

That was unexpected on several levels. She turned toward Sundown. "Is that on our side?"

He squinted as if trying to look into the heart of this

latest addition. "Looks like, but . . . hell, who knows at this point?"

Within seconds, the coyotes vanished into a mist. The wolf circled as if he was about to give chase. Until he turned into a man in the middle of the hallway.

Tall, blond, and extremely handsome, he still looked feral in his human form. There was a light in his eyes that said he wanted to taste blood.

She hoped it wasn't theirs.

Abigail held her breath as he moved forward with a deadly glower.

Here we go again. . . .

The wolf flipped the gun out of Sundown's hands. He cracked open the barrel to check its loaded status and shook his head. "Shells, cowboy? Really?"

Sundown shrugged. "Sometimes you just have to try even when it's wasted energy."

The wolf laughed, then handed it back. "I admire the tenacity, useless though it is."

Abigail relaxed as she realized the wolf was at the very least a frenemy.

Sundown leaned the gun against the wall. "What are you doing here?"

"Zarek sent me in, just in case."

Sundown scratched at the whiskers on his jaw. " 'Cause shit rolls downhill."

"Yeah, and what upsets Z gets my ass kicked. Have I

ever told you how much it chafes me that Astrid gave that psycho bastard god powers? I swear I go to bed every night with the one desire to rip out his throat, and I don't even live with them anymore. Sad, isn't it?"

Sundown bristled as if the wolf had struck a nerve. "Now, that's *my* boy you're talking about, and I don't want to get crossed up with you, Sasha. But you keep that tone and attitude about him, and we will."

Sasha held his hands up in surrender. "Sorry. I forget you and Ash are weird enough to actually like him. No accounting for taste." He turned that penetrating stare toward her. "And you must be the cause of this disaster."

Abigail was offended. What? Was there some cosmic social media feed somewhere with her photo on it, announcing her as the cause of the apocalypse? "I didn't do anything."

Sundown grinned. "She's in denial."

"Cool. We can feed her to the coyotes then, and I can go back to Sanctuary and continue scoping out this amazing brunette who keeps coming in with her friends."

She wasn't amused by that.

At all.

Sundown ignored her ire. "Speaking of friends . . . why did our new coyote buddies run from you?"

Sasha swaggered like a strutting peacock. "I'm *that* badass."

Sundown snorted. "Seriously."

"O ye of little faith. You doubt my rep? My skills?"

"And your brains."

Sasha tsked. "Fine. I'll be honest. . . . Absolutely no idea. They had me outnumbered. I should have been easy for them to rip into. Not that I wanted to be their early morning snack, but—"

"The wolf has always been a most natural enemy to the coyote. Wolves are one of the few predators known to hunt them when the season is right. And because of this, the coyote are wary of them by nature. Especially one from an unknown pantheon whose powers they can only guess at. No doubt, they thought retreat was the best course of action. As Sun Tzu would say, 'If ignorant both of your enemy and yourself, you are certain to be in peril.' "

Abigail turned at the voice of what sounded like an ancient Englishman standing behind them.

He wasn't English. Or anything like what she'd expected from his proper, thickly accented speech.

Barely taller than her, he wore a tan suede jacket with fringed sleeves and heavy Native American beadwork and carved bone all over it. His silver hair was parted into two braids that framed his withered face. However age hadn't dulled the sharpness of his hazel gold eyes, which stared at her with an accusation that cut her all the way to her soul.

She had a sudden desire to take a step back, but she refused to be a coward. So she stood her ground and put on the bravest face she could manage.

Sundown inclined his head respectfully to the man. "Choo Co La Tah, what are you doing here?"

Choo Co La Tah turned that frightening gaze from her to Sundown. "The Unfolding has started, and so I knew I couldn't wait, no matter Ren's protestations. As the Dineh would say, Coyote is always out there waiting, and Coyote is always hungry. I knew they would be after the woman as soon as they caught her scent. If they kill her before we reach the Valley, there will be no one to stop them. Hence my appearance here and now. The two of you must be protected, no matter what happens." He opened his jacket to show a crow that had been resting under his right arm. He pulled it out and, with a grace and dexterity that contradicted his apparent age, set it on the floor.

Letting out a caw, the bird flapped its wings, then manifested into a man. This one appeared to be in his early twenties with jet hair and eyes. Dressed all in black, he was stunningly sexy and even scarier than the coyotes had been.

He was also fanged.

And now all the men were staring at her, making her extremely uncomfortable and self-conscious. She felt like a mouse surrounded by hungry cats who were taking odds on who would be the first to pounce.

"Do you comprehend the gravity of your situation, my dear?" Choo Co La Tah asked her.

She did. But that didn't stop one cold, hard fact. "I don't want to die."

There was no sympathy in the old man's gaze. "As the

Duwamish would say, there is no death, only a change of worlds."

"I like *this* world."

"Then you should have thought of that before you took the life of Old Bear. I can assure you, even at his advanced age, he didn't want to change realms either. And he's only one of many you have killed who never once harmed you."

Her anger snapped at that. How dare he patronize her—something that was made even more pronounced by his accent and proper tone.

She hadn't stalked innocent people like some deranged serial killer. She was an avenger who was tallying a sickening score started by the true villains in all of this. "The Dark-Hunters have hunted my people for centuries."

"Your people, madam, are human . . . most of them qualify for that term, anyway. They are the ones the Dark-Hunters strive to protect."

"Yeah, right. They . . ." Her words broke off as images flashed in her mind. She heard countless humans begging for mercy as they were attacked.

Not by Dark-Hunters.

By Apollites who'd killed them so that they could take their human souls and feed on them and live past their twenty-seventh birthday—just as Sundown had told her. The horror of it slapped her hard as their screams resonated through her skull.

It couldn't be.

She shook her head in denial. "You planted those images in my head. They're not real."

Choo Co La Tah sighed. "My people have a saying. *Kirha tahanahna ditari sukenah.* To deny the presence of the sun doesn't escape its blister. I admire your loyalty. But sometimes you have to face the truth, even when it hurts."

No, she didn't. Because if he was right, if those images were the truth, then she was wrong on a level so profound that it made her sick. It would mean she'd done horrendous things to people who didn't deserve it.

People who'd been protecting the innocent from predators.

And if that was the case, she wasn't sure if she could live with herself.

I'm not a predator. I'm a protector.

Choo Co La Tah's eyes were filled with compassion. "I feel your pain, child. But you should have studied Confucius."

She frowned at his words. "How so?"

"Had you taken the time to learn his wisdom instead of war, you would have known that before you start down the road to revenge, dig two graves."

She bristled at that. "You don't understand."

"There you are quite wrong. Shamefully, all of us have wanted revenge on someone at some point for something. I've lived since before man and buffalo roamed this small planet. I have survived the beginning, bloom, and death of countless enemies, civilizations, and people. And the one truth I have learned most during all of these centuries is the old Japanese proverb. If you sit by the river long enough, you will see the body of your enemy float by."

That made her temper boil over. He made it sound so simple. But he was wrong, and she knew it. "Even if he's immortal?"

"Especially then. To quote the Tsalagi, you should never allow your yesterday to use up too much of today. The past is gone and tomorrow is at best a maybe. Live for this moment because it may be all you'll ever have."

She curled her lip in disgust. His pithy phrases were easy to spout, but living with her amount of pain was another story. And seeing your parents slaughtered was something no one got over. Ever. "What are you? A fortune cookie writer?"

The Native American Dark-Hunter started forward, but Choo Co La Tah stopped him before he could reach her. There was laughter in his tone as he spoke. "Respect must be earned, Ren. Not demanded. A questioning mind is the most cherished resource man has and the rarest. I admire her tenacity and her misplaced loyalty."

Those words embarrassed her, and somehow they made her feel like she was being childish.

"And I don't." Deep and resonant, Ren's voice rolled like thunder.

Choo Co La Tah placed a gentle hand on her shoulder.

"All feelings are valid, and I do not discount yours, Abigail. Our true journey will begin in a handful of hours after the sun sets. In the meantime, all of you need to rest and conserve your strength. Sasha and I will guard you while you slumber." He glanced to Sundown. "And I will notify Andy and make sure he, too, is safe."

Sasha arched a brow. "Why is the wolf always the one who's drafted?"

Choo Co La Tah smiled. "The wolf is the one who is most rested."

Sasha scoffed. "What? You want to toss logic into my emotional outburst? Where's the fairness of that?"

If she wasn't so upset, Abigail might have found Sasha amusing, but right now nothing was funny to her. Not when the agony of her past weighed on her and her conscience ripped at her with razor-sharp talons. *I'm not what they say.*

She wasn't. At least she hoped she wasn't.

But what if?

Sundown cleared his throat to get Choo Co La Tah's attention. "I agree we need to rest. But there is a small matter of scorpions in the basement, and that's the only safe place for me and Ren during daylight. No offense, I don't really want to nap with them crawling all over me."

Choo Co La Tah stepped away from her. "Ah yes, the scorpion infestation. Don't despair. I've taken care of your pest problem. All of them are gone now."

"You sent the snow?" Abigail asked.

He inclined his head. "The plagues that will come are designed to weaken me. The Coyote is forcing me to expend energy to protect mankind from his tools. For now, my strength holds. But I'm old and I must recharge my powers much more often than I did when I was young. If we don't make it to the Valley before I lose strength . . ."

It wouldn't be pretty for any of them.

And it will be all by my fault.

Jess saw the terrified look in Abigail's eyes before she hid it. That uncharacteristic frailty from her tugged at his heart. She wasn't the kind of woman to let her vulnerability show. The fact that she did . . .

She was in absolute agony, and he'd always been a sucker for a woman in pain.

"C'mon," he said to her gently. "I'll take you back downstairs."

For once, she didn't argue, and that told him exactly how torn up she really was. Ren followed after them while Choo Co La Tah and Sasha stayed topside to keep an eye out for any other enemies who might want to join them.

No one spoke until they were in the elevator. Ren folded his arms over his chest as he blocked the door and faced them. He glanced from Abigail to Jess. "You have no idea how much it bothers me to know that I was the man she meant to kill tonight and now I have to protect her."

Jess snorted. "Yeah, well, she tried to kill me, too, and I got over it."

"I'm not as good a man as you are, Sundown. I find it hard to give an enemy my back under any circumstance."

"Oh, I didn't say I was giving her my back. I'm not lacking all my noodle sense. But I'm not holding a grudge neither. Sometimes you just got to let the rattlesnake lay in the sun."

Ren muttered an obscenity about that under his breath.

Abigail cleared her throat. "Men? You do know I'm standing in this little box with you and can hear every word?"

They exchanged an arch look.

"We know," Ren said. "I merely don't care."

She rolled her eyes as the elevator stopped and Jess moved Ren aside so that he could open it.

Abigail hesitated before stepping out.

"Something wrong?" Jess held the door open for her with one arm.

She stuck her head out a little ways and squinted at the ground. "Making sure there's no scorpions on the floor."

He laughed at her uncharacteristic timidity. "Miraculously, they're all gone." The only proof of their ordeal was the hole in the ceiling that the coyotes had used to jump through earlier. "Looks safe."

Ren made a hostile noise before he pushed past them and took the rear bedroom suite.

Jess tsked at him. "You know, bud, that there's just plain rude."

Ren held his hand up over his shoulder to flip him off as he continued on without comment or pausing.

Abigail swallowed at his open hostility. Not that she blamed him, since he had been her target. Still . . .

"Don't take it too hard," Sundown said sheepishly. "Ren's . . . well . . . he's Ren. He don't mean nothing."

If it were only that simple, but she did appreciate his trying to make her feel better. "He hates me."

"He's wary of you. Big difference. Like he said, he was your target. Not exactly something a man gets over real fast."

"You seem to have adapted."

He flashed the most devilish and charming grin she'd ever seen before, and it did peculiar things to her stomach. "I'm not as bright as he is."

Oh yeah, he could be devastating when he wanted to. "I somehow doubt that."

"Is that a compliment?"

"Well, hell has indeed frozen over, in case you missed the snow on your front lawn."

He laughed as he led her toward the room he'd taken her to earlier. Now that they weren't in fear of their lives, she could appreciate the beauty of his home. The hallway was painted a peaceful ochre with white wainscoting. The wall sconces were baroque and seemed at odds with the down-home simplicity of Sundown Brady.

"Did you decorate this place?"

He cast a frown at her over his shoulder that said he

thought she was a few gallons shy of a load. "Yeah, no . . . decorating ain't exactly something I strive to do in my spare time. It came with the house."

"Why did you want to live here? No offense, but it doesn't really seem to be your style."

He paused at her room. "I think I might ought to be offended by that. What exactly are you saying about my style?"

She paused, too, then shrugged. "I don't know. You just seem to be the kind of guy to have a man cave, not something this . . ."

"Refined?"

She shook her head affirmatively.

"Well, that just shows what you know. For your information, I do like some fancy things."

"Like what? Lacy underwear?"

"On my women, yeah." He flashed that grin at her that she was learning to hate. Not for any reason other than the fact that it softened his features and made him terribly irresistible.

"And—?" she asked when he didn't continue.

He scratched at the back of his neck. "Well, opera for one and foreign films for another, especially French ones."

She scoffed. "No, you don't."

"I can show you my Opera Guild membership card if you want to see it. Been a season ticket holder for decades."

Out of all the things about him that took her by surprise, those actually floored her. She just couldn't imagine a man so large and tough wedging himself into an opera seat.

"Heck, I even play violin."

"You mean fiddle."

"Play that, too. But Mozart and Grieg are my favorite pieces that I like to unwind with after a hard night's work."

In the back of her mind was a vague memory of him playing Wagner on her toy piano and then showing her what the keys were. "You taught me 'Chopsticks.'"

"I did."

The thought of a man so huge and ripped handling such a delicate instrument was incongruous and yet . . .

Why can't I remember more?

Sundown opened the door for her.

Abigail went to the bed, then paused. Instead of leaving, Sundown pulled a blanket and pillow out of the closet and made a pallet on the floor.

"What are you doing?" she asked, dreading the obvious answer.

"We tore my room up, remember? I don't want to sleep with a big hole over my head. Plaster or something might fall down and scare me enough, I could scream like a woman and humiliate myself. I definitely don't want to do that with Sasha in the house. He'd laugh at me forever, and I'd have to skin him."

She started to protest, but honestly she was glad to have him in here. Just in case. After everything that had happened, her nerves were shot.

You should be running from him or at least trying to kill him.

Perhaps. But if the coyotes were really after her, the last thing she wanted to do was lead them home so that they could kill her adoptive family, too. Hannah and Kurt were all she had left. And while the Apollites were good, she wasn't sure they'd be enough to fight them. Not to mention Choo Co La Tah was right, she was exhausted to a level she'd never known before. She needed rest. At least for a couple of hours.

Then she might be up for an escape attempt.

Kicking off her shoes and pulling the band from her hair to release her ponytail, she climbed into bed. Before she could think better of it, she glanced to where Sundown lay on the floor. One thing she didn't miss was the fact that he had one foot against the door so that if anyone opened it, it would wake him immediately. And the shotgun was on the floor only millimeters from his fingertips.

Weird . . . she couldn't remember him picking it up again. Where had it come from?

Man, she must be tired to have missed that.

Pushing it out of her mind, she changed the topic. "You need another pillow?"

He covered his eyes with his arm. Something that caused his shirt to ride up and give her a glimpse of his rock-hard abs. Oh yeah, she could do laundry on that. "Nah, thanks. I'm good."

In more ways than one. He was definitely scrumptious, lying on the floor like that.

I have lost my mind. And then some. *You can't possibly find him attractive. He killed your family.*

Or had he? Could he have been telling her the truth earlier? If he really was a cold-blooded killer, why not murder her instead of bringing her back here? He could have abandoned her to the scorpions and coyotes.

Instead, he'd protected her.

He's a killer. You saw his face. You know his legend.

True. Her research of his human past had shown him to be the worst sort of humanity. Scum so foul that even bounty hunters and law enforcement had feared him.

But her personal experience with him refuted that.

What if she were wrong? She'd been so little at the time of her parents' deaths. Did she remember that night correctly? She could still see him so clearly in her mirror. And yet there were differences between the man on the floor and the one in her memory.

Why would he seem larger now than he had when she was a kid?

Even though she needed to sleep, she wanted answers.

Before she could stop herself, she asked the one that bothered her most. "What did you and my dad fight over the night they died?"

Jess fell quiet as her whispered question stirred old memories that cut him up deep inside. Things he'd tried not to think about. Things that had haunted him for years. As bad as those memories had been for him, he could only imagine how much harder they'd been for her. Damn shame for a mite to see such a thing as what had happened to her parents.

A part of him wanted to lie, but in the end, he spoke honestly. "Your mother."

She sat up in the bed to stare at him. "What?"

Lowering his arm, Jess sighed at the inevitable confession she deserved to hear. "Your pa thought I was trying to steal her affections away from him."

"Were you?"

"Hardly. Me and her were friends and nothing more."

"You're lying," she accused.

If only it'd been that simple. "No, sweet. I'm telling the truth. No need for me to lie about this."

"Why would my father think that unless you gave him reason to?"

'Cause he was fucking loco, but Jess would never say that to her. The man was her pa, and the last thing he wanted to do was taint her memory of him. The truth, though—her pa had been insanely jealous of any male in Laura's life who was over the age of five. He assumed every man was eat up with lust for her, and in his world someone couldn't just want to talk to her because she reminded him of someone else. Nah, and the worst of it was that he'd accused her of cheating on him. Something Laura would die before she did.

Since Jess couldn't say any of that, he went with the other simple truth. "'Cause I loved your mama, and there was nothing in the world I wouldn't have done for her or you."

Abigail felt tears sting her eyes as she remembered the beauty of her mother's face. She'd seen her as a wonderful angel with a smile that was filled with more warmth than the sun itself. Most of all, she remembered how safe and loved she'd felt every single time her mother wrapped her arms around her. God, to have one more second with her . . .

"If you were in love with—"

"Not *in* love, Abby. That's what your pa couldn't get through his thick skull. What I felt for her wasn't that. I just wanted to make her happy and keep her safe."

"Why?"

Jess felt the tic start in his jaw as a wave of agony swelled inside him. Laura had been a perfect physical copy of Matilda. Even some of her mannerisms. But she wasn't Tilly, and he'd known it. "She reminded me of someone I used to know." *Someone I once loved more than anything on this earth.*

"I don't understand."

And it was hard to explain. "I met your ma not long after she moved to Reno. She was a waitress in a restaurant where I used to go and eat sometimes." He hadn't been paying a bit of attention to the occupants as he took his usual seat in the small diner. He'd been staring out the window, skimming the crowd as people outside walked by, when a cup of coffee appeared on his table.

"Much obliged," he'd muttered, expecting it to be his usual waitress, Carla, who always brought him coffee the minute he sat down.

"You're welcome." The soft lilt of that unfamiliar voice had dragged his attention to her face. Even now, he could feel the shock of looking up and being sucked back in time.

"Are you all right?" she'd asked.

He'd sputtered and mumbled something back at her that was probably as stupid to her as he'd felt when he said it. Over the next hour, he'd coerced enough information out of her that he was able to get Ed to run a thorough background check on her.

That report had stunned him as much as seeing her in the diner. Laura was the great-great-granddaughter of the child Bart had fathered the day he raped Matilda.

A child Matilda had given up for adoption.

By the time the Squires told him about the infant a few years after it'd been born, he'd been unable to locate it. Records weren't kept the same way then as they were today. Until the night he'd stumbled across Laura and Ed had run his own check, he didn't even know that child had been a boy.

At first, he'd been livid with the discovery and angry at fate for dropping that living reminder slap-dab in the middle of his territory. Since he knew he'd never dishonored Matilda by taking her before their wedding, there was no doubt about the paternal sperm donor for Laura's line.

But by the next night, he'd chosen to focus on two things. One, it wasn't the baby's fault that he'd been conceived by violence, and there was no reason for Jess to hold that against the boy's descendants. Two, they were every bit as much a part of the woman he'd loved as the children she'd kept and raised, and the descendants he had the Squires watch over. It was only fair he take care of Laura, too.

In Laura, he'd only seen Matilda's genteel face.

In Abigail, he saw both. The woman he'd loved more than his life and the man he'd hated with every part of his being.

It was one hell of a combination.

"And?" Abigail prompted. "She was a waitress . . ."

"We became friends," he said simply. And it was the absolute truth. "I'd go in a few times a week, and we'd chat for a bit." He smiled at his bittersweet memories. Like Matilda, she'd been sweet and unassuming. "She was highly intelligent and quick-witted. Funny as all get out. I used to love listening to her banter with her friends and the other customers."

"Did you ever go out with her?"

"Never. Dark-Hunters aren't allowed to date, and I knew I had nothing to offer her. I just liked being in her company. She was good people, and there's not a lot of those around. I left big tips, and she threatened the life of anyone who dared try and wait on me anytime she was working."

"Then why was my father angry at you?"

He was a psychotic idiot.

But Jess didn't say that. "I made the mistake of giving your mother a butterfly necklace that I'd seen in a local shop on her birthday. I thought it was pretty, and the blue diamonds in it reminded me of her eyes. I meant nothing by it, but your pa didn't see it that way. Even though I'd known her long before she met and married him, he accused her of cheating on him with me, and I left before I physically hurt him."

Abigail searched her mind for some memory to either refute or sustain his words. All she could remember was the loud sounds of shouting voices. Her parents didn't fight a lot, but it'd been enough that she knew to hide whenever they did.

Her hiding over it was the very thing that had saved her life.

Sundown sighed. "I went out on my patrol, but I couldn't shake the bad feeling I had. I didn't want to leave her with him so mad. But I knew if I'd stayed, I'd have rearranged a few of his organs, and that would have only upset her more. I figured if I left, he'd calm down and everything would be all right. . . . At ten, I tried to call and got no answer. That worried me even more. So I headed back and . . ." He hesitated before he spoke again. "The police were already there and they wouldn't let me in. I looked around for you and asked about you, but there was no trace. They assumed that whoever killed your parents took you as well. We searched for you for a long time, but no one ever saw you again." He scowled at her. "So what happened to you, anyway? Where did you go?"

Abigail tried to recall when her adoptive father had shown up. But all she saw was Sundown walking out of her room. And then it'd seemed like forever before she heard a familiar voice call her name. "My adoptive father took me home with him. I don't remember seeing the police or really anything much about that night except you."

"What made you think I killed them?"

"I saw you in my room."

"I wasn't there, Abigail. I swear to you." There was so much conviction in his tone that he was either the best liar in the world . . .

Or he was telling the truth.

"He looked just like you. He even had on cowboy boots."

"A pair of shit-kickers in Reno is normal footwear. That don't mean nothing."

That much was true. Still . . .

"My adoptive father confirmed it. He said you slaughtered my parents because they were allies to the Apollites."

"I had no idea they even knew what an Apollite was. It's not something I normally talk about to anyone outside of the Dark-Hunter network, you know?"

That made a little too much sense. Abigail rubbed her forehead as she tried to discern the truth. Her feelings were so conflicted.

"So what do you believe now?" he asked.

Overwhelmed by everything, she lay back against the headboard. "I don't know, Sundown. I don't." Oh, how she hated being this tired. It made her an emotional wreck, and everything was so much worse right now. Tears started streaming quietly down her cheeks as everything crashed in on her. Her life had never been simple or easy.

But all of the past was like a ride on a merry-go-round compared to what it was right now. It was confusing and terrifying.

And if Choo Co La Tah was right, she only had an extremely short amount of time left to live.

Or the world would end.

What have I done?

What was she going to do?

Suddenly, Sundown was there, sitting on the bed. "Don't cry, Abby. It's all right."

It wasn't and they both knew it.

He gathered her into his arms and held her close. Something no one had done in a very long time. God, it felt so good. . . .

Abigail buried her face into his chest. His heartbeat was strong and sure, and in this moment, she needed that reassurance that she wasn't completely alone—even if it meant cuddling against her enemy. "I'm so sorry. I don't normally do this."

"Don't apologize. My ma used to say that crying is good for you. Tears are the path that free your mind of sorrowful thoughts."

"You sound like Choo Co La Tah now."

He nuzzled his face against her head while a gentle laugh rumbled deep in his chest. "He is kind of like Yoda.... 'There is only do or do not. There is no try.'"

That actually succeeded in making her laugh through her tears. "You're a *Star Wars* fan?"

"Oh yeah. May the Force be with you."

She sobered. "If what Choo Co La Tah said is true, I think we're going to need something a lot stronger than the Force to win this."

"Don't worry, we'll find a solution. There's always a way."

His positive attitude amazed her. "How can you be so sure?"

He shrugged. "You're talking to a man who came back from the dead just to even a score. You think I'm going to let something like Coyote win this? Hardly. One thing about Bradys . . . We don't run and we don't lose. Come hell or high water, no one gets the best of me. And I'll be damned if I let them take you. We'll find a way to keep you safe and save the world. You have my personal guarantee on that, and that's not something I give lightly."

His conviction stunned her. "Why do you even care? A few hours ago, I was trying to kill you."

"And not that long ago, you saved me from stepping into daylight. I haven't forgotten that either. Besides, I understand wanting retribution. Spent my whole human life in search of it. I won't hold that against you or anyone else."

That was so different from the things she'd read about him. Was it possible he wasn't as soulless as they claimed?

"But," he continued. "I would ask that if we do manage to save your butt and the world's that you find another hobby besides killing us."

How easy he made that sound. "Do you really think they'll let me live after what I've done?"

Jess paused as he considered it. She was right. The final decision wasn't his to make. The Powers were even more vengeful than his brethren were. Blood for blood. Tit for tat.

Still, things happened all the time that didn't make sense. And the Powers . . .

They were downright unpredictable.

"Have faith, Abigail. Sometimes the world surprises you."

Abigail swallowed at his words, wishing she could put

her faith in them. "Yeah, but it's never done so in a pleasant way. At least not for me."

And deep in her heart, she knew the truth. This wouldn't end until she'd paid for her actions.

She was going to die, and not even the infamous Jess Brady could stop it.

8

Abigail woke up to the sensation of someone cradling her against an impressively hard chest, as if she were unspeakably cherished. She honestly couldn't remember the last time a man had held her like this.

If ever.

He was wrapped completely around her.

Warm. Seductive. Inviting. Protective. It was the kind of sweet, loving embrace people dreamed of finding themselves in, but seldom did. For a full minute, she lay there in complete satiation.

Until she remembered who *he* was.

Sundown Brady.

Outlaw. Dark-Hunter. Killer.

Enemy.

She jerked involuntarily, which immediately caused him to awaken and push himself up on his arms to look around, as if expecting more coyotes to leap out of the walls and devour them.

When he didn't see an immediate threat, he scowled down at her. "Everything okay?"

Yes . . . He was so incredibly sexy in that pose. His hips were pressed intimately against hers, and his arms bulged with his raw strength. It made her ache for the very thing she would die before she gave him.

"No, you're on top of me." She pushed at his chest.

He rolled off her and onto his back with a taunting grin as he wiggled his hips to settle into his new position. "Now, that's not normally the way a woman reacts when I'm on top of her. I usually get a little more enthusiasm and welcome than that."

She gave him a withering stare to mask how incredibly yummy she thought he was right then. No need in feeding that ego. "Well, that's what happens when you pay women for sex."

To her surprise, he laughed good-naturedly. Damn, he was devastating when he did that, and he made it hard to remember she was supposed to hate his guts.

Stretching like a languid cat, he yawned. "Sorry about crushing you all morning. I think we fell asleep in the middle of a conversation."

They had. One she could barely recall now. What she did recall was how comforting he'd been while she'd cried, and that was the last thing she needed to think about. "Yeah, but I'm not sure which of us fell asleep first."

"I'm pretty sure it was you."

She had a suspicion he was right, and this was getting a little too familiar for her tastes. She wanted to keep a gap between them. A nice safe chasm that protected her from caring about anyone, especially him. So she changed the subject. "Your gun's still on the floor."

He scratched at the manly shadow on his cheek in a way that was boyish and somehow endearing. He was so nonchalant with her and she should be aggravated by that, not charmed. "Glad I didn't need it, since it's all the way over there."

No kidding. That could have been a bloody disaster. "So what time do you think it is?"

"Feels like it's still daylight. Not sure of the exact time, though."

"What do you mean it *feels* like daylight?"

He yawned before he answered. "Wicked power we have. We can sense when the sun's up. Which it still is."

No doubt they'd been given that to help keep them alive, since Apollo would kill any Dark-Hunter or Apollite he found in his domain. The Greek god was a real bastard that way.

And you killed two of Jess's brethren by trapping them in daylight. She didn't even want to think about how the others died.

Please, please don't let me have killed a protector. . . .

Trying not to think about that either, she got up and went to the bathroom.

Jess didn't speak as he watched her plod across the room. She had the most seductive walk he'd ever seen on any woman. Slow and sensual and full of sass. It was the kind of walk that made men turn and stare. Most of all, it made him ache to take a bite out of that hot little body of hers, especially that well-shaped ass.

Man, to have *that* naked and wrapped around him . . .

Uh, hello, cowboy? You're not supposed to have those thoughts about a human who's been offering your friends up as sacrifice to the dark gods.

Maybe not, but he was a man, and his body wasn't about to listen to his brain, especially since all the blood was now gathered into the part of him that craved her most. It wanted what it saw, and she was definitely worth an ass-whipping or two dozen.

Pushing that out of his mind before it got him into some serious trouble, he closed his eyes and used his powers to sense Ren. He knew the moment he made contact. Ren pushed back with his own telepathy.

"What, cowboy?"

He shook his head at Ren's surly tone in his head. He didn't like anyone near his thoughts—not the Jess blamed him. Mind readers weren't his favorite thing either. *"Wanted to see if you were awake yet."*

"I've been awake and meditating. And to answer your next question, it's almost four, so you have plenty of time to grab ass if you want."

Jess quickly blocked the image in his mind that those words conjured. Grabbing Abigail's ass was a lot more appealing to him than it should be. *"Stay out of my thoughts."*

"Believe me, I'm trying to. I don't want to throw up right after I brushed my teeth."

Bastard.

"By the way," Ren continued, ignoring the insult that questioned his parentage, *"I'm about as weak as I've ever been. Other than the telepathy, which I obviously know is working, how are your powers doing?"*

Jess winced as he realized his were down, too. *"Probably drained as much as yours are."*

"Guess we're going to pretend we're human for a bit."

Jess snorted. There were many folks, including Abigail, who would say that he'd never been human. *"Can you shape-shift at all?"*

"Never a problem."

Now, that was interesting. *"Care to tell me why that one isn't malfunctioning?"*

"It likes me best."

Jess shook his head. Smart-ass.

His attention shifted as he heard the water in his bathroom come on. Abigail was taking a shower. . . .

"I'm going to leave you to the thoughts of her naked, since I have no interest in being a voyeur to your fantasies, especially with a viper. Check in with me when you're focused on fighting and not—"

"Gotcha, Ren. I'll powwow with you later."

Jess lay alone on the bed, listening to the water run in the other room. In his mind, he had a perfect image of what Abigail would look like as she soaped her naked breasts. His body roared back to life with a vengeance. His hunger for her was unlike anything he'd ever experienced before. And it wasn't just because she was a beautiful woman.

There was something else. Something he hadn't felt since the first time he met Matilda. It was a deep-seated ache. An urge he had to be near her. To protect her.

To hold her.

It took every bit of his control not to go in there and make her slap his face. One corner of his mouth lifted as he imagined her outrage if he did.

Definitely worth the slap. But he wouldn't do that to

her. He was too much of a gentleman to horrify a woman. No matter how horny he was.

That being said, his thoughts of her were killing him.

Abigail *was trying* to sort through all the information she'd been given. She wanted to believe her family. She did.

But it was hard to refute what she'd been shown, and the fact that Sundown didn't act like a psychotic killer.

If only she knew the real truth of everything. Were there rogue Apollites who preyed on humans? It seemed preposterous, and yet so did the existence of Apollites altogether. If one was possible, wouldn't it stand to reason that so was the other?

But why had no one in her family ever mentioned them?

The only thing she knew for a fact was that she was being hunted by something she'd accidentally unleashed. And that she didn't doubt at all.

How could she have been so stupid?

Sighing, she reached for the soap, only to feel a vicious stabbing pain rip through her abdomen. It was a thousand times worse than the most wretched menstrual cramp. She tried to move, but it slammed her down to the ground as it continued to twist in her stomach. Her skin burned like it was on fire. The water was no longer soothing. Now it tore at her flesh like a razor. Tears gathered in her eyes.

Oh my God, I'm in an Alien *movie. . . .*

That was what it felt like. Some creature trying to claw its way out of her belly. Light and sound tortured her. Images flashed through her mind as if controlled by a psychedelic strobe.

Help me. . . .

She couldn't speak the words. They were frozen in her throat.

Suddenly, the shower door opened. Her breathing ragged, she looked up to find Sundown there.

"Abigail?" His tone was filled with concern.

"Help me," she choked out as tears coursed down her cheeks.

He turned the water off, then scooped her up in his arms to carry her back to bed.

Had she been able, she'd have protested his carrying her while she was wet and naked. But right now, she didn't care and he didn't seem to notice about either one.

She groaned out loud as more pain lacerated her.

"I've got you," he said comfortingly. He wrapped her in a blanket, then brushed her hair back from her face with a tenderness that was completely unexpected. "What's going on?"

"I—I don't know. It hurts."

"Where?"

"Everywhere. But my stomach's the worst of it."

Jess touched her stomach, and she screamed in agony.

He thought it might be appendicitis until he met her gaze. Her eyes glowed red. "Um, honey, is there something you want to tell me?"

"What? That I feel like I'm giving birth to a fire-breathing dragon?"

"Nah, more like . . . any idea why your eyes would be demon red?" They were the same color they'd turned when she was unconscious.

She opened her mouth as if to respond, but before she could, her incisors lengthened.

Holy shit.

Had she made a pact with Artemis? She definitely looked like a Hunter, but none that he knew of had red eyes. . . .

"Get away from her, Jess."

He glanced over his shoulder to see Choo Co La Tah there. "What's going on?"

Abigail went for Jess's throat with a force so fierce, she forced them both off the bed.

Jess caught her, but it was a struggle to keep her from biting him. Dang, she was strong. Inhumanly strong. He had to turn her around in his arms, and he held her there with her back pressed to him while she shrieked in outrage.

Choo Co La Tah crossed the room and took her face in his hands. He began chanting something Jess couldn't understand while Abigail fought him with everything she had. She slammed her head back into his, knocking him senseless. Still, he held on to her even while his jaw burned.

Her struggles increased until she let out another fierce scream. An instant later, she collapsed.

He lifted her up into his arms and cradled her against him once more. Her skin was suddenly so cold, it scared him. *Was she all right?* He returned her to bed while Choo Co La Tah continued with his melodic chant.

Her breathing was coming in short, hard gasps now.

Choo Co La Tah forced him away from the bed so that he could place one palm on her forehead. After a few seconds, she calmed down and appeared to sleep.

With his hands on his hips, Jess scowled. "What was that?"

"They have merged her blood with a demon's."

That hit him like another blow to the head, which was the last thing he needed. His senses were rattled as much as if he'd taken a header off a bronco onto a fence. "Come again?"

Choo Co La Tah nodded. "One could surmise that they thought to strengthen her abilities by combining her DNA with a demon's."

Now, that was about dumb. But then, most people weren't rocket scientists, and he could see an idiot Daimon thinking they'd found an upper hand by using her that way.

But damn, he'd have figured Abigail for having more sense than to try something so boneheaded.

Obviously not.

"So the demon's controlling her?"

Choo Co La Tah shook his head. "The demon is dead. Demons can control someone only when they're alive, and normally when the demon dies, the control over the person is broken. But this . . . They did something else to cause her to have the powers, and I don't know what it is."

"Beautiful." Well, at least that explained how she had the power to kill a Dark-Hunter. "Can she convert one of us if she bites us?"

Choo Co La Tah nodded grimly. "If her fangs are showing and she mixes her blood with anyone, it will bring them under her complete control. And the demon inside her will crave that control. The longer it's in there, the hungrier she'll become for a victim."

That was the scariest thought of all. "So what do we do?"

"We must get her to the Valley as soon as we can and perform the ritual."

"Then she'll be all right?"

Choo Co La Tah refused to answer—which could mean only one thing.

Abigail would die.

9

Abigail felt her heart rate slow down as she fell through a dark mist. Images flashed through her mind. She saw her parents again. Heard them laughing.

Suddenly, she found herself as a small child on the floor with Sundown, who was smiling at her. Dressed in a black button-down shirt and jeans, he wore his hair shorter, and he was freshly shaved. Still, he was devastating to look at, especially when he smiled.

"Now, look, Abby, you send the bunny under the bush and then down around the rabbit hole. Like this."

She watched in awe as he tied her red princess ballet bedroom shoe. "That's not a bunny, silly, that's a lace."

His smile widened but not so much that he showed his fangs. "Yeah, but we're pretending," he whispered like it was a big secret.

"Oh." She tried to repeat it with the other shoe.

"You need to find you a woman and settle down, Jess. You'd make a great father."

She saw the pain in his eyes that her mother's words evoked. His smile died instantly as he reached to pull his hat, which was filled with her Little Ponies, closer to them. "I don't believe in settling down. That's for folks like you." He held his hat out so that Abigail could take her ponies back.

"Yeah, but you don't want to grow old alone, do you?"

As a child, she'd missed the torment that flared deep in his black eyes while he faced her and had his back to her mother. But as a woman, she saw the demons that tortured him, and it made her ache for him. He ran his hand along the brim of his hat and swallowed before he answered. "Believe me, Laura, there are a lot of worse things in this world than growing old alone."

Abigail had looked up with wide eyes. "Like what?"

He gave her the forced smile that adults often give to kids when they don't want them to feel their pain. "Cookie monsters who sneak past you when you're tying your shoes and eat your chocolate chip yummies." He feigned a reach for the cookies on the floor next to her. Squealing, she threw herself over his arm to keep him from taking them.

He curled his arm, lifting her and bringing her straight to his chest so that he could catch her in his arms and swing her up. In one graceful move, he rose to his feet, then twirled her around.

"Airplane, airplane, airplane," she started chanting while Jess turned faster.

Her mother gaped at them. "You're going to be wearing those chocolate chips soon if you don't stop, Jess."

He laughed. "It'd be worth it to hear her laugh."

And Abigail did. . . . She laughed and squealed in delight.

How could she have ever forgotten how much she once loved that man?

"What's going on here?"

Jess stopped moving as her father's angry voice cut through their joy. He cradled her to his chest while she begged him to keep going. Patting her on the back to soothe her, he faced her outraged father. "I was just teaching Abby how to tie her shoes."

Her father forcefully yanked her out of his arms. "That's not *your* job, now, is it?"

She saw the anger in Jess's eyes, but he quickly hid it. "Nah, guess it's not."

Her mother stepped forward. "Baby, c'mon. Jess just stopped by for a second on his way to work to say happy birthday to me."

Her father's gaze narrowed on her mother's neck, where a beautiful diamond butterfly glittered in the light. Abigail reached to touch it, then protested when her father's grip on her tightened to the point of causing her pain. She cried out in protest and tried to squirm out of his hold.

Her father ignored her attempts to get free. "Long enough to give you *that*, huh? What? You think I can't afford you gifts like that? Is that it?"

Her mother's jaw dropped in shock and outrage as she took Abigail out of her father's arms and held her close to calm her. "What in the world is wrong with you?"

Jess stepped forward to wedge himself between her parents so that he could protect her and her mother from her father's anger. "Look, Stan, I wasn't trying to offend you. It was real pretty and all, and I just thought she'd like it. That's it. No slight to you was ever intended."

Even though her father was a full head shorter than Jess, he shoved him back, forcing her mother to step away from the men. Abigail saw the panic on her mother's face. She might not have known about Sundown's brutal past or his Dark-Hunter status, but it was obvious that he dwarfed her father, and that in a fight, he'd definitely be the victor.

Her father shoved him again. "You need to quit sniffing around my wife every time I leave."

Jess curled his lip and stood his ground. His expression promised a serious ass-whipping if her father didn't stand down. "I wasn't sniffing around her. We're friends. That's all."

"Then I suggest you go be friends with someone else's wife. My family is off-limits to you."

An angry tic beat a frenetic rhythm in Jess's jaw. It was obvious he was straining to ride herd on an urge to beat her father down. He glanced across the room to her mother. "I have to get to work. I'm sorry I caused you any trouble, Laura. I hope I didn't completely ruin your birthday, and I'm real sorry about the gift."

His words only enraged her father more. "Yeah, that's right. Rub it in how much better you are than I am at providing for her. We can't all be international investors and make millions doing it, can we?"

Jess paused, and Abigail saw the grim look on his face that said he was one step away from slamming her father's head through a wall. Instead, he pulled his Stetson off the floor and gently dumped her ponies on the coffee table. He picked up her favorite purple one and crossed the room to hand it to her. "Y'all have a good night." His eyes were dark and sorrowful as he met her mother's gaze. "Happy birthday, Laura." And then he put his hat on his head and walked out.

"Stan," her mother growled the moment he was gone. "That was unbelievably rude. What is wrong with you?"

He sneered at her. "How would you feel if you came home to find a woman in here alone with me?"

"I have many times. Tracy. Remember?"

He scoffed. "She's the babysitter."

"She's a very attractive woman."

"So?"

"That's exactly my point," her mother said in a disgusted tone. "I'm sorry you lost your job, but that's no reason to start hating a man who's been a good friend to me since before I met you."

"Yeah, right. I think it's more than friendship with you two."

Her mother gaped. "Are you completely out of your mind?"

Abigail covered her ears with her hands. "Please don't fight anymore. I don't like loud voices."

Her mother kissed her cheek and gave her a soothing cuddle. "Sorry, baby. Why don't you go play in your room?" She set her down.

Abigail ran to the hallway, then paused as her father grabbed her mother's arm and jerked her closer.

"I want you to give that necklace back to him," he said between clenched teeth.

"Why?"

"Because I don't want to see my wife wearing another man's gift. You hear me?"

Her mother rolled her eyes. "He's like a brother to me. Nothing more."

"Nothing more, huh? Then tell me why he carries a picture of you in his watch?"

Shock etched itself across her mother's face. "What?"

"You heard me. I saw it the last time he was over here. It's a photo of *you*. No man does that for his sister. Trust me."

"I don't believe you. He's never, ever said or done anything to act like he was interested in me in any way."

"And I know what I saw."

She wrested her arm out of his grip. "You're wrong about him."

"No, I'm not. It ain't natural for a man to want to come around someone else's family like this."

"You never had a problem with it before."

"I never saw that damn watch before."

Abigail frowned as she saw a shadow moving along the wall. It lifted up and crawled slowly toward her parents. Where was it coming from? There were no windows, and nothing that could cast it. It slinked down the hallway slowly. Methodically. But as a child, she was easily distracted, especially since her parents were escalating their argument. She scurried to her room to find her Scooter doll and hide.

She'd made a nest beneath her bed for just such occasions. It was where she felt safest. Her mother called it her princess hidey-hole. Abigail called it wonderful. With her blanket and dolls, she stayed there and lost track of time until she heard another familiar voice in the middle of their ongoing fight.

Jess's.

"You don't deserve her, you bastard."

"What are you doing here?" her father snarled, startling her from her play. "I told you not to come back."

"You don't tell me what to do."

Her mother's tone was much more reasonable. "Maybe you should go."

"So that's it, then?" her father shouted. "After all these years and everything I've done for you? You're just going to throw me out for this piece of random shit?"

Abigail covered her ears as the shouts grew louder and louder.

Her mother's scream rang out. "Stan! Put down the gun!" The next thing she heard was breaking furniture. Terrified, she dug deeper into her safety blanket and held her breath. She didn't know why she wasn't crying. But something told her not to even breathe audibly.

Four loud, deafening gunshots rang out.

Wide eyed, she'd been frozen in terror. *Mama* . . . That single word hovered in her mind as tears welled in her eyes. *Go check on her. . . .*

She couldn't. It felt as if someone or something held her down and kept her quiet.

Then there was the sound of lone boot heels clicking

eerily down the hallway toward her room. Chills raised on her arms.

Don't move, Abby. It sounded like her mother talking to her. *Whatever you do, stay silent and still. Pretend you're invisible.*

Her door opened with a slow arc.

Holding her breath, she peeped from beneath her bed to watch the boots move across her floor.

"Where are you, you little brat?" Jess snarled. He searched the room for her.

He's going to find me. . . . Every part of her seized with that fear. *I don't want to die.*

"Abigail!" he shouted as he searched through her closet. "Where are you?"

The sound of sirens filled the air, which made him tear through her room as he did his best to find her. She covered her head, terrified he'd overturn her bed.

"We need to go. Now!"

Abigail frowned at a voice that sounded familiar to her. Not as a little girl, but as an adult.

Whose was it?

"I can't find the brat."

The sirens were getting louder and louder.

"I'll take care of it," the voice whispered again. "But you need to go."

"Why? It might be better if they find me here."

"I have a better idea."

He let out a sound of extreme frustration as pulsating lights flashed through the windows. "Fine," he snarled. "I'll trust you, but if you're wrong, you'll be joining the other two in the living room."

"Don't worry, I have your back."

She watched as Sundown stormed out of the room, leaving nothing but bloody footprints in his wake. . . .

Abigail jerked awake to find herself in Sundown's house.

The memory of the night her parents had died lingered heavy in her heart as the sequence of events was clarified.

Sundown had killed her parents. He'd been lying to her when he denied it.

How do you know that?

Hello? I was there.

Still, there was a tiny part of her that doubted it. Her mind couldn't reconcile the two sides of Sundown that she'd seen. The fierce protector and the lethal killer.

You've killed, too.

But for a reason. Her parents hadn't deserved their deaths.

"You're awake."

She glanced over to the door where Sundown was standing. A wave of fury swelled through her, but she fought it down. The last thing she wanted was to warn him of her intentions.

"Yeah." Licking her dry lips, she glanced down to his right front pants pocket, which caused him to arch an inquisitive brow. Her face turned red as she realized he thought she was staring at his crotch and not the other, much smaller bump. "Not on your life, cowboy."

"Dang. Just when I got my hopes up, too."

For once, she didn't let his charm infiltrate her suspicions. She sat up on the bed. "Do you have the time?"

He pulled an old-fashioned pocket watch out and opened the cover to check it.

Before he could answer her question, she was off the bed and had it in her hand. Her breath caught as she saw the photo that had set her father off.

It *was* her mother.

"What are you doing with this?"

His face turned white. "It's not what you think."

She glared at him as she clutched the watch, wanting to strangle him. "What I think is that you're a liar." She held it up for him to see the picture. "This is my mother."

"It's not your mother."

"Bullshit. I know what she looked like."

Still, he shook his head in denial. "Look at it again. Your mother had short hair and never wore a dress like that one. Ever."

She turned it back toward her to study it.

He was right. The woman in the photograph had her hair piled up into an extravagant braided bun like a woman would have worn in the late 1800s. Her high-collar, white lace blouse was adorned at the neck by an antique cameo.

Like her mother's, the woman's eyes glowed with warmth and kindness.

But the most startling fact was that their features were eerily identical. The same sharp cheekbones and dark hair. Eyebrows that arched at an angle above kind eyes. But her mother's eyes had been blue. The woman in the photograph had dark eyes. Even so it was like staring at her mother all over again.

"I told you your ma reminded me of someone." Jess covered her hand with his. "Now you know."

That touch sent a chill down her spine. "Who is she?"

"Matilda Aponi." There was a catch in his voice that told her the mere mention of the name pained him.

"And what was she to you?"

He took the watch from her and closed it. "Does it matter?"

Obviously the woman had mattered a lot to him. "You loved her."

"More than my life."

Those heartfelt words actually made her ache. She'd never seen so much love in a man's eyes for any woman. It was so intense and unexpected that a part of her was actually jealous of it. She'd give anything to have a man love her so much. "Are we related to her?"

He started to turn away, but Abigail wouldn't let him. She reached out and touched his arm as a creepy suspicion filled her. *Please let me be wrong.*

"Am I related to you?"

"Oh God no," he said, his eyes widening in horror. "I'd have never let you kiss me like you did if you were."

That was a relief. "She married someone else, then?"

He inclined his head to her. "It wasn't meant to be between us."

Abigail didn't miss the way he stroked the watch as if it were a part of Matilda, or the agonized grief in his eyes as he talked about her.

"She was too good for me anyway. I'm just glad she found someone who made her happy." He slid the watch back into his pocket, then changed the subject. "Andy has some food for you. I'll go ring him to bring it."

Abigail didn't try to stop him from leaving this time as she digested everything.

Could a man capable of that much love for someone else be the monster she thought he was?

While she had no doubt he was more than capable of killing her father, she seriously doubted he would have slaughtered her mother. Not with the feelings he'd had for Matilda. It didn't seem to fit.

Could it have been a shape-shifter? There were plenty who could have worn his skin.

But who and, most important, why? What would anyone have to gain by framing him and not turning him over to the authorities? And why kill her parents?

Her head ached from trying to decipher it.

I have to find out the truth and make whoever killed them pay. She owed her parents that much.

She turned back toward the bed to get her shoes, when a disgusted sound made her pause.

"What do you mean I can't go?" It was a voice she was unfamiliar with that sounded like someone standing not too far from her room.

"I thought we'd settled this, mite," Jess said sternly.

"Ah hell no, we didn't. You let me go up to Alaska with you, and I was a lot younger then."

"And there were other Squires there to watch your back. Not to mention, I was dumb enough not to know how much danger was there. This time I know, and you're not going."

"I hate you, you decrepit bastard."

Sundown scoffed. "I hear you. Now take that to Abigail and mind your manners, pup."

"Yeah, yeah, yeah." A few seconds later, he knocked on her door.

"Come in." She couldn't wait to see Sundown's Squire.

Andy walked in with a tray that carried a bottled Coke, water, and a plate filled with chicken, roasted potatoes, and green beans. He paused to eye her suspiciously. Dressed in jeans and a red T-shirt, he appeared to be around her age and extremely cute. Except for the slight curl to his lip, as if it made him ill to be in her presence.

"You must be Andy."

"Yeah, and if you hurt Jess, so help me, I will hunt you down to the farthest corner of hell and make you wish to God you'd never breathed air. You hear me?"

Well, that was most unexpected. "You greet everyone this way?"

"No. I'm usually very nice. But you . . . you have no idea how much effort it's taking for me not to kill you where you stand."

She returned his sneer with one of her own. "Bring it, punk."

"Don't tempt me." He moved to set the tray at the foot of the bed. Closer to him now, she realized he was almost as tall as Sundown. Though without the massive muscles and aura of I-can-kick-the-crap-out-of-you, it wasn't quite so apparent at first glance. Unlike Sundown, he didn't dominate the room or her senses.

Andy started for the door.

"Why are you so protective of him, anyway? I thought Squires hated their Dark-Hunters."

He paused to give her a look that asked are-you-effing-nuts? "Our Dark-Hunters are our family. There's nothing we wouldn't do for them. Even die for them if we had to."

"That's not what I've heard."

He scowled at her. "From who? Daimons? Apollites? If the DH are so bad, explain to me why some of the above have been known to work and live with Dark-Hunters themselves."

She rolled her eyes. "Now I know you're lying to me. There's no way an Apollite would *ever* work for a Dark-Hunter."

Crossing his arms over his chest, he gave her a droll stare. "Babe, I know two of them who married one." He jerked his chin toward the door. "Ishtar Casino, here in Vegas, has a whole staff of Apollites who work for Sin Nana . . . who up until about four years ago was a Dark-Hunter, and he was doing his duties while they worked for him. Hell, half of them helped him, and when he was attacked, they and even a Daimon fought to protect him."

Abigail would argue, but she knew Apollites who'd worked there, and she knew Sin owned it. "How do I know Sin was ever a Dark-Hunter?"

"Why would I lie?"

"It could be pathological."

He rolled his eyes. "Whatever. I'm not going to argue with you. Don't like you enough to bother. But like I said, you hurt one hair on his head, and you will regret it. Jess *is* my family, and he's been through enough damage in his life. And in spite of all the shit people have done to him, including his best friend shooting him in the back and in his head on the day of his wedding at the feet of his fiancée, there's not a more decent human being ever born." He turned and was out the door before she had a chance to say anything else.

Stunned, she stood there as that last bit hit her like a fist.

Shot in the back on his wedding day? An image of Matilda and her mother went through her mind. For a full minute, she couldn't breathe. She could see it all in her head so clearly.

It wasn't meant to be. Sundown's words echoed in her ears. No wonder he'd been so sad when he talked about her.

To be with her mother, who looked so much like Matilda, must have killed him.

It's why he killed her and your father. He couldn't take it any more.

A psychotic break would make sense.

Andy and Jess were lying.

She wanted to believe that. It would be the easiest. Not to mention, it was the option that didn't leave her with a conscience that would flog her for the rest of her life.

However long that was.

Rubbing her hand over her eyes, she sat down on the bed and looked at the food. It turned her stomach.

No, not the food. What she'd done. The one thing no one had ever told her about was how to cope with the lives she'd taken. Even before Sundown had kidnapped her, her conscience had been there, telling her that she'd taken someone's life. Her anger kept her going, but it wasn't enough to drown out her actions.

"They deserved it. Think of how many of us they've killed over the centuries. Do you think they ever have a minute's worth of compassion when it comes to us? No, they don't. Kill the Apollite. We're animals to be butchered

to them. Wasn't it bad enough Apollo cursed us? Then his damned sister had to go and create a race to hunt and kill us as brutally as they can. They stab us in the hearts, Abby. And stand over our bodies while we die. Where is fair in all of that? We live twenty-seven years and hit full puberty at a time when most humans are still in grade school, learning their ABC's. Our lives are horrifically short, and you were there when my mother withered into dust. At twenty-seven. Remember that? Did you ever even hear her speak a bad word about anyone? No. She was kindness incarnate. We took you in and you've seen it firsthand. We don't hurt anyone. We are the victims." Kurt's indignation had fueled her vengeance quest, along with Perry and Jonah.

Even Hannah.

Kill the Dark-Hunters, Abby. That had been chanted to her since the moment Kurt's mother died. Even her adoptive father, on his deathbed, had begged her for retribution.

"*You're our only hope, Abs. Don't let us down. Remember what they did to us. What that animal did to your parents. Never forget it.*"

But her memories . . . Something in all of this didn't feel right. There were too many missing pieces.

If only she knew the truth.

You do know the truth. You were there.

Unable to sort through it, she looked up at the ceiling,

wishing the real answer would fall down and smack her hard enough to make her listen.

Your *coyotes just* came slinking back in the door with tucked tails. I would have killed them, but figured you'd want the honor. They claim there's a wolf helping your enemies now. But they don't know who he is, or if he's one of ours or from another pantheon. My guess is he's not one of ours."

Coyote narrowed his gaze on the huge bear of a man who dared to enter his den with such unwelcome news. And there was only one who would be so bold. Snake was a full head taller, which given the fact that Coyote was six feet two was impressive. While his own hair was short and black, Snake's was shaved bald and an intricate snake tattoo started at where his hairline would be on top of his head. It coiled down his neck and both of his beefy arms into a symbolic pattern that only one of their people could read. To most, Snake would appear like a criminal. But Coyote knew him for what he really was.

An ancient warrior who, like him, had lain dormant for far too long. Who would have thought when they agreed to their duties centuries ago that they, who had once made the very earth tremble in fear of their strength and skill, would be relegated to a role that was only one step above nursemaid?

"Did you hear me, Coyote?"

He gave a subtle nod. "They've grown fat and lazy. Unable to hunt. I weep for what has become of our people." Most of all, he wept for what had become of them.

"With Choo Co La Tah weakened, we'll have better luck after this."

He wished he were so optimistic. Choo Co La Tah had turned back his scorpions faster than he'd expected. But it'd drained the old man. With luck, his next plague would weaken him enough that they could kill him, too.

With Choo Co La Tah out of the way, there would be no stopping them.

He could almost smile at the unexpected gift the human had given them. He'd hoped she would kill Renegade and Brady. Taking out his other enemy was a bonus.

It'd been centuries since he stood this close to his goal. So close, he feel the breath of it on his face.

But nothing was certain. Nothing should ever be taken for granted.

And never, ever underestimate Choo Co La Tah. Even though he and Snake outnumbered the old man, they still had the problem that while Coyote was the Guardian for the East, he'd only obtained it by trickery.

It wasn't his right.

The legitimate Guardian still lived, even though it was as a Dark-Hunter and so long as he did, there was always the possibility that he'd step forward to claim his station and kill Coyote where he stood.

I would gladly step down. But the true Guardian had made it clear that he wouldn't allow it. Not at the price Coyote demanded.

Snake looked up at the sky above them. "The cycle is drawing close."

At last. He didn't say it. He didn't have to. They'd both been waiting for the Time Untime for far too long.

If the Butterfly and the Buffalo were to unite during the Time Untime, he and Snake would be destroyed. And all the Guardians replaced by those *they* chose.

But if he could stop it, he could rise on the eve of the Reset, and then he would have the power to select the new Guardians himself. With them under his control, they could unite their powers and return the world to their people. The Pale One would be defeated for once and for all.

The reign of the Coyote would be absolute. Uncontested.

Their enemies would be driven back into the sea.

And the elders and earth would weep for the wrong it had done to him. Blood would rain from the skies, and the Coyote would eat the sun and cover this earth with his vengeance.

He could already savor the taste. Soon this world would be his, and with his raised army, he would subjugate everyone.

The one thing he wanted most would then be his. No one would ever remove it again from his possession.

All he had to do was destroy one more Guardian.

So simple . . .

So damned hard.

But he wouldn't fail this time. This time, he would succeed and the world of man would finally understand what true misery meant.

The Reign of Coyote was about to begin, and the world would never be the same.

10

"You know, Jess. If something breaks in and eats me while you're gone, you're going to feel real bad about it. You've seen the movies. Read the books. You know it happens. Sidekick and girlfriend always get kidnapped, snuffed, or usually both by the bad guys after the good ones."

Jess rubbed his brow, trying to soothe the migraine Andy was causing. Not that Dark-Hunters could get migraines, but the boy was definitely putting that theory to the test.

It was either that . . .

Or a tumor.

Can't get those either.

Then what was the painful throb that wouldn't let up?

Oh yeah, it was Andy.

Jess sighed. "You're right, pup. So I'll be sending you over to the Ishtar for Sin to babysit until I get back. That'll make sure nothing bad happens to you."

Now, that was a nice shade of indignation mottling the boy's skin. Quite impressive, really. If he were tea kettle, he'd be whistling like a train. "I can take care of myself."

"Not what you just said."

"That don't mean—"

"Jess, we have a problem."

He glanced past Andy's shoulder to see Ren looking as flustered as the kid. Ren joined them in the kitchen.

A huge weight of dread fell right on top of Jess. "What's wrong?"

"Abigail's gone."

There was something Jess didn't want to hear. "Excuse me?"

Ren nodded. "I went to get her from downstairs, and there's no trace of her. She must have snuck up and out while we were preparing. Damn you for a house this big. Really, folks? Was it necessary?"

Andy snorted. "You try finding a house to accommodate a dozen horses with a large basement in Vegas that's not haunted, and that you can close on in two weeks and move in. I think I did pretty damn good."

Ignoring Andy's ornery outburst, Jess cursed. Both he and Ren were still plagued with their waned powers. And he could kick himself for not watching her closer. How could he have lulled his brain into forgetting she was a prisoner they intended to sacrifice?

Hell, he'd have run, too.

Andy arched a brow at them. "Why are you two freaking out, anyway? If she's in one of your cars, which I'm sure she is, she's LoJacked."

Jess scowled. "Come again?"

"I LoJack your ass every minute of the night, cowboy. Just in case." Andy went to the wall security monitor that tapped into all their camera feeds and pulled up the garage surveillance. Then he cursed even more foully than Jess had. "Forget yours, that bitch has taste. She's in my Audi R8 Spyder."

Jess growled at him. "Watch your mouth, pup. That's a lady you're talking about."

He grumbled under his breath, questioning that category. "You wouldn't feel that way if she'd run off on one of your stinking horses."

Ren crossed his arms over his chest. "Is it LoJacked?"

"Of course," Andy said indignantly. "That's my baby. I even have a kill switch on her."

"Then stop the engine."

Andy appeared downright horrified by Ren's suggestion. "Are you out of your mind? What if someone hits it for stalling? I had that thing on order for over a year. Custom hand built. The epitome of German engineering. I even paid extra for the paint on her. Ain't no way I'm going to chance someone denting my baby. Or, God forbid, totaling it."

Jess rolled his eyes at the boy's hissy fit. If he kept that up, he'd be putting Andy back in diapers.

He turned to Ren. "You take the air. I'll get a bike." Then he focused his attention on Andy again. "And you—"

Andy held his cell phone out to him. "Have an app. Track her down, get my car back, and beat the hell out of her. . . . In that precise order."

Jess would laugh if the entire fate of the world didn't hinge on his finding Abigail. Shaking his head, he went to the garage to get his red Hayabusa. It was the fastest thing he owned. Plus, it would synch to the tracker in Andy's phone—had to love the Squires and their toys.

He grabbed a full face helmet off the rack, along with the keys, and was on it in record time. While the garage door opened, he synched the phone. As soon as it was complete, he peeled out, leaving the stench of smoke and rubber behind him. He ducked to miss the door that hadn't gotten out of his way fast enough.

Opening the throttle, he shot through the gates that were also only partially parted and turned on to the street, heading south. The best part about the tracker was that it told him the speed the car was traveling. She didn't appear to be going too fast—she probably thought she was home free and didn't want to attract the attention of any police. Smart on her part.

But it wouldn't be enough to keep him from finding her.

Abigail regretted her choice of cars as she tried to navigate traffic. She'd thought the Audi, with its V10 engine, would be fast, but she couldn't have been more wrong. People actually cut her off or boxed her in so that they could slow her down to take pictures of the car with their camera phones. Good grief. She'd never seen anything like it.

Really people, it was a car with four tires like any other. She'd never understood how anyone could become so enthralled by a piece of metal transportation.

How did Sundown ever get anywhere with this much attention? It was so frustrating. She'd never been in a car before that affected traffic and drivers like this.

"I should have found something generic." Unfortunately, her choices had been limited to a Ferrari, an old classic Ford pickup from the 1940s, a Gator and this. The Audi was the only one that was street legal and wasn't a stick shift—something she couldn't drive.

The rest had been motorcycles, and since she'd never ridden one before, she didn't think her escape attempt should serve as her first learning experience. With her luck, she'd have wrecked it in the driveway.

Her heart raced as she habitually checked her rearview mirror, expecting to see Sundown catching up to her any second.

Don't discover I'm gone for a while. Please.

At least not until she had a chance to find out some truths. She wasn't running from what she'd done. She just wanted to understand her memories.

Who was lying to her?

She hated to be so confused. All her life, she'd had one clear-cut goal.

Kill Jess Brady.

Now . . . her emotions and memories were tangled into a knot she wasn't sure she could ever undo. If that wasn't bad enough, there was a bitter hunger inside her for . . .

She didn't know. The demon blood they'd mixed with hers was causing all kinds of problems. At times her senses would sharpen, then fall back to normal.

Beware the pathway that vengeance will take you down. The voice in her head sounded a lot like Sundown's.

His name had no more crossed her mind than something akin to lightning flashed behind her eyes. In that moment, she saw the past so clearly that it stole her breath.

It was Jess.

He kicked open the door to an old-fashioned room. The low, burning fire cast shadows across the cornflower blue scroll wallpaper that covered the walls. A man shot up from the old-fashioned sleigh bed with a gun in his hand. But as soon as he focused on Jess's face, he hesitated.

"I killed you."

Jess wore the mask of stone cold killer. Fierce. Terrifying. Gut-wrenching. "Yeah, you did, Bart. And I told you, you son of a bitch, that I'd be back for you." He spread his arms wide. "Here I am."

Bart came to his senses and unloaded all six of his bullets straight into Jess's body. The rounds left small puffs of smoke as they embedded in his chest without hurting him. He didn't even bleed that much.

Even with the chamber emptied, Bart continued to uselessly pull the trigger.

Jess laughed evilly as he stalked across the room to jerk the gun out of Bart's grasp with one hand. With his other, he grabbed him by the throat and held on so tight that Bart's eyes bulged while he knelt on the bed. Jess pulled him closer so that he could growl into his reddened face. "It was bad enough you killed me. I might have spared you for that. But you had no right to rape Matilda and kill her father in front of her, you worthless bastard. It's what you've done to her that will cost you your life. She was the only decent thing I've ever known. Damn you to hell for hurting her. You had *no* reason for it."

He waited until Bart was almost dead before he released him and slung him to the ground. Bart lay on the floor, wheezing while Jess went to the wooden washing stand in the corner and pulled the ceramic pitcher up and emptied it over Bart's head.

Now completely drenched, Bart sputtered and coughed.

Jess kicked him onto his back and planted his booted foot on his chest. He slammed the pitcher down on the floor, shattering it near Bart's face. Bart jerked, closing his eyes as shards rained down on him. Some of them even caught in his tousled hair.

"You didn't think I was going to kill you that easily, did you?" Jess taunted. "For what you did to her, you are going to suffer every second between now and dawn. I'm going to give you pain the likes of which my mama's people were famed for. And when I finally end your life, you will thank me for it."

"Go to hell!"

Jess scoffed. "You already sent me there. It's your turn now. Give the devil my regards."

Abigail jerked out of the memory as the sound of a horn blared. Blinking, she realized she was about to plow into an oncoming truck. She jerked the wheel and headed back into her lane.

Her breathing ragged, she rubbed at her forehead. Why was she seeing Jess's memories? And she knew that was what they were. It was too vivid to be something she created. She could still smell the fire and the stench of Bart's breath mixed with his sweat.

Jess had sold his soul not to avenge himself. He'd done it for Matilda.

Her gaze clouded as she saw another image. This one was a few years later. It was just after midnight, and Jess stood inside what appeared to be a lawyer's office. A man with a handlebar mustache and parted black hair sat behind a huge mahogany desk. He wore a dark gray suit over a bright burgundy brocade vest. Over his head was a large clock that ticked so loudly, it hurt Jess's hearing.

"I'm breaking all kinds of rules here," the man said as he passed a piece of paper across the clean desk to Jess. "But I did what you asked."

"She's happy?"

The lawyer nodded. "I transferred another half million into her account so that she could buy that house and land she wanted. She now has enough to do anything she wants for the rest of her life."

A tic worked in Jess's handsome jaw. "It's not enough. Keep adding to it every year like I said originally. I don't ever want her to have anything to worry about other than what dress looks best on her."

He inclined his head to the paper Jess held. "That's an

extra photograph I talked the photographer into making of her. Thought you'd like it."

There was no missing the love in his eyes, even though he kept his features completely stoic. "Does she need anything else?"

"No. She's married to a good man who owns the local mercantile."

Jess frowned as if the lawyer had said something wrong. "But?"

"I didn't say there was a but."

"She sits at her window at night and cries." Jess's tone was hollow.

"How did you—?"

"I can read your mind." Jess swallowed hard. "Thank you, Mr. Foster. I appreciate everything you've done." He went to the door and put his hat on his head before he left.

Outside, he tucked the photo into his jacket, and it was only then that she saw the moisture in his eyes.

He quickly blinked it away, then headed for his horse.

Abigail ached as she felt his pain like it was a part of her. He really had loved his Matilda.

"Stop it!" she snapped at herself. This was ridiculous. She didn't want to see Jess. Not now. She had more important things to do.

Slapping herself on the cheek, she focused her attention on the road that led her home. . . .

. . .

J*ess cursed as* he lost all trace of Abigail. The GPS literally flashed bright, then vanished altogether. It looked like something had burned it out.

What the hell?

He started to dial Ren, then remembered he was in crow mode so he wouldn't be able to answer. Instead, he rang Sasha, who picked it up immediately.

"Yell-oh?"

"I've lost her," Jess said without preamble. "Can you give me any guidance?"

Sasha snorted. "On what? A new personality? Car buying? I'm a Wolf, cowboy, not a life counselor."

That sarcasm snapped at his tolerance. "Can you track her, Scooby, or am I asking too much of you?"

"Now, *that* I can do. But it would leave Choo Co La Tah unguarded. Send birdbrain back, and I'll swap off."

"Fine." Jess hung up and mumbled under his breath how much he really hated shape-shifters.

Changing lanes to avoid a slow-moving Toyota, he used his powers to talk to Ren. He'd never tried to do this before when Ren was in crow form, so he had no idea if it would even work. While his powers were starting to recover from being in the house with Ren all day, they still weren't up to their usual strength.

"Talk to me, *penyo*. You there?"

Luckily, Ren came back fast. "I'm here."

Jess breathed a sigh of relief. "You wouldn't happen to know where Abigail got off to, would you?"

"No. I can't track her scent and I haven't had a visual on her yet."

Figured that would be too much to ask. "Then I need you to swap duties with Sasha so that he can track her down."

"Why isn't the GPS working?"

"Twenty-million-dollar question. No answer, and I have no idea who to call to get a clue. I'll keep heading in the direction she was and hope she doesn't turn off anytime soon."

"All right. I'm flashing back. Will get Sasha to you ASAP."

Jess slowed down and tried to use his own abilities to track her. He didn't really have that power, but . . . At this point, he was willing to try most anything.

Why? The bad feeling in his gut that said if he didn't find her quick, something awful would happen to her. It had nothing to do with needing to get her to the Valley to save the world. This was something else entirely. Something that made him desperate to locate her.

"Hang on, Abby. I'm coming."

A *bigail slowed as* she reached the modest home she shared with Hannah in Henderson. She cringed a bit as she scraped the front of the car on the angle of the aggregate driveway. *Hope Jess doesn't love this thing.*

He might kill her after all.

She parked outside and headed for the front door. But as she neared it, a strange red haze seemed to drop down over everything. It was like she was staring out of a pair of red glasses. She heard that strange thrumming sound again—the same she'd heard when they put the demon blood in her.

Like she was listening to the heartbeat of the world.

Shaking her head, she forced herself forward.

"If something's happened to her, Kurt, I swear I'll never forgive you."

"Shut up, Hannah, and sit down."

She knew they were inside the house, but she could hear them as clearly as if they were standing beside her. More than that, she could see them sitting at the table with Jonah.

"We know where Sundown lives," Hannah said. "Why can't we go get her?"

Kurt curled his lip. "Are you out of your mind? We march into a Dark-Hunter's home and do what? Tell him to hand her over?"

She lifted her chin defiantly. "Yes."

Looking up from the laptop where he was working, Jonah rolled his eyes. "I'm really sick of you two fighting. Take your sister out of here while I do this."

His voice . . .

There was something about it that tugged on the edge of her memory. But what?

Kurt grabbed Hannah by the arm and hauled her out of the room. As soon as they were gone, Jonah pulled out his phone and dialed it. "Hey. I've got her heartbeat on the monitor so we know she's still alive. Yeah, I think it's a good sign that the Hunter hasn't killed her yet."

At the sound of those words, Abigail felt a surge of some odd emotion throughout her entire body. Her teeth elongated. It was the demon again. It was reacting to being here.

Why?

Raw, unfettered rage followed the wave. The demon wanted to taste Jonah in the worst sort of way.

I can't do that.

Yet she salivated. The taste of warm, sweet blood filled her mouth, making her ache to take some from someone else. The haze turned brighter. She walked through the door without opening it. With no real understanding of moving, she found herself in the kitchen with Jonah.

He looked up and blanched. He dropped his phone straight to the floor, where it landed with a thud. "What's wrong?"

She licked at her fangs. *Taste him. . . . You know you want to.*

Strangely enough, she did.

Abigail reached for his throat, but he jumped to his feet and put distance between them.

He kept backing away from her. "What did they do to you, Abby?"

Abby . . .

No, that didn't seem right. She was . . .

Caught in a maelstrom. She could feel the winds whipping, howling, and tearing at her. The room spun around as more images flashed. She saw the past, the present, and a future filled with horrors that were indescribable.

But the one thing she saw clearest . . .

The night her parents died. And this time she knew why that voice had been familiar. Who had been there with "Sundown."

"You were there." She pointed her finger at Jonah, who stood before her, gaping.

"What are you talking about?"

She didn't answer as the demon swallowed her whole. Before she knew what she was doing, she was on him, biting into his neck. The moment she tasted his blood, she knew the truth.

Jonah was a Daimon. It was why the demon in her wanted to annihilate him.

The souls of his victims screamed in her head with a chorus that was deafening and sickening. They wanted their freedom.

And she wanted his blood.

"Abby! Stop!"

She recognized Kurt's voice, but there was no way she would listen to him. Not now. Not when the demon had her.

Kurt ran at her back and tried to knock her away. She turned on him and hissed, while she maintained her grip on Jonah, who was crying and begging for mercy.

Really? After all the people he'd ruthlessly killed to live, he had the nerve to beg for his own life? The hypocrisy sickened her even more.

"Coward," she breathed in his ear. "You could have saved my mother, and you didn't." He had swallowed her soul so that he could live. Damn him! Agony and fury bonded inside her to such a level that it was all she could do not to rip him apart.

Instead, she reached down to his boot, where he always kept a knife hidden. In slow motion, she saw Kurt lunging for her back. Before he could reach her, she stabbed Jonah in the heart.

He gasped, then burst apart into a shower of gold dust.

"No!" Kurt drew the word out, but it was too late.

Jonah was dead. She'd killed him.

Numb and dizzy, she stared down at her pristine hand. There was no blood there. Nothing left of Jonah except a shimmering film that graced the floor. Iridescent like the wings of a summer butterfly.

She could hear the laughter of the human souls as they

finally ascended to their rightful places. But more than that, she heard their gratitude. At least she had saved them. Too bad no one had saved her parents.

"What have you done?" His eyes wide, Kurt stared at her as if she was a stranger.

And she was. She didn't know herself any more than he did. "What have you made me?"

"You were supposed to be stronger. Not . . . not—" He gestured wildly at her. "—*this.*"

A weird odor filled her head. It was like sulfur, only stronger. It was . . .

"You took demon blood, too," she accused him as she understood what the demon was telling her.

He didn't deny it. "What was I supposed to do? I'll turn twenty-seven in a few months. I don't want to die any more than you do. At least it's better than killing a human."

Was it?

Hannah came out from the back of the house. She stared at Abigail with horrified eyes before she let out a shrill scream.

Abigail covered her ears as pain split her skull. She glared at her "brother." "You lied to me. *All* of you. You didn't tell me about Daimons."

Kurt narrowed his gaze on her. "You didn't need to know about them."

Oh, now there was an award-winning answer. "You told me the Dark-Hunters were our enemies."

"They are our enemies. They hunt and kill us."

It wasn't that simple. Not anymore. Jess had been right. They had lied to her. Used her. "You have no idea what you've done. What you've set into motion."

You will be known forever by the tracks you leave. Her mother's words haunted her now.

I will be known as the woman who ended the world. She felt so sick. Lost. Confused.

Betrayed.

Kurt grabbed her arm. "Abigail, listen to me. We're not your enemies. We took you in when no one else would have. My parents raised you like one of their own."

But there was more to it than that.

The truth hovered around the fringes of her mind like a ghost she could neither see nor touch. Only feel.

She stared at him as her conscience shredded her over her actions. "I don't trust you anymore."

Hannah stepped forward. "Abby—"

She moved away from Hannah's grasp.

I need to go. She didn't want to be here. It no longer felt like home.

It felt like hell.

She'd taken innocent lives. Killed an elder Guardian. Her life would never be the same. And it shouldn't be. Not after what she'd done. She stumbled back toward the door and went outside. The sky above twinkled with stars. It looked a thousand times brighter tonight than it ever had before.

Why?

Why would it be that way when everything was so wrong? Surely it should be storming. But it wasn't. The world appeared completely ignorant of the horrors to come.

"I have to fix this," she whispered. Before it was too late.

She would go with Choo Co La Tah to the Valley.

And there she would die.

11

Jess followed Sasha's directions as they sped toward Abigail's location. His stomach was knotted tight, and he had no idea why. It wasn't just that she was gone. He had a tangible need to find her and make sure she was all right.

To make sure no one hurt her.

He came around a corner right as a car rolled through the stop sign—straight into his path. Biting his lip, he tried to swerve to miss it, but because of the car's speed, it still managed to clip his back tire. His motorcycle came out from under him and dragged him down the street at a deadly pace.

Crap! The asphalt tore at his clothes and skin, reminding him why he wore a duster when he rode and why he was glad he was no longer mortal. Still, it hurt to kiss pavement, and his body was extremely unhappy with this predicament.

Abigail's heart stopped beating as she realized in her dazed stupor that she'd just hit someone. She slammed on the brakes and looked back to see the motorcycle and rider on the street, skidding sideways toward the curb.

Oh my God! What have I done now?

It wasn't until she'd put the car in park and opened the door that she recognized the sprawled-out man.

"Jess!" She ran toward him as fast as she could. She cringed at the length of how far he'd traveled over the road on his back. *He's a Dark-Hunter. A crash won't kill him.* In her mind, she knew it was the truth.

But her emotions weren't listening. Panic filled her as she drew closer and didn't see him moving.

Jess lay on the street, looking up through his helmet,

trying to figure out if he'd broken something other than his pride. Gah, it hurt to breathe. To move. He felt pretty banged up, but it was hard to tell just how bad.

And the damned billion-pound motorcycle was lying on his foot. That was going to leave a limp.

"Jess!" Out of nowhere, Abigail appeared, her face a mask of terrified fear. Before he could answer, she sank down beside him. "Oh my God! Oh my God! Oh my God! Are you all right? Are you alive? Did I hurt you?" She clutched at his body as if trying to find an injury. "Jess? Can you speak?"

It was so wrong, but he couldn't help grinning at her panic. No woman had been this scared for him in a long while. "Yeah, I can talk. But I kind of like the attention you're giving me. You want to grope a little lower, it'd be even better."

"Oh, you . . ." She shoved at him.

Pain cut through his body. "Ow!"

Her panic returned instantly. "Are you all right?"

He laughed. "Dang, you're easy."

"And you're completely evil."

Jess pulled his helmet off to stare up at her. The street-lights played in her dark hair, making it shimmer. Her eyes glowed with warmth, concern, and anger. It was a heady combination. "And you're completely beautiful."

Abigail's breath caught at those unexpected words. They settled something deep inside her. Made it calm in a way she'd never been calm before. And at the same time, her entire body was on fire from his nearness. A strange dichotomy that made no sense whatsoever.

He wrapped his arms around her and pulled her lips down to his so that he could give her the hottest kiss she'd ever received. One so unsettling that it made her entire body burn and caused her to forget where they were and what had happened. Nothing mattered in this moment except the sensation of his tongue sweeping against hers. Of his arms holding her close to his hard body.

Nothing had ever felt better.

"Excuse me, people. You're both lying in the middle of the street. Might want to move before someone else runs over both your damn fool selves."

Abigail pulled back, then turned to glare at Sasha, who stood on the curb, under the streetlamp, giving them an irritated grimace. She started to smart off, when all of a sudden, she heard a peculiar sound. It was like someone had let loose a herd of angry chainsaws.

Scowling, she looked back at Jess. "What is that?"

Sasha's face blanched. "Wasps . . . A shitload of them." He pointed down the street.

Following the direction of his arm, Abigail gaped at the sight of what appeared to be a thick, dancing cloud rolling toward them.

"Next plague." Jess jumped to his feet and pulled her up. He met Sasha's gaze. "Can you get the bike home?"

"On it. I'll see you back in your compound."

Jess inclined his head to him before he took her hand and ran with her back to the Audi. Abigail was still gaping as she watched the wasps draw closer and closer at an abnormal pace. The cloud rose and dived like some giant, lumbering, solid beast.

She ran to the passenger side while Jess wedged himself into the driver's seat and moved it back.

"I really hope you didn't damage this thing."

She slammed the door shut, grateful she'd left it running, then buckled herself in. "You that attached to it, cowboy?"

He put it in gear. "Nope. Not mine. It's Andy's pride and joy. If there's so much as a scratch on this thing, I'll never hear the end of it."

Great. Now the Squire had another reason to hate her. "I can't win for losing with him, can I?"

Jess didn't answer as the wasps literally enveloped the car. They landed on the windshield so thick that he had to turn the wipers on to try and dislodge them.

It didn't work. All it did was piss them off.

Disgusted and scared, Abigail hissed as she realized they were also crawling in through the vents.

"Close them quick," Jess said, snatching his shut.

She complied and held them in place to make sure the wasps didn't push them open again. "This is getting ugly."

"Like my great-aunt's underpants."

She arched a brow at his strange and unexpected comment. Okay . . .

Jess tried to navigate the streets, but it was far from easy going. Cars were swerving everywhere, trying to avoid the wasps. Horns blared and people screamed so loudly that it was deafening. She'd never seen anything like it.

What were they going to do?

She sighed. "I'm getting a little tired of this."

Jess flashed a fanged grin. "Not my fave thing either, I have to say. You wouldn't happen to have a can of Raid, would you?"

"I wish. What else don't they like?"

"Apparently us . . . and a little brown Audi."

She shook her head. "How can you find humor right now?"

"Damned if I know. I must be one sick SOB. There's definitely something in my noodle that's shorted out."

And how could she find that charming?

More than that, her entire life was falling apart, and the only comfort she had was him. Maybe he wasn't the sick one after all.

Maybe it was her.

Yeah, there's definitely something wrong with me. And it wasn't just the wasps trying to break into the car and sting them or the demon that had made her eat a friend. "This is definitely one of those days when you're praying it's a dream. Only you never wake up from the nightmare."

"I've had a few of those in my time. But this one here's not so bad."

"How do you figure?" she asked, flabbergasted by his words.

He flashed a fanged grin at her. "I might have lost some skin, but I got kissed by a beautiful woman who was happy to see me. I gotta say that's pretty epic in my book. Definitely not a worst-case day here."

Given what she'd seen of his past, she knew that for a fact. Still . . .

"Thank you."

He frowned. "For what?"

Being here.

Being you. Things she couldn't say out loud without embarrassing herself to the deepest level. But she felt that gratitude so much that it made tears prick at her eyes.

After a few seconds when she didn't respond, Jess looked over at her. She was staring at her hands as if they belonged to a stranger. A cloak of sadness enveloped her. "You okay?"

She nodded. And still she looked at her hands. "I killed a . . . Daimon tonight."

"What?"

Swallowing, she glanced over at him. "You were right. They'd lied to me my whole life and kept that knowledge from me. I don't know what to believe now."

"Believe in yourself. Trust your instincts."

"Is that what you do?"

Jess snorted as old memories burned. "No. Not doing it is what got me shot in the back by a man I thought was my brother. I like to think I learn a little as I go."

But sometimes he wondered. Like right now, there was a part of him that wanted to trust her, and if ever someone should know better than that, it was him. She'd already proved that she was willing to hurt him to get what she wanted.

And she'd also run to him when he was hurt to make sure he was still alive.

After she hit him with a car, of course. Yeah, okay, so that part sucked. But she *had* come back when she didn't have to. It was more than a lot of people would do.

"We're not going to make it back to your house, are we?" He heard the fearful undercurrent in her voice.

"Don't get maudlin on me. We're not dead yet . . . any chance those demon powers of yours have anything to help with this?"

"Not that . . ." Her voice trailed off as if an idea suddenly occurred to her. "Don't wasps hate bad smells?"

"I'm not fond of them neither. Is there something you need to tell me? 'Cause right now, I really can't open a window."

She made a sound of disgust at his offbeat humor. "Whenever the powers surge, they put off an awful smell. I was thinking—"

"I prefer the idea of me driving through the worst BOB ever than having you smell up the car with demon funk to choke us down. No offense, my sight and hearing aren't the only things my Dark-Hunter powers boost."

"BOB?"

He loved that out of all that, she'd gotten only one word. "Baked on bugs. Or in this case, I guess I should have said BOW—baked on wasps."

She started to laugh, but something slammed into them so hard, it snapped her forcefully to the right.

Jess cursed as he lost control of the car and they spun around. He wasn't sure what had struck them, but it felt like a semi.

On steroids.

All of a sudden, there was a lone howl.

Coyote. He'd know that sound anywhere. The only question was if he meant it as a taunt or an order for his servants. When the car finally stopped moving, it ended up embedded against a pole.

"You all right?" he asked Abigail.

She nodded. "I think so. You?"

"Brain's a mite rattled, but that's nothing new for me."

She jerked up in her seat as if someone had shocked her. "You hear that?"

He strained, then shook his head. The only sound in his ears was a bad inner buzzing and the wasps outside. "Hear what?"

"I can't make out the words, but it sounds like some-one whispering."

He tried again, and again he heard nothing. "I only hear you."

"You really don't hear that?"

"Sorry. My medium powers are on the fritz, and I can't channel spirits or bells right now. I'll get them worked on later. For—"

"Shh," she said, touching his arm with her hand. "The wasps are talking to someone. I hear them so clearly."

Okay, time to get someone to a psych ward.

"It says to kill the buffalo."

His scowl deepened. "There's no buffalo in Vegas. At least not that I know of."

"That's what they're saying, though."

Maybe what she heard was that weird tendency people had to make ambient noise and other obnoxious things tolerable by incorporating them into understand-able sounds and syllables. He didn't know for sure.

At least not until he felt something else strike the car and land on the hood. It struck the windshield repeat-edly.

The wasps pulled back enough for them to see a giant mountain lion. It was trying to break through the wind-shield to get them.

"Oh, this ain't good," Jess muttered under his breath. He put the car into reverse and backed up at a scary pace.

Cutting the wheel, he sent the mountain lion flying. Then he put it in drive and floored it.

Abigail held her breath as panic seized every part of her. She didn't see any way out of this. "You think Choo Co La Tah can save us again?"

"Eventually, he can stop it. I just don't know how long we have to hold out. Not to mention, the mountain lion is new. Man, what I wouldn't give for some catnip right now."

Cars were still running off the road as their drivers were swarmed.

As Jess passed a gas station, an idea hit him. It was lunacy, but . . .

It was all he had. He headed for another gas station down the street.

Abigail cringed as they pulled into the station and she saw the bodies on the ground of people who'd been caught outside by the wasps and who were now dead from their stings. There were others trapped in cars who screamed for help while the wasps continued to swarm, looking for new victims.

"Is there anything we can do for them?"

"Yeah. Stop Coyote."

That was much easier said than done.

Jess took them to the carwash and pulled inside. She started to ask him what he was doing when all of a sudden, the doors closed, sealing them in. The mountain lion slammed into the door, but couldn't reach them through the tough plastic.

Waving his hand, Jess appeared to make the water come on.

The wasps around their car went crazy as they were sprayed.

Her heart lightened. It was a brilliant idea. They were going to drown the wasps.

Laughing, she turned to Jess and kissed him on the cheek. "You're a genius!"

"Ah now, don't be going on like that. I might actually think you like me, and where would we be then?"

He was right. That was even more terrifying than being assaulted by killer wasps and angry mountain lions. And as that thought went through her head, she was struck with another realization.

"You have telekinesis."

He nodded. "A little, but it's not always reliable."

"How so?"

"I've had a few mishaps with it. I used to try and control it more, but after an embarrassing incident, I learned to leave it be."

This she wanted to hear. "What embarrassing incident?"

He actually blushed. "Really don't want to share or relive it. Suffice it to say, it learned me a thing or two that I've never forgotten."

All righty, then. She leaned back in the seat while the water and suds took care of their menace for them. It slid the wasps around and made a nice thick ick on the ground. And as she sat there watching them go down the drains and fall away, the horror of her actions hit her fully.

She'd killed a friend tonight.

And she'd lost her family.

I'm alone. But it was so much worse than that . . .

Jess felt her sadness as if it were inside him. He watched her in the dim light while emotions flitted across her face and darkened her eyes. "It'll be all right." He tried to reassure her.

She shook her head in denial. "No. Everything I've ever known. Everything I've been told by the people I loved was a lie." She held her hand up, grateful it was human and not demon, and yet she knew the truth. . . . . "I let them mix me with a demon and my adoptive brother did the same, too. I don't know what I am now. I don't know what he is. It was all so clear before. Kill you. Avenge my parents, and then protect my family and the Apollites and humans from the Dark-Hunters." A single tear went down her cheek as she met his gaze. "I'm a monster, Jess. I've destroyed myself."

Those words tugged at his heart and reminded him of the day he'd come to that same realization. It was so hard to see the truth in yourself.

Harder still to face it.

"You're not a monster, Abby. Confused, I'll give you. But not a monster. Believe me. I've seen those enough to know."

"Yeah, right."

He cupped her cheek and turned her head to face him so that she could see his sincerity. "Look at me, Abby. I know what it's like to wake up every single day, angry at the world. Angry at God and humanity for what they've done to you and to want to make them pay for it. To feel like the entire world sees you as nothing but its whipping boy. Like you, my mother died when I was a little kid. She was the only thing good I had. The only one who'd ever made me feel like I was human. My father hated me, and he never hid that fact from anyone. He took his own anger at the world out on me, and it left a lot of scars, inside and out. To this day, I can still hear him and that hatred in my head, trying to poison my thoughts. Trying to poison me. I ran away from home after he almost killed me. Thirteen, I was. I tried to find decent work or someplace to stay and call home. What I found out was that people like to kick others when they're down, even when they're just kids. They get a sick thrill out of it. Makes them feel big and powerful while it destroys the heart and soul of their unfortunate victim."

He swallowed as some of his harshest lessons resurfaced and he saw the faces of those who'd wronged him. But this wasn't about him—it was about her.

"I learned human decency is probably the rarest creature out there. And I couldn't find anyone who didn't want to take advantage of me or hurt me even worse than my pa had. And it hardened me even more. By the time I was sixteen, that poison had rotted me from the inside out. It colored everything about me. I justified what I did to other people by reminding myself of how they'd treated me. They deserved whatever I did to them. Do unto others before they do unto you."

"You became a killer."

He nodded. "Until the day I killed a boy, thinking he was a man. He'd wanted to avenge his pa, and for the first time in my life, I saw someone else capable of love and sacrifice. Believe it or not, it was something I hadn't seen except from my mother. And as stupid as it sounds, I'd convinced myself that it was unique to her and that no one else had it in them. But after that, I saw the difference between love and loyalty. Most of all, I saw what I'd become. What my hatred had turned me into."

His dark gaze was filled with torment. "Don't talk to me about monsters. I was one of the worst."

A few days ago, she'd have agreed completely. Hell, a few hours ago, she'd have agreed. Now . . .

"You told me you never killed a woman or child."

"Just that one time, and I never got over it. One stupid mistake that has lived with me every day since. Bart told me I was an idiot to let it bother me. Better he give up the ghost than I be the one lying in a grave. But that boy didn't give up the ghost. Not really. It followed me from town to town, and no matter what I did, I couldn't escape it. Until the day a beautiful woman smiled at me. She didn't see the ugliness I kept inside. For the first time in my life, she saw the man I wanted to be, and she helped me to find him. Because of her, I learned that, yeah, people are selfish assholes for the most part, but not everyone is. That there are some rare beings out there who will help others and not abuse them. People who really don't want anything from you."

He stroked her cheek with his thumb. "Acheron always says that our scars are there to remind us of our pasts, of where we've been and what we've gone through. But that pain doesn't have to drive or determine our future. We can rise above it if we let ourselves. It's not easy, but nothing in life ever is."

Those words haunted her. Like he said, she'd allowed her past to color everything about her and to infect any part of happiness she might try to find. She'd worn her scars like a badge, and her family had used them against her. Not for her best interest.

For theirs.

His warm hand felt so good as he soothed her. "I don't see the monster in you, Abby. Monsters don't care about other people, and they don't care who they hurt. In you, I see a woman who is strong. One who knows what's right and who will do whatever she has to to protect the ones she loves."

"I killed your friends," she reminded him.

"And I'm not happy about that. But your head wasn't

screwed on right. It's easy to let the enemies in and listen to them sometimes, especially when they're pretending to be your best friends who only want the best for you. At least that's what they claim. They're insidious bastards, telling you what you want to hear and using your emotions to manipulate you into doing their bidding. I did it with Bart. I thought he was the only person in the world who gave a shit about me, and I would have protected him with my life."

That was how she'd felt about Kurt.

"Sooner or later, usually out of jealousy, their real colors come out and you see the truth that makes you feel like a fool. I know that betrayal, Abigail. That sting that's so deep inside, it leaves a permanent scar on your soul. But you don't have to be like them. And *you're* not."

She felt her tears start falling at his words. He made her feel so much better, and she wasn't sure she had a right to. Honestly. She'd hurt so many people. Destroyed lives.

Over a lie . . .

Before she realized what she was doing, she had her belt unhooked and crawled into his lap.

Jess slid the seat back so that he could hold her in the darkness. The scent of her hair filled his head as his heart thumped wildly. He held her close, wishing he could take away the pain.

Only time could do that.

And it sucked at it. "It'll be all right, Abigail."

"Yeah, after I sacrifice myself for my stupidity."

"I told you, I'm not going to let that happen."

Abigail wanted to believe him. She did. But she knew better. "There's nothing to be done. It is what it is."

He scoffed at that. "You're talking to a man who sold his soul to a goddess to get revenge on the man who killed him. Really? You think *this* is impossible?"

She smiled against his chest. The way he said that, she could almost believe in a miracle. For the first time, she wanted to. She buried her face against his shoulder, inhaling his scent. Why was it that here, she finally felt safe? Even though there were enemies all around and a vicious mountain lion waiting outside to devour them, she felt safe. It defied all logic and sense.

Jess kissed the top of her head while his own emotions flared deep. He'd forgotten what it was like to look into a woman's eyes and see a future he craved. To be this close to one and to share things about his past that he told to no one.

Not even Matilda had known what he told to Abigail tonight. While he'd loved her, he'd always lived with the fear that she'd find out about his past and be horrified by it. That she'd cast him aside as everyone else had and hate him for the very things he'd done to survive.

But Abigail knew his ugliness.

She felt his scars.

It made him feel all the closer to her. Appreciate her more for not judging him. At least not now. She understood how easy it was to get sucked into a nightmare and how hard it was to get out. To do things you thought were justified and then wake up and realize you'd been duped. Lied to.

Used.

He'd woken up as a Dark-Hunter only to feel like a whore. Like he'd sold his life away for pocket change. And for what? To die alone in the gutter at the hands of his best friend.

He could hide his past from everyone, except himself. That was the hardest part. Even when you tried, forgiveness didn't come easy.

Some days it didn't come at all.

Maybe it would be kinder to let her die so that she wouldn't have to face that agony.

Life ain't supposed to be kind.

True. And God knew, it'd been nothing but a kick in his groin most days. But then there were moments like this one. Perfect moments of feeling close to someone. Of letting their warmth soothe you.

That was what living was about. That was being human. When everything hurt and everything was wrong, to have that one person who could make you smile even when all you wanted to do was cry.

These were the moments that got you through the bad.

Abigail looked up at him. He stared into those clear eyes as her breath tickled his skin.

And in that heartbeat, he knew he would die to protect her.

God help me.

The last time he felt this way, he had died. Leaning his head down, he pressed his forehead against hers and tried to see the future.

If there was one after all of this.

But he knew the truth. He was a Dark-Hunter, and she was . . .

Unique. There was nothing in the Dark-Hunter handbook about this situation.

He looked outside the car wash to see the wasps still swarming as they tried to find a way in. He didn't know how long this wave would last. How much time they had for anything.

Abigail cupped his head with her hand as her thoughts warred with each other. In spite of what Jess said, she couldn't see anyway out of this.

Except for death.

She'd really screwed up this time. In a life marked by mistakes, this had been the mother lode. And she'd dragged a good man into the nightmare with her.

Emotions ripped through her so fast, she couldn't even sort them out. She wanted to feel grounded again. To feel like she had a future.

But the only thing that kept her anchored was Jess.

Her heart swelling, she pulled his lips to hers and kissed

him. This was probably the last night of her life. She'd be lucky if any of them were alive by dawn.

And all because she'd been an idiot.

She owed him a debt more than she could pay for standing by her and saving her life. But it wasn't just obligation she felt for him. There was something so much more. Deeper.

She felt like she was a part of him. And she didn't want to die without letting him know.

Rising up in the seat, she straddled his hips.

Jess frowned as he looked up into Abigail's eyes. There was a hungry fire there he'd never seen before. And as she started unbuttoning her shirt, his breath caught. "Um . . . Abigail—"

She stopped his words by pressing her forefinger to his lips. Then she slid it slowly down his chest, heading south until she reached his fly.

"I know we don't have long, Jess. But this may be the only time we'll ever have. And I don't want to die without making amends to you."

"You don't have to do *this*."

She smiled. "I know. I want to do this."

And all his arguments and thoughts scattered as she slid her hand into his jeans and touched him. Oh yeah, he was lost now.

He knew that after this, he would never be the same again.

12

Abigail had never done anything like this a day in her life. She'd never even fantasized about it. But as they waited here, so close to death and with her mortality breathing down her neck, she couldn't help herself.

Jess didn't love her—she knew that. But it didn't matter. She'd seen inside his heart to the man he'd been and to the one he currently was. And the woman in her wanted to touch that part of him and share it. Once she was gone from this earth, he'd remember her.

For eternity.

She wanted him to remember her as someone who'd been decent and caring. Not the soulless monster she currently felt like.

Please see the real me.

Just once.

No one ever had. She'd always been so strong around Hannah and Kurt. Never let them see her fears. She'd strived to be a perfect sister and to help them with whatever problem they had, no matter what was going on in her own life, no matter how badly she ached inside.

They had come first.

And of course, to be a dutiful daughter to her adoptive parents, she'd learned to bury herself and her emotions and let no one ever see them. Her one fear had always been that they would regret taking a human into their home and turn her out into the streets if she caused them any problem whatsoever.

Most Apollites tried to hide their distaste about her unfortunate human birth, but she saw through the hollow smiles and false offers of friendship, especially her adoptive father's. Like the others, he'd tried to hide it. But he couldn't.

The truth had been forever etched in his eyes, and it had cut her to her soul.

They weren't her people, and they never forgot that fact. No matter how hard she'd tried to fit in and convince them that she was on their side. That she would fight to the death for them. No matter how many Hunters she pursued for them. There was still a wall they kept in place that she wasn't allowed to climb.

You're a human, and that's all you'll ever be to them.

But she'd always wanted to be more. In spite of it all, she'd loved them like the family they were to her. She'd always wanted to be accepted by them. To not feel like that needy child staring through a window at a world that would never welcome her in. That isolation had always stung and hurt.

Until now. Now, for the first time, all that desolate pain was gone.

Sundown made her feel like she belonged. Like she was wanted. It was as if he'd opened the door and finally said that it was okay for her to come inside. That he didn't mind being with her.

That she was welcome here.

For that, she would sell her soul.

Jess lifted his hand to cup her face. Smiling at him, she kissed his palm before she nuzzled the calluses there. His skin was so much tougher than hers. So manly. But that was what she loved about it. She leaned forward to nip at his whiskered chin while she stroked his cock. He was so hard and yet velvety soft.

He watched her from beneath lashes so thick, they should be illegal. "Be a hell of a time for a bee sting, wouldn't it?" he whispered against her lips.

She laughed. "You're so not right."

He kissed the tip of her nose. "Yeah, well, you're pretty damn perfect from where I'm sitting."

Those words made her heart soar. No one had ever said anything kinder to her. Closing her eyes, she leaned into him and held him tight. Why couldn't they have met under different circumstances? He was someone she could have loved. Had he not been a Dark-Hunter. Had her parents not been murdered.

Now . . .

There was nothing for them. If they survived, they couldn't stay together. No hope for any kind of future. This was all they'd ever have.

And she wanted to hold on to this moment forever. To pretend that they weren't who they were. Just two normal people who meant something to each other, who'd met by mere happenstance.

"Why are you so sad?"

She swallowed at his question. "I'm not sad, Jess. I'm scared."

"I won't hurt you."

And that made her ache all the more as guilt stabbed

her hard. Before she knew the truth, she would have hurt him in an instant. "I know."

He captured her lips as he slid his hand beneath her bra. His fingers teased her skin, sending chills the length of her body. It had been so long since she'd been with any man. Her training had always taken precedence, leaving her very little time to focus on something she'd always considered trivial. Relationships had seemed wasted. You never got as much out as you put in. It was a recipe for disaster and heartbreak, and she'd never wanted to waste her time with it.

Jess would have been worth the effort, though. The way he'd cherished Matilda . . .

That was what it was all about. Putting someone above you. Loving them with everything you had. Living for the sole reason of seeing them happy even if it meant you suffering for their well-being.

It was so rare that she'd never once allowed herself to contemplate the fact that it might be real. She'd relegated it to the realm of unicorns and fairies. A nice story to hear, but a total pipe dream.

Why couldn't she have been worth a love like his?

Had Matilda really appreciated what she'd been given?

I hope so. It made the tragedy of their doomed love seem less severe.

Jess cradled Abigail against him. She was shivering, and he wasn't sure why. Yeah, he could read her mind and find out, but he didn't like doing that to people. It was downright rude. And something he reserved for necessary times only.

This wasn't one of those.

A woman's mind was her own. Matilda had taught him that. It was something to be respected, as was her will. Still, it pained him to have her hurting while she was making love to him. It didn't seem right.

"Is there anything I can do for you?"

The look on her face gut-punched him as she traced the line of his lips with her fingertip. It sent chills over him, but not nearly as many as the adoring look in her eyes as she stared at him. "You're already doing it."

"Well, I got a fear here that I ain't doing it right, and I don't want this to be wrong."

She smiled then. A real one that reached all the way to her eyes and warmed him to his toes. Licking her lips, she lifted herself up so that he could undo her pants. "I promise you, it's all good."

Maybe, but wrangling her pants off her was another matter entirely. She actually elbowed him in the eye as he tried to maneuver.

She gasped in horror at what she'd done as she cupped her hands around her mouth. "Oh my God, are you okay?"

He rubbed at his eye and considered knifing his Squire when he got home. "Andy needs a bigger car." Damn it. Why did pain have to intrude right now?

She laughed again. "You poor baby." She leaned forward to kiss his eye, and that drove away most of the pain.

When she leaned into the passenger seat and pulled her pants off, it took the rest of it. She had long, shapely legs that begged for a tongue bath. Another thing he couldn't do in this infernally small car.

I'm torching this thing when I get it home. . . .

She hesitated at the waistband of her black panties. It was sheer torture for him.

"You changing your mind?" *Please, don't change your mind.* That'd be downright cruel, and he wasn't sure he could survive it. Not after they'd come this far.

Shaking her head, she slid them down her legs slowly. Seductively.

Dayam . . .

He thought he was going to die as he saw her naked. She was exquisite. And he was so hard now, he felt like he was about to explode. Before he could catch another thought, she was back in his seat, straddling him again as if she was as eager for him as he was for her.

Ah yeah . . . he could die right now without regret. This was what he'd been craving.

She raised up on her knees and pulled at his shirt.

Gladly, Jess let her strip him. He was as desperate to feel her skin on his as she was. Never in his life had he seen anything hotter or felt anything sexier than her breasts pressing against his bare flesh. He ran his hands through her hair, inhaling the scent of it as it stirred around them.

While he was far from celibate, he'd never been with a woman before who knew him. As a human, because of Bart, he'd been branded an outlaw at age thirteen. So by the time he was with a woman, he'd known better than to let her know his real identity. Or anything about him that she could tell or sell to someone out to put a bullet in him.

Then after he'd become a Dark-Hunter, he'd been expressly forbidden from telling anyone about their existence. He'd had to hide his fangs, his age.

Everything.

Only Abigail knew the truth about him. And it made this moment all the hotter. There was no fear of slipping up by letting her tongue brush against his fangs. Or having to be careful when he nibbled her since she might notice his longer teeth.

For once he could be himself, and that was the most incredible feeling of all.

He ran his tongue over her breast, savoring the ridges in her hardened nipple. Her skin smelled like the sweetest nectar imaginable. And the sensation of her hands in his hair . . .

If he died tonight, it'd be worth it.

She would be worth it.

All of a sudden, she let out a soft giggle. The uncharacteristic sound surprised him. "What are you laughing at?"

Her face turned bright red. "It's too cheesy to even mention."

Yeah, there was something a man didn't want to hear in this situation. *What did I do?* "Now, hon, you can't leave me hanging like that. I have to know."

Please don't be laughing at me.

She bit her lip. The expression was so playful and adorable that it made his stomach flutter. "I was thinking of the phrase, save a horse, ride a cowboy."

He laughed. "Well, baby, you can ride me any time you get the urge." He feigned deadly earnest. "I'm here *for* you."

She wrinkled her nose as she leaned him back in the seat. Damn if she wasn't the most beautiful thing he'd ever seen.

He slid his hand up her thigh until he found what he was seeking. She was warm and wet and she let out a deep moan as he lightly fingered her.

Abigail couldn't breathe as Jess slid his fingers deep into her body. Oh yeah, that was what she'd been desperate for. And it set her entire body on fire. Kissing his lips, she rose up and allowed him to guide her down onto him.

She sucked her breath in sharply at the sensation of him hard and full inside her.

This . . . this was heaven.

Her heart pounding, she rode him slow and gentle, savoring every inch of him. She laved his neck as she ran her hands over his muscled chest. He had a number of scars marring his flesh. Most looked like knife wounds or from barb wire. But a few were obvious bullet wounds.

Anger whipped through her that anyone would hurt him like that.

Until she remembered that she would have killed him, too.

Thank God, I didn't. And she was grateful to whatever power had brought them together. Most importantly to the one that had kept her from hurting him.

Not even the sight of the double bow and arrow mark of a Dark-Hunter on his arm could detract from this moment. Even it looked like it had hurt when he received it.

She'd never thought about that before. Dark-Hunters had their souls stripped from them. How much agony did Artemis put them through when she took it?

Abigail knew from her own experience, when her own soul had withered and died the night she lost her parents, how bad it hurt to lose one. Her scar had never healed.

Neither had his . . .

Jess let her take control of their pleasure as he ran the back of his hand across her breast. He enjoyed watching her love him, watching the light in her eyes that touched a part of him he liked to pretend didn't exist. It made him remember long forgotten things that he'd buried deep inside.

As a human, all he'd ever really wanted was a calm,

peaceful home with a good woman by his side. Someone he could grow old with, who would make him laugh and give him a reason to look forward to the next day.

And the ones thereafter.

A woman like Abigail.

She was a little more challenging than what he'd had in mind. But sometimes, cravings left out important, if not irritating, details. He actually liked her stubbornness. Most of all, her spirit.

More than that, there was a spark inside her. A fire that warmed him through and through.

Abigail smiled as Jess took her hand and led it to his lips so that he could kiss and nibble her knuckles. It was so sweet. Until he nipped her flesh with his fangs. Not too hard, but enough to send a quick rush through her.

There was nothing sexier than her cowboy. Nothing hotter than feeling him inside and outside her body while he held her close and loved her.

It was the headiest of mixtures. One so hot that it sent her straight over the edge. Throwing her head back, she felt her body release. She lost herself to that one moment of sheer perfection.

Jess smiled as he saw and felt her climax on top of him. Her body clutched his, heightening his own pleasure. He lifted his hips, driving himself in even deeper while taking care not to bump her head against the low-hanging roof.

She cried out in ecstasy.

And he quickly joined her there. His head reeled as wave after wave of pleasure rolled through him. Yeah, he needed this a lot more than he'd thought. For the first time in weeks, his head was clear and his body calm.

Right now, he was the happiest man on the planet. *That's right, all you badass punks. Bring it.*

'Cause right now, he felt like he could take on anything or anyone. And he was more than ready to.

Abigail lay flat against Jess's bare chest, listening to his heart pounding under her ear. A fine sheet of sweat covered them both as she slowly came to her senses.

I'm sitting naked in a car wash surrounded by angry wasps trying to kill us . . . with a man I've only known about forty hours.

Yeah, this was one for the books. And she definitely deserved the I-Have-No-Shame and What-the-Hell-Was-*I*-Thinking Award.

I can't believe I just did this.

But then, she'd have it no other way. She really didn't regret it. *And at least I don't have to worry about getting pregnant or diseased.* The one good thing about a Dark-Hunter was that they couldn't have children or carry any kind of STD or other illness.

Still, it was embarrassing. Anyone could walk in on them. Any minute. *I would die if anyone did.*

Jess kissed the top of her head. "We're all right, Abs. I have the doors sealed, and no one's coming."

That went over her like an ice water plunge. Her entire body locked up in horror.

"You heard that?"

"Um, yeah," he answered without reservation.

She shot up to stare at him as a new terror went through her. No . . . she better be wrong.

Surely . . .

"You can hear my thoughts?"

Now his gaze turned panicked. He glanced around as if trying to access some cosmic database in his head that would funnel a correct answer to him and get him out of this. "Uh . . ."

Good answer . . .

Not. His inner computer must be on the fritz, and her fury was mounting by the heartbeat. She could absolutely kill him! This was awful. Horrible!

Why didn't he tell me?

Abigail curled her lip. Yeah, okay, she vaguely remembered seeing that ability in one of those weird psychotic flashbacks of his past, but it hadn't sunk in and stayed with her.

Now it did.

"Oh my God, you can hear my thoughts!" She was thoroughly humiliated. Anger whipped through her as she returned to her seat and snatched for her underwear. *Oh, don't even get me started on the indignity of this. . . .* She wanted to crawl under the seat and die. *I should throw myself outside and let the wasps have me.*

Oh wait, he can hear me. He's probably listening in right now like some psychic pervert, getting his jollies off my embarrassment.

You suck, Sundown. You. Suck.

That she hoped he could hear.

She glared at him. "Why didn't you tell me you could do that?"

He held his hands up in surrender. "It's all right, Abby." His tone was soothing, but his eyes still showed panic.

And she wasn't ready to listen to any form of reason. She was too humiliated. Gah, if he'd heard everything she'd thought . . .

She couldn't stand it. "It's not all right. How dare you not tell me about this. What kind of sicko are you? I can't believe you'd do that. It's so intrusive and . . . and . . ." She couldn't think of a word bad enough to convey how very bad it was, and she was too angry to have full access to her vocabulary, anyway. "Have you been spying on me the whole time?"

Jess silently cursed as she continued to rant at him and snatch her clothes on. Damn, the woman was hotheaded. Not that he fully blamed her for it. He'd be pissed, too, if someone was traipsing in his mind.

Still . . .

"Abby, listen to me. I can hear thoughts—"

"Little late now, bucko." The last word was said with

such snapping venom, it oddly reminded him of a chicken clucking. She snatched her head up to pierce him with a look that really should have splintered him into pieces. Damn, someone should bottle that. It'd make entire armies drop arms. "I noticed. Thanks for volunteering *that*. Let me give you a Hero Award for your first confession. Big flippin' hairy doo dah . . ." Then she added an extremely sarcastic, "Woo. Hoo."

"But," he continued in what he hoped was a calming tone while he ignored her outburst and go-to-hell-and-roast-your-nuts glare. Now, that was what he deserved a Hero Award for. Took guts to face a woman this angry. "I don't. Not normally. Just every now and again, something comes through and pops into my head like your question. I don't know how it got past my defenses. Maybe 'cause I was in my zone and not thinking of anything other than how good you felt."

She covered herself with her jeans. "Like I believe that. How stupid do you think I am?"

"I don't think you're stupid at all." *He* was the rank idiot who'd opened his mouth when he should have kept it closed. His mama had always said 90% of intelligence was knowing when to shut up.

Other 10% was knowing when to nut up—which he was trying to do, but it wasn't easy.

She finally paused and locked gazes with him. That look paralyzed him because he knew if he so much as blinked wrong, it would set her off again, and that was the last thing he wanted.

Don't smile. Don't sweat. Don't do nothing.

Don't even breathe.

It was like watching a salivating bear you knew would either lumber past and go on its way . . .

Or rip your arm off and beat you with it.

"How do I know you're not in my head right now?"

He ran various answers through his mind. *'Cause I said so.* Nah, that'd get him bitch-slapped for sure. *I wouldn't dare.* Made him sound like a coward.

Think, Jess, think.

Finally he opted for the simple truth. "It's rude, and I wouldn't want anyone to do it to me, so I try hard not to do it to others. Honestly, it ain't my favorite power. You have no idea how sick people are, and I really don't want to know most days. The world can have their thoughts. I got enough of my own to deal with."

Abigail hesitated as she considered his words. For reasons that made no sense whatsoever, she believed him. Not to mention, what he said made a lot of sense. She wouldn't want to look into other people's minds and find out their psychoses and insecurities either.

And he hadn't said or done anything previously that led her to believe he had that ability. Her only clue had been that one snippet with him and the lawyer.

He'd been stressed then, too.

Okay, I'm going to trust him. But if she ever found him near her thoughts again without her permission . . . It definitely wouldn't pay to be in his boots.

"Don't do it again," she warned.

"Trust me, I won't. At least not on purpose. Like I said, I can't always control it, but I do most of the time, and I will definitely be more on guard around you, especially any time you're going near the more tender parts of my body."

She didn't want to be amused by that last bit at all. Unfortunately, she was.

Even so, it didn't mean she had to let him know it.

Forcing herself to stay stern, she nodded. "Good. Now what other evil powers do you have that I should know about?"

"I can roll my tongue," he said proudly.

Gah, he was such a goofball sometimes. Hard to believe a man with such a fierce, lethal reputation who'd been wanted and hunted voraciously by every branch of law enforcement in the Old West, could be so irreverent and playful. She wondered what those enemies would have thought of him had they ever seen this side of his personality. They certainly wouldn't have been so scared of him.

Which made her wonder if he'd been like this as a human. Or had he developed his humor as a Dark-Hunter?

In the grand scheme, it didn't matter. Right now, she

needed to know who and what, exactly, she was dealing with. "I'm serious, Jess."

"So am I. Not everyone can do it. It's a genetic thing, you know."

Abigail let out a tired sigh as she fought down the need to choke him.

He gave her a teasing grin, then finally took mercy on her and answered the question. "I have some telekinesis, which you already discovered. Premonitions. Can see auras and . . . I make a killer omelette."

That was an impressive list—including the omelette tidbit. But what made her sick to her stomach was that she'd stupidly gone up against him without knowing any of that.

Thanks, Jonah, for the extensive research you didn't do. It was a wonder Jess hadn't killed her.

Maybe that had been Jonah's intent all along. *"Believe me, Abigail. I've found every bit of detail on Sundown that's ever been documented or thought. There's nothing about him I don't know. We have all we need and then some to kill him.*

A clue about his powers would have been a nice addition to their arsenal.

Jess leaned forward and kissed her bare shoulder. "Am I forgiven yet?"

Dragging a slow gaze down his lush body, she hesitated. One because she basically lost her train of thought to how much she'd like to take another bite out of him. No man should be so sexy. Even naked, he exuded such power and confidence that it raised a chill on her skin. And two, she did have to think about the possibility of forgiving him. She still wasn't sure she should.

But really, what choice did she have? Could she really hold mind-reading against him when it was something he hadn't asked for?

She made him wait a few seconds more before she answered. "Fine. But only because you look good naked."

His grin turned evil. "I'll take that."

"Good. Now, let's get dressed before we do get discovered by some nosy clerk."

He tsked as he pulled his pants up and fastened them. "Remind me to kill Coyote for rushing this when I'd rather lay naked with you than fight wasps and coyotes and all the other crap he's throwing at us."

"Don't worry. I think we have many reasons to kill him." Abigail finished buttoning her shirt, then looked outside. The wasps were still everywhere. It was a sickening sight, and she was getting tired of listening to them buzz. "What are we going to do about our friends out there?"

Jess had no idea. But before he could respond, his phone rang. He fished it out of his pocket and answered it.

"Where are you?"

He arched a brow at Ren's angry tone. "We got trapped by the wasps. Where are *you*?"

"At your house with Choo Co La Tah. He was trying to chant the wasps into submission when something happened."

That can't be good. Dread ripped through Jess. They couldn't afford to lose him at this point. He was the only guide they had who actually had a clue about what was going on and how to correct it. The only other Guardian around was Snake . . . and he was on Coyote's side.

"What happened?" he asked Ren.

"I don't know. He's in some form of coma. I've never seen anything like this."

Jess winced. If Ren was panicked over this, then there was a good reason to be panicked over it. The man had ice water for blood and wasn't prone to any form of overreaction.

"Can we wake him out of it?"

Ren lost his patience. "Well, you know, cowboy, that's a really good idea. Damn shame *I* didn't think of it, huh?"

"Cut the sarcasm. Are you're sure it's not a vision quest?"

"For the sake of our long-term friendship, I'm not even going to dignify that with the response it deserves."

Because it, too, was a stupid question. Jess had known that before he asked it.

Still . . .

He ran his hand over his face as he tried to think of some kind of plan or action to save Choo Co La Tah and get rid of their current pest problem. "We need someone else who can control the weather. You know anyone?"

"I do." Jess heard Sasha in the background. "Give me a few, and I'll be back with help."

Ren said something muffled to Sasha, then uncovered the receiver so that Jess could hear again. "I have to say, Sister Fortune has ridden out of town on us, and I don't like it."

"Gotta say, I don't blame you. I'm not exactly sending roses to her either." He let out an aggravated breath. "So do we have any intel or insight as to what we need to do for Choo Co La Tah and to stop Coyote?"

"Not really. I don't know what else Coyote will come up with. He's unpredictable at best. A bastard at worst. And when cornered, he's lethal beyond measure and will do whatever he must to win. His heart lives in a place best left untrodden. All I know is we have to get to the Valley by sunrise."

"I know."

"No, Jess. You don't. We have to beat Coyote to Old Bear's magic. If we do, we might be able to keep him from unlocking the next set of plagues."

That would be good. But it wouldn't be easy. "What exactly is his magic? Other than the Grizzly?"

Ren sighed. "You should have listened more to your mother's stories, boy. Your lack of education offends me."

He glanced over to Abigail, who watched him with a

penetrating stare that said she was dying to know what they were talking about. He was grateful she didn't interrupt them. That was something he'd always found rude and extremely annoying.

Jess returned his attention to Ren. "My mother didn't talk that much about her beliefs or tell me many stories." She'd been too sick for too long. For the last three years of her life, every breath had been a precious struggle for her. So she'd conserved them for living and not for talking. "And when she did, it was in a hushed tone." Because she'd been terrified of anyone hurting him over their heritage.

Better to blend in than stand out, penyo. *The one who flies against the flock is always flying into opposition. No matter how strong the beast, sooner or later, he tires from his ragged journey.*

And when he falls, he falls alone.

His mother's words were still with him.

Even so, he'd never been one to conform. But all that had done was prove to him how wise and right his mother had been. In the end, he had died alone and he was tired.

Then and now.

He cleared his throat. "So you'll have to forgive me my ignorance."

"A wise man never argues a mother's decision for her child. Not unless he wants to face her claw, and there is nothing sharper than a mother defending her young."

Jess definitely concurred with that.

"You probably want to put me on speaker so that Abigail can hear it, too."

"All right." Jess pulled the phone back to comply. "We're here."

Abigail frowned.

"At the beginning of time when the Code of Order was being established, the First Guardian locked away all the evil he'd found in the world. Things that had been created by the Dark One for no other purpose than to plague man and hurt him. The First Guardian knew that mankind wasn't strong enough to fight it. So he banished it all to the West Lands where the sun lay down on that evil every night and kept it weak."

Ren paused. "But Evil is always resilient and ever resourceful. In time, it bred with Father Sun, and a tiny piece escaped to find an embittered warrior whose heart was blackened by jealousy over his own brother. He took the evil into him and was seduced by its promise that if he hurt others enough, their pain would make him stronger and drive his pain away. It succored him like a lover, and he embraced its insanity with everything he had. And so he went on a killing rage, and he consumed the lands until he ruled all from his bloodied fists."

"The Grizzly Spirit," Jess said quietly. He knew this legend from Choo Co La Tah.

Ren continued. "His war brought him to the realm of

the Guardian, and the two of them fought for a year and a day—a battle so violent, it left a permanent scar on Mother Earth."

The Grand Canyon. It was said the red color came from the blood of the wounds they'd given to each other while they fought.

"Finally, the warrior made a mistake and the Guardian was able to pin him down. He stripped the evil from the warrior, but it was too late. They had sweated and bled so much over that year on the earth that the very fabric of Mother Earth's gown, the granules of sand that carry man on his life's journey, was saturated with it and forever stained by it. There was no way to take all the evil back or to make her gown white again. The damage was done."

"What did he do?"

Jess smiled at the way Abigail was completely absorbed by the tale.

"The Guardian realized his mistake. There was no way to keep evil locked away forever. It's as pure an essence as good, and like good, it can't be denied or held back. And as Night and Day divide the sky between them, so must good and evil divide the world. Only then can there be balance and harmony for humans. Only then can there be any semblance of peace. So the Guardian banished the Grizzly Spirit that had infected the warrior and locked it behind the West Land Gate so that it could rage without harming man. He then took from Mother Earth eight jars to hold the plagues that had helped the Dark One escape and sealed them with his tears so that they could never again be used by the Grizzly. Those jars, he turned over to four Guardian protectors. North. South. East. West. The strongest corners of the earth who could be called on to defend should the West Gate ever be opened. Two of those Guardians were ruled by the Dark and two ruled by the Light. Perfect balance."

"How did he choose them?" Abigail asked.

"All but the East Guardian went through a trial created by the First Guardian to see who was the worthiest. The top three were the chosen ones."

"And the one from the East?"

"He was the warrior who'd been owned by the Grizzly Spirit. The First Guardian thought that if anyone would understand why they had to protect the West Gate, he would be the one. And that he would stand strongest against all threats to keep it from happening again. Not to mention, given their fight, he knew the warrior would be a worthy opponent for anyone who dared to breach his gate."

"That makes sense."

"Once they were given their jars, the First Guardian warned them of how serious their duties were and that they should never waver or falter. They were to stand together and to keep each other in line. Then he retired into the West Land so that he could rest after his battle. They say he still slumbers there even today."

"And the Guardians?"

Ren let out a light laugh. "Each took his jars deep into the sacred land where the Fire touches the Earth and hid them so that no one would be able to use the plagues against them or man."

Jess sighed as it all started coming together. "Coyote released his jars already." The scorpions and the wasps.

"Yes. Coyote has been trying for centuries to find the key to unlock the Gate and free the Grizzly Spirit. He knew as long as Old Bear and Choo Co La Tah were joined, there was no way for him to overpower either of them and open the Gate. Now that one has fallen, he and Snake can join together."

"And screw us royally," Jess said under his breath.

"You've no idea, my brother."

"But why?" Abigail asked. "Why would Snake join him?"

"Snake by nature is, and has always been, a follower. And he's served the Dark One too long. It was something the First Guardian feared the moment he assigned the two Dark Guardians their posts. He knew how insidious the Dark would be and how corruptible even the most noble of heart is. He'd hoped that the East Guardian would watch after and counsel Snake away from the darker side of his personality. But just in case the East Guardian failed, it was why he put a finite limit on the service of the Guardians. Next year, during the Time Untime when our calendar resets, the feathered rattlesnake will bear his color, and on the night when the evening star comes first, new Guardians are to be chosen by the one who holds the key. Old Bear. With him dead, that choice moves to Choo Co La Tah. If Coyote and Snake can kill him, they can choose the new Guardians."

Abigail frowned. "Why is that important?"

Jess answered before Ren had a chance. "Whoever assigns the Guardians, controls them and most importantly, controls the West Land."

"Ultimate power," Ren said. "Your every wish granted. You own the entire world."

Who wouldn't want that?

Well, okay, Jess didn't. He had enough trouble managing his own life. Last thing he wanted was to be responsible for everyone else.

Unfortunately for all the world, Coyote didn't feel the same way.

"Snake is now a loyal servant to Coyote and has been for a long time," Ren continued. "The only thing that kept them at bay was the Light Guardians."

Abigail winced.

And Jess didn't miss the heavy dread in Ren's tone. "What haven't you told us?"

"One of Old Bear's jars contains the Wind Seer which

is the one plague that can open the West Gate and free the Grizzly Spirit."

Crap. Crap. Crap. Jess flinched at the very thought.

Abigail drew her brow together in confusion. "I don't understand. If the First Guardian is there, can't he stop the Grizzly Spirit from escaping again?"

"It's not that easy, Abigail. No one has heard from him in countless centuries. For all we know, the Grizzly might have killed him when he went behind the Gate or he could have possessed him. You have no idea what the Grizzly is capable of. Trust me. We have to stop them from opening that jar. If the Grizzly gets out again—"

"It'll be a fun time in Disneyland," Jess mumbled. "Y'all think we could arm Mickey? He might be badass with a gun."

Abigail slapped him lightly on the arm. "What do we have to do, Ren?"

"Get his jars before they do."

It amazed Jess that Ren could make the impossible sound easy. Too bad reality didn't go that way. "Does Coyote know where it is?"

"I don't think so. But then, neither do we. Choo Co La Tah should be able to track it . . . if we can get *him* to wake up. However, the one who spilled Guardian blood has to make an offering on the sacred ground to appease the ancient elements before sunrise. Otherwise all of the jars will open . . . at once . . . which would then also blow open the Gate and all that concentrated evil would pour out of it."

Oh yeah, that would seriously suck. "Did they launch that last space shuttle yet?"

"I don't follow," Ren said.

"I'm just thinking maybe we should evacuate the whole planet. I've heard the moon is kind of nice this time of year."

Both Abigail and Ren let out mutual sounds of aggravation.

"Focus your ADD, Jess."

He rolled his eyes at Ren's quip. "I gotcha, brother. What you're forecasting is six more plagues coming out of the northwest at maximum velocity with a mild chance of survival. Followed by the world getting swallowed whole into a vat of evil."

"Well, yeah. That's exactly what I'm saying."

"Nice to know I didn't misunderstand and all." He purposefully exaggerated his drawl on that. "Ah, hell, y'all lucky I can follow anything, especially given how many times I got kicked in the head when I's a kid." Sobering, Jess let out an irritated breath.

Instead of Renegade, his name should be Mary Sunshine. "I'll get Abigail to you as soon as I can."

"I'll keep working on Choo Co La Tah. You be careful."

"Same to you. Let me know if anything changes. I could really use some good news right about now." Jess hung up and turned to face Abigail. Unfortunately, she had her clothes buttoned up all the way to her neck.

Damn.

She let out an exaggerated breath. "I don't want to know about Choo Co La Tah, do I?"

"Not really. Kind of wish I didn't know." Jess toyed with the keys that dangled from the ignition while he watched the wasps continue to swarm outside. He didn't like the idea of being trapped, and he wasn't keen on the idea of being beholden to Sasha for anything.

"Ah, screw this. I'm not going to wait for rescue like a puppy on a float. Buckle up. We're going for it."

Abigail wasn't sure she liked the sound of that. But what choice did she have? Jess was in the driver's seat.

Besides, she was with him on this. No need in waiting around when they could at least be trying to get home.

She snapped the belt over her lap and braced herself. "All right, cowboy. Let's do it."

Jess put the car in gear, then opened the garage door with his powers. The wasps immediately swarmed inside. Something that didn't faze Jess at all. She admired that.

He gripped the wheel, then tore out of the garage as fast as he could. The lights were dimmed by the number of wasps gathering around them.

But that wasn't the worst part.

She cringed at what awaited them on the street. Every-

thing had gotten worse. There was no movement from anyone, anywhere. Businesses and homes had their windows
drawn shut, and most were dark—as if afraid that the
light might attract more wasps.

It terrified her.

But at least there was no sign of the mountain lion. He
appeared to have moved on.

Needing to understand what was going on in the world
around them, she turned the car radio on and scanned the
channels until she found the local news.

The reporter's voice was thick with concern, and it
made her own throat tighten. "There's no explanation for
this rash of insect uprisings or these unprecedented weather
fronts that keep moving in. The authorities are advising
everyone to stay calm and in their homes until the experts
have figured out what's causing it. As of now, several
roads and highways are being closed, and everyone is being told to watch out for flash flooding. They also want us
to remind everyone that wasps can and do sting even after
death, so please don't pick up any of their remains without
gloves or some other form of protection. Officials are advising everyone to turn off any light that might attract
more wasps. And if you have pets in your yard, please do
not venture out to get them."

Flash flooding? The dark sky above them was completely clear.

She turned the radio off. That hadn't been very helpful.

"Guess they can't report that it's the end of the world, huh?"

"It's not the end."

She stared at the wrecked cars and bodies they passed. The people who'd posted handmade signs in the windows of their homes asking for God's forgiveness and warning others to repent. "It sure looks like it from my seat."

"Ah, now," Jess said in that exaggerated drawl she was beginning to recognize as his way of keeping things either in perspective or light. "Buck up, little camper. It ain't over yet. We're far from out of this."

That was the problem. They had a long way to go, and she didn't see an escape for them.

Jess kept his attention on the road as he navigated hazards every inch of the way. He was trying to be positive for her, but inside, he was worried fierce. Why had Old Bear been holding the key to the West Gate? Why take the chance? It should have been cast out to sea or something.

For that matter, couldn't the First Guardian have locked up butterflies or something equally harmless in those jars?

No. People had to have their misery, and Old Bear would have to have the pimp daddy of plagues waiting for discovery.

Give me locusts and boils. Hell, he'd even prefer pimples on his private parts. Anything would be better than Coyote taking over the world.

At this point, they were mired so deep in the mud of Shit City, he might as well have his mail forwarded.

I swear, Coyote. If I live through this . . .

You won't.

13

Jess let out a relieved breath as he pulled into his driveway while rain pelted the car so hard, it sounded like a sledgehammer pounding on metal and glass. Man, what a night. He was exhausted already, and it wasn't even late yet.

Of course, another round with Abigail and he'd definitely perk up.

Don't go there.

Please, go there. . . .

'Cause honestly, he'd much rather think about her naked in his arms than think about doing what they were going to have to do and then walking away and never seeing her again.

I thought the good guy was supposed to get the girl. That was the theory, anyway. Too bad he had enough life experience to know that it definitely wasn't the case.

Nice guys got shot by their best friend.

He shook his head to clear it of *that* nightmare and turned his attention where it needed to go.

Their friendly neighborhood plague.

At least it was raining heavy enough to drive the wasps back into submission and disperse them. Especially since Talon had added a little god power to it to shock and numb them.

Things were almost back to normal.

Yeah, right. Things were about as normal as a Luddite working for Bill Gates. But then, wishful thinking was about all he had left right now. That and the fierce desire to find Coyote and beat the ever-loving shit out of him.

He parked in the garage and looked over at Abigail. Her features were pinched by dread and determination, and still she was the most beautiful woman he'd ever seen. What he wouldn't give to be able to crawl into bed with her for a week and not come up for air until they both were near dead from lack of food.

Yeah, she'd be worth starvation.

And as he met her gaze, regret slammed hard into his gut. How he wished they'd had more time tonight. More time to explore and taste her.

More time to just . . .

He forced his thoughts away from that train wreck. What good were druthers, anyway? They just made you ache for things you couldn't have. And the one thing his childhood had taught him was not to dwell on what-ifs.

What was it Nietzsche had said? Hope was the worst of all evils, for it prolonged the torment of man?

Props to the philosopher. The man was definitely right in this case. Hoping for something better wouldn't make it manifest. It would only remind him of decisions he'd made that he couldn't undo.

He had a job to do, and it wasn't just to protect her. He had to save the rest of the world, too.

Steeling his own determination, he inclined his head to Abigail. "You ready for the next part?"

Apprehension lined her brow as she stared at her hands held clenched in her lap. "Like an adrenaline shot straight into my heart via my eyes." Her voice was faint and pain filled. "Weirdly, I think I dread meeting Andy more than fighting off Coyote."

He would laugh if she wasn't right. He had the same

rock in his stomach at the thought of how the kid would react to seeing his car mangled in its current condition. Definitely not something he was looking forward to.

Time to face the music.

After turning the engine off, he opened the door and got out while Abigail followed suit. He'd barely shut the car door behind him before he heard the agonized scream coming from the house.

"What have you monsters done?"

Abigail's face blanched as she froze in place.

He quickly moved past her to intercept Andy on his way to the car. He tried to shield the car with his body, but Andy was having none of that. Andy dodged left. Jess went right. Andy pivoted right. . . .

Jess held his arms out to stop him before he saw all the damage. Dang, the kid should have played ball. He'd seen less slippery piglets.

He offered his Squire a sympathetic nod. "You might want to order a new one."

Andy groaned in pain, then raked his hands through his hair in a way that would make James Dean proud. "I can't believe you tore up my car! My car! My precious baby. Sheez, Jess. What did you do?"

Well, there was one thing he definitely wasn't going to mention. That would only wig the kid out even more, and he would definitely never hear the end of that.

Not to mention Abigail would probably gut him if he told anyone what they'd done.

Jess dropped his arms and shrugged. "All I can say is, it got hairy for us."

"Hairy?" Andy covered his eyes with his fists and made the sound of ultimate suffering. Damn, the boy knew how to overreact. It was actually impressive. If the Squire gig failed, he could always get a job playing Oedipus. All he needed was to plunge two brooches into his eyes and stumble offstage. "My car looks like the stunt double for the Charger in *Burn Notice*. How could you? Jeez, Jess. Really?" He gestured toward the car. *"Really?"*

Abigail took a brave step forward. "I'm so sorry, Andy. It's all my fault."

He glared at her as if he was imagining her in little bloody pieces spread out through the house. He raised one hand as if about to lecture her, but honestly, he was so upset that all he could do was sputter indignantly.

Jess clapped him on the back. "You'll live. It's just a car, kid."

"And hell is just a sauna." Each word dripped with indignation and outrage.

Wincing, Andy sucked in a deep breath and appeared to get a hold of himself. "Fine," he said in a falsetto. "You're right. I'll live, even though right now it feels as if my guts have been yanked out through my nostrils and laid on the floor for your bitter amusement. You insensitive bastard! Just wait till I pick up your bike from the Ishtar. Let's see who laughs then."

"You hurt that bike, and I'll rip out your spine."

Andy paused. "Point taken." He looked at his car and sighed. "It could be worse. No one threw up in it. . . ." He widened his eyes, as if even more disturbed. "Did they?"

"No," Jess reassured him. "No one tossed cookies."

"All right." He straightened up and seemed to be true to his promise to let it go. "I will be a man about this."

That lasted until he saw the scratches on the hood from the mountain lion and the front fender, where Abigail had dragged it off the driveway.

Wailing, he went to it and sank to his knees. He sprawled over the hood and laid his head on the damaged fender. "I'm so sorry, Bets. I should have hidden the keys. Booted your tires. Something. I had no idea anyone would abuse you so, baby. I swear I'll never let anyone hurt you again. Ayyy, how could they do this to you? How? Oh the humanity!"

Jess let out a deep *heh* as he locked gazes with Abigail. "I really need to get that boy a girlfriend—" He glanced over to where Andy was now stroking the hood. "—or at least laid."

Abigail laughed.

Pushing himself back, Andy hissed at them. "You mock my pain, sir."

"Nah," Jess drawled. "I mock your idiocy."

Andy curled his lip. "Go on. Get in the house. Leave me to my suffering, you insensitive monster. You've done enough damage."

Jess shook his head. "Too bad the Razzie committee can't see this performance. We might actually have a winner if they did."

Hoping the boy would get over it without needing a therapist, he headed toward the house.

Abigail went over to Andy. "I really am sorry about your car. I mean it."

He looked up with a sincere stare that gave Jess hope Andy wasn't completely shot in the head. "It's all right. It's just . . . a . . . car. I'll get over it eventually." He pushed his bottom lip out to pout like a two-year-old.

In a weird way, it was almost adorable.

Abigail wanted to reach out and soothe poor Andy, even though his reaction was way over the top. Maybe it was ridiculous, but she felt terrible about it.

Because of her past, she tended to bond to objects more than to people, too. Objects could be stolen, but they didn't leave voluntarily. They were always there when you needed them, and they didn't say or do anything to hurt your feelings.

It killed her that she'd damaged something that obviously meant so much to him.

I'm becoming a massive walking disaster area. She was the opposite of Midas. Instead of turning to gold, everything she touched turned to dust.

Even her best friend . . .

Her heart caught on that. She still couldn't believe

everything that had happened tonight. Her friends were her enemies, and she was depending on her enemy to help save her life. Nothing in the world made sense right now.

Honestly, she just needed a few minutes of peace before the next catastrophe. A moment to ground herself before another storm blew through and swept her over the edge of insanity. But that was a luxury none of them had.

Unwilling to think about what was coming for her next, she followed after Jess, who'd already vanished into the house.

By the time Abigail caught up to him in the kitchen, he was standing with Sasha and a blond man she'd never seen before. Not quite as well muscled as Jess, the newcomer was by no means small. He had short tousled blond hair and tiny braids that fell from one temple. Dressed in jeans and a gray T-shirt, he had arms covered with black Celtic tribal tattoos. There was something about him that screamed ultimate badass.

And he pierced her with a suspicious look the moment he sensed her presence. That look pinned her feet to the floor and kept her from taking another step.

At least until Jess turned around and offered her a kind smile. By the friendly expression on his face, she knew it was safe to approach the other man.

She hoped.

Jess motioned her forward. "Abigail meet Talon. Talon, Abigail."

Relaxing a bit from his tough man stance, Talon inclined his head to her. "Hi."

Well, at least he was friendlier toward her than Zarek had been. Not that that was saying much. *They'd probably be a lot friendlier if you hadn't killed their brethren.*

In all honesty, she was lucky he wasn't attacking her, and she wouldn't blame him if he did. There was no telling how long he'd known the ones she'd killed. How close they'd been.

I'm so sorry.

Life seriously needed an undo button. The coward in her wanted to turn around and run. But she'd never been craven a day in her life, and she wasn't about to start now when they needed her to stand strong.

Clearing her throat, she forced herself to join them at the stainless steel island. "Are you the one responsible for the rain?"

"Yeah." Talon glanced at Jess and cracked a devilish grin that said there was an inside joke between them.

Jess made a face of supreme pain. "You're not still busting on Storm, are you?"

"Ah, hell yeah, you know it." Talon let out an evil laugh. "There are truly few things that give me more pleasure."

"You are all kinds of wrong." Jess shook his head before he explained it to her and Sasha. "Talon's brother-in-law is a professional rainmaker. So every time poor Storm tries to make it rain, Talon stops it. At this point, he's beginning to get a complex over it."

Pride gleamed bright in Talon's eyes. "I know it's cruel, but I can't help myself. Little bastard deserves it after all the grief he gives me over his sister. Not to mention I really like the little girl sound he makes when he fails."

Sasha snorted. "And you people think I'm twisted. Damn, that's so cold."

"Speaking of, Weatherman," Jess said. "You can probably kill the rain now. I think the wasps are pretty much shocked and driven back."

A loud clap of thunder shook the house. "Yeah, but it's fun."

"Might be, but you're flooding out parts of the city."

Talon grimaced. "Make me feel bad, why don't you? Fine, it's canned."

Abigail was intrigued by his powers. It was one she hadn't known a Dark-Hunter could have. "So can you summon tornadoes or earthquakes?"

"Earthquakes aren't weather related." Talon winked at her, then sobered as if he caught himself being too friendly. "And no offense, I don't feel comfortable discussing my powers with someone who might try and use them against me one day. So I'll be keeping all details close."

Pain stabbed her hard in the chest. "You're right. I deserve that. I shouldn't have asked."

The expression on his face said that he felt as bad about his words as she did.

Jess put his arm around her shoulders. "Go easy on her, Celt. She was protecting her family. We've all done things we regret while trying to help the people we love. It doesn't make her an enemy."

"True. It just makes her human." Talon held his hand out to her. "Truce?"

Offering him a shy smile, she took his hand in hers and shook it. "Truce." The moment she touched his skin, she felt something strange on his palm. Scowling, she turned his hand over to see a nasty burn scar there. "That looks really painful."

Talon actually smiled as if the memory warmed him. He pulled his hand away. "A very small price to pay for all I gained. Trust me. Had it been necessary, I'd have given the whole arm." He passed a look from her to Jess that sent a shiver down her spine.

It was like he knew what they'd done.

A light smile played at the edges of his lips. "Speaking of, I need to be getting back home. Last thing I want to do is stress out Sunny. My luck, she'd show up here and in her condition I'd have to kill someone if they upset her. Since I don't want to kill myself . . ." He scanned the three of them. "Good luck. For the gods's sakes, don't fail."

"Don't intend to," Jess assured him.

Talon vanished.

Abigail shifted nervously as Sasha arched a brow over the fact that Jess still had his arm around her. She'd shrug it off, but didn't want to do anything to make it stand out more. Besides, she liked it.

Ignoring Sasha's curiosity, she spoke to Jess. "I take it Sunny is his wife and she's pregnant?"

"Very."

She nodded as she absorbed that. Along with a new fear for herself. "I didn't think Dark-Hunters could have families or make someone pregnant."

A light appeared in his eyes that said he might actually be reading her thoughts.

She gave him a stern glare.

Panic flared deep in his dark gaze before he stepped away from her as if wanting to put distance between her and his so-called tender parts. "Didn't do it. I swear, and no we can't. Talon's no longer one of us and hasn't been for some time. Sunshine freed him."

Really . . . there was another thing she'd never known was possible.

Before she could speak again, Ren's deep, stern voice rang out. "You need to take it slowly."

"I say, stop mothering me, Ren. I'm not an invalid, you know? Fall into one little trance while taking care of something, and now I have a hen on top of me. I swear if you don't stop, I shall rename you."

Abigail quickly hid her amusement as Choo Co La Tah came into the kitchen with Ren. The expression on Ren's face could freeze fire.

Unlike her, Jess had no problem laughing at them both. "Anything I should know about?"

Choo Co La Tah stiffened indignantly. "Yes. Your friend here is a bit of a faffer, and I've had enough of it for one day, thank you very much."

Ren sighed in irritation. When he spoke, it was to Jess, not Choo Co La Tah. "Talon brought him out of the trance. I'm thinking now, though, that we should have left him there."

Abigail hated to interrupt, but . . . "Off topic—what's a faffer?"

Ren's face turned bright red.

Luckily, Choo Co La Tah smiled at her. "Someone who fusses, my dear."

Ah. No wonder Ren was so furious. Not the manliest of descriptions, by any means.

"May I also ask why you speak with an English accent? It seems . . ." She couldn't say *odd* without offending him, and that was the last thing she wanted to do. She actually liked the old elder a lot, even if he wasn't always the most likable of people. "Different."

Ren put his hands on his hips. "He learned to speak English from the original British settlers and never quite adapted to the modern accent."

Choo Co La Tah gave him a withering stare, as if he didn't appreciate Ren's explanation. "I like the way it sounds better. Besides, it throws everyone off balance when they hear it, and I like that even more. Always keep them guessing about you, my dear. Nothing ever makes them so crazy."

She appreciated that thought.

"How are you feeling?" Jess asked Choo Co La Tah, changing the subject.

"Weary. And we've wasted enough time. We need to get going so that we can reach the high point before dawn, make our offering, and secure the jars."

A tendril of fear went through her as she realized that the offering most likely would be her life. *I'm not ready for this. . . .*

Jess saw the fear in Abigail's eyes. Wanting only to soothe her, he took her hand in his and squeezed her fingers in a silent promise that he wouldn't let anything happen to her. He meant that, too. So long as he had breath inside him, nothing would get to her.

Choo Co La Tah dropped his gaze to their hands, and something akin to approval crossed his face.

Weird.

But Jess didn't have time to think about that. "Let's head to the Bronco and get started. It's a little over an hour to get there from here. We should have plenty of time before dawn, but with what all Coyote's been throwing at us, who knows."

Ren hesitated. "My powers are waning. I think I'll fly in and meet you."

He had a point, but . . . "You sure about that? Snake

could open a can of whoop-ass on us, too, and we don't know what his plagues are. Do we?"

"Flesh-eating virus," Choo Co La Tah said. "And bloodfire."

Sasha screwed his face up. "Bloodfire?"

"My personal fave." Ren's tone was thick with sarcasm. "It's blood drops that fall from the sky and explode like wet dynamite."

Jess nodded as Ren proved his point. "Not exactly something you want to have hit you when you're out in the open."

"True, but I'm stupid enough to chance it. I need to recharge if we have to fight, and I'm sure you do, too."

Jess cursed the man's stubbornness.

And his sacrifice.

"You be *really* careful," he warned.

Ren gave him a cocky grin. "Always. You have to be careful when you fly, or you end up smeared on the side of a building."

"You're not funny."

"I'm hilarious, crabass." Ren's gaze went to Abigail, and a shadow passed across his face. One that Jess sensed was extremely important. But as quickly as it came, Ren covered it. "Save our girl. Won't do us any good to get there without her."

"Don't worry." He wasn't about to let her go. Not yet, anyway. "Peaceful journey, *penyo*."

Ren saluted him, then went to the front door. He opened it before he turned into a crow and flew away.

Sasha let out a sound of disgust. "What? Was he raised in a barn? Didn't he ever learn how to close a door?" He flung his hand at the door and slammed it shut without touching it. "Amateur shape-shifters . . . No manners whatsoever."

Jess was puzzled by the lycanthrope's distemper. "Do we need to get you a Midol before we go?"

"I'm not that easy to soothe, cowboy. My peeves are on a cellular level."

Jess shook his head, then fell silent as he looked at Abigail and saw the tiniest spark of red in her eyes. The demon was trying to surface again. He wondered if she could feel it when it did that. "Are you all right?"

"Yeah, why?" Well, that answered his question. Obviously, she had no idea.

The red faded out.

His gut drew tight. That couldn't be good either. He'd be more concerned with it, but right now, they were on a tight schedule.

"Never mind." Taking her hand, he led them out of the kitchen and down the barrel-vaulted hallway to the other side of the house.

Abigail was floored as they kept walking and walking. In the back of her mind, she'd noted that his house was huge, but it wasn't until now that the full size of it hit her.

Dang . . .

He opened the door to another garage that housed a huge collection of cars and motorcycles. It had more in common with a warehouse than a garage, except for the fact that it was immaculate and ornate. The gold trim even appeared to be gilded. "Just how big is this house?"

Jess grinned sheepishly. "Andy's doing, not mine. Don't ask, 'cause it's just obscene. And no, with the exception of the black Bronco, nothing in here belongs to me. Since Andy lives in the apartment over the garage, this is his domain."

"And how big is Mr. Andy's apartment?"

He actually blushed. "Sixty-two hundred square feet, and I'm pretty sure it's why he picked out this house. Though he denies it."

Holy snikes . . . Well, that explained the huge feel of the place. Her house was one quarter of the size of Andy's apartment.

"And why's your Bronco in here?"

Jess continued on through the huge place toward his truck. "He was hauling tack earlier, and he didn't want to risk dinging or scraping one of his darlings. Since I don't drive it all that much, he left it over here."

She was strangely amused as she counted Andy's impressive super car collection. "If he has sixteen cars, why does he care about the Audi so?"

He opened the door for the Bronco and passed her a defiant grin that set fire to her blood. Oh, to have five minutes to nibble those lips. "That's his newest, and honestly,

I think the boy just wants something to moan about. Pay him no heed."

Abigail climbed into the backseat, leaving Choo Co La Tah to sit up front with Jess while Sasha climbed in beside her.

Jess adjusted the seat and mirrors to accommodate his size. Before he started it, he pinned a meaningful glare at Sasha through the rearview mirror. "Everyone buckled in?"

Sasha snorted, then gaped as he realized Jess wasn't joking about it. "Really? Is there anyone here one hundred percent human? No. I think dying from an unbuckled belt is the least of our concerns right now."

"And I don't put it in drive until everyone's secure. That means you, wolfboy."

Sasha's exasperated expression was priceless. "Unfrakkin'-believable. I'm in hell. With a lunatic. Might as well have stayed with Zarek. Next thing you know, you'll be drowning pancakes with syrup, too." He made a grand showing of buckling himself in. "Hope you get fleas," he mumbled under his breath.

"Thank you." Jess pulled out of the garage.

She pressed her lips together to keep from laughing at them. No doubt they'd take turns beating her if she did.

Curling his lip, Sasha sarcastically mocked his words in silence. "By the way, cowboy, you do know that if we were to wreck, I can teleport out of this thing. Right?"

"Is Scooby still bitching?" Jess asked Choo Co La Tah. "Remind me to check his vet record when we get back. I think he might have distemper or rabies or something."

Choo Co La Tah laughed.

Abigail shook her head at their antics. She wasn't used to people so at ease with danger. They were either the bravest creatures ever born . . .

Or the most reckless.

And as they headed back out into the darkness, she felt a chill run down her arm. *I'm being watched.*

It's Ren. Don't worry about it.

Maybe, but it didn't feel like Ren.

It felt like evil.

Coyote felt the fire in front of him flare as he walked with his mind through the realm of shadows to spy on his enemies. Even with his eyes closed, he could see himself in the cavern. The fire licked against the logs in front of him, casting eerie shadows from the stalagmites and stalactites onto the rock walls around him.

But that wasn't what held his focus. His enemies did.

They were together, and that made him seethe so deep inside, he was sure it burned a groove into his soul. "Why won't you die," he snarled. "All of you."

How many times did he have to kill Buffalo before he stayed dead?

As for Ren . . .

"What's happening?"

He opened his eyes to find Snake walking toward him from the dark opening that let out onto the hills he'd called home for centuries. "They're heading to the Valley."

Snake cursed. "We have to stop them."

Like he didn't know that? "Why are *you* panicking when I'm the one who has everything to lose?"

"You're not the only one, Coyote. I don't want to retire any more than you do."

But this wasn't about retirement. It was about payback. A betrayal so foul that no amount of time had lessened the burn of it.

How could I have been so stupid?

The First Guardian was still tormenting him. He could feel it. Why else would he have made the mistake he made all those years ago?

I killed the wrong one. Only the First Guardian could have pulled off that deception and protected the girl from him after he killed her mother.

And he needed that key. It was the only way to have his vengeance. The only way to survive this.

I will not fail. Not this time. He'd waited for centuries, and it was the season for his patience to be rewarded.

He rose to his feet and started for the entrance.

Snake caught him and held him by his side. "What are you doing?"

"I'm going after them."

"You can't. Outside of the Valley, we're like gods."

Inside, they weren't. It still mystified Coyote that the woman had been able to kill Old Bear. Something that should have been impossible even for her.

And if she could kill a Guardian outside of the Valley, then Buffalo most likely could do it, too. "I have to stop them."

"Then stop them, my brother . . . with others."

Coyote shook his head. "I've unleashed my plagues."

"Then I will unleash mine." Snake placed his hand on Coyote's shoulder in brotherly solidarity. "We are in this to the end."

Snake for the power.

Coyote for blood.

He nodded to the South Guardian. "At dawn we will feast on the hearts of our enemies."

"And bathe in their blood."

A warrior's bond.

Snake tightened the grip on his shoulder before he released him. "I will summon the bounty hunters." He started away.

"Wait." Coyote hesitated to say more. He didn't want to show his weakness to anyone. Ever. But he had no choice. "Tell them not to harm the woman. I want her brought back to me."

"Intact?"

"Preferably."

"May I ask why?"

The answer smoldered inside him like a pressure cooker that was about to explode. "It's personal."

Confusion marred his brow, but Snake didn't pursue it. "I'll make sure it's done."

Good. Coyote watched Snake make his exit while his emotions churned inside him. But it was his rage that flared brightest. "You owe me!" he shouted, his voice ringing through the cavern. And this time, he would collect on that balance.

Jess Brady would die, and he would finally have the reward he'd been promised.

14

Jess cursed as he swerved to miss a pedestrian while they drove down the Great Basin Highway toward the Valley of Fire. All over the interstate, people had abandoned their cars which had been wrecked during either the wasp attack or subsequent storm Talon had sent.

In spite of the media telling everyone to remain in their homes, thousands of people had tried to evacuate and were now walking on the side of the road. Many were screaming that it was the end of the world while others trudged on in grim determination to get wherever they were headed.

It was an ugly sight, and it made Abigail pray that whatever plague Coyote unleashed next didn't make it to them.

Cell phone lines were completely jammed, which only added to everyone's panic. There was no way to reach anyone inside or outside the city. Maybe that was what had caused them to try and leave. That need to find your family and hold on to them in a crisis.

Even though she'd lost her parents as a child, she still had that urge to crawl into her mother's arms whenever something awful happened. That burning need to talk to her and have her chase away all the monsters and fears.

It never went away.

Abigail wanted to weep over what she saw. She wanted to weep for the people who'd been hurt because of her stupidity. "I can't believe I did all this." Surely, she would burn in hell for it.

Choo Co La Tah turned in the seat to face her. "It's not entirely your fault, dear. Don't take that guilt into your heart. The Balance is fragile, and it controls everything in the cosmos. If the scales ever tip—"

"We get screwed," Sasha said in a chipper tone with a big grin.

"You're not funny, Sasha," Jess snapped.

"Sorry. Trying to lighten the mood." He met Abigail's gaze. "If it makes you feel any better, this isn't my first apocalypse. There is hope."

She wasn't sure what to make of that. "Obviously the world survived."

Even in the darkness, she could see the pain those words brought to him. "Yeah, not really. It kind of blew everything back to the Stone Age. The good news is, people are resilient, and that which doesn't kill you merely serves as a cautionary tale for others." He glanced out the window and sighed. "It also makes one hell of a bedtime story, especially if the Crypt-Keeper's your audience."

She sucked her breath in sharply at the unspoken agony that lay beneath those words. "What happened?"

"What always happens when preternatural powers are unleashed or go to war, and no one cares about the collateral damage during the battle." He gestured toward the people on the street. "I lost my entire family in the blink of an eye. But hey, I saved a lot of money on not having to buy Christmas cards."

How could he make light of something that was obviously so painful for him?

Without thinking, she reached out and touched his hand.

Sasha didn't look at her, but he closed his fingers around hers and gave a light squeeze that said he appreciated it.

Sasha cleared his throat. "So, Choo? How many apocalypses have *you* survived?"

"More than you, Wolf. More than you."

Abigail was humbled by their experience. The misery they'd seen. It was easy to lose sight of other people's pain when your own was so strong. What was it that Plato said? Be kind to all you meet, for everyone is fighting a hard battle?

It was so true.

"Are you all right?" Jess asked.

She caught his gaze in the rearview mirror. "Yeah."

No. Not really. Her guilt ate at her.

And one question hung heaviest in her mind. "How did you learn to live with being a hired killer?"

"It's just like any other act of cruelty. You lie to yourself. You say that they deserved it. You create stories to justify why they needed to die and tell yourself that if you hadn't struck first, they'd have done it to you. In the end, you do your damnedest not to think about it all."

Yeah, people did have a nasty tendency to excuse their bad behavior and then to hold it against others whenever they did the same thing.

Sasha let go of her hand. "Hey, Choo? Wanna take odds on our survival tonight? We are in Vegas, after all. I think we should up the ante and have a huge payout for whoever calls it." When Choo Co La Tah failed to respond, he turned his attention to Jess. "What about you, cowboy?"

Jess scoffed. "I only gamble with my life."

"Ah . . . explains so much about you. And off on a random topic in an attempt to divert our attention from the fact that we're all most likely speeding to our impending doom, how did you get the name Sundown, anyway?"

"You want to know that now?" His tone was incredulous.

"Why not?"

Jess shook his head. "Why?"

"It's just an odd moniker for an outlaw. Figured it had some deeper meaning."

"A newspaper reporter gave it to him," Abigail said quietly. She'd read the article in something Jonah found years ago. "The man wrote that everyone called him Sundown because he did his best and most gruesome work after dark."

"You believe everything you read in the papers?" The anger in Jess's tone cut through the truck as an angry tic beat a fierce rhythm in his sculpted jaw. "They get all the facts screwed up, and I think most of them are so crooked, they have to screw their pants on in the morning. Hell, most of them have to go diagonal just to walk in a straight line."

Obviously that had struck a nerve with him. "It was wrong?"

Sasha gave her a no-duh stare.

"Yeah." Venom saturated his voice. "It was wrong. Some . . ." He paused as if he was about to say something offensive and then caught himself. "Trying to take credit for something that has nothing to do with anything he did. My real name is Manee Ya Doy Ay . . . it means 'sundown' in my mother's language."

How beautiful. She doubted she could ever say it properly, but it sounded wonderful as it rolled off his tongue. "Really?"

He gave a subtle nod. "It was her favorite time of day. When the sun must make peace with the moon and for a few brief moments, the two touch in mutual friendship and respect. Perfect balance between the light and dark. A time for reflection and for preparation."

What a wonderful way of looking at things, and it made her ache for his loss. A woman so kind shouldn't be taken from her loved ones. No more than her own mother had. "She sounds incredible."

"She was."

"She was Cherokee, right?"

"Tsalagi," he corrected. "It's what they call themselves."

Abigail frowned as she saw a strange expression cross Choo Co La Tah's face. It was like he wanted to say something, but knew that he shouldn't.

Before she could ask him about it, something hit the car. Hard.

And set it on fire.

"What the—?" Jess swerved again as more fire rained down on them. It hit the hood like a gel egg and splattered, spraying flames that clung to the metal.

Abigail gasped as some hit the window, staining it red. Blood red. "Is that bloodfire?"

Choo Co La Tah nodded. "The worst part? It burns in water."

Lovely. Couldn't anyone ever invent a friendly plague? Something like raining daisies? Euphoria? Dancing flying pigs?

Nah. They always had to be nasty.

"Uh, guys?" Sasha said in a droll tone. "It's not just a plague."

Abigail understood what he meant a heartbeat later when the Bronco was literally swatted off the road so hard that it bounced over the concrete bridge wall on Interstate 15 to land them beneath it on Highway 93. Even after the jarring crash, the Bronco continued to roll fast and furiously toward the area where several tractor trailers were parked.

By the time they stopped moving, she was completely disoriented.

And upside down.

She lifted her hand to her brow and touched something wet along her eyebrow. Crap, she was bleeding. At least that explained her sudden headache. She glanced to Jess to make sure he was all right. Like her, he had a head injury on his temple, and his left hand was bleeding. Other than that, he appeared fine. Choo Co La Tah seemed to be the one with the least injuries. He held one arm over his head, bracing it against the ceiling to hold his weight so that his belt wasn't cutting in to him the way hers was.

Gravity was a definitely a bitch right now.

Sasha groaned from beside her as he struggled with his belt. "I think I'm going to barf a hairball."

Jess let out a frustrated breath as he tried to loosen himself. "You can't. You're canine."

"Tell that to the hairball in my stomach."

Jess cursed as his hand slipped while he was trying to get loose. "Bet you're glad I made you fasten that seat belt now, aren't you, Mr. I-can-flash-myself-out-if-we-get-hit?"

Sasha groaned. "Shut up, asshole." He glared at Jess. "And I would have flashed out of the car, but because we were rolling, I didn't want to get hit by it. Damn those Rytis laws."

Abigail wanted to ask what that was, but there was no time as they were hammered with more bloodfire. The smell of gas was thick. If the Bronco wasn't currently on fire, it wouldn't be long before it ignited from the rain.

"We have to get out of here." Jess kicked at the broken windshield with his booted feet.

Sasha flashed out.

Abigail tried to undo her seat belt, but she couldn't. The buckle had broken during the crash. "I hate to be all girly, but I'm trapped."

"Where's Sasha?" Jess asked.

The answer came from just outside her window. "Getting his ass kicked while deflecting this asshole from you. Any time you want to help me, Jess. Step right up."

Jess snorted at the acerbic shape-shifter as he cut his belt, then slammed down to the ceiling. "Whatever you do, keep him busy."

"No problemo. Using my face as his punching bag seems to be working. I'll just need you to help me find all my teeth later."

Abigail saw Sasha hit the ground near them. Oooh, that looked really painful. His face turned deadly before he pushed himself up and vanished out of her line of sight again.

Choo Co La Tah was strangely calm while the scent of gas grew stronger. And her breathing became more labored. It was hard to draw a breath while the nylon belt dug into her.

"Guys!" Sasha shouted. "You might want to think about getting out now. Flames are spreading all over the bottom of the truck."

She could hear the fire and feel the heat of it. *I'm going to die.*

And yet she had no fear. No idea why. It made no sense whatsoever. In fact, she was strangely calm, too. Like a part of her might even crave it.

Lying on his back, Jess kicked furiously at the windshield. "Damn. It. Break. Already. You. Sorry. Son. Of. A.

Biscuit. Eating. Cat." He had the most colorful way of speaking as he punctuated every word with a solid kick.

Something let out a high-pitched whine. A second later, the windshield flew out onto the ground. Jess moved toward her.

She shook her head. "Get Choo Co La Tah first."

He hesitated.

"No," Choo Co La Tah snapped. "Free her. I'll be out in a second."

She saw the indecision in those lush dark eyes. "He's more important than I am."

Not to me he isn't. Jess barely bit those words back before he said them out loud. Every part of him cringed at the thought of her being hurt any worse. He couldn't stand to see her trapped and bleeding. It brought back memories he didn't understand.

Not memories of Matilda. These were something else. Faded images of a time and place he didn't understand.

But he saw her face so clearly.

Her face. Same black hair and that sassy smile that dared him as she crooked her finger for him to follow after her.

I will always come for you, Kianini. Nothing will keep me from it.

She laughed as she pulled him into her arms and stared up at him coyly from beneath her lashes. *And I will never leave you, my heart. Forever yours.*

Those words whispered in his ears.

"Get her free."

It took him a moment to register Choo Co La Tah's words, which had been spoken in a language he'd never heard before. Yet he completely understood them.

Blinking, he moved to comply as Choo Co La Tah crawled out through the missing windshield.

Abigail met Jess's determined gaze, and the horror in his eyes told her that the clock was ticking down for them. The sound of fire was now deafening. More than that, the pungent gas odor clung to them so thickly that she tasted it and it made it even harder to breathe.

Undaunted by the danger, Jess struggled to cut through the belt. The car thudded and popped.

Her time could be counted in heartbeats now. But it touched her that Jess was still helping her.

Moronic, but touching.

She put her hand over his to stop him from cutting the belt. "Go. There's no need in both of us dying."

He lifted her hand to his lips and kissed her knuckles. "I'm not leaving you. If we go, we go together."

"Don't be stupid, Jess."

He scoffed as he returned to sawing on the belt. "Brains don't exactly run in my family. Suicidal lunacy, on the other hand . . ."

"Runs thick?"

He grinned at her. "Move back."

The metal whined a warning to them as the belt finally snapped.

Jess caught her against him and took a second to savor the feeling of her there before he kissed her temple, then pulled her from the wreckage.

They barely cleared the Bronco before it exploded into one impressive display of pyrotechnics. Fire shot up to the dark sky while pieces of the truck rained down all over them. Jess snatched Abigail under him to protect her from the shrapnel.

Abigail couldn't breathe with his heavy weight pressing down on her. But she was grateful to have him as her shield. Her only hope was that nothing hit him.

Jess froze the moment their eyes met, and he caught the full force of the adoration in her gaze. It stole his breath. She lifted her hand and laid it gently against his cheek. The warmth of her hand set him on fire.

Suddenly, the sound of a loud dragonesque call caught his attention and shattered the spell.

Abigail turned her head in synch with Jess. She gaped at the sight of Choo Co La Tah, Ren, and Sasha embroiled in a bitter fight with the most hideous thing she'd seen since Kurt's attempt to cut Hannah's hair when they were kids.

Solid black, it was extremely tall and thin with spidery limbs that twisted out like living tendrils. Whatever it was, it could sling its arm out like a whip and crack it against their friends. It moved so fast, it was hard to follow, and it said a lot about their fighting skills that they were able to stand toe to toe with these new creatures.

Jess pushed himself off her and ran to join the fight.

Rolling over, Abigail got up, intending to join them in battle. But before she could move or Jess reached the fight, Ren appeared in front of him.

"Get back."

Jess shook his head. "We can't let Choo Co La Tah get hurt."

"He's expendable, Jess. You and Abigail aren't."

That news floored her.

Jess scowled. "What?"

"Do what he says!" Choo Co La Tah shouted as he drove one of the creatures back while another one moved forward to fight him. "Both of you have to live."

Jess would argue, but honestly he wanted to protect her. Fine. He would trust them.

"What are these things?" she asked him as he returned to her side.

"A good fable gone bad."

"What?"

Ren kicked the one he was fighting away from him. "They're tsi-nooks."

He said that like she should understand it. "Gibberish is not my native tongue, Ren. What's a tsi-nook?"

No one answered, as they were a little occupied by fighting them, and while they were getting in some good blows, they didn't appear to be winning.

Abigail hated the feeling of being so vulnerable. She had no idea what she was up against or if she should poke out their eyes or kick them in the knees. Though to be honest, she wasn't sure they had either one. "Okay, I don't care what they are. How do we kill them?"

"With great skill, my girl. With great skill." Choo Co La Tah uncoiled his feathered bracelet from his arm. As he unwound it, it grew into a staff almost as tall as he was. One that expanded so that he could attack the tsi-nook nearest him.

But that didn't work. It seemed to only upset the beast. The tsi-nook fell on the ground. On its back. At least that's what she thought was its back. Their forms were so twisted, it was hard to tell for sure.

After it landed, she saw its face clearly for the first time. Strangely, it reminded her of a wooden mask. Weathered with deep lines all over its features, the eyes were nothing more than slits, and it didn't appear to have eyelids. For that matter, it didn't seem to blink.

In one word, they were ugly.

As if it sensed what she thought about it, it turned to face her and let out a piercing shriek. Apparently in freakspeak, that was some kind of rallying call because the moment it started, the others stopped to glare at her and Jess.

It was never a good thing to be the center of unwanted attention, and right now she felt like Carrie at the prom. Or more to the point, the only steak in a dog kennel.

Her heart pounded as fear tackled her to the ground and held her there.

Moving with an eerie fluid grace and a speed that shouldn't be possible, they ran in her direction. Jess went to fight them, but they actually ran past him and kept going full speed.

At *her*.

Abigail's eyes widened as she realized they didn't care about the men. She was the target.

The only target.

C-r-a-p.

She braced herself for the fight. *What am I doing?* There were more than a dozen of them, and there was only one her. One. While it was noble to be brave, it was stupid to be suicidal. Fighting a dozen . . . when she didn't have a weapon and didn't know how to kill them flew right past the realm of noble and landed solidly in the kingdom of stupid.

To quote her favorite play of all time . . . *Run away!* She turned and headed for the desert as fast as she could.

Jess went cold as the tsi-nooks ran for Abigail. His vision darkened at the same time fear for her rushed through him. For one second, he was mortal again, and then the sensation was gone.

"Oh no you don't." His powers surged in a way they hadn't in decades. Suddenly, he felt stronger than he ever had before. Something deep inside him snapped, and out came what he could only describe as an inner warrior. One who knew the taste and feel of the tsi-nooks' blood on its hands.

No one would harm Abigail.

He went after them. And as he neared her, he realized her eyes were turning red. The demon was taking possession of her again.

It could be a good thing.

Or a really bad one.

Since the tsi-nooks, much like a traditional Daimon, preyed primarily on human souls, they might not want any part of a gallu demon. Or if they were like the new generation of Daimons, eating her soul might charge their powers and make them stronger.

Either way, he wasn't going to chance it. Not tonight.

Jess reached deep inside and tapped the only other power he did his best not to use. One so strong and painful that later it would make him wish he were dead.

But first, it would save their lives.

Closing his eyes, he conjured a gun—and not just any gun. The one that had made him infamous. An 1887 lever-action Winchester with a five-round tubular magazine. Not that it would need that tonight. His powers would make sure he didn't run out of rounds.

The smell of blood permeated his nostrils. His nose always bled whenever he accessed this power, which was why he almost never used it. That and the vicious headache he'd have later from it. So much for Dark-Hunters not getting those.

But if it kept her safe, it was worth it.

Abigail froze as she caught sight of Jess approaching her with long, determined strides. The desert wind whipped at his long black duster, stirring it back from his muscled body. The grim lethal glare on his chiseled features promised the tsi-nooks hell wrath and then some. This wasn't the tender man who'd made love to her while cramped in a tiny car. Nor was it the goofball who joked with and teased her.

This was the fierce, cold-blooded killer who'd left legions of dead and a legend so terrifying that one marshal had surrendered his badge rather than take Jess's horse into custody.

True story.

And Jess had been only seventeen at the time.

No wonder his partner had shot him in the back. She doubted anyone with a brain would ever assault this version of Jess Brady while he was facing them. Even she had a chill running down her spine as the hairs along her arms and neck raised. While she was pretty sure he wouldn't hurt her, she really didn't want to find out for sure.

Without breaking stride, he cocked the lever of the shotgun across his chest, took aim, and blew the tsi-nook closest to her apart.

She flinched in reaction to the ringing sound of the gun

followed by the shrill scream of the tsi-nook. Blood from the creature sprayed all over her body. She tensed, unsure of what to expect from the blood touching her skin. Luckily, nothing happened.

Before she could think to breathe again, Jess kept firing, rapidly blowing apart every one of them in turn. Their screams echoed around her until the night swallowed the sound and silenced it forever.

Until he took aim at her head.

Eyes wide, she seized in terror. *What did I do? Why would he kill her now?* She stared straight into the barrel. Black and evil, it gave her a profound understanding of the people he'd killed.

Don't. The word caught in her throat.

His features stone cold, he fired.

Abigail sucked her breath in sharply at the sound, expecting pain and a recoil that would knock her off her feet. Instead, she remained intact.

No pain. No impact.

Jess continued toward her, taking aim again. It wasn't until he fired another round that she realized he was shooting past her and not *at* her.

Thank God, she hadn't moved. Then he might have really killed her.

In fact, he didn't stop shooting until he was standing right beside her. Only then did he put the gun down and scan the darkness to make sure there was nothing else out there.

The wind whistled around them, and out in the distance, she heard the cry of a single coyote. Though to be honest, she was amazed she could hear anything, given the last few minutes.

"Is that our friend?" she asked Jess.

"No." Jess tilted his head back and sniffed the air like a lycanthrope might if he was tracking someone. "They're bounty hunters."

"Pardon?"

Jess's memories burned as he was pulled back in time to age fifteen. Then, as now, there had been a chill in the warm air. But no one except him could feel it. Bart had left him holed up in a small dugout on the side of a mountain out in the middle of nowhere Arizona. A posse had been chasing after them, and he'd had nothing more than a handful of bullets.

He'd been dead asleep and then awakened to nothing other than his heart racing. As he tried to force himself back to sleep, he'd smelled that haunting stench that defied explanation.

It was the same odor he smelled on the wind now. He glanced over to Choo Co La Tah. "What's going on?"

"We must get to the Valley. Quickly. Coyote is growing desperate."

Putting his hands on his hips, Sasha stopped in front of them. "Coyote got boys." He jerked his chin toward the bodies. "And a lot of them. What the hell did we just fight?"

Abigail was even more grateful to the wolf. "Thank you for asking. That's what *I* wanted to know."

Jess didn't answer as he locked gazes with Choo Co La Tah. "What is out there?"

"You're asking me a question you already know the answer to. And yes, they have been after you before. . . . Many times."

Ren sighed. "They're skinwalkers who lost wagers to Coyote. Now they serve as his bounty hunters."

"They're the same as you?" Abigail asked.

Ren shook his head. "I'm a shape-shifter, not a skin-walker. They are the nastiest of creatures. Evil so foul that it rots them from the inside out." He turned to Jess. "That's the odor you smell. Nothing else like it."

Sasha growled. "What are their powers?"

"They can track as well as you do. Maybe better. They can shift forms, but only so long as they hold the pelt or feather of the animal they want to become next to their skin. Superhuman strength."

Choo Co La Tah agreed. "And halitosis so bad, it could knock down a building."

Great. Just great. Jess was really getting tired of being hunted. "I understand why they're after us tonight. But I remember them chasing me when I was human."

Sasha whistled. "Let's come back to the why in a few. First things first. What the hell is lying in pieces on the ground around us? I'm Greek, remember? So all this is . . .

non-Greek to me, which means I know nothing about it. And I need to know in the event I have to fight it again. Obviously shotguns are effective against them. What else?"

Jess rested his shotgun over his shoulder. "The term is tsi-noo. Tsi-nooks for the plural. Not to be confused with the Chinook Nation, because they have nothing to do with each other. . . . In short, they're our version of Daimons."

"Apollo curse them, too?"

Jess snorted at Sasha's irreverent question. "No. They were humans who committed crimes so unspeakable and horrific that the winter winds turned their hearts to ice. Now they can only live off the souls of humans."

"And they were one of Snake's plagues," Ren added. "Which means he and Coyote will be even more hell-bent on finding Old Bear's."

Sasha nodded as he listened. "Point taken there. Now, the important question, so pay attention, ye ADD degenerates. How the *F* do I kill them? 'Cause no offense, I was trying and they were kicking my ass all over the place. It really wasn't pretty and didn't do much for my ego either. My only reprieve is that no one I have to face on a regular basis witnessed my beating. Don't know why you wanted me here when I'm about as useful as a wart on Artemis's bum."

Smiling at his rant, Choo Co La Tah melted his staff back down to the bracelet, then coiled it around his wrist again. "Simple, Wolf. Like a Daimon, pierce the heart and the ice shatters inside. They die instantly. As you saw from Sundown, a shotgun will blow the heart apart and end them."

Sasha narrowed his gaze on Jess. "How you know that, cowboy?"

"Didn't. But a twelve-gauge round to the head or heart will take down just about anything. And if doesn't, kiss your ass good-bye and run like hell."

Abigail crossed her arms over her chest and drummed her fingernails on her biceps. "By the way, you and I need to talk about how you got that gun when I know it wasn't in the truck." She raked him with a glance from head to toe that succeeded in making him flinch. "You've been holding out on me."

Help . . .

How in the world could he be more afraid of her, a tiny little slip of a woman, than he'd been of the tsi-nooks?

"Um . . ."

"What was that?"

They all turned to look at Sasha who was staring into the darkness.

Jess frowned. "What?"

Ren stepped back as if he might have heard it, too. "We need to get going."

Sasha gestured toward the smoldering remains of the Bronco. "How? Are you an African swallow in another form or something?"

Choo Co La Tah scowled. "African swallow? What are you going on about now?"

"Oh c'mon, surely all of you get the Mon . . . ty . . . Python . . ." Sasha paused as if he remembered his audience. "Never mind."

Jess rubbed at his jaw. "He's right. It's too far to walk, and with the exception of Sasha and Ren, we don't have a ride."

Choo Co La Tah pointed to the parked tractor trailers. "What about one of those?"

Jess considered it. "Someone might have left keys in one. Let's go see."

Abigail walked in the center of the men while she listened for another attack. It was so dark, she could barely see. There was a low-lying cloud cover that held back the stars. It made the air feel heavy. Ominous. Or maybe that was from the fact that she knew what was out to get her.

Without thinking, she reached out and took Jess's rough hand. When he laced his fingers with hers, it warmed her in spite of the cold desert wind. She took strength from his nearness, and it made her wish that they didn't have to do this.

Made her wish that she could find some way to end the nightmare and return to a normal life.

Your life was never normal.

That was certainly true. But for the first time, she

wanted normality. She craved it now that it was too late to claim it. She'd already cast her die and come up bust.

One way or the other, her life was over. If by some miracle she did survive all of this and convince Choo Co La Tah not to sacrifice her to the spirits she'd offended, she had no doubt that one of the other Dark-Hunters would kill her for what she'd done.

There was no hope. Not now.

How could I have screwed up my life so badly?

The same way everyone did. She'd listened to and trusted the wrong people. Had put her faith and energy into the wrong things, only to learn too late that she shouldn't have harbored hatred.

I'm so stupid.

Jess paused as they reached the trucks. He and Abigail searched the first one for keys while the others spread out to check the rest.

One by one, they reported failure.

"Hey!" Sasha shouted after a minute. "I don't have keys, but this one's open. Anyone know how to hot-wire?"

Ren gave him an arch stare. "Can't you use your powers to start it?"

Sasha raked him with an equally offended sweep. "Can't you?"

Abigail held her hands up. "Step aside, boys. I have the evil powers for this."

Jess smiled as she climbed inside the cab and vanished

under the dash. "My lady got mad skills," he said, imitating the slang Sasha used.

Then he sobered as he realized what he'd done.

He'd claimed her. Publicly. But that wasn't what shocked him. The fact that he truly thought of her like that did. She was a part of him now. Even though they hadn't known each other long, she had breached his defenses and wormed her way into his heart.

Oh my God. The very idea terrified him.

He wouldn't call it love.

Would he?

It wasn't what he felt for Matilda by a long shot, and yet there were enough similarities that it left him wondering. When had he known he loved Matilda?

The day he'd realized he couldn't live without her.

Bart had told him that he wanted to move on. That it was time for them to find a new base of operations. Normally, Jess would have been packed up in a few hours and been ready to ride. Instead, an excruciating pain had ripped him apart when he thought about not seeing Matilda again. It'd been so debilitating that it brought him to his knees.

Nothing had struck him like that since.

Not until he'd seen the tsi-nooks going after Abigail.

I would die for her. That fact hit him like a punch in the jaw. He really would. She had a power over him that not even Matilda had possessed. *I'm so screwed.*

The semi started up, startling him away from his train of thought.

Blinking, he realized the other men were staring at him like he'd grown a third head. "What?" he asked defensively.

Sasha snorted. "I have never in my extremely long life seen anyone take so long to answer a question. It's like you went into your mind and got lost. You need a bread crumb, buddy?" He made a noise like he was calling his pet. "Here, Lassie, here. Come back, girl."

Jess shoved at him. "Shut up. What did you ask me, anyway?"

Sasha slapped himself on the forehead and groaned. "Really? Good thing I didn't tell you to duck a bomb."

He started to respond, but Abigail's frantic voice stopped him.

"Gentlemen. We have company."

15

The men climbed up the sides of the truck to see why Abigail had called them. Ren and Sasha on the passenger side. Choo Co La Tah and Jess on hers.

Jess stood in the open door with one hand braced against the top, looking down at her. "What is it, babe?"

Stunned, all she could do was point at the herd of . . . whatever it was, speeding toward them. The group was stirring up a huge cloud of dust in their wake. Not even the darkness could conceal their presence. Mostly because their number was just that impressive.

Some she knew to be tsi-nooks. Others were definitely coyotes and the last group she assumed were the bounty hunters they'd been talking about.

Ren's jaw went slack.

Jess's tensed.

Sasha outdid them all. He laughed. "Now there's something you don't see everyday. Gah, I hope there's no human roaming around with a video recorder or cell phone. Be a bitch to explain that. Easier just to kill them."

Ren ignored him. "Did they open the Gate already?"

That would explain it.

But Choo Co La Tah shook his head. "They're trying to scare us."

"Working. 'Cause the wolf here is definitely feeling an 'oh shit' moment." He glanced over to Abigail. "You wouldn't want to change my diaper, would you?"

Jess shook his head at the wolf. He started to take the wheel from Abigail, then paused. "You know this is one of those moments when you think about the fact that you didn't quite complete the plan."

She frowned. "How so?"

He glanced around their small group. "Anyone know how to drive a semi?"

Ugh! She could kick herself for not thinking of that. Since they'd trained her to go after Dark-Hunters, Jonah had taught her the skill of hot-wiring—just in case she needed a quick getaway. She even knew how to start electronic and digital ignitions.

Why hadn't she ever taken the time to learn a standard transmission?

Sasha and Ren exchanged a bemused stare. "I don't drive," they said simultaneously.

Her heart sank. Of course they didn't. Ren flew as a bird and Sasha did that flashing thing. When would *they* have ever needed a driver's license?

"Can't you flash us out?" she asked Sasha.

He let out a fake, hysterical laugh. "My powers were strangled by a bitch-goddess as punishment for my gross stupidity. I'm lucky I can still flash myself, never mind other people. All I have is raw power and sexy, fighting prowess. Well, okay, if I had to, I might teleport one, maybe two others. But I wouldn't bet my better body parts on it."

Ren frowned. "I didn't think you could lose psychic powers."

"*You* can't, Dark-Hunter boy. But mine weren't a gift. I was born with them. Total different standard. Lucky me."

Jess arched a brow at her. "Can you drive it?"

"No. I can't drive a stick at all. It's why I took Andy's car and not one of yours."

"Oh people, for goodness' sake . . . Move over." Choo Co La Tah pushed past Jess to take the driver's seat.

Curious about that, she slid over to make room for the ancient.

Jess hesitated. "Do you know what you're doing?"

Choo Co La Tah gave him a withering glare. "Not at all. But I figured someone needed to learn and no one else was volunteering. Step in and get situated. Time is of the essence."

Abigail's heart pounded. "I hope he's joking about that." If not, it would be a very short trip.

Ren changed into his crow form before he took flight.

Jess and Sasha climbed in, then moved to the compartment behind the seat. A pall hung over all of them while Choo Co La Tah adjusted the seat and mirrors.

By all means, please take your time. Not like they were all about to die or anything . . .

She couldn't speak as she watched their enemies rapidly closing the distance between them. This was by far the scariest thing she'd seen. Unlike the wasps and scorpions, this horde could think and adapt.

They even had opposable thumbs.

Whole different ball game.

Choo Co La Tah shifted into gear. Or at least he tried. The truck made a fierce grinding sound that caused Jess to screw his face up as it lurched violently and shook like a dog coming in from the rain.

"You sure you don't want me to try?" Jess offered.

Choo Co La Tah waved him away. "I'm a little rusty. Just give me a second to get used to it again."

Abigail swallowed hard. "How long has it been?"

Choo Co La Tah eased off the clutch and they shuddered forward at the most impressive speed of two whole miles an hour. About the same speed as a limping turtle. "Hmm, probably sometime around nineteen hundred and . . ."

They all waited with bated breath while he ground his way through more gears. With every shift, the engine audibly protested his skills.

Silently, so did she.

The truck was really moving along now. They reached a staggering fifteen miles an hour. At this rate, they might be able to overtake a loaded school bus . . .

By tomorrow.

Or at the very least, the day after that.

". . . must have been the summer of . . . hmm . . . let me think a moment. Fifty-three. Yes, that was it. 1953. The year they came out with color teles. It was a good year as I recall. Same year Bill Gates was born."

The look on Jess's and Sasha's faces would have made her laugh if she wasn't every bit as horrified. *Oh my God, who put him behind the wheel?*

Sasha visibly cringed as he saw how close their pursuers were to their bumper. "Should I get out and push?"

Jess cursed under his breath as he saw them, too. "I'd get out and run at this point. I think you'd go faster."

Choo Co La Tah took their comments in stride. "Now, now, gentlemen. All is well. See, I'm getting better." He finally made a gear without the truck spazzing or the gears grinding.

Abigail cringed as she saw the whites of the eyes of their pursuers. "They're almost at our tailgate."

"Excuse me, darling." Jess slid over her lap to roll down the window.

She started to ask him what he was doing, but before she could, he held his hand out toward Sasha.

"Gun."

Sasha handed it over like a surgical assistant.

Jess leaned against the door with one leg braced over her lap. He pressed his thigh lightly against her stomach as he started shooting at the ones chasing them. The rapid fire rang in her ears as she felt his muscles contracting with each movement. He leaned out further.

Choo Co La Tah snatched the wheel to avoid an abandoned car in the road.

The motion tipped Jess so fast that he lost his balance and fell forward, through the window. Terrified he was about to fall to the street, Abigail wrapped herself around him to hold him in place.

Jess couldn't breathe for a second. He'd bruised the shit out of his ribs when he'd slipped and slammed his side into the door. Not to mention, Abigail had him pinned in a bear hug so tight he was amazed he wasn't turning blue.

But he didn't mind the pain. She felt so good, he was willing to suffer.

Unfortunately, he couldn't shoot this way.

"Sweetie?"

She looked up at him.

"I need my arm back."

Her face turned bright red. "Sorry." She quickly released it, but she kept her arms around his waist, anchoring him to her.

His heart pounded at the sight she made holding on to him to keep him safe. He wanted to kiss her so badly, he could taste her lips.

First, he had to protect her. Returning to his post, he started picking off their pursuers while Choo Co La Tah floored it. They were finally going fast and putting some distance between the truck and their pursuers.

Jess kept firing as the wind rushed around him. A tsi-noo screamed in frustration. *Yeah, that's right. Cry, baby, cry. Go home to your daddy and tell him you failed. Let him kick your ass.*

"Jess?"

He felt Abigail tugging hard at his shirt. Ducking back into the cab, he arched a brow. "Yeah?"

Choo Co La Tah cleared his throat then asked in the

calmest of tones. "You wouldn't happen to know how to stop one of these devices, would you?"

Oh please no . . .

Surely he'd misheard that. "Come again?"

Choo Co La Tah pressed the brake pedal all the way to the floor. A loud sound echoed

Nothing happened. The truck didn't slow in the least. Jess's stomach sank to his feet.

His arms spread wide over the giant steering wheel, Choo Co La Tah held on with a grip so tight his knuckles blanched. "I'm sorry to say, there seems to be a little bit of a problem. As you can see, it doesn't respond when I apply the brake."

And they were approaching an almost ninety degree turn they'd have to make onto the Valley of Fire Highway.

Jess considered their options. "Keep going straight. Don't try to make the off ramp."

"And again I say we have a bit of a problem."

Jess dreaded the next word. "Yeah?"

Abigail swallowed hard before she pointed down the road. "There are two jack-knifed trucks blocking it."

Shit.

And they were going way too fast. He'd say to ram the trucks, but one was hauling gas. They'd go up like a Roman candle.

Why, Lord, why?

Sasha leaned forward. "Hit the brake again."

Choo Co La Tah complied. Air blew back on him as a loud *sssshhhh* sound filled the cab. "I fear they're in ill repair, my boy."

"Yeah, but I think I know what it is." Sasha dove at the floorboard and started pounding against it with his fist. "C'mon, you little bastard. Work." He hit the brake with his hand.

As before, nothing happened.

Sasha growled low in his throat. "Send the wolf to watch them," he mocked in a falsetto. His nostrils flared. "I swear Z, if I live, I'm going to rip that damned goatee off your face and stick your shaving cream in the fridge." He locked gazes with Jess. "I'll be right back."

Abigail bit her lip as fear darkened her eyes. "Where's he going?"

Jess shrugged. "No idea."

"Oh dear . . ."

Since his back was to the windshield, Jess really didn't want to look at what had alarmed the ancient spirit. He'd much rather stare at Abigail.

But the compulsion was too great.

He turned, then wished he'd listened to himself. *Ay carumba!* They were way too close to the wrecked trucks. One lay on its side like it'd fainted while the other was sideways on the highway. No way to avoid them.

We're going to burn . . .

Suddenly, something was slamming hard at the floorboard underneath Choo Co La Tah's feet.

"Hit the brakes!" Sasha's muffled shout was barely audible even with Jess's super hearing.

Choo Co La Tah stomped the brakes and everyone held their collective breath and prayed.

Nothing happened. Jess felt his heart stop as he realized they were going to crash. He wasn't worried about himself. He would survive.

Abigail might not.

"Again!" Sasha shouted.

Choo Co La Tah obeyed. Jess tensed in expectation of their oncoming crash.

Then, to his utmost shock, the truck finally began to slow. He couldn't believe it. Sasha flashed back into the cab with a proud grin on his face.

Abigail leaned her head back on the seat and returned his smile. She high-fived Sasha.

Until Choo Co La Tah cursed—something he never did. "Hold on everyone."

Jess was tossed forward as they left the interstate and flew down the exit ramp at a speed that would have probably gotten them arrested had a cop seen it. Luckily there were no concrete barriers or anything significant around. Only small road markers that warned of the drop off the shoulder that they plowed over.

Please don't tip, please don't tip.

And don't plow into the Casino Smoke Shop Truck

Stop. The owner definitely wouldn't appreciate it. That had now become his biggest concern. Killing someone other than them.

The truck shimmied and shook as if it wanted to flip. But through some miracle, it didn't and in a few seconds, they were slowed to a safe speed while Choo Co La Tah headed toward the Valley.

Sasha fell back and laughed. "All right, everyone. Fess up. Who just shat in their pants? C'mon. Admit it." He raised his hand. "I know I did and I'm wolf enough to own it."

Jess ignored him. "Are you all right?" he asked Abigail. She was still a little too pale for his tastes.

"I think I'm going to own Sasha's question. Definitely put me on your list."

Jess laughed, then looked over at Sasha. "So Wolf, what did you do?"

"You mean before or after I soiled my jeans? Which, by the way, I want kudos for coming back in the cab when I could have gone home." Sasha sobered. "The foot valve was stuck. It doesn't happen often. But it can happen as you just saw. If you're lucky you can pop it back out from the cab. Obviously, given the horrors of this night, I wasn't lucky so I had to crawl under the damn thing at ninety miles an hour and pound it out from underneath. I don't *ever* want to hang like that under a speeding vehicle again. I swear I lost eight of my nine lives."

"What is it with you and the cat analogies?"

"Long, really not boring story. Anyway, I'm just glad I knew what it was."

Impressive, but . . .

"How did you know?"

"Video games," Sasha said proudly. "Never let it be said they're a waste of time. But for them, we'd be toasting some better parts or flipped and bleeding. And speaking of, we probably want to leave a note for whoever owns this thing so they can get it fixed. We don't want a human getting hurt over bad maintenance."

Choo Co La Tah checked the side view mirror. "I hate to be the one to cut in on the reverie and congratulatory sentiments, but we still have our friends following behind us."

Jess let out a long breath at their persistence. "What I wouldn't give for a case of C-4." And then the worst thing happened.

The pain from conjuring his gun hit.

Abigail gasped as Jess pressed his hand to his forehead and doubled over in the seat. "Jess?"

"It's okay," he said between clenched teeth. "I'll be all right."

In spite of those words, fear gripped her. "You don't look all right."

His nose started pouring blood.

She widened her eyes. "Honey?"

Sasha manifested a small hand towel and threw it over him.

Jess held it to his nose and tilted his head back. Terrified, Abigail ran her hand through his hair. "Is there anything I can do?"

He shook his head.

"All right, my boy. Now that we're on the back road . . ." Choo Co La Tah begin chanting something under his breath. Light in tone at first and then in crescendo. Louder and louder it went like a frenetic dance. Acapulco and harmonious, she couldn't understand a word of it. Only the beauty of the sound.

And as he spoke, the dirt outside began to swirl and spin, rising higher like small tornados.

Abigail was floored by what she saw. In a matter of seconds, they had a dust cloud surrounding them. The only problem was, their sight was limited by it.

"Why didn't you do this before?" Sasha asked. "When it could have really helped us?"

Jess shifted the towel that was fast becoming drenched in blood. "He needed to be close to the Valley to draw the sand."

And it wasn't just any sand. It rose up into the shape of an angry fist and rushed back toward their enemies like a landlocked tsunami. She could hear their screams as the sand blasted and pelted them.

Yeah, that had to sting.

In a matter of minutes, the swirling sands had settled and there was no one on the road but them.

Abigail took that moment to relax, hoping that this time it would last a little bit longer than a few ragged heartbeats. She needed a small break. They all did. This had been an incredible nonstop journey.

Jess watched the relief play across Abigail's delicate features as she lay back with her eyes half closed. The light of the cab cast shadows over her face. Her soft hands stroked his hair while he tried to breathe through the pain pounding in his skull. He had no idea why this power took its toll on him. For that he'd like to beat Artemis.

But if it meant being held so tenderly by Abigail, he was willing to suffer.

No one spoke as they traveled down the lonely desert road. They were all too relieved to be alive and not have to fight for it. The silence seduced them with her well needed tranquility. Only the sound of the engine and the tires rolling on asphalt reached them.

But all too soon they reached the Valley—something he'd been dreading for hours. Choo Co La Tah slowed down even more so that he could scan the surrounding landscape.

"What are you looking for?" Jess asked.

"The mound that marks our trail."

Abigail looked around at the dips and crevices of land and rock that now lined both sides of the highway. She'd never been to the Valley before. It was spooky at night.

Skeletal bushes and shrubs rose out of the ground to tower like evil spirits. A part of her even felt like they were watching her.

"Do you feel it?"

She glanced over at Choo Co La Tah. "Feel what?"

"The manitou? The energy of the earth that flows through everyone and everything. It's a living creature that can feel our pain and our joy. Everything we are, feeds into it and it leaves a lasting impression on the earth after we're gone."

Sasha sat up. "So it's like a ghost?"

Smiling, he shook his head. "It's hard to explain. You must feel it."

Abigail tried, but the only thing she felt was the weight of Jess's head in her lap and the heaviness of her conscience that still flogged her over all of this.

Choo Co La Tah's words didn't help her any, either. If anything, they made her feel worse. Her lasting impression was four plagues and untold horrors played out on innocent people.

Part of her wished she was twisted enough to not care. But sadly, she did.

Choo Co La Tah pulled over to the side of the road and parked the truck.

Jess sat up slowly.

"Are you any better?"

He pulled the towel down and she cringed. He was

still bleeding pretty badly. "Sasha? I need some tissue to pack my nose with."

The wolf gave him a suspicious stare. "Is that hygienically sound?"

"Sasha . . ."

"Fine, but if you get toxic shock up your nose, buddy, remember I warned you." He held his hand palm up and a box of Kleenex appeared.

Jess pulled a couple out and wedged them into his nostrils. He gave Abigail a sheepish smile. "Sexy, right?"

"Oh yeah, baby. You're so hot right now, if I was chicken I'd lay hard-boiled eggs."

Sasha fell back laughing.

Jess chucked the box of tissues at him. "At least I don't lick my own crotch."

"Hey!" Sasha snapped. "That's just rude. And for the record, I don't. We do have full cognitive functioning in our animal forms and that's all I'm going to say on the matter. I refute your mean lies." He sat up again and laughed at Jess. "By the way, you really need to check yourself out in the mirror."

"I'm really not going to." There were some things a man didn't need to know about himself. How much a goober he appeared to a woman he had the hots for was one of them. His imagination was bad enough. God forbid the reality be worse than the image he had in his head.

He wouldn't be able to recover from that blow.

Sasha flashed out of the cab while the rest of them climbed down.

Jess made sure to take his gun.

They met up at the back of the trailer while Ren swooped down from the sky and returned to his human form.

Abigail was impressed at how he did that. One second he was a bird and then after a small flash of light that could be easily missed if you weren't paying attention, he was human again.

Ren shook his head at Choo Co La Tah. "Nice driving. I honestly thought you guys were dead, especially when you hit that off-ramp at warp speed."

Sasha snorted. "So did we. Be glad you weren't there for the screaming."

Abigail rubbed her hands down her arms, trying to banish a sudden chill. "So what do we do now?"

Choo Co La Tah pinned her with sinister stare. "We find the sacred rock and you make your sacrifice."

16

Abigail took a deep breath to quell her rising fears. This was what she'd come here to do. Trade her life for the world.

You can do this.

No, I can't. I can't. I don't want to die. Not now that she had a real reason to live. She wanted to hang on to every heartbeat.

Every breath. Because every one of them meant something now in a way they never had before. After a lifetime of waiting for something, anything special, each second with Jess was an extraordinary adventure in discovery . . .

Of him.

Most of all, herself. She'd learned about a whole new side of her that she never knew existed. He brought out a sense of wonder and showed her miracles in the smallest things, and she didn't want to leave that. Not so soon.

One more day, please . . .

Panic set its steely talons against her courage, and it wouldn't let go of her.

Until she met Jess's dark gaze. That centered and calmed her nerves. Yeah, he looked like a silly kid with his nose packed full of Kleenex. Still, it didn't detract from how gorgeous he was with his dark windswept hair falling gently into his eyes. Those sharp cheekbones and soft lips that she could nibble on until her mouth was numb. From that tough aura of I-am-here-to-kick-your-ass-and-make-it-count.

Only Jess could make Kleenex sexy.

And that brought home one simple truth. *I won't die to save the world.*

But she would die for him.

He didn't deserve to pay for her stupidity. He'd suffered enough in his life. It was her turn to make a sacrifice. To grow up and face the consequences of her actions. Yes, she'd been lied to, but she'd let them deceive her. There was no one else to blame.

She'd dragged an innocent man into all of this . . . True, she'd seen his face that night in her room, but the woman in her now knew the man, and while she had no doubt he could have murdered her father without a second thought, Sundown would never have been able to hurt her mother.

Not like that. And there was absolutely no way he would *ever* search for a child to kill it. He was lethal, but never intentionally cruel.

Jess was innocent and she most definitely wasn't. She deserved to be punished for what she'd done.

Her entire body quaked from fear, yet she refused to let anyone know that. She wouldn't be a hypocrite. Lifting her chin, she nodded at Choo Co La Tah. "Where do you need me?"

"Follow me, my dear."

She took a step forward.

Jess cut her off. "We don't need to do this. I can fight Coyote. We have the ability to defeat him."

Sasha laughed hysterically. "Are you out of your effing mind? Hello? Where have you been for the last two days? I want whatever screwed-up glasses you're looking through. 'Cause from where I've been standing, we've been getting our asses seriously kicked around the block. Up a few stairs and down again."

Jess let out a sound of supreme exasperation as he cut a killing glare toward the wolf. "We're not dead yet."

"*Yet* is the operative word. If that's all that's in the way, I'll kill you and end it. Ren? Give me your knife."

Ren shook his head. "It's their decision."

Sasha curled his lip in repugnance. "Oh, that's it. You're fired, buddy. Get off my island until you learn to be a team player."

Abigail ignored his tirade. The only one who had her attention right now was Sundown. "It's okay, Jess. I'm ready."

"I'm not." Those dark eyes scorched her with emotions she couldn't even begin to understand. Was it possible she might mean something to him after all?

Dare she even hope for it?

She walked into his arms and held him close against her, wishing they had one more night together. *I would give anything for it.*

But it wasn't meant to be. And for that alone, she wanted to weep.

Jess couldn't breathe as he held on to her and pain ripped him apart. Every inch of her body was pressed against his, making him hunger for her in a way he'd never hungered for anything.

How could he lose her now when he'd only just found her? The depth of his feelings for her didn't make any sense. She had knocked him senseless, literally, from the first time he'd laid eyes on her and she kept him off-kilter.

There was no denying the agony that blistered him from the inside out at the thought of not seeing her again. The very concept of losing her staggered him.

He couldn't let go. Not of this.

Not of her.

I'm not strong enough to lose another woman I love. Yeah, he could take a savage beating and not blink. He could walk through hell itself and taunt the devil while Lucifer's demons flogged him every step of the way.

But living without her would break him. As bad as losing Matilda had hurt, this was so much worse. He wouldn't just lose the woman he loved.

He'd lose the only woman who'd ever seen the real him. The only person who knew his true feelings. He'd never been so honest with anyone.

Not even himself.

I can't let you go. . . .

Abigail ran her hands over his muscled back and savored this last connection to the one person she'd waited her entire life to meet.

The man she loved with every part of her.

Squeezing him tight, she forced herself to let go and step back. He stared down at her while she reached into his front pocket and pulled out his watch. Opening it, she stared at the face that had changed him forever. The face that had saved him from himself and given him back his soul.

The woman he'd sold his soul to avenge.

His was the face she would carry in her watch if she had one.

Heartsick and weary, she shut the watch and placed it in his palm, then folded his fingers around it. Lifting his hand to her lips, she inhaled the deep masculine scent of his skin, then kissed his scarred knuckles. A permanent reminder of how difficult his life had been and how hard he'd fought for it. "You will always belong to Matilda, Jess. I understand that now." Just as she understood what Jess had told her about his relationship with her mother.

Being in love was vastly different from loving someone. When you were *in* love, it consumed you. Devoured you.

And made you deliriously happy.

That was what he did for her.

Take care of our boy, Matilda. I won't fight you for his affections.

She'd been lucky enough just to know him for a short time.

Holding back her tears, she stepped around him and climbed up the dark ground to where Choo Co La Tah waited for her.

Don't look back. Don't torture yourself. But she couldn't help it. She had to see him one last time.

Her throat tight, she turned to find those dark eyes

never wavering. The look of tormented pain on his face seared her, and it made her wish she could steal every bad memory from him and replace it with only happiness.

Time seemed suspended as they stared at each other. Even her heart seemed to stop.

"Abigail . . ." Jess started forward, but Ren stopped him.

"She has to do this alone, *penyo*."

That familiar tic thumped against his lean jaw. She watched the battle he waged with himself. The indecision he had. Finally, he shoved Ren aside and sprinted up the hill to where she stood.

He took her hand into his and placed his watch in her palm. It was still warm from his touch.

She frowned at him. "What are you doing?"

"I don't want you to be alone anymore." He closed her fingers around the watch and kissed her hand just like she'd kissed his.

Those words and that single action brought her to her knees. They shattered her facade and succeeded in wrenching a sob from her. She understood exactly what he was saying. He was giving her his most prized possession.

He loved her.

And that made her cry all the harder. "Damn you, Jess," she breathed, despising her weakness in front of the others. "I hate you."

He flashed that charming grin that was as much a part

of him as his slow Southern drawl. "I know . . . Me, too."
He clutched her hand in his.

Don't let go of me.

"Abigail? We must go."

She wiped the tears away with the back of her hand.
There was so much she wanted to say to him. So much to
tell.

I love you. How could three small words like that become lodged in her throat?

Jess had been right. The hardest words to live with
were the ones you didn't say that you should have.

Summoning her courage, she pulled away and went to
Choo Co La Tah.

Jess couldn't breathe as he watched her vanish into the
landscape. *How could you let her go?*

Duty. Honor. He could come up with "noble" reasons
all night long. But none of them made this tolerable.

One life to save the world. It was a fair exchange. The
only problem was that one life had become the entire world
to him.

And he'd just sent her off to her death.

Alone.

A*bigail clutched Jess's* watch to her heart and held it there
as she followed Choo Co La Tah into a cave that looked
like something other than nature had hand-carved it out of

the hills. Once the darkness had swallowed them whole, he clapped his hands together three times, and on the last one, a fire ignited between his palms. He spread his arms wide, allowing the light to arc between his hands. It grew taller, stretching for the earthen ceiling far above them. Blues, greens, reds, and oranges burned in the fire, entrancing her like a melody for the eyes.

Then it shot around the room, lighting sconces she hadn't even known were there. A living entity, the candlelight danced against the walls in a way that made it appear the myriad of petroglyphs were moving.

The one on the far west side drew her attention. It showed a man with a buffalo skin holding the hand of a woman with butterfly wings. But what kept her spellbound was the design of the wings.

She'd seen that before.

Where?

Choo Co La Tah moved to stand behind her. "Open your mind, Abigail. Don't be afraid."

Something about his voice lulled her senses. Suddenly her eyelids were heavy. So heavy, it was hard to keep them open.

Stay awake.

She couldn't. Against her will, they closed and the images continued to play behind her eyelids.

Cool wind blew on her face as she ran by a small pond, searching for something.

No, she was searching for some*one*.

"Where are you?" she called in a loud whisper.

When no one appeared, she became frantic with worry. Where was he? Had something happened? He was never late. Terror flooded every part of her body. What would she do if he was gone?

"I would never leave you, precious."

She laughed at the deep, resonant voice that breathed in her ear. "You know not to do that to me."

He laid his lightly whiskered cheek against her smooth one, then enveloped her in his arms. Ahh . . . This was what she'd been craving all day. Smiling, she allowed him to rock her while they listened to the waves lap against the edges of the pool and the birds serenade one another.

He kissed her neck. "Have you told him yet?"

That question pierced her happiness with an arrow of sorrow. "No. I dare not."

"Then you will marry him?"

"No," she said, dipping her chin coyly. "That I cannot."

He tightened his arms around her. "Those are your only two choices."

But she knew better. There was a third option as well. "We could run away together." She pressed his hands closer to her skin. "Just the two of us. We'd be free, and no one—"

"I have responsibilities." His tone sharpened to a dagger's edge. "Would you have me turn my back on them?"

"Yes," she answered honestly.

He clenched his teeth. "No."

That word wounded her deep in the heart that beat only for him. "Don't you love me?"

"Of course I do."

She turned in his arms so that he could see her desperation for himself. "Then come away with me. Now. Today."

His eyes glowed with warmth as he watched her giddy playfulness, and that succeeded in taking the anger from his tone. "I can't." He gave her chin a gentle caress. "You have to tell him about us."

Guilt stabbed her breast as she thought about the man who loved her as much as she loved the one before her. A man who had proven exactly how much she meant to him in a way no one ever had.

Why can't I love him? It would be so much easier if she did, and she'd tried. She really had.

Unfortunately, the heart played its own tune, and it was deaf to what the head tried to tell it.

"It will crush him, and that's the last thing I want to do. He's given me so much and been so kind . . ."

Anger slapped at her from his dark eyes. "Then marry *him.*"

Those words stung her like a slap. And she didn't deserve them. "You shouldn't say that if you don't mean it. What if I did what you said?"

His nostrils flared. "I would cut his heart out and feed it to him."

Now he scared her. Was this the real him that he was showing to her because her love had made him comfortable? "What's happening to you?"

"The woman I love won't come to her senses. That's all."

She shook her head as every instinct she possessed denied his words. "There's something else. You're . . . different."

"I'm the same as ever."

But she knew better. This wasn't the man who'd conquered her defenses and laid siege to what no other man had ever claimed. "Is your post corrupting you?"

He scoffed. "I'm stronger than that."

Everyone had a weakness. Everyone. "Where is your arrogance coming from?" She didn't understand it.

"The truth isn't arrogance."

She gaped at him. "Who are you?"

"I'm the man you love."

And those words hurt her most of all. "Are you not the man who loves me?"

"Of course."

She shook her head in denial. "No, that's not what you said. You put the order there that matters most to you. All you care about it is you."

"I did not say that."

"You don't have to." Tears began to flood her eyes

until her vision drowned in misery. "Your words betray your thoughts." She tried to leave him, but he stopped her. She tried to gain her release. "Let me go!"

"Not until you learn to be reasonable."

Learn? She was not some infant who needed lessons. She was a woman full grown. How dare he not see that. "I'm not the one who's changing. There's something dark inside you that wasn't there before."

He scoffed. "You don't know what you're talking about."

But she did, and that knowledge beat painfully inside her.

He leaned down, his eyes glacial and foreign. "If you love me, you will tell him."

Why did she have to prove her love? Was it not enough that he saw it with his own vision?

She wrested her arm from his grasp. "I must go."

He didn't speak as he watched her walk away.

A shadow unwrapped itself from his and peeled itself from the wall. As full figured as a man, it walked toward him to stand behind his shoulder and whisper in his ear. "I told you so, didn't I? Women are ever fickle. There's no man who can keep one forever satisfied."

"Butterfly is different. She is all things good."

"And you are not."

No, he wasn't. He was a warrior, and his skin had been bathed in blood more times than he could count. It didn't pay for him to show mercy or patience. He wasn't supposed to.

At the right hand of his chief, he had slain innocents aplenty. It was his job. But now that they were at peace, he was lost.

Until he'd seen the Butterfly. She had tamed the savage inside him. Made it content to sit before hearth and watch her gentle ways. He didn't understand it. But so long as she was with him, he had no desire to pick up knife or spear.

He wanted only to please her.

Abigail blinked as the vision faded. When it was gone completely, she realized she was still standing in front of the wall with Choo Co La Tah behind her.

"Now you know," he said quietly.

Baffled, she turned to meet his kind gaze. "Know what?"

"Who you really are. Who Jess is."

More images flashed in her mind like a short-circuiting strobe trying to drive her mad. They came so fast that she could barely see them, and yet somehow her mind registered it all. "I don't understand."

He placed his hands on each of her arms. "You are the Butterfly, and Jess is the Buffalo. Peace and war. Two halves who were supposed to make one."

She shook her head in denial. "What have you been smoking or snorting or inhaling?"

"Do you not feel the connection here?"

Weirdly enough, she did. But that only freaked her out more.

Choo Co La Tah sighed as he realized she still wasn't ready for the truth. For all these centuries, he'd hidden her and waited for her to find a way to free herself from the curse. And still she was bound.

What a pity.

Maybe in her next life . . .

"Come." He gestured toward the rock in the center of the room that lay like a bed beneath a cluster of shimmering stalactites. She was strong in this lifetime. Stronger than she'd ever been before. He saw the rebellion in her eyes that he'd waited a millennium for.

She squelched it and then went to obey. Even so, it was obvious that her submission grated against every part of her being. Her teeth thoroughly clenched, she climbed up and lay back against the cold stone slab.

Choo Co La Tah began chanting as he summoned the sacred breath to cleanse them both.

Abigail listened to his song, but she zoned out as she conjured an image of Jess in her mind. A smile spread across her face as she saw him in the car again. As she felt the memory of his touch on her body. She cupped his pocket watch in her hands and held it on her stomach.

"Choo Co La Tah?" She hated to interrupt his ceremony, but this needed to be done.

"Yes?"

"Once I'm dead, would you please return Jess's watch to him?"

"Why?"

She ran the pad of her thumb over the engraved scrollwork. "He loves it."

"Is his happiness all that matters to you?"

"No. But I don't want him to have any regrets. Not about me."

He inclined his head to her, then went back to his chanting.

Abigail was patient at first, but as it dragged on and on, it began to wear on her nerves. Why couldn't he kill her already? Was the torture part of it?

Perv.

When he started on another chant with no letup in sight, she lost all semblance of manners.

"Choo? Really? Is all this necessary?"

He paused midsyllable. "You're ready to die, then?"

Oh . . . there was that.

She turned her head to look at him. "May I have what's behind door number two?"

He actually laughed. "You already chose."

"I know." She swallowed hard and closed her eyes. "I'm ready."

She felt Choo Co La Tah move to stand by her shoulder. The faintest whisper of metal scraping leather let her

know he was drawing a knife. Bracing herself, she conjured Jess's face and imagined herself in his arms.

No, on a beach. A little difficult, granted, since he
couldn't be in daylight without bursting into flames, but
she'd loved the beach when she was a kid. And since the
Apollites had the same spontaneous combustion issue with
the silken sands, she hadn't been on one since her mother
took her there for her fourth birthday.

But she was there now. Jess in a Speedo.

Just kidding. That was too bold a look even for him.
Maybe a . . .

Naked. Yeah, naked. She liked that best of all. The two
of them lying in the surf like the old movie her mother
had loved, *From Here to Eternity*.

Something cold and sharp touched her throat. Tens-
ing, she braced herself for the cut that would end her
life.

"Do you not want to fight me to live?"

Hold on to Jess. Naked. Beach. Naked.

"Answer me, Abigail. Do you want to live?"

"Of course I do." What kind of question was that?

"Then why don't you fight me?"

Abigail didn't answer. She had to hold on to Jess's face
or she would be fighting him with everything she had.

"Why don't you fight?"

She opened her eyes to glare at him. "Don't you understand? I *am* saving my life."

"I don't follow. You're doing this to save the world?"

She shook her head. "I'm doing this to save Jess."

"For him I can cut your throat?" He laid the knife across her neck. So close, she couldn't swallow without cutting herself. She kept her eyes open this time.

Screw it. If he was going to kill her, he could do it looking at her.

"Yes."

His gaze softened immediately as a slow smile spread across his face. "That's the right answer." He pulled the knife away.

Completely confused, she scowled at him. "What are you doing?"

"You made your sacrifice. You can get up now."

She still didn't understand. "I have to die. Don't I?"

"Not all sacrifices involve death, child. As the Enapay used to say, the noblest sacrifice of all is to open your heart up completely to another person and give them the dagger with which to slay you. . . . You were willing to die for Jess. Bravely. You proved it. That's enough for the Spirit to see and be appeased."

Incredulous, she gaped at him. "Get out." Could it really be that easy?

"No getting out, I'm afraid, my dear. All we need to do now is make your offering and then locate those jars to protect them."

She bolted upright. "I really don't have to die?"

"Are we going to be doing this all night? Should I book us a reservation at Redundancy?"

She laughed. Until her gaze went past his shoulder to . . .

It took a moment for her eyes to see it again and then to realize what it was. . . .

That familiar shadow she'd seen on her wall as a child. The one that had whispered to Buffalo.

And before she could make a single sound of warning, it attacked.

17

Jess paced back and forth like a caged cougar on steroids. Every time he started to go after Abigail, Ren grabbed his arm and stopped him.

The bastard was about to get a boot kicked so far up his ass, he'd be burping shoe leather for the rest of his immortal life.

Jess started for the cave again.

Ren cut him off. "You can't."

"Bull. Shit. What I can't do is leave her. Don't you understand?"

Ren laughed bitterly. "Yeah, I understand better than you can ever imagine. I know exactly what it's like to want something so bad, you can taste it and to have to watch as it voluntarily goes to someone else and then wish them both the best and try to mean it. I know the bitter taste of gall as they sit down at your table and you have to smile while inside you die every time they touch or exchange love-saturated glances. Don't talk to me about torment, Jess. I wrote the fucking book on it."

Now, that was something Ren had never shared with him before. He had no idea his friend had been through an experience like that. Ren never talked about his past. Hell, Jess didn't even know why Ren was a Dark-Hunter.

Because of his own past, he'd never wanted to pry into someone else's. He figured they'd tell him what they wanted him to know, and if they didn't volunteer it, then there was probably a real good reason why.

Far be it from him to stick his nose in it.

Jess inclined his head respectfully. "I'm sorry, Ren."

Ren wore an expression that said, *You have no idea.*

From up the hill where the cavern was, a fierce battle cry rang out. One that sounded like Choo Co La Tah's. Jess's heart seized as a bad feeling tore through him.

Please let me be wrong.

As fast as he could, he ran up the red-soiled hill while Ren turned into a bird to fly and Sasha took his wolf form.

By the time Jess reached Choo Co La Tah's private cave, Sasha, still in wolf form, was fighting a coyote and Ren was nowhere to be seen.

Neither was Abigail.

That didn't make him happy at all. Was she dead?

He ground his teeth as agony poured through him. It was the same aching, desolate feeling he'd had the night he sold his soul to Artemis.

Abigail was gone.

Please don't be dead.

"Jess?" Choo Co La Tah's voice pulled him back to their present situation. They were in the middle of an attack, and he had to focus if they were to survive. Six bodies of coyotes lay nearby as a gruesome reminder of everything at stake. Blood was splattered on the walls and pooled on the floor, under the bodies.

Choo Co La Tah took a step toward him, then slipped and fell on the blood-drenched ground.

He didn't get back up.

Jess sprinted toward the elder, who lay in a small crevice on his side. A quick visual skim of his injuries said that it was a miracle he was still alive.

Coyote had been playing for keeps. But by the looks of it, so had Choo Co La Tah.

Jess reached down to gently roll him over so that he could see the extent of his injuries. And they were extensive. The coyotes had torn him up badly. "What happened?"

He swallowed hard. "They jumped us."

"Us?"

Choo Co La Tah cleared his throat. "They took Abigail before I could complete the ritual. We have to make the offering by dawn . . . or else."

Hell would rain down on them in biblical proportions. Boy, would his snooty neighbors be pissed. They didn't like him on his best day anyway. Not that he cared.

"Do you know where they took her?"

Choo Co La Tah rubbed at his bleeding forehead while Jess tried to tend the wound. "Most likely, Coyote's den . . . and you can't kill him there, Jess. We have to get him here in the Valley."

Jess glanced around to see Sasha defeating his playmate. "Where's Ren?"

"He went after Coyote and Abigail. You have to find them, Jess. Bring them back."

"Don't worry. I won't fail."

He hoped.

Abigail *fought hard* against the ropes that bound her hands and feet together, but there was no give with them. As Jess would say, she was bound up and dressed like a Christmas goose.

And in total darkness. If only she knew where she was.

Then she heard a deep voice from the other side of whatever she was in.

"I'll deal with him later," a man growled in a voice that was familiar, yet she couldn't identify it.

A second later, the door opened and relief poured through her at the sight of a friendly face. And here she'd thought she was in danger.

Thank God.

She smiled at him. "Ren. It's so good to see you. You won't believe what happened."

He curled his lip at her, silencing her happy greeting. "Do I look like that piece of shit?"

Okay . . . Obviously he equated Ren with something bad. Which was strange, since they were virtually identical. Same black hair, dark eyes. Refined features. But now that he mentioned it, there was a difference.

Ren wasn't crazy. This man was.

Did he have multiple personality disorder?

"Are you a shape-shifter?" she tried again.

"Are you stupid? Of course I am."

He acted like she should know him and yet claimed he wasn't Ren. What was she dealing with? "Are we playing a game?"

He snatched her closer to him. "I don't play games. Ever."

Psycho it was. She would take that category and run with it.

And he got even weirder a few heartbeats later when he leaned over her and brushed his hand through her hair. He picked a handful of it up and held it to his nose so that he could sniff it. "So beautiful."

Ew . . . where's my Perv Be Gone? Had she known she'd be facing him, she'd have brought extra.

He brushed his lips against her forehead. The moment he touched her, a bright image appeared in her mind.

She saw the Butterfly again, and this time she was talking to . . .

Ren?

"I can't marry you, Coyote."

That name slammed into her like a truck. For a full minute, she couldn't breathe.

Coyote was an identical match for Ren? WTF? Why hadn't Ren mentioned that fact? Wouldn't something like that be a *little* important?

Especially since they were at war.

That thought made her blood run cold as another one followed right behind it. Was Ren a spy for Coyote?

It made total sense. No wonder Coyote kept finding them and Ren kept vanishing. He was probably heading straight to his brother every time he took flight.

She was the only one who knew. *I can't die until I let the others know, too.*

And still the images of the past played in her mind. . . .

Coyote's handsome face was a mixture of equal parts

horror and hurt over Butterfly breaking up with him. His breathing ragged, he shook his head in denial. "I don't understand. More than anything, I love you. Why would you want to leave me?"

Guilt hung heavy in her heart. The last thing she'd wanted to do was make him hurt. "I love someone else."

Coyote shot to his feet to confront her. "No. It's not possible."

Of course it was possible. It'd already happened. She started crying. "I'm so sorry, Cy. I never meant for this to happen. I did want to marry you, but then we met and . . . and . . . I haven't been the same. Please be happy for us." Her smile turned dreamy through her tears. "He understands me in a way no one ever has. I feel so alive, and all I have to do is think of him."

Coyote's face turned beet red from his fury, and for a second, she thought he might actually strike her.

Girl, get out of there. This was the part where Freddy Krueger or some other ghoul jumped out and killed the hapless victim.

Why wasn't Butterfly standing up for herself?

Coyote sneered in her face. "Never meant for this to happen?" He mocked her tone of voice. "Is that the lie you tell, you whore? Where did you meet him? Was it before or after I was tortured for over a year for protecting you?"

Guilt gnawed her into pieces. He was right. He had suffered so much for her.

But it was wrong to throw that in her face, and she knew it. "I'm sorry. I am. I didn't mean to hurt you. Please understand. I know in time you will."

She turned and walked across the floor, toward the door.

"I'll win you back, Butterfly!" he shouted after her. "Watch me. You'll see. You're mine. Now and always."

What a jerk . . .

"Shhh," Coyote whispered to her as he rubbed her forehead and her dreams of the past dissipated. He traced the line of her brow. Something that made her skin crawl.

"What do you want with me?" she asked him.

"For you to fulfill your promise."

Abigail widened her eyes. "I didn't promise anything."

He gave her an evil smirk. "You always had trouble remembering your promises. Keeping your word. But not this time. You *owe* me. And I intend to collect it."

Yeah, she had something she was going to pay him with. But she could pretty much bet he wouldn't like it.

He definitely wouldn't enjoy it.

Pulling away from her, he cocked his head as if he heard something. He shoved her back into the darkness and withdrew, then shut the door.

That's right. Run, Coyote, run. No matter what Choo Co La Tah or Coyote thought, she wasn't Butterfly. She was Abigail Yager. And she didn't give up or give in.

Yes, she'd spent her childhood in fearful submission to

her Apollite parents. But that had ended when they died. From that day forward, she'd been reborn as an assertive woman who refused to cower to anyone.

"Abby?"

She stopped her tirade as she heard the most wonderful voice in the world in her head.

"Sundown?"

"Yeah. Are you okay, baby?"

She definitely was now. *"Didn't I tell you to stay out of my thoughts?"*

"You can beat me later. Just do it naked."

In spite of the danger and her being tied up, she laughed at his humor.

Until she remembered Ren might be with him. *"Jess, listen. We have a spy in our midst."*

"What?"

"It's true. Did you know Coyote is Ren's brother?"

"No. No way. It's not possible."

"It's definitely possible and extremely creepy. Keep your eye on Ren. Whatever you do, don't turn your back on him."

"Okay. Are you somewhere safe?"

She glanced around her jet black prison. *"I really can't answer that. I'm tied up in some kind of little room without any light whatsoever."*

"All right. I have Sasha tracking you. I'm going to stay here in your head with you until we get there . . . if that's all right with you, that is. I don't want to intrude."

Those words made her smile in spite of her danger. *"Thank you, Jess."*

"There's no reason to thank me, Abby. You say the word, and I will always come for you. No matter what."

That promise choked her and brought tears to her eyes. Never in her life had she had that kind of security.

Not even with Kurt or Hannah. As the oldest of the three of them, she'd allowed them to rely on her. Not the other way around.

The closest thing she'd had, had been Jonah. But even he hadn't been reliable.

I love you, Jess.

How she wished she could say that to him. But she knew she couldn't. He would always be a Dark-Hunter, and they couldn't marry.

"You still with me, Abby?"

"I'm here. How many more hours till dawn?"

"Less than two."

Ouch. They were running out of time. Choo Co La Tah needed to finish his ceremony and make an offering of her blood to Mother Earth.

"Where are you guys right now?" she asked.

"Not close enough to you for my money."

"How close would that be?"

"By your side."

"You keep talking to me like that, cowboy, and you might get lucky tonight."

"I already got lucky tonight."

"Mmm, so you're a one-shot-a-night guy, huh?"

He laughed in her head. *"Ah, now, sugar, I didn't say that. The stallion never minds an all-night ride, especially when it's a wild one."*

"Stallion? That's some ego you have there."

"It's not ego when it's true."

A chill went down her spine at that phrase. It was the same one Buffalo had used with Butterfly.

Could it be true?

Before she could pursue that thought, she heard a strange noise outside her door. Was Coyote coming back?

Something large struck the door hard a split second before it was wrenched open. Reacting purely on instinct, she charged the newcomer and kicked out with every-thing she had, hoping it would be enough to overpower him.

He fell straight to the ground, where he rolled back and forth on his shoulders in utter agony. A loud groan filled her ears. She moved to kick his groin again.

"Abigail!" he snapped, lifting his arm to prevent her infamous nut-cracker stomp. "Stop!"

Unsure whom she was dealing with, she narrowed her gaze on the man. "Are you Ren or Coyote?"

He flashed into the body of the crow. But it didn't last long. A heartbeat later, he returned to his male form.

Granted, he was still a little green around the gills . . . and cupping himself. But he was Ren again. And he was whimpering.

"Oh, come on, you big baby. I didn't hit you that hard."

"I completely disagree. You kick like a damn mule, and I swear both my testicles are now lodged in my throat." He let out a long breath as he pressed his hand to his groin. Then slowly, he rose to his feet. Biting his lip, he let out several sounds of severe pain before he stood and glared angrily at her.

She backed up, unsure of his intent. Would he kill her for his brother?

"What's wrong with you?"

Abigail hesitated. "I'm fine. What's wrong with *you?*"

"You kicked me in the balls."

There was that. And then there was the other matter. "What are you doing here?"

"I was trying to rescue you, but I'm thinking it was bad idea. And damn, you're still bundled up. I'd hate to see what you could do with unrestricted access."

Likely story. Who would have ever questioned him coming in to save her? But she wasn't that stupid. "How did you know where I was?"

"I tracked one of the coyotes back here." He pulled a knife out of his pocket and took a step toward her.

Abigail backed up in trepidation. "I'd rather wait till Jess gets here."

He didn't listen. Instead, he sliced through her bindings and let them fall to the floor. "We don't have time to wait. . . . Are you sure you're okay? You're as skittish as a cat in a Doberman factory."

She hesitated. Was he leading her home?

Or somewhere far more sinister?

"Abigail?"

"I don't want to go with you."

He recoiled as if she'd slapped him. "You don't have to worry about your privacy. I won't betray you."

"That's not what I'm worried about."

"What, then?"

"*Your* loyalty. You want to talk to me about Coyote and explain why he looks just like you?"

Busted. It was written all over his face. She could almost see the gears grinding in his head.

"Yeah," she accused. "That's what I thought."

He shook his head. "No. It's not what you think."

"I think you've teamed up with your brother and sold all of us down Shit Creek. Paddles are extra."

"I didn't. You remember the story I told you about the warrior and the Gate?"

"Yeah?"

"*I* was the warrior."

Her mind reeled with that knowledge. "No."

He nodded. "My brother hates me to this day, and I don't blame him. I was out of control."

"But why?"

"I told you why. Jealousy. I'd spent my entire life living in Coyote's shadow. Others flocked to him. And for the most part, I was good with that."

Ren clenched his teeth. "Until the day he brought you

home." He winced as if the pain was still too much to bear. "I'd never seen a more beautiful woman. For our people, butterflies are a symbol of hope. It's said that if you capture one in your hands and whisper your dreams to it, it will carry them up to the heavens so that the wish can be granted."

Sarcastic applause rang out from behind him.

Ren turned to find Coyote there.

"Nice, brother. You're still trying to get into her bed, eh?"

Abigail noted the pain in Ren's expression.

"I put it aside, Coyote. It's time for you to do the same."

Coyote shook his head. "No. The Butterfly belongs to me. I captured her. I tamed her. Most of all, I protected her."

"She's not a possession."

He smiled evilly. "Yes, she is. She's the most precious possession."

Abigail's head spun as the words they were saying now caused her mind to flash back to a time and place she still couldn't identify.

She saw Ren and Coyote in a meadow, where they were fighting just like now. Even the subject was the same.

Coyote sneered at Ren. "This is all your fault. You and your petty jealousy. Why couldn't you have been happy for me? Just once. Why? Had you left us alone, none of this would have ever happened. There would have been no Grizzly Spirit. No need for Guardians and he—" Coyote gestured to the floor with a knife. "—would never have come here."

Ren didn't respond. His gaze was fastened to the red on Coyote's hands. It went from there to the ground, where . . .

Buffalo lay dead in a pool of blood.

Ren winced. "How could you do this? He was a Guardian." *And my best friend in the world.* The one and only person who'd stood by him without question.

Even when evil had claimed possession of his body and he'd served it willingly, Buffalo had stayed with him. Protecting him.

Now he lay slain by Ren's own brother.

My cruelty drove him mad. . . .

Coyote spit on Buffalo's back. "He was a bastard, and he stole her heart from me."

Ren shook his head slowly as guilt and sorrow ripped him apart. "Hearts can never be stolen, Cy. They can only be given."

Coyote sneered at him. "You're wrong! That's your jealousy speaking."

But it wasn't. Ren had learned to banish that.

Now it was too late. He'd destroyed everything that was good in his life.

Everything.

Sick to his stomach, he went to Buffalo and knelt beside him to whisper a small prayer over his body.

A shrill scream echoed. Looking up, Ren saw Butterfly

as she ran to her Buffalo. She sobbed hysterically, throwing herself down on top of him.

"Why? Why? Why would you hurt me so?"

Coyote curled his lip. "You tore my heart out."

"And you killed mine." She laid herself over the Buffalo and wept.

Ren rose to his feet and left her there to grieve while he confronted his brother.

That was his mistake. He didn't think about what would happen if Butterfly was allowed to cry her misery out to the gods and spirits. To wail and shriek for her lost Buffalo.

But it was too late now. A howling wind came screaming through the woods, dancing around their whitebuckskin–covered bodies. Those winds joined together to form two trumpeters who blew their horns to announce the most feared creature of all.

The Avenging Spirit. Something that could be summoned only by the cries of a wronged woman who wanted vengeance against the ones who'd hurt her.

Nebulous in form, he was bathed all in white. His hair, the translucent skin that covered his skeletal features. His feathers and buckskin. The only break from the color was the dark blue beadwork along his neck.

"Why was I called forth?" he demanded.

Butterfly looked up. Her beautiful face contorted by grief, she looked old and haggard now. Her hair blew around her body as her gaze pierced them with her fury.

"The Coyote killed my heart. So I want his as payment for what he took."

The Avenging Spirit bowed to her. Then he turned toward the men. His face changed from an old gaunt man with stringy hair to the face of ultimate evil. He opened his mouth and it dropped to the floor, contorting and elongating his features. Abigail shivered in terror.

Out of his mouth flew a giant eagle with a lone ghostly warrior on its back. The warrior lifted his spear.

Ren stepped back to give the warrior room.

With a discordant cry of vengeance that shook the very fabric of Mother Earth's gown, he let fly his spear at Coyote's heart.

One moment Ren was standing out of the way. In the next, he was across the room, where Coyote had been a heartbeat earlier. Before he could gather his wits and move, the spear flew through the center of his chest, piercing his heart. The force of it lifted him off his feet and pinned him to a tree.

Pain exploded through his body as he gasped for breath. The taste of blood filled his mouth. His eyesight dimmed.

He was dying.

The warrior turned his eagle around and flew back into the Avenging Spirit's mouth. As quickly as they'd come, they were gone.

His breathing labored, Ren stared at his brother. "I would have given you my life had you asked for it."

"You taught me to take what I wanted." Coyote closed the distance between them and snatched the bone necklace from Ren's throat that held his Guardian seal. He untied the pouch from Ren's belt where he kept his strongest magic. "And I want your Guardianship."

"You weren't chosen."

"And neither were you." Coyote seized the spear and drove it in even deeper. He laughed in triumph as Ren choked on his own blood.

With one last gasp, he fell silent.

The pride on Coyote's face was sickening as he turned his attention to Butterfly. "I'm a Guardian now. You can love me again."

She curled her lip in repugnance. "I could never love you after what you've done. You're a monster."

He snatched her up by her arm. "You are mine, and I will never share you. Make yourself ready for our wedding."

"No."

He slapped her across the face. "You do not argue with me, woman. You obey." He let go of her so fast that she fell back across Buffalo's body, where she wept until she had no more tears.

She was still there when the maids came and dressed her for Coyote.

At sundown, he returned for her. But before they could begin the ceremony that would join them together, the

Keeper appeared in the middle of the meadow. His dark eyes radiated fury.

"I am here to claim the life of the one responsible for killing two Guardians."

Coyote gasped in terror. His mind whirled as he tried to think of some trick that could save his life. And while his brother's magic was powerful, it wasn't enough.

The Keeper crossed the room in a determined stride that promised retribution. From his belt, he drew the Dagger of Justice and without hesitating, plunged it straight into the heart of the one who'd caused such turmoil and misery.

Butterfly staggered back as blood saturated her dress and ran across her braids. Instead of showing pain, she sighed in relief. Blood ran from her lips as she turned to Coyote. "I will be with my love now. Forever in his arms." She sank to the ground, where she died with the most blissful of looks on her face.

Coyote sputtered. "I don't understand."

The Keeper shrugged. "You were the tool. Butterfly was the cause. Had she not been born, you wouldn't have acted."

"No, no, no, no. This isn't right. This wasn't how it was supposed to end." Raking his hands through his hair, he went to his one true love and cradled her in his arms one last time. She was so tiny and light. Her blood stained his wedding clothes, and he wept at the loss of her.

And it was his loss.

She wouldn't be waiting for him on the other side. Not now. The pain of that knowledge tore him apart. She would greet Buffalo.

Throwing his head back, he screamed in outrage. No, it wouldn't end like this. He'd been a good man. Decent. And one by one, all of them had killed that. His brother, Buffalo and Butterfly.

They'd ruined his life. There was no way he would let them live a happy eternity. Not after the way they'd tortured him. He reached into his pouch and summoned the strongest elements there.

"I curse you, Buffalo. You will live a thousand lives and never be happy in any of them. You will walk this earth, betrayed by all who look upon you. There will be no one place you call home. Not in any human lifetime. And you will never have my Butterfly." He blew his magic from his palm into the air so that it could be carried to the spirits who would make it so.

Then he looked down at the serene beauty of the Butterfly. So gentle. So sweet. The thought of cursing her stung him deep.

But she had scorned him.

"Because of what you did to me, you will never marry the one you love. He will always die on his way to unite with you, and you will spend your life mourning him over and over again. No peace. Not until you accept me. And if you do marry another, he will never trust you. You will never be happy in any marriage. Not so long as you have human blood within you." He reached into his pouch and drew the last of his magic, then sent it into the wind.

"Do you know what you've done?"

Coyote looked up at Choo Co La Tah's approach. "I settled the score."

Choo Co La Tah laughed. "Such magic always comes back on the one who wields it."

"How so?"

He gestured toward the sky and the trees. "You know the law. Do no harm, and yet you have done much harm here today."

"They hurt me first."

Choo Co La Tah sighed. "And you have sown the seeds of your ultimate demise. When you curse two people together, you bind them. With that combined strength, they will have the ability to break their curse and kill *you*."

"You don't know what you're talking about."

"Arrogance. The number one cause of death among both peasant and king. Beware its sharp blade. More times than not, it injures the one who wields it most of all."

Coyote dismissed the Guardian's words. He had no interest in them. He would never suffer.

But he would ensure that they did.

Abigail *came out* of her trance with a full understanding of everything around them.

Ren and Coyote were now in full combat mode, and they were going at it like nobody's business. They took turns pummeling each other through the tunnels of Coyote's den. She'd never seen a bloodier fight, which given the number of fights she'd been to over the years said a lot.

Glancing around, she looked for a weapon she might use that could help them.

Unfortunately, there wasn't one. But if arrogant belligerence could take down an opponent . . .

There was no telling who would win. It would definitely be close. But she knew which side she was pulling for.

Go Red Sox.

"Abigail?"

"I'm here, Jess."

"So are we."

Now, that was the best news she'd heard in days. Leaving Ren and Coyote to their bashing, she ran for the opening. At least she hoped that was where she was headed.

She knew she was going in the right direction when an explosion echoed and blew pieces of rock everywhere.

Yeah, her boys had arrived. Leave it to them to make a grand entrance.

She ran to launch herself at Jess.

Jess smiled as he felt her soft curves pressed up against his hard body. And when she kissed him, he held on to her tight. Until he sensed something that shouldn't be here.

Pulling back, he cocked his head to listen.

"What's wrong?" she asked.

"There are Daimons here."

She scowled. "No. Why would there be?"

"I don't know. But I can feel it. It's like a nest of them are nearby."

But that didn't make any sense. Why would Daimons be here with Coyote?

Unless . . .

"Coyote's a trickster."

Jess cursed as he came to the same realization she did. How could they have been so ever-loving stupid?

This was a trap, and they'd just barreled right into it.

18

Jess would laugh if it weren't so damn ironic. One of his powers was the ability to know when he was about to be ambushed. And the den they were in had a damper on psychic powers. Not that he and Ren needed that right now, since they'd been draining each other for the last few days.

At best, his powers were working only at

half-mast. And it wouldn't have mattered if they hadn't been. He still would have walked right into this.

For one simple reason.

He'd been so fixated on getting to Abigail and making sure she was safe, that he'd have been blind to everything else.

Oh, well . . .

Die and learn.

Cupping her face and soaking in that gleam in her eyes, he leaned his forehead against hers and took a moment to inhale the sweet scent of her skin. Yeah, this gave him strength.

"Um, guys?" Sasha said from beside them. "I hate to toss ice water on your mood, but we have a situation here, and you might want to look up and prepare or sneeze or something. Just saying."

Jess didn't have to look up. He could feel every pair of eyes on him. The three of them were standing in the center of a large round room deep inside a cavern. Pristine white and trimmed in black, the walls around them reminded him of a palace. Kind of place he'd never thought to see in real life back in the day when he'd been human.

Things changed. Not always for the good and not always for the bad.

Sasha stood on his left and Abigail in front. Because of his injuries, Choo Co La Tah wasn't with them, and Ren seemed to have disappeared entirely.

Again.

There were six Daimons coming at them. Three to his right, four to his left. And a herd of them in the back tunnel.

Ah hell, he'd had worst odds.

And that was just yesterday.

Abigail took a second longer to stare into those dark eyes that haunted her. Rising on her tiptoes, she kissed the tip of his delectable nose. "Thank you for coming for me."

"My pleasure."

She hugged him close. "And in case we don't make it out alive . . . I love you, Jess Brady. I just wanted you to know it."

Jess felt his heart swell over words he'd never thought to hear from another pair of lips that set his world on fire. "I love you, too."

She smiled.

Until Sasha barked. "They're attacking."

Jess savored the sensation of her skin against his for one second longer. "Aim for the heart."

Inclining her head to let him know she understood, she reached around his waist to pull the two weapons he had on the back part of his holster. He drew the ones in front.

They turned in synch and opened fire on their enemies. The first one he struck, flipped and landed at his feet. It didn't explode, so he took that to mean it wasn't dead or it was one of the new breed of killing machines.

Daimons were coming at them from every direction. It reminded him of the *Alien* video game. The more he shot, the more they grew. Only difference? Daimons didn't drop from the ceiling.

Yet.

Who knew what power they might develop at a later date. Every time he got it halfway figured out, they discovered something new—like eating a gallu to augment their powers. Who the hell thought of that?

Probably the same sick SOB who saw a chicken shoot an egg out its nether region and said, "Hey, y'all, I think I'm gonna fry that up and eat it. Wish me luck. If I get sick from it, someone fetch a doctor."

Abigail fired her last round and blew one of the Daimons into dust. She was having a serious crisis of conscience about killing people she'd have died to defend a week ago. But the fact that they were so determined to kill her if she didn't kill them made it a little easier to do.

She pivoted to her right and froze as she caught sight of Jess fighting. He fired a round from his shotgun, then used the stock to swat another. Turning in a graceful arc, he fired again at a new target, then ducked, slid along the ground on his knees to reach another bad guy that he slugged with the gunstock, then stabbed. He moved so fast that he was already two steps ahead of her before she'd done anything at all.

Incredible.

Another Daimon wielding an ax attacked. Completely calm . . . *freakishly* calm, Jess leaned his head back from the swing, letting the ax fly clear of his throat Still, it'd been so close that she didn't know how he could trust himself not to have misjudged the swing.

Thank God he didn't. Otherwise, she'd be picking his head up right now.

As their ammunition ran low and the Daimons kept coming, Jess put himself between Sasha, who was in wolf form, and her. She loved the fierce protector in him.

Still he fought like a ninja. She was extremely impressed. And if the truth were told, she was amazed she'd been able to hold her own against him when they'd fought. Until now, she hadn't realized just how accomplished he was.

That boy had mad skills.

In no time, their rounds were spent, and they were retreating to the back part of the cavern while beating Daimons down as hard as they could.

Jess was really starting to miss his ability to reload his weapons. And create them. Damn his drained powers. It would make things easier, especially since Coyote had nothing here that could be used as a weapon.

Bastard.

"Can you hear the human souls releasing when you kill them?" Abigail asked.

"No."

But by the look on her face, he could tell that she did. "Are you all right about it?"

She nodded. "No," she said, contradicting the nod. "I keep thinking about the fact that my mother's soul was taken and consumed by a Daimon. No one freed hers."

"I'm sorry."

"Not your fault."

Maybe, but he felt bad for her anyway.

Sasha's powers were as limited by the damper as his were. They were fighting with their hands behind their backs, and the Daimons were all at their full psychic capacity.

Abigail began to panic as more Daimons showed up. They were breeding like cockroaches. "We're going to die, aren't we?"

"Hope not. I still have another episode of *No Ordinary Family* downloaded on my computer that I haven't had a chance to watch yet. Be a damn shame to miss it. Might have to hurt them if that happens."

She shook her head at him. "You're so not right." But that was what she loved about him.

They were backing up through the cavern and quickly running out of places to go.

When they got to the last of it, they formed a small circle.

Sasha sighed. "So this is it, huh? Not how I thought I'd go out." He glanced around at the extremely green cavern walls. "Well, at least we'll be all minty fresh when we go."

"Psst!"

Sasha turned around in a circle, looking for the source of the sound.

Jess arched a brow at Abigail.

"I didn't do it."

They looked at Sasha. "What? Some freak noise gets made, and you blame the dog? That ain't right. Next thing you know, I'll get blamed for gas attacks, too. I didn't do it."

"Psst! Abby!"

Abigail froze as she recognized Hannah's voice. She turned around to find her sister in a small hole in the wall. Dressed all in black, she looked like Spy Doll Barbie. If the point was to make her fierce, it was failing miserably. Hannah was too tiny, too blond, and too sweet looking to make anyone afraid of her.

"What are you doing here, H?"

"Saving your asses. Come on."

Abigail followed her without reservation.

"Keep your voices real low," Hannah warned in a whisper. "Some of the Daimons have really good ears, and the walls are thin."

"Do you know where Ren is?" Jess asked.

She nodded. "They're planning to sacrifice him at midnight. Right now, Coyote is torturing him."

Abigail frowned. Hannah acted like she was at home here and knew the schedule for everything. Best of all, she knew about this hidden passage. "I don't understand. How did you guys get hooked up with Coyote?"

"Jonah."

That unexpected response startled her so badly that she actually stumbled. "What?"

"You remember how Jonah did all that research into trying to find a cure for us?"

Abigail nodded. Everyone who'd ever met Jonah knew this story. He'd found some obscure text that said one of the local Nevada tribes had hidden a serum in the mountains that could cure any illness and transform someone's DNA into perfect structure.

Jonah had taken that to mean that it would repair whatever physiological damage Apollo had done to them when he cursed them.

Both she and Hannah had thought it was a load, but Jonah had insisted, and for years, he'd take night trips out to the desert to look for it.

"Jonah didn't find the serum. He found Coyote, who told him that the legend was real and that if he'd help Coyote find the two jars that contained it, Coyote would share. They were still looking for it when . . ." She passed a harsh stare to Abigail. "Jonah died. Anyway, they've been working together for decades now. So when Coyote called Kurt and asked him to round up Daimons to kill a Dark-Hunter, we came."

Abigail's heart stopped beating. "We?"

"I took gallu blood with Kurt. I don't want to kill humans, Abby, but I don't want to die either. I figure no one will miss a demon."

Grateful for her compassion and humanity, Abigail hugged her. "I love you, little sister."

"I love you, too. It's why I couldn't let them kill you. Even if you are with the enemy." Hannah pulled a small box out of her jacket and pressed a button on it.

Jess breathed a sigh of relief. She'd turned off the damper.

Hannah hung her head down. "I feel like I've just betrayed one family member for another."

Abigail shook her head. "You haven't betrayed Kurt. He doesn't want me dead, does he?"

"I don't know. He's so angry and hard to read. Especially when it comes to Jonah. You know how close the two of them were. But I don't want to live like that. It takes too much energy to hate. I'd rather get on with my life than worry about someone else's."

Jess cleared his throat. "Sorry to interrupt, but we need to find Ren."

"He's probably in the lower chamber."

Abigail arched her brow at that. Hannah had responded without any thought whatsoever. "How much time have you spent here?"

"Too much. Coyote . . ." Hannah paused as if seeking the right adjective for him.

"What?" Abigail prompted.

She squirmed like she used to do as a kid whenever she'd done something she thought their parents might punish her for. "Promise you won't hate me if I tell you something."

Abigail went cold with dread. What was wrong now? "Tell me what?"

"Promise me first."

Oh, she could wring her little sister's neck whenever she played these stupid games. "All right. I promise."

Hannah licked her lips and glanced about nervously. "Coyote was the one who killed your parents."

That news slammed into her with the force of gale winds and left her reeling. "What?"

She nodded. "He wanted your mom, but she wouldn't have anything to do with him. He'd gone to see her in various disguises and tried to seduce her. No matter what he did, she wouldn't look at him. Apparently the last time, she said something she shouldn't have and he killed them for it."

Abigail was flabbergasted. And she would have denied it, but it all made sense now. It hadn't been Jess in her room. It'd been Coyote wearing his skin. "How do you know this?"

"Jonah. He got drunk one night back when we were dating and told me all about it. He was there with Coyote when he did it."

It was just as she'd seen in her house. That was why the voice had seemed so familiar to her.

"I should have told you when I found out, but Kurt and the others were in love with the idea of turning you into their own personal Terminator to slay the evil Dark-Hunters. It's all they talked about. They saw you as the perfect weapon against our enemies."

The sad thing was, she had been.

And Abigail didn't know what to say to that. Raw emotions warred inside her. Anger, hatred, betrayal. And even relief. At least she finally knew the truth about the night her parents died.

"Thank you, Hannah."

"You're not mad?"

"Not at you." Kurt and the others, she could kill over it.

Most of all, it was Coyote blood she wanted. That need was so strong that it bubbled up inside her like a volcano.

"Hey, Jess?"

Jess turned his attention to Sasha. "Yeah?"

He pointed to Abigail.

Jess looked over at her, then actually jumped when he saw what she looked like.

Holy shit. She barely looked human right now.

In fact, all three of them took a step back as they saw her eyes. They weren't just red. They had stripes of orange laced through them.

Her teeth grew longer, and there was an evil aura around her that said she was open for business.

Jess approached her slowly. Any sudden movement might make her gut him. "Baby?"

Abigail put her hand on his chest to stop him from coming any closer. "Not this time, Jess." Her voice sounded like it had reverb on it. "I want the blood of Coyote, and I won't be stopped."

Normally, he'd have stopped her anyway. *But you know what?*

Payback's a bitch, and this one was way overdue. If she wanted to rip Coyote's head off and play basketball with it, he'd bring the net.

"I've got your back, Abs."

Sasha screwed his face up. "You're going to make me get her back, too, aren't you?"

He gave the wolf a droll stare. "You wanna live?"

"Some days." Sasha let out a long, tired groan. "Fine. I'll follow even if it kills me, and it better not."

When Abigail started toward the lower chamber, Hannah fell in line to go with them.

As soon as Abigail noticed her slinking behind Sasha, she stopped her. "I want you to sit this one out."

Hannah scowled. "I don't understand."

"If anyone sees you aiding a Dark-Hunter . . ."

"I'm aiding my sister."

Abigail was touched by the offer. But she knew exactly

what kind of repercussions Hannah would have. From everyone. "They won't see it that way, and you know it." They would make her life a living hell, and they might even drive her out of their community.

Hannah sighed. "Fine. Take care of you." It was a line from their favorite girl movie, *Pretty Woman*.

Abigail hugged her again. "Take care of you." Then she set her sister aside and accessed the part of her that was still foreign and terrifying.

The demon.

Jess exchanged a wary grimace with Sasha. The old school cowboy in him didn't like giving such a tiny woman the lead in anything so dangerous. His job was to protect the woman he loved. Not put her in the line of fire.

But he knew if he said that out loud, she'd have his boys for jewelry and make him pay for eternity for his chauvinistic ways. So he rode herd on his tongue, but stayed extra vigilant where she was concerned.

If anyone came for her, they'd answer to him.

And he'd gut them for it.

He didn't know how she did it, but she went straight to where Coyote held Ren like she'd lived here for years.

Jess winced as he saw the holding cell where Ren was strapped to a metal rod. Coyote had put him in with Tesla coils that were sending shock after shock to Renegade, who screamed when they hit him.

Yeah, that was the drawback to being immortal. If

someone wanted to torture you, you couldn't die to escape it.

Jess opened his mouth to ask Abigail what her plan was, but he never got the chance. His hotheaded woman stormed into Coyote's workspace without preamble and seized the ancient being by the throat. When Coyote moved to fight, she backhanded him so hard, he dented the wall.

Remind me not to make her mad.

Jess rushed to turn the electricity off in Ren's cell and stop the pain of his being electrocuted.

Sasha fell back away from the switchboard and room. "Don't shock me, man." It had really nasty consequences for Were-Hunters.

"Check on Ren."

Sasha snorted. "In the electricity cube? What kind of psycho are you?"

"Sasha . . ."

He bared his teeth in a purely canine gesture of defiance. "Fine. I get shocked, you better start checking shoes before you put them on." He went to comply.

Jess rushed to watch Abigail mop the floor with Coyote.

"How could you kill my mother? You bastard!" She slammed his head down on the ground repeatedly.

Coyote twisted and sent her flying. "I only wanted her to love *me*."

"So you killed her when she didn't? That's not love. That's sick."

Coyote kicked her across the chamber. "Don't you dare lecture me. I thought her soul was yours. You. You're the one who betrayed me."

"I have no memory of you, and I'm grateful for that."

The fury in his eyes was scorching. "You can't kill me."

Abigail glanced over to where Sasha was helping Ren. "Torture works for me. Besides, I've already killed one Guardian. What's another?"

He shoved the lab table at her.

Abigail caught it and sent flying back at his head.

Jess widened his eyes at her strength, but wisely stayed out of it.

"You're an animal," she snarled. "You've done nothing but destroy everyone around you."

"Me?" Coyote asked indignantly. "I'm not the animal." He glared at Ren. "He is."

Abigail pulled a knife from her boot. "Yeah, well, from where I call home, we put down rabid animals."

Snake entered the room at the same time Coyote ran.

All Abigail could see was her mother's killer getting away. Without a second thought, she threw her knife at his fleeing back.

One second he was there.

The next, he'd changed places with Snake, just like he'd done with Ren. Her knife buried itself straight into Snake's heart.

No!

Snake blanched as he looked down and saw the knife

sticking out of his chest. His breathing labored, he gave her such a sad, pathetic look that it wrung her heart.

"I'm so sorry."

He said something in a language she didn't know, then sank to the floor.

Abigail ran to him with Jess one step behind her. "Don't die, Snake. We can help you." She looked at Jess. "Can't we?"

But it was too late. His eyes turned cloudy and his last breath left him.

Abigail covered her eyes as the horror of it ripped through her. "I thought the Guardians were immortal. How could I have killed another?"

"They don't die of natural causes." Only unnatural ones.

She ground her teeth in frustration.

Sasha brought Ren over to them. Ren collapsed on the floor and leaned against the wall. "It wasn't your fault, Abigail. Trust me. He killed me the same way. Coyote's a trickster. It's what he does."

Jess growled as his own need for vengeance overwhelmed him. "We'll find him."

Ren shook his head "No. You won't. Not for a while. Not until the Reset of the Time Untime. He'll be in hiding now. Plotting for a way to get his Butterfly back."

"I won't let him."

"I know, but it won't stop him from trying." Ren sank

his hand in his pocket and pulled out a necklace. He handed it Abigail.

Her heart pounded as she saw the necklace Jess had given her mother on the day she died. "Where did you get this?"

"I ripped it off Coyote's neck while we were fighting. I thought you'd want it back."

She nodded as she clutched it to her chest. "Thank you."

"I would say no problem, but it really was." Ren let out a long breath and closed his eyes.

Jess cursed.

Abigail was almost too afraid to ask. "What?"

"It's dawn," he said in synch with Ren.

Jess sighed. "We missed the deadline for the offering."

Abigail groaned as she heard those dreaded words. "What do we do now?"

To her chagrin, both Jess and Ren started laughing.

Jess pulled her against him. "We do what we've always done. We protect . . ."

"And we fight," Ren finished. "But only after I have a nap, preferably away from electricity and daylight."

Sasha helped him to his feet. "Come on, Dark-Hunter badass." He looked at Abigail. "I'll take this one if you take yours."

"It's a deal."

She watched as Sasha and Ren limped away from them. Then she turned back to Jess. "Is it over?"

"For now. You've stopped your first apocalypse. You should be proud."

"I'm too tired to be proud."

He laughed. "I know that feeling." He fished his phone out of his pocket and called his Squire.

Abigail stood in silence as she listened to Jess negotiate a ride home for them in something that wouldn't cause him to burst into flames. From what she overheard, Andy wasn't willing to haul them anywhere since he was still mourning the mangling of his Audi.

After a few minutes of asking politely, then threatening his Squire with bodily harm, Jess hung up the phone. "Andy will be here shortly."

Yeah, right . . . She could see Andy taking his sweet time getting here and grumbling every inch of the way. They'd be lucky if he didn't let them starve to death before he made it out here.

Jess's gaze went past her to see something behind her that made his jaw go slack.

Her stomach shrank with dread. *How bad is it this time?* More to the point, how many whatevers were about to attack them?

Not quite ready for another round, she turned to find . . .

Her own jaw hit the floor.

Was that Choo Co La Tah? Gone was the old man and in his place was the younger version of him that she'd seen in her visions of the past. Strange that she hadn't noticed before how handsome a man he'd been. He wore his long black hair loose around his shoulders and walked with the swagger of a predator.

This was a warrior in the prime of his youth and that fact was evident in every bulging muscle and most of all in a stance that said he could kill you in a heartbeat.

Jess put himself between them as if to protect her.

Choo Co La Tah smiled. "Stand down, Jess. I'm not here to harm either of you." He held his hands out to his sides to prove his intent. "I do have to say 'thank you' to our Butterfly though."

Abigail frowned. "How so?"

"It appears we didn't miss the deadline as we feared. When they attacked us earlier and you protected me, you shed some of your blood on the cavern floor. Because of that the seals are still intact."

She wasn't sure if she should be grateful or ticked off at him. One day, they'd have to do something about Choo Co La Tah's penchant for withholding important details. "That was the offering I had to make?"

He nodded. "It also restored my youth and health. For that, my dear, I offer a resounding debt of gratitude. I haven't felt this strong in centuries."

Jess stepped aside as she moved forward to eye the ancient Guardian with respect.

"I don't understand," Jess drawled. "Why did you and Old Bear age while neither Snake nor Coyote did?"

Choo Co La Tah lowered his arms. "It takes more energy to not give in to the Dark One they chose to serve. Fighting them and staying true to our duties takes its toll. It's another reason why our posts are finite. There's only so long you can hold them back before the body wears out and leaves you defenseless." He swept his gaze to where Snake lay dead on the ground. Pain flickered deep in his dark eyes. "You were ever a fool, my friend. Ever led astray and for that I am truly sorry. May your soul find the peace your body never could." He looked back at Abigail. "You may lay your fear aside, child. I can hear it even from here. The ancients never held you responsible for the death of Old Bear nor will they for Snake."

His words confused her. "I don't understand. You said—"

"I implied and you inferred. You were only a tool Coyote used for his own purposes. The ancients are able to look past the event to see the true causation and who set it in motion. All of which go back to Coyote and his actions and greed. Just as I was trying to use you and Sundown to lure him to the Valley so that we could trap him. I knew he would follow you. But unfortunately, he's escaped again."

"We can follow once the sun sets," Jess offered.

Choo Co La Tah sighed. "We won't find him. He's clever that way and he will go to ground to lick his wounds and plot his next move."

Abigail felt a tingle of hope inside her at his words as another idea occurred to her. "Isn't the balance restored now that Snake is dead?"

"In theory."

She didn't care for his tone that told her it would never be so easy. "Theory?"

Choo Co La Tah fell silent for a bit as if thinking on how best to answer. "The balance is a very delicate thing. While Coyote and I may contain each other, we are still missing two Guardians. The jars aren't open, but their seals are weakened by the death of their Guardians. The Wind Seer could free herself now and then go after the Grizzly Spirit on her own. If she were to unite with him, they will rain down an apocalyptic hell that would impress even Sasha."

Great. But she wasn't ready to give up. "What of Jess and Ren? They were the original Guardians, right? Can't they step in and replace Old Bear and Snake?"

He shook his head. "Until the Reset, no new Guardians are allowed to be appointed."

Jess scowled. "Ren told me earlier that Coyote's actions had caused that to speed up."

"They have indeed. And we will have to stand strong against him to keep the Dark One from reigning during the next cycle."

"I'm ready," Jess said with conviction.

Choo Co La Tah smiled. "While I appreciate that, the last chapter isn't yours to write."

"What do you mean?"

"This is now between Ren and his brother. Your job was to stop him before he claimed the Butterfly and tainted her bloodline. You've done that and you kept him from claiming Old Bear's magic."

Abigail was even more confused by his words. "Tainted me how?"

"The Butterfly people were the guardians of the soul. They were born of the Light while the Coyote and Crow are the Dark that would cover the soul and turn it evil. While they, like all of us, were drawn to the Butterfly because of her magic and beauty, she was never theirs to have. The Butterfly can be captured, but never claimed. Her love is a gift that only she can bestow on her chosen one." He gestured to the petroglyphs on the wall where a butterfly flew around a white buffalo. "The Buffalo were the strongest warriors ever known. Intuitive. Brazen. They were fearless. Their job was to protect all of the people, especially those charged with our souls. It's why the two of you were forever drawn together—you were destined to join the two bloodlines. But in the first lifetime, Butterfly was too weak to stand with the Buffalo. She had to learn to fight for herself. To stand up and let the world know she was unafraid." He turned to Jess. "Buffalo was arrogant and egocentric. He had to learn to put the Butterfly before himself and to realize that she was the most vital part of him." He paused. "You both have done that. You understand that while you're strong alone, you're so much stronger to-gether. So long as you stand together, no one can tear you down."

Abigail swallowed. "We're still cursed."

"Yes and no. You two have confronted the Coyote over his evil and you no longer have human blood in you. Coy-ote's curse only applied so long as you were human."

She seriously regretted that decision. If only she could go back . . . "What about the demon inside me?"

"You're controlling it and you have Jess to help."

He made it sound so much easier than it was. Even now she could feel it inside her, salivating. It wanted to feed and it was hard to deny that craving. "But when it wants to feed . . . What do I do then?"

"You do what all of us should do when evil beckons. You beat it back into submission and rise above it. You are more than strong enough to succeed. I know it."

She wasn't sure she liked that answer.

Choo Co La Tah closed the distance between them and took her hands into his. "The Buffalo people had a saying. There is purpose in all things no matter how random they seem. Mother Fate is ever watching and ever working to aid us." He looked at Jess. "Your mother was the last of her people. She knew the Coyote wanted you and it's why she never told you who you really were. Who her people really were. She hid your true tribe from you and married your father, hoping his lineage would disguise you and give you a fighting chance to fulfill your destiny." He tightened his grip on their hands. "It did and because of your mother's sacrifice, you evolved into what you needed to be. It's why you came so close to marrying your true Butterfly then. Unfortunately, she hadn't metamorphosed enough. Matilda was still too weak to stand by your side." He reached for Abigail's. "Now you are ready."

He put their hands together between his. "In spite of all the enemies who would seek to destroy you, you two have found each other again. As the Tsalagi would say, the future path is the one you choose to follow. The journey what you make of it. You both have come so far in this lifetime and those before. I know that this time you will have the life you've dreamed of." He squeezed their hands, then released them. "Now I must go and rest. The fight between the Dark and Pale One is upon us. We will need all of our strength for the battle to come." With those words spoken, he vanished.

Abigail stood there for several heartbeats, absorbing everything that had happened. She didn't know what the future held and that terrified her. For a woman who'd had her entire life mapped out, it was scary to stand here with no clear cut path to follow. She'd chosen the wrong way so many times that she wasn't sure she trusted her instincts anymore.

But she trusted Jess.

She looked down at their combined hands. Who would

have thought? While looking for her enemy, she'd found her best friend. "So where does this leave us?"

Jess froze at a word he hadn't thought about in a long time.

Us. Two united beings.

For the first time in over a century, he wasn't alone.

He stared at how delicate the bones in her fingers were. At how warm her touch made him. It was a sensation, he never wanted to lose again. "I hope it leaves us together."

"Is that what you want?"

"Absolutely." How could she ever doubt it? "Marry me, Abigail, and I swear this time, curse or no curse, I will make it to that damned altar. Even if I drag the devil with me to be there on time."

She offered him a smile. "I will definitely marry you, Sundown Brady. And this time, I will kill anyone who tries to stop you from making it to that altar."

He leaned in and gave her the sweetest kiss of her life. And when he pulled back, her lips were still burning.

"So tell me . . ." she whispered. "How do we get you free from Artemis's service?"

19

A week later

*The hardest part of living is making peace
with your past. Most of all, it's making peace
with yourself.* Ash's words hung in Jess's mind
as a sober reminder of how hard the journey
had been to get to this one perfect moment.

He'd never thought to have that peace, but as he watched Abigail napping on his couch after an entire day of exploring each other, he knew the past no longer mattered to him at all.

Only tomorrow did.

Smiling, he got up to find a blanket for her.

Abigail knew the moment Jess had left the room even though she was sound asleep. She wasn't sure where that power came from. But it was there.

And it let her know that something else was here with her.

Her eyes flew open as she jumped to her feet to find an unknown man in front of her. She started to attack until she saw the double bow and arrow mark of a Dark-Hunter on his cheek. He was one of them and yet . . .

The demon in her recognized the demon in him. He was much more than what he appeared and what he appeared to be was a vicious predator. He wore his dark hair swept back from a handsome face that could only be described as pitiless. There was no compassion or even kindness evident in any part of him.

"Nick? What are you doing here?"

She turned to see Jess rejoining them.

That dark, scary gaze left hers to meet Jess's. "I was told you wanted your soul back."

"I thought Ash would be the one to bring it."

Nick curled his lip at the mention of Ash's name, but

he didn't say anything about him. He merely reached into his long black coat to pull out a small wooden box. Delicate scroll work decorated the top of it.

Without preamble, he handed it to Abigail. "Make sure you truly love him before you even attempt to restore it. If you fail, you will kill him and there are no second chances."

Before either of them could speak, Nick vanished.

Abigail shivered at the sudden coldness Nick had left in the air. "Is it just me or was that creepy and weird?"

"Yeah, Nick isn't exactly . . . right. He's the youngest of our kind and I guess he hasn't settled in yet."

She started to mention the demon inside Nick that she'd sensed, but then thought better of it. If Nick didn't want anyone else knowing about it, he might go to war with her over it. The last thing they needed was another enemy coming for them.

Curious about the contents, she opened the box. There on a nest of black velvet was the glowing red medallion that housed Jess's soul. It was so beautiful that she instinctively wanted to touch it. But Jess had already warned her that it would sear her skin and leave a scar on her hand like the one Talon had.

Jess moved to stand in front of her. "What are you thinking?"

She smiled at the fact that he didn't pry into her thoughts. "How much I love you."

"I love you, too." He peered over the lid to see the medallion. "You'll have to kill me to restore my soul into my body."

"I know, but . . ."

He arched a brow at her hesitation. "But what?"

"I'm not so sure about this. We still have Coyote out there, gunning for both of us. If I put this in you, you'll be mortal again and you'll be able to die."

"I can die now."

She shook her head. "Not as easily and you know that."

"I'll still have my powers though."

True, but she wasn't sure it would be enough. There was no telling what tricks Coyote might come up with next. "It's not the same. Do we have to do this?"

"No. I have my soul back. Technically, I'm out of Artemis's service. As far as I know, there's nothing that says I have to restore my soul once I have it again. But we won't be able to start a family without it."

"We already have a family. You, me . . . and one irritated Squire."

He laughed at that. "Yeah, I guess Andy is our ill-mannered adopted son."

Abigail closed the box. She had a bad feeling deep inside that wouldn't ease. Something more was out there and it would be coming for them. "I don't want to take a chance on losing you, Jess. Not again. Let's wait on this."

He took the box from her hand. "All right. We'll wait."

That was one of the things she loved most about him. He never pushed his will onto hers. The decisions they made, they made as a team. Together.

She looked down at the simple wedding band that rested on her left hand. Even though Dark-Hunters couldn't marry, they'd eloped six nights ago. It was Vegas, after all. And Sin had a small chapel inside his casino that had provided a perfect setting. Zarek had been the best man and Hannah her maid of honor. Kat, Sin, Sasha, Choo Co La Tah, Ren and Andy had also been there as witnesses.

Yes, they'd jumped the gun, but given everything that had happened to them, it'd seemed most appropriate. And neither of them had wanted to take a chance on anything else going wrong.

Carpe Noctem. Seize the night. That was exactly what they'd done.

"You sure you don't want a diamond to go with that?" Jess had been nagging her about that since she'd declined an engagement ring. But that wasn't her style.

"I have everything I need and he's standing right in front of me."

Jess savored those words that had been her wedding vow. Even with her in front of him, he couldn't believe she was here and that they were finally together. That it was her face he now carried in the watch she'd returned to him. "I will spend the rest of my life, however long it is, making damn sure you always feel that way."

In the deepest part of himself, he sensed that Coyote would be coming for them again. He didn't know what tomorrow would hold, but today he knew what he would be holding.

Her.

And that was all he needed.

Bonus Scene

New Orleans
April 16, 2011

Holding on to her husband's huge, strong hand for dear life while they were surrounded by their closest friends and family in the bedroom of their home, Soteria Parthenopaeus leaned her head against the stacked pillows behind her and pushed with everything she had.

Ah, gah, it hurt.

It really, *really* hurt!

And it hadn't stopped for hours or was it days or weeks? Funny thing about labor, it made time slow down so that one minute in human time equaled three hours to a laboring mom. Maybe longer.

Yeah, definitely longer.

She reverted to her breathing techniques that all three (because her husband's paranoia feared one might not be good enough) of her midwives had taught her, but that was about as useful as all the pushing she'd been doing.

And the breathing was making her feel like a hyperventilating dog after a long race. Not to mention dizzy. She glanced at her husband who was coated in as much sweat as she was. He hadn't left her side for a single second since it started. His long black hair was pulled back into a sleek ponytail and his swirling silver eyes stared at her with pride and love.

She adored, loved, and worshiped him so incredibly much, would crawl naked over broken glass just to see him smile, but right now in the throes of ten hours of hard labor pains, she really wanted to grab the most tender part of his body in a set of pliers and squeeze his junk until he could fully understand how much childbirth sucked. "I swear if that's a pair of demon horns digging into my belly and stabbing me right now, Ash, I'm going to beat you after it's born."

'Cause face it, horns on the head didn't come from my *side of the family or genetic code.*

He actually had the nerve to laugh at her threat. Was he out of his mind? Just because he was an eleven-thousand-year-old Atlantean god with omnipotent powers didn't mean she couldn't make him suffer. Not that she ever would, but still. The least he could do was pretend to be afraid of her.

He kissed her cheek and brushed her hair back from her face. "It's all right, Sota. I have you."

"Apostolos, adjust her pillows higher," her mother-in-law snapped at her husband. "She doesn't look comfortable. I don't want my daughter in any more pain than necessary. You men have no idea what you put us through." While Apollymi couldn't physically leave her prison realm, her astral projection could travel without her. And it'd been pacing near Ash's oldest daughter Simi since the labor had started.

Simi rolled back and forth and spun around on Ash's wheeled desk chair. Dressed in a neon pink lab coat and black and white striped leggings with thigh high laced platform boots that went all the way up to her black lace miniskirt, she was adorable. Her face was mostly covered by a black surgical mask with a matching pink skull and crossbones on the right side of it. Her glowing red eyes were empathized by her solid jet-black pigtails and dark purple eyeliner. She'd been so excited about the impending birth of the baby, that she'd been dressing that way for a month and shadowing Tory's every step. If Tory so much as hiccuped, Simi had whipped out a black baseball glove and asked, "is it time yet? The Simi's gots her glove all ready to catch it if it is, 'cause sometimes they come out flying."

Simi couldn't wait to be a big sister again.

Kat, Ash's other daughter who was married to Sin Nana, sat in the window seat, holding her sleeping daughter on her lap. Her long flowing blue jersey dress was as serene as she was. "Grandma, please. It's okay. Dad's doing a great job. I give him kudos for at least being calm and rational, and not losing his temper with everyone around him who isn't in childbirth. And he has yet to start shooting lightning bolts at people. Poor Damien still has a burn scar."

That thought actually made Soteria laugh as she pictured it. Sin did have a temper where his wife was concerned.

Breathtaking, blond, and statuesque as the daughter of two gods should be, Kat smiled at Tory. "If it makes you feel any better Tory, they were just as bad when Mia was born. At least you don't have Sin, Kish *and* Damien running around, trying to boil water for no other reason than that's what someone had told Sin husbands are supposed to do and since Sin doesn't know how to boil water, he had to micromanage the other two incompetents who'd never done it either. I'm amazed they didn't band together to kill him during it or burn down the casino. And don't get me started on my mother trying to murder my husband in the middle of it or her fighting with grandma over whose labors were more painful. Or," she cast a meaningful glance to Simi, "someone setting my mother's hair on fire and trying to barbecue her to celebrate the birth."

Simi stopped rolling and pulled her black surgical mask down to show them her proud fanged grin. "That an old Charonte custom that go back forever 'cause we a really old race of demons who go back even before forever." She looked over to where Danger's shade glittered in the opposite corner while the former Dark-Huntress was assisting Pam and Kim with the birth, and explained the custom to her. "When a new baby is born you kill off an old annoying family member who gets on everyone's nerves which for all of us would be the heifer-goddess 'cause the only person who like her be you, Akra-Kat. I know she you mother and all, but sometimes you just gotta say no thank you. You a mean old heifer-goddess who need to go play in traffic and get run over by something big like a steamroller or bus or something else really painful that would hurt her a lot and make the rest of us laugh." She put her mask back on. "Not to mention the Simi barbecue would have been fun too if someone, Akra-Kat, hadn't stopped the Simi from it. I personally think it would have been a most magnificent gift for the baby. Barbecued heifer-goddess Artemis. Yum! No better meal. Oh then again baby got a delicate constitution and that might give the poor thing indigestion. Artemis definitely give the Simi indigestion and I ain't even ate her yet."

Kat let out an exaggerated sigh as she passed a bemused stare to Tory. "There's a reason Mia is currently an only child. Family drama takes on a whole new meaning when they're feuding gods who can't stand the sight of each other and always try to kill one another whenever they're in the same room."

Tory laughed, knowing just how right Kat was. It was why Xirena was downstairs with Alexian and Urian, eating her out of house and home. Simi's older sister couldn't stand Apollymi and the two of them had been fighting so badly that Alexian had volunteered to babysit the demon downstairs until the birth.

Tory loved her huge family, quirks, thorns, fangs, horns and all. She only wished her cousin, Geary, who was like a sister to her could have been here too. But Geary was about to give birth herself and was on bed rest for it.

She couldn't wait. Their babies would be like twins.

Acheron brushed her damp hair back from her face and started massaging her temples. "Is there anything I can do for you?"

She grimaced as more agony lacerated her abdomen. "Stop the pain."

He pressed his cheek against hers and gave her a gentle squeeze. "You know I can't."

Because they weren't sure what it might do to the baby or how it might unknowingly affect it and they'd decided together, as a family, that no one was going to lay a preternatural hand on the infant no matter what.

Not after what had been done to Acheron when he'd been born.

"Fine," she breathed. "But next time you're the one who's doing labor duty. I get to sit there and hold *your* hand."

And again he laughed.

She glared at him. "You have no sense of self preservation, do you?"

"Not really."

"Akra-Tory want some of my barbecue sauce to use on akri if he don't behave?"

Tory laughed again. "It's all right, Simi. I'll . . ." she screamed as something twisted inside her that felt like a broken bottle scraping her stomach lining.

Ash went pale. "Tory? Is something wrong?"

She couldn't answer. All she could do was try to breathe.

Ash looked at Tory's best friend Kim who was their lead midwife. Her features were drawn tight as she and Tory's other best friend, Pam talked in a low whisper.

"What's going on?" Ash demanded.

Kim turned to Danger. "Hon, can you go get Essie

from downstairs?" Esmerelda Deveraux was another friend who was practically family. While Kim was a medical practitioner and experienced midwife, Essie was a medical doctor with an additional twelve years of experience with delivering babies at home.

Danger left immediately.

Tory screamed as the pain worsened.

Acheron's skin turned from olive to mottled blue as his panic rose. "Answer me, Kim. What's happening?" Oh yeah, the god tone came out. It was so deep a growl that it vibrated the room.

Luckily, Kim knew he was a god and she never panicked over anything. "I don't know, sweetie. I've never delivered a nonhuman infant before. I don't know if this is normal or not. That's why I want a second opinion."

"How about a third?" Menyara asked as she, Essie, and Danger spilled into the room.

Ash stood up. "Don't touch the baby, Mennie."

Menyara cocked her hip and head at his concern. Dressed in a flowing orange skirt and cream peasant blouse, she had her sisterlocks held back from her face by a striped red scarf. "Now I know you didn't just come at me with your attitude, Mr. High And Mighty Atlantean God. Believe you me, if there's one thing I know how to do it's birth nonhuman infants. Been doing it since before even your old ass was born."

"Men—"

She held up her hand, cutting him off. "You know me better than that. I would never do *anything* to harm your baby and I'm not about to curse or mark it. Now let me take a look and see what's going on."

Ash stood down. "I'm sorry, Mennie."

"It's all right. I know where you're coming from and I know you're stressed. But don't worry. We'll take care of it."

Ash returned to Tory's side.

Tory took his hand again and did her best not to scream out anymore. Her poor baby. From the moment she'd told him she was pregnant, he'd been terrified. He didn't say it, but she knew. His childhood had been made so violent and traumatic by those who sought to destroy him that it'd left scars inside him that not even eleven thousand years could ease.

And all because his goddess aunt had touched his skin when she delivered him.

"It's okay, baby," she said to him.

But still she saw the fear in his eyes. *I can't lose you, Sota. I can't.* He sent those words to her and her alone.

She smiled at him through her pain as she used the powers he'd given her to respond. *I have no intention of leaving you. Ever.*

"Is it supposed to do that?" Kim asked Menyara.

Menyara swallowed. "I've never seen anything like this."

"What's wrong?" Tory's heart pounded as her panic rose. For Menyara to say something like that . . .

It was bad.

"We need to do a c-section." Menyara directed the others as they scrambled to make preparations.

Ash went to look, then stepped back.

Tory panicked even more. "What is it?"

"Stay calm," Apollymi said. "It's fine."

But it wasn't fine and she knew it. That fact was etched in the horror on all their faces. More pain stabbed at her.

Within minutes, they had her prepped. But when Essie went to make the cut, the blade snapped in two.

The room began to shake.

Tory screamed as the baby rolled inside her. It was as if he was angry at all of them and taking it out on her.

The midwives looked hopelessly at each other. "What do we do?"

Tory's vision dimmed. She was shaking uncontrollably.

"Do something!" Acheron shouted.

Essie swallowed. "We don't know what to do."

They couldn't take her to a hospital because of the fact that the baby wasn't human. If he were like his father and had mottled blue skin and horns, it was going to be a little difficult to explain.

Apollymi gestured to Menyara and Acheron. "Use your powers to pull it out."

Ash paled even more. "What if it damages the baby?"

"Oh for goodness sakes, child. The baby will never be left alone and unprotected." She gestured to the crowded room. "There's not a being here who wouldn't lay their life down for him. He is not you, Apostolos. We don't have to hide him."

Pam looked up from the monitors. "Tory's blood pressure's too high. We have to calm her down or she's going to have a stroke."

"Calm her down? How?"

Tory screamed as the baby moved again. It felt like he was trying to rip her in half.

Kim blanched. "We're going to lose them both."

Ash couldn't breathe as he heard those words.

In all of his extremely long life, he'd never been more terrified. He couldn't lose his wife. He couldn't.

Hoping he didn't do it wrong, he reached with his powers to pull the baby out.

Lightning burst in the room, ricocheting all over it. He had to duck to keep from getting blasted.

Tory screamed even louder.

And the baby stayed inside her.

"Oh that's not good," Menyara whispered. She moved him aside. "Let me try."

This time, the lightning slammed her into the wall.

Ash looked at his mother who shook her head. "I've never seen anything like this."

Pam turned the monitors toward them. "She can't take much more."

Ash met Tory's gaze. The utter agony and terror there stabbed him. What were they going to do?

"Her heart's failing."

Tears welled in his eyes. If she died because of this, because of him, he'd never forgive himself.

"Call Mom."

Ash frowned at Kat. "What?"

"She's a goddess of childbirth. She was only a few hours old when she delivered Apollo from her own mother. If anyone knows what to do . . ."

Yes, but she was also his worst enemy. They hated each other. Why would she help?

And then another fear stabbed him. What if Artemis was doing this? She'd been known to kill women in the throes of labor. Could she hate him so much that she would kill Tory just to get back at him?

Of course she would

Tory screamed again.

Wincing, Ash teleported himself from his home to Artemis's temple on Mount Olympus. He would rather be flayed, which he'd been many times, than come here. Only fear for Tory's life would have him in this hated place.

Her receiving hall was completely empty. "Artemis!" he called, heading toward her bedroom. If she did have something to do with this, he would turn Simi loose on her. Fate and order be damned.

Artemis appeared in front of the doors.

Ash hesitated. There was something different about her. She still had the flawless beauty that had always been hers. The long curly red hair and eyes so green they betrayed her divine status, but there was a serenity to her that had never been there before.

"Are you all right?" She actually managed to look concerned.

"Tory . . ." he choked at saying her name as unimaginable fear and pain ripped him apart. "She's in trouble. The baby won't come and she can't survive it. I need your help."

Her eyes darkened. "You would dare come here about that after all you've put me through?"

Oh yeah, there was the old Artemis he knew and hated. No mention of the fact that she'd stood and watched while her brother disemboweled him at her feet. Or of all the times he'd been beaten and humiliated while she watched on.

But none of that mattered to him.

Only Tory did.

Swallowing his pride, he kept the hatred from his gaze. "Please. Whatever price you demand of me, I will pay it. Anything, Artie. Just don't let her die."

"She, a pathetic human, really means that much to you?"

"I would die for her."

Artemis pressed her lips together as tears glistened in her eyes. "You loved me like that once."

And he'd paid for that love in the most violent ways

imaginable. "Please, Artemis. If you ever loved me, don't make Tory pay. I'm the one who wronged you. Not her."

A single tear slid down her cheek. "Would you have ever begged for my life?"

"When I was human. Yes."

She reached out and laid her hand on his cheek. "I did love you, Acheron. As I have never loved anything else, other than the child you gave me. And you're right to hate me. Because I'd never loved anything, I didn't know how to take care of it. I didn't know how to take care of you." She pulled his head down to hers and whispered softly in his ear. "I'm sorry." She placed her lips to his cheek and kissed it.

Then she vanished.

Ash scanned the room, trying to locate her. "Artemis?" Where had she gone? He shoved open the doors to her bedroom. "Artie?"

Still no answer.

Had her apology meant that she was sorry she wouldn't help? Terror tore through him.

What have I done?

Ash raked his hands through his hair as he fought down his panic and rage. Fine, if Artemis wanted to be a bitch, he'd find some way to save his wife.

Closing his eyes, he went home.

And froze in the corner as he saw the most shocking thing of all time.

Artemis with Tory.

"That's it, Soteria. Breathe easy." Artemis had one hand on Tory's forehead while she gently rubbed the other over Tory's stomach. "See how calm he is now?"

Tory nodded.

"He feels what you feel. He's trying to protect you both." Artemis looked at the others. "All of you need to leave."

Kat stood up slowly. "Mom . . ."

"Leave, Katra. The baby wants peace."

"We'll be downstairs," Menyara said.

Ash hesitated. "Am I to leave too?"

Artemis shook her head. "If you go, you'll always think I've done something to the child to get back at you. Stay and know that I'm not hurting him."

One by one, she pulled all the monitoring devices from Tory. Then she cupped Tory's face in her hand.

"Breathe slow and easy, then push. Not hard, but gently. Let him know that it's safe and that you want him here to be loved."

Licking her lips, Tory nodded and did what she ordered.

"Again."

After the fourth time, Artemis went to her feet. Then turned toward Ash. "Come, Acheron. Be the first to welcome your son into his new life."

She was right, he was still suspicious of her. All their

centuries together, the only thing he'd ever been able to count on was her willingness to hurt him anyway she could.

But he did as she said. He went to Tory and with one more push, his son slid into his hands.

For a full minute, he couldn't breathe as he stared at the tiniest, most perfect creature he'd ever seen in his life.

"Is it a smurf?" Tory asked.

Ash laughed. Since he was blue in his natural god skin, Tory had been joking with him that she wasn't having a baby, but rather a smurf. Artemis cut and sealed the cord, then took the baby and woke him.

He let loose a wail that would have shamed Simi.

Artemis wrapped him in a blanket, then took him to Tory. "Meet your son, Soteria."

Tory stared in wonder at the tiny baby who, even now, looked just like her husband. He was perfect in every way. From the top of his head that was covered with blond fuzz to the bottom of his itsy bitsy toes.

Artemis started to move away.

Tory took her hand to stop her. Her emotions swelled inside, choking her. "Thank you, Artemis. Thank you."

Artemis smiled at her. "I hope he brings you as much happiness and pride as Katra has always brought me."

Ash came closer. "Thank you, Artie."

She inclined her head to him, then moved to leave.

"Aren't you forgetting something?"

She paused at Ash's question. "What?"

"Your payment."

Artemis shook her head. "The happiness on your face when first you touched him was enough. I only wish you'd been there when your daughter was born, but that was my fault. I've had a lifetime of joy, hugs and love from her and you missed all of that because of my stupidity and fear. His life is my gift to both of you. Let's hope the future is much kinder to all of us than the past has been." And then she was gone.

Tory stared in confounded disbelief. "What did you do to her?"

Ash shook his head. "I don't think it was my influence."

"Then who? 'Cause that's not the Artemis who came at me over you."

Ash shrugged. "I don't know. She's been hanging out with Nick."

"Nick? As in I-hate-your-guts-Ash-go-die Nick?"

He nodded.

"Whoa." Tory looked down at her son while he kicked and squirmed. There was no way to describe what she felt in that moment. This was her baby. A part of her and Ash. The best part of them.

Ash held his hand so that the baby could wrap his tiny hand around his pinky. "So what are we going call him?"

"Bob."

Ash laughed at the name Zarek used for his son because he detested the name Astrid had picked out. "Really?"

Her smile set his entire world on fire. "No. I think I'd like to name him Sebastos Eudorus."

Ash arched a brow at her choice. "Why that?"

"Sebastos was the name my parents picked out for me, had I been a boy and I always thought it would make a great name for my son. And Eudorus because he was the son of Hermes and Polymele. As a boy he danced in Artemis's chair to celebrate her. When he grew up, he was one of the fiercest, most venerated of Achilles' Myrmidons and Homer wrote more lines about him than anyone else. Plus it means gift of joy, which he is. And while we've had our issues with Artemis, but for her I wouldn't have you and neither of us would have had the baby today. "

Only his wife would know all of that off the top of her head. Ash laughed. "Sebastos Eudorus Parthenopaeus. He is really going to hate us when he has to learn to spell all that."

"Probably, but I think I'll call him Sebastian. That way he can grow up and confuse people with his name just like his father does."

"Yeah well, I still haven't figured out how you got Tory out of Soteria." He leaned down and kissed her gently. "Thank you for my son."

Her eyes glistened and the love he saw there never ceased to amaze him. "Thank you for my life."

He could stare into her beautiful face all day.

She patted him lightly on the cheek. "You should probably let the thundering horde in from downstairs. Let them know Artemis didn't kill us."

"All right. You sure you're ready?"

"Absolutely. And before you start posting photos on Facebook for the rest of the Dark-Hunters to see, make sure I have on makeup."

He scoffed. "You don't need makeup to be beautiful."

"And that's part of why I love you so much. But the rest of the world doesn't look at me through silver swirling eyes."

"I love you, Tory. I know I say it a lot, but . . ."

"I know, baby. I feel the same way about you. Those words never convey what goes through my mind and heart every time I look up and see you sitting in my house. Funny thing is, I always thought my house was full and that there was nothing missing in my life. I had a job I loved. Family who loved me. Good friends to keep me sane. Everything a human could want. And then I met an infuriating, impossible man who added the one thing I didn't know wasn't there."

"Dirty socks on the floor?"

She laughed. "No, the other part of my heart. The last face I see before I go to sleep and the first one I see when I get up. I'm so glad it was you."

Those words both thrilled and scared him. Mostly

because he knew firsthand that if love went untended it turned into profound hatred. "And I hope you never change your mind about that."

"Never."

Foolish or not, he believed her. But the one thing he knew for certain. He would never be able to live without her.

Author's Note

As a woman of mixed Tsalagi (Cherokee)
heritage, I've always been fascinated by the
beliefs and legends of all the Native American Nations. I spent untold hours as a child,
combing through the library, reading any and
everything I could find that would give me
insight into that part of my family history as

well as listening to countless stories told to me by my family, all of whom wove great magic with their words.

When I first started writing the Dark-Hunter series back in college, I decided to base it around Greek mythology with one notable exception. The Daimons. A cursed vampire-like demon that wasn't immortal and rather than feed from blood, they fed from something a little more . . . robust.

The human soul.

While I created the curse and the mythos around the Atlanteans, Apollites and Daimons from my own mind, there was one thing I did borrow from my ancestors. Part of the tsi-noo (chenoo) legend.

When I was a child, the tsi-noo was the bogeyman my mother would threaten me with if I didn't behave (she also used the Manitou, but that's another story).

A Wabanaki legend, the tsi-noo began life as a human who was either possessed by an evil demon or one who committed some atrocious crime (usually cannibalism) that caused his heart to turn to ice. Also known as an Ice Cannibal, the tsi-noo stayed alive and grew stronger by consuming humans, especially their souls. This was why my mother told me it was imperative to say my prayers at night and to ask God to keep my soul safe while I slept. If I failed to do so, one could slip into my bed (or my dreams) and steal it away from me . . . because everyone knew that a child's soul was the most coveted by the tsi-noo and if you weren't careful, you could easily give your soul to one. I'm pretty sure all of that last bit was made up by my mother for the sheer fear factor of it as I haven't been able to find any corroborating story about it.

But as a little girl, the idea of having my soul stolen or being able to lock one up fascinated me and as an adult, I decided to borrow it for my Daimons.

I also incorporated the tsi-noo, as well as several other monsters, into this book. It's something I've been wanting to do for a very long time. I introduced Sunshine Running-wolf into the series at the beginning (she was the heroine of the second published Dark-Hunter novel, *Night Embrace*). A woman of mixed Native American heritage, she, like me, treasures both sides of her ancestry. And from the moment, I completed that novel, I've been aching to return to my roots and explore them more.

Finally, in this book, I was able to pay homage to many different Native American legends and beliefs, including those of my family, and to explore them more fully.

That being said, I've also created my own Native American history for the purpose of the book. The original tribes/clans, creators and Guardians I've used, as well as some of the monsters, are not taken from any Native American belief system or religion. This was done out of respect and on purpose.

As a very spiritual person who comes from a mixed

religious background, I have a deep and abiding love and respect for all religions and points of view. I would never intentionally insult or otherwise offend anyone.

The Time Untime is a real Cherokee belief that I couldn't resist borrowing a bit from and it was another story I grew up with. However, I have tweaked it a bit and will continue it on in the 2012 Dark-Hunter novel that will follow this one.

I can't tell you how much I've enjoyed my foray into another pantheon. I knew when I sat down to start Jess's story that it would grab my heart and make me laugh and cry. It did both many times.

As with all of my books, I'm very proud of this one and I hope you enjoy taking this journey with me. Now I must get back to the voices in my head who, I pray, will never leave me alone and who will sing their songs to me for many years to come.

But before I go, I'd like to leave you with the first words my uncle taught me to say in Tsalagi. *Wa-do* (wah doe). Thank you.

OEDIPUS THE KING
ELECTRA

WIDELY regarded in both ancient and modern times as the most sublime of the tragic poets, the life of Sophocles the Athenian (*c*.495–405 BC) spanned the century of his city's greatness as an imperial democracy and the leading state of the Greek-speaking world. He was a popular and prominent figure in the public affairs of Athens, acting as both treasurer and general in the late 440s, and as a magistrate in the civic crisis which resulted from the Athenians' catastrophic invasion of Sicily in 413 BC. His first tragedy was produced in 468 BC, when he was in his late twenties, and he seems to have worked right up until his death, achieving a prodigious output of well over a hundred plays. Seven of his tragedies survive, of which only two, products of his old age, are firmly dated. *Philoctetes* was first produced in 409 BC, and *Oedipus at Colonus* was put on posthumously by Sophocles' grandson in 402 or 401 BC. *Ajax* and *Women of Trachis* may be the earliest of his surviving works: the three contained in this volume, *Antigone*, *Oedipus the King*, and *Electra*, were all probably composed after he had reached the age of 50. They have proved to be the most influential of his works and are generally regarded as his masterpieces.

The debt owed by western drama to Sophocles is incalculable. He was believed by the ancients to have been the first tragic poet to use painted scenery and three actors, and Aristotle bestowed the highest praise on him in his treatise on tragic poetry, the *Poetics*, singling out the economy of his plot construction, the nobility of his characters, and his excellent handling of the chorus. But Sophocles' name means 'renowned for wisdom', and few if any tragedies have ever rivalled his works in intellectual depth, luminosity of language, precision of imagery, and sheer emotional power.

EDITH HALL is Leverhulme Professor of Greek Cultural History at the University of Durham and co-director of the Archive of Performances of Greek and Roman Drama at the University of Oxford; her books include *Inventing the Barbarian* (Oxford, 1989). For Oxford World's Classics she has introduced five volumes of Euripides' plays.

OXFORD WORLD'S CLASSICS

SOPHOCLES

Antigone
Oedipus the King
Electra

Translated by
H. D. F. KITTO

Edited with an Introduction and Notes by
EDITH HALL

OXFORD
UNIVERSITY PRESS

OXFORD
UNIVERSITY PRESS

Great Clarendon Street, Oxford OX2 6DP

Oxford University Press is a department of the University of Oxford.
It furthers the University's objective of excellence in research, scholarship,
and education by publishing worldwide in

Oxford New York

Auckland Bangkok Buenos Aires Cape Town Chennai
Dar es Salaam Delhi Hong Kong Istanbul Karachi Kolkata
Kuala Lumpur Madrid Melbourne Mexico City Mumbai Nairobi
São Paulo Shanghai Singapore Taipei Tokyo Toronto

Oxford is a registered trade mark of Oxford University Press
in the UK and in certain other countries

Published in the United States
by Oxford University Press Inc., New York

English translation © Oxford University Press 1962
Editorial material © Edith Hall 1994

British Library Cataloguing in Publication Data

Data available

Library of Congress Cataloging in Publication Data

Data available

ISBN 0-19-283588-2

14

Printed in Great Britain by
Clays Ltd., St Ives plc

ACKNOWLEDGEMENTS

SEVERAL people have helped me in the preparation of this edition. John Betts, Nicholas Hammond, Christopher Robinson, Christopher Rowe, George Rowell, and Glynne Wickham all helped me to track down the history of the genesis and first performances of the translations. My students at Reading made it quite clear to me what they would wish to find in an edited translation of Sophocles. I would also like to record my heartfelt thanks to Linda Holt, Fiona Macintosh, Oliver Taplin, and especially Richard Poynder, for invaluable assistance of other kinds.

CONTENTS

INTRODUCTION

Time is a recurrent topic in Sophoclean tragedy. Of Oedipus, so recently so fortunate, the chorus sings, 'Time sees all, and Time, in your despite, | Disclosed and punished your unnatural marriage' (p. 91). Within the stark temporal economy of these tragedies, whose actions commence at dawn and are consummated within a single day, human fortunes are completely overturned. Antigone dies, Oedipus the king becomes a blinded outcast, and Electra is reunited with her long-lost brother Orestes, who slaughters the incumbents of the Mycenaean throne. Time is the only conceptual benchmark by which Sophocles' mortals can fully understand their difference from divinity. Unlike the power held by Creon or Oedipus or Clytemnestra, the sovereignty of the gods is immune to time's passing. The chorus of *Antigone* praises Zeus' immortality: 'Sleep ... cannot overcome Thee, | Nor can the never-wearied | Years, but throughout | Time Thou art strong and ageless' (p. 23).

Sophoclean drama has proved to be as 'strong and ageless' as its immortal gods. These plays in this volume do not die; they are merely reinterpreted. The inventory of Sophocles' admirers and imitators, in the English-speaking world alone, includes John Milton, Samuel Johnson, Percy Shelley (who translated *Oedipus the King* and drowned with a text of Sophocles in his pocket), Matthew Arnold, George Eliot, Virginia Woolf, W. B. Yeats, Ezra Pound, and more recently Seamus Heaney and Tony Harrison.[1]

Sophocles' influence extends beyond literature to philosophy and psychology. Hegel's dialectic and view of tragic conflict are inseparable from his understanding of *Antigone*;[2] Sigmund Freud's most famous theory is named after the

[1] See further Stuart Gillespie, *The Poets on the Classics: An Anthology* (London/New York, 1988), 202–6.

[2] See esp. Michelle Gellrich, *Tragedy and Theory: The Problem of Conflict since Aristotle* (Princeton, NJ, 1988).

protagonist of *Oedipus the King*.[3] Nor, for over 400 years, has this poet been confined to the academy. The earliest-attested performance of a Greek tragedy in modern translation presented an audience of Italian humanists, in Vicenza, with a production of *Oedipus the King* on 3 March 1585.[4] Although the performance of Sophoclean drama was, in nineteenth-century Britain, generally proscribed on moral grounds by the Lord Chamberlain,[5] this playwright has never enjoyed so many revivals as in the period since the Second World War. During 1992, as this edition was in preparation, every play in it was performed by the Royal Shakespeare Company on the English stage.[6]

Their enduring popularity makes it hard to remember that they were first performed 2,500 years ago, by exclusively male actors, in the quite different context of a day-lit theatre in Athens. Dramas were produced at sacred festivals in honour of Dionysus, god of wine, dancing, and illusion. Every year three tragedians competed against each other with a group of four plays, three tragedies and a satyr play (a hybrid dramatic form mixing tragic and comic elements), with the aim of persuading a democratically selected jury to award their group of works the first prize; with it came vast prestige and fame around the whole Greek-speaking world.[7]

The decision to present these particular three of the seven surviving tragedies by Sophocles together in a single volume, although unusual, has great advantages. By detaching

[3] For a critique of Freud's (ab)use of Sophocles, especially with regard to *Oedipus the King*, see Jean-Pierre Vernant, 'Oedipus Without the Complex', in Jean-Pierre Vernant and Pierre Vidal-Naquet, *Myth and Tragedy in Ancient Greece* (Eng. trans. New York, 1988), 85–111.

[4] Hellmut Flashar, *Inszenierung der Antike: Das griechische Drama auf der Bühne der Neuzeit 1585–1990* (Munich, 1991), 27–9.

[5] See F. Macintosh, 'Tragedy in Performance', in P. Easterling, *The Cambridge Companion to Greek Tragedy* (Cambridge, 1995).

[6] *Oedipus the King* and *Antigone* were performed together with *Oedipus at Colonus* under the title *The Thebans*. The director was Adrian Noble. *Electra* was directed by Deborah Warner. (Kitto's translations were not the versions used for these productions.)

[7] See A. W. Pickard-Cambridge, *The Dramatic Festivals of Athens*, reissue, with new supplement, of the second edition, revised by J. Gould and D. M. Lewis (Oxford, 1988).

Oedipus the King and *Antigone* from *Oedipus at Colonus*, which is not included, the misleading latter-day myth of a Theban 'trilogy' or 'cycle' is exploded. For the three surviving plays by Sophocles set at Thebes and focusing on the family of Oedipus were not designed to be performed together sequentially. They were independently conceived, composed over a period of perhaps nearly forty years, and were first produced separately, each in a group with other, unknown, tragedies. *Antigone* and *Oedipus the King*, are, however, at least consistent with each other, whereas *Antigone* and *Oedipus at Colonus* contain one important factual difference. *Antigone* assumes that Oedipus died ingloriously at Thebes, whereas *Oedipus at Colonus* brings him to a beatific death at Athens.

The selection has other merits, however. A distinctive feature of Sophoclean tragedy is a titanic central heroic figure defiantly refusing to compromise and bend to other people's different perceptions of reality.[8] These characters' intransigent stances, while ennobling them, bring them into collision with, at best, misery (Electra) and, at worst, catastrophe (Oedipus): this volume brings together the two surviving Sophoclean tragedies, *Antigone* and *Electra*, in which the dominant heroic figure is a woman.

Another significant link connecting the three is the similarity of their perspective on familial relationships. Discord abounds between husbands and wives. Creon drives his wife to suicide; Oedipus wants to kill his mother/wife; Clytemnestra murdered her husband. Siblings of the same sex are vulnerable to dissension; in *Antigone* two brothers have killed each other; in both *Antigone* and *Electra* pairs of sisters are in powerful disagreement. Oedipus killed his father, and mother–child enmity leads to matricide in *Electra*. All three plays, however, privilege, indeed idealize, two particular bonds—between daughter and father and between sister and brother: in the case of Antigone and Oedipus the bond is famously and bizarrely identical.

[8] For a discussion of this aspect of Sophoclean drama see the definitive, but controversial, study by B. M. W. Knox, *The Heroic Temper: Studies in Sophoclean Tragedy* (Berkeley/Los Angeles, 1964).

Antigone, torn as a child from her father's arms at the end of *Oedipus the King*, later brings death upon herself out of loyalty to her dead brother Polyneices; Electra awaits the return of her adored younger brother Orestes to avenge the death of a father to whose memory she is quite obsessively attached. Sophoclean women are only defined, and can only achieve heroic status, in the contexts of their relationships with men.

Sophocles

Sophocles was enormously popular within his own lifetime, and had his place in the gallery of the greatest poets of all time canonized by the generations immediately succeeding him. Even Plato, who was to banish dramatists from his ideal Republic, was gentle in his assessment of Sophocles (*Republic* 1. 329 b–c), and in his *Poetics* Aristotle expressed the view that Sophoclean drama brought the genre of tragedy to its consummate achievements, especially in *Oedipus the King*. The general consensus of Sophocles' contemporaries and successors was that he was a man blessed with a virtuous disposition and, unlike his characters, a remarkably trouble-free life. A charming epitaph occurred in a fragmentary comedy entitled *The Muses*, by Phrynichus: 'fortunate Sophocles lived a long life, made many beautiful tragedies, and, in the end, died without suffering any evil'.[9]

The facts of Sophocles' life must, however, be pieced together from diverse sources of varying reliability.[10] Inscriptions can usually be trusted; ancient librarians and scholars had access to sources of information now lost to us, but many allusions in ancient authors have little claim to veracity. The 'Chronology' in this edition therefore confines itself to those few dates which are almost certainly trustworthy.

Ancient poets attracted anecdotes and sayings which were

---

[9] Phrynichus, fr. 32, in R. Kassel and C. Austin (eds.), *Poetae Comici Graeci*, vol. vii (Berlin, 1989).

[10] All the evidence is compiled in S. Radt, *Tragicorum Graecorum Fragmenta* iv (Berlin, 1977), 29–95.

compiled in later antiquity into 'biographies'. The *Life of Sophocles* contains numerous pieces of information which it would be delightful to be able to believe. He is alleged to have led with his lyre the Athenian chorus which celebrated the victory over the Persians at the battle of Salamis, to have acted leading roles in his own plays, and to have died either while reciting a long sentence from *Antigone* without pause for breath, or by choking on a grape (the fruit of Dionysus, the tutelary deity of drama). Unfortunately such anecdotes reveal more about the biographers' imaginations than about the poet himself.[11]

Sophocles son of Sophilus was born at the Colonus of his *Oedipus at Colonus*, a district of the Athenian city-state, in the middle of the first decade of the fifth century BC. He is said to have married one Nicostrate, and both a son (Iophon) and a grandson (also named Sophocles) followed him by becoming tragic poets. He lived until about 405 BC, just before the Athenians' defeat in the disastrous Peloponnesian War, which had thrown the Greek-speaking world into divisive chaos for nearly three decades. His life thus began and ended commensurately with the century of Athens' greatness as an imperial democracy and the leading city-state of the Hellenic world.[12]

He composed at least 120 dramas, of which only seven tragedies survive; a certain amount is known, however, about many of his other productions.[13] In the three plays translated here mythical parallels are often drawn from other stories we know he was sufficiently interested in to dramatize. He wrote, for example, a *Niobe*, about a tragically bereaved mother, with whose misery both Antigone and Electra emotionally identify (see pp. 29 and 109 with explanatory notes).

[11] The ancient *Life of Sophocles* is reproduced in English translation and well discussed by Mary R. Lefkowitz in *The Lives of the Greek Poets* (London, 1981), 74–87 and 160–3. See also J. Fairweather, 'Fiction in the biographies of ancient writers', *Ancient Society* v (1974), 231–75.

[12] An admirably clear account of fifth-century Athenian history is to be found in J.K. Davies, *Democracy and Classical Greece* (Glasgow, second edition, 1993).

[13] See D. F. Sutton, *The Lost Sophocles* (Lanham, 1984), and A. Kiso, *The Lost Sophocles* (New York, 1984).

He was victorious in the dramatic competitions about twenty times, and apparently never came last; he is thought to have won in the year he produced *Antigone*, but the group of plays which included *Oedipus the King* was astonishingly awarded only second place. Whether or not *Electra* and its companion dramas won the first prize is not even known. A portion of *Trackers*, a satyr play, has been discovered on papyrus: its pastoral content—an enormous newborn Hermes, greedy satyrs, an indignant nymph, and cattle dung— has granted the twentieth century a precious glimpse into this sombre tragedian's sense of humour.[14]

Sophoclean scholarship is hampered by the lack of evidence concerning the dates of his works. He won his first victory in 468 BC, defeating the great Aeschylus, when he was approaching the age of thirty;[15] the victorious plays may have included his (lost) *Triptolemus*. *Philoctetes* was awarded first place in 409,[16] and *Oedipus at Colonus* was produced posthumously in 402/1.[17] But of the other five extant tragedies, namely *Ajax*, *Women of Trachis*, and those published here, not one is firmly dated. The dramatic technique and style of *Ajax* and *Women of Trachis* may suggest that they are fairly early, but this assumes that a writer's works must evolve in a smooth linear progression. An ancient, but unreliable, tradition implies that *Antigone* may have been produced in the late 440s.[18] Scholars have tried hard to place *Oedipus the King* in the mid-420s[19] and *Electra*

---

[14] Recently incorporated by Tony Harrison into his drama *The Trackers of Oxyrhynchus* (2nd edn., London, 1991). The fragment, which is of considerable length and interest, was edited by Richard Walker (*The Ichneutae of Sophocles*, London, 1919); a prosaic, but faithful, translation may be found in D. L. Page (ed.), *Select Papyri*, vol. iii (Cambridge, Mass./London, 1941), 27–53.

[15] Plutarch, *Life of Cimon* 8. 8.

[16] 'Hypothesis' (ancient scholarly note of introduction) to *Philoctetes*.

[17] Second 'hypothesis' to *Oedipus at Colonus*.

[18] See below and n. 27.

[19] Bernard Knox ('The date of the *Oedipus Tyrannus* of Sophocles', in *Word and Action: Essays on the Ancient Theater*, Baltimore/London, 1979, 112–24), argues for a production in 425 BC. He compares the plague blighting Thebes in the play with the outbreaks of plague which had beset Athens from 430 to 426 BC. This seems persuasive, until it is remembered that the earliest and greatest work of Greek literature, the *Iliad*, likewise opens with a plague sent by Apollo.

about a decade later,[20] but such conjectural dating should not be treated with anything but rampant scepticism.[21]

It is fairly certain that Sophocles dedicated a cult of the healing hero Asclepius in his own home,[22] but the biographical tradition makes extravagant claims about the poet's personal piety. He is supposed to have been loved more than others by the gods, to have been a favourite of Heracles, and to have held a priesthood himself. Such dubious testimony has resulted in scholarly quests for evidence of religious conviction in his plays.[23] But the only generalization that can safely be made applies equally to all Greek tragedy: divine will is always eventually done.

Antigone affirms that the laws of heaven are 'Unwritten and unchanging. Not of today | Or yesterday is their authority; | They are eternal' (p. 17). These 'Unwritten Laws' encoded archaic taboos and imperatives regulating familial and social relations; they proscribed murder within the family, the breaking of oaths, incest, and disrespect towards the dead—for example, the failure to bury them.[24] Mortals who in tragedy transgress these immortal edicts must come to see the error of their ways. Creon may have justification in *Antigone* for the measures by which he attempts to deter possible traitors to his city, but the play reveals that human reasoning faculties are not sufficient means by which to apprehend an inexplicable universe. Iocasta derides oracles as hocus-pocus, but they all come true in the end. Oedipus attempts to save his city from its disastrous plight by means of his intellect, but his detective trail leads him to the discovery that the gods had ordained that he break, by parricide and incest, two of the 'Unwritten Laws'. In *Electra* Clytemnestra may have had a perfectly understandable motive

[20] See e.g. A. M. Dale (ed.), *Euripides' Helen* (Oxford, 1967), xxiv–v.

[21] For a succinct and sensibly agnostic discussion of Sophoclean chronology see R. G. A. Buxton, *Sophocles* (*Greece & Rome*, New Surveys in the Classics, xvi, Oxford, 1984), 3–5.

[22] *Inscriptiones Graecae* ii[2]. 1252.4.

[23] See e.g. E. R. Dodds, *The Greeks and the Irrational* (Berkeley, 1951), 193.

[24] On the 'Unwritten Laws' see V. Ehrenberg, *Sophocles and Pericles* (Oxford, 1954), 22–50 and 167–72.

for killing her husband, Agamemnon—he was responsible for the death of their daughter Iphigeneia—but divine law dictates that as a murderer within the family, she must give her life in return.

The only other pertinent biographical information, which in this case is reasonably reliable, concerns Sophocles' public life.[25] He served as an ambassador, held office under the Athenian democracy as a treasurer in 443-2 BC, as a general (not a narrowly military office) in 441-0, and as a magistrate in 413 after the disastrous Athenian expedition to Sicily.[26] Such practical experiences are not inconsistent with the continuous investigation running through all three plays of the ease with which political authority can turn into tyranny, and with the artistic exploration, through the dilemmas facing Creon and Oedipus, of the anxieties inherent in the possession of political power.

Antigone

Of all Sophocles' tragedies _Antigone_ is the most overtly political, in that it directly confronts problems involved in running a _polis_, a city-state. The ancients already recognized this; a tradition emerged that Sophocles' election to the generalship in 441/0 was a direct result of the success of the play.[27] In modern times the political element has inspired numerous adaptations and productions, often anachronistically portraying Antigone as a liberal individualist shaking her little fist against a totalitarian state: she has been made to protest against everything from Nazism (especially in the versions by Jean Anouilh of 1944 and Bertolt Brecht of

[25] For an attempted reconstruction of Sophocles' political career see Ehrenberg (n. 24 above).

[26] _Inscriptiones Graecae_ i³. 269.36; first 'hypothesis' to _Antigone_; Androtion 324, fr. 38, in F. Jacoby (ed.), _Die Fragmente der griechischen Historiker_, vol. IIIb (Leiden, 1950), 69; Aristotle, _Rhetoric_ 1419ª25.

[27] Recorded in the first 'hypothesis' to _Antigone_. L. Woodbury argued that the tradition was credible ('Sophocles among the Generals', _Phoenix_ xxiv, 1970, 209–24); for a more sceptical view see Karl Reinhardt, _Sophocles_ (Eng. trans. Oxford, 1979), 240.

1948) to eastern-bloc communism, South African apartheid, and British imperialism in Ireland.[28]

The action of the play, although occupying first place in this volume, should, according to a strict observance of 'mythical time', occur later than that of *Oedipus the King*. It is set in Thebes, a mainland Greek city-state to the north of Athens and in reality anti-democratic and hostile to her; the Athenian dramatists typically displaced or 'expatriated' to Thebes political strife, tyranny, and domestic chaos.[29] *Antigone* opens at a moment of political crisis caused directly by internecine warfare. King Oedipus and Iocasta, now deceased, had four children, Polyneices, Eteocles, Antigone, and Ismene. The two sons quarrelled over the kingship of Thebes, and Polyneices was driven into exile; Eteocles was left ruling Thebes, apparently with the support of the brothers' maternal uncle Creon. Polyneices formed an alliance with the king of the important Peloponnesian city of Argos (where *Electra* is set), and raised a force with which to attack his own city. The assault failed, but in the battle Polyneices and Eteocles killed each other.

The tragedy begins at dawn after the Theban victory; Creon, as the nearest surviving male relative of the two sons of Oedipus, has now assumed power. The play enacts the catastrophic events which take place on his first day in office; it ironically demonstrates the truth of his own inaugural speech, in which he pronounces that no man's character can be known 'Until he has been proved by government | And lawgiving' (p. 8). For the very first law which Creon passes— that the body of the traitor Polyneices is to be refused burial— is in direct contravention of the 'Unwritten Law' protecting the rights of the dead; it precipitates, moreover, not only the death of his disobedient niece Antigone, who buries the corpse, but also the suicides of his own son Haemon and of Creon's wife Eurydice.

Butler too?

[28] On the 'afterlife' of *Antigone* see the illuminating discussion by George Steiner in *Antigones* (Oxford, 1984).

[29] See Froma Zeitlin, 'Thebes: Theater of Self and Society in Athenian Drama', in J. Peter Euben (ed.), *Greek Tragedy and Political Theory* (Berkeley/Los Angeles/London, 1986), 101–41.

Antigone explores the difficult path any head of state must tread between clear leadership and despotism. It has sometimes been argued that Creon's law was defensible, given the divisive nature of the civil war which had blighted Thebes and the urgent need for a firm hand on the rudder of government.[30] Funerals, as politicians everywhere know, can spark off insurrection. It is even possible to see Creon's failure to achieve heroic stature, at least in human terms, as a result simply of his unsteadiness in the face of opposition. For he is, above all, erratic: having decided that Ismene is as guilty as Antigone, he then changes his mind about her. He vacillates wildly about Antigone's fate: the original edict decreed death by stoning, but at one point he is going to have her executed publicly in front of Haemon; finally he opts for entombing her alive, but eventually revokes even this decision. He is the perfect example of the type of tragic character Aristotle described as 'consistently inconsistent' (*Poetics*, ch. 15).

Thinkers contemporary with Sophocles were involved in the development of a political theory to match the needs of the new Athenian democracy. One concept being developed was that of *homonoia* or 'same-mindedness', according to which laws are ideally the results of a consensual or contractual agreement made by all the citizens of a state.[31] Creon's law was passed autocratically, without *homonoia*, and his increasingly domineering attitude towards the views of others renders the disastrous outcome of his reign, and of the play, inevitable. As his own son puts it, 'The man | Who thinks that he alone is wise, that he | Is best in speech or counsel, such a man | Brought to the proof is found but emptiness' (pp. 25–6).

Creon is 'brought to the proof', however, not by civic disagreement articulated in the male arenas of council or assembly, but by a young female relative. This completely incenses him. Her goal is not political influence; she is simply obeying the divine law which laid on family members—

[30] See e.g. W. M. Calder, 'Sophocles' political tragedy, *Antigone*', *Greek, Roman and Byzantine Studies* ix (1968), 389–407.

[31] See G. B. Kerferd, *The Sophistic Movement* (Cambridge, 1981), 149–50.

especially women—the solemn duty of performing funeral rites for their kin. The mysterious, and often arrogant, Antigone is as inflexible as Creon is erratic; as the chorus comments, 'The daughter shows her father's temper—fierce, | Defiant; she will not yield to any storm' (p. 17). It is Creon's misfortune that she happens to be not only Oedipus' daughter, but Creon's own niece and his son's fiancée. This calls the conventional dichotomy of public and private life into profound question; Creon cannot keep his two worlds separate, and the drama shows that they are as inextricably intertwined as the corpses of Antigone and Haemon, locked in a bizarre travesty of a nuptial embrace. If the play has a moral, it is that when political expediency cannot accommodate familial obligations and ritual observance of ancestral law, its advocates are courting disaster.

Oedipus the King

In recent times this definitive tragedy has been brought to a wider audience than ever before by a cinematic adaptation, Pier Paolo Pasolini's atmospheric *Edipo Re* (1967), which, appropriately in our post-Freudian era, concentrates on the hero's private psychological and emotional self-discovery.[32] But *Oedipus the King* (sometimes known by its Latinized name as *Oedipus Rex*) was previously reinvented, especially in pre-revolutionary France, as a treatise on government.[33] And indeed, although less transparently political than *Antigone*, it meditates on a similar difficult issue in statecraft: the *via media* between decisive leadership and excessive self-confidence.

This aspect of the play is somewhat obscured in translation: the Greek title and several passages actually call Oedipus a *turannos*. This is an ambiguous word, from which

[32] For a discussion of this and other film versions of Sophoclean tragedy see Kenneth MacKinnon, *Greek Tragedy into Film* (London/Sydney, 1986), esp. 126–46.

[33] See Pierre Vidal-Naquet, 'Oedipus in Vicenza and in Paris: Two Turning Points in the History of Oedipus', in Vernant and Vidal-Naquet (n. 3 above), 361–80.

our 'tyrant' is derived, but whose meaning in Sophocles' time was unstable. It oscillated between 'a ruler who has attained to power, not by inheritance, but by popular support' (which Oedipus *thinks* he has, although he is ironically later revealed as the true son of the former hereditary king of Thebes), and the more value-laden and pejorative 'despot' (which Oedipus is in danger of becoming). The play's interest in the psychology of the *turannos* is expressed in Oedipus' monologue on the fears besetting those in power (pp. 61–2), and culminates in the enigmatic central ode, in which the chorus sings, 'Pride makes the tyrant—pride of wealth | And power, too great for wisdom and restraint' (p. 78).

The action takes place perhaps a decade earlier in mythical time than that of *Antigone*. It also opens with the city of Thebes in crisis, but on this occasion the reason is plague. The opening tableau portrays the priests and other Thebans entreating their king, Oedipus, who had previously saved them from the monstrous Sphinx by solving her famous riddle, to find a way to cure the disease. It is the irony of the play that in this he is successful, but only by bringing utter catastrophe upon himself, for it is none but he who has unwittingly caused the city's afflictions.

Twentieth-century scholarship has continually reassessed the relationships in Sophocles between fate and freewill, character and action.[34] The litmus test is always the unforgettable story of the lame king who becomes a scapegoat, and who blinds himself at the precise point when he is no longer blind to the truth of which his audience, in this paradigmatic exercise in dramatic irony, has been painfully aware all along. Oedipus was doomed *before he was born* to kill his father and marry his mother, and commits both crimes unwittingly. Some interpreters see him as a virtuous man, through whom Sophocles shows the absolute injustice

---

[34] e.g. John Jones, *On Aristotle and Greek Tragedy* (London, 1962); P. E. Easterling, 'Character in Sophocles', *Greece & Rome* xxiv (1977), 121–9; J. Gould, 'Dramatic character and "human intelligibility" in Greek tragedy', *Proceedings of the Cambridge Philological Society* cciv (1978), 43–67.

(from a human perspective) of divine preordinance; others point to the unattractive sides of his character—his temper, his paranoia, the way he threatens Teiresias, Creon, and the Theban with arbitrary punishment, and his arrogant conviction that his intellect can surmount any obstacles in his, or his city's path. This view renders Oedipus somehow culpable after the event; his fate is rendered justifiable by his abrasive personality.

Yet both views oversimplify the sophisticated dialectics of the Sophoclean negotiations between character, action, and responsibility. Although the Greeks had none of the Christian cognitive machinery which lies behind, for example, Renaissance drama, a limited psychological vocabulary, and only an embryonic notion of the autonomous individual will, Sophocles still makes it entirely plausible that tragic victims can only bring their fates upon themselves because of the type of people that they are. If Oedipus had not been a self-sufficient individual, confident in his ability to escape the dreadful destiny the Delphic oracle had revealed to him as a youth, he would never have left Corinth, the city in which he grew up, and the couple he believed to be his natural parents. If he had not been a proud and daring man, he would not have retaliated single-handedly against the travellers, including his real father Laius, who tried to push him off the road at the triple junction between Thebes and Delphi. He certainly would not have killed them. If he had not been a man of searching intellect and sense of civic responsibility, he could never have solved the riddle of the supernatural Sphinx and released Thebes from servitude, thus meriting election to kingship of the very city of his birth and marriage to its queen. It is the same public spirit and curiosity which drives Oedipus on to solve the new riddle—who killed king Laius?—and thence to the discovery of the horrifying truth. The play's agonizingly slow accumulation of the 'facts' of the past simultaneously builds up a picture of Oedipus' egregious personality. The magisterial subtlety of Sophoclean characterization thus lends credibility to the breathtaking coincidences which led to his hero's unconscious breaching of fundamental taboos. Oedipus can only fulfil his exceptional god-ordained destiny because Oedipus is a pre-eminently capable and intelligent human being.

Electra

Sophocles' *Electra*, of whose numerous adaptations perhaps the most familiar today is Richard Strauss's searing opera *Elektra* (1909),[35] is the only surviving Sophoclean tragedy set at Mycenae, somewhat inaccurately conflated with another Peloponnesian city-state, Argos. The fortunes of the Argive dynasty were popular with the ancient dramatists: Aeschylus and Euripides, the other two great Athenian tragedians, portrayed their versions of the same myth in their *Libation Bearers* (458 BC, the second play of the *Oresteia*) and *Electra* (undated, though possibly earlier than Sophocles' play), respectively. The action of Sophocles' tragedy takes place on a day perhaps fifteen years after the king of the city, Agamemnon, returned from the Trojan war to be murdered by his wife Clytemnestra and her lover Aegisthus (also Agamemnon's first cousin), who had jointly usurped his power. The crisis awaiting resolution in this play is less political than domestic; Agamemnon and Clytemnestra's son Orestes, with his sister Electra's fullest co-operation, takes vengeance on his father's murderers by killing them in return.

The central question in the other two playwrights' versions of the story of Orestes' revenge is the justice of his actions. In Aeschylus' *Oresteia* he is pursued by his mother's vengeance spirits (known in Greek as 'Erinyes' though more familiar in their Latin guise as 'Furies'), but is eventually tried for the murder, and acquitted by Athena, who is carrying out the will of her father Zeus. In the torrid psychological world of Euripides, on the other hand, the two siblings decline into guilt, remorse, and misery. Yet Sophocles appears, on a superficial reading, to have put his individual stamp on the story by completely exonerating the matricide; there is no explicit prediction in the text that Orestes is to be hounded

---

[35] See P. E. Easterling, 'Electra's Story', in Derrick Puffett (ed.), *Richard Strauss: Elektra* (Cambridge, 1989), 10–16.

by the Erinyes, put on trial, or that he or Electra will suffer any consequences at all.

The play has therefore usually been seen as a morally uncomplicated vindication of the divine law that a death within the family must be punished by another death, and a fulfilment of the matricidal injunction given to Orestes by Apollo at Delphi. This view asserts that the play's focus is, rather, on the psychological disturbances undergone by Electra. Sophocles certainly found an effective dramatic vehicle in this remarkable figure, driven by deprivation and cruelty into near-psychotic extremes of behaviour; no other character in his extant dramas dominates the stage to such an extent. In contrast, Orestes seems two-dimensional. Sophocles seduces his audience into a quasi-voyeuristic enjoyment of Electra's obsession with the past, her despair, her anger, her embarrassingly demonstrative recognition of her brother and her correspondingly bloodthirsty exultation at the deaths of her persecutors.

This line of interpretation fails, however, to do justice to the irony and ambivalence of the play's comment on the ancient story. Electra's speech in her great debate with her mother, for example, throws up several hints that the play's ethics are not as simple as they seem. She is quite shockingly dismissive of her mother's claim that her murder of Agamemnon was an act of retribution for his sacrifice of their daughter Iphigeneia. She also articulates the principle of retributive killing, '*Blood in return for blood*' (p. 123); an attentive audience must realize that intra-familial murder, by this law, is bound to result in an endless cycle of violence down the generations. If Clytemnestra is killed, her blood too must ultimately be avenged. Sophocles even obliquely suggests candidates to take on this responsibility, by attributing children to her by Aegisthus; according to Electra's own principle, they must sooner or later avenge their own parents' deaths.

Even more sinister are the words of Aegisthus (unusually credited with prophetic powers), which reverberate around the theatre at the end of the play. Just before he enters the palace to his death, he enigmatically laments that it must 'behold | Death upon death, those now *and those to come*' (p. 155). Sophocles provides no solution to the contradictions inherent in the archaic system of reciprocal murder. He neither condemns nor condones the killing of Clytemnestra and Aegisthus. But he does ironically undermine the apparently complacent closure of his portrayal of this outstandingly familiar myth. Surely Nabokov was correct in commenting that the 'effect of a play cannot be final when it ends with murder'.[36]

Background

The texts seem to inhabit a time-warp between fifth-century Athens and the present. Since Aristotle, critics have stressed the universality of their meanings and the timelessness of their imports; but there are more rigorous ways of explaining their apparent modernity. One is to appeal to historical relativism. Every generation listens to the ancient world and hears new resonances in tune with its own contingent preoccupations; perhaps it is tragedy's very susceptibility to reinterpretation which lends it its aura of universality. Another approach is to concede that the influence of these archetypal dramas has actually allowed them to transcend history. They seem familiar precisely because they have been so consistently emulated. Despite the changes which have taken place in drama, the alterations in perspective which are connected with the historical contexts of its later practitioners, it remains umbilically attached to the ancient theatre. Greek tragedy has exerted such a profound influence on European aesthetic categories—often via its Latin adaptations by Seneca—that it has moulded all later drama. The great classical scholar Jean-Pierre Vernant compares the legacy of Greek thought. Philosophers must still use the vocabulary and types of argument which first took shape in ancient Greece; similarly, subsequent western dramatists have not been able to avoid locating themselves, whether by

---

[36] Quoted in Richard Reid (ed.), *Elektra: A Play by Ezra Pound and Rudd Fleming* (Princeton, NJ, 1989), p. xiii.

imitation or rejection, in or against a tradition founded by the playwrights of classical Athens.[37]

Recent criticism has, however, tried to scrape off the barnacles of meaning with which reinterpretation and their status as Classics have encrusted these texts, and to relocate them in their own time and place.[38] However powerful their impact may still be, the social structures implicit within them to a varying degree have vanished from western experience.

Tragedy was invented in Athens a few decades before the birth of Sophocles. Albert Camus said that a necessary condition for the production of tragedy was a time of transition 'between a sacred society and a society built by man',[39] and in the case of Athenian tragedy this perception is strikingly apposite. The rise of tragedy coincided historically with the Athenian democratic revolution. Rich and prominent families were forced by a series of uprisings and reforms, notably those of Cleisthenes in 508 BC, to transfer much of their power to the body of Athenian citizens. The central institution of pre-democratic Athens had been the extended family; with the rise of the democracy the claims of the state, the collective citizenship, began to challenge the claims of blood-kinship. With this radical change in the political and social situation there had to come changes in the values, ideas, and ideals of the community. As the notion of the citizen was forced into the centre of the conceptual universe, as the natural rights of the aristocracy to ascendancy began to be questioned, so the archaic religious imperatives were increasingly eroded and humanity took central place on the intellectual and ideological stage. Democracy was a man-made political order; the Athenians became increasingly aware of their own power to create their own destiny. Some thinkers even began to question, if not the existence of

---

[37] Jean-Pierre Vernant, 'The Tragic Subject: Historicity and Transhistoricity', in Vernant and Vidal-Naquet (n. 3 above), 237–47.

[38] An approach exemplified by the essays in John J. Winkler and Froma Zeitlin (eds.), *Nothing to do with Dionysos? Athenian Drama in its Social Context* (Princeton, NJ, 1990).

[39] Albert Camus, *Selected Essays and Notebooks*, trans. P. Thody (Harmondsworth, 1970), 199.

the gods, then certainly their power to affect human life: Protagoras, for example, a philosopher working in Athens, whose ideas have come down to us in the form of a Platonic dialogue named after him, famously declared that man was the measure of all things. He traced the evolution of human-kind from the status of victim of nature to master of nature, in a linear progression towards the civilization of the demo-cratic city-state—an idea which seems to have influenced Sophocles and finds expression in the great second choral ode of *Antigone*, 'Wonders are many, yet of all | Things is Man the most wonderful' (p. 13).

see also Adorno the Enlighten

Tragedy was enacted before the collective body of Athenian citizens; it examined the religious and ethical problems to which the new socio-political order had given rise, albeit through the mediated symbolic language of archaic myth. The kings and queens whose crises it represents are con-fronted with problems directly related to those facing the Athenian democracy; the conflicts enacted crystallize tensions underlying Athenian life.[40] Sophoclean tragedy repeatedly portrays the clash between the archaic family-centred order and the secular pragmatism of the new citizen. Creon can decree what 'human' edicts he will, but Antigone, who is obsessively aware of the nobility of her lineage and her special status as an aristocrat, is interested only in protecting her family's interests and the antique canons of religion. Oedipus, however talented a human being, cannot elude his divinely ordained destiny. Orestes fulfils his archaic duty in murdering his father's murderer, but the audience of the tragedy was well aware that in its own society aristocratic blood feuds were not immune to the jurisdiction of the state, and that Orestes would himself have been tried for murder by a democratically selected jury of ordinary citizens.

The economic system underpinning the famous Athenian democracy was slavery; the producers of raw materials, of arms and artefacts, the labourers who sweated to create the Athenians' wealth and build their buildings, were, for the

[40] See Jean-Pierre Vernant, 'The Historical Moment of Tragedy in Greece', in Vernant and Vidal-Naquet (n. 3 above), 23–8.

most part, slaves. And in the mythical pasts of Thebes and Argos Sophocles assumes the existence of the uncrossable social boundary dividing slave and free. One ground on which Antigone defends burying Polyneices is that it was not some slave, but a brother, who had died (p. 19); Oedipus wants to know who his mother was, even if she was a third-generation slave (p. 85); Electra's plight is that, although a princess, she is dressed, fed, and treated like a slave (p. 110). The expectations of women implied in these plays similarly reflect the dominant ideology of Sophoclean Athens, a city-state in which women were nearly silenced in public discourse, excluded from political institutions, and remained legally under the guardianship of a male, usually a father or husband, throughout their lives.[41] Respectable women of the citizen class were married at an early age, and exemplary paragons of wifehood remained at home as inconspicuously as possible. Sophocles' contemporary and friend, the Athenian statesman Pericles, is supposed to have said, 'the greatest glory of a woman is to be least talked about by men, whether in praise or in criticism' (Thucydides 2. 46). Eurydice, Creon's enigmatic wife in *Antigone*, nearly fits the template of the perfect wife. She is never mentioned, either in praise or in criticism, until her appearance nine-tenths of the way through the play. In the end she makes a single defiant gesture of self-assertion, in stabbing herself to death in her grief for her sons and her anger at her husband, but at no point has she disrupted the male world of city-state management in which women should not intervene. For her husband is present, and it is a generic convention with profound social significance that women in Greek tragedy rarely become vocally or actively transgressive except in the physical absence of their male guardians.

The Greeks, moreover, believed that after puberty women were prone to both physical and psychic disorders, and could become social liabilities until, on marriage, their conduct came under the regulation of legitimate husbands. Antigone and Electra are both fatherless virgins of marriageable age,

[41] See in general R. Just, *Women in Athenian Law and Life* (London, 1989).

and their obstreperous conduct is not to be dissociated from this socio-sexual status. Antigone openly flouts the authority of her nearest surviving male relative, Creon. Electra, it is stressed, would not be wandering about outside the palace were Aegisthus, her stepfather, present to keep her in a woman's rightful place: indoors, unseen, and unheard.[42]

An aspect of the world portrayed in Sophoclean drama totally alien to the modern western mind, conditioned by monotheistic and messianic faiths, is its pluralist theology. This becomes much easier to approach if it is appreciated that there is always a specific reason why a particular deity is singled out for mention.[43] Classical Greek polytheism attributed to its gods, for example, discrete topographical areas of influence. Dionysus is praised in the sixth choral ode of *Antigone*, and Ares the war god is prominent in *Oedipus the King*, because they were the recipients of important cults in the city-state of Thebes, where these two plays are set, just as Athena was central to Athenian religion. Similarly, the prologue to *Electra* draws attention to the nearby temple of Hera, who was from earliest times the tutelary deity of the city where the action takes place.

The gods also had separate spheres of practical competence and responsibility which transcended the geographical boundaries of these local city-state cults. Hera was goddess of Argos, but also of marriage, an institution whose defilement by adultery and murder is the topic of *Electra*. Zeus, as the father of the gods and senior male Olympian, is everywhere ultimately responsible for the Unwritten Laws

---

[42] Sophoclean women are discussed by R. P. Winnington-Ingram, 'Sophocles and women', in *Sofocle, Entretiens sur l'antiquité classique*, vol. xix (Fondation Hardt, Geneva, 1983), 233–49, and S. Wiersma, 'Women in Sophocles', *Mnemosyne* xxxvii (1984) 25–55. On the relation between the portrayal of women in tragedy and the realities of life for women in classical Athens see John Gould, 'Law, Custom and Myth: Aspects of the Social Position of Women in Classical Athens', *Journal of Hellenic Studies* c (1980), 39–59, and H. P. Foley, 'The Conception of Women in Athenian Drama', in H. P. Foley (ed.), *Reflections of Women in Antiquity* (New York, 1981), 127–68.

[43] See Walter Burkert, *Greek Religion: Archaic and Classical* (Oxford, 1985), especially ch. 3, and Jon D. Mikalson, *Honor thy Gods: Popular Religion in Greek Tragedy* (North Carolina, 1992).

and the punishment of those who transgress them. Sitting on a tripod at Apollo's panhellenic cult centre at Delphi, his priestess absorbed vapours and expressed them as oracles to visitors from all over the Greek world, and both *Oedipus the King* and *Electra* prove the veracity of her utterances. But Apollo was a god of healing as much as of prophecy, and it is to this aspect of his divine personality that the plague-ridden Thebans appeal in *Oedipus the King* (pp. 54–5).

Another feature liable to estrange the modern reader is the prominence of the chorus, which can seem intrusive and irrelevant. Yet it was from a form of ritual choral song, in honour of Dionysus, that tragedy almost certainly first evolved (Aristotle, *Poetics*, ch. 6); to the ancient audience the choral songs were highlights of a tragedy. Although in the classical period the role of the chorus was beginning to diminish, in Sophocles it remains central to the intellectual, religious, ethical, and emotional impact of the plays.[44] He was so admired for his skilful handling of the chorus that antiquity ascribed to him a (lost or apocryphal) prose treatise on the subject. The chorus, always an anonymous collective, is an intermediary between actors and audience; it is simultaneously a spectator of the action and deeply affected by it. Occasionally it even intervenes actively within it: in *Antigone* it is in consultation with the chorus of Theban elders that Creon decides (too late) to relent and release his niece (pp. 38–9). Aristotle commends such organic participation in the action by Sophocles' choruses (*Poetics*, ch. 19).

A dramatist made a crucial choice in the identity of his chorus. The political significance of the principals' actions is emphasized in both *Antigone* and *Oedipus the King* by the selection of male Theban citizens, for the audience is invited to interpret the events from the perspective of the civic community; it is emotionally important, however, that Sophocles selected a chorus of older women to consort with Electra. Their tender parental attitude towards her, and her depen-

---

[44] For detailed studies of Sophocles' use of the chorus see R. W. B. Burton, *The Chorus in Sophocles' Tragedies* (Oxford, 1980), and C. P. Gardiner, *The Sophoclean Chorus: A Study of Character and Function* (Iowa City, 1987).

dence on them, are comments on her psychological isolation and estrangement from her own natural mother.

The chorus performed an important role in dramaturgical terms, providing the playwright with a means of filling in the necessary time while the three available actors changed costume, mask, and role behind the scenes, and describing or responding to unseen events taking place inside.[45] Sometimes a chorus may sing a transparently hymn-like religious song, appropriate to the emotions of the moment, which has clear roots in one of the ritual genres of archaic choral performance. Examples are the first odes of both *Antigone* (a song of thanksgiving for military victory and salvation, pp. 6–8) and *Oedipus the King* (a prayer summoning the assistance of numerous gods in the face of plague and catastrophe, pp. 54–5).

In Sophocles' hands, however, the chorus transcended such formal restraints and conventions of the genre. It is in the choral odes that the finest poetry is often found and the most illuminating perspectives on the individuals' activities expressed. The chorus complements the action and often guides the audience's responses; it uses a lyric register and an elevated poetic idiom with a tendency towards the articulation of proverbial wisdom. In *Antigone*, for example, the chorus concludes the scene in which Haemon tries to save his betrothed by musing on the potentially destructive power of sexual passion (p. 28). It can guess at the future or recount events prior to the action of the play, as the chorus of *Electra* predicts the murder of Clytemnestra and traces her death to the origins of the family curse (pp. 120–1). It illuminates experiences by drawing mythical parallels: when Antigone has been led from the stage to her death by entombment within a cave, the chorus adduces several examples of other heroic figures of myth who endured some form of incarceration (pp. 33–5). Often a choral song meditates in a generalizing manner on the scene which directly precedes it. At the climactic moment when the truth has been revealed in

---

[45] On Sophoclean stagecraft see O. Taplin, 'Sophocles in his Theatre', in *Sofocle* (n. 42 above), 155–74.

Oedipus the King, the chorus sings a great ode, 'Alas! You generations of men', reflecting on the mutability of human fortune and the transience of wealth and power (p. 91); indeed, in this play the chorus provides something approaching an abstract metaphysical commentary on the issues raised by the specific events they are witnessing.

The least recoverable aspect of ancient tragedy is its performative dimension. This has been signally underestimated ever since Aristotle, who read tragedies as much as he watched them, and relegated music and spectacle to last place in his catalogue of the elements of tragedy (*Poetics*, ch. 6): the popular image of a sombre recitation of eternal verities by static sages from white-columned porticoes is a post-classical fantasy. The scenery and costumes were vibrant with forgotten colour; Sophocles is supposed to have been the first playwright to use painted scenery (Aristotle, *Poetics*, ch. 4), and contemporary vase-paintings can offer faint clues as to the appearance of the costumes and masks.[46] The chorus danced in steps and postures of which we understand little; large portions of the plays were sung to music at which we can scarcely guess.[47] Tragedy was not only a cerebral genre, but 'an astounding aural and visual experience' (Plutarch, *de gloria Athenarum* 348 BC). Our legacy, however, amounts to little more than the words on these printed pages. The reader must usually reconstruct in imagination the extra dramatic meanings and nuances which the visual and musical dimensions lent to a play, although it is occasionally apparent that Sophocles used props with devastating precision. In *Electra*, for example, they appropriately link its morbid main character firmly with the dead: they include the funeral urn in which she believes her brother's ashes are incinerated, her own virginal girdle, which she dedicates to her dead father's memory, his signet ring, and the funeral shroud veiling her murdered mother's face.[48]

---

[46] Pickard-Cambridge (n. 7 above), 190–204.

[47] See Pickard-Cambridge (n. 7 above), 257–62; M. L. West, *Ancient Greek Music* (Oxford, 1992), especially 350–5.

[48] D. Seale, *Vision and Stagecraft in Sophocles* (London, 1982), discusses the visual dimension of Sophoclean tragedy.

The Translator

The translations are the work of Humphrey Davy Findley Kitto (1897–1982), perhaps the last of the English romantic philhellenes; at his funeral no god was allowed to be mentioned except those of the classical pantheon, and the readings were taken from his own translations, reproduced here, of choral odes from *Antigone*. Kitto was one of the most idiosyncratic, yet influential, twentieth-century authorities on Greek tragedy. He was educated at the Crypt Grammar School, Gloucester, and, after rejection from military service (his eyesight was dreadful), at St John's College, Cambridge. He taught at the University of Glasgow from 1921 to 1944, and was then appointed Professor of Greek at the University of Bristol, where he remained until his retirement in 1962, the year in which these translations were first published by Oxford University Press.[49]

He is best known for his books on tragic drama— *Greek Tragedy: A Literary Study* (London, 1939), *Sophocles: Dramatist and Philosopher* (London, 1958), *Form and Meaning in Drama: A Study of Six Greek Plays and of Hamlet* (London, 1956), and *Poiesis: Structure and Thought* (Berkeley, 1966). He also wrote an introductory study to ancient Hellas, *The Greeks* (London, 1951), which is still widely read. His romantic apprehension of Greece emerges from his account of a walking holiday he took there, published under the title *In the Mountains of Greece* (London, 1933). It conveys the inspiration he took from ancient sites (Sparta, Olympia, and the temple of Apollo at Bassae), and contains many allusions to ancient authors, especially his beloved Sophocles.

Kitto was fanatically committed to theatre, and was partially responsible for the establishment of the important Chair of Drama at the University of Bristol in 1947. The Classics and Drama departments there used annually to collaborate in productions of Greek plays; oral tradition

[49] For an appreciation of Kitto's life and work see N. G. L. Hammond's memoir in *Proceedings of the British Academy*, lxi (1982), 585–90.

records his own memorable performance, suspended from a basket, in the role of the eccentric philosopher Socrates in a production in 1962 of Aristophanes' comedy *The Clouds*. It is touching to note that his outstanding translations of *Antigone* and *Electra* were written for these modest amateur performances. Kitto attended rehearsals, revising the English as he heard it delivered, which helps to account for the satisfying fluency and sheer performability of his translations; with his wife he composed the original musical scores. The Library at Bristol University retains a photograph of the first production of Kitto's version of *Antigone* in May 1951; the *Electra* followed it in 1955. *Oedipus the King* was translated for performance by the local Classical Association in the late 1950s.

The Translations

The ancient critic Dio Chrysostom described Sophocles' verse as 'dignified and grand, tragic and euphonius to the highest degree, combining great charm with sublimity and dignity' (*Oration* 52). It is also remarkable for its lapidary precision and its imagery, which is simultaneously muscular, subtle, and economical. Conveying such qualities in another language represents an astonishing challenge. Unusually for an academic, Kitto was a fine poet, and his translations are notable for their lucidity, accuracy, and vigour. His lifelong passion for Shakespearean drama bears rich fruit in his rendering of Sophocles' standard Attic iambics of the speeches and dialogue into the graceful iambic pentameters of English blank verse.

But Greek tragedy was an inclusive genre, alternating spoken iambic sections with dance and song, accompanied by pipe music, in numerous complicated metres.[50] Kitto's translation succeeds in the ambitious project of reproducing in lyrics some of the effects of the elaborate shifts and changes in the original metres of the musical sections. They comprise both choral song and passages in which individual characters sing either on their own or antiphonally in response to the chorus. This important aspect of tragedy, far from being a matter simply of technical formality, has been disastrously neglected in most modern translations. For a poet's choice of song or speech for a particular section can, especially in performance, radically affect its impact. Song is a mark of social status: besides the chorus, only royal individuals (as opposed to guards, messengers, and servants) are awarded the privilege. But when characters sing, it also signifies drastically heightened emotion. Antigone sings her own funeral lament (pp. 29–31); when Oedipus emerges blinded from his palace, he expresses his agony in song (pp. 94–6); the actor who played Electra needed to be vocally gifted, for she frequently resorts to the musical medium to articulate her fluctuating feelings.

Metrical authenticity is ultimately unattainable in translation from ancient Greek, not least because its metres were shaped by vowel length and, not, as in English verse, by accentual stress. This edition therefore simply marks those sections of the tragedies which are thought to have been either sung or chanted (depending on the nature of the metre) rather than spoken. Speech is the correct medium unless otherwise indicated.

The basic rhythmic unit of sung sections, whether delivered by the chorus alone, or by a character or characters, or antiphonally by both chorus and characters, often comprises a pair of stanzas metrically (and originally no doubt melodically) corresponding with each other (AA). Sometimes more than one pair of such corresponding stanzas is accumulated sequentially, producing an overall metrical pattern AABB, or even AABBCC. The tragic chorus danced as it sang, and is believed to have marked the end of each stanza by some kind of physical turn, perhaps to face the opposite side of the circular dancing area (*orchēstra*). The two parts of each pair thus came to be known traditionally by the Greek terms *strophē* ('turn'), and *antistrophē* ('counter-turn'), respectively. Some antistrophic sung sections conclude with the addition of a metrically independent *epōdē* ('after-song'), which gives

[50] See A. M. Dale, *The Lyric Metres of Greek Drama*[2] (Cambridge, 1968).

a pattern, for example in the second choral section of *Electra*, of AAB (pp. 120–1). This feature of the original Greek lyric verse, important in performance, has been conveyed particularly well by Kitto's translation, and so the present edition has retained the labels in the sung sections marking each stanza as a 'strophe', 'antistrophe', or 'epode'.

Kitto's renderings compress the plays into fewer metrical lines than are contained in the Greek texts of Sophocles now in use; they all adopt the same standard system of numeration. The line numbering in this edition therefore marks not the lines of the translation itself, but those of the standard Greek texts. This is intended to enable the user to compare the translation with others, or with the original Greek, or quickly to locate passages discussed in secondary criticism. When an article or book cites, for example, '*Electra*, lines 820–2', it will certainly be using the same orthodox numerical system as this volume.

No authentic stage directions survive from the ancient world. The text therefore marks only exits, entrances, and the few other actions and gestures that can be indisputably inferred from the spoken words.

Spelling and Pronunciation

Any translation of a Greek author must address the problem presented by the spelling of proper names. Established usage has made many of the ancient Greek mythical names familiar in either Latinized or Anglicized forms. Although it is becoming increasingly fashionable to present proper names in a faithful transliteration from the Greek (rendering the familiar 'Clytemnestra' as 'Klutaimnēstra', for example), it can alienate the reader or listener who is not conversant with the ancient language. In the interests of euphony and intelligibility, Kitto wisely chose, therefore, an unashamed mixture of transliterated Greek ('Phokis'), Latinized forms where they are extremely familiar ('Oedipus' rather than 'Oidipous', and 'Laius' rather than 'Laios'), English renderings where anything else would jar on the modern ear (notably 'Thebes' and 'Athens' rather than 'Thēbai' and 'Athēnai'), and his own hybrid mixture of Greek and English in the instance of Iocasta, traditionally Anglicized as 'Jocasta' but actually *Iokastē* in Greek.

Pronunciation of ancient proper names presents a related problem. Here I have taken the liberty of reproducing a slightly adapted version of Kitto's own sensible note in the original edition: '*Ch* should always be made hard, unless an aspirated *k* (as in *loch*) is preferred. The diphthong *ae* is the Latinization of *ai*; pronunciation in English varies between a long *e* ("see") and *i* (as in *high*). *Oe* regularly becomes the long *e*, and final *eus* rhymes with *deuce*.'[51] I would add that the final vowel *e*, common in feminine proper names (Antigone, Ismene, and Danae, for example), is always long. The letter *c* is often used in place of the Greek *k* (as in *Polyneices* and *Mycenae*), and many prefer to pronounce it inauthentically like the English *s*.

The Explanatory Notes

These have been kept as simple as possible. I have tried to elucidate mythical and topographical references which might be unfamiliar to the modern reader and to explain terminology relating to obscure ancient Greek beliefs, customs, religion, and ritual. Where there is significant dispute as to the text of the original Greek, it has been noted. I have also indicated points where Kitto's translation, although in the main faithful to the original, omits, paraphrases, or adds to features present in the Greek, especially where it could affect interpretation of the plays; an important example is his omission of the seven lines which in the manuscripts conclude *Oedipus the King* (see p. 101 with note). The attribution of lines to different characters, obviously crucial to the interpretation of a passage, is also sometimes questionable. Where there is significant doubt, it has been registered (see especially p. 21 with notes).

---

[51] *Sophocles: Three Tragedies* (Oxford, 1962), 154.

NOTE ON THE TEXTS

THE first authoritative text of Sophocles' plays was established in the century after he lived by the Athenian statesman Lycurgus (see [Plutarch], *Lives of the Ten Orators* 841–2). Alexandrian scholars in Hellenistic Egypt assembled a fairly comprehensive library of Sophoclean texts and scholarship, but by the time of the Byzantines, who were the conduit through which the MSS of Sophoclean drama reached Renaissance Europe and eventually their first printed edition (Venice, 1502),[1] only seven complete tragedies—those we now possess—survived.

An obstacle in the path of any editor of Sophocles' Greek text is the unreliability of the MSS, which are approximately 200 in number.[2] Although one tenth-century MS in Florence, the Laurentianus 32.9, is generally agreed to be the most important, any editor of the Greek text faces a bewildering variety of alternative readings, omissions, and interpolations. Kitto, as a translator, did not normally refer to the MSS, but selected readings from three texts of the Greek which were then available to him. First, the magisterial editions of Richard Jebb, whose *Antigone* was first published by Cambridge University Press in 1888 (3rd edn. 1900), *Oedipus* in 1883 (3rd edn. 1893), and *Electra* in 1894. These volumes include detailed commentaries and faithful prose translations to which Kitto is at many times indebted. The second Greek edition he used was A. C. Pearson's Oxford Classical Text, *Sophoclis Fabulae*, first published in 1924 (corrected edn. 1928). The last was the Budé edition, with French translation, by A. Dain and P. Mazon (Paris, 1955–60).

Those equipped with ancient Greek who wish to consult

---

[1] See L. D. Reynolds and N. G. Wilson, *Scribes and Scholars: A Guide to the Transmission of Greek and Latin Literature* (Oxford, 1968), 129–32.

[2] For a discussion see Alexander Turyn, *Studies in the Manuscript Tradition of the Tragedies of Sophocles* (Urbana, Ill., 1952).

the original Sophoclean texts of the plays should be aware that since the first publication in 1962 of Kitto's translation, two important new editions of the Greek text have appeared which supersede those mentioned above: R. D. Dawe's Teubner text (2nd edn. Leipzig, 1984–5), and the new Oxford Classical Text, *Sophoclis Fabulae*, by H. Lloyd-Jones and Nigel Wilson (1990).

SELECT BIBLIOGRAPHY

THIS list largely avoids works in languages other than English. For a comprehensive general survey of Sophoclean studies until 1959 the reader is directed to H. F. Johansen, 'Sophocles 1939–1959', *Lustrum* vii (1962), 94–288. S. Said updates this to 1988 in *Théâtre grec et tragique* (= *Métis* iii. 1–2, Paris, 1988), 416–18 and 468–84.

(1) *Editions and Commentaries*

Jebb's seminal commentaries (Cambridge, 1883 onwards, see above, p. xxxviii) are still mines of fascinating information. All of Sophocles' tragedies have more recently been treated to detailed commentaries in English (without text or translation) by J. C. Kamerbeek, including *Oedipus* (Leiden, 1967), *Electra* (Leiden, 1974), and *Antigone* (Leiden, 1978). Other important modern commentaries on individual plays include A. L. Brown, *Sophocles: Antigone* (Warminster, 1987), R. D. Dawe, *Sophocles' Oedipus Rex* (Cambridge, 1982), J. H. Kells, *Sophocles' Electra* (Cambridge, 1973), P. E. Easterling, *Sophocles' Trachiniae* (Cambridge, 1982), W. B. Stanford, *Sophocles' Ajax* (London, 1963), and T. B. L. Webster, *Sophocles' Philoctetes* (Cambridge, 1970). The standard edition of the fragments of Sophocles is S. Radt's *Tragicorum Graecorum Fragmenta* iv (Berlin, 1977), although A. C. Pearson's three-volume edition, *The Fragments of Sophocles* (Cambridge, 1917), is still useful.

(2) *General Studies*

C. M. Bowra, *Sophoclean Tragedy* (Oxford, 1944); R. G. A. Buxton, *Sophocles* (*Greece & Rome*, New Surveys in the Classics, xvi (Oxford, 1984). H. Diller (ed.), *Sophokles* (*Wege der Forschung* xcv, Darmstadt, 1967); G. H. Gellie, *Sophocles: A Reading* (Melbourne, 1972); G. M. Kirkwood, *A Study of Sophoclean Drama* (Ithaca, 1958); H. D. F. Kitto, *Sophocles: Dramatist and Philosopher* (London, 1958); B. M. W. Knox, *The Heroic Temper: Studies in Sophoclean Tragedy* (Berkeley/Los Angeles, 1964); K. Reinhardt, *Sophocles* (Eng. trans. Oxford, 1979); C. P. Segal, *Tragedy and Civilization: An Interpretation of Sophocles* (Cambridge, Mass., 1981); *Sofocle, Entretiens sur l'antiquité classique* xix (Fondation Hardt, Geneva, 1983); R. M. Torrance, 'Sophocles: Some Bearings',

Harvard Studies in Classical Philology lxix (1965), 269–327; A. J. A. Waldock, *Sophocles the Dramatist* (Cambridge, 1951); T. B. L. Webster, *An Introduction to Sophocles*[2] (London, 1969); C. Whitman, *Sophocles: A Study in Heroic Humanism* (Cambridge, Mass., 1951); R. P. Winnington-Ingram, *Sophocles: An Interpretation* (Cambridge, 1980); T. Woodard (ed.), *Sophocles: A Collection of Critical Essays* (Englewood Cliffs, 1966).

(3) *Specific Aspects*

M. W. Blundell, *Helping Friends and Harming Enemies: A Study in Sophocles and Greek Ethics* (Cambridge, 1989); R. W. B. Burton, *The Chorus in Sophocles' Tragedies* (Oxford, 1980); R. G. A. Buxton, 'Blindness and Limits: Sophokles and the Logic of Myth', *Journal of Hellenic Studies* c (1980), 22–37; P. E. Easterling, 'Character in Sophocles', *Greece & Rome* xxiv (1977), 121–9; V. Ehrenberg, *Sophocles and Pericles* (Oxford, 1954); G. H. Gellie, 'Motivation in Sophocles', *Bulletin of the Institute of Classical Studies* xi (1694), 1–14; C. P. Gardiner, *The Sophoclean Chorus: A Study of Character and Function* (Iowa City, 1987); A. E. Hinds, 'Binary Action in Sophocles', *Hermathena* cxxix (1980), 51–7; A. O. Hulton, 'The Prologues of Sophocles', *Greece & Rome* xvi (1969), 49–59; G. M. Kirkwood, 'The Dramatic Role of the Chorus in Sophocles', *Phoenix* xiii (1954), 1–22; H. D. F. Kitto, 'The Idea of God in Aeschylus and Sophocles', in H. J. Rose (ed.), *La Notion du divin* (Berne, 1955), 169–89; A. A. Long, *Language and Thought in Sophocles* (London, 1968); J. C. Opstelten, *Sophocles and Greek Pessimism* (Eng. trans. Amsterdam, 1952); D. Seale, *Vision and Stagecraft in Sophocles* (London, 1982); O. Taplin, 'Lyric Dialogue and Dramatic Construction in Later Sophocles', *Dioniso* lv (1984–5), 115–22; S. Wiersma, 'Women in Sophocles', *Mnemosyne* xxxvii (1984), 25–55.

(4) *Other books including interesting discussions of Sophocles*

J. P. Euben (ed.), *Greek Tragedy and Political Theory* (Berkeley, Calif., 1986); John Jones, *On Aristotle and Greek Tragedy* (London, 1962); Bernard Knox, *Word and Action: Essays on the Ancient Theater* (Baltimore/London 1979); J.-P. Vernant and P. Vidal-Naquet, *Myth and Tragedy in Ancient Greece* (Eng. trans. New York, 1988).

(5) *Antigone*

S. Bernadete, 'A Reading of Sophocles' *Antigone*', *Interpretation: A Journal of Political Philosophy* iv (1975), 148–96; v (1975), 1–55 and 148–84; W. M. Calder, 'Sophocles' Political Tragedy: *Antigone*', *Greek, Roman and Byzantine Studies* ix (1968), 389–407; R. Coleman, 'The Role of the Chorus in Sophocles' *Antigone*', *Proceedings of the Cambridge Philological Society* xviii (1972), 4–27; P. E. Easterling, 'The Second Stasimon of Sophocles' *Antigone*', in R. D. Dawe, J. Diggle, and P. E. Easterling (eds.), *Dionysiaca* (Cambridge, 1978), 141–58; R. F. Goheen, *The Imagery of Sophocles'* Antigone (Princeton, NJ, 1951); D. A. Hester, 'Sophocles the Unphilosophical', *Mnemosyne* xxiv (1971), 11–59; J. C. Hogan, 'The Protagonists of the *Antigone*', *Arethusa* v (1972), 93–100; I. M. Linforth, 'Antigone and Creon', *University of California Publications in Classical Philology* xv (1961), 183–260; M. MacCall, 'Divine and Human Action in Sophocles: The Two Burials of the *Antigone*', *Yale Classical Studies* xxii (1972), 103–17; T.-C. Oudemans and A. P. M. H. Lardinois, *Tragic Ambiguity: Anthropology, Philosophy, and Sophocles'* Antigone (Leiden, 1987); V. Rosivach, 'On Creon, Antigone, and Not Burying the Dead', *Rheinisches Museum* cxxvi (1983), 16–26; M. Santirocco, 'Justice in Sophocles' *Antigone*', *Philosophy and Literature* iv (1980), 180–98.

(6) *Oedipus the King*

Rebecca W. Bushnell, *Prophesying Tragedy: Sign and Voice in Sophocles' Theban Plays* (Ithaca, NY, 1988); A. Cameron, *The Identity of Oedipus the King: Five Essays on the* Oedipus Tyrannus (New York, 1968); M. W. Champlin, '*Oedipus Tyrannus* and the problem of knowledge', *Classical Journal* lxiv (1969), 337–45; E. R. Dodds, 'On Misunderstanding the *Oedipus Rex*', in *Greece & Rome* xiii (1966), 37–49, repr. in his *The Ancient Concept of Progress* (Oxford, 1973), 64–77; P. W. Harsh, 'Implicit and Explicit in the *Oedipus Tyrannus*', *American Journal of Philology* lxxix (1958), 243–58; D. A. Hester, 'Oedipus and Jonah', *Proceedings of the Cambridge Philological Society* xxiii (1977), 32–61; H. P. Houghton, 'Jocasta in the *Oedipus Tyrannus*', *Euphrosyne* ii (1959), 3–28; B. M. W. Knox, *Oedipus at Thebes* (New Haven/London, 1957); M. J. O'Brien (ed.), *Twentieth-Century Interpretations of* Oedipus Rex (Englewood Cliffs, 1968); Pietro Pucci, 'The Tragic *Pharmakos* of the *Oedipus Rex*', *Helios* xvii (1990), 41–9; W. B.

SELECT BIBLIOGRAPHY

Stanford, 'Ambiguities in the *Oedipus Tyrannus*', in *Ambiguity in Greek Literature* (Oxford, 1939), 163–73.

(7) *Electra*

B. Alexanderson, 'On Sophocles' *Electra*', *Classica et Mediaevelia* xxvii (1966), 78–98; A. M. Dale, 'The *Electra* of Sophocles', in *Collected Papers* (Cambridge, 1969), 221–9; I. M. Linforth, 'Electra's Day in the Tragedy of Sophocles', *University of California Publications in Classical Philology* xix (1963), 89–125; R. W. Minadeo, 'Plot, Theme and Meaning in Sophocles' *Electra*', *Classica et Mediaevelia* xxviii (1967), 114–42; R. Seaford, 'The Destruction of Limits in Sophocles' *Elektra*', *Classical Quarterly* xxxv (1985), 315–23; C. P. Segal, 'The *Electra* of Sophocles', *Transaction and Proceedings of the American Philological Association* xcvii (1966), 473–545; J. T. Sheppard, 'The Tragedy of Electra According to Sophocles', *Classical Quarterly* xii (1918), 80–8; id., 'Electra: a Defence of Sophocles', *Classical Review* xli (1927), 2–9; F. Solmsen, *Electra and Orestes: Three Recognitions in Greek Tragedy* (Amsterdam, 1967); P. T. Stevens, 'Sophocles: *Elektra*, Doom or Triumph?', *Greece & Rome* xxv (1978), 111–20; T. M. Woodard, '*Electra* by Sophocles: The Dialectical Design', *Harvard Studies in Classical Philology* lxviii (1964), 163–205; lxx (1965), 195–233; Virginia Woolf, 'On Not Knowing Greek', in *The Common Reader* (London, 1925).

(8) *Reception*

For Sophocles' influence see Stuart Gillespie, *The Poets on the Classics: An Anthology of English Poets' Writings on the Classical Poets and Dramatists from Chaucer to the Present* (London/New York, 1988), 202–6; H. D. F. Kitto, 'The Vitality of Sophocles', in Whitney J. Oates (ed.), *From Sophocles to Picasso: The Present-Day Vitality of the Classical Tradition* (Bloomington, Ind., 1962), 39–67; A. T. Sheppard, *Aeschylus and Sophocles: Their Work and Influence* (= *Our Debt to Greece and Rome* xxiii, Boston, 1927). On the performance history of Sophocles' plays see Hellmut Flashar, *Inszenierung der Antike: Das griechische Drama auf der Bühne der Neuzeit 1585–1990* (Munich, 1991).

On the reception of *Antigone* see Simone Fraisse, *Le Mythe d'Antigone* (Paris, 1974); L. A. MacKay, 'Antigone, Coriolanus and Hegel', *Transactions and Proceedings of the American Philological Associ-*

ation xciii (1962), 166–74; A. and H. Paolucci (eds.), *Hegel on Tragedy* (New York, 1962); G. Steiner, *Antigones* (Oxford, 1984). On *Oedipus the King* see Colette Astier, *Le Mythe d'Oedipe* (Paris, 1974); L. Edmunds, *Oedipus: The Ancient Legend and its Later Analogues* (Baltimore, 1985); and B. Gentili and R. Pretagostini (eds.), *Edipo: il teatro greco e la cultura europea* (Rome, 1986). For *Electra* see Henriette Booneric, *La Famille des Atrides dans la littérature française* (Paris, 1986); Pierre Brunel, *Le Mythe d'Électre* (Paris, 1971); H.-J. Newiger, 'Hofmannsthals *Elektra* und die griechische Tragödie', *Arcadia* 4 (1969), 138–63; Brenda J. Powell, *The Metaphysical Quality of the Tragic: A Study of Sophocles, Giraudoux, and Sartre* (New York, 1990).

CHRONOLOGY
(all dates BC)

508	Cleisthenes' democratic reforms at Athens.
497–494	Birth of Sophocles.
480	Persians defeated at the battle of Salamis.
468	Sophocles' victory in first dramatic competition, defeating Aeschylus.
443/2	Sophocles holds office of Treasurer.
442?	*Antigone*?
441/0	Sophocles elected general in Samian campaign.
438	His victory in dramatic competition, defeating a group of plays by Euripides, including *Alcestis*.
431	Sophocles awarded second place in dramatic competition. The obscure Euphorion won first prize, and Euripides came last with plays including *Medea*. Outbreak of the Peloponnesian war.
420/19	Sophocles instals cult of Asclepius in his home.
413	Magistrate at Athens after defeat of Athenian expedition to Sicily.
409	Victory with *Philoctetes*.
406/5	Death.
404	Peloponnesian war ends with the defeat of Athens.
402/1	*Oedipus at Colonus* produced posthumously by Sophocles' grandson, also named Sophocles.

ANTIGONE

DRAMATIS PERSONAE

ANTIGONE, *daughter of Oedipus and Iocasta*
ISMENE, *her sister*
CREON, *King of Thebes, brother of Iocasta*
HAEMON, *his son*
A GUARD
TEIRESIAS, *a Seer*
MESSENGER
EURYDICE, *wife to Creon*
CHORUS *of Theban elders*
Guards, Attendants, etc.

Scene: Thebes, before the royal palace

Your - nid - jee

Poly - ree - sca

Is - many

ANTIGONE[1]

Enter, from the palace, ANTIGONE *and* ISMENE

ANTIGONE. Ismene, my own sister, dear Ismene,
  How many miseries our father caused!
  And is there one of them that does not fall
  On us while yet we live? Unhappiness,
  Calamity, disgrace, dishonour—which
  Of these have you and I not known? And now
  Again: there is the order which they say
  Brave Creon* has proclaimed to all the city.
  You understand? or do you not yet know
  What outrage threatens one of those we love?   10

ISMENE. Of them, Antigone, I have not heard
  Good news or bad—nothing, since we two sisters
  Were robbed of our two brothers on one day
  When each destroyed the other. During the night
  The enemy* has fled: so much I know,
  But nothing more, either for grief or joy.

can only hear news from men?

ANTIGONE. I knew it; therefore I have brought you
      here,
  Outside the doors, to tell you secretly.

ISMENE. What is it? Some dark shadow is upon you.   20

ANTIGONE. Our brother's burial.—Creon has ordained
  Honour for one, dishonour for the other.
  Eteocles, they say, has been entombed
  With every solemn rite and ceremony
  To do him honour in the world below;
  But as for Polyneices, Creon has ordered
  That none shall bury him* or mourn for him;
  He must be left to lie unwept, unburied,

---

[1] Verse lines are numbered according to the Greek text (see Introduction, p. xxxv).

3

For hungry birds of prey to swoop and feast
On his poor body. So he has decreed,   30
Our noble Creon, to all the citizens:
To you, to me. To me! And he is coming
To make it public here, that no one may
Be left in ignorance; nor does he hold it
Of little moment: he who disobeys
In any detail shall be put to death
By public stoning* in the streets of Thebes.
So it is now for you to show if you
Are worthy, or unworthy, of your birth.

ISMENE. O my poor sister! If it has come to this
What can I do, either to help or hinder?   40

ANTIGONE. Will you join hands with me and share my
    task?

ISMENE. What dangerous enterprise have you in mind?

ANTIGONE. Will you join me in taking up the body?

ISMENE. What? Would you bury him, against the law?

ANTIGONE. No one shall say *I* failed him! I will bury
    My brother—and yours too, if you will not.

ISMENE. You reckless girl! When Creon has forbidden?

ANTIGONE. He has no right to keep me from my own!

ISMENE. Think of our father, dear Antigone,
    And how we saw him die, hated and scorned,
    When his own hands had blinded his own eyes   50
    Because of sins which he himself disclosed;
    And how his mother-wife, two names in one,
    Knotted a rope, and so destroyed herself.*
    And, last of all, upon a single day
    Our brothers fought each other to the death
    And shed upon the ground the blood that joined
        them.
    Now you and I are left, alone; and think:
    If we defy the King's prerogative

4

And break the law, our death will be more shameful   60
Even than theirs. Remember too that we
Are women, not made to fight with men. Since they
Who rule us now are stronger far than we,
In this and worse than this we must obey them.
Therefore, beseeching pardon from the dead,*
Since what I do is done on hard compulsion,
I yield to those who have authority;
For useless meddling has no sense at all.

ANTIGONE. I will not urge you. Even if you should wish
To give your help I would not take it now.   70
Your choice is made. But I shall bury him.
And if I have to die for this pure crime,
I am content, for I shall rest beside him;
His love will answer mine. I have to please
The dead far longer than I need to please
The living; with them, I have to dwell for ever.
But you, if so you choose, you may dishonour
The sacred laws* that Heaven holds in honour.

ISMENE. I do them no dishonour, but to act
Against the city's will I am too weak.

ANTIGONE. Make that your pretext! I will go and heap   80
The earth upon the brother whom I love.

ISMENE. You reckless girl! I tremble for your life.

ANTIGONE. Look to yourself and do not fear for me.

ISMENE. At least let no one hear of it, but keep
Your purpose secret, and so too will I.

ANTIGONE. Go and denounce me! I shall hate you more
If you keep silent and do not proclaim it.

ISMENE. Your heart is hot upon a wintry work!

ANTIGONE. I know I please whom most I ought to
please.

ISMENE. But can you do it? It is impossible!   90

5

ANTIGONE. When I can do no more, then I will stop.

ISMENE. But why attempt a hopeless task at all?

ANTIGONE. O stop, or I shall hate you! He will hate
You too, for ever, justly. Let me be,
Me and my folly! I will face the danger
That so dismays you, for it cannot be
So dreadful as to die a coward's death.

ISMENE. Then go and do it, if you must. It is
Blind folly—but those who love you love you dearly.

[*Exeunt severally*

Strophe 1

CHORUS [*sings*]. Welcome, light of the Sun, the fairest   100
Sun that ever has dawned upon
Thebes, the city of seven gates!*
At last thou art arisen, great
Orb of shining day, pouring
Light across the gleaming water of Dirke.*
Thou hast turned into headlong flight,
Galloping faster and faster, the foe who
Bearing a snow-white shield* in full
Panoply came from Argos.

He* had come to destroy us, in Polyneices'   110
Fierce quarrel.* *He* brought them against our land;
And like some eagle* screaming his rage
From the sky he descended upon us,
With his armour about him, shining like snow,
    With spear upon spear,
And with plumes that swayed on their helmets.

Antistrophe 1 (Counter - Turn)

Close he hovered above our houses,
Circling around our seven gates, with
Spears that thirsted to drink our blood.
He's gone! gone before ever his jaws

6

Snapped on our flesh, before he sated   120
Himself with our blood, before his blazing fire-brand
Seized with its fire our city's towers.
Terrible clangour of arms repelled him,
Driving him back, for hard it is to
Strive with the sons of a Dragon.*

For the arrogant boast of an impious man
Zeus hateth exceedingly. So, when he saw
This army advancing in swollen flood
In the pride of its gilded equipment,   130
He struck them down from the rampart's edge
    With a fiery bolt*
In the midst of their shout of 'Triumph!'

Strophe 2

Heavily down to the earth did he fall, and lie there,
He who with torch in his hand and possessed with
        frenzy*
    Breathed forth bitterest hate
    Like some fierce tempestuous wind.
        So it fared then with him;
And of the rest, each met his own terrible doom,
Given by the great War-god,* our deliverer.   140
Seven foemen* appointed to our seven gates
Each fell to a Theban, and Argive arms
Shall grace our Theban temple of Zeus:*
Save two, those two of unnatural hate,
Two sons of one mother, two sons of one King;
They strove for the crown, and shared with the
        sword
Their estate, each slain by his brother.

Antistrophe 2

Yet do we see in our midst, and acclaim with
        gladness,
Victory, glorious Victory,* smiling, welcome.
    Now, since danger is past,

7

Thoughts of war shall pass from our minds.   150
    Come! let all thank the gods,
Dancing before temple and shrine all through the
    night,
Following Thee, Theban Dionysus.*

CHORUS. But here comes Creon, the new king of
    Thebes,
In these new fortunes that the gods have given us.
What purpose is he furthering, that he   160
Has called this gathering of his Counsellors?

Suspense function

    Enter CREON, *attended*

CREON. My lords: for what concerns the state, the gods
Who tossed it on the angry surge of strife
Have righted it again; and therefore you
By royal edict I have summoned here,
Chosen from all our number. I know well
How you revered the throne of Laius;*
And then, when Oedipus maintained our state,
And when he perished, round his sons you rallied,
Still firm and steadfast in your loyalty.
Since they have fallen by a double doom   170
Upon a single day, two brothers each
Killing the other with polluted sword,*
I now possess the throne and royal power
By right of nearest kinship* with the dead.
    There is no art that teaches us to know
The temper, mind or spirit of any man
Until he has been proved by government
And lawgiving. A man who rules a state
And will not ever steer the wisest course,
But is afraid, and says not what he thinks,   180
That man is worthless; and if any holds
A friend of more account than his own city,
I scorn him; for if I should see destruction
Threatening the safety of my citizens,
I would not hold my peace, nor would I count
That man my friend who was my country's foe,

(Zeus be my witness.)For be sure of this:
It is the city that protects us all;
She bears us through the storm; only when she
Rides safe and sound can we make loyal friends.   190
    This I believe, and thus will I maintain
Our city's greatness.—Now, conformably,
Of Oedipus' two sons I have proclaimed
This edict: he who in his country's cause
Fought gloriously and so laid down his life,
Shall be entombed and graced with every rite
That men can pay to those who die with honour;
But for his brother, him called Polyneices,
Who came from exile to lay waste his land,
To burn the temples of his native gods,   200
To drink his kindred blood,* and to enslave
The rest, I have proclaimed to Thebes that none
Shall give him funeral honours or lament him,
But leave him there unburied, to be devoured
By dogs and birds, mangled most hideously.
Such is my will; never shall I allow
The villain to win more honour than the upright;
But any who show love to this our city
In life and death alike shall win my praise.   210

CHORUS. Such is your will, my lord; so you requite
    Our city's champion and our city's foe.
    You, being sovereign, make what laws you will
    Both for the dead and those of us who live.

CREON. See then that you defend the law now made.

CHORUS. No, lay that burden on some younger men.

CREON. I have appointed guards to watch the body.

CHORUS. What further charge, then, do you lay on us?

CREON. Not to connive at those that disobey me.
CHORUS. None are so foolish as to long for death.   220

CREON. Death is indeed the price, but love of gain
    Has often lured a man to his destruction.

Enter a GUARD

GUARD. My lord: I cannot say that I am come
  All out of breath with running. More than once
  I stopped and thought and turned round in my path
  And started to go back. My mind had much
  To say to me. One time it said 'You fool!
  Why do you go to certain punishment?'
  Another time 'What? Standing still, you wretch?
  You'll smart for it, if Creon comes to hear
  From someone else.' And so I went along   230
  Debating with myself, not swift nor sure.
  This way, a short road soon becomes a long one.
  At last this was the verdict: I must come
  And tell you. It may be worse than nothing; still,
  I'll tell you. I can suffer nothing more
  Than what is in my fate. There is my comfort!

CREON. And what is this that makes you so
    despondent?

GUARD. First for myself: I did not see it done,
  I do not know who did it. Plainly then,
  I cannot rightly come to any harm.   240

CREON. You are a cautious fellow, building up
  This barricade. You bring unpleasant news?

GUARD. I do, and peril makes a man pause long.

CREON. O, won't you tell your story and be gone?

GUARD. Then, here it is. The body: someone has
  Just buried it, and gone away. He sprinkled
  Dry dust on it, with all the sacred rites.

CREON. What? Buried it? What man has so defied me?

GUARD. How can I tell? There was no mark of pickaxe,
  No sign of digging; the earth was hard and dry   250
  And undisturbed; no waggon had been there;
  He who had done it left no trace at all.
  So, when the first day-watchman showed it to us,

We were appalled. We could not see the body;
It was not buried but was thinly covered
With dust, as if by someone who had sought
To avoid a curse.* Although we looked, we saw
No sign that any dog or bird had come
And torn the body. Angry accusations
Flew up between us; each man blamed another,   260
And in the end it would have come to blows,
For there was none to stop it. Each single man
Seemed guilty, yet proclaimed his ignorance)
And could not be convicted. We were all
Ready to take hot iron in our hands,
To walk through fire,* to swear by all the gods
We had not done it, nor had secret knowledge
Of any man who did it or contrived it.
We could not find a clue. Then one man spoke:
It made us hang our heads in terror, yet   270
No one could answer him, nor could we see
Much profit for ourselves if we should do it.
He said 'We must report this thing to Creon;
We dare not hide it';* and his word prevailed.
I am the unlucky man who drew the prize
When we cast lots, and therefore I am come
Unwilling and, for certain, most unwelcome:
Nobody loves the bringer of bad news.

CHORUS. My lord, the thought has risen in my mind:
Do we not see in this the hand of God?

CREON. Silence! or you will anger me. You are   280
An old man: must you be a fool as well?
Intolerable, that you suppose the gods
Should have a single thought for this dead body.
What? should they honour him with burial
As one who served them well, when he had come
To burn their pillared temples, to destroy
Their treasuries, to devastate their land
And overturn its laws? Or have you noticed
The gods prefer the vile? No, from the first
There was a muttering against my edict,   290

11

Wagging of heads in secret, restiveness
And discontent with my authority.
I know that some of these perverted others
And bribed them to this act. Of all vile things
Current on earth, none is so vile as money.
For money opens wide the city-gates
To ravishers, it drives the citizens
To exile, it perverts the honest mind
To shamefulness, it teaches men to practise   300
All forms of wickedness and impiety.
These criminals who sold themselves for money
Have bought with it their certain punishment;
For, as I reverence the throne of Zeus,
I tell you plainly, and confirm it with
My oath: unless you find, and bring before me,
The very author of this burial-rite
Mere death shall not suffice; you shall be hanged
Alive,* until you have disclosed the crime,
That for the future you may ply your trade   310
More cleverly, and learn not every pocket
Is safely to be picked. Ill-gotten gains
More often lead to ruin than to safety.

GUARD. May I reply? Or must I turn and go?

CREON. Now, as before, your very voice offends me.

GUARD. Is it your ears that feel it, or your mind?

CREON. Why must you probe the seat of our
    displeasure?

GUARD. The rebel hurts your mind; I but your ears.

CREON. No more of this! You are a babbling fool!   320

GUARD. If so, I cannot be the one who did it.

CREON. Yes, but you did—selling your life for money!

GUARD. It's bad, to judge at random, and judge wrong!

CREON. You judge my judgement as you will—but
    bring

12

The man who did it, or you shall proclaim
What punishment is earned by crooked dealings.

GUARD. God grant he may be found! But whether he
Be found or not—for this must lie with chance—
You will not see me coming *here* again.
Alive beyond my hope and expectation,   330
I thank the gods who have delivered me.
                    [*Exeunt severally* CREON *and* GUARD

Strophe 1

CHORUS [*sings*]. Wonders are many, yet of all
Things is Man the most wonderful.
    He can sail on the stormy sea
    Though the tempest rage, and the loud
    Waves roar around, as he makes his
    Path amid the towering surge.

Earth inexhaustible, ageless, he wearies, as
Backwards and forwards, from season to season, his   340
    Ox-team* drives along the ploughshare.

Antistrophe 1

    He can entrap the cheerful birds,
    Setting a snare, and all the wild
    Beasts of the earth he has learned to catch, and
    Fish that teem in the deep sea, with
    Nets knotted of stout cords; of
    Such inventiveness is man.
    Through his inventions he becomes lord
Even of the beasts of the mountain: the long-haired
Horse he subdues to the yoke on his neck, and the   350
    Hill-bred bull, of strength untiring.

man masters
nature =
"Enlightenment

Strophe 2

And speech he has learned, and thought
So swift, and the temper of mind

13

To dwell within cities, and not to lie bare
Amid the keen, biting frosts
Or cower beneath pelting rain;
Full of resource against all that comes to him   360
Is Man. Against Death alone
He is left with no defence.
But painful sickness he can cure
  By his own skill.

Antistrophe 2

Surpassing belief, the device and
Cunning that Man has attained,
And it bringeth him now to evil, now to good.
If he observe Law,* and tread
The righteous path God ordained,
Honoured is he; dishonoured, the man whose   370
    reckless heart
Shall make him join hands with sin:
May I not think like him,
Nor may such an impious man
  Dwell in my house.

Enter GUARD, with ANTIGONE

CHORUS. What evil spirit is abroad? I know
  Her well: Antigone. But how can I
  Believe it? Why, O you unlucky daughter
  Of an unlucky father,* what is this?   380
  Can it be you, so mad and so defiant,
  So disobedient to a King's decree?

GUARD. Here is the one who did the deed, this girl;
  We caught her burying him.—But where is Creon?

CHORUS. He comes, just as you need him, from the
  palace.

Enter CREON, attended

CREON. How? What occasion makes my coming
  timely?

GUARD. Sir, against nothing should a man take oath,
    For second thoughts belie him. Under your threats   390
    That lashed me like a hailstorm, I'd have said
    I would not quickly have come here again;
    But joy that comes beyond our dearest hope
    Surpasses all in magnitude. So I
    Return, though I had sworn I never would,
    Bringing this girl detected in the act
    Of honouring the body. This time no lot
    Was cast; the windfall is my very own.
    And so, my lord, do as you please: take her
    Yourself, examine her, cross-question her.
    I claim the right of free and final quittance.   400

CREON. Why do you bring this girl? Where was she
    taken?

GUARD. In burying the body. That is all.

CREON. You know what you are saying? Do you mean
    it?

GUARD. I saw her giving burial to the corpse
    You had forbidden. Is that plain and clear?

CREON. How did you see and take her so red-handed?

GUARD. It was like this. When we had reached the
    place,
    Those dreadful threats of yours upon our heads,
    We swept aside each grain of dust that hid
    The clammy body, leaving it quite bare,   410
    And sat down on a hill, to the windward side
    That so we might avoid the smell of it.
    We kept sharp look-out; each man roundly cursed
    His neighbour, if he should neglect his duty.
    So the time passed, until the blazing sun
    Reached his mid-course and burned us with his heat.
    Then, suddenly, a whirlwind came from heaven
    And raised a storm of dust, which blotted out
    The earth and sky; the air was filled with sand
    And leaves ripped from the trees. We closed our eyes

15

And bore this visitation* as we could.   420
At last it ended; then we saw the girl.
She raised a bitter cry, as will a bird
Returning to its nest and finding it
Despoiled, a cradle empty of its young.
So, when she saw the body bare, she raised
A cry of anguish mixed with imprecations
Laid upon those who did it; then at once
Brought handfuls of dry dust, and raised aloft
A shapely vase of bronze, and three times poured   430
The funeral libation for the dead.
We rushed upon her swiftly, seized our prey,
And charged her both with this offence and that.*
She faced us calmly; she did not disown
The double crime. How glad I was!—and yet
How sorry too; it is a painful thing
To bring a friend to ruin. Still, for me,
My own escape comes before everything.   440

CREON. You there, who keep your eyes fixed on the
    ground,
Do you admit this, or do you deny it?

ANTIGONE. No, I do not deny it. I admit it.

CREON [to Guard]. Then you may go; go where you
    like. You have
Been fully cleared of that grave accusation.
                                    [Exit GUARD

You: tell me briefly—I want no long speech:
Did you not know that this had been forbidden?

ANTIGONE. Of course I knew. There was a
    proclamation.

CREON. And so you dared to disobey the law?

ANTIGONE. It was not Zeus who published this decree,   450
Nor have the Powers who rule among the dead*
Imposed such laws as this upon mankind;
Nor could I think that a decree of yours—

16

A man—could override the laws of Heaven*
Unwritten and unchanging. Not of today
Or yesterday is their authority;
They are eternal; no man saw their birth.
Was I to stand before the gods' tribunal
For disobeying *them*, because I feared
A man? I knew that I should have to die,   460
Even without your edict; if I die
Before my time, why then, I count it gain;
To one who lives as I do, ringed about
With countless miseries, why, death is welcome.
For me to meet this doom is little grief;
But when my mother's son lay dead, had I
Neglected him and left him there unburied,
That would have caused me grief; this causes none.
And if you think it folly, then perhaps
I am accused of folly by the fool.   470

CHORUS. The daughter shows her father's temper—
    fierce,
    Defiant; she will not yield to any storm.

CREON. But it is those that are most obstinate
    Suffer the greatest fall; the hardest iron,
    Most fiercely tempered in the fire, that is
    Most often snapped and splintered. I have seen
    The wildest horses tamed, and only by
    The tiny bit. There is no room for pride
    In one who is a slave! This girl already
    Had fully learned the art of insolence   480
    When she transgressed the laws that I established;
    And now to that she adds a second outrage—
    To boast of what she did, and laugh at us.
    Now she would be the man, not I, if she
    Defeated me and did not pay for it.   (see Butler, pg. 9)
    But though she be my niece, or closer still
    Than all our family,* she shall not escape
    The direst penalty; no, nor shall her sister:
    I judge her guilty too; she played her part
    In burying the body. Summon her.   490

17

Just now I saw her raving and distracted
Within the palace. So it often is:
Those who plan crime in secret are betrayed
Despite themselves; they show it in their faces.
But this is worst of all: to be convicted
And then to glorify the crime as virtue.

[*Exeunt some* GUARDS

ANTIGONE. Would you do more than simply take and
    kill me?

CREON. I will have nothing more, and nothing less.

ANTIGONE. Then why delay? To me no word of yours
Is pleasing—God forbid it should be so!—   500
And everything in me displeases you.
Yet what could I have done to win renown
More glorious than giving burial
To my own brother? These men too would say it,
Except that terror cows them into silence.
A king has many a privilege: the greatest,
That he can say and do all that he will.

CREON. You are the only one in Thebes to think it!

ANTIGONE. These think as I do—but they dare not
    speak.

CREON. Have you no shame, not to conform with
    others?   510

ANTIGONE. To reverence a brother is no shame.

CREON. Was he no brother, he who died for Thebes?

ANTIGONE. One mother and one father gave them
    birth.

CREON. Honouring the traitor, you dishonour *him*.*

ANTIGONE. He will not bear this testimony, in death.

CREON. Yes! if the traitor fare the same as he.

ANTIGONE. It was a brother, not a slave who died!

18

CREON. He died attacking Thebes; the other saved us.

ANTIGONE. Even so, the god of Death* demands these
rites.

CREON. The good demand more honour than the
. wicked.   520

ANTIGONE. Who knows? In death they may be
reconciled.

CREON. Death does not make an enemy a friend!

ANTIGONE. Even so, I give both love, not share their
hatred.

CREON. Down then to Hell! Love there, if love you
must.
While I am living, no woman shall have rule.

Enter GUARDS, *with* ISMENE

CHORUS [*chants*]. See where Ismene leaves the palace-
gate,
In tears shed for her sister. On her brow
A cloud of grief has blotted out her sun,
And breaks in rain upon her comeliness.   530

CREON. You, lurking like a serpent in my house,
Drinking my life-blood unawares; nor did
I know that I was cherishing two fiends,
Subverters of my throne; come, tell me this:
Do you confess you shared this burial,
Or will you swear you had no knowledge of it?

ISMENE. I did it too, if she allows my claim;
I share the burden of this heavy charge.

ANTIGONE. No! Justice will not suffer that; for you
Refused, and I gave you no part in it.

ISMENE. But in your stormy voyage I am glad   540
To share the danger, travelling at your side.

19

ANTIGONE. Whose was the deed the god of Death
  knows well;
I love not those who love in words alone.

ISMENE. My sister, do not scorn me, nor refuse
  That I may die with you, honouring the dead.

ANTIGONE. You shall not die with me, nor claim as
  yours
What you rejected. My death will be enough.

ISMENE. What life is left to me if I lose you?

ANTIGONE. Ask Creon! It was Creon that you cared
  for.

ISMENE. O why taunt me, when it does not help you?　550

ANTIGONE. If I do taunt you, it is to my pain.

ISMENE. Can I not help you, even at this late hour?

ANTIGONE. Save your own life. I grudge not your
  escape.

ISMENE. Alas! Can I not join you in your fate?

ANTIGONE. You cannot: you chose life, and I chose
  death.

ISMENE. But not without the warning that I gave you!

ANTIGONE. Some thought *you* wise; the dead
  commended me.

ISMENE. But my offence has been as great as yours.

ANTIGONE. Be comforted; you live, but I have given
  My life already, in service of the dead.　560

CREON. Of these two girls, one has been driven frantic,
  The other has been frantic since her birth.

ISMENE. Not so, my lord; but when disaster comes
  The reason that one has can not stand firm.

CREON. Yours did not, when you chose to partner
  crime!

ISMENE. But what is life to me, without my sister?

CREON. Say not 'my sister': sister you have none.

ISMENE. But she is Haemon's bride—and can you kill
    her?

CREON. Is she the only woman he can bed with?

ISMENE. The only one so joined in love with him.   570

CREON. I hate a son to have an evil wife.

ANTIGONE. O my dear Haemon! How your father
    wrongs you!*

CREON. I hear too much of you and of your marriage.

ISMENE. He is your son; how can you take her from
    him?*

CREON. It is not I, but Death, that stops this wedding.

CHORUS. It is determined, then, that she must die?*

CREON. For you, and me, determined. [*To the* GUARDS.]
    Take them in
  At once; no more delay. Henceforward let
  Them stay at home, like women, not roam abroad.
  Even the bold, you know, will seek escape   580
  When they see death at last standing beside them.
[*Exeunt* ANTIGONE *and* ISMENE *into the palace,*
                        guarded. CREON *remains*.

Strophe 1

CHORUS [*sings*]. Thrice happy are they who have never
    known disaster!
  Once a house is shaken of Heaven, disaster
  Never leaves it, from generation to generation.
    'Tis even as the swelling sea,
    When the roaring wind from Thrace*
  Drives blustering over the water and makes it black: 590
    It bears up from below
    A thick, dark cloud of mud,

21

And groaning cliffs repel the smack of wind and
   angry breakers.

Antistrophe 1

I see, in the house of our kings, how ancient sorrows
Rise again; disaster is linked with disaster.
Woe again must each generation inherit. Some god
   Besets them, nor will give release.
    On the last of royal blood
There gleamed a shimmering light in the house of
    Oedipus.   600
   But Death comes once again
   With blood-stained axe, and hews
The sapling down; and Frenzy lends her aid, and
   vengeful Madness.

Strophe 2

Thy power, Zeus, is almighty! No
Mortal insolence can oppose Thee!
Sleep, which conquers all else, cannot overcome
   Thee,
   Nor can the never-wearied
   Years, but throughout
Time Thou art strong and ageless,
   In thy own Olympus
Ruling in radiant splendour.   610
For today, and in all past time,
And through all time to come,
This is the law: that in Man's
Life every success brings with it some disaster.

Antistrophe 2

Hope springs high, and to many a man
   Hope brings comfort and consolation;
Yet she is to some nothing but fond illusion:
   Swiftly they come to ruin,

As when a man
Treads unawares on hot fire.
  For it was a wise man   620
First made that ancient saying:
To the man whom God will ruin
One day shall evil seem
  Good, in his twisted judgement
He comes in a short time to fell disaster.

CHORUS. See, here comes Haemon, last-born of your
    children,*
  Grieving, it may be, for Antigone.*   630

CREON. Soon we shall know, better than seers can tell
us.

Enter HAEMON

My son:
You have not come in rage against your father
Because your bride must die? Or are you still
My loyal son, whatever I may do?

HAEMON. Father, I am your son; may your wise
    judgement
Rule me, and may I always follow it.
No marriage shall be thought a greater prize
For me to win than your good government.

CREON. So may you ever be resolved, my son,
  In all things to be guided by your father.   640
It is for this men pray that they may have
Obedient children, that they may requite
Their father's enemy with enmity
And honour whom their father loves to honour.
One who begets unprofitable children
Makes trouble for himself, and gives his foes
Nothing but laughter. Therefore do not let
Your pleasure in a woman overcome
Your judgement, knowing this, that if you have
An evil wife to share your house, you'll find
Cold comfort in your bed. What other wound   650

Can cut so deep as treachery at home?
So, think this girl your enemy; spit on her,
And let her find her husband down in Hell!
She is the only one that I have found
In all the city disobedient.
I will not make myself a liar. I
Have caught her; I will kill her. Let her sing
Her hymns to Sacred Kinship!* If I breed
Rebellion in the house, then it is certain
There'll be no lack of rebels out of doors.   660
No man can rule a city uprightly
Who is not just in ruling his own household.
Never will I approve of one who breaks
And violates the law, or would dictate
To those who rule. Lawful authority
Must be obeyed in all things, great or small,
Just and unjust alike; and such a man
Would win my confidence both in command
And as a subject; standing at my side
In the storm of battle he would hold his ground,   670
Not leave me unprotected. But there is
No greater curse than disobedience.
This brings destruction on a city, this
Drives men from hearth and home, this brings about
A sudden panic in the battle-front.
Where all goes well, obedience is the cause.
So we must vindicate the law; we must not be
Defeated by a woman. Better far
Be overthrown, if need be, by a man
Than to be called the victim of a woman.   680

CHORUS. Unless the years have stolen away our wits,
  All you say is said most prudently.

HAEMON. Father, it is the gods who give us wisdom;
  No gift of theirs more precious. I cannot say
  That you are wrong, nor would I ever learn
  That impudence, although perhaps another
  Might fairly say it. But it falls to me,
  Being your son, to note what others say,

24

Or do, or censure in you, for your glance
Intimidates the common citizen;   690
He will not say, before your face, what might
Displease you; I can listen freely, how
The city mourns this girl. 'No other woman',
So they are saying, 'so undeservedly
Has been condemned for such a glorious deed.
When her own brother had been slain in battle
She would not let his body lie unburied
To be devoured by dogs or birds of prey.
Is not this worthy of a crown of gold?'—
Such is the muttering that spreads everywhere.   700
   Father, no greater treasure can I have
Than your prosperity; no son can find
A greater prize than his own father's fame,
No father than his son's. Therefore let not
This single thought possess you: only what
You say is right, and nothing else. The man
Who thinks that he alone is wise, that he
Is best in speech or counsel, such a man
Brought to the proof is found but emptiness.
There's no disgrace, even if one is wise,   710
In learning more, and knowing when to yield.
See how the trees that grow beside a torrent
Preserve their branches, if they bend; the others,
Those that resist, are torn out, root and branch.
So too the captain of a ship; let him
Refuse to shorten sail, despite the storm—
He'll end his voyage bottom uppermost.
No, let your anger cool, and be persuaded.
If one who is still young can speak with sense,
Then I would say that he does best who has   720
Most understanding; second best, the man
Who profits from the wisdom of another.

CHORUS. My lord, he has not spoken foolishly;
   You each can learn some wisdom from the other.

CREON. What? men of our age go to school again
   And take a lesson from a very boy?

HAEMON. If it is worth the taking. I am young,
But think what should be done, not of my age.

CREON. What should be done! To honour
disobedience! 730

HAEMON. I would not have you honour criminals.

CREON. And is this girl then not a criminal?

HAEMON. The city with a single voice denies it. *) personified*

CREON. Must I give orders then by their permission?

HAEMON. If youth is folly, this is childishness.

CREON. Am I to rule for them, not for myself?

HAEMON. That is not government, but tyranny.

CREON. The king is lord and master of his city.

HAEMON. Then you had better rule a desert island!

CREON. This man, it seems, is the ally of the woman. 740

HAEMON. If you're the woman, yes! I fight for you.

CREON. Villain! Do you oppose your father's will?

HAEMON. Only because you are opposing Justice.

CREON. When I regard my own prerogative?

HAEMON. Opposing God's, you disregard your own.

CREON. Scoundrel, so to surrender to a woman! *(see Butler 8)*

HAEMON. But not to anything that brings me shame.

CREON. Your every word is in defence of her.

HAEMON. And me, and you—and of the gods below.

CREON. You shall not marry her this side the grave! 750

HAEMON. So, she must die—and will not die alone.

CREON. What? Threaten me? Are you so insolent?

HAEMON. It is no threat, if I reply to folly.

CREON. The fool would teach me sense! You'll pay for
  it.

HAEMON. I'd call you mad, if you were not my father.

CREON. I'll hear no chatter from a woman's plaything.

HAEMON. Would you have all the talk, and hear no
  answer?

CREON. So?
  I swear to God, you shall not bandy words
  With me and not repent it! Bring her out,
  That loathsome creature! I will have her killed   760
  At once, before her bridegroom's very eyes.

HAEMON. How can you think it? I will not see that,
  Nor shall you ever see my face again.
  Those friends of yours who can must tolerate
  Your raging madness; I will not endure it.

                                       [*Exit* HAEMON

CHORUS. How angrily he went, my lord! The young,
  When they are greatly hurt, grow desperate.

CREON. Then let his pride and folly do their worst!
  He shall not save these women from their doom.

CHORUS. Is it your purpose then to kill them both?   770

CREON. Not her who had no part in it.—I thank you.

CHORUS. And for the other: how is she to die?

CREON. I'll find a cave in some deserted spot,
  And there I will imprison her alive
  With so much food—no more—as will avert
  Pollution and a curse upon the city.*
  There let her pray to Death, the only god
  Whom she reveres, to rescue her from death,
  Or learn at last, though it be late, that it
  Is wanton folly to respect the dead.   780
                            [CREON *remains on the stage*

27

Strophe

CHORUS [*sings*]. Invincible, implacable Love,* O
   Love, that makes havoc of all wealth;
   That peacefully keeps his night-watch
   On tender cheek of a maiden:
   The Sea is no barrier, nor
   Mountainous waste to Love's flight; for
   No one can escape Love's domination,
   Man, no, nor immortal god. Love's
   Prey is possessed by madness.   790

Antistrophe

By Love, the mind even of the just
   Is bent awry; he becomes unjust.
   So here: it is Love that stirred up
   This quarrel of son with father.
   The kindling light of Love in the soft
   Eye of a bride conquers, for
   Love sits on his throne, one of the great Powers;
   Nought else can prevail against   800
   Invincible Aphrodite.*

Enter ANTIGONE, *under guard.* [*From this point up to line
     987 everything is sung, except lines 883–928.*]

CHORUS. I too, when I see this sight, cannot stay
   Within bounds; I cannot keep back my tears
   Which rise like a flood. For behold, they bring
   Antigone here, on the journey that all
   Must make, to the silence of Hades.*

Strophe 1

ANTIGONE. Behold me, O lords of my native city!
   Now do I make my last journey;
   Now do I see the last
   Sun that ever I shall behold.
   Never another! Death, that lulls   810

All to sleep, takes me while I live
Down to the grim shore of Acheron.*
   No wedding day can be
Mine, no hymn will be raised to honour
Marriage of mine; for I
Go to espouse the bridegroom, Death.

CHORUS. Yet a glorious death, and rich in fame
   Is yours; you go to the silent tomb
   Not smitten with wasting sickness, nor
   Repaying a debt to the sharp-edged sword;   820
   But alone among mortals* you go to the home
   Of the dead while yet you are living.

Antistrophe 1

ANTIGONE. They tell of how cruelly she did perish,
   Niobe, Queen in Thebes;*
   For, as ivy grows on a tree,
   Strangling it, so she slowly turned to
   Stone on a Phrygian mountain-top.
   Now the rain-storms wear her away—
     So does the story run—and
   Snow clings to her always: 830
   Tears fall from her weeping eyes for
   Ever and ever. Like to hers, the
   Cruel death that now awaits me.

CHORUS. But she was a goddess, and born of the
     gods;*
   We are but mortals, of mortals born.
   For a mortal to share in the doom of a god,
   That brings her renown while yet she lives,
   And a glory that long will outlive her.

Strophe 2

ANTIGONE. Alas, they laugh! O by the gods of Thebes,
   my native city,   840

Mock me, if you must, when I am gone, not to my
    face!
O Thebes my city, O you lordly men of Thebes!
O water of Dirke's stream!* Holy soil where our
    chariots run!
You, you do I call upon; you, you shall testify
How all unwept of friends, by what harsh decree,
They send me to the cavern that shall be my
    everlasting grave.
Ah, cruel doom! to be banished from earth, nor
    welcomed   850
Among the dead, set apart, for ever!

CHORUS. Too bold, too reckless, you affronted
    Justice. Now that awful power
Takes terrible vengeance, O my child.
For some old sin you make atonement.

Antistrophe 2

ANTIGONE. My father's sin! There is the source of all
    my anguish.
Harsh fate that befell my father! Harsh fate that has
    held
Fast in its grip the whole renowned race of
    Labdacus!*   860
O the blind madness of my father's and my mother's
    marriage!
O cursed union of a son with his own mother!
From such as those I draw my own unhappy life;
And now I go to dwell with them, unwedded and
    accursed.
O brother,* through an evil marriage you were slain;
    and I   870
Live—but your dead hand destroys me.

CHORUS. Such loyalty is a holy thing.
    Yet none that holds authority
Can brook disobedience, O my child.
Your self-willed pride has been your ruin.

Epode

ANTIGONE. Unwept, unwedded and unbefriended,
Alone, pitilessly used,
Now they drag me to death.
Never again, O thou Sun in the heavens,
May I look on thy holy radiance!   880
Such is my fate, and no one laments it;
No friend is here to mourn me.

CREON [*speaks*]. Enough of this! If tears and
    lamentations
Could stave off death they would go on for ever.
Take her away at once, and wall her up
Inside a cavern, as I have commanded,
And leave her there, alone, in solitude.
Her home shall be her tomb; there she may live
Or die, as she may choose: my hands are clean;
But she shall live no more among the living.   890

ANTIGONE [*speaks*]. O grave, my bridal-chamber,
    everlasting
Prison within a rock: now I must go
To join my own, those many who have died
And whom Persephone* has welcomed home;
And now to me, the last of all, so young,
Death comes, so cruelly. And yet I go
In the sure hope that you will welcome me,
Father, and you, my mother; you, my brother.*
For when you died* it was my hands that washed   900
And dressed you, laid you in your graves, and
    poured
The last libations. Now, because to you,
Polyneices, I have given burial,
To me they give a recompense like this!
Yet what I did,* the wise will all approve.
For had I lost a son, or lost a husband,
Never would I have ventured such an act
Against the city's will. And wherefore so?
My husband dead, I might have found another;

31

Another son from him, if I had lost 910
A son. But since my mother and my father
Have both gone to the grave, there can be none
Henceforth that I can ever call my brother.
It was for this I paid you such an honour,
Dear Polyneices, and in Creon's eyes
Thus wantonly and gravely have offended.
So with rude hands he drags me to my death.
No chanted wedding-hymn, no bridal-joy,
No tender care of children can be mine;
But like an outcast, and without a friend,
They take me to the cavernous home of death. 920
What ordinance of the gods have I transgressed?
Why should I look to Heaven any more
For help, or seek an ally among men?
If this is what the gods approve, why then,
When I am dead I shall discern my fault;
If theirs the sin, may they endure a doom
No worse than mine, so wantonly inflicted!

CHORUS. Still from the same quarter the same wild
    winds
Blow fiercely, and shake her stubborn soul. 930

CREON. And therefore, for this, these men shall have
    cause,
Bitter cause, to lament their tardiness.

CHORUS. I fear these words bring us closer yet
To the verge of death.*

CREON. I have nothing to say, no comfort to give:
The sentence is passed, and the end is here.

ANTIGONE. O city of Thebes where my fathers dwelt,
    O gods of our race,
Now at last their hands are upon me!
You princes of Thebes, O look upon me, 940
The last that remain of a line of kings!
How savagely impious men use me,
For keeping a law that is holy.
       [*Exit* ANTIGONE, *under guard.* CREON *remains*

Strophe 1

CHORUS. There was one in days of old who was
    imprisoned
  In a chamber like a grave, within a tower:
  Fair Danae,* who in darkness was held, and never
    saw the pure daylight.
  Yet she too, O my child, was of an ancient line,
  Entrusted with divine seed* that had come in shower
    of gold.   950
  Mysterious, overmastering, is the power of Fate.
    From this, nor wealth nor force of arms
    Nor strong encircling city-walls
    Nor storm-tossed ship can give deliverance.

Antistrophe 1

Close bondage was ordained by Dionysus
For one who in a frenzy had denied
His godhead: in a cavern Lycurgus,* for his sin, was
    imprisoned.
In such wise did his madness bear a bitter fruit,   960
Which withered in a dungeon. So he learned it was a
    god
He had ventured in his blindness to revile and taunt.
    The sacred dances he had tried
    To quell, and end the Bacchic rite,
    Offending all the tuneful Muses.*

Strophe 2

There is a town by the rocks where a sea meets
    another sea,
Two black rocks by the Bosphorus, near the
    Thracian coast,
Salmydessus;* and there a wife had been spurned,   970
    Held close in bitter constraint.*
    Then upon both her children
    A blinding wound fell from her cruel rival:

With shuttle in hand she smote the open eyes with
    sharp
And blood-stained point, and brought to Phineus'
Two sons a darkness that cried for vengeance.*

Antistrophe 2

In bitter grief and despair they bewailed their unhappy
    lot,
Children born to a mother whose marriage proved
    accursed.   980
Yet she came of a race of ancient kings,*
    Her sire the offspring of gods.*
    Reared in a distant country,*
  Among her fierce, northern father's tempests,
She went, a Boread, swift as horses, over the lofty
Mountains.* Yet not even she was
Safe against the long-lived Fates, my daughter.

Enter TEIRESIAS, *led by a boy*

TEIRESIAS. My lords, I share my journey with this boy
  Whose eyes must see for both; for so the blind
  Must move abroad, with one to guide their steps.   990

CREON. Why, what is this? Why are *you* here,
  Teiresias?

TEIRESIAS. I will explain; you will do well to listen.

CREON. Have I not always followed your good counsel?

TEIRESIAS. You have; therefore we have been guided
  well.

CREON. I have had much experience of your wisdom.

TEIRESIAS. Then think: once more you tread the razor's
  edge.

CREON. You make me tremble! What is it you mean?

TEIRESIAS. What divination has revealed to me,
  That I will tell you. To my ancient seat

Of augury* I went, where all the birds   1000
Foregather. There I sat, and heard a clamour
Strange and unnatural—birds screaming in rage.
I knew that they were tearing at each other
With murderous claws: the beating of their wings
Meant nothing less than that; and I was frightened.
I made a blazing fire upon the altar
And offered sacrifice:* it would not burn;
The melting fat oozed out upon the embers
And smoked and bubbled; high into the air
The bladder spirted gall, and from the bones   1010
The fatty meat slid off and left them bare.
Such omens, baffling, indistinct, I learned
From him who guides me,* as I am guide to others.
Sickness has come upon us, and the cause
Is you: our altars and our sacred hearths
Are all polluted by the dogs and birds
That have been gorging on the fallen body
Of Polyneices. Therefore heaven will not
Accept from us our prayers, no fire will burn   1020
Our offerings, nor will birds give out clear sounds,
For they are glutted with the blood of men.
Be warned, my son. No man alive is free
From error, but the wise and prudent man
When he has fallen into evil courses
Does not persist, but tries to find amendment.
It is the stubborn man who is the fool.
Yield to the dead, forbear to strike the fallen;
To slay the slain, is that a deed of valour?   1030
Your good is what I seek; and that instruction
Is best that comes from wisdom, and brings profit.

CREON. Sir, all of you, like bowmen at a target,
Let fly your shafts at me. Now they have turned
Even diviners on me! By that tribe
I am bought and sold and stowed away on board.
Go, make your profits, drive your trade
In Lydian silver* or in Indian gold,
But him you shall not bury in a tomb,

35

No, not though Zeus' own eagles* eat the corpse   1040
And bear the carrion to their master's throne:
Not even so, for fear of that defilement,
Will I permit his burial—for well I know
That mortal man can not defile the gods.
But, old Teiresias, even the cleverest men
Fall shamefully when for a little money
They use fair words to mask their villainy.

TEIRESIAS. Does any man reflect, does any know . . .

CREON. Know *what*? Why do you preach at me like
    this?

TEIRESIAS. How much the greatest blessing is good
    counsel?   1050

CREON. As much, I think, as folly is his plague.

TEIRESIAS. Yet with this plague you are yourself
    infected.

CREON. I will not bandy words with any prophet.

TEIRESIAS. And yet you say my prophecies are
    dishonest!

CREON. Prophets have always been too fond of gold.

TEIRESIAS. And tyrants, of the shameful use of power.

CREON. You know it is your King of whom you speak?

TEIRESIAS. King of the land I saved from mortal
    danger.*

CREON. A clever prophet—but an evil one.

TEIRESIAS. You'll rouse me to awaken my dark secret.   1060

CREON. Awaken it, but do not speak for money.

TEIRESIAS. And do you think that I am come to *that*?

CREON. You shall not buy and sell *my* policy.

TEIRESIAS. Then I will tell you this: you will not live
    Through many circuits of the racing sun

Before you give a child of your own body
To make amends for murder, death for death;
Because you have thrust down within the earth
One who should walk upon it,* and have lodged
A living soul dishonourably in a tomb;
And impiously have kept upon the earth   1070
Unburied and unblest one who belongs
Neither to you nor to the upper gods
But to the gods below, who are despoiled
By you. Therefore the gods arouse against you
Their sure avengers;* they lie in your path
Even now to trap you and to make you pay
Their price.—Now think: do I say *this* for money?
Not many hours will pass before your house
Rings loud with lamentation, men and women.
Hatred for you is moving in those cities   1080
Whose mangled sons* had funeral-rites from dogs
Or from some bird of prey, whose wings have
   carried
The taint of dead men's flesh to their own homes,
Polluting hearth and altar.
These are the arrows that I launch at you,
Because you anger me. I shall not miss
My aim, and you shall not escape their smart.
Boy, lead me home again, that he may vent
His rage upon some younger man, and learn
To moderate his violent tongue, and find
More understanding than he has today.   1090

[*Exit* TEIRESIAS *and boy*

CHORUS. And so, my lord, he leaves us, with a threat
   Of doom. I have lived long,* but I am sure
   Of this: no single prophecy that he
   Has made to Thebes has gone without fulfilment.

CREON. I know it too, and I am terrified.
   To yield is very hard, but to resist
   And meet disaster, that is harder still.

CHORUS. Creon, this is no time for wrong decision.

37

CREON. What shall I do? Advise me; I will listen.

CHORUS. Release Antigone from her rock-hewn
    dungeon,   1100
  And lay the unburied body in a tomb.

CREON. Is this your counsel? You would have me yield?

CHORUS. I would, and quickly. The destroying hand
  Of Heaven is quick to punish human error.

CREON. How hard it is! And yet one cannot fight
  Against Necessity.*—I will give way.

CHORUS. Go then and do it; leave it not to others.

CREON. Just as I am I go.—You men-at-arms,
  You here, and those within: away at once
  Up to the hill, and take your implements.   1110
  Now that my resolution is reversed
  I who imprisoned her will set her free.—
    I fear it may be wisest to observe
  Throughout one's life the laws that are established.
                      [Exit CREON *and guards*

Strophe 1

CHORUS [*sings*]. Thou Spirit whose names are many,*
    Dionysus,
    Born to Zeus the loud-thunderer,
    Joy of thy Theban mother-nymph,*
    Lover of famous Italy:*
    King art thou in the crowded shrine   1120
    Where Demeter has her abode,* O
    Bacchus! Here is thy mother's home,
    Here is thine, by the smooth Is-
    menus' flood,* here where the savage
    Dragon's teeth had offspring.*

Antistrophe 1

  Thou art seen by the nymphs amid the smoky
    torchlight,

Where, upon Parnassus' height,*
They hold revels to honour Thee
Close to the spring of Castaly.*   1130
Thou art come from the ivy-clad
Slopes of Asian hills,* and vineyards
Hanging thick with clustering grapes.
Mystic voices chant: 'O
Bacchus! O Bacchus!' in
The roads and ways of Thebe.

Strophe 2

Here is thy chosen home,
In Thebes above all lands,
With thy mother, bride of Zeus.
Wherefore, since a pollution holds   1140
All our people fast in its grip,
O come with swift healing* across the wall of high
Parnassus,
Or over the rough Euripus.*

Antistrophe 2

Stars that move, breathing flame,
Honour Thee as they dance;
Voices cry to Thee in the night.
Son begotten of Zeus, appear!
Come, Lord, with thy company,   1150
Thy own nymphs, who with wild, nightlong dances
praise Thee,
Bountiful Dionysus!

Enter a MESSENGER

MESSENGER. You noblemen of Thebes, how insecure
Is human fortune! Chance will overthrow
The great, and raise the lowly; nothing's firm,
Either for confidence or for despair;
No one can prophesy what lies in store.   1160
An hour ago, how much I envied Creon!

He had saved Thebes, we had accorded him
The sovereign power; he ruled our land
Supported by a noble prince, his son.
Now all is lost, and he who forfeits joy
Forfeits his life; he is a breathing corpse.
Heap treasures in your palace, if you will,
And wear the pomp of royalty; but if
You have no happiness, I would not give   1170
A straw for all of it, compared with joy.

CHORUS. What is this weight of heavy news you bring?

MESSENGER. Death!—and the blood-guilt rests upon
   the living.

CHORUS. Death? Who is dead? And who has killed
   him? Tell me.

MESSENGER. Haemon is dead, and by no stranger's
   hand.

CHORUS. But by his father's? Or was it his own?

MESSENGER. His own—inflamed with anger at his
   father.

CHORUS. Yours was no idle prophecy, Teiresias!

MESSENGER. That is my news. What next, remains with
   you.

CHORUS. But look! There is his wife, Eurydice;   1180
   She is coming from the palace. Has she heard
   About her son, or is she here by chance?

Enter EURYDICE

EURYDICE. You citizens of Thebes, I overheard
   When I was standing at the gates, for I
   Had come to make an offering at the shrine
   Of Pallas,* and my hand was on the bar
   That holds the gate, to draw it; then there fell
   Upon my ears a voice that spoke of death.
   My terror took away my strength; I fell
   Into my servants' arms and swooned away.

But tell it me once more; I can endure   1190
To listen; I am no stranger to bad news.*

MESSENGER. Dear lady, I was there, and I will tell
The truth; I will not keep it back from you.
Why should I gloze it over? You would hear
From someone else, and I should seem a liar.
The truth is always best.
                        I went with Creon
Up to the hill where Polyneices' body
Still lay, unpitied, torn by animals.
We gave it holy washing, and we prayed
To Hecate and Pluto* that they would
Restrain their anger and be merciful.   1200
And then we cut some branches, and we burned
What little had been left, and built a mound
Over his ashes of his native soil.
Then, to the cavern, to the home of death,
The bridal-chamber with its bed of stone.
One of us heard a cry of lamentation
From that unhallowed place; he went to Creon
And told him. On the wind, as he came near,
Cries of despair were borne. He groaned aloud   1210
In anguish: 'O, and are my fears come true?
Of all the journeys I have made, am I
To find this one the most calamitous?
It is my son's voice greets me. Hurry, men;
Run to the place, and when you reach the tomb
Creep in between the gaping stones and see
If it be Haemon there, or if the gods
Are cheating me.' Upon this desperate order
We ran and looked. Within the furthest chamber   1220
We saw her hanging, dead; strips from her dress
Had served her for a rope. Haemon we saw
Embracing her dead body and lamenting
His loss, his father's deed, and her destruction.
When Creon saw him he cried out in anguish,
Went in, and called to him: 'My son! my son!
O why? What have you done? What brought you
  here?

41

What is this madness? O come out, my son,
Come, I implore you!' Haemon glared at him   1230
With anger in his eyes, spat in his face,
Said nothing, drew his double-hilted sword,
But missed his aim as Creon leapt aside.
Then in remorse he leaned upon the blade
And drove it half its length into his body.
While yet the life was in him he embraced
The girl with failing arms, and breathing hard
Poured out his life-blood on to her white face.
So side by side they lie, and both are dead.   1240
Not in this world but in the world below
He wins his bride, and shows to all mankind
That folly is the worst of human evils.

                                        [*Exit* EURYDICE

CHORUS. What can we think of this? The Queen is
    gone
Without one word of good or evil omen.

MESSENGER. What can it mean? But yet we may sustain
The hope that she would not display her grief
In public, but will rouse the sad lament
For Haemon's death among her serving-women
Inside the palace. She has true discretion,
And she would never do what is unseemly.   1250

CHORUS. I cannot say, but wild lament would be
Less ominous than this unnatural silence.

MESSENGER. It *is* unnatural; there may be danger.
I'll follow her; it may be she is hiding
Some secret purpose in her passionate heart.

                        [*Exit* MESSENGER, *into the palace*

CHORUS [*chants*]. Look, Creon draws near, and the
    burden he bears
Gives witness to his misdeeds; the cause
    Lies only in his blind error.   1260

Enter CREON *and the* GUARDS, *with the body of* HAEMON

Strophe 1 (Turn 1)

CREON [*sings*]. Alas!
The wrongs I have done by ill-counselling!
Cruel and fraught with death.
You behold, men of Thebes,
The slayer, the slain; a father, a son.
My own stubborn ways have borne bitter fruit.
My son! Dead, my son! So soon torn from me,
So young, so young!
The fault only mine, not yours, O my son.

CHORUS. Too late, too late you see the path of wisdom. 1270

CREON [*sings*]. Alas!
A bitter lesson I have learned! The god
Coming with all his weight has borne down on me,
And smitten me with all his cruelty;
My joy overturned, trampled beneath his feet.
What suffering besets the whole race of men!

Enter MESSENGER,* *from the palace*

MESSENGER. My master, when you came you brought a burden
Of sorrow with you; now, within your house,
A second store of misery confronts you. 1280

CREON. Another sorrow come to crown my sorrow?

MESSENGER. The Queen, true mother of her son, is dead;
In grief she drove a blade into her heart.*

Antistrophe 1 (Counter-turn 1)

CREON [*sings*]. Alas!
Thou grim hand of death, greedy and unappeased,
Why so implacable?
Voice of doom, you who bring
Such dire news of grief, O, can it be true?
What have you said, my son? O, you have slain the slain! 1290

43

Tell me, can it be true? Is death crowning death?
  My wife! my wife!
My son dead, and now my wife taken too!

EURYDICE's *body is revealed*

CHORUS. But raise your eyes: there is her lifeless body.

CREON [*sings*]. Alas!
  Here is a sorrow that redoubles sorrow.
  Where will it end? What else can Fate hold in store?
  While yet I clasp my dead son in my arms
  Before me there lies another struck by death.
  Alas cruel doom! the mother's and the son's.   1300

MESSENGER. She took a sharp-edged knife, stood by the
    altar,
  And made lament for Megareus* who was killed
  Of old, and next for Haemon. Then at last,
  Invoking evil upon you, the slayer
  Of both her sons, she closed her eyes in death.

Strophe 2 (Turn 2)

CREON [*sings*]. A curse, a thing of terror! O, is there
    none
  Will unsheathe a sword to end all my woes   1310
  With one deadly thrust? My grief crushes me.

MESSENGER. She cursed you for the guilt of Haemon's
    death
  And of the other son who died before.

CREON. What did she do? How did she end her life?

MESSENGER. She heard my bitter story; then she put
  A dagger to her heart and drove it home.

CREON [*sings*]. The guilt falls on me alone; none but I
  Have slain her; no other shares in the sin.
  'Twas I dealt the blow. This is the truth, my friends.   1320
  Away, take me away, far from the sight of men!
  My life now is death. Lead me away from here.

CHORUS. That would be well, if anything is well.
Briefest is best when such disaster comes.

Antistrophe 2 (Counter-turn 2)

CREON [*sings*]. O come, best of all the days I can see,
The last day of all, the day that brings death.   1330
O come quickly! Come, thou night with no dawn!

CHORUS. That's for the future; here and now are duties
That fall on those to whom they are allotted.

CREON. I prayed for death; I wish for nothing else.

CHORUS. Then pray no more; from suffering that has
been
Decreed no man will ever find escape.

CREON [*sings*]. Lead me away, a rash, a misguided
man,
Whose blindness has killed a wife and a son.*   1340
O where can I look? What strength can I find?
On me has fallen a doom greater than I can bear.
                    [*Exeunt* CREON *and* GUARDS *into the palace*

CHORUS [*chants*]. Of happiness, far the greatest part
Is wisdom, and reverence towards the gods.
Proud words of the arrogant man, in the end,   1350
Meet punishment, great as his pride was great,
Till at last he is schooled in wisdom.

OEDIPUS THE KING

DRAMATIS PERSONAE

OEDIPUS, *King of Thebes*
PRIEST OF ZEUS
CREON, *brother of Iocasta*
TEIRESIAS, *a Seer*
IOCASTA, *Queen of Thebes*
A CORINTHIAN SHEPHERD
A THEBAN SHEPHERD
A MESSENGER
CHORUS *of Theban citizens*
ANTIGONE ⎫ daughters of Oedipus and Iocasta (*they have no*
ISMENE ⎭ *speaking parts.*)
Priests, Attendants, etc.

Scene: Thebes, before the royal palace

OEDIPUS THE KING[1]

OEDIPUS. My children,* latest brood of ancient
    Cadmus,*
  What purpose brings you here, a multitude
  Bearing the boughs that mark the suppliant?*
  Why is our air so full of frankincense,
  So full of hymns and prayers* and lamentations?
  This, children, was no matter to entrust
  To others: therefore I myself am come
  Whose fame is known to all—I, Oedipus.
  —You, Sir, are pointed out by length of years
  To be the spokesman: tell me, what is in   10
  Your hearts? What fear? What sorrow? Count on all
  That I can do, for I am not so hard
  As not to pity such a supplication.

PRIEST. Great King of Thebes, and sovereign Oedipus,
  Look on us, who now stand before the altars—*
  Some young, still weak of wing; some bowed with
    age—
  The priests, as I, of Zeus; and these, the best
  Of our young men; and in the market-place,
  And by Athena's temples and the shrine
  Of fiery divination,* there is kneeling,   20
  Each with his suppliant branch, the rest of Thebes.
  The city, as you see yourself, is now
  Storm-tossed, and can no longer raise its head
  Above the waves and angry surge of death.
  The fruitful blossoms of the land are barren,
  The herds upon our pastures, and our wives
  In childbirth, barren. Last, and worst of all,
  The withering god of fever* swoops on us
  To empty Cadmus' city and enrich

---

[1] Verse lines are numbered according to the Greek text (see Introduction,
p. xxxv).

Dark Hades with our groans and lamentations.　　　30
No god we count you,* that we bring our prayers,
I and these children, to your palace-door,
But wise above all other men to read
Life's riddles, and the hidden ways of Heaven;
For it was you who came and set us free
From the blood-tribute that the cruel Sphinx*
Had laid upon our city; without our aid
Or our instruction, but, as we believe,
With god as ally, you gave us back our life.
So now, most dear, most mighty Oedipus,　　　40
We all entreat you on our bended knees,*
Come to our rescue, whether from the gods
Or from some man you can find means to save.
For I have noted, *that* man's counsel is
Of best effect, who has been tried in action.
Come, noble Oedipus! Come, save our city.
Be well advised; for that past service given
This city calls you Saviour; of your kingship
Let not the record be that first we rose
From ruin, then to ruin fell again.　　　50
No, save our city, let it stand secure.
You brought us gladness and deliverance
Before; now do no less. You rule this land;
Better to rule it full of living men
Than rule a desert; citadel or ship
Without its company of men is nothing.

OEDIPUS. My children, what you long for, that I know
Indeed, and pity you. I know how cruelly
You suffer; yet, though sick, not one of you　　　60
Suffers a sickness half as great as mine.
Yours is a single pain; each man of you
Feels but his own. My heart is heavy with
The city's pain, my own, and yours together.
You come to me not as to one asleep
And needing to be wakened; many a tear
I have been shedding, every path of thought
Have I been pacing; and what remedy,

What single hope my anxious thought has found
That I have tried. Creon, Menoeceus' son,
My own wife's brother, I have sent to Delphi   70
To ask in Phoebus' house* what act of mine,
What word of mine, may bring deliverance.
Now, as I count the days, it troubles me
What he is doing; his absence is prolonged
Beyond the proper time. But when he comes
Then write me down a villain, if I do
Not each particular that the god discloses.

PRIEST. You give us hope.—And here is more, for they
Are signalling* that Creon has returned.

OEDIPUS. O Lord Apollo, even as Creon smiles,   80
Smile now on us, and let it be deliverance!

PRIEST. The news is good; or he would not be wearing
That ample wreath of richly-berried laurel.

OEDIPUS. We soon shall know; my voice will reach so
far:
Creon my lord, my kinsman, what response
Do you bring with you from the god of Delphi?

Enter CREON

CREON. Good news! Our sufferings, if they are guided
right,
Can even yet turn to a happy issue.

OEDIPUS. This only leaves my fear and confidence
In equal balance: what did Phoebus say?   90

CREON. Is it your wish to hear it now, in public,
Or in the palace? I am at your service.

OEDIPUS. Let them all hear! Their sufferings distress
Me more than if my own life were at stake.

CREON. Then I will tell you what Apollo said—
And it was very clear. There is pollution*
Here in our midst, long-standing. This must we
Expel, nor let it grow past remedy.

OEDIPUS. What has defiled us? and how are we to
  purge it?

CREON. By banishing or killing one who murdered,   100
  And so called down this pestilence upon us.

OEDIPUS. Who is the man whose death the god
  denounces?

CREON. Before the city passed into your care,
  My lord, we had a king called Laius.*

OEDIPUS. So have I often heard.—I never saw him.

CREON. His death, Apollo clearly charges us,
  We must avenge upon his murderers.

OEDIPUS. Where are they now? And where shall we
  disclose
  The unseen traces of that ancient crime?

CREON. The god said, Here.—A man who hunts with
  care   110
  May often find what other men will miss.

OEDIPUS. Where was he murdered?* In the palace
  here?
  Or in the country? Or was he abroad?

CREON. He made a journey to consult the god,
  He said—and never came back home again.

OEDIPUS. But was there no report? no fellow traveller
  Whose knowledge might have helped you in your
  search?

CREON. All died, except one terror-stricken man,
  And he could tell us nothing—next to nothing.

OEDIPUS. And what was that? One thing might lead to
  much,   120
  If only we could find one ray of light.

CREON. He said they met with brigands—not with one,
  But a whole company; they killed Laius.

OEDIPUS. A brigand would not *dare*—unless perhaps
  Conspirators in Thebes had bribed the man.

CREON. There *was* conjecture; but disaster came
  And we were leaderless, without our king.

OEDIPUS. Disaster? With a king cut down like that
  You did not seek the cause? Where was the
    hindrance?

CREON. The Sphinx. *Her* riddle* pressed us harder still;
  For Laius—out of sight was out of mind.   130

OEDIPUS. I will begin again; *I*'ll find the truth.
  The dead man's cause has found a true defender
  In Phoebus, and in you. And I will join you
  In seeking vengeance on behalf of Thebes
  And Phoebus too; indeed, I must: if I
  Remove this taint, it is not for a stranger,
  But for myself: the man who murdered him
  Might make the same attempt on me; and so,   140
  Avenging him, I shall protect myself.—
    Now you, my sons, without delay, arise,
  Take up your suppliant branches.—Someone, go
  And call the people here, for I will do
  What can be done; and either, by the grace
  Of God we shall be saved—or we shall fall.

PRIEST. My children, we will go; the King has promised
  All that we came to ask.—O Phoebus, thou
  Hast given us an answer: give us too
  Protection! grant remission of the plague!   150
    [*Exeunt* CREON, PRIESTS, *etc*. OEDIPUS *remains*

Enter the CHORUS *representing the citizens of Thebes*

Strophe 1

CHORUS [*sings*]. Sweet is the voice of the god,* that
  sounds in the
  Golden shrine of Delphi.

What message has it sent to Thebes? My trembling
Heart is torn with anguish.
Thou god of Healing, Phoebus Apollo,
How do I fear! What hast thou in mind
To bring upon us now? what is to be fulfilled
From days of old?
Tell me this, O Voice divine,
Thou child of golden Hope.

Antistrophe 1

First on the Daughter of Zeus I call for
Help, divine Athena;
And Artemis, whose throne is all the earth, whose   160
Shrine is in our city;
Apollo too, who shoots from afar:*
Trinity of Powers, come to our defence!
If ever in the past, when ruin threatened us,
You stayed its course
And turned aside the flood of Death,
O then, protect us now!

Strophe 2

Past counting are the woes we suffer;
Affliction bears on all the city, and
Nowhere is any defence against destruction.   170
The holy soil can bring no increase,
Our women suffer and cry in childbirth
But do not bring forth living children.
The souls of those who perish, one by one,
Unceasingly, swift as raging fire,
Rise and take their flight to the dark realms of the
   dead.*

Antistrophe 2

Past counting, those of us who perish:
They lie upon the ground, unpitied,   180

Unburied, infecting the air with deadly pollution.
Young wives, and grey-haired mothers with them,
From every quarter approach the altars
And cry aloud in supplication.
The prayer for healing, the loud wail of lament,
Together are heard in dissonance:
O thou golden Daughter of Zeus,* grant thy aid!

Strophe 3

The fierce god of War* has laid aside   190
His spear; but yet his terrible cry
Rings in our ears; he spreads death and destruction.
Ye gods, drive him back to his distant home!*
   For what the light of day has spared,
   That the darkness of night destroys.
   Zeus our father! All power is thine: 200
The lightning-flash is thine: hurl upon him
Thy thunderbolt, and quell this god of War!

Antistrophe 3

We pray, Lord Apollo: draw thy bow
In our defence. Thy quiver is full of
Arrows unerring: shoot! slay the destroyer!
And thou, radiant Artemis, lend thy aid!
   Thou whose hair is bound in gold,
   Bacchus, lord of the sacred dance,*   210
   Theban Bacchus! Come, show thyself!
Display thy blazing torch; drive from our midst
The savage god,* abhorred by other gods!

OEDIPUS. Would you have answer to these prayers?
   Then hear
My words; give heed; your help may bring
Deliverance, and the end of all our troubles.
Here do I stand before you all, a stranger
Both to the deed and to the story.—What   220
Could I have done alone, without a clue?

But I was yet a foreigner; it was later
That I became a Theban among Thebans.
So now do I proclaim to all the city:
If any Theban knows by what man's hand
He perished, Laius, son of Labdacus,
Him I command to tell me all he can;
And if he is afraid, let him annul
Himself the charge he fears; no punishment
Shall fall on him, save only to depart
Unharmed from Thebes. Further, if any knows   230
The slayer to be a stranger from abroad,
Let him speak out; I will reward him, and
Besides, he will have all my gratitude.
But if you still keep silent, if any man
Fearing for self or friend shall disobey me,
This will I do—and listen to my words:
Whoever he may be, I do forbid
All in this realm, of which I am the King
And high authority, to shelter in their houses
Or speak to him, or let him be their partner
In prayers or sacrifices to the gods, or give
Him lustral water;* I command you all   240
To drive him from your doors; for he it is
That brings this plague upon us, as the god
Of Delphi has but now declared to me.—
So stern an ally do I make myself
Both of the god and of our murdered king.—
And for the man that slew him, whether he
Slew him alone, or with a band of helpers,
I lay this curse upon him, that the wretch
In wretchedness and misery may live.
And more: if with my knowledge he be found   250
To share my hearth and home, then upon me
Descend that doom that I invoke on him.
This charge I lay upon you, to observe
All my commands: to aid myself, the god,
And this our land, so spurned of Heaven, so ravaged.
For such a taint we should not leave unpurged—
The death of such a man, and he your king—

56

Even if Heaven had not commanded us,
But we should search it out. Now, since 'tis I
That wear the crown that he had worn before me,
And have his Queen to wife, and common children   260
Were born to us, but that his own did perish,
And sudden death has carried him away—
Because of this, I will defend his cause
As if it were my father's; nothing I
Will leave undone to find the man who killed
The son of Labdacus, and offspring of
Polydorus, Cadmus, and of old Agenor.*
On those that disobey, this is my curse:
May never field of theirs give increase, nor   270
Their wives have children; may our present plagues,
And worse, be ever theirs, for their destruction.
But for the others, all with whom my words
Find favour, this I pray: Justice* and all
The gods be ever at your side to help you.

CHORUS. Your curse constrains me; therefore will I
    speak.
  I did not kill him, neither can I tell
  Who did. It is for Phoebus, since he laid
  The task upon us, to declare the man.

OEDIPUS. True; but to force the gods against their
    will—   280
  That is a thing beyond all human power.

CHORUS. All I could say is but a second best.

OEDIPUS. Though it were third best, do not hold it
    back.

CHORUS. I know of none that reads Apollo's mind
  So surely as the lord Teiresias;
  Consulting him you best might learn the truth.

OEDIPUS. Not even this have I neglected: Creon
  Advised me, and already I have sent
  Two messengers.—Strange he has not come.

CHORUS. There's nothing else but old and idle gossip.   290

OEDIPUS. And what was that? I clutch at any straw.

CHORUS. They said that he was killed by travellers.

OEDIPUS. So I have heard; but no one knows a witness.

CHORUS. But if he is not proof against *all* fear
  He'll not keep silent when he hears your curse.

OEDIPUS. And will they fear a curse, who dared to kill?

CHORUS. Here is the one to find him, for at last
  They bring the prophet here. He is inspired,
  The only man whose heart is filled with truth.

Enter TEIRESIAS, *led by a boy*

OEDIPUS. Teiresias, by your art you read the signs   300
  And secrets of the earth and of the sky;
  Therefore you know, although you cannot see,
  The plague that is besetting us; from this
  No other man but you, my lord, can save us.
  Phoebus has said—you may have heard already—
  In answer to our question, that this plague
  Will never cease unless we can discover
  What men they were who murdered Laius,
  And punish them with death or banishment.
  Therefore give freely all that you have learned   310
  From birds or other form of divination;*
  Save us; save me, the city, and yourself,
  From the pollution that his bloodshed causes.
  No finer task, than to give all one has
  In helping others; we are in your hands.

TEIRESIAS. Ah! what a burden knowledge is, when
    knowledge
  Can be of no avail! I knew this well,
  And yet forgot, or I should not have come.

OEDIPUS. Why, what is this? Why are you so
    despondent?

58

TEIRESIAS. Let me go home! It will be best for you,   320
    And best for me, if you will let me go.

OEDIPUS. But to withhold your knowledge! This is
    wrong,
    Disloyal to the city of your birth.

TEIRESIAS. I know that what you say will lead you on
    To ruin; therefore, lest the same befall me too . . .

OEDIPUS. No, by the gods! Say all you know, for we
    Go down upon our knees, your suppliants.

TEIRESIAS. Because *you* do *not* know! I never shall
    Reveal my burden—I will not say *yours*.

OEDIPUS. You know, and will not tell us? Do you wish
    To ruin Thebes and to destroy us all?   330

TEIRESIAS. *My* pain, and yours, will not be caused by
    me.
    Why these vain questions?—for I will not speak.

OEDIPUS. You villain!—for you would provoke a stone
    To anger: you'll not speak, but show yourself
    So hard of heart and so inflexible?

TEIRESIAS. You heap the blame on me; but what is
    yours
    You do not know—therefore *I* am the villain!

OEDIPUS. And who would not be angry, finding that
    You treat our people with such cold disdain?   340

TEIRESIAS. The truth will come to light, without *my*
    help.

OEDIPUS. If it is bound to come, you ought to speak it.

TEIRESIAS. I'll say no more, and you, if so you choose,
    May rage and bluster on without restraint.

OEDIPUS. Restraint? Then I'll show none! I'll tell you
    all
    That I can see in you: I do believe

This crime was planned and carried out by you,
All but the killing; and were you not blind
I'd say your hand alone had done the murder.

TEIRESIAS. So? Then I tell you this: submit yourself   350
To that decree that you have made; from now
Address no word to these men nor to me:
You are the man whose crimes pollute our city.

OEDIPUS. What, does your impudence extend thus far?
And do you hope that it will go scot-free?

TEIRESIAS. It will. I have a champion—the truth.

OEDIPUS. Who taught you that? For it was not your
art.

TEIRESIAS. No; you! You made me speak, against my
will.

OEDIPUS. Speak what? Say it again, and say it clearly.

TEIRESIAS. Was I not clear? Or are you tempting me?   360

OEDIPUS. Not clear enough for me. Say it again.

TEIRESIAS. You are yourself the murderer you seek.

OEDIPUS. You'll not affront me twice and go
unpunished!

TEIRESIAS. Then shall I give you still more cause for
rage?

OEDIPUS. Say what you will; you'll say it to no
purpose.

TEIRESIAS. *I* know, *you* do not know, the hideous life
Of shame you lead with those most near to you.

OEDIPUS. You'll pay most dearly for this insolence!

TEIRESIAS. No, not if Truth is strong, and can prevail.

OEDIPUS. It is—except in you; for you are blind   370
In eyes and ears and brains and everything.

TEIRESIAS. You'll not forget these insults that you
    throw
  At me, when all men throw the same at you.

OEDIPUS. You live in darkness; you can do no harm
  To me or any man who has his eyes.

TEIRESIAS. No; *I* am not to bring you down, because
  Apollo is enough; he'll see to it.

OEDIPUS. Creon, or you? Which of you made this plot?

TEIRESIAS. Creon's no enemy of yours; you are your
    own.

OEDIPUS. O Wealth! O Royalty! whose commanding   380
    art
  Outstrips all other arts in life's contentions!
  How great a store of envy lies upon you,
  If for this sceptre, that the city gave
  Freely to me, unasked—if now my friend,
  The trusty Creon, burns to drive me hence
  And steal it from me! So he has suborned
  This crafty schemer here, this mountebank,
  Whose purse alone has eyes, whose art is blind.—
  Come, prophet, show your title! When the Sphinx   390
  Chanted her music here, why did not *you*
  Speak out and save the city? Yet such a question
  Was one for augury, not for mother wit.
  You were no prophet then; your birds, your voice
  From Heaven, were dumb. But I, who came by
    chance,
  I, knowing nothing, put the Sphinx to flight,
  Thanks to my wit—no thanks to divination!
  And now you try to drive me out; you hope
  When Creon's king to bask in Creon's favour.   400
  You'll expiate the curse? Ay, and repent it,
  Both you and your accomplice. But that you
  Seem old, I'd teach you what you gain by treason!

CHORUS. My lord, he spoke in anger; so, I think,
  Did you. What help in angry speeches? Come,

This is the task, how we can best discharge
The duty that the god has laid on us.

TEIRESIAS. King though you are, I claim the privilege
Of equal answer. No, I have the right;
I am no slave of yours—I serve Apollo,   410
And therefore am not listed *Creon's* man.
Listen—since you have taunted me with blindness!
You have your sight, and yet you cannot see
Where, nor with whom, you live, nor in what
    horror.
Your parents—do you know them? or that you
Are enemy to your kin, alive or dead?
And that a father's and a mother's curse
Shall join to drive you headlong out of Thebes
And change the light that now you see to darkness?
Your cries of agony, where will they not reach?   420
Where on Cithaeron* will they not re-echo?
When you have learned what meant the marriage-
    song
Which bore you to an evil haven here
After so fair a voyage? And you are blind
To other horrors, which shall make you one
With your own children. Therefore, heap your scorn
On Creon and on me, for no man living
Will meet a doom more terrible than yours.

OEDIPUS. What? Am I to suffer words like this from
    him?
Ruin, damnation seize you! Off at once   430
Out of our sight! Go! Get you whence you came!

TEIRESIAS. Had you not called me, I should not be here.

OEDIPUS. And had I known that you would talk such
    folly,
I'd not have called you to a house of mine.

TEIRESIAS. To you I seem a fool, but to your parents,
To those who did beget you, I was wise.

OEDIPUS. Stop! Who were they? Who *were* my
parents? Tell me!

TEIRESIAS. This day will show your birth and your
destruction.

OEDIPUS. You are too fond of dark obscurities.

TEIRESIAS. But do you not excel in reading riddles?　　440

OEDIPUS. I scorn your taunts; my skill has brought me
glory.

TEIRESIAS. And this success brought you to ruin too.

OEDIPUS. I am content, if so I saved this city.

TEIRESIAS. Then I will leave you. Come, boy, take my
hand.

OEDIPUS. Yes, let him take it. You are nothing but
Vexation here. Begone, and give me peace!

TEIRESIAS. When I have had my say. No frown of yours
Shall frighten *me*; you cannot injure me.
Here is my message: that man whom you seek
With threats and proclamations for the death　　450
Of Laius, he is living here; he's thought
To be a foreigner, but shall be found
Theban by birth—and little joy will this
Bring *him*; when, with his eyesight turned to
blindness,
His wealth to beggary, on foreign soil
With staff* in hand he'll tap his way along,
His children with him; and he will be known
Himself to be their father and their brother,
The husband of the mother who gave him birth,
Supplanter of his father, and his slayer.　　460
—There! Go, and think on this; and if you find
That I'm deceived, say then—and not before—
That I am ignorant in divination.

　　　　[*Exeunt severally* OEDIPUS, TEIRESIAS, *and boy*

Strophe 1

CHORUS [*sings*]. The voice of god* rang out in the holy
    cavern,
  Denouncing one who has killed a King—the crime
    of crimes.
    Who is the man? Let him begone in
    Headlong flight, swift as a horse!

  For the terrible god,* like a warrior armed,
  Stands ready to strike with a lightning-flash: 470
    The Furies who punish crime,* and never fail,
    Are hot in their pursuit.

Antistrophe 1

The snow is white on the cliffs of high Parnassus.*
It has flashed a message: Let every Theban join the
    hunt!
    Lurking in caves among the mountains,
    Deep in the woods—where is the man?

In wearisome flight, unresting, alone,
An outlaw, he shuns Apollo's shrine;   480
    But ever the living menace of the god
    Hovers around his head.

Strophe 2

Strange, disturbing, what the wise
Prophet has said. What can he mean?
Neither can I believe, nor can I disbelieve;
I do not know what to say.
I look here, and there; nothing can I find—
No strife, either now or in the past,
Between the kings of Thebes and Corinth.*   490
A hand unknown struck down the King;
Though I would learn who it was dealt the blow,
That *he* is guilty whom all revere—
How can I believe this with no proof?

Antistrophe 2

Zeus, Apollo—they have knowledge;
They understand the ways of life.
Prophets are men, like me; that they can understand
More than is revealed to me—   500
Of that, I can find nowhere certain proof,
Though one man is wise, another foolish.
Until the charge is manifest
I will not credit his accusers.
I saw myself how the Sphinx challenged him:
He proved his wisdom; he saved our city;   510
Therefore how can I now condemn him?

Enter CREON

CREON. They tell me, Sirs, that Oedipus the King
　　Has made against me such an accusation
　　That I will not endure. For if he thinks
　　That in this present trouble I have done
　　Or said a single thing to do him harm,
　　Then let me die, and not drag out my days
　　With such a name as that. For it is not
　　One injury this accusation does me;   520
　　It touches my whole life, if you, my friends,
　　And all the city are to call me traitor.

CHORUS. The accusation may perhaps have come
　　From heat of temper, not from sober judgement.

CREON. What was it made him think contrivances
　　Of mine suborned the seer to tell his lies?

CHORUS. Those were his words; I do not know his
　　　　reasons.

CREON. Was he in earnest, master of himself,
　　When he attacked me with this accusation?

CHORUS. I do not closely scan what kings are doing.—   530
　　But here he comes in person from the palace.

Enter OEDIPUS

OEDIPUS. What, *you*? You dare come here? How can
    you find
    The impudence to show yourself before
    My house, when you are clearly proven
    To have sought my life and tried to steal my crown?
    Why, do you think me then a coward, or
    A fool, that you should try to lay this plot?
    Or that I should not see what you were scheming,
    And so fall unresisting, blindly, to you?
    But you were mad, so to attempt the throne,   540
    Poor and unaided; this is not encompassed
    Without the strong support of friends and money!

CREON. This you must do: now you have had your say
    Hear my reply; then yourself shall judge.

OEDIPUS. A ready tongue! But I am bad at listening—
    To you. For I have found how much you hate me.

CREON. One thing: first listen to what I have to say.

OEDIPUS. One thing: do not pretend you're not a
    villain.

CREON. If you believe it is a thing worth having,
    Insensate stubbornness, then you are wrong.   550

OEDIPUS. If you believe that one can harm a kinsman
    Without retaliation, you are wrong.

CREON. With this I have no quarrel; but explain
    What injury you say that I have done you.

OEDIPUS. Did you advise, or did you not, that I
    Should send a man for that most reverend prophet?

CREON. I did, and I am still of that advice.

OEDIPUS. How long a time is it since Laius . . .

CREON. Since Laius did *what*? How can I say?

OEDIPUS. Was seen no more, but met a violent death?   560

CREON. It would be many years now past and gone.

OEDIPUS. And had this prophet learned his art already?

CREON. Yes; his repute was great—as it is now.

OEDIPUS. Did he make any mention then of me?

CREON. He never spoke of you within my hearing.

OEDIPUS. Touching the murder: did you make no
   search?

CREON. No search? Of course we did; but we found
   nothing.

OEDIPUS. And why did this wise prophet not speak
   then?

CREON. Who knows? Where I know nothing I say
   nothing.

OEDIPUS. This much you know—and you'll do well to
   answer: 570

CREON. What is it? If I know, I'll tell you freely.

OEDIPUS. That if he had not joined with you, he'd not
   Have said that I was Laius' murderer.

CREON. If he said this, I did not know.—But I
   May rightly question you, as you have me.

OEDIPUS. Ask what you will. You'll never prove *I*
   killed him.

CREON. Why then: are you not married to my sister?

OEDIPUS. I am indeed; it cannot be denied.

CREON. You share with her the sovereignty of Thebes?

OEDIPUS. She need but ask, and anything is hers.   580

CREON. And am I not myself conjoined with you?

OEDIPUS. You are; not rebel therefore, but a traitor!

CREON. Not so, if you will reason with yourself,
   As I with you. This first: would any man,

67

To gain no increase of authority,
Choose kingship, with its fears and sleepless nights?
Not I. What I desire, what every man
Desires, if he has wisdom, is to take
The substance, not the show, of royalty.
For now, through you, I have both power and ease,   590
But were I king, I'd be oppressed with cares.
Not so: while I have ample sovereignty
And rule in peace, why should I want the crown?
I am not yet so made as to give up
All that which brings me honour and advantage.
Now, every man greets me, and I greet him;
Those who have need of you make much of me,
Since I can make or mar them. Why should I
Surrender this to load myself with that?
A man of sense was never yet a traitor;   600
I have no taste for that, nor could I force
Myself to aid another's treachery.
    But you can test me: go to Delphi; ask
If I reported rightly what was said.
And further: if you find that I had dealings
With that diviner, you may take and kill me
Not with your single vote, but yours and mine,
But not on bare suspicion, unsupported.
How wrong it is, to use a random judgement
And think the false man true, the true man false!   610
To spurn a loyal friend, that is no better
Than to destroy the life to which we cling.
This you will learn in time, for Time alone
Reveals the upright man; a single day
Suffices to unmask the treacherous.

CHORUS. My lord, he speaks with caution, to avoid
    Grave error. Hasty judgement is not sure.

OEDIPUS. But when an enemy is quick to plot
    And strike, I must be quick in answer too.
    If I am slow, and wait, then I shall find   620
    That he has gained his end, and I am lost.

68

CREON. What do you wish? To drive me into exile?

OEDIPUS. No, more than exile: I will have your life.

CREON. 〈When will it cease, this monstrous rage of
　　yours?〉*

OEDIPUS. When your example shows what comes of
　　envy.

CREON. Must you be stubborn? Cannot you believe
　　me?

OEDIPUS. 〈You speak to me as if I were a fool!〉

CREON. Because I know you're wrong.

OEDIPUS.　　　　　　　　　　Right, for myself!

CREON. It is not right for me!

OEDIPUS.　　　　　　　　　　But you're a traitor.

CREON. What if your charge is false?

OEDIPUS.　　　　　　　　　　I have to govern.

CREON. Not govern badly!

OEDIPUS.　　　　　　　Listen to him, Thebes!

CREON. You're not the city! I am Theban too.　　　630

CHORUS. My lords, no more! Here comes the Queen,
　　and not
　Too soon, to join you. With her help, you must
　Compose the bitter strife that now divides you.

Enter IOCASTA

IOCASTA. You frantic men! What has aroused this wild
　Dispute? Have you no shame, when such a plague
　Afflicts us, to indulge in private quarrels?
　Creon, go home, I pray. You, Oedipus,
　Come in; do not make much of what is nothing.

CREON. My sister: Oedipus, your husband here,
　Has thought it right to punish me with one　　　640
　Of two most awful dooms: exile, or death.

69

OEDIPUS. I have: I have convicted him, Iocasta,
  Of plotting secretly against my life.

CREON. If I am guilty in a single point
  Of such a crime, then may I die accursed.

IOCASTA. O, by the gods, believe him, Oedipus!
  Respect the oath that he has sworn, and have
  Regard for me, and for these citizens.

[*Until line 697 the parts given to the chorus are sung, the rest,
  presumably, spoken.*]

Strophe

CHORUS. My lord, I pray, give consent.
  Yield to us; ponder well.   650

OEDIPUS. What is it you would have me yield?

CHORUS. Respect a man ripe in years,
  Bound by this mighty oath he has sworn.

OEDIPUS. Your wish is clear?

CHORUS.   It is.

OEDIPUS.   Then tell it me.

CHORUS. Not to repel, and drive out of our midst a
    friend,
  Scorning a solemn curse, for uncertain cause.

OEDIPUS. I tell you this: your prayer will mean for me
  My banishment from Thebes, or else my death.

CHORUS. No, no! by the Sun, the chief of gods,*   660
    Ruin and desolation and all evil come upon me
  If I harbour thoughts such as these!
  No; our land racked with plague breaks my heart.
    Do not now deal a new wound on Thebes to
    crown the old!

OEDIPUS. Then let him be, though I must die twice
  over,

Or be dishonoured, spurned and driven out.   670
It's your entreaty, and not his, that moves
My pity; he shall have my lasting hatred.

CREON. You yield ungenerously; but when your wrath
Has cooled, how it will prick you! Natures such
As yours give most vexation to themselves.

OEDIPUS. O, let me be! Get from my sight.

CREON.   I go,
Misjudged by you—but these will judge me better
                              [*indicating* CHORUS].
                                    [*Exit* CREON

Antistrophe

CHORUS. My lady, why now delay?
Let the King go in with you.

IOCASTA. When you have told me what has passed.   680

CHORUS. Suspicion came.—Random words,
   undeserved,
Will provoke men to wrath.

IOCASTA. It was from both?

CHORUS.   It was.

IOCASTA.   And what was said?

CHORUS. It is enough for me, more than enough, when
   I
Think of our ills, that this should rest where it lies.

OEDIPUS. You and your wise advice, blunting my
   wrath,
Frustrated me—and it has come to this!

CHORUS. This, O my King, I said, and say again:
   I should be mad, distraught,   690
   I should be a fool, and worse,
   If I sought to drive you away.
   Thebes was near sinking; you brought her safe

71

Through the storm. Now again we pray that you
    may save us.

IOCASTA. In Heaven's name, my lord, I too must know
    What was the reason for this blazing anger.

OEDIPUS. There's none to whom I more defer; and so,   700
    I'll tell you: Creon and his vile plot against me.

IOCASTA. What has he done, that you are so incensed?

OEDIPUS. He says that I am Laius' murderer.

IOCASTA. From his own knowledge? Or has someone
    told him?

OEDIPUS. No; that suspicion should not fall upon
    Himself, he used a tool—a crafty prophet.

IOCASTA. Why, have no fear of *that*. Listen to me,
    And you will learn that the prophetic art
    Touches our human fortunes not at all.
    I soon can give you proof.—An oracle   710
    Once came to Laius—from the god himself
    I do not say, but from his ministers:
    His fate it was, that should he have a son
    By me, that son would take his father's life.
    But he was killed—or so they said—by strangers,
    By brigands, at a place where three ways meet.
    As for the child, it was not three days old
    When Laius fastened both its feet together
    And had it cast over a precipice.*
    Therefore Apollo failed; for neither did   720
    His son kill Laius, nor did Laius meet
    The awful end he feared, killed by his son.
      So much for what prophetic voices uttered.
    Have no regard for them. The god will bring
    To light himself whatever thing he chooses.

OEDIPUS. Iocasta, terror seizes me, and shakes
    My very soul, at one thing you have said.

IOCASTA. Why so? What have I said to frighten you?

OEDIPUS. I think I heard you say that Laius
Was murdered at a place where three ways meet?   730

IOCASTA. So it was said—indeed, they say it still.

OEDIPUS. Where is the place where this encounter
happened?

IOCASTA. They call the country Phokis, and a road
From Delphi joins a road from Daulia.*

OEDIPUS. Since that was done, how many years have
passed?

IOCASTA. It was proclaimed in Thebes a little time
Before the city offered you the crown.

OEDIPUS. O Zeus, what fate hast thou ordained for
me?

IOCASTA. What is the fear that so oppresses you?

OEDIPUS. One moment yet: tell me of Laius.   740
What age was he? and what was his appearance?

IOCASTA. A tall man, and his hair was touched with
white;
In figure he was not unlike yourself.

OEDIPUS. O God! Did I, then, in my ignorance,
Proclaim that awful curse against myself?

IOCASTA. What are you saying? How you frighten me!

OEDIPUS. I greatly fear that prophet was not blind.
But yet one question; that will show me more.

IOCASTA. For all my fear, I'll tell you what I can.

OEDIPUS. Was he alone, or did he have with him   750
A royal bodyguard of men-at-arms?

IOCASTA. The company in all were five; the King
Rode in a carriage, and there was a Herald.*

OEDIPUS. Ah God! How clear the picture is! . . . But
who,

73

Iocasta, brought report of this to Thebes?

IOCASTA. A slave, the only man that was not killed.

OEDIPUS. And is he round about the palace now?

IOCASTA. No, he is not. When he returned, and saw
You ruling in the place of the dead King,
He begged me, on his bended knees, to send him   760
Into the hills as shepherd, out of sight,
As far as could be from the city here.
I sent him, for he was a loyal slave;
He well deserved this favour—and much more.

OEDIPUS. Could he be brought back here—at once—
to see me?

IOCASTA. He could; but why do you desire his
coming?

OEDIPUS. I fear I have already said, Iocasta,
More than enough; and therefore I will see him.

IOCASTA. Then he shall come. But, as your wife, I ask
you,
What is the terror that possesses you?   770

OEDIPUS. And you shall know it, since my fears have
grown
So great; for who is more to me than you,
That I should speak to *him* at such a moment?
   My father, then, was Polybus of Corinth;
My mother, Merope.* My station there
Was high as any man's—until a thing
Befell me that was strange indeed, though not
Deserving of the thought I gave to it.
A man said at a banquet—he was full
Of wine—that I was not my father's son.   780
It angered me; but I restrained myself
That day. The next I went and questioned both
My parents. They were much incensed with him
Who had let fall the insult. So, from them,
I had assurance. Yet the slander spread

74

And always chafed me. Therefore secretly,
My mother and my father unaware,
I went to Delphi. Phoebus would return
No answer to my question, but declared
A thing most horrible: he foretold that I   790
Should mate with my own mother, and beget
A brood that men would shudder to behold,
And that I was to be the murderer
Of my own father.
              Therefore, back to Corinth
I never went—the stars alone have told me*
Where Corinth lies—that I might never see
Cruel fulfilment of that oracle.
So journeying, I came to that same spot
Where, as you say, this King was killed. And now,
This is the truth, Iocasta: when I reached   800
The place where three ways meet, I met a herald,
And in a carriage drawn by colts was such
A man as you describe. By violence
The herald and the older man attempted
To push me off the road, I, in my rage,
Struck at the driver, who was hustling me.
The old man, when he saw me level with him,
Taking a double-goad, aimed at my head
A murderous blow. He paid for that, full measure.   810
Swiftly I hit him with my staff; he rolled
Out of his carriage, flat upon his back.
I killed them all.—But if, between this stranger
And Laius there was any bond of kinship,*
Who could be in more desperate plight than I?
Who more accursèd in the eyes of Heaven?
For neither citizen nor stranger may
Receive me in his house, nor speak to me,
But he must bar the door. And it was none
But I invoked this curse on my own head!   820
And I pollute the bed of him I slew
With my own hands! Say, am I vile? Am I
Not all impure? Seeing I must be exiled,
And even in my exile must not go

And see my parents, nor set foot upon
My native land; or, if I do, I must
Marry my mother, and kill Polybus
My father, who engendered me and reared me.
If one should say it was a cruel god
Brought this upon me, would he not speak right?
    No, no, you holy powers above! Let me   830
Not see that day! but rather let me pass
Beyond the sight of men, before I see
The stain of such pollution come upon me!

CHORUS. My lord, this frightens me. But you must
   hope,
Until we hear the tale from him that saw it.

OEDIPUS. That is the only hope that's left to me;
   We must await the coming of the shepherd.

IOCASTA. What do you hope from him, when he is
   here?

OEDIPUS. I'll tell you; if his story shall be found
   The same as yours, then I am free of guilt.   840

IOCASTA. But what have *I* said of especial note?

OEDIPUS. You said that he reported it was brigands
   Who killed the King. If he still speaks of 'men',
   It was not I; a single man, and 'men',
   Are not the same. But if he says it was
   A traveller journeying alone, why then,
   The burden of the guilt must fall on me.

IOCASTA. But that *is* what he said, I do assure you!
   He cannot take it back again! Not I
   Alone, but the whole city heard him say it!   850
   But even if he should revoke the tale
   He told before, not even so, my lord,
   Will he establish that the King was slain
   According to the prophecy. For that was clear:
   His son, and mine, should slay him.—He, poor
     thing,

Was killed himself, and never killed his father.
Therefore, so far as divination goes,
Or prophecy, I'll take no notice of it.

OEDIPUS. And that is wise. But send a man to bring
The shepherd; I would not have that neglected.   860

IOCASTA. I'll send at once.—But come with me; for I
Would not do anything that could displease you.
                    [*Exeunt* OEDIPUS *and* IOCASTA

Strophe 1

CHORUS [*sings*]. I pray that I may pass my life
  In reverent holiness of word and deed.
  For there are laws* enthroned above;
  Heaven created them,
  Olympus was their father,
  And mortal men had no part in their birth;
  Nor ever shall their power pass from sight   870
  In dull forgetfulness;
  A god* moves in them; he grows not old.

Antistrophe 1

  Pride makes the tyrant*—pride of wealth
  And power, too great for wisdom and restraint;
  For Pride will climb the topmost height;
  Then is the man cast down
  To uttermost destruction.
  There he finds no escape, no resource.
  But high contention for the city's good   880
  May the gods preserve.
  For me—may the gods be my defence!

Strophe 2

  If there is one who walks in pride
  Of word or deed, and has no fear of Justice,
  No reverence for holy shrines—

May utter ruin fall on him!
So may his ill-starred pride be given its reward.
Those who seek dishonourable advantage
And lay violent hands on holy things   890
And do not shun impiety—
Who among these will secure himself from the
   wrath of God?
If deeds like these are honoured,
Why should I join in the sacred dance?*

Antistrophe 2

No longer shall Apollo's shrine,
The holy centre of the Earth, receive my worship;
No, nor his seat at Abae,* nor   900
The temple of Olympian Zeus,*
If what the god foretold does not come to pass.
Mighty Zeus—if so I should address Thee—
O great Ruler of all things, look on this!
Now are thy oracles* falling into contempt, and
   men
Deny Apollo's power.
Worship of the gods is passing away.   910

Enter IOCASTA, *attended by a girl carrying a wreath
and incense*

IOCASTA. My lords of Thebes, I have bethought myself
   To approach the altars of the gods, and lay
   These wreaths on them, and burn this frankincense.
   For every kind of terror has laid hold
   On Oedipus; his judgement is distracted.
   He will not read the future by the past
   But yields himself to any who speaks fear.
   Since then no words of mine suffice to calm him
   I turn to Thee, Apollo—Thou art nearest—
   Thy suppliant, with these votive offerings.   920
   Grant us deliverance and peace, for now
   Fear is on all, when we see Oedipus,
   The helmsman of the ship, so terrified.

[*A reverent silence, while* IOCASTA *lays the wreath at the altar and sets fire to the incense.*]

Enter a SHEPHERD FROM CORINTH

CORINTHIAN. Might I inquire of you where I may find
The royal palace of King Oedipus?
Or, better, where himself is to be found?

CHORUS. There is the palace; himself, Sir, is within,
But here his wife and mother of his children.

CORINTHIAN. Ever may happiness attend on her,
And hers, the wedded wife of such a man.   930

IOCASTA. May you enjoy the same; your gentle words
Deserve no less.—Now, Sir, declare your purpose;
With what request, what message have you come?

CORINTHIAN. With good news for your husband and
his house.

IOCASTA. What news is this? And who has sent you
here?

CORINTHIAN. I come from Corinth, and the news I
bring
Will give you joy, though joy be crossed with grief.

IOCASTA. What is this, with its two-fold influence?

CORINTHIAN. The common talk in Corinth is that they
Will call on Oedipus to be their king.   940

IOCASTA. What? Does old Polybus no longer reign?

CORINTHIAN. Not now, for Death has laid him in his
grave.*

IOCASTA. Go quickly to your master, girl; give him
The news.—You oracles, where are you now?
This is the man whom Oedipus so long
Has shunned, fearing to kill him; now he's dead,
And killed by Fortune, not by Oedipus.

Enter OEDIPUS

79

OEDIPUS. My dear Iocasta, tell me, my dear wife,   950
Why have you sent to fetch me from the palace?

IOCASTA. Listen to *him*, and as you hear, reflect
What has become of all those oracles.

OEDIPUS. Who is this man?—What has he to tell me?

IOCASTA. He is from Corinth, and he brings you news
About your father. Polybus is dead.

OEDIPUS. What say you, sir? Tell me the news
yourself.

CORINTHIAN. If you would have me first report on
this,
I tell you; death has carried him away.

OEDIPUS. By treachery? Or did sickness come to him?   960

CORINTHIAN. A small mischance will lay an old man
low.

OEDIPUS. Poor Polybus! He died, then, of a sickness?

CORINTHIAN. That, and the measure of his many years.

OEDIPUS. Ah me! Why then, Iocasta, should a man
Regard the Pythian house of oracles,
Or screaming birds, on whose authority
I was to slay my father? But he is dead;
The earth has covered him; and here am I,
My sword undrawn—unless perchance *my* loss
Has killed him; so might I be called his slayer.   970
But for those oracles about my father,
Those he has taken with him to the grave
Wherein he lies, and they are come to nothing.

IOCASTA. Did I not say long since it would be so?

OEDIPUS. You did; but I was led astray by fear.

IOCASTA. So none of this deserves another thought.

OEDIPUS. Yet how can I not fear my mother's bed?

80

IOCASTA. Why should we fear, seeing that man is ruled
By chance, and there is room for no clear
    forethought?
No; live at random, live as best one can.
So do not fear this marriage with your mother;   980
Many a man has suffered this before—
But only in his dreams. Whoever thinks
The least of this, he lives most comfortably.

OEDIPUS. Your every word I do accept, if she
That bore me did not live; but as she does—
Despite your wisdom, how can I but tremble?

IOCASTA. Yet there is comfort in your father's death.

OEDIPUS. Great comfort, but still fear of her who lives.

CORINTHIAN. And who is this who makes you so
    afraid?

OEDIPUS. Merope, my man, the wife of Polybus.   990

CORINTHIAN. And what in *her* gives cause of fear in
    you?

OEDIPUS. There was an awful warning from the gods.

CORINTHIAN. Can it be told, or must it be kept secret?

OEDIPUS. No secret. Once Apollo said that I
Was doomed to lie with my own mother, and
Defile my own hands with my father's blood.
Wherefore has Corinth been, these many years,
My home no more. My fortunes have been fair.—
But it is good to see a parent's face.

CORINTHIAN. It was for fear of *this* you fled the city?   1000

OEDIPUS. This, and the shedding of my father's blood.

CORINTHIAN. Why then, my lord, since I am come in
    friendship,
I'll rid you here and now of that misgiving.

OEDIPUS. Be sure, your recompense would be in
    keeping.

CORINTHIAN. It was the chief cause of my coming here
That your return might bring me some advantage.

OEDIPUS. Back to my parents I will never go.

CORINTHIAN. My son, it is clear, you know not what
you do. . . .

OEDIPUS. Not know? What is this? Tell me what you
mean.

CORINTHIAN. If for this reason you avoid your home.   1010

OEDIPUS. Fearing Apollo's oracle may come true.

CORINTHIAN. And you incur pollution from your
parents?

OEDIPUS. That is the thought that makes me live in
terror.

CORINTHIAN. I tell you then, this fear of yours is idle.

OEDIPUS. How? Am I not their child, and they my
parents?

CORINTHIAN. Because there's none of Polybus in you.

OEDIPUS. How can you say so? Was he not my father?

CORINTHIAN. I am your father just as much as he!

OEDIPUS. A stranger equal to the father? How?

CORINTHIAN. Neither did he beget you, nor did I.   1020

OEDIPUS. Then for what reason did he call me son?

CORINTHIAN. He had you as a gift—from my own
hands.

OEDIPUS. And showed such love to me? Me, not his
own?

CORINTHIAN. Yes; his own childlessness so worked on
him.

OEDIPUS. You, when you gave me: had you bought, or
found me?

82

CORINTHIAN. I found you in the woods upon
Cithaeron.

OEDIPUS. Why were you travelling in that
neighbourhood?

CORINTHIAN. I tended flocks of sheep upon the
mountain.

OEDIPUS. You were a shepherd, then, wandering for
hire?

CORINTHIAN. I was, my son; but that day, your
preserver. 1030

OEDIPUS. How so? What ailed me when you took me
up?

CORINTHIAN. For that, your ankles might give evidence.

OEDIPUS. Alas! why speak of this, my life-long trouble?

CORINTHIAN. I loosed the fetters clamped upon your
feet.

OEDIPUS. A pretty gift to carry from the cradle!*

CORINTHIAN. It was for this they named you Oedipus.*

OEDIPUS. Who did, my father or my mother? Tell me.

CORINTHIAN. I cannot; he knows more, from whom I
had you.

OEDIPUS. It was another, not yourself, that found me?

CORINTHIAN. Yes, you were given me by another
shepherd. 1040

OEDIPUS. Who? Do you know him? Can you name the
man?

CORINTHIAN. They said that he belonged to Laius.

OEDIPUS. What—him who once was ruler here in
Thebes?

OEDIPUS. Yes, he it was for whom this man was
  shepherd.

OEDIPUS. And is he still alive, that I can see him?

CORINTHIAN [*turning to the Chorus*].
  You that are native here would know that best.

OEDIPUS. Has any man of you now present here
  Acquaintance with this shepherd, him he speaks of?
  Has any seen him, here, or in the fields?
  Speak; on this moment hangs discovery.   1050

CHORUS. It is, I think, the man that you have sent for,
  The slave now in the country. But who should know
  The truth of this more than Iocasta here?

OEDIPUS. The man he speaks of: do you think, Iocasta,
  He is the one I have already summoned?

IOCASTA. What matters who he is? Pay no regard.—
  The tale is idle; it is best forgotten.

OEDIPUS. It cannot be that I should have this clue
  And then not find the secret of my birth.

IOCASTA. In God's name stop, if you have any thought

                                                 1060
  For your own life! My ruin is enough.

OEDIPUS. Be not dismayed; nothing can prove you
  base.
  Not though I find my mother thrice a slave.*

IOCASTA. O, I beseech you, do not! Seek no more!

OEDIPUS. You cannot move me. I *will* know the truth.

IOCASTA. I know that what I say is for the best.

OEDIPUS. This 'best' of yours! I have no patience with
  it.

IOCASTA. O may you never learn what man you are!

OEDIPUS. Go, someone, bring the herdsman here to me,
  And leave her to enjoy her pride of birth.   1070

IOCASTA. O man of doom! For by no other name
  Can I address you now or evermore.

                  [*Exit* IOCASTA *and girl*

CHORUS. The Queen has fled, my lord, as if before
  Some driving storm of grief. I fear that from
  Her silence may break forth some great disaster.

OEDIPUS. Break forth what will! My birth, however
    humble,
  I am resolved to find. But she, perhaps,
  Is proud, as women will be; is ashamed
  Of my low birth. But I do rate myself
  The child of Fortune,* giver of all good,   1080
  And I shall not be put to shame, for I
  Am born of Her; the Years who are my kinsmen
  Distinguished my estate, now high, now low;
  So born, I could not make me someone else,
  And not do all to find my parentage.

Strophe 1

CHORUS [*sings*]. If I have power of prophecy,
  If I have judgement wise and sure, Cithaeron
  (I swear by Olympus),
  Thou shalt be honoured when the moon
  Next is full,* as mother and foster-nurse   1090
  And birth-place of Oedipus, with festival and
  dancing,
  For thou hast given great blessings to our King.
  To Thee, Apollo, now we raise our cry:
  O grant our prayer find favour in thy sight!

Antistrophe

Who is thy mother, O my son?
Is she an ageless nymph among the mountains,
That bore thee to Pan?*   1100
Or did Apollo father thee?
For dear to him are the pastures in the hills.

Or Hermes, who ruleth from the summit of
    Kyllene?*
Or Dionysus on the mountain-tops,
Did he receive thee from thy mother's arms,
A nymph who follows him on Helicon?*

OEDIPUS. If I, who never yet have met the man,   1110
    May risk conjecture, I think I see the herdsman
    Whom we have long been seeking. In his age
    He well accords; and more, I recognize
    Those who are with him as of my own household.
    But as for knowing, you will have advantage
    Of me, if you have seen the man before.

CHORUS. 'Tis he, for certain—one of Laius' men,
    One of the shepherds whom he trusted most.

Enter the THEBAN SHEPHERD

OEDIPUS. You first I ask, you who have come from
    Corinth:
    Is that the man you mean?

CORINTHIAN.   That very man. 1120

OEDIPUS. Come here, my man; look at me; answer me
    My questions. Were you ever Laius' man?

THEBAN. I was; his slave—born in the house, not
    bought.*

OEDIPUS. What was your charge, or what your way of
    life?

THEBAN. Tending the sheep, the most part of my life.

OEDIPUS. And to what regions did you most resort?

THEBAN. Now it was Cithaeron, now the country
    round.

OEDIPUS. And was this man of your acquaintance
    there?

THEBAN. In what employment? Which is the man you
    mean?

86

OEDIPUS. Him yonder. Had you any dealings with   1130
                        him?

THEBAN. Not such that I can quickly call to mind.

CORINTHIAN. No wonder, Sir, but though he has
    forgotten
  I can remind him. I am very sure,
  He knows the time when, round about Cithaeron,
  He with a double flock, and I with one,
  We spent together three whole summer seasons,
  From spring until the rising of Arcturus.*
  Then, with the coming on of winter, I
  Drove my flocks home, he his, to Laius' folds.
  Is this the truth? or am I telling lies?   1140

THEBAN. It is true, although it happened long ago.

CORINTHIAN. Then tell me: do you recollect a baby
  You gave me once to bring up for my own?

THEBAN. Why this? Why are you asking me this
    question?

CORINTHIAN. My friend, *here* is the man who was that
    baby!

THEBAN. O, devil take you! Cannot you keep silent?

OEDIPUS. Here, Sir! This man needs no reproof from
    you.
  Your tongue needs chastisement much more than
    his.

THEBAN. O best of masters, how am I offending?

OEDIPUS. Not telling of the child of whom he speaks.   1150

THEBAN. He? He knows nothing. He is wasting time.

OEDIPUS [*threatening*]. If you'll not speak from
    pleasure, speak from pain.

THEBAN. No, no, I pray! Not torture an old man!

OEDIPUS. Here, someone, quickly! Twist this fellow's arms!

THEBAN. Why, wretched man? What would you know besides?

OEDIPUS. That child: you gave it him, the one he speaks of?

THEBAN. I did. Ah God, would I had died instead!

OEDIPUS. And die you shall, unless you speak the truth.

THEBAN. And if I do, then death is still more certain.

OEDIPUS. This man, I think, is trying to delay me.　　1160

THEBAN. Not I! I said I gave the child—just now.

OEDIPUS. And got it—where? Your own? or someone else's?

THEBAN. No, not my own. Someone had given it me.

OEDIPUS. Who? Which of these our citizens? From what house?

THEBAN. No, I implore you, master! Do not ask!

OEDIPUS. You die if I must question you again.

THEBAN. Then, 'twas a child of one in Laius' house.

OEDIPUS. You mean a slave? Or someone of his kin?

THEBAN. God! I am on the verge of saying it.

OEDIPUS. And I of hearing it, but hear I must.　　1170

THEBAN. His own, or so they said. But she within
Could tell you best—your wife—the truth of it.

OEDIPUS. What, did she give you it?

THEBAN.　　　　　　　　　　　　She did, my lord.

OEDIPUS. With what intention?

THEBAN.　　　　　　　　　　That I should destroy it.

OEDIPUS. Her own?—How could she?

THEBAN.   Frightened by oracles.

OEDIPUS. What oracles?

THEBAN.   That it would kill its parents.*

OEDIPUS. Why did you let it go to this man here?

THEBAN. I pitied it, my lord. I thought to send
  The child abroad, whence this man came. And he
  Saved it, for utter doom. For if you are   1180
  The man he says, then you were born for ruin.

OEDIPUS. Ah God! Ah God!* This is the truth, at last!
  O Sun,* let me behold thee this once more,
  I who am proved accursed in my conception,
  And in my marriage, and in him I slew.

  [*Exeunt severally* OEDIPUS, CORINTHIAN, THEBAN

Strophe 1

CHORUS [*sings*]. Alas! you generations of men!
  Even while you live you are next to nothing!
  Has any man won for himself
  More than the shadow of happiness,   1190
  A shadow that swiftly fades away?
  Oedipus, now as I look on you,
  See your ruin, how can I say that
  Mortal man can be happy?

Antistrophe 1

For who won greater prosperity?
Sovereignty and wealth beyond all desiring?*
The crooked-clawed, riddling Sphinx,
Maiden and bird, you overcame;   1200
You stood like a tower of strength to Thebes.
So you received our crown, received the
Highest honours that we could give—
King in our mighty city.

Strophe 2

Who more wretched, more afflicted now,
With cruel misery, with fell disaster,
Your life in dust and ashes?
  O noble Oedipus!
  How could it be? to come again
A bridegroom of her who gave you birth!　　　　1210
How could such a monstrous thing
Endure so long, unknown?

Antistrophe 2

Time sees all, and Time, in your despite,
Disclosed and punished your unnatural marriage—
A child, and then a husband.
  O son of Laius,
  Would I had never looked on you!
I mourn you as one who mourns the dead.　　　　1220
First you gave me back my life,
And now, that life is death.

Enter, from the palace, a MESSENGER

MESSENGER. My Lords, most honoured citizens of
    Thebes,
What deeds am I to tell of, you to see!
What heavy grief to bear, if still remains
Your native loyalty to our line of kings.
For not the Ister,* no, nor Phasis' flood*
Could purify this house, such things it hides,
Such others will it soon display to all,
Evils self-sought.* Of all our sufferings　　　　1230
Those hurt the most that we ourselves inflict.

CHORUS. Sorrow enough—too much—in what was
    known
Already. What new sorrow do you bring?

MESSENGER. Quickest for me to say and you to hear:
It is the Queen, Iocasta—she is dead.

CHORUS. Iocasta, dead? But how? What was the cause?

MESSENGER. By her own hand. Of what has passed, the
   worst
  Cannot be yours: that was, to see it.
  But you shall hear, so far as memory serves,
  The cruel story.—In her agony   1240
  She ran across the courtyard, snatching at
  Her hair with both her hands. She made her way
  Straight to her chamber; she barred fast the doors
  And called on Laius, these long years dead,
  Remembering their by-gone procreation.
  'Through this did you meet death yourself, and leave
  To me, the mother, child-bearing accursed
  To my own child.'* She cried aloud upon
  The bed where she had borne a double brood,
  Husband from husband, children from a child.   1250
  And thereupon she died, I know not how;
  For, groaning, Oedipus burst in, and we,
  For watching him, saw not *her* agony
  And how it ended. He, ranging through the palace,
  Came up to each man calling for a sword,
  Calling for her whom he had called his wife,
  Asking where was she who had borne them all,
  Himself and his own children. So he raved.
  And then some deity* showed him the way,
  For it was none of us that stood around;
  He cried aloud, as if to someone who   1260
  Was leading him; he leapt upon the doors,
  Burst from their sockets the yielding bars, and fell
  Into the room; and there, hanged by the neck,
  We saw his wife, held in a swinging cord.
  He, when he saw it, groaned in misery
  And loosed her body from the rope. When now
  She lay upon the ground, awful to see
  Was that which followed: from her dress he tore
  The golden brooches that she had been wearing,
  Raised them, and with their points struck his own
    eyes,   1270

Crying aloud that they should never see
What he had suffered and what he had done,
But in the dark henceforth they should behold
Those whom they ought not; nor should recognize
Those whom he longed to see. To such refrain
He smote his eyeballs with the pins, not once,
Nor twice; and as he smote them, blood ran down
His face, not dripping slowly, but there fell
Showers of black rain and blood-red hail together.

    Not on his head alone, but on them both,   1280
Husband and wife, this common storm has broken.
Their ancient happiness of early days
Was happiness indeed; but now, today,
Death, ruin, lamentation, shame—of all
The ills there are, not one is wanting here.

CHORUS. Now is there intermission in his agony?

MESSENGER. He shouts for someone to unbar the gates,
And to display to Thebes the parricide,
His mother's—no, I cannot speak the words;
For, by the doom he uttered, he will cast
Himself beyond our borders, nor remain   1290
To be a curse at home. But he needs strength,
And one to guide him; for these wounds are greater
Than he can bear—as you shall see; for look!
They draw the bolts. A sight you will behold
To move the pity even of an enemy.

    The doors open. OEDIPUS *slowly advances*

CHORUS [*chants*]. O horrible, dreadful sight. More
    dreadful far
Than any I have yet seen. What cruel frenzy
Came over you? What spirit* with superhuman leap 1300
Came to assist your grim destiny?
Ah, most unhappy man!
But no! I cannot bear even to look at you,
Though there is much that I would ask and see and
    hear.
But I shudder at the very sight of you.

OEDIPUS [*sings*]. Alas! alas! and woe for my misery!
   Where are my steps taking me?
   My random voice is lost in the air.   1310
   O God!* how hast thou crushed me!

CHORUS [*speaks*]. Too terribly for us to hear or see.

OEDIPUS [*sings*]. O cloud of darkness abominable,
   My enemy unspeakable,
   In cruel onset insuperable.
   Alas! alas! Assailed at once by pain
   Of pin-points and of memory of crimes.

CHORUS [*speaks*]. In such tormenting pains you well
     may cry
   A double grief and feel a double woe.   1320

OEDIPUS [*sings*]. Ah, my friend!
   Still at my side? Still steadfast?
   Still can you endure me?
   Still care for me, a blind man?*
   [*speaks*] For it is you, my friend; I know 'tis you;
   Though all is darkness, yet I know your voice.

CHORUS [*speaks*]. O, to destroy your sight! How could
    you bring
   Yourself to do it? What god* incited you?

OEDIPUS [*sings*]. It was Apollo, friends, Apollo.
   He decreed that I should suffer what I suffer;   1330
   But the hand that struck, alas! was my own,
   And not another's.
   For why should I have sight.
   When sight of nothing could give me pleasure?

CHORUS [*speaks*]. It was even as you say.

OEDIPUS [*sings*]. What have I left, my friends, to see,
   To cherish, whom to speak with, or
   To listen to, with joy?
   Lead me away at once, far from Thebes;   1340
   Lead me away, my friends!

I have destroyed; I am accursed, and, what is more,
Hateful to Heaven, as no other.

CHORUS [*speaks*]. Unhappy your intention, and
    unhappy
Your fate. O would that I had never known you!

OEDIPUS [*sings*]. Curses on him, whoever he was,
    Who took the savage fetters from my feet,   1350
        Snatched me from death, and saved me.
        No thanks I owe him,
        For had I died that day
Less ruin had I brought on me and mine.

CHORUS [*speaks*]. That wish is my wish too.

OEDIPUS [*sings*]. I had not then come and slain my
    father.
        Nor then would men have called me
        Husband of her that bore me.
    Now am I God's enemy, child of the guilty,   1360
    And she that bore me has borne too my children;
    And if there is evil surpassing evil,
        That has come to Oedipus.

CHORUS [*speaks*]. How can I say that you have
    counselled well?
Far better to be dead than to be blind.

OEDIPUS [*speaks*]. That what is done was not done for
    the best
Seek not to teach me: counsel me no more.   1370
I know not how I could have gone to Hades
And with these eyes have looked upon my father
Or on my mother;* such things have I done
To them, death* is no worthy punishment.
Or could I look for pleasure in the sight
Of my own children, born as they were born?
Never! No pleasure there, for eyes of mine,
Nor in this city, nor its battlements
Nor sacred images. From these—ah, miserable!—
I, the most nobly born of any Theban   1380

Am banned for ever by my own decree
That the defiler should be driven forth,
The man accursed of Heaven and Laius' house.
Was I to find such taint in me, and then
With level eyes to look *them** in the face?
Nay more: if for my ears I could have built
Some dam to stay the flood of sound, that I
Might lose both sight and hearing, and seal up
My wretched body—that I would have done.
How good to dwell beyond the reach of pain! 1390
   Cithaeron! Why did you accept me? Why
Did you not take and kill me? Never then
Should I have come to dwell among the Thebans.*
   O Polybus! Corinth! and that ancient home
I thought my father's—what a thing you nurtured!
How fair, how foul beneath! For I am found
Foul in myself and in my parentage.
   O you three ways, that in a hidden glen
Do meet: you narrow branching roads within
The forest—you, through my own hands, did drink 1400
My father's blood, that was my own.—Ah! do you
Remember what you saw me do? And what
I did again in Thebes? You marriages!
You did beget me: then, having begotten,
Bore the same crop again, and brought to light
Commingled blood of fathers, brothers, sons,
Brides, mothers, wives; all that there can be
Among the human kind most horrible!
   But that which it is foul to do, it is
Not fair to speak of. Quick as you can, I beg, 1410
Banish me, hide me, slay me! Throw me forth
Into the sea, where I may sink from view.
I pray you, deign to touch one so afflicted,
And do not fear: there is no man alive
Can bear this load of evil but myself.

CHORUS. To listen to your prayers, Creon is here,
   For act or guidance opportune; for he,
   In your defection, is our champion.

Enter CREON

OEDIPUS. Alas! alas! How can I speak to him?
 What word of credit find? In all my commerce   1420
 With him aforetime I am proven false.

CREON. No exultation, Oedipus, and no reproach
 Of injuries inflicted brings me here;
 But if the face of men moves not your shame,
 Then reverence show to that all-nurturing fire,
 The holy Sun, that he be not polluted
 By such accursèd sight, which neither Earth
 Nor rain from Heaven nor sunlight can endure.*
  Take him within, and quickly: it is right
 His kinsmen only should behold and hear   1430
 Evils that chiefly on his kinsmen fall.

OEDIPUS. In Heaven's name—since you cheat my
  expectation,
 So noble towards my baseness—grant me this:
 It is for you I ask it, not myself.

CREON. What is this supplication that you make?

OEDIPUS. Drive me at once beyond your bounds, where
  I
 Shall be alone, and no one speak to me.

CREON. I would have done it; but I first desired
 To ask the God what he would have me do.

OEDIPUS. No, his command was given in full, to slay 1440
 Me, the polluter and the parricide.

CREON. Those were his words; but in our present need
 It would be wise to ask what we should do.

OEDIPUS. You will inquire for such a wretch as I?

CREON. I will; for now *you* may believe the god.

OEDIPUS. Yes; and on you I lay this charge and duty:
 Give burial, as you will, to her who lies
 Within—for she is yours,* and this is proper;

And, while I live, let not my father's city
Endure to have me as a citizen.   1450
My home must be the mountains—on Cithaeron,
Which, while they lived, my parents chose to be
My tomb: they wished to slay me; now they shall.
For this I know: sickness can never kill me,
Nor any other evil; I was not saved
That day from death, except for some strange
    doom.*
My fate must take the course it will.—Now, for my
    sons,
Be not concerned for them: they can, being men,   1460
Fend for themselves, wherever they may be:
But my unhappy daughters, my two girls,
Whose chairs were always set beside my own
At table—they who shared in every dish
That was prepared for me—oh Creon! these
Do I commend to you. And grant me this:
To take them in my arms, and weep for them.
My lord! most noble Creon! could I now
But hold them in my arms, then I should think
I had them as I had when I could see them.   1470

Enter ANTIGONE *and* ISMENE

Ah! what is this?
Ah Heaven! do I not hear my dear ones, sobbing?
Has Creon, in his pity, sent to me
My darling children? Has he? Is it true?

CREON. It is; they have been always your delight;
    So, knowing this, I had them brought to you.

OEDIPUS. Then Heaven reward you, and for this kind
    service
    Protect you better than it protected me!
        Where are you, children? Where? O come to me!   1480
    Come, let me clasp you with a brother's arms,
    These hands, which helped your father's eyes, once
        bright,
    To look upon you as they see you now—

97

Your father who, not seeing, nor inquiring,
Gave you for mother her who bore himself.
See you I cannot; but I weep for you,
For the unhappiness that must be yours,
And for the bitter life that you must lead.
What gathering of the citizens, what festivals,
Will you have part in? Your high celebrations   1490
Will be to go back home, and sit in tears.
And when the time for marriage comes, what man
Will stake upon the ruin and the shame
That *I* am to my parents and to you!
Nothing is wanting there: your father slew
His father, married her who gave him birth,
And then, from that same source whence he himself
Had sprung, got you.—With these things they will
    taunt you;
And who will take you then in marriage?—Nobody; 1500
But you must waste, unwedded and unfruitful.
    Ah, Creon! Since they have no parent* now
But you—for both of us who gave them life
Have perished—suffer them not to be cast out
Homeless and beggars; for they are your kin.*
Have pity on them, for they are so young,
So desolate, except for you alone.
Say 'Yes', good Creon! Let your hand confirm it.   1510
    And now, my children, for my exhortation
You are too young; but you can pray that I
May live henceforward—where I should; and you
More happily than the father who begot you.

CREON. Now make an end of tears, and go within.

OEDIPUS. Then I must go—against my will.

CREON. There is a time for everything.

OEDIPUS. You know what I would have you do?

CREON. If you will tell me, I shall know.

OEDIPUS. Send me away, away from Thebes.

CREON. The God, not I, must grant you this.

OEDIPUS. The gods hate no man more than me!

CREON. Then what you ask they soon will give.

OEDIPUS. You promise this?

CREON.   Ah no! When I
   Am ignorant, I do not speak.   1520

OEDIPUS. Then lead me in; I say no more.

CREON. Release the children then, and come.

OEDIPUS. What? Take these children from me? No!

CREON. Seek not to have your way in all things:
   Where you had your way before,
   Your mastery broke before the end.*

ELECTRA

DRAMATIS PERSONAE

ORESTES, *only son of Agamemnon and Clytemnestra*
PYLADES, *his friend (he has no speaking part)*
TUTOR, *personal attendant of Orestes*
ELECTRA, *daughter of Agamemnon and Clytemnestra*
CHRYSOTHEMIS, *her sister*
CLYTEMNESTRA
AEGISTHUS
CHORUS *of women of Mycenae*
Attendants etc.

Scene: Mycenae, in Argos, before the royal palace

ELECTRA[1]

Enter ORESTES, PYLADES *and the* TUTOR, *with two attendants*

TUTOR. Here is the land of Argos. From this place
    Your father Agamemnon led the Greeks
    To Troy. How many years have you been longing
    To see what now your eyes can look upon:
    The ancient city Argos, once the home
    Of Io and her father Inachus.*
    Now look upon it: there, the market-place
    That bears Apollo's name,* and to the left
    Is Hera's famous temple.* The place where we
    Are standing now—my son, this is Mycenae,
    Golden Mycenae, and the blood-drenched palace
    Of Pelops' dynasty* is here, the place   10
    From which your sister saved you, as a baby,*
    When they had murdered Agamemnon. I
    Took you to safety, I have brought you up
    To manhood. Now you must avenge your father.
      So now, Orestes, you and Pylades
    Your loyal friend, resolve with no delay
    What you will do. For dawn has come; the stars
    Have vanished from the darkness of the sky;
    The birds are striking up their morning songs;
    People will soon be stirring. Little time   20
    Is left to you; the hour has come for action.

ORESTES. My friend, my loyal servant:* everything
    You say or do proclaims your true devotion.
    Just as a horse, if he is thoroughbred,
    Will keep his mettle even in old age,
    Will never flinch, but in the face of danger
    Prick up his ears, so you are ever first
    To proffer help and to encourage me.

---

[1] Verse lines are numbered according to the Greek text (see Introduction, p. xxxv).

You then shall hear my plan, and as you listen
Give it your sharp attention, to amend   30
Whatever seems amiss.
I went to Delphi,* and I asked Apollo
How best I might avenge my father's death
On these who murdered him. The god's reply
Was brief; it went like this: *Not with an army
But with your own right hand, by stratagem
Give them what they have earned, and kill them both.*
Therefore, since this is what the god has said,
Your part shall be to have yourself admitted
Inside the palace when the moment favours.
Find out what is afoot; return to me   40
And tell me what you can.—They will not know
    you;
You have grown old, so many years have passed;
Your silver hair will keep them from suspecting.
Your story shall be this, that you have come
From foreign parts, from Phanoteus of Phokis*—
For he is one of their most trusted allies;
Tell them Orestes has been killed, and give
Your oath that it is true: he met his death
Competing in the Pythian Games at Delphi,*
Flung from his racing-chariot. Let this be   50
The tale. And for myself, the god commanded
That I should first go to my father's tomb
And pay my tribute with a lock of hair
And wine-libation. This then will I do;
And I will find the urn which you have told me
Lies hidden in a thicket, and with that
I will come back. This urn of beaten bronze
Shall bring them joy—though not for long; for it
(So we will tell them) holds the ash and cinders
Of this my body that the fire consumed.—
Why should I fear an omen,* if I say that I
Am dead, then by this story I fulfil
My life's true purpose, to secure my vengeance?   60
No need to fear a tale that brings me gain.
For I have heard of those philosophers*

Who were reported dead: when they returned,
Each to his city, they were honoured more.
And so, I trust, may I, through this pretence,
Look down triumphant like the sun* in heaven
Upon my enemies.
Only do thou, my native soil; you, gods of Argos,
Receive and prosper me. House of my fathers,
Receive me with your blessing! The gods have sent
    me,   70
And I have come to purify and purge you.
Do not reject me, drive me not away,
But let me enter into my possessions;
Let me rebuild my father's fallen house.
   Such is my prayer. My friend, go to your task
And do it well. We go to ours; for Time
Calls only once, and that determines all.

ELECTRA [*within*]. Ah me! Ah me!

TUTOR. Listen, my son: I thought I heard a cry
  From near the gates, a cry of bitter grief.*

ORESTES. Electra, my unhappy sister! Could   80
  It be her cry?—Let us wait and listen.

TUTOR. No. The command that God has given us,
  That must come first, to offer your libations
  At Agamemnon's tomb. His aid will bring
  Victory to us, and ruin to his foes.
    [*Exeunt* ORESTES, PYLADES, *the* TUTOR, *and*
    attendants

Enter ELECTRA

ELECTRA [*chants*]. Thou holy light,
  Thou sky that art earth's canopy,
  How many bitter cries of mine   90
  Have you not heard,* when shadowy night
  Has given place to days of mourning!
  And when the night has come again
  My hateful bed alone can tell

The tears that I have shed within
This cruel palace. O my father!
No Trojan spear,* no god of war,*
Brought death to you on foreign soil.
My mother killed you, and her mate
Aegisthus! As a woodman fells
An oak, they took a murderous axe
   And cut you down.
And yet no other voice but mine   100
Cries out upon this bloody deed.
I only, father, mourn your death.
   Nor ever will
I cease from dirge and sad lament
So long as I behold the sun
By day and see the stars by night;
But like the sorrowing nightingale*
Who mourns her young unceasingly,
Here at the very gates will I
Proclaim my grief for all to hear.

You powers of Death! you gods below!*   110
Avenging Spirits, who behold
Each deed of blood, each faithless act
Dishonouring the marriage-vow,*
Desert me not. Come to my aid!
Avenge my father's death!
And send my brother; bring to me Orestes! For I can
   no more
Sustain this grief; it crushes me.   120

Enter the CHORUS

[*From here until line 250 everything is sung.*]

Strophe 1

CHORUS. Electra, child of a most pitiless mother,
   Why are you so wasting your life in unceasing
   Grief and despair? Agamemnon
   Died long ago. Treachery filled the heart,
   Your mother's heart, that gave him,

Snared, entrapped, to a shameful supplanter who killed him.
  If I may dare to say it, may
  Those who did such a thing
  Suffer the same themselves.

ELECTRA. O my noble, generous friends,
  You are here, I know, to comfort me in my sorrow.   130
  Welcome to me, most welcome, is your coming.
  But ask me not to abandon my grief
    Or cease to mourn my father.
  No, my friends; give, as always you give me, your
    love and devotion,
  But bear with my grief; I cannot betray my sorrow.

Antistrophe 1

CHORUS. But he has gone to the land to which we all
  must
  Go. Neither by tears nor by mourning can
  He be restored from the land of the dead.
  Yours is a grief beyond the common measure,   140
    A grief that knows no ending,
  Consuming your own life, and all in vain.
    For how can mourning end wrong?
  Cannot you part yourself from your long
    Sorrow and suffering?

ELECTRA. Hard the heart, unfeeling the mind,
  Of one who should forget a father, cruelly slain.
  Her will my heart follow, the sad nightingale,*
    Bird of grief, always lamenting
    Itys, Itys,* her child.
  And O, Niobe,* Queen of Sorrow, to thee do I turn,
    as a goddess   150
  Weeping for ever, in thy mountain-tomb.

Strophe 2

CHORUS. Not upon you alone, my child,
  Has come the heavy burden of grief

That chafes you more than those with whom you
    live,
The two bound to you by kindred blood.
See how Chrysothemis lives, and Iphianassa,*
    Your two sisters within.
    He also lives, your brother,
    Although in exile, suffering grief;   160
    And glory awaits Orestes, for
He will come by the kindly guidance of Zeus, and be
Received with honour and welcome, here in
    Mycenae.

ELECTRA. But I, year after year, waiting for him,
    Tread my weary path, unwedded, childless,
    Bathed in tears, burdened with endless sorrow.
    For the wrongs he has suffered, the crimes of which
        I have told him,
    He cares nothing. Messages come; all are belied;   170
    He longs to be here, but not enough to come!

Antistrophe 2

CHORUS. Comfort yourself, take comfort, child;
    Zeus is still King in the heavens.
He sees all; he overrules all things.
Leave this bitter grief and anger to him.
Do not go too far in hatred with those you hate,
    Nor be forgetful of him.
    Time has power to heal all wounds.
    Nor will he who lives in the rich   180
    Plain of Crisa,* near the sea,
Agamemnon's son, neglect his own father.*

ELECTRA. But how much of my life has now been spent,
    Spent in despair! My strength will soon be gone.
    I am alone, without the comfort of children; no
    Husband to stand beside me, and share the burden; 190
    Spurned like a slave, dressed like a slave, fed on the
        scraps,
    I serve, disdained by all—in the house of my fathers!

Strophe 3

CHORUS. Pitiful the cry at his return,
　　Your father's cry in the banquet-hall,
　When the straight, sharp blow of an axe was
　　launched at him.
　　　Guile was the plotter, lust was the slayer,
　　　Hideous begetters of a hideous crime,
　　　Whether the hand that wrought the deed
　Was a mortal hand, or a Spirit loosed from Hell.*　　200

ELECTRA. That day of horrors beyond all other
　　horrors!
　Hateful and bitter beyond all other days!
　　That accursed night of banqueting
　　Filled with fear and blood!
　My father looked, and saw two murderers aiming
　　A deadly, cowardly blow at him,
　　A blow that has betrayed my life
　　To slavery, to ruin.
　　O God that rulest Heaven and Earth,*
　　Make retribution fall on them!　　210
　What they have done, that may they suffer.
　　Leave them not to triumph!

Antistrophe 3

CHORUS. Yet you should be wise, and say no more,
　　It is yourself and what you do
　That brings upon yourself this cruel outrage.
　Your sullen, irreconcilable heart,
　　Breeding strife and enmity,
　　Adds to your own misery.
　To fight with those that hold the power is folly.　　220

ELECTRA. I know, I know my bitter and hateful temper;
　But see what I have to suffer! That constrains me.
　　Because of that, I cannot help
　　But give myself to frenzied hate
　So long as life shall last. My gentle friends,

What words of comfort or persuasion
Can prevail, to reconcile
My spirit with this evil?
No; leave me, leave me; do not try.
These are ills past remedy.   230
Never shall I depart from sorrow
And tears and lamentation.

Epode

CHORUS. In love and friendship, like a mother,
    I beg you: do not make, my child,
        Trouble on top of trouble.

ELECTRA. In what I suffer, is there moderation?
    To be neglectful of the dead, can that be right?
    Where among men is that accounted honour?
        I'll not accept praise from them!
        Whatever happiness is mine,   240
    I'll not enjoy dishonourable ease,
        Forget my grief, or cease to pay
        Tribute of mourning to my father.
    For if the dead shall lie there, nothing but dust and
        ashes,
    And they who killed him do not suffer death in
        return,
        Then, for all mankind,
    Fear of the gods, respect for men, have vanished.   250

CHORUS. Your cause I make my own. So, if my words
    Displease you, I recall them and let yours
    Prevail; for I will always follow you.

ELECTRA. My friends, these lamentations are a sore
    Vexation to you, and I am ashamed.
    But bear with me: I can do nothing else.
    What woman would not cry to Heaven, if she
    Had any trace of spirit,* when she saw
    Her father suffering outrage such as I
    Must look on every day—and every night?

And it does not decrease, but always grows 260
More insolent. There is my mother: she,
My mother! has become my bitterest enemy.
And then, I have to share my house with those
Who murdered my own father; I am ruled
By them, and what I get, what I must do
Without, depends on them. What happy days,
Think you, mine are, when I must see Aegisthus
Sitting upon my father's throne, wearing
My father's robes, and pouring his libations
Beside the hearth-stone* where they murdered him? 270
And I must look upon the crowning outrage,
The murderer lying in my father's bed
With my abandoned mother—if I must
Call her a mother who dares sleep with him!
She is so brazen that she lives with that
Defiler; vengeance from the gods is not
A thought that frightens her! As if exulting
In what she did she noted carefully
The day on which she treacherously killed
My father, and each month, when that day comes,
She holds high festival and sacrifices 280
Sheep to the Gods her Saviours.* I look on
In misery, and weep with breaking heart.
This cruel mockery, her Festival
Of Agamemnon, is to me a day
Of bitter grief—and I must grieve alone.
And then, I cannot even weep in peace:
This noble lady bids me stop, reviles
Me bitterly: 'You god-forsaken creature!
You hateful thing! Are you the only one
Who ever lost a father? Has none but you 290
Ever worn black? A curse upon you! May
The gods of Hades give you ample cause
To weep for evermore!'—So she reviles me.
But when she hears from someone that Orestes
May come, she flies into a frenzied rage,
Stands over me and screams: 'It's you I have
To thank for this, my girl! This is your work!

111

You stole Orestes from my hands, and sent
Him secretly away. But let me tell you,
I'll make you pay for this as you deserve.'
So, like a dog, she yelps, encouraged by
That glorious bridegroom who stands at her side,   300
That milksop coward, that abomination,
That warrior who shelters behind women.
　My cry is for Orestes and his coming
To put an end to this. O, I am sick
At heart from waiting; he is holding back,
And his delay has broken all my hopes.
Enduring this, my friends, how can I follow
Wisdom and piety? Among such evils
How can my conduct not be evil too?

CHORUS. Come, tell me: is Aegisthus here, that you   310
　Say this to us, or is he gone from home?

ELECTRA. If he were here, I'd not have dared to come
　Outside the palace. No, he's in the country.

CHORUS. If that is so, why then, I might perhaps
　Myself be bold, and speak with you more freely.

ELECTRA. Say what you will; Aegisthus is not here.

CHORUS. Then tell me of your brother: is there news
　That he is coming, or is he still waiting?

ELECTRA. He promises—and that is all he does.

CHORUS. So great an enterprise is not done quickly.   320

ELECTRA. Yet I was quick enough when I saved him!

CHORUS. He'll not desert his friends. Have confidence.

ELECTRA. I have. If I had not I should have died.

CHORUS. Hush, say no more! Chrysothemis is coming,
　Your sister,* from the palace, carrying
　Grave-offerings, that are given to the dead.

Enter CHRYSOTHEMIS

112

CHRYSOTHEMIS. Why have you come again outside the
    gate,
  Spreading your talk? O, will you never learn?
  Will nothing teach you? Why do you indulge   330
  This vain resentment? I am sure of this:
  Mine is as great as yours. If I could find
  The power, they soon would learn how much I hate
    them.
  But we are helpless; we should ride the storm
  With shortened sail, not show our enmity
  When we are impotent to do them harm.
  Will you not do the same? The right may lie
  On your side, not on mine, but since *they* rule,
  I must submit, or lose all liberty.   340

ELECTRA. Shameful! that you, the child of such a father
  Should have no thought for him, but only for
  Your mother! All the wise advice you give me
  You learn of her; none of it is your own.
  But you must make your choice: to be a fool,
  Like me, or to be prudent, and abandon
  Those dearest to you. If you had the power,
  You say, you'd show them how you hate them
    both—
  And yet when I do all I can to avenge
  Our father, do you help me? No; you try   350
  To thwart me, adding cowardice on top
  Of misery. Come, tell me—or let me
  Tell you: if I give up my grief, what should
  I gain? Do I not live? Barely, I know,
  But well enough for me; and I give *them*
  Continual vexation, and thereby
  Honour the dead, if there is any feeling
  Beyond the grave. You hate them, so you tell me:
  Your tongue may hate them; what you do supports
  Our father's enemies and murderers.
  I will not yield to them, no, not for all
  The toys and trinkets that give you such pleasure. 360
  Enjoy your luxuries, your delicate food!

113

It is enough for me if I may eat
What does not turn my stomach. I have no
Desire to share in your high privileges.
And you would scorn them, if you knew your duty.
You might be known as Agamemnon's child,
But let them call you Clytemnestra's daughter,
And recognize your treason, who abandon
Your murdered father and your family.

CHORUS. Do not give way to anger. Each of you
Can with advantage listen to the other.   370

CHRYSOTHEMIS. I am well used to her tirades, my
    friends;
I would not have provoked her, but that I
Know that the gravest danger threatens her:
They are resolved to end her long complaints.

ELECTRA. What is this awful thing? If it is worse
Than *this* I will not say another word.

CHRYSOTHEMIS. I'll tell you everything I know.—
    They have determined,
If you will not give up these protestations,
To imprison you in such a place that you
Will never see the sun again, but live   380
To sing your own laments in some dark dungeon.*
So think on this, or, when the blow has fallen,
Do not blame me. Now is the time for prudence.

ELECTRA. Will they do *that* to me?

CHRYSOTHEMIS.   They will; it is
Decreed, the moment that Aegisthus has returned.

ELECTRA. Then let him come at once, for all I care!

CHRYSOTHEMIS. How can you say it? Are you mad?   390

ELECTRA.   At least,
I shall be out of sight of all of you.

CHRYSOTHEMIS. But to give up the life you lead with
    us!

114

ELECTRA. A marvellous existence! One to envy!

CHRYSOTHEMIS. It could be, if you would behave with
sense.

ELECTRA. You'll not teach *me* to abandon those I love.

CHRYSOTHEMIS. Not that, but to give in to those who
rule us.

ELECTRA. Let that be your excuse; I will not make it!

CHRYSOTHEMIS. It is a duty, not to fall through folly.

ELECTRA. I'll fall, if fall I must, avenging *him*.

CHRYSOTHEMIS. Our father will not blame me, I am
sure.   400

ELECTRA. Only a coward would rely on that!

CHRYSOTHEMIS. Will you not listen, and let me
persuade you?

ELECTRA. Never! I hope my judgement will not fall
As low as that.

CHRYSOTHEMIS. Then I will say no more.
I'll leave you now, and go upon my errand.

ELECTRA. Where are you going, with those offerings?

CHRYSOTHEMIS. I am to lay them on our father's tomb;
Our mother sent me.

ELECTRA.   She? Give offerings
To him who is her deadliest enemy?

CHRYSOTHEMIS. Say next: 'The husband slain by her own
hand'!

ELECTRA. Who thought of this? Or who persuaded her?

CHRYSOTHEMIS. She had a dream, I think, that
frightened her.   410

ELECTRA. Gods of our race! Be with us now, at last!

115

CHRYSOTHEMIS. Do you find cause of hope in this bad
  dream?

ELECTRA. Tell me the dream, and then perhaps I'll
  know.

CHRYSOTHEMIS. I cannot tell you much.

ELECTRA.   But tell me *that*!
  The safety or the ruin of a house
  Will often turn upon a little thing.

CHRYSOTHEMIS. They say that in her dream she saw
    our father
  Returned to life and standing at her side;
  He took the sceptre which he used to hold
  Himself—the one that now Aegisthus carries—   420
  And planted it beside the hearth; from that
  There grew, and spread, an over-arching tree
  That gave its shelter to the whole of Argos.
  At sunrise, to allay her fear, she told
  Her vision to the sun-god:* one who stood
  Nearby and heard reported it to me.
  I cannot tell you more, except that I
  Am sent because the dream has frightened her.
    So now, I beg you, in the name of all
  The gods we worship, do as I advise:
  Give up this folly which will be your ruin.
  If you reject me now, you will return
  To me when nothing I can do will help you.   430

ELECTRA. Dear sister, do not let these offerings
  Come near his tomb; it is a thing that law
  And piety forbid, to dedicate
  To him gifts and libations that are sent
  By her, his deadliest, bitterest enemy.
  Bury them in the ground, or throw them to
  The random winds, that none of them may reach
    him.
  No; let them all be kept in store for her
  In Hell, a treasure for her when she dies.

If she were not the most insensate woman
The world has ever seen, she'd not have dared   440
To try to crown the tomb of him she killed
With gifts inspired by enmity. Think: would they
Cause any gratitude in him? Did she not kill him?
And with such hatred, and with such dishonour,
That she attacked even his lifeless body
And mangled it?* You cannot think that gifts
Will gain her absolution from her crime?
Impossible! No, let them be, and make
A different offering at our father's grave:
Give him a lock of hair for token, one
Of yours, and one of mine*—no lordly gifts,   450
But all I have; and give him too this girdle,
Poor, unadorned; and as you give them, kneel
Upon his grave; beseech him, from the world
Below, to look with favour on us, and
To give his aid against our enemies;
And that his son Orestes may be saved
To come in triumph and to trample on
His foes, that in the days to come we may
Grace him with gifts more splendid far than those
That we can offer now. For I believe,
I do believe, that in this dream, to her
So terrifying, the spirit of our father   460
Has played some part. However that may be,
My sister, do this service to yourself,
To me, and to the one we love beyond
All others, him who now is dead—our father.

CHORUS. My child, if you are wise, you will do all
    She bids you, for she speaks in piety.

CHRYSOTHEMIS. Do it I will; when duty's clear, there is
    No cause to argue, but to do it quickly.
    But, O my friends, I beg you, keep it secret,
    This that I undertake. If it should come
    To Clytemnestra's knowledge, then I fear   470
    I should pay dearly for this enterprise.
                                [*Exit* CHRYSOTHEMIS

117

Strophe 1

CHORUS [*sings*]. If I have any foresight, any judgement
    to be trusted,
  Retribution* is at hand; her shadow falls before she
    comes.
  She is coming, and she brings with her a power
    invincible.
    Confidence rises in my heart;
    The dream is good; it makes me glad.   480
  The King, your father, is not sunk in dull
    forgetfulness,
  Nor does the rusty two-edged axe* forget the foul
    blow.

Antistrophe 1

She will come swiftly and strongly, springing on   490
    them from an ambush,
The Vengeance of the gods, coming in might. For
    they were swept
By a passion for a lawless and bloody mating into
    crime.
    Therefore I feel glad confidence;
    The omen has not come in vain.
For evil doers must pay. Oracles and prophecies   500
Only deceive, if this dream is not now fulfilled.

Epode

That chariot-race of Pelops*
Has become the cause of sorrow
And of suffering without end.
Since Myrtilus* was thrown from
His golden car, and dashed to death into   510
The sea that roared beneath him,
Cruel violence and bloodshed
Have been quartered on this house.

        Enter CLYTEMNESTRA, *with a servant carrying
        materials for a sacrifice*

118

CLYTEMNESTRA. At large again, it seems—because Aegisthus
Is not at home to stop you. So you go
Roaming about, putting us all to shame!
But in *his* absence, you are not afraid
Of me! And yet you say to everyone   520
That I am cruel and tyrannical,
That I heap outrage both on you and yours.
I do no outrage; if my tongue reviles you,
It is because my tongue must answer yours.
Your father: that is always your excuse,
That he was killed by me.—By me! Of course;
I know he was, and I do not deny it—
Because his own crime killed him, and not I
Alone. And you, if you had known your duty,
Ought to have helped, for I was helping Justice.
This father of yours, whom you are always   530
    mourning,
Had killed your sister,* sacrificing her
To Artemis,* the only Greek* who could endure
To do it—though his part, when he begot her,
Was so much less than mine, who bore the child.
So tell me why, in deference to whom,
He sacrificed her? For the Greeks, you say?
What right had they to kill a child of mine?
But if you say he killed *my* child to serve
His brother Menelaus, should not he
Pay me for that? Did not this brother have
Two sons, and should they rather not have died,   540
The sons of Helen* who had caused the war
And Menelaus who had started it?
Or had the god of death some strange desire
To feast on mine, and not on Helen's children?
Or did this most unnatural father love
His brother's children, not the one I bore him?
Was not this father monstrous, criminal?
You will say No, but I declare he was,
And so would she who died—if she could speak.
Therefore at what has happened I am not

Dismayed; and if you think me wrong, correct 550
Your own mistakes before you censure mine.

ELECTRA. This time at least you will not say that I
    Attacked you first, and then got such an answer.
    If you allow it, I'll declare the truth
    On his behalf and on my sister's* too.

CLYTEMNESTRA. I do allow it. Had you always spoken
    Like this, you would have given less offence.

ELECTRA. Then listen. You admit you killed my
                                    father:
    Justly or not, could you say anything
    More foul? But I can prove to you it was 560
    No love of Justice that inspired the deed,
    But the suggestions of that criminal
    With whom you now are living. Go and ask
    The Huntress Artemis why she becalmed
    The fleet at windy Aulis.*—No; *I* will tell you;
    We may not question gods.
    My father once, they tell me, hunting in
    A forest that was sacred to the goddess,*
    Started an antlered stag. He aimed, and shot it,
    Then made a foolish boast, of such a kind
    As angered Artemis. Therefore she held up 570
    The fleet, to make my father sacrifice
    His daughter to her in requital for
    The stag he'd killed. So came the sacrifice:
    The Greeks were prisoners, they could neither sail
    To Troy nor go back home; and so, in anguish,
    And after long refusal, being compelled,
    He sacrificed her. It was not to help
    His brother. But even had it been for that,
    As you pretend, what right had you to kill him?
    Under what law? Be careful; if you set 580
    This up for law, *Blood in return for blood*,
    You may repent it; you would be the first
    To die, if you were given your deserts.
    But this is nothing but an empty pretext;

For tell me—if you will—why you are doing
What is of all things most abominable.
You take the murderer with whose help you killed
My father, sleep with him and bear him children;*
Those born to you before, in lawful wedlock,
You have cast out. Is this to be applauded?   590
Will you declare this too is retribution?
You'll not say that; most shameful if you do—
Marrying enemies to avenge a daughter!
But there, one cannot even warn you, for
You shout aloud that I revile my mother.
You are no daughter's *mother*, but a slave's
Mistress to me! You and your paramour
Enforce on me a life of misery.   600
Your son Orestes, whom you nearly killed,
Is dragging out a weary life in exile.
You say I am sustaining him that he
May come as an avenger: would to God
I were! Go then, denounce me where you like—
Unfilial, disloyal, shameless, impudent.
I may be skilled in all these arts; if so,
I am at least a credit to my mother!

CHORUS. She is so furious that she is beyond   610
   All caring whether she be right or wrong.

CLYTEMNESTRA. Then why should I care what I say to
      her,
   When she so brazenly insults her mother,
   At her age too?* She is so impudent
   That there is nothing that she would not do.*

ELECTRA. Then let me tell you, though you'll not
      believe it:
   I *am* ashamed at what I do; I hate it.
   But it is forced on me, despite myself,
   By your malignity and wickedness.   620
   Evil in one breeds evil in another.

CLYTEMNESTRA. You shameless creature! What I say, it
      seems,

121

And what I do give you too much to say.

ELECTRA. 'Tis you that say it, not I. You do the deeds,
And your ungodly deeds find me the words.*

CLYTEMNESTRA. I swear by Artemis* that when
    Aegisthus comes
Back home you'll suffer for this insolence.

ELECTRA. You see? You give me leave to speak my
    mind,
Then fly into a rage and will not listen.

CLYTEMNESTRA. Will you not even keep a decent
    silence   630
And let me offer sacrifice in peace
When I have let you rage without restraint?

ELECTRA. Begin your sacrifice. I will not speak
Another word. You shall not say I stopped you.

CLYTEMNESTRA [to the servant]. Lift up the rich fruit-
    offering to Apollo
As I lift up my prayers to him, that he
Will give deliverance from the fears that now
Possess me.
Phoebus Apollo, god of our defence:
Hear my petition, though I keep it secret;
There is one present who has little love
For me. Should I speak openly, her sour   640
And clamorous tongue would spread malicious
    rumour
Throughout the city. Therefore, as I may
Not speak, give ear to my unspoken prayer.
Those visions of the doubtful dreams that came
When I was sleeping, if they bring good omen,
Then grant, O Lord Apollo, that they be
Fulfilled; if evil omen, then avert
That evil; let it fall upon my foes.
If there be any who, by trickery,
Would wrest from me the wealth I now enjoy,
Frustrate them. Let this royal power be mine,   650

122

This house of Atreus.* So, until I die,
My peace untroubled, my prosperity
Unbroken, let me live with those with whom
I now am living, with my children round me—
Those who are not my bitter enemies.
    Such is my prayer; accept it graciously,
O Lord Apollo; give to all of us
Even as we ask. And there is something more.
I say not what it is; I must be silent;
But thou, being a god, wilt understand.
Nothing is hidden from the sons of Zeus.
    A silence, while CLYTEMNESTRA *makes her sacrifice.*

Enter the TUTOR

TUTOR [*to the chorus*]. Might I inquire of you if I have
    come   660
    To the royal palace of the lord Aegisthus?

CHORUS. You have made no mistake, sir; this is it.

TUTOR. The lady standing there perhaps might be
    Aegisthus' wife? She well might be a queen!

CHORUS. She is indeed the queen.

TUTOR.   My lady, greeting!
    One whom you know—a friend—has sent me here
    To you and to Aegisthus with good news.

CLYTEMNESTRA. Then you are very welcome. Tell me
    first,
    Who is the friend who sent you?

TUTOR.   Phanoteus
    Of Phokis.—The news is of importance.   670

CLYTEMNESTRA. Then sir, what is it? Tell me. Coming
    from
    So good a friend, the news, I'm sure, is good.

TUTOR. In short, it is Orestes. He is dead.

ELECTRA. Orestes, dead? O this is death to me!

123

CLYTEMNESTRA. What, dead?—Take no account of
   her.

TUTOR. That is the news. Orestes has been killed.

ELECTRA. Orestes! Dead! Then what have I to live for?

CLYTEMNESTRA. That's your affair!—Now let me hear
   the truth,
   Stranger. What was the manner of his death?

TUTOR. That was my errand, and I'll tell you all.   680
   He came to Delphi for the Pythian Games,
   That pride and glory of the land of Greece.
   So, when he heard the herald's voice proclaim
   The foot-race, which was first to be contested,
   He stepped into the course, admired by all.
   And soon he showed that he was swift and strong
   No less than beautiful, for he returned
   Crowned with the glory of a victory.
   But though there's much to tell, I will be brief:
   That man was never known who did the like.
   Of every contest in the Festival*   690
   He won the prize, triumphantly. His name
   Time and again was heard proclaimed: 'Victor:
   Orestes, citizen of Argos, son
   Of Agamemnon, who commanded all
   The Greeks at Troy.' And so far, all was well.
   But when the gods are adverse, human strength
   Cannot prevail; and so it was with him.
   For when upon another day, at dawn,
   There was to be a contest of swift chariots,
   He took his place—and he was one of many: 700
   One from Achaea,* one from Sparta, two
   From Libya,* charioteers of skill; Orestes
   Was next—the fifth—driving Thessalian mares;*
   Then an Aetolian* with a team of chestnuts;
   The seventh was from Magnesia;* the eighth
   From Aenia*—he was driving bays;
   The ninth was from that ancient city Athens;
   The tenth and last was a Boeotian.

They drew their places. Then the umpire set them
Each at the station that had been allotted.   710
The brazen trumpet sounded; they were off.
They shouted to their horses, shook the reins;
You could hear nothing but the rattling din
Of chariots; clouds of dust arose; they all
Were bunched together; every driver
Goaded his horses, hoping so to pass
His rival's wheels and then his panting horses.
Foam from the horses' mouths was everywhere—
On one man's wheels, upon another's back.

   So far no chariot had been overturned.   720
But now, the sixth lap finished and the seventh
Begun, the Aenian driver lost control:
His horses, hard of mouth, swerved suddenly
And dashed against a Libyan team. From this
Single mishap there followed crash on crash;
The course* was full of wreckage. Seeing this,   730
The Athenian—a clever charioteer—
Drew out and waited, till the struggling mass
Had passed him by. Orestes was behind,
Relying on the finish. When he saw
That only the Athenian was left
He gave his team a ringing cry, and they
Responded. Now the two of them raced level;
First one and then the other gained the lead,
But only by a head. And as he drove,
Each time he turned the pillar at the end,   740
Checking the inside horse he gave full rein
To the outer one, and so he almost grazed
The stone.* Eleven circuits now he had
Safely accomplished; still he stood erect,
And still the chariot ran. But then, as he
Came to the turn, slackening the left-hand rein
Too soon, he struck the pillar. The axle-shaft
Was snapped in two, and he was flung headlong,
Entangled in the reins. The horses ran
Amok into mid-course and dragged Orestes
Along the ground. O, what a cry arose

From all the company when they saw him thrown!   750
That he, who had achieved so much, should meet
With such disaster, dashed to the ground, and now
Tossed high, until the other charioteers,
After a struggle with the horses, checked them
And loosed him, torn and bleeding, from the reins,
So mangled that his friends would not have known

                                                    him.

    A funeral-pyre was made; they burned the body.
Two men of Phokis, chosen for the task,
Are bringing home his ashes in an urn—
A little urn, to hold so tall a man*—
That in his native soil he may find burial.   760
Such is my tale, painful enough to hear;
For those of us who saw it, how much worse!
Far worse than anything I yet have seen.

CHORUS. And so the ancient line of Argive kings
    Has reached its end, in such calamity!

CLYTEMNESTRA. O Zeus! Am I to call this happy
    news,
    Or sorrowful, but good? What bitterness,
    If I must lose a son to save my life!

TUTOR. My lady, why so sad?

CLYTEMNESTRA.   There is strange power
    In motherhood: however terrible   770
    Her wrongs, a mother never hates her child.

TUTOR. So then it seems that I have come in vain.

CLYTEMNESTRA. No, not in vain! How can you say 'In
    vain'
    When you have brought to me the certain news
    That he is dead who drew his life from mine
    But then deserted me, who suckled him
    And reared him, and in exile has become
    A stranger to me? Since he left this country
    I have not seen him; but he charged me with
    His father's murder, and he threatened me*

Such that by day or night I could not sleep   780
Except in terror; each single hour that came
Cast over me the shadow of my death.
    But now . . . ! This day removes my fear of him—
And her! She was the worse affliction; she
Lived with me, draining me of life. But now
Her threats are harmless; I can live in peace.

ELECTRA. O my Orestes! Here is double cause
    For grief: you dead, and your unnatural mother
    Exulting in your death! O, is it just?   790

CLYTEMNESTRA. You are not! He is—being as he is!

ELECTRA. Nemesis!* Listen, and avenge Orestes.

CLYTEMNESTRA. She has heard already, and has rightly
    judged.

ELECTRA. Do outrage to me now: your hour has
    come.

CLYTEMNESTRA. But you will silence me, you and
    Orestes!

ELECTRA. Not now, alas! It is we that have been
    silenced.

CLYTEMNESTRA. My man, if you have stopped her
    mouth, you do
Indeed deserve a very rich reward.

TUTOR. Then I may go back home, if all is well?

CLYTEMNESTRA. Back home? By no means! That would
    not be worthy   800
Of me, or of the friend who sent you here.
No, come inside, and leave this woman here
To shout her sorrows—and her brother's too!
                    [*Exeunt* CLYTEMNESTRA, *her servant and the*
                                    TUTOR *into the palace*

ELECTRA. What grief and pain she suffered! Did you see
    it?

127

How bitterly she wept, how wildly mourned
Her son's destruction! Did you see it? No,
She left us laughing. O my brother! O
My dear Orestes! You are dead; your death
Has killed me too, for it has torn from me
The only hope I had, that you would come   810
At last in might, to be the avenger of
Your father, and my champion. But now
Where can I turn? For I am left alone,
Robbed of my father, and of you. Henceforth
I must go back again, for ever, into bondage
To those whom most I hate, the murderers
Who killed my father. O, can this be justice?
Never again will I consent to go
Under their roof; I'll lie down here, and starve,
Outside their doors; and if *that* vexes them,
Let them come out and kill me. If they do,   820
I shall be glad; it will be misery
To go on living; I would rather die.

[*From here until line 870 everything is sung.*]

Strophe 1

CHORUS. Zeus, where are thy thunderbolts?
   Where is the bright eye of the Sun-
   God? if they look down upon this
      And see it not.

ELECTRA.   [*An inarticulate cry of woe*]

CHORUS. My daughter, do not weep.

ELECTRA.   [*Cry, as before*]

CHORUS. My child, say nothing impious.   830

ELECTRA. You break my heart.

CHORUS.   But how?

ELECTRA. By holding out an empty hope.
   Who now can avenge *him*?
   His son Orestes is in his grave.

128

There is no comfort. O, let me be!
You do but make my grief the more.

Antistrophe 1

CHORUS. But yet, there was a king of old,
Amphiareus:* his wicked wife
Tempted by gold killed him, and yet
Though he is dead . . .

ELECTRA.   [*Cry, as before*]   840

CHORUS. He lives and reigns below.

ELECTRA.   [*Cry, as before*]

CHORUS. Alas indeed! The murderess . . .

ELECTRA. But she was killed!

CHORUS.   She was.

ELECTRA. I know! I know! Amphiareus
Had a champion* to avenge him;
But I have none now left to me.
The one I had is in his grave.

Strophe 2

CHORUS. Your fate is hard and cruel.

ELECTRA. How well I know it! Sorrow, pain,   850
Year upon year of bitter grief!

CHORUS. Yes, we have seen it all.

ELECTRA. O offer not, I beg you,*
An empty consolation.
No longer can I look for help
From my noble and loyal brother.

Antistrophe 2

CHORUS. Yet death must come to all men.   860

129

ELECTRA. But not like this! Dragged along,
Trampled on by horses' hooves!

CHORUS. No, do not think of it!

ELECTRA. O what an end! In exile,*
Without a loving sister
To lay him in his grave, with none
To pay tribute of tears and mourning.   870

Enter CHRYSOTHEMIS

CHRYSOTHEMIS. Great happiness, dear sister, is the
  cause
Of my unseemly haste; good news for you,
And joy. Release has come at last from all
The sufferings that you have so long endured.

ELECTRA. And where can you find any help for my
Afflictions? They have grown past remedy.

CHRYSOTHEMIS. Orestes has come back to us! I know it
As surely as I stand before you now.

ELECTRA. What, are you mad, poor girl? Do you make
  fun
Of your calamity, and mine as well?   880

CHRYSOTHEMIS. I am not mocking you! I swear it by
Our father's memory.* He is here, among us.

ELECTRA. You foolish girl! You have been listening to
Some idle rumour. Who has told it you?

CHRYSOTHEMIS. No one has told me anything. I know
From proof that I have seen with my own eyes.

ELECTRA. What proof, unhappy girl? What have you
  seen
To be inflamed with this disastrous hope?

CHRYSOTHEMIS. Do listen, I implore you; then you'll
  know
If I am talking foolishly or not.   890

ELECTRA. Then tell me, if it gives you any pleasure.

130

CHRYSOTHEMIS. I'll tell you everything I saw. When I
   Came near the tomb, I saw that offerings
   Of milk had just been poured upon the mound,
   And it was wreathed with flowers. I looked, and
     wondered;
   I peered about, to see if anyone
   Was standing near; then, as I seemed alone,
   I crept a little nearer to the tomb,   900
   And there, upon the edge, I saw a lock
   Of hair; it had been newly cut.
   Upon the moment, as I looked, there fell
   Across my mind a picture, one that I
   Have often dreamed of, and I knew that these
   Were offerings given by our beloved brother.
   I took them up with reverence; my eyes
   Were filled with tears of joy; for I was sure,
   As I am now, that none but he has laid
   This tribute on the grave. Who else should do it
   But he, or you, or I? It was not I,   910
   That is quite certain. You have not been there;
   How could you? Even to worship at a shrine
   They do not let you leave the house, unpunished.
   As for our mother, she has little mind
   To make such offerings—and we should have
     known it.
   No, dear Electra, they are from Orestes.
   Therefore take courage! There is no such thing
   As joy unbroken, or unbroken sorrow.
   We have known sorrow—nothing else; perhaps
   Today great happiness begins for us.

ELECTRA. O you unhappy girl! You little know!   920

CHRYSOTHEMIS. Unhappy? Is this not the best of news?

ELECTRA. The truth is very different from your fancy.

CHRYSOTHEMIS. This is the truth. Mayn't I believe my
   eyes?

ELECTRA. Poor girl! He's dead! We cannot look to him
   For our deliverance; our hopes are gone.

131

CHRYSOTHEMIS. Alas, alas! . . . Who told you this?

ELECTRA. One who was there; a man who saw him
    killed.

CHRYSOTHEMIS. Where is the man? This fills me with
    dismay!

ELECTRA. At home; and, to our mother, very welcome.

CHRYSOTHEMIS. Alas, alas! Who could it then have
    been
    Who put those many offerings on the tomb? 930

ELECTRA. It will be someone who has laid them there
    As a memorial of Orestes' death.

CHRYSOTHEMIS. O, this is ruin! I came hurrying back,
    So happy, with my news, not knowing this
    Calamity. But all the woes we had
    Before are with us still, and worse are added!

ELECTRA. Yet even so, if you will work with me,
    We can throw off the weight that wears us down.

CHRYSOTHEMIS. What, can I bring the dead to life
    again? 940

ELECTRA. That's not my meaning; I am not a fool.

CHRYSOTHEMIS. Then what assistance can I give to
    you?

ELECTRA. I need your courage in a certain venture.

CHRYSOTHEMIS. If it will help us, I will not refuse.

ELECTRA. Remember: nothing prospers without effort.

CHRYSOTHEMIS. You may command whatever strength
    I have.

ELECTRA. This then is what I have resolved to do.
    You know, as I do, we have no support
    Of friends; of what we had we have been stripped
    By death. We two are left; we are alone. 950

For me, while I had news about our brother,
That he was well and strong, I lived in hope
That he would some time come and punish those
Who killed our father. Now that he is dead,
I turn to you, that you will join your hand
With mine, your sister's; help me, do not flinch:
Aegisthus, who has murdered our dear father—
We'll kill him! There's no reason now to keep
It back from you. You cannot wait, inactive,
Hoping for—nothing. What hope was left to you
That is not shattered? This is what you have:
Lasting resentment that you have been robbed
Of all the wealth that rightly should be yours;   960
Anger that they have let you live so long
Unmarried—and do not think that this will change:
Aegisthus is no fool; he can foresee,
If you or I had children, they would take
Revenge on him. Marriage is not for us.
Therefore be with me in my resolution.
This you will win: the praise of our dead father,
And of our brother, for your loyalty;
The freedom that is yours by right of birth;   970
A marriage worthy of your station, since
All look admiringly upon the brave.
Do you not see what glory you will win
Both for yourself and me by doing this?
For all will cry, Argive or foreigner,
When they behold us: 'See! there are the sisters
Who saved their father's house from desolation;
Who, when their enemies were firmly set
In power, avenged a murder, risking all.   980
Love and respect and honour are their due;
At festivals and public gatherings
Give them pre-eminence, for their bravery.'
So we shall be acclaimed by everyone;
As long as we shall live our glory will
Endure, and will not fade when we are dead.
  My sister, give consent! Stand by your father,
Work with your brother, put an end to my

Calamities and yours; for to the noble
A life of shameful suffering is disgraceful.

CHORUS. In such a case, in speech or in reply,   990
　Forethought and prudence are the best of helpers.

CHRYSOTHEMIS. Before she spoke at all, my friends, if
　　she
　Had any prudence she might have preserved
　Some caution, not have thrown it to the winds.
　For what can you be thinking of, to arm
　Yourself with utter recklessness, and call
　On me to help you? Do you not reflect
　You are a woman, not a man? how weak
　You are, how strong your foes? that day by day
　Their cause grows stronger, ours diminishes
　And dwindles into nothing? Who can hope,   1000
　Plotting to overthrow so powerful
　A man, not to be overwhelmed himself
　In utter ruin? Our plight is desperate
　Already; you will make it worse, far worse,
　If you are heard saying such things as this.
　It brings us nothing, if when we have won
　That glorious repute, we die ignobly.
　Mere death is not the worst; this is the worst,
　To long for death and be compelled to live.
　No, I implore you, keep your rage in check
　Before you bring destruction on us both   1010
　And devastation to our father's house.
　What you have said shall be as if unsaid,
　Of no effect; and you, before it is
　Too late, must learn that since you have no strength
　You have to yield to those that are in power.

CHORUS. You must indeed. There is no better thing
　For anyone than forethought and good sense.

ELECTRA. I had expected this; I thought that you
　Would spurn the offer that I made. And so
　My hand alone must do it—for be sure,
　It is a task that cannot be neglected.   1020

134

CHRYSOTHEMIS. A pity you were not as bold as this
Before! You might have thwarted the assassins!

ELECTRA. I was too young to act. I had the will!

CHRYSOTHEMIS. Then try once more to be too young to
act.

ELECTRA. It seems you are determined not to help me.

CHRYSOTHEMIS. Not in a venture that would be our
ruin.

ELECTRA. How wise you are! And what a coward too.

CHRYSOTHEMIS. Some day you'll praise my wisdom. I
will bear it!

ELECTRA. I'll never trouble you so far as that!

CHRYSOTHEMIS. Who's wise, and who is foolish, time
will show.   1030

ELECTRA. Out of my sight! You are no use to me.

CHRYSOTHEMIS. I am, if you were wise enough to
listen.

ELECTRA. Go to your mother; tell her everything!

CHRYSOTHEMIS. No; I refuse my help, but not from
hatred.

ELECTRA. But in contempt! You make that very plain.

CHRYSOTHEMIS. Trying to save your life! Is that
contempt?

ELECTRA. Am I to do what you imagine right?

CHRYSOTHEMIS. Yes; and when you are right, I'll
follow you.

ELECTRA. To be so plausible—and be so wrong!

CHRYSOTHEMIS. These are the very words I'd use of
you.   1040

ELECTRA. The right is on my side. Do you deny it?

CHRYSOTHEMIS. The right may lead a man to his
  destruction.

ELECTRA. That is no principle for me to follow.

CHRYSOTHEMIS. You'll think the same as I—when you
  have done it.

ELECTRA. Do it I will. You shall not frighten me.

CHRYSOTHEMIS. Give up this folly! Be advised by me!

ELECTRA. No! There is nothing worse than bad advice.

CHRYSOTHEMIS. Can I say nothing that you will
  accept?

ELECTRA. I have considered, and I have determined.

CHRYSOTHEMIS. Then I will go, since you do not
  approve   1050
  Of what I say, nor I of what you do.

ELECTRA. Go then, for your ways never can be mine
  However much you wish. It is mere folly
  To go in quest of the impossible.

CHRYSOTHEMIS. If this, to you, is wisdom, follow it;
  But when it leads you to disaster, then
  At last you'll learn mine was the better wisdom.
                              [*Exit* CHRYSOTHEMIS

Strophe 1

CHORUS [*sings*]. We see the birds of the air, with what
  Sure instinct they protect and nourish
  Those who brought them to life and tended them.   1060
    How can man disobey the laws of Nature?
    The anger of the gods, the law established,
    Enthroned in Heaven,* will bring them
    retribution.
    There is a Voice the dead can hear:
  Speak, O Voice, to the King, to Agamemnon,
  A message of shame and sorrow and deep dishonour.

136

Antistrophe 1

His house already was near to falling;   1070
Now a new cause of ruin threatens:
Discord comes to divide his champions.
  Now no longer is daughter joined with daughter
  In loyalty and love, but strife divides them.
  Electra stands alone to face the tempest.
  Never has she ceased to mourn,*
Faithful, careless of life, if she may purge this   1080
Palace of those two Furies,* a foul pollution.*

Strophe 2

He that is noble in spirit scorns
A life ignoble, darkened by shame,
And chooses honour, my daughter,
As you chose to cleave to your father,
Accepting a life of sorrow.
Spurning dishonour, you have won a double fame:
  Courage is yours, and wisdom.

Antistrophe 2

Still may I see you triumph, raised   1090
Above your foes, restored to the power
And wealth of which they have robbed you.
You have known nothing but sorrow;
And yet by observing those great
Laws of the gods,* in piety* and reverence,
  You crown your sorrow with glory.

    Enter ORESTES, PYLADES, *and attendants*

ORESTES. Ladies, we wish to know if we have been
  Rightly directed to the place we look for.

CHORUS. What is that you wish to find?   1100

ORESTES.   Aegisthus,
  If you could tell us where to find his palace?

137

CHORUS. But it is here. You have been guided well.

ORESTES. Could one of you perhaps tell those within
   That we have come, whom they have long awaited?

CHORUS [*indicating* ELECTRA]. She best might do it;
      she is nearest to them.*

ORESTES. Madam, we are from Phokis; tell them, pray,
   That we have certain business with Aegisthus.

ELECTRA. Alas, alas! You have not come with
      something
   To prove it true—the rumour that we heard?

ORESTES. Of 'rumours' I know nothing. I am sent   1110
   By Strophius,* Orestes' friend, with news.

ELECTRA. O, tell me what it is! You frighten me.

ORESTES. We bring him home; this little urn contains
   What now is left of him; for he is dead.

ELECTRA. Ah, this is what I feared! I see your burden;
   Small weight for you, but heavy grief to me.

ORESTES. It is—if that which moves your sorrow is
   Orestes' death: in *that* we bring his ashes.

ELECTRA. Then give it me, I beg you! If this vessel
   Now holds him, let me take it in my arms.*   1120

ORESTES. Men, give it her, whoever she may be:
   A friend; perhaps, one of his family.
   This is no prayer of one who wished him evil.
         [ELECTRA *advances to the front of the stage.*
      ORESTES *and* PYLADES *retire near the palace gate*

ELECTRA. Orestes! my Orestes! you have come
   To this! The hopes with which I sent you forth
   Are come to this! How radiant you were!
   And now I hold you—so: a little dust!   1130
   O, would to God that I had died myself,
   And had not snatched *you* from the edge of death
   To have you sent into a foreign land!

138

They would have killed you—but you would have
    shared
Your father's death and burial; not been killed
Far from your home, an exile, pitiably,
Alone, without your sister. Not for you,
The last sad tribute of a sister's hand!
Some stranger washed your wounds, and laid your
    body
On the devouring fire; the charity   1140
Of strangers brings you home—so light a burden,
And in so small a vessel!
                    O, my brother,
What love and tenderness I spent on you!
For you were my child rather than your mother's;
I was your nurse—or you would not have had
A nurse; *I* was the one you always called
Your *sister*—and it has come to nothing.
One single day has made it all in vain,
And, like a blast of wind, has swept it all   1150
To ruin. You are dead; my father too
Lies in his grave; your death is death to me,
Joy to our enemies: our mother—if
She *is* a mother!—dances in delight,
When you had sent me many a secret promise
That you would come and be revenged on her.
But no! A cruel fate has ruined you,
And ruined me, and brought it all to nothing:
The brother that I loved is gone, and in
His place are ashes, and an empty shadow.
O pity! pity, grief and sorrow!*   1160
How cruel, cruel, is your home-coming,
My dearest brother! I can live no longer.
O take me with you! You are nothing; I
Am nothing, now. Let me henceforward be
A shade among the shades, with you. We lived
As one; so now in death, let us be one,
And share a common grave, as while you lived
We shared a common life. O, let me die;
For death alone can put an end to grief.   1170

139

CHORUS. Your father died, Electra; he was mortal:
So has Orestes died; so shall we all.
Remember this, and do not grieve too much.

ORESTES. What answer can I make to this? What *can*
I say? I must, and yet I cannot, speak.

ELECTRA. Sir, what has troubled you? Why speak like
this?

ORESTES. Are *you* the Princess? Can you be Electra?

ELECTRA. I *am* Electra, though I look so mean.

ORESTES. To think that it has gone so far as this!

ELECTRA. But why such words of pity over *me*?   1180

ORESTES.—Treated so harshly and with such
dishonour!

ELECTRA. Ill words well spoken, stranger—of Electra.

ORESTES.—How cruel! Kept unmarried, and ill-used!

ELECTRA. Sir, why do you look at me so fixedly,
And in such pity?

ORESTES.   Little did I know
My own unhappiness, how great it was.

ELECTRA. What words of mine have made you think of
that?

ORESTES. No words; it is the sight of all you suffer.

ELECTRA. The sight of it? What you can see is nothing!

ORESTES. How? What can be more terrible than this?

ELECTRA. To live, as I do, with the murderers.   1190

ORESTES. What murderers? Who are these guilty men?

ELECTRA. My father's.—And they treat me as their
slave!

ORESTES. But who has forced you to this servitude?

140

ELECTRA. She who has the name of mother—nothing
else!

ORESTES. What does she do? Oppression? Violence?

ELECTRA. Violence, oppression, everything that's evil!

ORESTES. You have no champion? no one to oppose
them?

ELECTRA. The one I had is dead: here are his ashes.

ORESTES. A cruel life! How much I pity you.

ELECTRA. You are the only one who pities me!   1200

ORESTES. I am the only one who shares your sorrow.

ELECTRA. Who are you? Can it be you are some
kinsman?

ORESTES. If I may trust these women I would tell you.

ELECTRA. Yes, you may trust them: they are friends,
and loyal.

ORESTES. Give back the urn, and I will tell you all.

ELECTRA. No, no, I beg you; do not be so cruel!

ORESTES. Do as I ask; you will do nothing wrong.

ELECTRA. It is all I have! You cannot take it from me!

ORESTES. You may not keep it.

ELECTRA.   O, my dear Orestes,
How cruel! I may not even bury you.   1210

ORESTES. Your talk of burial, your tears, are wrong.

ELECTRA. How is it wrong to mourn my brother's
death?

ORESTES. You must not speak of him in words like
these.

ELECTRA. Must I be robbed of *all* my rights in him?

ORESTES. You are robbed of nothing! *This* is not for you.

ELECTRA. Yes, if I hold Orestes in my arms!

ORESTES. This is Orestes only by a fiction.

ELECTRA. Then *where* is my unhappy brother's grave?

ORESTES. Nowhere. The living do not have a *grave!*

ELECTRA. My friend!* What do you mean?

ORESTES.   I mean—   1220
   the truth.

ELECTRA. My brother is *alive?*

ORESTES.   If *I'm* alive!

ELECTRA. *You* are *Orestes?*

ORESTES.   Look upon this ring—
  Our father's ring.*—Do you believe me now?

ELECTRA. O day of happiness!

ORESTES.   Great happiness!

ELECTRA. It is *your* voice?—And have you come?

ORESTES.   My voice,
  And I am here!

ELECTRA.   I hold you in my arms?

ORESTES. You do—and may we nevermore be parted.

ELECTRA. O look, my friends! My friends of Argos,
  look!
  It is Orestes!—dead, by artifice,
  And by that artifice restored to us.

CHORUS. To see him, and to see your happiness,   1230
  My child, brings tears of joy into my eyes.

   [*From here until line 1288,* ELECTRA *sings,* ORESTES *speaks.*]

Strophe

ELECTRA. My brother is here! the son of my own dear
  father!
  You longed to see me, and now, at last,
  You have found me! O, you have come to me!

ORESTES. Yes, I have come: but wait;* contain your joy
  In silence; they will hear us in the palace.

ELECTRA. O by the virgin-goddess, by Artemis,
  I despise them, those in the palace—   1240
  Women, useless and helpless!
  O, why should I fear them?

ORESTES. Remember: women may not be too weak
  To strike a blow.* You have seen proof of it.

ELECTRA. Ah me! The foul crime, that no
  Darkness can ever hide, that no
  Oblivion can wash away, no
  Power on earth remove.   1250

ORESTES. All this I know; but we will speak of it
  When we can speak of it without restraint.

Antistrophe

ELECTRA. Each moment of time, now or to come, is
  time
  To proclaim aloud the abomination.
  At last, at last, I can speak with freedom.

ORESTES. You can; and yet,* until the hour has come,
  By speaking freely we may lose our freedom.

ELECTRA. How can I chain my tongue and repress my   1260
  joy?
  Can I look upon you and be silent,
  Safe returned, my brother?
  It is more than I dared hope.

ORESTES. I waited long, but when the voice of God
  Spoke, then I made no more delay.*

ELECTRA. O, this is joy crowning joy, if
    Heaven has brought you home to me!
    I see the hand of God
    Working along with us.   1270

ORESTES. To stem your flood of joy is hard, but yet
  There is some danger in this long rejoicing.

Epode

ELECTRA. So weary was the time of waiting!
    Now when you have come at last
    And all my sorrows have reached their end,*
    O, do not check my happiness.

ORESTES. Nor would I do it—but we must be   1280
    prudent.*

ELECTRA. My friends, I heard my brother's voice,
    And I had thought
  That I would never hear his voice again:
    How could I restrain my joy?
  Ah, now I have you; I can look upon
  The well-loved face that I could not forget
    Even in darkest sorrow.

ORESTES. How much there is to hear!—our mother's
    sin
  And cruelty, that our ancestral wealth
  Is plundered, ravished, wantonly misused   1290
  By that usurper. Yet our time is short
  And their misdeeds are more than can be told.
  But tell me what may help our present venture:
  Where can I hide, or where can I confront
  Our foes, to turn their laughter into silence?
  And see to this: our mother must not read
  Our secret in your face. Conceal your joy
  When we go in; look sad, and mourn, as if
  The tale that you have heard were true. There will
  Be time enough to smile when we have conquered.   1300

ELECTRA. My brother, what seems good to you shall be
   My law; your pleasure shall be mine, for mine
   Is nothing, except what you have brought to me,
   And to win all there is I would not cause
   A moment's pain to you, nor would that serve
   The favour of the gods, which now is with us.
     Now as to what you ask.—You surely know
   Aegisthus is abroad, not in the palace;
   But she is there, and you need have no fear
   That she will see a look of happiness   1310
   Upon my face. The settled hatred which
   I have for her will banish any smile.
   I shall be weeping!—though my tears will be
   Of joy at your return. My tears today
   Flow in abundance; I have seen you dead,
   And now alive. So strange the day has been
   That if our father came and greeted us
   I should not think it was a ghost; I should
   Believe it. Therefore, being yourself a miracle
   In your return, command me as you will;
   For had you died, had I been left alone,
   I should myself have ventured all, and found   1320
   Glorious deliverance, or a glorious death.

ORESTES. Hush! I can hear the steps of someone
    coming
   Out of the palace.

ELECTRA.   You are welcome, strangers.
   Enter; the burden that you bring is such
   As no one could reject—and no one welcome.

Enter the TUTOR, *from the palace*

TUTOR. You reckless fools! What, have you got no
    sense?
   Do you not care whether you live or die?
   Are you demented? Don't you understand
   The peril you are in? Not one that *threatens*;   1330
   No, it is here! Had I not stood on guard
   Inside the door they would have known your plot

Before they saw you. As it is, I took
Good care of that. So, make an end of talk
And these interminable cries of joy.
Go in; delay is dangerous at such
A moment. You must act, and make an end.

ORESTES. When I go in, how shall I find it there?

TUTOR. All's well. Rely on this: they will not know
   you.   1340

ORESTES. You have reported, then, that I am dead?

TUTOR. I have; in their eyes you are dead and gone.

ORESTES. And are they glad? Or what have they been
   saying?

TUTOR. We'll speak of that hereafter. All is well
   Within the palace—even what is shameful.

ELECTRA. In Heaven's name, who is this man, Orestes?

ORESTES. Do you not know him?

ELECTRA.   I cannot even guess.

ORESTES. You know the man to whom you gave me
   once?

ELECTRA. Which man? What are you saying?

ORESTES.   The man
   by whom
You had me secretly conveyed to Phokis.   1350

ELECTRA. What, this is *he*?—the only one I found
   Remaining loyal at our father's murder?

ORESTES. That is the man; no need to ask for proof.

ELECTRA. How glad I am! Dear friend, to you alone
   The house of Agamemnon owes deliverance.
   How come you here? Can you be really he
   That saved us both from all that threatened us?
   Come, let me take your hands, those faithful hands,*

My friend! How could I not have known you, when
You came to bring me joy—but joy concealed   1360
In words of deadly grief? I'll call you father,
Give you a daughter's greeting—for to me
You are a father. How I hated you
A while ago; how much I love you now!

TUTOR. It is enough. Though there is much to tell,
  There will be many days and many nights
  In which, Electra, you may tell it all.
    One word with you, Orestes, Pylades:
  This is your moment; now she is alone,
  No men-at-arms are near. But if you wait,
  Then you will have to face not only them,   1370
  But many more—men trained to use their weapons.

ORESTES. Pylades, there is no longer time for talk;
  It seems the hour has come. So, let us go;
  And as I go I give my reverence
  To all the gods that stand before the house.*
    [ORESTES *enters the palace with* PYLADES, *praying
    before images on either side of the gate.* ELECTRA
    *goes to the altar where Clytemnestra's offerings
    are still visible.*   Exit the TUTOR

ELECTRA. O Lord Apollo, listen to their prayers,
  Be gracious to them! Listen too to mine!
  How often have I been thy suppliant
  Bringing what gifts I had; and therefore now,
  Although my hands are empty, I beseech thee,
  I beg thee, I implore thee, Lord Apollo: 1380
  Give us thy favour, help our purposes,
  And show mankind what chastisement the gods
  Inflict on those who practise wickedness.
            [*Exit* ELECTRA, *into the palace*

Strophe

CHORUS [*sings*]. Look where the god of death* makes
  his way,

Fierce and implacable.
The Furies, champions of Justice,
Hounds of the gods, hot on the trail of crime,
   Have entered the palace.
   Before me rises a vision:
   Soon shall I see fulfilment.   1390

Antistrophe

The minister of the gods,* with stealthy foot,
   Ushered within the palace,
   The ancient home of his fathers,
Holds in his hand a keen whetted sword,
   With Hermes to guide him,*
   To shroud his designs in darkness
   And lead him straight to vengeance.

Enter ELECTRA

ELECTRA. My friends, keep silent; wait. It will not be
  For long. Their hands are ready; soon they'll strike.

CHORUS. What are they doing now?

ELECTRA.   She has the urn,   1400
  Preparing it for burial; they are near her.

CHORUS. And why have you come out?

ELECTRA.   To stand on
  guard;*
  To give the warning if Aegisthus comes.

CLYTEMNESTRA [*within*]. Ah . . . ! So many
  Murderers, and not a single friend!

ELECTRA. Someone inside is screaming. Do you hear it?

CHORUS. I heard. . . . It makes me shudder; it is fearful.

CLYTEMNESTRA. Aegisthus! O where are you? They will
  kill me!

ELECTRA. There, yet another scream!

CLYTEMNESTRA.   My son, my son! 1410
 Take pity on your mother!

ELECTRA.   You had none
 For him, nor for his father!

CHORUS [*sings*]. O my city! Ill-starred race of our
  kings!
 So many years a doom has lain on you:
  Now it is passing away.

CLYTEMNESTRA. Ah! . . . They have struck me!

ELECTRA. Strike her again, if you have strength enough!

CLYTEMNESTRA. Another blow!

ELECTRA.   Pray God there'll be a third,
 And that one for Aegisthus!

CHORUS [*sings*]. The cry for vengeance is at work; the
  dead are stirring.
   Those who were killed of old now   1420
  Drink in return the blood of those who killed
               them.

CHORUS [*speaks*]. See, they are coming, and the blood-
  stained arm
 Drips sacrifice of death. It was deserved.

Enter ORESTES *and* PYLADES

ELECTRA. How is it with you both?

ORESTES.   All's well, within
 The palace, if Apollo's oracle was well.

ELECTRA. Then she is dead?

ORESTES.   No longer need you fear
 Your mother's insolence and cruelty.*

CHORUS. Be silent! I can see Aegisthus coming.

ELECTRA. Stand back, Orestes.

ORESTES.   Are you sure you see   1430
                                         him?

ELECTRA. Yes, he is coming from the town. He smiles;
    We have him in our hands.

CHORUS [*sings*]. Back to the doorway quickly! One
    Task is accomplished; may the second prosper
                                       too!

ORESTES. It will. No fear of that.

ELECTRA.   Then, to your station.

ORESTES. I go at once.

ELECTRA.   And leave the rest to me.
        [ORESTES *and* PYLADES *enter the palace*

CHORUS [*sings*]. Speak some gentle words to him
     That he may fall, unawares,   1440
   Into the retribution that awaits him.

Enter AEGISTHUS

AEGISTHUS. They tell me that some men have come
    from Phokis
    With news about Orestes; dead, they say,
    Killed in a chariot-race. Where are these men?
    Will someone tell me? [*To* ELECTRA.] You! Yes, you
      should know;*
    It will have special interest for you!

ELECTRA. I know. Of course I know. I loved my
    brother;
    How then should I make little of his death?

AEGISTHUS. Then tell me where these men are to be
    found.   1450

ELECTRA. In there.
    They've won their way to Clytemnestra's heart.

AEGISTHUS. And is it true that they have brought this
    message?

ELECTRA. More than the message: they brought Orestes
  too.

AEGISTHUS. What, is the very body to be seen?

ELECTRA. It is; I do not envy you the sight.

AEGISTHUS. Our meetings have not always been so
  pleasant!

ELECTRA. If this proves to your liking, you are
  welcome.

AEGISTHUS. I bid you all keep silence. Let the doors
  Be opened.

> *The palace doors open to disclose* ORESTES *and*
> PYLADES, *standing over the shrouded body of*
> CLYTEMNESTRA

           Citizens of Argos, look!
  If there is any who had hopes in him,   1460
  That hope lies shattered. Look upon this body
  And learn that I am master—or the weight
  Of my strong arm will make him learn the lesson.

ELECTRA. I need no teaching; I have learned, at last,
  That I must live at peace with those that rule.

AEGISTHUS. Zeus! Here is one laid low, before our eyes,
  By the angry gods—and may no Nemesis
  Attend my words, or I unsay them.—Now,
  Turn back the shroud, and let me see the face.
  It was a kinsman, and I too must mourn.

ORESTES. This you should do; it is for you, not me,   1470
  To look upon this face and take farewell.

AEGISTHUS. It is indeed for me, and I will do it.—
  Call Clytemnestra, if she is at hand.

ORESTES. She is not far away; look straight before you.
                [AEGISTHUS *takes the shroud from the face*

AEGISTHUS. God! What is this?

ORESTES.   Some stranger,
                                 frightening you?

AEGISTHUS. Who are you, that have got me in your
    clutches

    For my destruction?

ORESTES.   Have you not seen already?
    Someone you thought was dead is still alive.

AEGISTHUS. Ah. . . . Now I understand.—You, who
    speak,   1480
    You are Orestes!

ORESTES.   You could read the future
    So well,* yet were so blind.

AEGISTHUS.   Ah. . . . You have come
    To kill me! Give me time, a little time,
    To speak.

ELECTRA. No, by the gods, Orestes! No
    Long speech from him! No, not a single word!
    He's face to face with death; there's nothing gained
    In gaining time. Kill him at once! And when
    You've killed him, throw the body out of sight,
    And let him have the funeral he deserves.
    Animals shall eat him! Nothing less than this
    Will compensate for all that he has done.   1490

ORESTES. Sir, come with me into the house; this is
    No time for talk. My business is your life.

AEGISTHUS. Why to the house? If you are not ashamed
    At what you do, then do it openly.

ORESTES. You shall not order me. Go in, and die
    On the same spot on which you killed my father.

AEGISTHUS. This house of Atreus* must, it seems,
    behold
    Death upon death, those now and those to come.*

ORESTES. It will see yours; so much I can foresee.

AEGISTHUS. You did not get this foresight from your 1500
 father!

ORESTES. You have too much to say; the time is
 passing.
 Go!

AEGISTHUS. Lead the way.

ORESTES.   You must go before me.

AEGISTHUS. That I may not escape you?

ORESTES.   That you may not
 Be killed where *you* would choose. You shall taste all
 The bitterness of death.—If retribution
 Were swift and certain, and the lawless man
 Paid with his life, there would be fewer villains.
   [*Exeunt* ORESTES, PYLADES, ELECTRA, AEGISTHUS

CHORUS [*chants*]. Children of Atreus, now at last
 Your sufferings are ended. You have won
 Your own deliverance; now once more
 Is the line of your fathers restored.   1510

EXPLANATORY NOTES

ANTIGONE

3 *Creon*: he is not named in the Greek, which here designates him simply *stratēgos*, 'general'.

The enemy: the Greek says 'the Argive army', the troops Polyneices, one of Antigone and Ismene's two brothers, had raised in support of his cause.

That none shall bury him: lines 1080–4, indicate that burial was refused to all the Argive dead. Antigone is concentrating on the corpse which concerns her personally. Denial of burial was an outrage; according to *Iliad* 23. 71, the souls of the dead refused to allow the unburied to join their company.

4 *public stoning*: a punishment associated particularly with treachery.

his own hands...destroyed herself: Ismene summarizes the appalling events recounted at much greater length by the messenger in *Oedipus the King*, see pp. 90–2, with one important difference. In *Antigone* Sophocles assumes a version of the myth in which Oedipus had died 'hated and scorned', whereas in *Oedipus the King* it is left unclear how and when he is to die. See further below, note to p. 97.

5 *the dead*: the Greek says 'those beneath the earth', although Ismene is presumably including the unburied Polyneices.

The sacred laws: archaic socio-religious rules also described as the 'unwritten laws', the 'ancestral laws', and the 'common laws of Greece'. They protected the relationships between family members, between hosts and guests, and between the living and the dead. They are often articulated negatively as taboos on intra-familial murder, incest, murder of guest or host, and disrespect towards the dead.

6 *of seven gates*: a traditional epithet of Thebes (*Odyssey* 11. 263).

Dirke: the name of a river running to the west of Thebes, named after the wife of Zethus, an early co-ruler of the city with his brother Amphion.

155

6 *a snow-white shield*: Argive soldiers were traditionally imagined bearing shields painted white. This may have arisen from a confusion of the toponym 'Argos' with the adjective *argos*, 'white'.

He: the generalized Argive soldier.

in Polyneices' | Fierce quarrel: in the Greek there is a play on the word for 'quarrel' (*neikos*), which supplied the latter part of Polyneices' name *Polu-neikēs*, 'much-quarrelling'.

like some eagle: the figure equating Polyneices and his army with a predatory bird descending on Thebes is continued into the antistrophe.

7 *the sons of a Dragon*: the Thebans. Cadmus, the mythical founder of Thebes and the dynasty ending in Antigone and Ismene, was thought to have slain a dragon and sown its teeth in the earth, from which sprang a harvest of 'sown men', the ancestors of the Theban aristocracy. The image of a dragon and an eagle in combat was traditional in Greek epic poetry (*Iliad* 12. 201).

With a fiery bolt: tradition made Zeus strike down with a thunderbolt the Argive leader Capaneus, the first to scale the Theban ramparts, who had delivered the 'arrogant boast' obliquely alluded to in line 127. The story was too familiar for Capaneus to need naming by Sophocles: he is often depicted in the visual arts falling from his ladder after being struck by lightning.

possessed with frenzy: in the Greek Capaneus is explicitly likened to a maenad.

the great War-god: Ares, the Greek god of martial violence. Thebes was one of the few Greek cities where Ares received an important cult; in myth he fathered both Harmonia whom Cadmus married and the dragon which Cadmus killed.

Seven foemen: none of Polyneices' six allies is mentioned by name in Sophocles' *Antigone*. In *Oedipus at Colonus* they are catalogued as Amphiareus, Tydeus, Eteoclus, Hippomedon, Capaneus, and Parthenopaeus (1313–20). Their respective fates at the hands of Theban heroes is recounted fully in Aeschylus' *Seven against Thebes*.

Argive arms . . . temple of Zeus: after victory in battle it was established practice to honour the gods by fastening military spoils to temple walls. The Greek here explicitly honours Zeus in his capacity as Zeus *tropaios*, the god who causes a rout (*tropē*) of the enemy.

Victory: originally an offshoot of Athena, Victory (*Nikē*) was conceptualized as a winged female deity.

8 *Theban Dionysus*: For several reasons it is appropriate to suggest that the end of the battle be marked by a night-long celebration of Dionysus, the god of wine and dancing; he was an important deity at Thebes, particularly associated with nocturnal festivals (Euripides, *Bacchae* 486), and he led in his entourage Eirene, the divine personification of peace.

Laius: previous king of Thebes, the son of Labdacus and father of Oedipus.

with polluted sword: the weapons with which the brothers killed each other are described as polluted because a special pollution (*miasma*) attached to intra-familial murder.

nearest kinship: Creon is only related to the sons of Oedipus by marriage, as the brother of their mother Iocasta. Sophocles chooses to present Polyneices and Eteocles as childless, ignoring alternative traditions which attributed sons to them (e.g. Herodotus 4. 147; 5. 61).

9 *To drink his kindred blood*: imagery connected with anthropophagy was used traditionally in Greek poetry to denote extremes of hatred (e.g. *Iliad* 4. 35, Theognis 349). It is not to be taken literally.

11 *To avoid a curse*: it was believed that guilt fell on anyone who passed a corpse without throwing earth upon it.

hot iron . . . To walk through fire: the guard refers to archaic ordeals connected with the sanctioning of oaths.

'*We must report . . . We dare not hide it*': in the Greek there is no direct speech here.

12 *you shall be hanged | Alive*: evidence from slaves was believed to be more reliable if exacted under torture (see e.g. Isaeus 8. 12).

13 *Ox-team*: the Greek actually says 'mules', believed to be superior to oxen for ploughing (*Iliad* 10. 352).

14 *If he observe Law*: the Greek actually says 'the laws of the land', providing an important contrast with the divine law mentioned subsequently.

an unlucky father: Sophocles explicitly names Oedipus here.

16 *this visitation*: the Greek makes it clear that the guard believed that the whirlwind was sent by the gods.

this offence and that: i.e. Antigone's present and previous attempts to provide the corpse with burial.

the Powers who rule among the dead: the Greek names *Dikē*, the divine personification of 'Justice', a daughter of Zeus.

17 *the laws of Heaven*: see above, note to p. 5.

closer still | Than all our family: the Greek says 'closer to me in blood than anyone who worships Zeus at our family altar'.

18 *him*: i.e. Eteocles.

19 *the god of Death*: Hades, explicitly named in the Greek.

21 *O my dear Haemon . . . wrongs you!*: the manuscripts attribute this line to Ismene. Nowhere else does Antigone name her fiancé.

He is your son . . . from him: many editors attribute this line to the chorus.

It is determined . . . she must die: some manuscripts attribute this line to Ismene.

wind from Thrace: Boreas, the god of the north wind, was believed to live in Thrace, a country bordering on northern Greece approximately equivalent to the modern Bulgaria. See further below, note to p. 34.

23 *last-born of your children*: the significance of this detail will become painfully clear, below p. 44.

for Antigone: the Greek adds, 'and for the disappointment with regards to his marriage'.

24 *to Sacred Kinship*: the Greek actually says 'to Zeus who presides over the family'.

27 *as will avert . . . a curse upon the city*: Creon does not inflict the threatened punishment of stoning on Antigone, choosing starvation instead. The token supply of food with which she is to be imprisoned is intended to avert the pollution which the killing of a kinswoman would normally be supposed to incur, but may also be seen as an offering to the gods of the underworld.

28 *Love*: the Greeks had several different words customarily translated as 'love'. Here the Greek term is the personified force exclusively of sexual love, Eros, usually depicted as a boy.

Aphrodite: goddess of sexual love, and mother of Eros.

Hades: the Greek suggests that Antigone is going to a nuptial chamber, introducing the motif of the 'bride of death' which becomes prominent henceforward.

29 *Acheron*: a river of the underworld, usually conceptualized as a stagnant lake, whose name was derived from a word meaning 'lamentation'.

alone among mortals: the translation omits the important point that Antigone goes to her death 'autonomously' (*autonomos*), i.e., of her own free will.

Niobe: a princess from Phrygia in Asia Minor, the daughter of Tantalus. Niobe married Amphion, an early ruler of Thebes. She boasted that she had borne many beautiful children, whereas Leto, the mother of Apollo and Artemis, had borne only two. The divine siblings killed Niobe's sons and daughters in recompense. The bereaved mother was subsequently transformed into stone on Mount Sipylus back in her homeland, her tears symbolized in perpetuity by the rivers which course down the mountain side. Both Aeschylus and Sophocles dramatized her tragic story.

a goddess, and born of the gods: the former is not strictly speaking true, but Niobe was of divine descent. Her paternal grandfather was Zeus.

30 *Dirke's stream*: see above, note to p. 6.

Labdacus: Oedipus' paternal grandfather.

O brother: some have thought that this is a macabre address to Oedipus, simultaneously Antigone's father and her brother. It is more likely, however, that it refers to Polyneices, whose armed assault on Thebes with an Argive army, and consequently both his death and Antigone's, were precipitated by his marriage with Argeia, daughter of the Argive king Adrastus.

31 *Persephone*: the daughter of Demeter and Zeus (Hesiod, *Theogony* 912–13), and, in her capacity as wife to Hades, goddess of the underworld.

my brother: here Antigone means Eteocles.

For when you died . . .: the 'you' here is plural, encompassing Oedipus, Iocasta, and Eteocles. As above, p. 4, Sophocles is supposing a version of the myth in which Oedipus died at Thebes, rather than, as in his *Oedipus at Colonus*, at Athens.

31 *Yet what I did*: The authenticity of the whole of the remainder of this speech has been questioned. Some scholars have deleted it all, others various individual verses. But if the speech includes lines which were not written by Sophocles, they had been interpolated by the time Aristotle published his *Rhetoric* in the fourth century BC, because he quotes lines 911–12 (*Rhet.* 3. 16. 9), 'But since my mother and my father │ Have both gone to the grave, there can be none │ Henceforth that I can ever call my brother.' The main ground on which deletions have been suggested is ethical: it has been objected that Antigone's declaration that she would not have contravened a civic edict to bury a husband or child is 'unbecoming' and inconsistent with her obedience to the 'unwritten law' pertaining to burial avowed elsewhere. But the lines can equally well be defended by their being seen as an extreme expression of Antigone's obsessive fidelity to her natal family, and therefore entirely in keeping with her overall characterization.

32 *I fear these words . . . the verge of death*: the manuscripts attribute these two lines to Antigone.

33 *Fair Danae*: Danae was an Argive princess, daughter of King Acrisius. He received an oracle from Delphi informing him that he would be killed by a son of hers. To prevent her from conceiving he therefore imprisoned her in a room built for the purpose within his palace. Both Sophocles and Euripides composed plays about Acrisius and Danae. This choral ode provides several examples of mythical characters who, like Antigone, suffered from incarceration.

divine seed: Acrisius' plan was foiled because Zeus (named in the Greek here), taking the form of a shower of gold, visited Danae in her prison and impregnated her. She subsequently gave birth to Perseus (famous for slaying the Gorgon), who did eventually kill his grandfather.

Lycurgus: king of the Edonians in Thrace, Lycurgus rejected the worship of the god Dionysus. As a result, he was driven mad, committed various crimes, and was eventually imprisoned in a cave on Mount Pangaeum. This story was dramatized by Aeschylus.

the tuneful Muses: although more usually connected with the god Apollo, the Muses are sometimes imagined as forming part of Dionysus' entourage.

160

Salmydessus: a town lying about 60 miles up the western coast of the Black Sea from the Bosphorus. The Greek adds that it was the domain of Ares, the god of war.

a wife ... bitter constraint: Cleopatra, the wife of Phineus, king of Salmydessus. She was imprisoned after he had put her aside in favour of a new wife, Idaea or Eidothea.

34 *a darkness that cried for vengeance*: the translation of this whole strophe is a loose paraphrase of the Greek, which refers elliptically to a myth undoubtedly familiar to its original audience (Sophocles himself composed at least two tragedies on the theme). The stepmother, jealous of her rival Cleopatra's two sons by Phineus, blinded them with a shuttle.

a race of ancient kings: the descendants of the early Athenian king Erechtheus. Cleopatra's mother Oreithyia was Erechtheus' daughter.

Her sire the offspring of gods: Cleopatra's father was Boreas, the god of the north wind, himself the son of Eos, goddess of the Dawn.

in a distant country: Thrace. Boreas abducted Oreithyia from Athens to his northern home, where their children were reared.

the lofty | Mountains: the translation omits the important point made in the original that, unlike Antigone, Cleopatra was 'a child of the gods'.

35 *my ancient seat | Of augury*: Teiresias' 'bird-watching shrine' could still be seen at Thebes by tourists in the second century AD (Pausanias 9. 16. 1).

offered sacrifice: Teiresias, baffled by the ominous clamour of the birds, attempts another form of divination, by setting alight an offering of bones wrapped in fat. The auspice was deduced from the manner in which the offering did or did not burn when set alight.

from him who guides me: his boy attendant (not Apollo).

Lydian silver: Lydia in Asia Minor was famous for its metal ore, and believed to be the country where money had been invented.

36 *Zeus' own eagles*: in the *Iliad* the eagle is described as Zeus' 'swift messenger', because, as the strongest of all birds, it is his favourite (24. 310–11).

36 *the land I saved from mortal danger*: this probably alludes to
Teiresias' advice, given earlier to Creon and Eteocles when
Polyneices was besieging Thebes. A version of the story is given
in Euripides' *Phoenician Women* (930–1018). Teiresias had
explained that Ares was angry with the city because Cadmus
had long ago killed a child of the god, the dragon from whose
teeth, when sown in the earth, the Theban aristocracy had
sprung. If the city were to be saved from Polyneices, one of the
descendants of the 'sown men' must die in order to propitiate
Ares. As a result, Creon's elder son, called Menoeceus by
Euripides, but Megareus in *Antigone* (below, line 1302), had
patriotically committed suicide.

37 *One who should walk upon it*: the translation does not make
it entirely clear that both this and the subsequent phrase refer
to Antigone.

Their sure avengers: the Erinyes (singular: Erinys), often translated into English as 'Furies', divinities whose special responsibility was to avenge crimes of blood, especially within
the family. They were the agents of *Dikē*, 'Justice' or
'Retribution'.

Whose mangled sons: there has been no previous suggestion
that funeral rites were to be denied to any of the enemy corpses
except that of Polyneices. The recovery and burial of the remaining bodies, at the instigation of the Athenian king Theseus,
was a familiar story, dramatized by Euripides in his *Suppliant
Women*.

I have lived long: the Greek actually says that Teiresias has
never been wrong either when the chorus had dark hair or
since it has become grey—that is, in all their lifetime.

38 *Necessity*: the divine personification of absolute and ineluc-
table destiny, the goddess *Anankē* was, like Zeus, a daughter of
Cronus.

whose names are many: the Greek gods had many different
titles. Some were toponymics, referring to the different places
in which they were worshipped, and some were descriptive of
the particular capacity or function of the divinity in which
he or she was being invoked. Dionysus had a large number
of titles, including 'Bacchus' and 'Iacchus'. This particular
hymn meditates on the numerous places in which his cult was
practised.

thy Theban mother-nymph: Dionysus was the son by Zeus to Semele, daughter of Cadmus and Harmonia.

Italy: some editors have doubted the manuscripts' reference to *Italia*, substituting *Icaria*, a district north of Athens with an important local cult of Dionysus. But the Greeks had colonized southern Italy, taking their gods with them, and the reference to Italy emphasizes the universality of the worship of Dionysus which is the underlying theme of this ode.

Where Demeter has her abode: Demeter, goddess of arable farming and mother of Persephone, the queen of the underworld, received at her shrine in the Attic town of Eleusis—the 'abode' mentioned here—a famous mystery cult in which Dionysus also played a prominent role.

Ismenus' flood: a river flowing to the east of Thebes, after which Ismene is named.

the savage | Dragon's teeth had offspring: see above, note to p. 7.

39 *Parnassus' height*: Parnassus is a mountain in Phokis with a steep face on which the Delphic oracle, sacred to Apollo, was built. Dionysus was believed to hold revels on the mountain (Euripides, *Ion* 716).

the spring of Castaly: the Castalia is a stream flowing from the cliffs above Delphi.

Asian hills: the translation departs considerably from the Greek, which names Nysa, a mountain traditionally associated with Dionysus, but located in many different places. Here the Mount Nysa of Euboea in mainland Greece is probably meant.

with swift healing: the Greek refers to Dionysus' familiar function as *katharsios*, 'purifier'.

Euripus: the straits between Euboea and Boeotia, the district in which the city of Thebes lay.

40 *Pallas*: the goddess Athena, whose temples at Thebes are mentioned in *Oedipus the King* (line 19). In the aftermath of the siege Eurydice was presumably thanking Athena in her capacity as the goddess who protects citadels.

41 *no stranger to bad news*: Sophocles again hints at the death, prior to the action of the play, of Creon and Eurydice's elder son (see above, note to p. 23).

163

41 *Hecate and Pluto*: it is important for Creon, having failed to send Polyneices' corpse to the world below with due burial, to appease these gods' wrath. Hecate was a wandering goddess of crossroads, but also the divine representative on earth of the underworld; Pluto was a ritual title of Hades.

42 *Inside the palace*: excessive public displays of mourning were frowned upon in Sophocles' time, and, indeed, at Athens actually outlawed.

43 *Enter* MESSENGER: there is no indication in the Greek as to whether this messenger is male or female. The character is probably meant, however, to be the same (male) messenger who followed Eurydice into the palace after line 1255.

a blade into her heart: it is comparatively rare for women in tragedy to stab themselves. Most females, for example Antigone and Iocasta, commit suicide by hanging themselves.

44 *Megareus*: the elder son of Creon and Eurydice, to whose death oblique allusion has already been made (see above, note to p. 41), is finally named.

45 *a wife and a son*: the translation reduces the pathos of the original, in which Creon addresses both characters vocatively in the second person singular.

OEDIPUS THE KING

49 *My children*: it is unusual for rulers in Greek tragedy to address their citizens in this way; it implies the 'benevolent paternalism' of Oedipus' rule, but also his absolute power.

Cadmus: the founder of Thebes and its royal dynasty.

the boughs that mark the suppliant: branches of laurel or olive, entwined with wool.

hymns and prayers: the Greek names explicitly the *paian*, the prayer to Apollo the Healer.

before the altars: the altars in front of the palace, including certainly that of Apollo (see below, line 919).

the shrine | Of fiery divination: the Greek makes it clear that the Theban temple of Apollo Ismenios is meant. Divination by means of burnt offerings was practised there.

The withering god of fever: at this stage no particular god is named as responsible for the plague afflicting Thebes, although

164

later it is unusually identified with Ares, the god of war (line 190).

50 *No god we count you*: it is important to establish that although Oedipus is an autocrat (unlike the democratically-minded Athenian kings in tragedy), he does not sacrilegiously expect to be regarded by his citizens as divine.

the cruel Sphinx: the Greek here does not actually name the Sphinx, but calls her simply 'the cruel singer'.

on our bended knees: i.e. assuming the traditional posture of supplication.

51 *in Phoebus' house*: in Apollo's temple.

for they | Are signalling: presumably some of the suppliants attending the priest.

There is pollution: the Greeks believed that homicides were afflicted by pollution, *miasma*, which could communicate itself to all who came in to contact with them.

52 *Laius*: previous king of Thebes and husband of Iocasta. He was the son of Labdacus and a descendant of Cadmus, the founder of Thebes.

Where was he murdered? It is Aristotle's only criticism of this, his favourite tragedy, that Oedipus is here implausibly characterized as totally ignorant of the circumstances surrounding his predecessor's death (*Poetics* 1460ª30).

53 Her *riddle*: the Sphinx's famous riddle asked what thing goes on four legs in the morning, two at noon, and three in the evening. The answer to the riddle is 'man'. It is noteworthy that Sophocles at no point in the play recounts the riddle explicitly, although tracing Oedipus' own progress from a helpless baby to a man in his prime to a blinded cripple, who can walk only with the aid of his 'third leg'—a walking-stick.

the god: named in the Greek as Zeus.

54 *Apollo too, who shoots from afar*: the chorus invokes three of Zeus' Olympian children to assist them in their plight. Athena, goddess of cunning intelligence, Artemis, the goddess who presides over the Theban market-place (but is also responsible for childbirth), and Apollo 'who shoots from afar', the archer-god whose arrows can bring both disease and remission from it.

to the dark realms of the dead: the Greek actually says 'to the shore of the western god', for the home of the shades of the dead was traditionally located towards the setting sun (e.g. Homer, *Odyssey* 12. 81).

55 *Daughter of Zeus*: either Athena or Artemis may be meant here.

god of War: Ares, named in the Greek, unusually in this play held responsible for physical afflictions resulting not from violence, but from plague.

to his distant home: this is a reductive adaptation of the Greek, which graphically specifies 'either to the great deep of Amphitrite [a sea-goddess, probably here to be associated with the Atlantic] or to the hostile waves of Thrace [a country bordering on northern Greece, probably here suggestive of the Black Sea] where it is difficult to anchor'.

lord of the sacred dance: Dionysus, otherwise known as Bacchus, was the patron deity of dancing. See above, note to p. 8.

The savage god: Ares once again. In the *Iliad* Zeus describes him as 'the most hated of the gods to me' (5. 890).

56 *lustral water*: collective sacrifices made by a household included the sprinkling of its members with consecrated water. Denial of access to this ritual meant, effectively, excommunication.

57 *Agenor*: a Phoenician king, whose son Cadmus came to Greece and founded Thebes. He was succeeded by his son Polydorus, his grandson Labdacus, and his great-grandson Laius. The enumeration of Laius' ancestors adds weight and solemnity to the curse Oedipus is about to pronounce.

Justice: Dikē. See above, note to p. 17.

58 *or other form of divination*: e.g. by fire, as attempted by Teiresias in *Antigone*, above, note to p. 35.

62 *Cithaeron*: a mountain range sacred to Zeus lying near Thebes, and dividing Attica and Plataea. It was there that Oedipus was exposed in infancy.

63 *staff*: it is impossible for any translation to convey the effect in the Greek attained by the use of the same word, *skēptron*, for the sceptre which grants Oedipus his royal authority, for the weapon with which he killed Laius, and for the staff on which he will lean, blinded, at the close of the play.

64 *The voice of god*: here the oracular voice of Apollo at Delphi.

the terrible god: Apollo, armed with his father Zeus' lightning, is here envisaged as the executor of punishment.

The Furies who punish crime: here the Greek names the *Kēres*, agents of divine vengeance, often identified with the Erinyes (see above, note to p. 37).

Parnassus: see above, note to p. 39.

Thebes and Corinth: the chorus has no conception that Oedipus' Corinthian birth and provenance might be in doubt.

69 *rage of yours*: this and the following three lines, as they stand in the MSS, make little sense. Two lines have probably been lost. The translation offers an intelligible and performable text reconstructed by guesswork: the lines printed in brackets were supplied by the translator.

70 *the chief of gods*: the sun-god, Helios, is foremost among the gods not in terms of power, but in that he is the most conspicuous and apparent to men. It was customary to swear oaths by him.

72 *over a precipice*: this detail is not in the Greek, which states that the baby was simply cast out on a 'trackless mountain'.

73 *Daulia*: a district south-east of Parnassus. The place where the three roads meet is the point on the road from Thebes to Delphi, leading westward, where a branch diverges off to the north-west in the direction of Daulia.

a Herald: at line 114 the audience was told that Laius was killed while on a pilgrimage to Delphi. The company of a Herald, to lend solemnity to the sacred mission, would have been appropriate.

74 *Merope*: the Greek adds that she was of 'Dorian' stock—a noble lineage which could trace itself back to Hellen, the eponymous ancestor of the Greek people.

75 *the stars alone have told me*: Oedipus has only been able to locate the land in which he grew up by calculations from the stars, as a sailor uses the heavens to navigate.

any bond of kinship: at this point Oedipus is only hypothesizing a distant blood relationship with Laius.

77 *laws*: see above, note to p. 5.

A god: the Greek implies a mysterious, but unnamed, divine presence.

77 *Pride makes the tyrant*: this is one of the most hotly disputed textual points in Greek tragedy. Some editors believe that the sentence should read 'a tyrant produces pride'. 'Pride' here translates *hubris*.

78 *the sacred dance*: dancing was so central a component of the cults of Apollo, Dionysus, and other gods that this question really implies, 'Why should I participate in public worship at all?'

Abae: the location of an important shrine of Apollo, mentioned by Herodotus (8. 33), in north-west Phokis.

Olympian Zeus: the famous cult centre of Zeus at Olympia in the Peloponnese is meant.

thy oracles: a misleading translation of the Greek, which explicitly says 'oracles concerning Laius'.

79 *in his grave*: the translation omits two suspect lines after this. Iocasta asks 'What are you saying? Has Polybus died?', and the Corinthian responds 'If I am not telling the truth, then I am worthy to die'.

83 *from the cradle*: the Greek says literally 'from my swaddling-clothes'.

they named you Oedipus: Oedipus' name means, literally, 'Swollen-foot'.

84 *thrice a slave*: i.e. a slave whose mother and grandmother had also been slaves.

85 *Fortune*: the goddess *Tuchē*, who personified random chance. She was a daughter of Zeus and had a local cult in Thebes.

when the moon | Next is full: the Greek may mean 'at tomorrow's full moon'.

Pan: as a god of the countryside, who oversaw the reproduction of flocks, Pan was invested with considerable sexual energy, often expressed in chasing nymphs. He would therefore be a plausible divine candidate for fathering Oedipus on Mount Cithaeron.

86 *Kyllene*: a mountain in Arcadia on which Hermes was supposed to have been born—a story dramatized by Sophocles in his satyric *Trackers*.

Helicon: a mountain range in western Boeotia, associated primarily with the Muses.

not bought: slaves who were born and bred in the house of their owners, rather than purchased, were regarded as more loyal to their masters. This fits the characterization of the Theban shepherd.

87 *Arcturus*: the leading star of the constellation Boötes (Ursa Major), appearing as a morning star in September shortly before the autumnal equinox.

89 *parents*: the masculine-plural Greek term *tekontas* is ambiguous. The plural could be used honorifically in place of the singular, in which case this occurrence should be translated 'father'. But, as in this translation, the Greek can equally well be interpreted as meaning both parents, raising in the audience's mind the question of the extent to which Oedipus is to be responsible for Iocasta's death.

Ah God! Ah God!: this is an over-translation of the Greek, in which Oedipus utters two meaningless cries of woe, '*iou iou*'.

O Sun: in the Greek Oedipus apostrophizes rather the light.

all desiring: the loose translation omits an important appeal to Zeus.

90 *Ister*: the ancient name for the river Danube.

Phasis' flood: now called the river Rion, running through Colchis (approximately equivalent to the modern Georgia) into the south-eastern end of the Black Sea.

Evils self-sought: the suicide of Iocasta and the self-blinding of Oedipus are deliberate and conscious acts based on true knowledge. The messenger thus distinguishes them from the previous calamitous deeds (parricide and incest) which were performed unwittingly.

91 '*Through this ... To my own child*': there is no direct speech in the original.

some deity: the messenger's speech implies that Oedipus was guided by some unidentified supernatural agent, for which the Greek term is *daimōn*, often translated as 'spirit'. This word is used repeatedly until the climactic moment when Oedipus names Apollo at line 1329.

92 *spirit*: the Greek term, again, is the anonymous *daimōn*.

93 *O God*: the Greek refrains from naming the divine agent, which is still referred to as a *daimōn*.

93 *a blind man*: the translation omits Oedipus' twice repeated utterance here of 'alas'.

What god: the Greek yet again uses the ambiguous term *daimōn*.

94 *Or on my mother*: Oedipus anticipates that he will not have recovered his sight after death when he encounters his parents in the underworld. In the *Odyssey*, similarly, Teiresias is conceptualized as remaining blind in Hades (12. 266).

death: the Greek actually says 'hanging'—suicide by the same means as Iocasta.

95 *them*: it is not clear to whom Oedipus here refers. It may be the members of his own family, or the Thebans in general.

to dwell among the Thebans: the translation wanders far from the Greek. Oedipus actually says that if he had died on Cithaeron he would never have revealed his origins to mankind.

96 *nor sunlight can endure*: Oedipus' pollution is so great that it threatens the very purity of the elements, represented by Earth, the rain, and the light respectively.

for she is yours: as Iocasta's brother, Creon is to be responsible for her burial. It is noteworthy that Oedipus does not name her.

97 *some strange doom*: it is not made clear in this play how, when, and where Oedipus is to die. In *Antigone* he had been buried, apparently, at Thebes; in *Oedipus at Colonus* he dies a supernatural death at Athens.

98 *parent*: the Greek says 'father'. Oedipus is officially handing over to Creon the guardianship (a responsibility which could only devolve upon a male) of his daughters.

your kin: the translation omits a whole line after this, in which Oedipus asks Creon not to let the girls be reduced to the same level of misery as himself.

99 *the end*: the translation omits the concluding utterance, as contained in the MSS, delivered by the chorus. It is possible that it is a spurious interpolation and should be omitted; it is also possible that it should be attributed to Oedipus himself. The seven lines can be translated thus: 'Inhabitants of our native Thebes, behold here Oedipus, who understood the famous riddle and was a most powerful man. Which citizen did not look enviously upon his fortunes? But see the dreadful

wave of disaster he has encountered! Therefore let no mortal
be called happy until the final fated day when he has crossed
life's border without enduring pain.'

ELECTRA

103 *Io and her father Inachus*: Inachus was the earliest king of
Argos known to Greek mythology. Zeus became enamoured
with his daughter Io, but turned her into a heifer in order to
protect her from the jealousy of his wife Hera. Sophocles
dramatized this story in his lost *Inachus*: Io makes an appearance in her bovine form in the *Prometheus* tragedy attributed
to Aeschylus.

the market-place | That bears Apollo's name: corroborative
evidence that a temple of Apollo stood in the market-place at
Argos is to be found in Pausanias 2. 19. 3.

Hera's famous temple: Hera was the tutelary deity of Argos
and intimately associated with the city in mythology.

Pelops' dynasty: Pelops was the father of Atreus, grandfather
of Agamemnon, and therefore great-grandfather of Orestes.
See further below, note to p. 118.

as a baby: the translation is misleading. The Greek here implies
that Orestes was a child when he was given by Electra to the
tutor, but it is clear from Clytemnestra's words at 778–80 that
the boy had already been capable of threatening her.

my loyal servant: boys were entrusted to the care of male
slaves whose duty was to oversee their upbringing and education. In tragedy they act as the equivalent of the 'nurses' who
often attend aristocratic females. 'Tutor' is an approximate
translation of the Greek term *paidagōgos*, 'pedagogue'.

104 *I went to Delphi*: i.e. to consult the famous oracle of Apollo.

Phanoteus of Phokis: this obscure mythical figure was thought
to have had a feud with his brother Crisus, beginning with a
fight in their mother's womb. Since Crisus fathered Strophius,
who had taken in the exiled Orestes, Phanoteus would be a
natural choice for an ally of Orestes' enemies, Clytemnestra
and Aegisthus.

The Pythian games at Delphi: from 582 BC athletics competitions modelled on the more famous games at Olympia were

held every four years as part of the festival of Pythian Apollo at Delphi.

104 *Why should I fear an omen*: it would normally be considered an inauspicious invitation to disaster for a living person to be described as dead.

those philosophers | Who were reported dead: there were several stories of this type. Pythagoras, for example, was reputed to have reappeared after concealing himself in a chamber beneath the earth, thus engendering rumours that he was dead.

105 *like the sun*: the Greek actually says 'like a star'.

a cry of bitter grief: in the Greek the tutor suggests that the cry is specifically that of a slave-woman.

Have you not heard: the translation omits the gruesome detail which Electra adds here. She describes the wild blows she strikes against her breast, making it bleed—a conventional sign of mourning.

106 *No Trojan spear*: Electra regrets that her father was not killed in battle at Troy, in which case he would have received the honour of a warrior's funeral.

no god of war: the Greek explicitly names Ares.

the sorrowing nightingale: in myth Procne, an Athenian princess, was supposed to have been turned into a nightingale after murdering her son Itys. She killed the boy in order to avenge herself on her husband Tereus, who had raped and mutilated her sister Philomela. The nightingale's song was explained as her unceasing laments for Itys. Sophocles wrote a famous drama portraying this story, his *Tereus*.

You powers of Death! You gods below!: The Greek text mentions by name Hades, Persephone, Hermes (the only Olympian who could pass between the upper and lower worlds) and a personified Curse.

Avenging spirits . . . marriage-vow: the Erinyes (see above, note to p. 37). These agents of divine retribution were responsible for the punishment of misdemeanours to do with the family, both intra-familial murder and, as here, adultery.

107 *the sad nightingale*: Procne. See above, note to p. 106.

Itys: son of Procne and Tereus. See above, note to p. 106.

Niobe: see above, note to p. 29.

108 *Iphianassa*: this is the only mention in the play of a living sister of Electra other than Chrysothemis. She is named as a daughter of Agamemnon in the *Iliad* (9. 145).

Plain of Crisa: an area of land to the south-west of Delphi which was kept unploughed as sacred to Apollo, and on which the horse races at the Pythian games are later said to have been run (see below, note to p. 124).

his own father: the Greek adds that along with Orestes neither the dead Agamemnon nor Hades himself will neglect the situation in Mycenae.

109 *a Spirit loosed from Hell*: an extravagant paraphrase of the plain Greek 'a god'.

O God that rulest Heaven and Earth: Zeus, the chief Olympian.

110 *Had any trace of spirit*: the Greek is more accurately rendered 'was a woman of high birth and character'.

111 *the hearth-stone*: banquets were customarily opened and closed with libations poured to Hestia, goddess of the family hearth.

the Gods her Saviours: especially Zeus in his capacity as Saviour (*Sōtēr*) and Apollo, to whom Clytemnestra later prays for protection (p. 122).

112 *Your sister*: the Greek adds for clarity 'by the same father and mother', thus distinguishing Chrysothemis from Electra's half-siblings borne by Clytemnestra to Aegisthus (see line 588).

114 *in some dark dungeon*: in the Greek the punishment is to be even worse. Electra is to be held captive in exile, 'beyond the borders of this land'.

116 *the sun-god*: Helios. It was conventional to narrate frightening dreams to him, as the god whose light dispels nocturnal fears and expiates them. Compare Euripides, *Iphigeneia in Tauris* 42–3.

117 *mangled it*: the Greek term makes it clear that Agamemnon's corpse had been subjected to a ritual mutilation practised by murderers, probably taking the form of having his extremities removed and hung from his arm-pits and neck. This custom may have been intended to prevent the victim from retaliation after death, or to provide a gesture towards atonement.

and one of mine: the Greek adds the pathetic detail that Electra's hair is unkempt.

173

118 *Retribution*: a rough translation of the Greek *Dikē* (see above, note to p. 16).

two-edged axe: even the murder weapon is imagined as bearing a grudge against its users. In Athenian law inanimate objects could be put on trial for causing death (Aeschines 3. 244).

chariot-race of Pelops: Sophocles is using a version of the myth which referred the recurrent disasters afflicting this royal house back to a curse incurred by Pelops, Agamemnon's grandfather (see also above, note to p. 105). He had competed in a chariot-race against Oenomaus, king of Pisa, for the hand of Oenomaus' daughter Hippodameia. He won the race and the woman by treachery; he had bribed Myrtilus, Oenomaus' charioteer, to sabotage the rival chariot. Oenomaus died in the ensuing accident; Myrtilus was thrown into the sea and drowned, but not before he had cursed Pelops. This myth may have suggested to Sophocles the means by which Orestes is said to have died in the 'false' messenger speech delivered by the tutor, pp. 124–6.

Myrtilus: see note above.

119 *your sister*: Iphigeneia, the eldest of Agamemnon's daughters.

Artemis: the virgin goddess, in charge of female rites of passage, hunting, and wild animals. She is not, however, named here in the Greek, which says only vaguely 'to gods'.

the only Greek: human sacrifice was regarded by Sophocles' contemporaries as a barbarism permitted only in uncivilized, non-Greek lands.

The sons of Helen: in Homer Helen and Menelaus had only one child, a daughter (*Odyssey* 4. 14). There was, however, another attested tradition older than Sophocles that they had *one* son, Nicostratus.

120 *my sister's*: Iphigeneia's (not Chrysothemis').

windy Aulis: a site on the eastern coast of Greece in Boeotia with a large natural harbour, at which the Greek forces had traditionally mustered before their expedition to Troy.

a forest that was sacred to the goddess: probably meant to be understood as the precinct of Artemis close to her temple at Aulis.

121 *bear him children*: different versions of the myth variously give Aegisthus and Clytemnestra a son Aletes and a daughter

174

Erigone. Sophocles composed plays about both. This ambiguous reference could be taken to imply that vengeance for the deaths of Clytemnestra and Aegisthus might await Orestes; it is one of several subtle ways in which Sophocles subverts the apparently satisfactory situation at the end of *Electra*.

At her age too: i.e. at her stage of maturity (not of youthfulness).

She is so impudent . . . not do: This sentence takes the form of a direct question in the Greek.

122 *'Tis you that say it . . . find me the words*: the translation of these two lines has been borrowed from John Milton's *An Apology Against a Pamphlet* (Otherwise known as *Apology for Smectymnus*), in Douglas Bush *et al.* (eds.), *Complete Prose Works of John Milton* (New Haven/London 1953), i. 905.

by Artemis: Artemis was the divinity thought to be responsible for the deaths of women. This adds weight to Clytemnestra's threat.

123 *Atreus*: the father of Agamemnon and uncle of Aegisthus.

124 *in the Festival*: the translation here omits a corrupt line, which cited two events—some kind of race and the pentathlon.

Achaea: the term here designates a specific area in southern Thessaly.

Libya: the generic name for the Greek colonies in North Africa.

Thessalian mares: Orestes is given horses from Thessaly, which reputedly produced the finest horses and most skilled cavalry in the Greek world (see e.g. Herodotus 7. 196).

an Aetolian: Aetolia was a large inland district of mainland Greece.

Magnesia: a mountainous district on the east coast of Thessaly.

Aenia: an area in southern Thessaly.

125 *The course*: the Greek says 'the plain of Crisa' (see above, note to p. 108).

And as he drove . . . The stone: These lines have been transposed, following many editors, from after line 719.

126 *so tall a man*: ancient heroes were thought to have been far greater than later people in size and strength (Homer, *Iliad* 5. 303, Herodotus 1. 68—specifically on Orestes' extraordinary stature).

175

126 *he threatened me*: this implies that Orestes had outgrown infancy when Electra had him sent away. See above, note to p. 103.

127 *Nemesis*: the goddess Nemesis' special responsibility was to oversee the rights of the dead, and avenge any wrong done to them.

129 *Amphiareus*: an Argive hero. He married Eriphyle, sister of Adrastus, king of Argos. When Amphiareus refused to help Polyneices (Antigone's brother) in the campaign against Thebes, Polyneices bribed Eriphyle with a golden necklace. She then cajoled her husband into joining the expedition, which resulted in his death.

a champion: Alcmaeon. Amphiareus' death was eventually avenged by his son Alcmaeon, who killed his mother Eriphyle. Sophocles composed plays bearing the names of all three mythical figures.

I beg you: the translation omits here an interjection by the chorus, 'What are you saying?'

130 *In exile*: the translation omits another choral interjection, 'Alas!'

Our father's memory: the Greek says literally 'our father's hearth'. See above, note to p. 111.

136 *The anger of the gods...Enthroned in Heaven*: this is a periphrasis diverging greatly from the Greek, which names the lightning-bolt of Zeus (with which he punishes miscreants), and Themis, a female divinity responsible for the safeguarding of law and order, often conceptualized as enthroned beside Zeus and sometimes described as a wife of his.

137 *Never has she ceased to mourn*: the Greek once again likens Electra to a nightingale, engaged in incessant lamentation (see above, note to p. 106).

those two Furies: Aegisthus and Clytemnestra. The Greek language could transfer the name of the Furies or 'Erinyes', the spirits who oversee acts of blood-vengeance, to both the victims of a crime and to those who had perpetrated it.

a foul pollution: the translation omits a hypothetical question delivered by the chorus here, 'Who else would be so noble?' (i.e. as Electra).

Laws of the gods: once again Sophocles refers to the supreme 'unwritten laws', as at *Antigone* 454–5 (see also above, note to p. 5) and *Oedipus the King* 865–7.

in piety: the Greek adds 'towards Zeus', the supreme overseer of the 'unwritten laws'.

138 *nearest to them*: i.e. she is their nearest relation by blood.

Strophius: Pylades' father, the old friend of Agamemnon to whom the exiled Orestes had been entrusted, named only here in this play. See above, note to p. 104.

in my arms: the translation omits two lines here. Electra continues, 'so that I may weep and wail, not only for these ashes but along with them for myself and for my entire family.'

139 *sorrow*: in the Greek the metre changes for this line, probably indicating that in the emotion of the moment Electra briefly begins to chant rather than speak.

142 *friend*: the Greek word should be translated 'child' or 'son', which is more appropriate to the pathos of this recognition scene.

Our father's ring: the Greek makes it explicit that it is a signet ring with a recognizable seal-mark.

143 *but wait*: the translation here omits a lyrical interjection by Electra, 'What is the matter?'

women . . . To strike a blow: the Greek actually says 'Ares dwells in women too.'

and yet: the translation omits another lyrical interjection by Electra, 'What shall I do?'

then I made no more delay: these words have been supplied by the translator to fill in a line missing from the Greek.

144 *their end*: the translation here omits an interjection by Orestes, 'What are you asking of me?'

be prudent: the translation here omits two lines. Electra asks, 'Do you grant what I ask?', and Orestes responds, 'Why not?'

146 *those faithful hands*: the translation, perhaps prudently, omits here a remark by Electra referring to the tutor's feet as 'kindly messengers'.

147 *the gods that stand before the house*: images of gods placed at the front of the palace. They included Apollo (addressed by Clytemnestra at line 637) and Hermes, the god who always presided over entrances.

147 *the god of death*: the Greek names rather Ares, the god of war and violence.

148 *The minister of the gods*: i.e. Orestes.

With Hermes to guide him: the chorus prays that Hermes will assist Orestes in his capacity as Hermes *dolios* (the god of trickery).

To stand on guard: Sophocles finds a reason to have Electra on stage during the murder of Clytemnestra, so that her blood-thirsty reactions can be fully appreciated.

149 *cruelty*: at least three lines are probably missing from the Greek between here and Orestes' question at line 1430, 'Are you sure you see him?' The translation has been designed to offer a performable text.

150 *you should know*: the translation here omits a harsh phrase addressing Electra as 'you who were formerly so bold'.

152 *You could read the future | So well*: there appears to have been a tradition that Aegisthus had some special mantic powers.

This house of Atreus: the Greek names, rather, the house of Pelops, in accordance with the play's tracing of the sufferings of the family back to the original curse on Pelops' head (see above, note to p. 118. Aegisthus, as son of Thyestes, Atreus' brother, was of course also a Pelopid.

those to come: an implication that the deaths of Aegisthus and Clytemnestra may not put an end to the family's calamities. See above, note to p. 121.

The Oxford World's Classics Website

www.worldsclassics.co.uk

- Information about new titles
- Explore the full range of Oxford World's Classics
- Links to other literary sites and the main OUP webpage
- Imaginative competitions, with bookish prizes
- Peruse the Oxford World's Classics Magazine
- Articles by editors
- Extracts from Introductions
- A forum for discussion and feedback on the series
- Special information for teachers and lecturers

www.worldsclassics.co.uk

American Literature

British and Irish Literature

Children's Literature

Classics and Ancient Literature

Colonial Literature

Eastern Literature

European Literature

History

Medieval Literature

Oxford English Drama

Poetry

Philosophy

Politics

Religion

The Oxford Shakespeare

A complete list of Oxford Paperbacks, including Oxford World's Classics, Oxford Shakespeare, Oxford Drama, and Oxford Paperback Reference, is available in the UK from the Academic Division Publicity Department, Oxford University Press, Great Clarendon Street, Oxford OX2 6DP.

In the USA, complete lists are available from the Paperbacks Marketing Manager, Oxford University Press, 198 Madison Avenue, New York, NY 10016.

Oxford Paperbacks are available from all good bookshops. In case of difficulty, customers in the UK can order direct from Oxford University Press Bookshop, Freepost, 116 High Street, Oxford OX1 4BR, enclosing full payment. Please add 10 per cent of published price for postage and packing.

The Emily Carr
Mystery

Hi Isabella!

Eric Wilson

Victoria 2009

Books by Eric Wilson

The Tom and Liz Austen Mysteries

Also available by Eric Wilson

The Emily Carr Mystery

A Liz Austen Mystery

by

ERIC WILSON

HarperCollins*Publishers*Ltd

As in his other mysteries, Eric Wilson writes here about imaginary people in a real landscape.

Find Eric Wilson at www.ericwilson.com

The Emily Carr Mystery
Text copyright © 2001 by Eric Hamilton Wilson. Copyright renewed 2003 by Eric Wilson Enterprises, Inc. All rights reserved.

Published by HarperCollins Publishers Ltd

HarperCollins books may be purchased for educational, business, or sales promotional use through our Special Markets Department.

HarperCollins Publishers Ltd
2 Bloor Street East, 20th Floor
Toronto, Ontario, Canada
M4W 1A8

www.harpercollins.ca

Library and Archives Canada Cataloguing in Publication

Wilson, Eric, 1940–
The Emily Carr mystery / Eric Wilson.

ISBN 978-0-00-639190-6

I. Title.

PS8595.I583E55 2002   jC813'.54   C2002-902417-X PZ7

EPC 9 8 7 6 5 4 3 2 1

Printed and bound in Canada

cover design: Richard Bingham
cover and chapter illustrations: Richard Row
author photograph: Heath Moffat © 2003 ewelnc.

For my dear wife, Flo,
and our friend Sadie

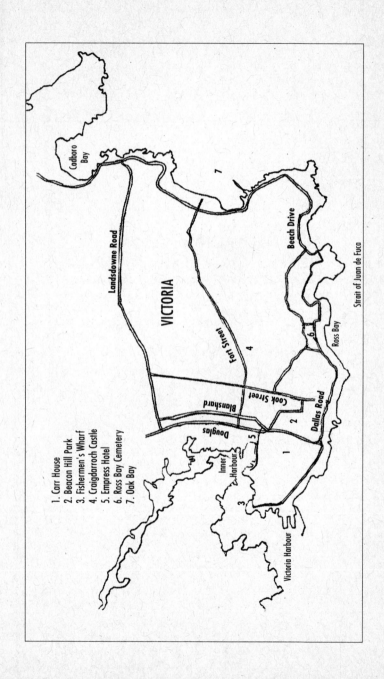

1. Carr House
2. Beacon Hill Park
3. Fishermen's Wharf
4. Craigdarroch Castle
5. Empress Hotel
6. Ross Bay Cemetery
7. Oak Bay

VICTORIA

Landsdowne Road

Fort Street

Cook Street

Blanshard

Douglas

Dallas Road

Beach Drive

Cadboro Bay

Ross Bay

Strait of Juan de Fuca

Inner Harbour

Victoria Harbour

1

Our boat was the greatest—a classic cruiser called the *Amor de Cosmos*.

But I wasn't happy.

I almost screamed as our cruiser heeled over. Cold spray whipped my face as we raced through the night. I grabbed for support, thinking I'd tumble into the dark sea waters.

From above, on the command bridge, came laughter. It was my friend Tiffany, who was feeling good. Tiff was beside the man she soon would marry—Paris de-Mornay. As I watched, Paris fed more horsepower to the twin turbocharged diesels—our cruiser leapt forward even faster through the waves, making me stagger.

Paris was movie-star handsome. A spotlight shone on his perfect face as he smiled at Tiffany. Paris was

22 and wore shorts, a sweater, and a gold necklace. Apparently his deck shoes had been shipped from an exclusive shop in Hawaii; Paris bought almost everything on the Internet.

The deMornay family was very wealthy, and so was Tiff's. The families were a unit, bonded together by the friendship of the two mothers. Paris was three years old when Tiffany was born; at the time the mothers quipped that eventually Paris and Tiffany should marry.

Then the family joke turned into reality. Tiff fell totally in love with Paris during her teens. It happened so easily—the families spent a lot of time together. Tiff and Paris made a natural couple.

Recently, though, tragedy had struck. Two years ago Paris lost his parents in a terrible car crash. He was especially devastated about his father, and Tiff had spent a lot of time consoling Paris. Then one day I learned that Tiffany had accepted his marriage proposal.

Now I was in Victoria for the wedding. But I was feeling upset—somehow, things didn't seem right. Sighing, I looked at the sky. A silvery moon watched from the glorious heavens; below, whitecaps raced across the waters.

"The lights of Victoria look so pretty from out here," I said to Tiffany, as she climbed down a ladder from the bridge. "Thanks for inviting me to British Columbia for your wedding. Imagine, two full weeks in Victoria—and I love it here."

Tiffany flashed her blue eyes my way. "That's wonderful, Liz." Tiny, blonde and pretty, 19 years old, she'd been raised in the exclusive world of the ultra-wealthy. With her own personal fortune Tiff could have bought and sold some countries, but she was the sweetest and most natural person. We'd met volunteering at a children's hospital in Winnipeg, and our friendship was the best. Tiff was two years older than me, but it didn't matter.

"Tiff," I said, "remember all those times Paris came to Winnipeg to see you? He was such a fun guy, and I was so happy about your wedding. But . . . somehow he's changed."

"Of course he has!" There was an edge to Tiff's voice, and I realized I'd touched a nerve. "How would you feel, Liz? His parents have died, and he's still grieving."

I braced myself against the rolling of the sea. "I guess you're right, Tiff. You know what? You always find the good in people."

"Liz, he needs me. Besides, I want children and a husband. I like the West Coast—I can be happy here." She lovingly touched her engagement ring. "Paris and I are in this together. Through the good times and the bad. We've got so much in common—"

Then Tiffany screamed. "*Look out*," she yelled at Paris. Tiff pointed across the sea. "That's the *Clipper*, and we're going straight at it!"

I stared at the *Clipper* as it raced out of the night. A high-speed catamaran carrying tourists between Seattle and Victoria, the *Clipper* rode above the water on two pontoons with an open space between.

Now I saw what Paris had planned—he was trying a daredevil stunt, aiming our boat directly at the space between the pontoons. "We'll never make it," I yelled into the shrieking wind. "Don't be crazy, Paris!"

Grinning, he fed more power to the diesels. From the *Clipper*, a loud horn split the night air—warning us of the danger. Tiffany and I grabbed the railing, horrified at the vision of the *Clipper* coming swiftly at us.

Suddenly our boat heeled over, changing course. With a laugh, and an arrogant wave of his hand at the other vessel, Paris took the *Amor de Cosmos* safely out of danger.

Grabbing the steel rungs of the ladder, I climbed to the command bridge. It rolled and pitched as Paris hotdogged the cruiser across the sea. Before him, on the control console, blue dials glowed.

"Listen, Paris," I said, "how about cutting back on the throttle."

"Sure, Liz, no problem."

The engines slowed, right down to a low growl. I heard whitecaps crashing against each other in the night.

"I was just having some fun," Paris added.

I didn't want to object once again to one of his stunts, so I said nothing about the *Clipper*. Instead, I commented, "This is a beautiful boat."

"It belonged to my father."

"You miss him, eh?"

"Yeah." Paris sighed.

"Listen," I said, "thanks for letting me stay at your estate while I'm in Victoria. That's generous of you, Paris."

"Hey, Liz, you're my fiancée's closest friend and one of her bridesmaids. I'm only sorry you can't be maid of honour. Why's that, anyway? Tiffany never told me."

"The maid of honour has to be at least 18 to sign the wedding register. I'm a year too young."

"I'm sorry about that," Paris said with genuine sympathy.

"Robbed of the chance to be maid of honour at my best friend's wedding. Gee, you could have waited a year! But Tiff wants wedding bells, and the pitter-patter of little feet."

Paris grinned. "Tiffany sure loves kids. Me, too. I want a son and heir. We'll name him for my father."

Then Paris opened his cell phone; it had commanded attention by loudly playing "Jingle Bells."

"Yes?" Paris said. He listened for a moment, then replied, "Four K on Bigoted Earl. That's all I can manage. Goodbye, now."

Turning to me, Paris smiled. "I was going to mention, Liz, a lot of smuggling happens here. I thought you'd be interested."

Paris looked across the water at the lights of a distant city, sparkling on the shoreline of the United States. Above, the Olympic Mountains rose into the night sky. White snow glowed on some peaks, even though it was summer.

"That's Port Angeles over there," Paris explained. "It's in the state of Washington." He turned toward Victoria. "I can always spot the smugglers—maybe we'll see one tonight. They come out of Canada, moving fast, with no running lights. They carry drugs, forged credit cards, illegal immigrants. If someone can make a buck smuggling, they'll do it. Personally, I think it's crazy."

Tiffany joined us on the command bridge. As she

cuddled against Paris, I took the other seat. From here, the view was beyond awesome. It was a total panorama—not a single tree or building blocked the horizon. I could see every star, even little faint ones. It was so romantic.

Tiffany snuggled closer to Paris. "Remember when you called me 'princess'? When we were kids? I loved that, Paris." She smiled at me. "We used to play wedding, and Paris would be the groom. I was Lady Diana."

Paris kissed her cheek. "Tiff, you'll always be my princess."

I smiled at him. "How'd you come up with your boat's name?"

"Amor de Cosmos was an actual dude, long ago. He arrived in British Columbia in the 19th century and ended up as premier, running the place. He started life as William Smith, then picked a new name—cool idea, eh? *Amor de cosmos* means 'lover of the universe.'"

Tiffany touched his dark hair. "That's a perfect description of you, sweetheart."

"My dad was quite the guy," Paris told me proudly. "A sports champion in his time, and adored by all the cuties. He bought this classic cruiser when he was young. The *Amor* has a cedar-strip hull on oak. I added the twin diesels for real power. They're turbocharged."

Tiffany glanced at her Rolex. "Let's head home, Paris. Daddy will be calling soon."

"Phone him on your cell, and we'll stay out longer."

Tiffany shook her head. "Daddy needs to know I'm safely home from the sea. Otherwise he won't be able to sleep."

"He's staying downtown at the Empress Hotel?" I asked.

Tiffany nodded. "Daddy loves that place."

Before long we approached Oak Bay, Victoria's luxurious neighbour. Through binoculars I studied the Oak Bay Beach Hotel, then the expensive mansions, houses, and condos along the shoreline. Lights glowed from the windows, looking cosy.

"What a sight under a full moon," Tiffany said. "It's like being in a dream."

"*Hey*," Paris exclaimed. Grabbing the binoculars from me, he looked north along the water in the direction of Thirteen Oaks, the estate owned by his family. "I see some boat, stopped abeam of my house. No running lights. Let's check this out."

"Could it be a smuggler?" I asked excitedly.

"Possibly."

"Be careful," Tiffany warned, as Paris fed maximum RPMs to the twin beasts that roared below decks. "This could be dangerous!"

We moved north along the shoreline, feeling the wind on our faces. As we approached the mystery craft, Paris studied it through his state-of-the-art night binoculars. "It's called the *Outlaw*. There's an open deck and a wheelhouse. Some guy's inside—I can see him. He's got blond hair and two gold earrings. Looks maybe 20 years old, 25 max."

Above the cliff stood an ancient mansion. Moonlight glowed on the ivy embracing its walls. The stone building was very large, dominating the enormous estate known as Thirteen Oaks. There were several chimneys; smoke curled from one. From the gardens of the estate, a crooked path led down to a beach. Nearby was a small island with no signs of habitation.

The *Amor de Cosmos* powered forward, moving in on the mysterious *Outlaw*. Suddenly a spotlight glared across the water. A man's voice yelled, "Clear away."

Paris swore angrily. Veins bulged in his throat as he screamed, "Forget it, jerk. And what exactly are you doing? I live in that house up there." The engines rumbled as Paris moved our craft closer. "Who are you, anyway?" he cried across the water. "Identify yourself."

Silence from the *Outlaw*. I gripped the railing, aware of the painful throbbing of my heart. I was so scared.

Then Tiffany screamed. "A gun! Paris, he's got a gun!"

I stared across the tossing waves. "Holy Hannah." A nickel-plated revolver shone in the spotlight's glow. "That thing looks real. Let's—"

Fire burst from the muzzle. Something hummed past into the night, and then I heard the shot. It was total confusion on our boat as I dove for cover beside Tiffany while Paris grabbed for the throttle, and our cruiser leapt away across the waves.

"That was a real bullet," I yelled.

Paris looked behind. "He's coming after us, but we'll outrun him. This baby can really move."

The other boat fell away into the night as we escaped north. Then, without warning, the mighty roar of our engines turned to a coughing gasp, followed by utter silence. Out in the night, we heard the *Outlaw* coming our way.

2

"We're out of fuel," Paris yelled. "We'll have to swim for it."

Paris hurried forward to drop the anchor. Kicking off his deck shoes, he glanced toward the nearby shoreline. Then he dove into the night. His body describing a perfect arc, Paris sliced down into the sea—then surfaced.

"You next, Tiffany," he cried from the waves. "I'll swim with you, but hurry. I can see the spotlight. He's coming fast!"

Moments later, Tiffany was in the water and swimming toward safety. The other boat was getting close—the spotlight beam swept back and forth, searching. I was freaked out of my mind!

Kicking away from the *Amor*, I sailed out over the

waves. I flinched, then cut deep into the freezing waters of the Pacific.

Surfacing, I gasped for air. Wiping salty water from my eyes, I watched the spotlight play across the command bridge of the *Amor de Cosmos*. The other boat moved closer to the *Amor*; on its deck was a young man.

Whatever he held was on fire. A bottle stuffed with a flaming rag? Then I understood. *A Molotov cocktail*, I thought. *There's gasoline in that bottle.*

The weapon flew through the air, smashing on the deck of our boat. Almost immediately, it began to burn. Flames licked greedily across the hardwood. From the *Outlaw*, a voice called, "Don't mess with me."

As the *Outlaw* powered away, I started swimming toward shore. I was so cold, but I forced myself to keep moving. Seawater was in my eyes and getting down my throat, but finally I stumbled up a rocky beach. Tiffany and Paris were hiding behind a bush. Tiffany waved me over; her teeth were chattering.

"Are you okay?" I asked anxiously.

"Sure, I'm just so cold . . ."

Paris had his arms around Tiffany. "That's one serious dude. We were lucky to get out alive." His sombre eyes gazed across the water. Orange and red flames were eating into the wooden deck and up the deckhouse of the *Amor de Cosmos*. The fire spread quickly; black smoke smeared the stars.

"What would my dad say?" Paris groaned.

Tiffany squeezed his hand.

I looked at Paris. "Do you think that guy was planning a break-in at your estate?"

He nodded. "That's probably it."

On the sea, flames chased each other across the doomed vessel. They were reflected in the eyes of Paris deMornay. "I can't believe what I'm seeing. The *Amor* is finished."

"Honey, we're safe," Tiffany said gently. "That's what matters. The *Amor de Cosmos* was only a boat."

"Sure," Paris said, hanging his head. "But it was my father's boat."

* * *

The next evening, thunder boomed and lightning exploded across the sky. What drama! I was at Thirteen Oaks, sitting with Tiffany, Paris, and Paris's younger brother, Hart, on stone benches in the garden. We were watching an awesome light show illuminate the dark ocean waters. So far, rain had not fallen.

"Thunderstorms are unusual for Victoria," said Hart deMornay, smiling at me. Hart was 20, and there was also a younger teenage sister named Pepper. These were the deMornays; their parents' death had left them a large fortune that was controlled by a family trust.

Hart had luminous grey eyes and chestnut-brown hair; a lock fell across his lightly freckled face. He seemed really West Coast, like he'd been hiking through forests and windsurfing since childhood—which was true. "Wow," Hart exclaimed as a lightning bolt shot down, scattering bright colours across the sea. "What a spectacle."

"Here comes the rain," Paris said, as large drops

pattered on the leaves above us. "Let's make a run for the house. Dinner will be served soon."

As we approached the front door, Paris signalled to a servant who stood waiting. Immediately the heavy wooden entrance swung open, and we all rushed inside. I was beside Tiffany, who was beautiful as always. My friend closely resembled Grace Kelly, the movie star who became a famous princess; all Tiff needed was a sparkling diamond tiara on her blonde head—and she'd probably get one as a wedding gift from her wealthy dad.

Tonight Paris was very stylish, wearing a white dress shirt and pleated light wool trousers. "What's the story on your estate?" I asked him. "It's an amazing place."

"This part of Victoria is called the Uplands," he explained. "It's super classy. One of my ancestors built this big old mansion. The deMornays are a famous family in Britain. My great-grandfather came out to Canada and made a fortune."

"Your name sounds French."

"Maybe"—Paris shrugged—"but I'm British aristocracy. If I lived in England, people would call me Lord Paris deMornay. Impressive, eh?"

"I saw the story in today's *Times Colonist* about your boat going down. I hope the police find that guy."

"The chances are slim," Paris replied. "A high-speed boat like the *Outlaw* would be difficult to capture."

We were walking along a wide hallway past old-fashioned furniture and oil portraits of the deMornay ancestors. What a gloomy bunch. Then I heard the opening notes of "Jingle Bells." Paris grabbed his cell phone, and fell back to answer. The others kept walking, but I hesitated. I remembered the phone call to the *Amor*. Some might call me nosy, but it comes with the territory. I was born to be a detective.

"I'll join you later," I whispered to Tiffany.

Pretending to adjust my shoe strap, I glanced at Paris as he listened to the person who had called. A frown creased his face. "I'll call you back," Paris said, snapping shut the phone.

Paris disappeared through a doorway. I counted to 10, then followed. Finding stairs, I climbed up past cold cement walls. In the upper hallway, small yellow lights gleamed above the oil portraits lining the walls.

I heard a voice from behind a door. It was Paris, talking on the phone. I tiptoed closer.

"Don't threaten me," I heard Paris say angrily. "You'll get every dollar, very soon. Yes, plus your exorbitant interest."

I held my breath, listening.

Then I heard a noise from down the hallway. Footsteps—someone was coming my way!

* * *

I was motionless, frozen, as a tall man approached. He wore formal clothing. His cheeks were hollow, his white hair was thin. It was Cambridge, the butler at Thirteen Oaks.

"Good evening, Miss Austen," Cambridge said with a dusty voice as he walked past.

A door opened, and Paris stared at me. The cell phone was in his hand. "Liz? Why aren't you at the dining room?"

"I . . . I'm lost."

"Huh?"

"I can't find my room."

Paris shook his head, looking impatient. "There's a map of Thirteen Oaks. Ask Pepper for a copy."

"Is that your office?" I asked, looking at the room behind Paris. "May I take a look?"

"Sure, I suppose so." Paris closed his cell phone, not bothering to say goodbye to his caller.

Meanwhile I began looking around. A portrait of Paris's father hung above the desk; clearly he'd once been handsome, but in the portrait looked stern and unfriendly.

I liked the large mahogany desk and the electronic gear, but I was highly offended by the sight of real animal heads mounted on the wall. A deer, a mountain goat—even a beautiful polar bear.

"That is so depressing," I exclaimed.

Paris glanced at the heads. "Hart and Pepper don't like them, either. My father bagged those trophies. He was quite the hunter. I inherited this office from him."

"You're getting rid of them, of course."

Paris shook his head. "Not a chance. Those trophies were my dad's pride and joy."

I decided to abandon the subject—Paris could be stubborn. Instead I asked a question. "What's your job, Paris?"

"Spending my share of the family fortune. Believe me, it's a full-time occupation. The deMornay family trust has plenty in the bank. Our ancestors made big money in British Columbia from lumber and coal and fish. Back then, the pickings were easy. Unions were weak or non-existent. We got rich."

I looked at the wastebasket, which contained a bunch of ripped-up lottery tickets. "How's your luck?"

"Not good, but my horoscope predicts a big win soon." Paris looked at me. "Tiffany says you're into arts."

I wondered if he was changing the subject.

Then I nodded. "I've learned some martial arts. Occasionally they come in handy."

"No, I mean stuff like painting. The Group of Seven and other famous artists."

"We studied those guys in school," I replied, "but I can't say I'm an expert."

"Care to see a unique treasure?"

"Sure thing."

At the ground floor we followed a long hallway. "I haven't been in this wing of the house," I told Paris.

He smiled. "It would take days to explore Thirteen Oaks. It's a big place—but my parents were happy here."

"Hey," I exclaimed, "what's with the laser beams?" We stopped at the door of a large library. Red beams, pencil-thin, shone from wall to wall.

"Any intruder steps into here," Paris said, "and the beams trigger alarms everywhere."

"What are you protecting?"

"Can I swear you to secrecy?"

"Of course."

Paris punched numbers on a security panel outside the library door. (I couldn't help noticing the code.)

The red beams were instantly gone, although the room still seemed to glisten with their energy.

"You've heard of the acclaimed artist Emily Carr, of course," Paris said, as we stepped into the library. As well as lots of books, there were several leather sofas and mahogany writing desks.

I nodded. "She's really famous. Every Christmas my brother and I give Mom the new Emily Carr calendar. Mom loves her paintings."

"Miss Carr was born in Victoria in 1871," Paris said, "the same year that B.C. became the sixth province of Canada. For many years she travelled British Columbia by horseback and canoe, capturing totem poles and forest scenes and First Nations communities with her artistry. It's beautiful stuff. The way she did some forests, it's like the trees are actually moving—you can feel the power of the wind. Most of those old totem poles were collected by museums, or rotted and fell down, so it's good she recorded them in their original settings."

"In grade 10 we read Emily Carr's book *Klee Wyck*," I said. "Our teacher said that means 'Laughing One.' Klee Wyck was Emily Carr's honorary name, given to her by the First Nations. Mrs. Silsbe told us the people liked Emily Carr."

Paris turned to the fireplace, where no fire burned. Above the mantel was a large oil painting. It showed totems outside wooden longhouses; I could see people chatting, and canoes pulled up on shore. In the foreground, a woman laughed heartily. Beside her was a child with solemn eyes. The woman's face was radiant with life. Printed in a corner was *M. EMILY CARR*, followed by the date *1912*.

"Is that Emily Carr? The woman in the picture?"

"No," Paris replied. "I imagine she was a resident of that village back in 1912, when Miss Carr painted this picture."

"I haven't seen it before," I said. "It's never been in Mom's calendars."

"That's because it's a secret," Paris explained. "You're looking at Emily Carr's unknown masterpiece. It's called *Klee Wyck*."

"Just like her book," I commented.

Paris nodded. "Miss Carr gave the picture to my grandfather, in return for something she wanted from our family store downtown. She was usually broke—a typical artist. Her paintings didn't become really valuable until after her death." A smirk touched his perfect lips. "Emily Carr desperately needed furniture, so Grandfather traded some junky old stuff in return for this painting. Our family did well, and no one got hurt. Thanks to my clever grandfather, we own an Emily Carr original that is unknown to art collectors. Can you imagine its value?"

"Multi gazzilions, at least," I said, shaking my head. "No wonder all the security."

"I promised my father I'd protect this painting," Paris said, "and never sell it." In the hallway he punched in the code, and the red lasers bounced back to life. "It's time to eat."

"Where's the dining room?" I asked.

"I'll lead the way," Paris responded. "This is a big old house, eh, with lots of crooked hallways. I used to explore this place with Hart and Pepper when we were kids."

We turned a corner—and the others were visible in the distance. I could see Tiffany chatting with Hart and Pepper deMornay. The dining room was like something from an old horror movie. Outside tall windows, rain lashed down on a marble statue of a Greek goddess and blew in crooked streams across the glass. Thunder crackled and lightning split the sky. Around the table were solemn servants wearing white aprons over black dresses, with white caps on their heads. They were serving food to Tiffany and the others, who sat on hard chairs at a long table surrounded by the large, dark spaces of the bleak room.

A gust of wind, smelling of the sea, guttered tall candles along the table. I hurried to join Tiffany, who was giggling with Hart deMornay, who looked *really good* by candlelight.

"Sorry I'm late," I said.

Turning to Pepper, I smiled hello. Pepper deMornay was 17, like me. She was a single parent with an 18-month-old named Amanda. Pepper's eyes were big and brown, and she was very friendly. Pepper's chestnut-coloured hair fell to her shoulders, and was beautifully cut. She wore a nice blouse, jeans, and cowboy boots.

To my right, a face leaned in. It was sad-looking Cambridge, the family butler whom I had seen earlier upstairs. Cambridge was middle-aged, but acted older. He took my order for a glass of chocolate milk, then withdrew.

We were served B.C. salmon for dinner, and it was really toothsome. Tiffany and I talked to Hart about his love of the wilderness, and I could tell that Tiff was impressed by Hart's passion for life.

Then Tiffany accidentally dropped her fork; she looked embarrassed, but I just smiled. "That means a female visitor," I told her. "If you'd dropped a knife, Thirteen Oaks could expect a male visitor."

She grinned. "Oh, Liz. You and your superstitions."

Hart turned to Paris. "There was a call from the Royal Victoria Yacht Club. Your membership payment is way overdue, but I guess that doesn't matter now."

This upset Paris, and the brothers began arguing.

As they bickered, Pepper leaned close to me and murmured, "Did you see *Klee Wyck*?"

I nodded. "How'd you guess?"

"I told Paris to show you," Pepper replied. "I figured you'd be interested. Liz, is the security code still 7-7-6-6?"

When I hesitated, Pepper grinned. "So, it is, eh? I knew you'd notice. It's about time Paris changed the code. It's been used for weeks. All the servants probably know it by now."

She stopped talking as a servant presented us with frosted silver dishes of my favourite dessert, ice cream! "Did you know," Pepper said, "that Emily Carr was profiled on *Biography* in June? They did a week of famous artists." Pepper shook her head. "I bet the value of *Klee Wyck* rises by thousands of dollars every minute."

A deep *boom-boom-boom* came from the grandfather clock in a gloomy corner. Pepper jumped and nervously checked her watch before turning to Tiffany.

"Would you hold Amanda for a while?"

"For sure."

As my friend eagerly accepted the bundle of joy,

Pepper picked up her cell phone from the table and left the dining room. I smiled at Tiffany—she seemed totally at peace whenever she cuddled Amanda. Tiff adored babies and was looking forward to starting a family.

When Pepper returned to her chair, she glanced at Paris. "You still think my idea is stupid?"

"You mean the recording studio you're going to buy? The one that's vastly overpriced?"

"I'm going to become a music producer, Paris, and you can't stop me."

"Pepper, your idea is *so* bad, I've gotta laugh. You're always talking about stuff you're going to do. First it was producing for television, then lamebrain dot-com investments. Get a grip, Pepper. You're an unwed teenaged mother. How are you going to be a successful producer?"

"I'll have the money soon," Pepper declared. "You wait and see."

Hart leaned forward to squeeze her hand. "Personally, sis, I like your idea a lot. You could do anything, you're that smart."

Pepper blushed. "Thanks," she said, smiling shyly.

Tiffany looked at her fiancé. "Please stop arguing with Pepper and Hart, okay? Lately there's so much yelling. My nerves can't take it."

Pepper looked at her brother with hostility. "Ever since Mom and Dad died, you've been different. You're so crabby and jittery. Your friends were always phoning, and now you sit alone. What happened to all your snowboarding pals? When your money dried up, they did, too?"

Paris slammed his hand against the mahogany table. "Mind your own business, Pepper. Just leave me alone, okay?"

Standing up, he hurried from the room. Tiffany immediately went after him, and I followed. I found my friend in a dark hallway, staring moodily at the portraits lit by small lights. "Where'd Paris go?" I asked.

Tiffany shook her head. "He's disappeared. This old mansion is full of secret passages, and the deMornays know them all."

"Secret passages? Really?"

"That's what Pepper was saying."

"Tiff, *is* Paris different these days?"

"Sure, Liz, but he's under tremendous pressure. Cut him some slack, okay?"

"I'll try my best, Tiff," I replied, vowing to refrain from further comment.

We wandered in silence through the gloomy old mansion, and then I grabbed Tiffany by the arm. "Look," I whispered.

In the distance was the library, home to the highly prized painting by Emily Carr. But something was wrong—we couldn't see the lasers that provided security for the artwork.

Then a flashlight beam cut the darkness inside the library. It flickered and flashed—a spooky image. Next we saw a young man step into the hallway. He wore black jeans, a jacket, and a woollen cap. Two golden hoops glittered in his right ear.

He was carrying the painting.

3

Glancing at Tiffany, I put a warning finger to my lips as we shrank back against the wall. My heart was pounding overtime—what if the guy heard us?

Kneeling down in the hallway, he swiftly removed the painting from its frame. He used some kind of staple remover; each *kachunk* was a scary sound, echoing past us. Rolling up the painting, the intruder quickly slipped it inside a large metal tube. Then he was gone, disappearing down a hallway. It was all over in seconds.

Tiff stared at me in horror. "Liz, what should we do? Paris is going to be *freaked*. That painting meant everything to his father."

"Okay, Tiff, take it easy. Let's follow that guy."

Was this crazy? I wasn't sure, but my friend was highly agitated and I wanted to help. "This way," I said, leading Tiffany along the shadowy hallway. From the distance came sounds; we followed for what seemed an eternity. Down one hallway we went, then another.

Eventually we felt fresh air on our faces and smelled the ocean. We reached an open door—outside, the rain was pouring down. A concrete path led to the nearby shore, where I saw an old wharf. On the sea was a boat I recognized. It was the *Outlaw*.

Almost for sure, the stolen painting was on board.

As the vessel raced away into the night, Tiffany stared after it. She looked so sad. "We've lost the Emily Carr. I can't believe this has happened."

* * *

Tiffany and I were silent as we returned to the library. The laser beams remained down, their mission in ruins. The others had discovered the theft and were standing outside the library. Hart, Pepper, Paris, even Cambridge and several servants—they all clustered around us. Everyone kept saying, *What happened . . . What happened?* Paris was so upset; he didn't say a word, but his fists were curled up hard.

The abandoned frame lay in the hallway outside the library. "Don't touch the frame," I warned. "The police will want to dust it for fingerprints. That thief wasn't wearing gloves."

Paris started to speak, then changed his mind.

Everyone was glum as we went into the library. I looked at the large empty space above the mantel, then turned to the circle of watching faces. "This was an inside job," I declared. "Someone helped that thief."

Hart stared at me. Then he asked Cambridge to bring some coffee to the library.

"Have you called the police?" I asked Paris.

He gazed into the empty fireplace. "No."

"But why?" I asked.

"The police weren't called because we don't want publicity. No one knows about our painting—and that's how it stays. This information stays inside the family."

"I know about it."

"Sure, because you're my fiancée's best friend and you're trustworthy. No one else must learn the secret."

I was amazed at such foolishness. Without police help, the family might never recover the *Klee Wyck*. I turned to the others, expecting astonishment equal to mine. But no one cared. Pepper looked bored and Hart was whispering something to Tiffany.

Then Tiff looked at me. "I agree with Paris. We must protect our families—that's what counts the most."

Not impressed, I shook my head at their folly. Paris smiled, obviously pleased that he'd demonstrated who was boss at Thirteen Oaks.

* * *

Tiffany and I left the library, heading for our rooms.

"Paris really should call the police," I commented. "After all—"

"Let's trust him," Tiff snapped. "Paris knows what he's doing."

"Okay," I replied. "I didn't mean to upset you."

"Don't worry about it, Liz. I'm just on edge."

We stood for a moment outside Tiffany's bedroom. "Lock your door," I urged her. Tiff smiled at me with huge angel eyes. She seemed so fragile, like the famous Tiffany glass designs that share her name.

"I like Hart," I said. "He's nice."

She smiled. "That guy has so much energy."

Saying goodnight, I opened the door to my bedroom. The storm was over. Bright moonlight shone through the tall windows, glinting from the crystal angel I'd hung there.

Crossing the large room, I looked at the midnight garden. The radiance of the silver moon filled the sky, spreading a shining lustre over bushes and trees. A driveway curved past rolling lawns toward the estate's main gate. Somewhere in the night a vehicle passed on Beach Drive; I heard its tires on the wet pavement, but tall trees hid it from view.

I yawned hugely—what an evening. Going into the bathroom, I brushed and flossed at the marble sink while thinking about the mansion's strange inhabitants. Wearing my favourite PJs, I crawled into the big four-poster bed, made notes about the case, and then fell sound asleep.

* * *

Up early the next morning, I went outside. The first gentle rays of sunshine lit the garden leaves, green and wet with dew. The grass was so beautiful—it looked like velvet. The garden was filled with honeyed scents.

Surrounded by roses and sweet honeysuckle, I

wandered through the gardens of the estate, then approached the ocean. The sea air was delicious—I snuffled the morning breezes like a cat and let sunshine warm my face.

"Hi there."

Turning, I saw Hart deMornay climbing a path from the shoreline below. His face was radiant. Grinning at me, Hart swept back a lock of wavy brown hair. Beyond him, sunshine sparkled on the ocean, where seagulls swooped and played.

"I was out in my kayak," Hart explained. "Hey, Liz, you look all sunshine and happiness."

"Thanks." I was pleased. "Actually, I've been feeling down."

"Because of the robbery?"

"I guess so."

"You're a private eye type, eh? Got any theories?"

I studied Hart's large eyes and pleasant face. He looked so trustworthy, and yet . . .

Then Hart spoke. "Liz, be careful. My brother has a short temper. Don't rattle him."

"Hey! Paris and I are best buddies."

"Maybe once," Hart said with a smile. "But not now."

Opening the door of a small shed, he stowed the kayak's paddle inside. I looked at the scuba gear on the walls. "Look at this stuff!"

"All my family scuba," Hart told me. "Pater taught us."

"Who?"

Hart grinned. "*Pater* means 'father' in Latin. It's a snobby way of saying Daddy, and my father was a snob. Worse, he was a rich snob." Hart glanced suddenly at me. "When the *Amor de Cosmos* was fire-bombed, did you recognize the person who threw the Molotov cocktail?"

"No," I replied.

"Are you sure?"

"Of course," I said, smiling. "I'm very observant."

"Because—"

A screen door slammed, then Pepper appeared on the porch with her baby. Pretty in pink, Amanda looked so cute in her mother's arms. "Hey, you two," Pepper said, "come for breakfast. Liz, please tell me again about the werewolf in New Brunswick. I like that story."

"Okay." I grinned. "But this will be the third time."

"I'll join you shortly," Hart said. "I've got an important phone call to make."

Pepper and I ate in a pleasant sunroom overlooking both the ocean and the driveway. Just offshore was the small island I'd noticed before, its many trees emerald green in the morning sunshine. "I'd love to explore that island," I said. "Is there a rowboat or something I could use to get there?"

Pepper surprised me with a warning. "Stay away from that island, Liz. During the last war it was used by the army for training exercises. There are unexploded bombs and mines, all over the place."

"Are you certain?"

"Of course. It's called Hidden Island. I know everything about Thirteen Oaks. I'm totally into the past, just like Hart." She paused, thinking. "I guess we're both curious, like our mom. She was always talking history." Pepper sighed. "I wish I'd lived back when Thirteen Oaks was built. All that luxury, and all those parties. Sometimes, these days, I get so bored."

* * *

Arriving at the sunroom, Hart poured us all a glass of organic apple juice. It was some good. As I was downing a second glass, we heard a car stop outside.

"It's Laura," Pepper said, immediately leaving the room.

"What a car," I exclaimed, gazing out the window at a top-of-the-line BMW. Behind the steering wheel was a woman in her 30s; her auburn hair was stylishly swept back from an intelligent face with large, expressive eyes. Her makeup was immaculate. "I told Tiffany there'd be a female guest," I said, smiling at Hart.

"That's our family lawyer," Hart said. "Her name is Laura Singlehurst. Laura is responsible for the family trust. All the expenses at Thirteen Oaks are paid by the trust, and we each receive a large allowance." Hart glanced at me. "I don't need extra money—I own a company that does well in ecotourism. So I donate my allowance to the Hospice Society."

"Laura looks so interesting," I said, as the lawyer stepped from her elegant vehicle. From the colour of her car to her earrings, dress, and shoes, Laura was totally coordinated. Everything was the same lovely shade of green.

"Laura's very pleasant," Hart said. "I like her, and Pepper does, too. Laura's kind of a mother figure—if someone that glamorous can be called Mom." Hart chuckled. "But Paris hates Laura because she refuses to increase his allowance. You've heard that a fool and his money are soon parted—well, Paris is a perfect example."

As I stood up from the kitchen table, I saw Pepper approach Laura. They had a short conversation that left Pepper scowling.

"Laura didn't approve of Pepper dropping out of school because of the baby," Hart explained to me. "Sometimes Laura gets too bossy with Pepper. She can take the mother figure stuff a bit too far, if you know what I mean."

"Why don't you say something to her?"

Hart gave me a rueful smile. He swept back a lock of chestnut-coloured hair. "I guess I'm not very assertive, Liz."

Outside, the summer air was warm. Hart introduced me to Laura, who was kind and charming. We chatted about the wedding, then Laura produced a copy of the Victoria *Times Colonist*. "Look at this, Hart," she said proudly, opening to a report on the city's social scene. "I'm mentioned again today by Jim Gibson." She thrust the newspaper into Hart's hand. "Keep this copy—I've got more."

"You're always in the newspaper, Laura. With all the publicity, you'd be a natural for politics."

"Not a chance." Laura leaned on the car horn. Its sharp sound vibrated off the stone walls of the house, making birds fly up from the garden.

The sleepy face of Paris deMornay looked down

from an upstairs window. "What's with the noise?"

"Get down here fast," Laura called to him. "I've got news about your stolen painting."

Paris stared at Laura in amazement, then he disappeared from the window.

Hart's face also registered astonishment. "How'd you know the *Klee Wyck* was stolen? My brother strong-armed us into silence on that one."

The lawyer held up her cell phone. "I just had a call from some guy demanding a ransom."

"Could you identify his voice?" I asked.

Laura shook her head. "Only that he sounded young. Maybe 20 or so."

"Have you got call display?"

Laura nodded. "It said Unknown Caller. He was at a pay phone, I think. I could hear traffic sounds. Then a construction jackhammer started pounding, and he cut the connection."

Paris joined us and heard the details. "We must pay the ransom," he declared. "How much is it?"

Laura produced a pocket notebook. She'd written the ransom demand in ink the same elegant colour as her car.

When Paris saw the ransom, his face turned white. "That's . . . it's so much, I . . ."

"It's a lot," Laura agreed, "but the trust has enough money. However, that's only if you three considerably reduce your allowances for the next two years."

Paris gulped. His skin was pale, and he hadn't shaved. "We'll pay the ransom," he said at last. "That painting was Pater's favourite thing, and I just can't face losing it."

"That's okay with me," Hart said, and Pepper nodded her agreement.

"What happens next?" I asked Laura.

"I was told to expect another phone call, but I don't know when."

Paris looked at us all. "Say nothing about the painting being gone. I don't want the media to get wind of this story."

"What about the police?" I asked. "Have you changed your mind about telling them?"

"No way," Paris replied vehemently.

* * *

Later that day, Tiffany and I left Oak Bay for downtown Victoria. Her father had arrived a week earlier from Winnipeg and was staying at the world-famous Empress Hotel. He was treating us to the hotel's celebrated Afternoon Tea at four o'clock.

Tiffany drove a candy-apple red Jeep, open to the sky. On the radio aerial, a Canadian flag whipped back and forth. The air was sweet as we zoomed along Rockland Avenue, Tiff's favourite route to downtown. Sometimes we'd detour past Craigdarroch Castle so we could gaze at the impressive setting for her forthcoming wedding.

"Victoria has police radar," I warned, noting the 30-kilometre speed limit.

As a gesture to me, Tiffany slowed down. Leafy trees shaded the road, which curved past ancient mansions featuring massive, amazing gardens. Every size of blossom seemed represented in the Rockland neighbourhood.

."Listen, Tiff," I said, "has Paris mentioned someone called Bigoted Earl?"

She nodded. "Paris often goes to Sandown to see the earl."

"What's Sandown?"

Tiffany shrugged. "I've no idea."

She glanced at her diamond—a big, honking solitaire. "The castle is up that street," she said, gesturing past the trees. "But I guess you know that."

"You always talked about a church wedding, Tiff. That was your dream."

She nodded. "Yeah, but Daddy insists on the castle for the wedding. He's showing off, I think—but what can you do?"

"I hate to repeat myself, but isn't 19 kind of young for marriage?"

Tiffany smiled comfortably. "Princess Victoria, daughter of Queen Victoria, was married at 17—"

"You've told me that, but . . ."

"In the upper classes, Liz, many young people are pledged to each other. I've known couples to marry the moment they're of legal age. That way the benefits can get started. Like combining families and fortunes, and maybe titles."

"And how do you feel about Paris? Still happy?"

Tiff produced a smile of sweet innocence. "Paris loves me, Liz. Since I was 12, I knew I really did want to marry him. We're so good together—and we understand each other." Her voice trailed off, and she frowned. Then she seemed to shake off her thoughts. "Anyway," she said brightly, "we've been through the same fires growing up. Both our fathers demanded a lot of us, right from childhood. It turned into a terrible burden for Paris. He could never meet his father's expectations. I understand that, and I help Paris with his feelings. He really needs me."

"What do *you* need, Tiff?"

She shrugged. "To have a family, and to know my parents are okay."

"What about college or university? You're very bright. You could have a career."

"I've got a lifetime supply of money, Liz. I don't need a career. I want my very own babies, a real family, and then I'm going to establish a charitable foundation. I'll help children, especially in war zones."

The Jeep hung a left, and we moved south under leafy boughs. In Cook Street Village the chestnut trees were glorious, shading little shops and wide sidewalks where people read newspapers outside coffee shops and lovers kissed.

As we approached the ocean I began to notice the wind, how it bent trees low. I saw whitecaps out on the sea racing toward shore.

"It's a windstorm," Tiff said. "Let's go watch."

She followed Dallas Road to St. Charles, where we found parking. "Hart brought me here during a storm," Tiffany said, as we left the Jeep. "It was so awesome. The waves were, like, huge."

The white buildings along the seashore reminded me of the Mediterranean, and so did the sea. The breakers were blue and green, tossed and turbulent. Spray flew away as they pounded ashore, noisily rattling stones when the waters ran back into the sea. In the distance, wave after wave crashed on the stony beach and came racing toward us along the shoreline.

I noticed that police had set up a roadblock, preventing vehicles from using this section of Dallas Road during the storm. Huge waves crashed against the concrete roadway, scattering ocean foam and seawater across the pavement.

I looked at the far side of the roadway. "What's there?"

"Ross Bay Cemetery. Cambridge told me it's the oldest burial ground in the city. Some famous people are in it, like Emily Carr."

"Wow," I suddenly exclaimed, pointing at the ocean pounding the roadway. "Look at that *vision*."

Out of the waves came a blond runner, a tall guy in his late teens. Head down, he plunged through the cascading waves with total determination. He was soaked but he kept moving.

"He's really something," I said, watching as the runner stopped at a small low-rider truck parked nearby on St. Charles. The windows were tinted; I couldn't see the driver. "Maybe that truck's from Seattle."

"How come?"

"It's got a Washington plate."

Tiff smiled. "You're so observant."

"I forgot my camera," I replied, "and I regret my foolishness. I could use a photo of that dreamboat. Maybe he's in movies. Lots of shows get made in B.C."

"Put that guy on the screen and he'll be the next big thing."

A window rolled down. I couldn't see the driver,

but it seemed he was speaking to the blond guy. Then the runner was handed a wad of bills. After carefully counting the money, he disappeared up St. Charles. The truck also took off. I never got a look at the driver.

4

Soon after, Tiffany parked the Jeep near downtown on Burdett. This was a pleasant street of apartment buildings and dignified mansions dominated by a massive cathedral. As Tiffany snapped a locking device on the steering wheel, I nodded my approval.

Sunlight filtered down through the leaves. A clergyman riding an old bicycle waved hello, and a young mother pushing a baby carriage smiled at us. "It's a friendly town," I commented to Tiffany, as we walked to Fort Street for some shopping on Antique Row.

Our mission was to purchase gifts for the wedding party, then meet Tiffany's dad for Afternoon Tea at the Empress Hotel. Many of the storefronts made me think of Olde England, back in the days of Scrooge and his creator, Charles Dickens. Displayed in windows along the street were many treasures, from antique jewellery to the finest furniture.

In a jewellery shop, Tiffany studied two large buttons on display. "Objects are different when they're old," she said. "These buttons are so heavy, eh? I bet they're from a soldier's uniform, back in the First World War."

Tiff studied the Latin inscription on the buttons. "You know something, Liz? I have a real emotional affinity for those times. Even when I was very small I was fascinated by images from the days of the British Empire." Tiffany paused. "If ever I lived before," she said, "it was then."

Back outside, we wandered past an upscale auction house. "Look at these classic train sets," I said, stopping at the window. "My brother Tom would love this place—"

"Liz, look!" Tiffany pointed into the auction house. "That painting—it's Lady deMornay. But I saw it at Thirteen Oaks, just days ago. It was in the morning room. That's where Lady deMornay used to sit, watching the sea."

Tiffany snapped open her miniaturized cell phone. "Hello, Paris?" she said, moments later. "Listen, that portrait of your mother has maybe been stolen. Liz and I just spotted it, up for auction."

As she listened to Paris, Tiffany frowned. "But she's your own mother, Paris. How could you auction her portrait? Hart and Pepper will be devastated." Tiffany kept talking, then stared at the phone.

"He hung up on me."

I started to comment, then pointed in the window of the auction house. "Tiffany, look who's in there."

"Oh, gosh—it's Cambridge, the butler."

"See how he's staring at the portrait of Lady deMornay? Like he's going to start crying."

We watched Cambridge for a few minutes, but nothing much happened. I felt impatient to do something—to make progress on this case. Opening a map of Victoria, I located the Maritime Museum. "We could check their records for information about the *Outlaw*. Like who's the owner and where it's registered."

"Sure, let's try that," Tiffany immediately replied. "Anything to find the painting. Paris was in a really bad mood this morning."

* * *

Without highrise towers to block the sun, the downtown streets were bright and attractive. They were crowded with tourists and shoppers and office workers. People looked so fit and healthy!

"Look at that crow," I said, pointing. It had landed on a bicycle that leaned against a lamp standard; in the bicycle basket was a shopping bag containing bagels. The crow took a bagel, then lifted off with it.

"Stop, thief," Tiffany called, laughing.

At Bastion Square we found a lively street market with booths selling artwork and wonderful crafts. I got started on my own gift list by finding something pretty for my mom (earrings made of cobalt-blue glass beads), then we went inside the Maritime Museum.

With luck, we happened to meet the museum's director, a nice woman named Yvonne. "We're looking for information about a boat called the *Outlaw*," I said.

"Can you help?"

"Perhaps," Yvonne said. "Let's try the library."

She escorted us into an unusual elevator. "This is the oldest operating birdcage elevator in Canada," Yvonne told us.

The double metal doors clanked closed, and our birdcage began to rise. I grinned. "This is cool."

At the top floor, Yvonne opened the elevator door. "There are some beautiful old buildings in Victoria, many dating back to the gold rush. This one is from the 19th century; it used to be the courthouse. You've heard of Matthew Begbie?"

We both shook our heads.

"They called him the Hanging Judge because of the number of people he sentenced to die. This is the actual building where he presided."

The ceiling of the library was high; above us, portraits of British royalty were displayed beside the Canadian coat of arms. "You know something I like about Victoria?" I said. "All the connections to England. Like those British candy shops we've seen."

The museum's librarian, Lynn, was smart like Yvonne. Diligently searching the archives and photo files, they managed to discover one vessel named the *Outlaw*. "It's listed in *Lloyd's Register* of ships," Yvonne said, studying a thick volume. "But it can't be your *Outlaw*. This one's a freighter, built in 1946 for general cargo and registered in Malta. I'm sorry, I guess you're out of luck. Probably the boat you're seeking has never been registered. It's an *Outlaw*, just like its name implies."

I smiled at them. "Thanks, anyway, for trying."

In the hallway we stopped at an original poster from 1911 showing the *Titanic* and her sister ship, the *Olympic*. A shiver went through me, thinking of the iceberg and that horrifying night.

Inside the birdcage elevator again, we descended noisily to the ground floor, where Yvonne introduced us to a bearded man named Richard, who also worked there. Richard wore a tie displaying nautical flags, and he was an expert on matters of the sea.

"My suggestion," he said, after hearing our story, "is to visit Fishermen's Wharf. Ask for Fossilized Pete. If anyone's heard of the *Outlaw*, it'll be Pete." Richard smiled at us. "Tell you what, I'll phone Pete and set up a meeting. He's a friend of mine."

I spoke to Pete, who sounded friendly, and we arranged to meet in the early evening. After thanking Richard, we returned to Bastion Square with Yvonne, who was going on a break. Above our heads, flags fluttered in the summer breeze. A few paces from the museum, Yvonne showed us a row of bricks embedded in the pavement. "The wall of Fort Victoria was here." Yvonne looked toward the city's nearby Inner Harbour. "The fort started at the ocean and ran past us to Government Street. Things were pretty calm in Victoria until the big gold rush of 1858. Twenty thousand prospectors came through here, heading for the goldfields."

Tiffany looked at Yvonne. "We're on Vancouver Island, right? But the city of Vancouver is over on the mainland. That's, like, totally confusing."

"I agree," Yvonne said. "George Vancouver was an English sea captain who mapped the waters of the Pacific Northwest. Adding to the confusion, in Washington state there's another city named Vancouver."

"Wasn't Captain Vancouver eaten by cannibals?"

"No." Yvonne shook hands goodbye. "Look for the statue of Captain James Cook near the Empress Hotel—he once explored these waters. You'll also see Captain Vancouver, high atop the Legislative Building. And good luck in finding the *Outlaw*."

"We'll do our best," I promised her.

* * *

At Government Street a busker was thumping a guitar, while his friend sang with a powerful voice. "They're great," Tiffany exclaimed at the end of the song. She gave them a generous donation.

"Wow, thanks," the boy said, staring at the money.

The singer hugged Tiffany. "You're so cool."

"Where's the food bank?" Tiffany asked.

The singer pointed north. "It's on Queens."

Soon we reached the Mustard Seed Food Bank, which was a busy place. "There are a lot of young families," I said in dismay. "Look at all the kids. It's shocking."

"I know," Tiffany replied sadly. "It's so wrong that a country as wealthy as Canada allows children to live in poverty. It's a national disgrace."

Tiffany asked to meet the manager of the Mustard Seed, then wrote out a cheque. The manager gasped when she saw the amount Tiffany was donating. "Thank you so much. Let me show you around the premises."

As we returned to sunshine, Tiffany consulted her watch. "Time to meet Daddy."

"Will your mother be attending the wedding?" A year earlier there'd been a divorce, and Tiff's mother now lived on Grand Cayman Island.

Tiff shook her head. "For some reason she no longer approves of Paris, and she and Daddy haven't been getting along lately, so it's probably for the best."

Tiffany was looking anxiously along Johnson Street. "Oh, good—there's a Kabuki Kab."

Kabukis are popular with tourists in Victoria. You sit in a cab attached behind a bicycle, and the driver describes why he loves this city while pedalling you to a destination.

Our driver was friendly, and I enjoyed the ride. Soon we arrived at Victoria's Inner Harbour, where the waters of the Pacific reach into the heart of the city. People were posing for pictures; beyond them was the spectacular sight of the provincial Legislative Buildings, where British Columbia's government holds its meetings. Above the imposing stone walls were many green domes, the tallest topped by a golden statue of Captain Vancouver. Many other buildings overlooked the water; some were brick and stone structures still surviving from the gold rush days, but we also saw the latest in luxury condos and upscale hotels.

Plus, of course, there was the fabled Empress.

A favourite of Hollywood stars and the very wealthy, the enormous hotel dominated the scene. Its walls rose high above to a giant Canadian flag that fluttered against the blue sky.

Two friendly doormen in fancy uniforms welcomed

us to the Empress; the lobby was filled with huge bouquets of fresh flowers radiating sweet fragrances. Right away I spotted Tiff's dad, Major Wright. His skull shone beneath grey, brushcut hair; the Major was short, resembling a small bulldog in a three-piece suit as he paced back and forth while glancing impatiently at his gold watch. Tiffany's father was proud to have served in the armed forces, and still liked to be called "the Major."

"Daddy," Tiffany cried, running to her father for a hug.

They were obviously pleased to see each other. I shook hands with the Major. "Thank you for inviting us," I said. "I'm looking forward to this."

Major Wright smiled at me. "It's good to see you again, Liz."

People were lined up, waiting their turn to enjoy the ceremony of "taking tea" in the grand hotel's original tea lobby. Portraits of long-ago British monarchs were displayed against elegant wallpaper. We saw many exquisite flowers and even some genuine palm trees. Silver spoons clinked inside china cups. I could smell the delicious tea, and my mouth watered at the sight of the goodies being served.

"Look at the whipped cream," I whispered to Tiffany. "For sure I'm having crumpets with jam and *dollops* of whipped cream."

Major Wright snapped his fingers at a waiter. "We have a table reserved."

Soon we were seated under a portrait of Queen Mary, who wore many diamonds. "This hotel was named in honour of Queen Victoria," the Major told us, as our waiter poured tea from a silver pot. "She was the Empress of India."

"These cucumber sandwiches are so good," I said, then took another bite.

Major Wright beamed at his daughter. "Great news. I've sold our house in Winnipeg. I'm moving to Victoria, to be close when my grandchildren start arriving. My life has changed for the best, Tiffany, all thanks to your forthcoming marriage."

"That's nice, Daddy."

"My own little girl will soon be Lady deMornay, chatelaine of Thirteen Oaks. Liz, isn't that great?"

"Major Wright, you're an expert on titles. Why can't Hart become Lord deMornay?"

Tiffany's blue eyes darted to her father. "That's an interesting idea."

But Major Wright threw cold water on my brainwave. "The title goes automatically to the eldest son." He turned to his daughter. "Wouldn't it be something to meet the Royal Family, Tiffany?" Major Wright's eyes grew bright with excitement. "Maybe when you're Lady deMornay, royalty will visit Thirteen Oaks, and even stay with you. Wouldn't the folks back home in Winnipeg be jealous?"

"I guess so, Daddy."

"Call me a sentimental old fool, but I can't wait for your marriage. Joining together the Wrights and the deMornays is so important for both families. Your marriage to Paris will unite us with Victoria's top society. You'll be living in the Uplands, at the number one address—Thirteen Oaks."

Eventually the Major's enthusiasm ran down, and for

a while nothing more was said. We munched the goodies and sipped delicious tea. Then Tiffany took a deep breath. "I've been thinking, Daddy, about the wedding."

"Yes?"

"Maybe I should postpone it? Even just a little bit?" Tiffany spoke rapidly; her voice seemed breathless. "It's just that . . ."

"Tiffany, sweetheart. What's wrong?"

"It's just that Paris, he's changed. I'm not sure . . ."

Major Wright took her hand; his eyes were as blue as Tiff's. "Of course he's different, sweetie pie. He's grieving for his parents. Wouldn't you be?"

"Of course, but—"

"Think about the grandchildren you and Paris will give me. Those kids are the next generation of the Wright and deMornay empire. With parents like you and Paris, they can't fail." He gently touched the side of Tiffany's face. "Think of the babies, honey. You're going to love them so much."

"That's true, but—"

"The invitations have been sent, Tiffany, and beautiful presents have arrived. You can't return those! Besides, calling off the wedding would look bad."

I looked at him. "Other people have cancelled weddings."

"Sure, but—"

Tiffany interrupted his response. "Liz, I understand what Daddy means. What would people think? That's important, you know."

"If you say so," I replied.

As the Major patted Tiffany's hand, his cell phone shrilled. He answered and spoke briefly, then looked at us. "Good news. Paris is joining us for tea. His limousine just arrived outside the Empress."

"That's wonderful," Tiffany exclaimed. She fluffed up her blonde curls and straightened her skirt, but a frown remained on her face.

I watched Paris approach across the hardwood floor, smiling at the women who glanced his way. He wore a suit the colour of vanilla ice cream, with a beautiful shirt and a tie of blue silk. In his ear was a small golden hoop. His dark hair was swept back dramatically.

Paris shook hands warmly with the Major, then sat down beside Tiffany and gazed into her eyes. "Sweetheart, it's so good to see you."

Tiffany smiled happily. "You, too, Paris."

Paris turned to the Major. "Sir, you'll recall I put your name forward for membership in the Union Club. It's very exclusive, but I've got wonderful news. You've been accepted as a member."

"Wonderful." The Major shook hands with Paris. "You're a fine young man." Then he turned to Tiffany with a smile. "My own dear Lady deMornay. I can hardly wait."

* * *

Outside the Empress we said goodbye to Major Wright and Paris. Then, before I could speak, Tiffany raised her hand. "Please, Liz, no advice about my marriage. This is important to Daddy and it's important to me."

"Still, I'm glad you mentioned your doubts, Tiff. Maybe that got your father thinking."

After shopping in Chinatown, Tiff and I enjoyed a

tour of the Legislative Buildings. Then we returned outside to the sight of the Inner Harbour as evening came to Victoria. The distant hills were lovely, turning dark and mysterious before our eyes.

The air was warm; many people were out this early evening, strolling arm in arm or passing in horse-drawn carriages. Stopping at a low stone wall, we gazed at the vessels cruising the Inner Harbour. There were luxury yachts and sleek kayaks and noisy sea-planes, plus a large Zodiac full of tourists returning to port from a whale-watching excursion.

The setting sun glowed on a huge sign reading WELCOME TO VICTORIA. The words were made entirely of flowers. "Excuse us, girls," a man said with a drawl, "but how's about taking our picture?"

"Sure."

Through the lens of his camera, I focused on a middle-aged couple dressed in shorts and "Victoria City of Gardens" T-shirts. Beyond them was a statue of Queen Victoria, the famed British monarch who gave the city its name.

"You're from out of town?" I commented, after capturing the couple's self-conscious grins for posterity.

The man's bushy eyebrows rose high. "Now, little lady, how'd you guess?"

"It was easy." I smiled. "You're carrying a copy of WHERE Victoria. That's a tourist guide."

"Shucks." The man laughed. "For a moment there, I was impressed."

Tiffany shook her finger at the man, but in a friendly manner. "Now, listen up. My friend's a successful detective. She's very smart."

"Say," the lady remarked to me, "ever met Nancy Drew?"

"Not so far!"

The man photographed the nearby Royal British Columbia Museum. "We're here on business, hoping to sell this town a hockey arena. But we might just move to Canada. Shucks, the air is so clean—why, you can taste it."

"Some of those big flowers are *amazing*," his wife added, "and folks are so friendly."

The man looked at the Legislative Buildings. "That fellow on top, the gold statue. He's holding something, maybe a hockey stick. Someone said that's the legendary star Wayne Gretzky. Is it true?"

I shook my head. "That's Captain George Vancouver."

After saying goodbye, we descended stone stairs to the Lower Causeway. Here people strolled, licking cones as they watched buskers perform and sidewalk artists paint and sketch. Young kids were blowing rainbow bubbles, which drifted lazily through the warm air. This seemed like a carnival by the sea.

On enormous white yachts, boaters sat chatting in deck chairs or panned their cameras across the enchanting scene. Red and gold sunset colours reflected from the water and I could smell the salty ocean.

I consulted my watch. "It's time for our meeting with Fossilized Pete at Fishermen's Wharf. Richard at the museum suggested getting there by harbour ferry."

"There's one," Tiffany said, pointing.

The ferries were loading passengers at a nearby wooden wharf, which creaked with the movement of the sea. The ferry was so cute—it looked like a tiny tugboat. We stepped down into a small cabin, where other passengers waited for the departure. Surrounded by windows, we could see everything.

"Please let us off at Fishermen's Wharf," I asked the captain, as he took our fares.

"Going for fish and chips?"

I shook my head. "We stuffed our faces at the Empress."

"Will this ride make us seasick?" Tiffany asked.

"Not a chance," our captain replied. "The Inner Harbour is almost totally enclosed by land. It's very calm. We're also protected by the Sooke Hills." He pronounced it *Sook*, with a silent e. "The first inhabitants of those hills were the Tsouke people."

Proudly displaying the flags of B.C. and Canada, the ferry plowed a furrow of small waves as its bow cut through the water. Our relaxing journey ended at Fishermen's Wharf, where various vessels were moored along the wooden wharves. Signs at Barb's seafood stand asked customers to refrain from feeding birds. But one guy totally ignored the warning, holding a juicy morsel aloft to tempt the gulls that wheeled and screamed above.

"He'll lose a finger," I predicted, but I was wrong.

We followed a series of wharves to the home of Fossilized Pete; it resembled a tiny house, floating on the sea. There was even a picket fence.

A porthole overlooked the houseboat's tiny porch. As I leaned close, hoping to see inside, the door opened and Fossilized Pete stood before us.

I had expected a grizzled type, white whiskers and weathered skin, but instead Pete was quite young. He had large eyes like those of a puppy dog, and neatly trimmed black hair turning to grey. He wore deck shoes, faded jeans, and a T-shirt reading "TerrifVic Jazz Party." I asked about the *Outlaw*, showing him a rough drawing I'd made. Then I held my breath. Surely Fossilized Pete could help us.

To our delight, Pete nodded his head. "Yes, I've seen this craft before."

"Wonderful," we both exclaimed.

Pete pointed across the water. "Last night I spotted the *Outlaw* heading toward the West Bay Marina. You can see the marina's lights from here."

I exchanged an excited glance with Tiffany. "How do we get there?" I asked Pete.

He gestured at a small boat moored beside the wharf. "That's my skiff. Hop aboard."

"Wonderful."

Minutes later we were skimming across the water, powered by an outboard in the stern of the skiff. I felt determined, yet nervous. Suppose we found the *Outlaw*—what would happen then?

5

"I'm a volunteer with the Victoria Marine Rescue Society," Pete told us, as our boat sped across the waters. "We're out a lot, helping boaters in trouble, that sort of thing."

"How'd you get your name?" I asked. "Fossilized Pete doesn't really suit you."

"Actually it's a nickname. I don't smoke, I don't drink, I don't do drugs. For that, some people back home called me a fossil—you know, old-fashioned. So I moved to the West Coast, where people are more accepting of differences. I'm not considered a fossil now, but I've kept my nickname, just for the memories."

"What's your T-shirt about?" I asked.

"The Jazz Party is an annual event in Victoria.

People come from all over the world. I've danced to some great bands—Zydeco, swing, you name it. And I volunteer at the special Saturday party for kids."

For a time I was silent, thinking.

"Is it dangerous on the open sea?"

"Sure," Pete replied. "Especially for the dunderheads, the ones with no training. They don't keep a weather eye out. Then suddenly they're overboard into bitterly cold water. People have died out there."

Looking down into the depths, I shivered. Night had closed around us; the breeze chilled my face. Directly ahead was the marina, where lights glowed inside houseboats and cabin cruisers. People on deck talked to each other across the water, and I could hear music and barking dogs. It was like entering a small town, afloat on the sea.

"I'll drop you here," Pete said.

"How do we get back?" I asked.

"Take a harbour ferry. They stop here."

Jumping onto a wharf, we waved goodbye to Fossilized Pete. Then we wandered around, hoping to spot the *Outlaw*. We showed the drawing to lots of people, but the search was doomed. It all seemed a big waste of time.

Until we spotted the thief.

He was on a nearby wharf. I his spiky bleach-blond hair and the two golden hoops in his ear. "That's him for sure."

"What'll we do?"

"Let's get closer."

Then his cell phone beeped. "Jason speaking," he

said. His voice came clearly to us. After listening to his caller, Jason nodded. "Thanks for the warning."

Jason dashed to a boathouse, opened the door, and disappeared inside. Moments later, we heard the throaty roar of a powerful engine as a cruiser appeared from the boathouse.

"Look," I cried. "It's the *Outlaw*."

* * *

Jason was inside, alone at the controls. "He's getting away," I said urgently. "Come on, let's stop him." I pointed along the wharf. "There's someone who can help."

We ran toward an open boat with an oversize outboard motor, mounted at its stern. The guy at the wheel had just started the motor when we reached him.

"Help us," I shouted. "We must stop that cruiser."

"O . . . kay," the guy replied. "Throw off the lines . . . and . . . and jump aboard."

The boat was stripped bare of seats and anything else that would slow it down. As we held tightly to a railing at the stern, it roared away from the marina. Many stars shone above. I could see the *Outlaw*, moving fast. I looked at the lights of condo towers, shining on the water, then felt our boat pick up speed. The motor was powerful; spray lashed back, soaking us. Lights blurred past—I shook saltwater out of my eyes, fighting to see.

"Hang on," Tiffany screamed, as the boat heeled to the side. Then I looked at the guy at the wheel—and understood our problem.

He was drinking from a vodka bottle, and it was almost empty.

* * *

The guy leered at us with bloodshot eyes. "Enjoying the ride, girls?" he yelled.

Laughing, he twisted the wheel. We both screamed as the boat almost overturned before the guy managed to right it.

I staggered forward, balancing myself, as the drunk twisted the wheel back and forth. "Keep back," he yelled at me.

"Be careful, Liz," Tiffany called.

We'd left the Inner Harbour behind and reached the open sea. Directly ahead was the massive bulk of the *Coho*, a large ferry carrying vehicles and passengers to Victoria. Its horn sounded a warning, startling the drunk. He weaved back and forth, holding tightly to the wheel, trying to watch the ferry and also watch me.

"Danger," I suddenly cried, pointing over his shoulder. "Right there!"

"*Huh*?" the drunk responded, turning to look.

I leapt for the wheel, determined to take control. But the drunk saw me coming and lashed out with his foot. Avoiding the kick, I hit the deck and rolled. Trying to aim another kick, the drunk accidentally released the wheel—and immediately the boat changed direction, veering sharply to starboard.

The drunk staggered, then fell. His head smacked against the deck, and he went silent. Stumbling forward, I managed to grab the wheel. Somehow I got the boat under control, and we zoomed safely away from the *Coho*.

"Is he breathing?" I yelled back at Tiffany.

"Yes, but he's out cold."

I turned the boat toward the Inner Harbour. A crisis had been averted, but I didn't feel good. Somewhere in the night, the *Outlaw* was getting away.

We'd lost our quarry.

* * *

We left the boat at a wharf near the Empress. When we walked away, the drunk was leaning against the bulkhead, head in his hands. He was groaning.

"When we get home," I said, "I'll phone the police about spotting the *Outlaw*. But I'm guessing Jason will move his boat to another location."

"I wonder who warned him about us," Tiff said.

"Good point."

A lot of young people were hanging out across the street from the Empress. One of them was Pepper. She was comforting a teenager who was crying; I saw tears on the girl's face. Nearby, three well-dressed teenagers were staring with hostility at Pepper.

As we approached, Pepper smiled. "Good to see you," she said. "Laura's arriving any minute now. She's giving me a ride home to Thirteen Oaks."

Laura's shiny BMW pulled smoothly to the curb. At the same moment, a city bus stopped nearby; Pepper escorted the forlorn girl to the bus, then waved goodbye as the bus pulled away.

We all climbed into the BMW. "Brother," Pepper

exclaimed. She was in the back; Tiffany was up front with Laura. "I hate gossip—I hate it. Words can cause so much pain."

"What happened?" I asked.

"That girl I was with—some boy started a rumour about her. He wrote lies on a wall, looking for revenge. You saw those three girls? They're treating the rumour like the truth and passing it along. I told them what I thought."

"You did the right thing," Laura said. "You didn't join the finger-pointers. The only way to stop that stuff is not to be one of the sheep. You showed courage, Pepper, giving friendship to an outcast."

"Thanks," Pepper said, looking embarrassed. "Anyway, no one tells me what to think. I make up my own mind about people."

* * *

We soon reached the Jeep. "Liz and I can drive Pepper home," Tiffany suggested to Laura. "It'll save you the trip."

Laura declined the offer. "I feel like a drive. I've worked hard today, and I need to unwind."

"Okay to go with you?" I asked Laura. "I'd like your advice about what happened tonight."

"You bet," Laura replied.

We all said good night to Tiffany, and the BMW purred smoothly away. As I gazed at the charming houses passing by, I told Laura and Pepper about the events at the West Bay Marina. "I feel like I'm getting somewhere on this case," I said.

"How so?" Laura enquired. She was remarkably beautiful.

"Well, Jason is clearly connected to the *Outlaw*, and he also stole the painting. I should tell the police, don't you think?"

As Laura pondered this, Pepper studied her face. Then Laura nodded. "Yes, do tell the police about Jason's link to the *Outlaw*. But you'd better not mention the painting. That would upset Paris."

"Okay," I replied, somewhat reluctantly. "Have you heard anything about the ransom?"

She shook her head. "Nothing so far."

"Do you think the caller was Jason?"

"Probably," Laura said. "You're a good detective, Liz."

I grinned. "Sleuthing's in my blood. My mom's a lawyer, just like you. She loves it."

"I went into law to have a career," said Laura. "That way I'd never be financially dependent on anyone else."

The BMW rolled quietly through the deeply shadowed streets of the Uplands district, until it reached the stone walls of the Thirteen Oaks estate. Stepping out of the luxurious car, I sniffed the fragrant breezes.

Laura waved to us from behind the wheel. "Goodnight, girls."

"Goodnight, Laura," I said. "Thanks for the ride."

The lights of the beemer disappeared into the night, and we entered the quiet gardens of the estate. The moon was lovely, and so were the glorious stars that twinkled across the heavens. "It's so perfect under the moon," I exclaimed to Pepper. "I love this place."

* * *

The next morning, Tiff and I wandered together through the gardens of Thirteen Oaks.

The garage stood at the edge of the estate. Cambridge was shining the chrome on the family limousine. The vehicle sparkled in the morning sunshine. It was a Daimler, manufactured in England. It had right-hand drive and a cream and navy two-tone finish—very nice indeed.

"The Daimler's for sale," Cambridge told us. "Master Paris has ordered me to spiff it up. He's ordered a new limousine from Detroit—it's got bulletproof glass."

"Where's the chauffeur?" Tiffany asked.

"He's quit, miss. A disagreement with Master Paris."

Cambridge then began talking about the Moss Street Paint-In. "Are you going?" he asked. "It's a famous event in Victoria, and very popular."

"What's it about?" Tiffany asked.

"All along Moss Street, local artists set up their easels. You can watch them painting, or ask questions. I go every year." For a moment Cambridge stared at the ground. "When I was young, I dreamed of being an artist. I had real talent—but it didn't work out."

"Do you still paint?" I asked.

"Oh, yes, miss. I have a small studio above the garage."

"May we visit sometime?" I asked.

Cambridge shook his head. "I don't like people to look at my work. It's . . . Well . . . Well, I do it because

. . ." His voice faded away, then he straightened up. "You'll see some good work today at the Paint-In. I suggest that you go."

* * *

It was a beautiful Saturday, and sunshine warmed our faces as we headed south in the Jeep on Beach Drive, admiring the view. Yards in the Uplands were big, big, big, and featured beautiful trees and flowering bushes, a lot of them taller than people. The hollyhocks were particularly sensational with their fat blossoms of pink and dark red. The careful landscaping in the Uplands was so elegant— many houses seemed to be set into nests of greenery. Big trees shaded us from the sun; south of Willows Beach we passed Glenlyon-Norfolk School, located beside the ocean. "According to Pepper," Tiffany said, "that place was originally a private home owned by a famous architect named Francis Rattenbury. He ended up murdered."

I stared at the building. "I wonder if there's a ghost."

"Probably not. The murder happened in England."

At Windsor Park we paused to watch a cricket match, then headed for town by way of Oak Bay Village. What a great place. The village totally reminded me of England, with its little shops selling chocolates and flowers and other delights.

One place was called the Blethering Place Tea Room. "What's a blethering place?" I wondered aloud.

"That's a Scottish expression," Tiffany explained. "It's a place where people gather for gossip and good food."

"Hey, we could ask people there if they know anything about the *Outlaw*."

Tiffany smiled. "Instead of always investigating, Liz, you could help me relax. I am getting so nervous. My wedding is exactly one week away."

People on the sidewalk watched us pass in the red Jeep, and then a beautifully dressed white-haired lady waved, and I returned her sweet smile. She was with a younger woman in an elegant outfit.

"This is a very nice area," I said, then turned to Tiffany to discuss something that had been on my mind. "I've been thinking—maybe Cambridge has been stealing artwork from Thirteen Oaks. He's got a background as an artist, so he'd know the value of the stuff."

"But Cambridge has been with the family forever. Why would he do something like that?"

I shrugged. "Could be he needs the money." It was amazing what people would do for money, I'd learned in my years of investigating.

Soon we reached Dallas Road, where a sleek cruise ship moved splendidly past on the sparkly blue ocean. In the distance, the snow-capped Olympic Mountains added grace and majesty to the scene. It was hard to believe that so recently we'd faced danger on those same waters.

Parking spots near Moss Street were at a premium, but Tiffany deftly manoeuvred the Jeep into a tiny place. Jumping out, we gazed at a welcoming scene. Sunshine splattered down through leafy trees—all along the street, artists were at work, while spectators strolled from easel to easel, sculpture to sculpture.

The atmosphere was pleasant. A girl with a French

horn played a love song, while young children passed by, their faces painted to resemble clowns and cats. The houses had wonderful gardens—one place reminded me of Snow White. Somehow I could just picture her, looking down from the tiny upstairs window with its leaded-glass panes and little curved roof.

After wandering for a while, we purchased lemonade from some kids and then joined a crowd watching a woman at work on her canvas. "The painting must have movement," she explained to us. "Without movement, art is nothing."

A yellow butterfly drifted past. I watched its serene passage through the warm air—then stared in shock.

"Tiff," I exclaimed. "Look who it is."

* * *

"It's him," Tiffany said. "From the storm."

We'd last seen this guy running through the waves as they crashed ashore on Dallas Road. He was one of the artists, and sat working on a canvas. His work was certainly impressive; several large canvases of B.C. scenery were on display. My personal favourite showed emerald forests sweeping down through a mountain valley. I longed to visit that place.

"How much?" I asked, smiling at the handsome blond artist.

He grinned. "For you, it would cost nothing. But unfortunately, it's from my private collection. This one's not for sale."

"My name is Liz," I said, "and this is my best friend, Tiffany Wright."

"I'm William. It's nice to know you."

"Well," I said reluctantly, "we'd better move along. I'm sure other fans want to talk with you."

"Hey, don't go." William studied me with his large, green eyes. "You know, my cousin has been showing my art today. I've been at my studio, working on a rush assignment—for real money, I might add. Anyway, I'm just here for an hour while my cousin gets a break. Luckily, it's the hour when you passed by."

I blushed.

"We're from Winnipeg," Tiffany explained to William, "but I'll be living here now. I'm getting married at Craigdarroch Castle."

"That's a cool place for a wedding." William turned to me. "It's totally out of the Victorian age. It's got stained-glass windows and a tower with an unforgettable view of the city. Hollywood producers have used the castle in some movies. The ballroom dancing in *Little Women*, for example."

"With Winona Ryder?"

"That's the one."

I examined William's artistry with admiration. "You're really talented. But you're, like, so young."

He smiled shyly. "My teacher says I have a gift, but I need to work, work, work. It's difficult, you know, trying to be an artist and also earn a living. When I'm not painting I'm on a Kabuki Kab, earning money for art lessons and supplies."

William told us about his admiration for Emily Carr. "My teacher is an expert on her," he explained. "Robert says some of Victoria is essentially unchanged from the days when Emily Carr lived here. You can walk the same streets, paint the same scenes."

I was dying to tell William about the theft of Emily Carr's unknown masterpiece from Thirteen Oaks, but of course I couldn't. Instead I asked, "What's her art worth?"

"Plenty," William replied. "There was an auction recently for one of her pieces called *War Canoes, Alert Bay*. It fetched more than a million dollars."

"Yikes."

"For more than 20 years Emily Carr struggled to earn money, and had little time for her art. She raised sheepdogs and operated a small apartment house."

William told us about Emily Carr's monkey named Woo, and how she'd take Woo for walks in a baby carriage. "Some people called her eccentric—but artists can be difficult to understand. Our challenge is to capture the essence of life, and that's a tall order."

"You're passionate about it," I said.

"Liz, my art is everything." Then William smiled. "Perhaps I'll see you again." He scribbled his phone number on a piece of paper. "Call me sometime, okay?"

"Sure," I replied, feeling amazed and happy.

Walking on, Tiff and I discussed William in detail. "He's going to be famous," I predicted. Then I grabbed Tiffany's arm. "Look, there's Hart. Who's his pretty friend?"

"I don't know." Tiff stared daggers in her direction. "Hart told me there's no one special in his life."

I glanced at Tiff. "You sound miffed."

"I doubt it."

"Methinks the lady doth protest too much."

Spotting us, Hart hurried over. "Tiff and Liz, please meet my cousin, Lorna Taft—she's arrived early for the wedding. Lorna's from Terrace, in northern B.C."

"Your cousin?" Tiff said, sounding relieved.

"Is the north a cool place to live?" I asked.

"You bet," Lorna laughed. "Especially in January."

I noticed a warm smile pass between Hart and Tiff. "We're going to visit Craigdarroch Castle," Hart explained.

Lorna nodded. "I want to see the castle where you're getting married, Tiffany."

"Come with us," Hart suggested. "The castle's a short walk from here."

"We'd love to go with you," Tiffany responded with great enthusiasm.

Chatting together, we walked through the festive Rockland neighbourhood. Every type had come for the Paint-In: grandmas and grandpas, parents and kids, yuppies and hippies, all having fun. Passing by the elegant houses, I daydreamed about being a famous artist who lived in Victoria and was adored by all.

Then the castle appeared, looming high above us. "The castle's Scottish name means 'Rocky Oak Place,'" Hart explained to us. "It was built for a man who got rich operating coal mines. Back then, the castle was surrounded by 28 acres of meadows with many Garry oaks and an artificial lake. It must have been so beautiful."

"The castle's still impressive," I said, staring at the

granite walls and tall chimneys. I could just imagine a princess brushing her hair at one of the arched windows, or gazing down at her curly-haired swain from a balcony far above.

"It's like we're in Scotland. I love the red-tiled roof."

We purchased admission tickets, then stepped into the opulent luxury of the Victorian era. Ahead was an enormous sandstone fireplace; a scene was carved inside. "Those are players in an opera by Wagner," Hart told us. "Much of the castle remains exactly the same as when the Dunsmuirs lived here. Just imagine—this place has 17 fireplaces."

"A life of abundance," his cousin commented.

Hart nodded. "The Victorians lived in a luxurious world of leather-bound books, Tiffany paperweights, stained-glass windows, and pianos by Steinway."

A wooden staircase spiralled above us to an alcove, where I could see a bouquet of flowers on an organ under a stained-glass window. "My father admires James Dunsmuir," Tiffany told us, "because of the power and prestige he commanded. That's why Daddy insists that I get married in Dunsmuir's castle." Her red lips pouted. "I was hoping for a church."

Tiff turned to me. "One of James Dunsmuir's daughters had 30 bridesmaids and flower girls— there's a picture upstairs of her wedding day."

Next we studied the drawing room. It featured a lovely chandelier, its crystals glittering blue like the sea and red like the most exquisite of rubies. In exactly one week Tiffany would be married here; the ceremony was planned for the evening, after the castle had closed to the public. Not for the first time, a wave of uneasiness passed over me as I thought of the wedding.

6

That evening Paris and Tiffany went out for supper. I
summoned my courage and phoned William. My heart
was beating hard, and I hoped I wouldn't sound too
anxious.

To my relief, William was happy to hear from me.
"I was just reading the newspaper," I said, my voice
trembling. "There's a special lantern ceremony
tonight. It starts at eight." I took a deep breath. "Care
to go with me?"

"You bet," William replied. "I've been working
hard and I could use a break."

"Wonderful."

We arranged to meet at a bus stop on Toronto Street
in the James Bay neighbourhood. Stepping from the
bus, I saw William waiting. He wore a "Kabuki Kabs"

T-shirt and long khaki shorts, and had a string of small shells around his neck. It felt so good to see him.

We walked south on Government Street, getting to know each other. "I've been worried about my mom," William told me. "Lately her bronchitis is so bad. I want Mom to spend time in Arizona, because of the dry air." William smiled happily. "The project I'm working on will pay for getting her to Arizona for the winter. What a relief."

We were walking past wooden houses that dated back to pioneer days. We admired the gingerbread decorations on Emily Carr's childhood home, then watched tourists pass in a graceful carriage pulled by a big horse.

"What's the story on this lantern ceremony?" William asked.

"It's apparently a tradition that began in Japan," I replied. "People are launching lanterns in paper boats to honour those who died when nuclear weapons ended the last world war."

"Now I remember—I heard about this on the radio. The boats are released on the water, while everyone prays for world peace. Right?"

I nodded. "It sounds very moving."

A lot of people had gathered beside a large, round pond. Many kids were there, carrying paper boats they'd made. A swallow darted past, moving fast in the gathering dusk; beyond the Sooke Hills, wispy clouds turned orange as the sun disappeared for the night.

William and I listened to speeches from a Japanese lady and a man wearing a white beret. Then a street person emerged from the darkness, wrapped in an old blanket, and disrupted the ceremony by making loud comments in a voice slurred by booze. People shifted uneasily, but nothing happened until William left my side and approached the man.

They spoke quietly, then William returned to me. The drunk said nothing more during the remaining speeches and the launching of the paper boats on the pond. Some were beautifully decorated, while others displayed only the single word *Peace* on their sails. Inside each boat, a candle burned; filled with light, the boats drifted together and then apart. Some people wept, while others closed their eyes in prayer.

After the ceremony ended, I looked at William. "That was wonderful. But what happened with that guy? You totally silenced him."

William shrugged. "I explained the importance of the ceremony. He understood."

I looked for the man, but he was gone.

William glanced at his watch. "Liz, I've got to run. I've really got to get back to work."

I was disappointed. I wondered if William was secretly a workaholic, but I didn't say anything.

He smiled with those big, green eyes. "My project must get finished, Liz. I have to deliver within days." He touched my arm. "I shouldn't have come out tonight. But I wanted to see you."

"Well, I understand. Perhaps we'll meet again?"

William nodded. "You'd better believe it."

* * *

Asleep that night, I thought I heard my cell phone ring. "William's calling," I mumbled to myself, stumbling around the room in search of the phone.

But the call was only a dream—I realized the phone had never rung. "Oh, William," I whispered, wandering to the window to gaze at the moon. "Are you thinking of me?"

In the morning I was anxious to tell Tiffany about William, but she'd gone downtown with the maid of honour. "Wedding errands," Pepper explained, as we ate breakfast together. "Tiff gave you the day off."

I yawned, still sleepy. "Maybe I'll phone William for a chat."

"Who's he?"

"This guy I met. Pepper, he's so cool. I hope you'll meet him."

"Feel like going to the park?" Pepper asked. "I'm taking Amanda to visit the Children's Zoo and see the ducks."

"Let's do it," I replied. "It's fun being with you."

I phoned William, but got his machine. *Please leave a message*, his recorded voice requested pleasantly, but I didn't. I knew I shouldn't be bothering William while he worked on his project.

The day was rainy, so the park was almost empty and virtually silent, except for the distant sound of slow-moving traffic. Above us, an eagle soared past. I wandered the pathways with Pepper, who had rain-proofed Amanda in her stroller. The flower beds were beautifully planted with many wonderful flowers. Many trees were *huge*.

"Emily Carr loved this place," Pepper said.

"Look." I pointed up at a huge nest. "There's a heron."

We watched the heron spread an enormous wing for a careful cleaning, then it lifted off from the nest. After a couple of flaps, the heron sailed gracefully down across a small lake to land near an elderly man who was feeding ducks from his park bench.

"Let's get closer," Pepper suggested.

Near a path beside the lake, we took shelter under a weeping willow. "This is more mist than rain," I whispered, watching it collect on leaves to form chubby raindrops that plopped to the ground.

We watched the man tossing birdseed to the noisy ducks crowded all around. His wooden cane was hooked over the park bench. My heart melted at the sweetness of the scene—until the man produced a package of cigarettes and lit up!

Shaking my head, I walked away with Pepper and Amanda. At Fountain Lake we stopped to watch ducks paddling in search of food amongst a carpet of lily pads. The petals of their flowers were pure white; each encircled at its heart a burst of yellow, as though the sun lived there.

"Even on a cloudy day," Pepper said, "that glow can warm your soul."

I watched a white-haired lady pass by, chatting happily with a younger man. Then I smiled fondly at Amanda, who was fascinated by the ducks. "Isn't it difficult, coping with a child? I mean, you're so young."

"Well, the servants help a lot."

"Any regrets?"

Pepper shook her head. "Amanda was born on February 14, and she'll always be my favourite Valentine. But I tell you, Liz, getting dates is tough. Lots of guys don't want a kid around."

At that moment the sun broke through the clouds, and as the day became warmer, steam began rising from the pathways. Drawn by the sound of music, we came upon an outdoor bandstand. A pretty woman with long hair was on the stage with her band, entertaining an appreciative audience seated on benches. *Music for the Trees,* read a banner behind the band. *Send a message of love to B.C.'s trees.*

We stopped to listen. Pepper and I were both impressed by the singer; I loved the idea of music serenading the trees.

"Maybe I could sign her to a contract," Pepper said. "You know, when I'm a music producer. It won't be long now."

After the concert we walked to the Inner Harbour, where Cambridge was waiting with the Daimler outside the Empress. Pepper got into the limo with Amanda, but I decided against returning to Thirteen Oaks. "You see that boat with the big sign?" I said to Pepper. "They offer a three-hour sail. I think I'll get a ticket. What a perfect day for riding the ocean waves."

We said goodbye, then I crossed Government to the Inner Harbour. There was a nice hum of activity, what with the boaters and buskers and lots of tourists. A nice-looking guy approached, smiling. It was Fossilized Pete, who'd taken us to the West Bay Marina.

"How'd that turn out?" Pete asked, after we'd exchanged hellos.

"We found the *Outlaw*."

Pete looked surprised. "Tell me more."

I decided not to mention Jason by name, but did describe his boat escaping into the night. I also told Pete about the drunk. When I finished my story, Pete smiled. "You know Laura Singlehurst, eh? She's a friend of mine. I saw Laura the other night—she was looking for someone named Pepper. She mentioned you."

We chatted for a few minutes, and then I said good-bye to Pete and climbed on board the boat. It was the *Thayne*, a 17-metre gaff-rigged ketch (as the captain told me). About a dozen tourists waited on the deck, and I said hello while searching for somewhere to sit. From below came the smell of fuel; a dinghy with an outboard was attached to the stern.

The captain was young and friendly. "We'll use the sails, once we've left port. This schooner was hand-built from bits of old Victoria houses, so it's got some nice vibes."

As we left port, I waved at people in a harbour ferry, then turned my face to the sun. As always, the water was heavy with vessels; on shore, people watched our passage from an oceanside pathway. I saw joggers and cyclists passing before some large buildings.

"Those are condos and townhouses," our captain explained to me. "It's a nice location, but the seaplanes can get noisy."

"Be careful your captain's cap doesn't blow off," I warned him, as the wind gusted briefly.

"Huh?"

"If your hat blows overboard, you're marked for drowning."

He grinned. "Hey, you're superstitious. Just like my wife."

We glided past a Coast Guard station, then a gigantic cruise ship moored at a wharf where a really big mural welcomed people to Victoria. "Cruise ships visit here every summer," our captain said. "This is a favourite stop on their journey to Alaska."

"I'd love to get on board." I felt smaller than an ant, staring up at the balconies on the many decks.

Out on the open sea, large orange sails were unfurled. Finding them, the breezes sent our vessel running swiftly forward. It was so quiet, with just the wind in our ears. One passenger felt seasick, but our captain told him to keep watching the horizon, and that seemed to help.

"Look," someone cried, pointing to starboard. "There's an orca, right beside us."

What a thrilling sight. For several minutes the whale swam near us, its dorsal fin, white "flash" and immense black body glistening each time it emerged from beneath the surface. "Sometimes this happens once we've turned off the engine," the captain told us. "There's no noise to frighten the orcas, and people say they're naturally friendly."

The captain watched me take some more photos of the beautiful whale. "Are you using colour film?"

"Sure."

"But why?" He grinned. "The orca's in black and white."

I chuckled at his joke. "Okay to use your binoculars?" I asked.

He passed me powerful Zeiss-Ikons. I trained them

on the distant Victoria shoreline, hoping to spot the *Outlaw* prowling along. I needed a break in the case, something to help crack it wide open. But luck wasn't with me.

The mysterious craft was nowhere to be seen.

* * *

On Monday I went downtown by bus. The sun was hot but the air was pleasantly free of humidity as I walked to the Cyber Station.

Inside its cool depths, I asked to use a computer terminal. There was something about Paris that had been niggling at me. I could have used a computer at Thirteen Oaks, but I needed to work away from prying eyes.

Lots of people sat at the terminals; some were tourists, speaking together in foreign languages as they read e-mail messages or surfed the Net. I read the news from my family and friends, answered everyone, then checked the Tourism Victoria Website for the name Sandown. Sure enough I found something, and soon had tracked down the truth about Bigoted Earl.

* * *

I was feeling pleased with myself as I rode beside Tiffany in the Jeep. We were heading out of Victoria on West Saanich Road, which wandered amid thick stands of trees and past scenic homes and small farms. Our destination was known only to me.

Tiffany glanced my way. "You're certain this mystery trip is necessary, Liz? I'm very busy, you know."

"Yes, yes, I do know. But you're going to see something important. Just follow my directions."

Eventually we approached a parking lot filled with vehicles. Beyond them, a large wooden grandstand rose into the air. We could hear loud cries from the spectators.

"What's this place?" Tiff asked.

"Sandown," I replied triumphantly. "It's a track. Horses race here. One's called Bigoted Earl, and it's running today." Before Tiffany could respond, I punched numbers into my cell phone. When a man answered, I gave him a short message.

"Now let's see what happens," I said to Tiffany. "This should be good."

* * *

A few minutes later, Paris came out of the grandstand. I waved at him, and he hurried forward. Then he saw Tiffany, and his face turned pale.

"Tiffany, why are you here? Liz told me there was an emergency, but she never mentioned your name."

Tiffany's blue eyes stared at Paris; she seemed confused and frightened.

He scowled at me. "I knew you'd betray me to Tiff."

"Well," I said briskly, "why not confess? You've been gambling money at Sandown Raceway. Today you're betting on Bigoted Earl, right?"

Tiffany was totally shocked. "Well, Paris?"

"I guess . . . I guess it's true."

I waited for Tiffany to throw her engagement ring at

his feet. Instead, she did nothing—absolutely nothing.

Then Paris said, "Listen, Tiff, how about a loan? I've got inside information on the race. Bigoted Earl can't fail. Let's win this one together."

I was shocked and appalled. Then, to my horror, Tiffany nodded her agreement. "Okay, I guess. But only this time, all right?"

Paris grinned. "You bet. Thanks, sweetheart."

Tiffany handed Paris a bunch of cash. As she did, my heart almost broke. What did the future hold for a girl as sweet and trusting as Tiff?

* * *

As I feared, Bigoted Earl ran out of the money. The horse was a loser, just like Paris. He stayed for more races, but we left the raceway.

"Tiffany," I pleaded, as we walked to the Jeep, "don't lend him more money. He'll just gamble it away."

"Paris needs me, Liz."

"He needs your bank account!"

"Since his father's death, I've been his constant strength."

Once again, I gave up. At Thirteen Oaks we collected Pepper, then headed to the Artful Needle for a dress fitting. After that we continued downtown for more errands. Tiff parked the Jeep at the Eaton Centre, a large mall with a British theme, and we wandered along tourist-thronged Government Street. Then I glanced east and saw that people had gathered at a nearby street.

We hurried to join the crowd. "What's going on?" Tiff asked a bicycle cop who was on traffic duty. "Is this the marathon for charity? I read about it in the newspaper."

She nodded. "A run across Canada is ending today in Victoria. The guy will pass here in a few minutes, heading for Mile Zero at the ocean."

"What charity is the runner supporting?" Pepper asked.

"This guy wants to help abused kids," the officer replied. "He was assaulted himself—by his coach when he played junior hockey. He kept the secret all through his years as an NHL player, but eventually he told and the coach went to prison."

"Telling takes such courage," Tiffany said. "It's so cool that he turned his problem into a way to help others. I like kids—I wish I could help."

She got her chance when we put donations into a can carried by a volunteer. All around us, people were cheering as the runner approached. He was young and handsome, and tears were streaming from his eyes. I started to cry, and so did the others, as everyone applauded the runner and shouted praise.

Then he was gone, trailed by TV cameras and media photographers and kids on bikes. Returning to Government Street, Tiffany talked nonstop about the runner's accomplishments. "Imagine telling on your coach. They're such authority figures, right? I mean, where'd he find the courage?"

"By taking one step at a time," Pepper replied.

7

Tiff dropped me in the Cook Street Village. I'd looked up William's address in the phone book, and decided to walk past. Just in case he was around—you know? But also because I was curious to see his home.

Thick, beautiful chestnut trees sheltered Cook Street. There was a fish and chips shop, a stationer, some food stores, and several of those ubiquitous West Coast coffee shops. I noticed a small low-rider truck pass by, throbbing with music; the driver was hidden behind tinted windows. The truck carried Washington plates.

I remembered William accepting money from someone in a similar truck, perhaps even this one. I wondered who the driver was.

Soon after, I reached William's address. He lived

near the park in a three-storey house divided into apartments. Big steps led to the building's front door. William sat on the steps.

He looked exhausted. As I approached, he hardly seemed to recognize me. Then William folded a thick envelope and stuck it away in his jeans pocket. "Hi, Liz," he said, managing a smile. "I'm so beat. I've been working around the clock."

"You got paid?"

"Yeah. Now I can send Mom to Arizona. I tell you . . ."

William stopped speaking. His eyes stared past me, down to the street corner. I followed his gaze, and saw the truck with Washington plates. William watched the truck pass by, but said nothing. When it was gone, he turned to me. "Liz, I'm dead tired. See you another time, okay?"

I was disappointed but not surprised. I'm familiar with workaholics. My dad can get totally absorbed during his police investigations, and Mom's often consumed by her cases.

I said goodnight to William and went home by bus.

* * *

I was feeling sorry for myself, but a surprise invitation soon cheered me up. Laura Singlehurst had phoned Thirteen Oaks, wanting everyone to join her at Butchart Gardens for an evening picnic.

"She especially asked for you, Liz," Pepper said, as we got ready. "There are fireworks tonight. It gets chilly after dark, so bring something warm to wear."

"Why the invitation?" I asked. "What's the occasion?"

Pepper grinned. "Who knows? Who cares?"

Tiffany stayed home with tummy problems. The rest of us piled into the Daimler; with Cambridge at the wheel, we drove north out of Victoria to Butchart Gardens.

Laura met us at the entrance. We all thanked her for the surprise, and she smiled happily. "Have you ever visited Butchart Gardens?" she asked me.

I shook my head.

"For flower lovers," Laura said, "this place is heaven on earth. There are thousands and thousands of blossoms, and they're so fragrant."

"Still nothing heard about the ransom?" Paris asked Laura.

"Not a word. The kid has gone silent. We still don't know exactly what he wants."

"I'm getting nervous," Paris said. "Maybe I should inform the police. I simply can't lose the Emily Carr— Dad treasured it."

"You're a bit late calling 911," I commented disapprovingly. "The painting could be anywhere by now— some crooked collector may have bought it."

Paris glared at me but said nothing. He was in a sulky mood, and I wished he'd stayed home.

Hart knew a lot about Butchart Gardens. "They were created by a remarkable woman named Jennie Butchart," he explained. "She loved adventures, like horseback riding and hot-air ballooning, but mostly she loved her gardens."

Hart pointed at an attractive, old-fashioned house surrounded by flowers. "Long ago, the family lived in that house. All around was the Butchart quarry, where limestone was dug to make cement."

He turned to a nearby vista of flowering plants, shrubs, and evergreens. "Jennie Butchart didn't like her view of the cement works. She planted gardens and trees to hide it, then she filled the abandoned quarries with gardens. She had a great talent for design. Pretty soon she was famous, and everyone came visiting."

Hart smiled. "In 1915 Jennie Butchart served 15,000 cups of tea to visitors. Her gardens became more and more popular, and now there's got to be easily a million visitors every year. It's beautiful here at Christmas, with the lights sparkling everywhere, but personally I love the summertime fireworks concerts. There's one tonight—they are amazing events."

"Concerts?" I said. "You mean, like a band has a concert?"

"Kind of," Hart replied. "We'll be watching fireworks set to music."

Cambridge returned from the gardens' dining room, carrying a picnic basket full of gourmet goodies Laura had ordered especially for the occasion. "We'll be eating soon," Laura promised us.

We posed for a picture with the picnic basket beside a giant boar fashioned from bronze. "Why's his nose so shiny?" I asked.

"People touch the statue for good luck," Laura explained.

"I could use some good luck," Pepper muttered, vigorously rubbing the boar's nose.

The comment caused Laura to glance at Pepper, but she said nothing.

A path beneath cedars and Douglas firs led to a lookout above the Sunken Garden. We leaned over a railing, amazed at the visual splendour spread out below. "This was a quarry," Hart explained. "Limestone from here was used to make cement. See the tall chimney in the distance? It's all that remains of the cement factory. The ivy on the quarry walls was part of Jennie Butchart's vision."

Laura looked at us. "My aunt says that Jennie used to be lowered by rope into the quarry with seeds and tools, then she spent the day creating her gardens."

"Look at that enormous dahlia," I exclaimed. "It's like a soccer ball—it's colossal."

"Wait till you see the Rose Garden," Hart said. "The West Coast has a perfect climate for growing roses. They love it here."

We watched the dancing waters of a pretty fountain located deep within the walls of the former quarry. Then we followed a pathway to grassy lawns where a large crowd was gathering for the fireworks.

"There's got to be three thousand people here," I exclaimed, with a whistle of astonishment. "Are the fireworks that good?"

Hart smiled. "Wait and see. They start at dusk."

Finding our way through the crowd, we located some open grass and spread out blankets. We were totally surrounded by beautiful flowers and many vibrant shades of green. It was a festive scene. I noticed flash cameras popping all over the crowd. People were having a good time together, their buzzing voices making them sound like a convention of gossiping locusts.

The scrumptious picnic was spread out, photographed, and drooled over. Then we dove at the food. My favourite was probably the chilled prawns with pesto mayonnaise, or maybe the teriyaki chicken, but *everything* was a fantastic taste sensation.

Since the fireworks wouldn't start until dusk, we played card games and read books. I was totally involved in a creepy tale when Pepper touched my shoulder, making me jump.

"I'm going to the snack bar, Liz. Come with me, okay?"

"Sure thing," I replied, reluctantly closing the book at an extremely suspenseful scene.

The delicate lights of Japanese lanterns shone close to the forest. The night was closing in, and I crossed my fingers for luck—a frequent habit of mine. We found our way through the chattering crowds, and then, at the snack bar, I got a surprise. A young guy behind the counter said, "You're Liz Austen, right?"

"Sure, but how'd you know?"

"Somebody left an envelope for you, and described your looks. They were right—you're gorgeous."

"Out of three thousand people," I said doubtfully, "you recognized me?"

"Well . . ."

"Come on, Liz," Pepper said impatiently. "Take the envelope, and let's get going. Otherwise we'll miss the fireworks."

"Okay," I replied.

My name was on the envelope; inside was a brief message written in emerald ink. *Liz*, it said, *Meet me at the Japanese Garden at exactly 10 tonight. Please don't be late. Don't tell anyone—this is very important.*

The message was signed with a single letter. My

heart skipped a beat when I saw it. It was a W—as in William.

* * *

As we returned to the others, slowly finding our way past the many blankets and lawn chairs, I glanced at Pepper. "You gave that guy at the snack bar a big tip. I guess you liked him."

She shrugged. "He was okay."

Pepper didn't ask about my message, and I didn't volunteer any information. I was confused by what it said, and needed time to think.

Our blankets were on a slope, facing a small lake. Beyond the water, the forest was silhouetted against a pale orange sky. Looking up, I searched for stars. Then I smiled at Laura. "Thanks for treating us all to Butchart Gardens. I'll never forget this—it's so lovely here."

"You're very welcome, Liz."

A starburst lit the pale sky. Thousands of voices went *oooooooh*, then everyone cheered as shooting stars exploded above—purple, white, blue, green, red, everything!

From the trees came beautiful music—violins, and the voice of a singer. More fireworks shot above us, then displays suddenly ignited. Multicoloured fountains arose at the lake, twirling sparkles into the night, while a huge golden hive came to life with artificial bees twirling noisily in the night air. Beyond the lake, a colourful train choo-chooed past, as cameras flashed from the crowd. Amazingly, everything was made of fireworks.

"How have they done this?" I exclaimed. "It's magical."

I looked at my watch. Almost 10 o'clock—time to go! "I'll be back soon," I said to Laura. "I've got someone to meet."

She looked surprised. "What's going on?"

I shrugged, trying to appear nonchalant. "I'm, um, meeting someone. I won't be long."

"I'm not so sure . . ."

"Please, Laura. This is important."

"Well, okay, but take my cell phone." Laura handed me a tiny ruby-coloured phone. Then she turned to Paris. "Got your cell here?"

"Yes," he replied.

"If you need us," Laura told me, "push Memory-1 on my cell. Paris will answer."

"Where should we meet?" I asked.

"At the parking lot, following the fireworks. You remember where the Daimler is parked?"

I nodded.

"We'll see you there."

Slowly I found a path through the throng while *ooooooohs* and *ahhhhhhhs* sounded from open mouths, cameras flashed, and deep *booms* echoed from the hills. Leaving the show behind, I was soon alone in the vast central gardens. I looked up at the fireworks and saw whirling colours and fireballs trailing diamonds in their wake, and even a comet burning across the sky.

"Totally cool," I whispered to myself.

The evening smelled of summer; all around, flowers slumbered in their beds. As I followed signposts along a cinder pathway, I discovered places where invisible pools of warm air had gathered, filled with sweet fragrances. Half expecting to meet the ghost of Jennie Butchart wandering her earthly paradise, I finally reached the Japanese Garden. Lights shone on delicate plants, and water trickled between ponds where small statues represented pagodas.

Where was William? I felt very alone, and was glad that Laura had provided her cell phone. Was this some kind of hoax? As I hesitated, wondering what to do, I heard my name.

Liz, a voice called from the trees. *Liz! Liz!*

* * *

I squinted, looking for movement. Light flashed—once, twice, three times. I was confused for a moment, then realized I was looking at reflectors on the heels of someone's joggers.

Someone who was running down a path, away from me.

I quickly followed. The path sloped down, following a zigzag pattern lower and lower through the trees. I became aware of the ocean's salty smell, and I could hear waves slapping against the shore.

The roar of an engine split the night. I was startled by the noise, but pressed on. Moments later, I reached the ocean. The path ended at a wooden dock. Out on the water I saw a boat zooming away under the stars; no name was visible. At the controls was a figure, impossible to identify.

A surprise awaited me—lying on the dock was a metal tube. "Wait a minute," I exclaimed to myself.

"The thief at Thirteen Oaks put *Klee Wyck* inside a tube just like this."

I opened the tube at one end. Something was in there. Working quickly, I soon was able to remove a painting and unroll it. To my utter astonishment, I found myself gazing at a picture of a woman with a laughing face.

"Wow," I exclaimed. "This is the missing painting! This is *Klee Wyck*."

* * *

Seconds later I punched Memory-1 on the cell phone. When Paris answered, I immediately asked for Laura. "Guess what?" I exclaimed, and quickly told the news.

"We'll be right there," Laura said. "Guard that painting."

I heard Paris yelp, "What painting?" followed by dead air. Switching off the phone, I contemplated the laughing face of *Klee Wyck*. How wonderful that she'd been found!

Voices soon approached through the trees, then I saw Hart and the others. Pushing Laura aside, Paris hurried forward to grab the painting from my hands. "Amazing," he exclaimed. "This is marvellous. *Klee Wyck* has actually been returned."

"But why give back the painting?" Laura demanded. "It doesn't make sense."

"I guess that kid got cold feet and decided to abandon the thing." Paris kissed the painting. "I'm so happy. This ranks with the time I hit the jackpot at Vegas. No—it's even better."

Laura turned to me. "Liz, what happened?"

They listened to my story, then Laura smiled. "You deserve a reward. Don't you agree, Paris?"

"I guess you're right, Laura. Liz did find the painting."

"But why me?" I said. "Why the voice calling my name, and why the message in the envelope? What's going on? Nothing makes sense."

"Who cares," Paris exclaimed happily. "I've got my painting back. That's what matters."

Hart looked at him. "It's *our* painting, Paris. It belongs to the family."

"Okay, sure." Paris looked around at us. "Remember, you're sworn to secrecy. Keep a tight lid on this, okay?"

* * *

On Tuesday evening, Paris summoned a family gathering in the library at Thirteen Oaks. He wanted everyone to see the *Klee Wyck*, safely returned to its place above the fireplace.

Laura Singlehurst was there, looking glorious in a spectacular fashion creation. Major Wright also attended, which was a surprise. Somehow he'd learned the truth about the brief disappearance of *Klee Wyck*.

I stood beside Tiff, admiring Emily Carr's painting; the totems and the longhouses were captured with such artistry. I smiled, looking at the spirited face of the Laughing One, then I snapped out of my revery when Paris began shouting at Hart.

"I told you—*no way*." I stared at Paris—a vein bulged at his temple.

"We do not involve the police. Not now, not ever."

"But things don't add up, Paris. Why steal the painting, then return it?"

"It would be hard to make money with a stolen painting," Laura suggested. "Maybe the thief gave up trying."

Paris nodded. "I agree with Laura. Jason stole the wrong thing."

"If so," Hart responded, "he'll be back, looking for the right thing. I agree with Liz—something is rotten in the state of Denmark."

"Huh?" Paris said. "What's that mean?"

"It's nothing," Hart replied disdainfully. "Forget it."

Paris laughed. "Hart, you are such a fool."

Laura looked at the deMornay brothers. "In my opinion, don't involve the police. What are your thoughts, Major Wright?"

The Major focused his attention on the family circle. "I agree with Miss Singlehurst and Paris. We can't risk informing the police. Liz Austen's got a hyperactive imagination. Everyone in Winnipeg knows that."

Tiffany turned to the Major, annoyed. "Liz and her brother are famous crime-busters, Daddy."

"Tiffany, this is not a crime. The painting is hanging on the wall, in front of our eyes. Let's stay focused— we can't let anything spoil my daughter's romantic wedding."

Glancing into the dark hallway, I saw the butler. Cambridge lurked in the shadows, listening to every word. Noticing my stare, however, he hastily entered the library with refreshments on a wheeled trolley.

* * *

The gathering broke up soon afterward, with Paris ordering us to remain silent about anything involving Emily Carr's unknown masterpiece.

"Let's keep this in the family," he said, repeating one of his favourite arguments.

Later that evening, Tiff and I were still in the library. The security lasers were off; Hart had promised to return later to enter the code. (After the theft Paris had changed the code from 7-7-6-6, a classic example of closing the barn door too late.) Hart and the others had scattered to distant corners of the moody old mansion, leaving us alone with *Klee Wyck*.

"It's good Emily Carr went to those villages," I said, studying the painting, "so we've got her take on British Columbia long ago. I wish I could have met her."

Tiff shivered. "I'd be scared the monkey would bite."

I wandered around the bookshelves, studying the titles. The deMornay family liked to read; recent bestsellers shared the shelves with some really old books.

"This is a history of Thirteen Oaks," I told Tiff, selecting a mouldy oldy from the shelf. "Hey, look. There's a map of the estate in here. Maybe we could learn something."

I settled down on a leather sofa to read. But moments later, Pepper rushed into the library. "Liz, Tiff. Put down that book and come quickly!"

Tossing it down, I jumped to my feet. The three of us hurried into the dark hallway.

"I've looked everywhere for you," Pepper said. "There's been a message from that guy Jason. From the *Outlaw*."

"That's amazing," I exclaimed.

We hurried through the old mansion. "We're going to the family office," Pepper explained. "Jason said to wait at the office, and he'd call back. It's you he's calling, Liz."

* * *

A long time passed while I paced back and forth in the office. I kept thinking about Jason's call—what could it mean?

"I'll make some lemonade," Pepper eventually offered, leaving for the kitchen.

When she returned, we glugged down the delicious, cold beverage. Then I stood up. "Forget Jason—he was pulling a hoax. It's time for bed."

"Are you sure?" Pepper asked.

"Yes—I'm sick of this. I'm going to the library to get that history of the estate. I need some bedtime reading."

The laser beams were still down at the library. I was looking forward to reading about Thirteen Oaks, but instead I got a surprise.

The book was gone.

8

I searched the library, but found nothing. The next day I returned with Pepper, and we both tried, again without success.

"This is so weird," I said, as we sat with glasses of lemonade. "First the painting disappears, and now a book. What gives?"

Pepper shook her head. "It beats me."

Later, driving downtown in the Jeep, I debated telling Tiffany about the Curious Incident of the Book in the Night. Only three days remained until her wedding, and Tiff was sometimes very agitated. Finally I decided against mentioning the book. Tiff looked tense, and I didn't want anything else to bother her.

We met Paris downtown at Ming's for a delicious Chinese meal with friends of theirs. I was the fifth wheel, but I didn't mind—I liked the other couple and, anyway, William had called, and I'd be seeing him later that evening. Nothing could bother me.

I have to admit that Paris was good for Tiff when she was moody. He whispered sweet nothings in her ear, and soon she was cheerful again. Leaving them at the table, I went to the washroom with their friend, Jennifer Scriver.

"Have you known Paris long?" I asked, as we combed our hair in front of the mirror.

Jennifer nodded. "I went to Shawnigan Lake School, same as Paris and Tiffany. He was a fun guy, but something's gone wrong."

"Meaning what?"

Jennifer looked at me in the mirror. "Paris went from grief about his dad to reckless behaviour. Now he's unstable, and looking for security. Someone to cling to."

"And Tiff is rock solid."

"You bet," Jennifer said. "Tiffany knows exactly what she wants—marriage and a family. She's also got a bank account. For Paris, it's the perfect package."

* * *

As we left the restaurant, Paris took Tiffany aside. I could see her shaking her head, then finally she frowned and handed him some money. Paris waved goodbye to me, and walked away with the other couple.

"They're heading for Sandown Raceway," Tiff said glumly. "I refused to go."

"I'm visiting William," I said. "Come with me. You need cheering up."

"You're sure William won't mind?"

"I doubt it."

I was right—William welcomed us warmly. His funky place was filled with objects and art that hinted at a unique personality. As I roamed the walls, studying everything, Tiff and William chatted in the tiny kitchen.

Heading downstairs, we met William's neighbour in the lobby; Sadie was the singer who'd been at the park, performing a concert for the trees. We enjoyed a friendly chat with her, then went outside.

"Sadie's multi-talented," William told us. "She paints miniatures—very beautiful. You should see the flowers with their tiny petals. Victoria is full of incredible artists."

Behind the house was a garage that William had converted into a studio. Inside, we saw his landscapes—he really loved British Columbia's forests, mountains and oceans. William concentrated on big vistas and filled his scenes with light.

"I love your art," I said. "It's so like Emily Carr."

"I certainly admire her work," William said, "and her courage. She didn't do things the easy way. She got into her canoe, and went out into nature. She went in pursuit of truth—to show the totems in their natural setting, in the forest and the villages, how they really looked. Emily Carr went through tremendous difficulties in pursuit of her art—you can imagine the social pressures against her. That's so admirable for a woman of her time, being brave enough to chase such a beautiful dream."

"I love listening to you," I said.

"That's good, Liz, because—"

A shrill *brrring* shattered the moment. I looked in annoyance at the phone, a paint-smeared relic with a rotary dial.

William picked it up and said, "William speaking."

Frowning, he listened to the caller. "You can have it back," he said angrily. "It's dirty."

Then William stared at the phone. "He hung up."

"Who was it?" I asked.

"No one important," William replied, avoiding my eyes. "Listen, I need a sweater. Wait here, okay? I'll get one from my apartment in the big house."

Tiff and I wandered around the studio, looking at canvases stacked against the walls. Then I stopped at a wooden desk in the corner; scattered across it were some photos, face down.

"I wonder what these are?" I reached toward the nearest photo. "Maybe preliminary studies for William's next project."

Then I heard William's voice. "Don't touch those."

Startled, I turned toward the sound. William stood in the doorway, pointing at me. "Liz, please don't touch those pictures."

"Sure," I replied, raising my hands. "No problem."

William scooped up the photos, dropped them into a drawer, and turned the key. "It's just," he said, pocketing the key, "that I'm . . . very superstitious."

"Me, too," I replied.

"Letting anyone see my next project would be really bad luck. You understand, Liz?"

"Of course." I studied William's handsome face.

His eyes flicked from me to the desk, then back to me.

Was I making a mistake here?

"My uncle works on the pilot boat," William told us. "It's going out tonight and he's invited us along. Care to go?"

We both happily agreed.

"What's a pilot boat?" I asked later from the Jeep's back seat, as Tiff reached Cook Street.

William turned to her. "Let's stop at the Chateau Victoria, and I'll explain."

At the upscale hotel we took an elevator to the 18th floor, where seagulls winged past large windows enclosing a restaurant high above the city streets. It was early evening, and the descending sun made every colour intense. Beyond an assortment of roofs, we saw the green trees of Beacon Hill Park and a big freighter on the beautiful waters of the ocean strait. Visible beneath the mountains on the strait's far side was the city of Port Angeles, Washington.

"Lots of oceangoing vessels pass along this strait," William said. "In these narrow waters they need a nautical pilot on the ship to guide the captain safely through. The pilot is taken out to the vessel from Victoria on board the pilot boat. Uncle Joe is the boat's captain. We're going out as his guests."

"Cool," Tiffany exclaimed. "I need a distraction from all the wedding talk."

"Thanks so much," I said, smiling at William. This time I thought to myself, *He's so nice.*

* * *

Soon we reached Ogden Point, home to the pilot boat. The small vessel was sheltered from storms by a large breakwater, where people strolled as darkness arrived. Scuba divers explored the waters near the breakwater; some had neon glow ropes, which looked eerie shining beneath the surface. Nearby were large wharves; at one was a U.S. navy vessel, in town for a visit.

On board the pilot boat we were introduced to its captain, William's friendly uncle Joe. "A cruise ship named the *Galaxy* is passing by tonight," he explained, "bound for Alaska. We're taking a pilot to board the *Galaxy*, out on the strait."

"Why doesn't it stop in Victoria and collect the pilot before it sails?"

"Not all cruise ships visit here. Some passengers prefer a bigger city like Vancouver, but others find our town very friendly. Some locals even dress up in old-fashioned garb and hand out flowers at the cruise ship wharf. The passengers love that."

"Is your work dangerous?" I asked.

"It can be, especially in a storm. Our boat is mighty small alongside some of those cruise ships."

The pilot boat was indeed small, with an open deck and an enclosed cabin where the pilot was working on some papers. As Uncle Joe started the engine, he pointed at a blue heron standing near the shore. It looked so regal, totally focused on the water as it hungrily awaited a passing meal. "We call that heron Doug," Uncle Joe explained. "Doug's lived in this basin for 23 years."

Reaching open waters, Uncle Joe opened the throttle. A powerful roar sounded from below decks as the boat gathered speed, leaving a plume of spray in its wake. The boat had a solid hull and lots of power, so it moved smoothly through the waves.

Wearing fluorescent life preservers, we stood beside William's uncle on the deck. He was at the wheel, controlling the boat with an effortless grace. Behind us, the lights of Victoria glowed along the shoreline. It was a warm night; stars lit the dark sky as surf rushed away across the restless depths.

I pointed at the Dallas Road cliffs. "I guess that's Beacon Hill Park, up on top. What's the other dark area, farther down Dallas Road? Is that Ross Bay Cemetery, where Emily Carr is buried?"

"Yup," William replied.

"Maybe I'll go visit her grave."

I asked Uncle Joe if he'd seen the *Outlaw*. "The name sounds familiar," he said, looking at my drawing of the mystery boat. He promised to watch for it, then answered more questions about his work. "The worst thing is the fog," he told us. "You can imagine—buried in swirling mists while you're rocking and rolling on heavy seas, trying to park this small craft beside a huge elephant like the *Galaxy*. That can get pretty hair-raising."

"Ever had a man overboard?" William asked.

He nodded. "Pilots have to jump between vessels— sometimes one lands in the drink. But we're quick to save them. We have a safety procedure which we practise frequently."

The cruise ship approached out of the night, glittering with lights. It looked like a birthday cake with every candle glowing, and it was soooo big. My heart pounded with excitement; this was an amazing experience.

We moved in close to the *Galaxy*. It was impossible to see the upper decks, so far above; down at the water level, a large open door awaited the pilot. He wore a shirt and tie, plus a corduroy jacket and tan trousers. As we moved in on the cruise ship, the pilot tensed, ready to leap across the cold waters.

"Now," William exclaimed, as the vessels met. Immediately the pilot sailed through the air, landing nimbly inside the cruise ship. We three cheered and applauded; the grinning pilot bowed deeply, as Uncle Joe powered our vessel away from the *Galaxy*.

"Gosh," I said dreamily, watching the cruise ship's radiant lights twinkle away into the night. "That is such a vision."

* * *

The next morning I awoke long before dawn. Unable to sleep, I went to the kitchen. Cambridge was already there, moodily preparing coffee. Outside the window, birdsong heralded the coming day. "They're up early," I commented, glancing into the garden. "What a sweet sound they make."

A grunt was the butler's only reply. I pressed on, determined to remain cheerful. "Do local buses run this early?"

He glanced at the clock. "Yes, Miss Austen."

"How would I catch a bus to Dallas Road? I'm thinking of walking the cliffs, then visiting Emily Carr's grave."

The butler's shaggy eyebrows rose. "Why Emily Carr?"

I shrugged. "I'm a fan."

Cambridge disappeared from the room, then returned with a well-thumbed paperback. "This is the John Adams guide to Ross Bay Cemetery," he told me. "Take it with you—there are lots of fascinating stories about the people in that cemetery. It dates back to 1873, so you'll find the graves of many famous types. The quirky ones usually have the best stories. Like Emily Carr, for example."

"Thanks, Cambridge. You're very kind."

"It's no problem," he replied. "You see—"

Cambridge was interrupted by a plaintive *meow*. Opening the outside door, he looked down at a scrawny cat with ragged fur. "This stray's been coming by for food," Cambridge said, preparing a dish of leftovers, as the waif rubbed around his ankles, purring. "My brother owns a pet store in the Fairfield Plaza. He's always pleading with people—don't give pets as Christmas presents, because they can get abandoned once the festivities are over."

Cambridge watched the cat hungrily devour its feast. "Buy a pet in January, once you're certain it's not just a holiday whim."

What a nice man, I thought a little later, while hurrying through the quiet Uplands to the nearest bus stop. After a pleasant journey, I stepped from the bus in the quiet James Bay neighbourhood. At Dallas Road a sign pointed the way to a beach named for marathon runner Steve Fonyo. I photographed the sign, then moved on.

A paved walkway wandered along the clifftop, with the occasional path or stairs providing access to the ocean far below. In the pale sky, swallows flitted past, appearing to play, but probably chasing McInsects for breakfast. Over at the western hills the newborn sun reflected from the windows of homes, transforming the glass into sparkling jewels.

I wandered along the pathway, pausing to watch the pilot boat heading toward a large freighter. The tide was out, exposing wet seaweed on the rocks below; in the distance were the mountains, pale blue under the pink sky of early morning.

The path led to Beacon Hill Park, where a large sign announced this as Mile Zero of the Trans-Canada Highway. Inside the park, thick bushes and trees grew along the pathway. I studied a tugboat on the water; it looked motionless, straining against the mighty weight of the logs it towed. I watched birds winging across the water on important business, and heard pleasant whistling cries from within the trees. Yellow broom was scattered everywhere, lending its sweet fragrance to the morning air.

I then spotted the world's tallest totem pole, which I remembered from researching Victoria on the Net. Nearby was the hill that probably gave this park its name; in the days before lighthouses, a beacon up there would have warned boats away from the cliffs.

Before long I left Beacon Hill Park behind, but continued walking above the cliff. The early morning sun was on the ocean, shining a golden path for my pleasure. Beside me was a large green space, then a road and some small houses. White and purple wildflowers scattered their colours along the cliff. A kayaker was out, enjoying the good life, B.C. style. Seagulls called across the water, and waves lapped softly against the rocky beaches below. A blue heron lifted away from the water, circled, and was slowly airborne on impressive wings.

Finally I reached Ross Bay Cemetery, an oasis of shady trees beside the blue ocean. I opened my packsack, looking for water and more film, then leaned against a marble tombstone while I flipped through the cemetery guidebook. It was loaded with interesting stories.

At Emily Carr's grave, I was touched by the inscription, *Artist and author, lover of nature.* I took a photo, then wandered on. I stayed on the paved walkways, wanting to avoid crossing an unmarked grave (as many people know, doing so can cause your body to develop a serious rash). I studied a holly tree and then a monkey puzzle tree, its curved branches so like the tails of playful monkeys. One tombstone was called Pooley's marble angel; it was said to cry on nights with a full moon, according to the guidebook.

"I should check this out with William," I murmured to myself. "Too bad we missed the full moon."

In the guidebook, Cambridge had underlined several notes in green ink. Walking west, I studied the notes, trying to find a pattern. One note referred to a teenager who'd drowned in the Gorge waterway, so perhaps Cambridge—

Somewhere in the cemetery, a stick cracked loudly. I lifted my head and looked around—there were a lot of big tombstones. Bushes and trees also provided hiding places.

I could feel my heart thumping. For moments I

waited. Nothing stirred but the occasional leaf drifting to earth.

I stared at a cobweb, shining on a stone cross—it was beautiful, but I felt frightened. I decided to go home; closing the guidebook, I lowered my packsack to stuff the book away. But my camera accidentally fell, smacking hard against the paved walkway. Annoyed, I picked up the camera—had it been damaged?

He came out of nowhere, a blur of motion.

Energy pumped through my body. I rolled swiftly aside to avoid the attack, then sprang into the ready position I knew from martial arts. Behind me, a hill fell down to Dallas Road. I breathed deeply, centring my energy and power in my torso.

The attacker wore a ski mask—all I could see were his eyes. For a moment he stared, then he lunged at me. Stepping swiftly aside and bringing up my foot, I kicked out at his leg. He yelled in pain and surprise, then went over the side. As he disappeared, I heard branches breaking and rocks pouring down the slope.

Running to the edge, I looked down. The guy stood up, painfully and slowly, and gave me a malignant stare before limping quickly away. Then he was gone from sight.

I knew what I had to do. I was going straight to the police.

9

I called Laura from a pay phone at the nearby Fairfield
Plaza. She answered on the first ring and promised to join
me ASAP. While waiting for Laura, I kept an eye on Fairfield Road; a car passed with Paris at the wheel, and that
surprised me. He didn't seem the early-morning type.

Nervously I paced, watching shopkeepers opening
their premises for the day. They were a relaxed crowd,
exchanging greetings in the sunshine as they got ready,
and I felt slightly better.

I saw Laura's BMW pull into the lot. As she stepped
from the car, tall and elegant and so in control, I ran
quickly to her. I guess I needed a hug more than I'd
realized.

"I was so scared," I told Laura, as we headed for police headquarters in her car.

She patted my hand. "I know how you feel, Liz. I went through a similar experience."

After parking, we walked to the ultramodern police station on Caledonia Street. A detective took us into her office, where she poured coffee for Laura and bottled water for me. She listened carefully to all the details, then told us she'd be in touch if anything came up.

Back outside, I walked with Laura to her car. She'd offered to take me to the Inner Harbour. "I probably won't mention the attack to anyone," I said. "Tiffany would be really upset."

"That's a good idea," Laura agreed.

"Do you think this wedding makes sense?"

Laura smiled. "I've got an opinion, Liz, but I won't comment publicly."

* * *

At the Inner Harbour all kinds of people were out strolling, enjoying the musicians and artists. Boats of every type lined the wharves near the Empress Hotel, which glowed in the warmth of the sun. Some people were having their picture taken in front of the hotel, and other tourists were boarding red double-decker buses for tours of the city.

As arranged, I met Pepper at the statue of Captain Cook. We leaned against a stone wall, checking out the yachts and people below. The happy scene made me feel better. Four young men were singing "The Lion Sleeps Tonight." They harmonized without musical instruments, and received loud applause when the song ended. Everyone's mood seemed good—this was a beautiful place to be sharing.

I looked at the Empress. "Tiffany's in there right now, meeting with Major Wright. Tiff told me she's got news for her father, but she wouldn't tell me what it is."

Descending stone stairs, Pepper and I joined the crowd strolling the Lower Causeway. "I can't believe all the languages I'm hearing," I commented. "People must visit Victoria from the entire globe."

We paused to watch musicians from Peru performing on the causeway against the backdrop of the Legislative Buildings. Two men played panpipes—the music sweet and haunting—while another thumped a drum. The musicians were having fun, occasionally dancing in a circle around an open instrument case that awaited donations from onlookers.

We moved on. "I was interested in the band members' shoes," I said. "They seemed to fit each guy's personality, except for the tall one. He was heavy-set, but he wore paper-thin dancing shoes."

"You're quite the detective," Pepper said. Then she glanced at me. "How do you think the painting was stolen from Thirteen Oaks, Liz? Got any theories?"

"Someone inside the house must have been involved. Otherwise, how did the thief get past the security codes at the library?"

"Who do you think it was?"

I shook my head. "I can't say. There are too many suspects, and there's no real evidence."

As we continued our short walk, Pepper hummed a cheerful tune. A number of tents had been set up for a FolkFest, not far from the Empress. Arts and crafts were on display from all over the province. Pottery, jewellery, sweet-smelling soaps—even a First Nations raven mask with copper eyes.

A feature of the FolkFest was free entertainment on a large stage. Sitting on aluminum stands, we watched young Ukrainian dancers high-kick in bright costumes, while tiny girls from the audience joined in the fun, bouncing around in front of the stage to the rousing music, their parents watching from close by.

"I'm so lucky the servants help with Amanda," Pepper said. "Kids are so much work."

"What about her father helping?"

"He left town," Pepper replied. "You know, Liz, I can't imagine being a teenager alone with a baby, carrying diaper bags everywhere. I never realized the work involved—and the worry. I'm always freaked about Amanda—like, is she safe?"

"You mean from kidnappers?"

"I guess so," Pepper replied. "But I never thought about kidnappers before now. I just meant being safe from falling down. That kind of thing."

"Sorry," I said, feeling foolish.

"Don't worry, Liz," Pepper replied. "You're nice, and so is Tiffany. I wish she wouldn't marry Paris."

"Why?"

"For starters, he's a control freak. He's lucky that Tiffany is so sweet-natured—other women would tell Paris to take a hike." Pepper sighed. "Everything changed for Paris when our parents died. Pater's will contained a large cash payment for each kid. Hart made a smart investment with his legacy, but I lost mine buying into a dot-com company that failed."

"That's too bad."

Tiffany shrugged. "Anyway, Paris totally went stupid with his legacy. My brother's lifestyle was wild—you can't imagine the parties at Thirteen Oaks. The clothes he bought—incredible. Plus crazy stunts, very expensive stuff. Like flying his friends in chartered helicopters to Whistler for snowboarding and more parties. I've seen him burn through so much, so fast."

"Does Tiffany know about this?"

Pepper nodded. "Anyway, I guess Paris blew all Pater's money. Now he's back to his allowance from the family trust. For me the allowance is plenty to live on, but Paris is a different breed of cat."

"Tiffany is so trusting," I said. "She always looks for the good side in people. Major Wright is a pretty nice guy, but basically an emotional manipulator. He's decided this marriage makes sense for Tiffany, and he thinks her doubts are just pre-wedding jitters."

"She's bought into that?"

"So far," I replied. "Tiff really loves and respects her dad. She values his opinion." Lost in thought, I absent-mindedly ran my fingers through my hair. Then I turned to Pepper. "You know what Tiff believes? If she gives Paris enough love, he'll get over his problems. And I'm just not certain it's possible."

* * *

We visited the food stands, where the goodies looked scrumptious and the smells were so delicious. I settled on a vegetarian pita from the Mediterranean stand, perogies from the Polish White Eagle Association, and

Rose's "Awesome" chocolate cake from the Jewish Community Centre.

People were eating at outdoor tables. "I'll tell you the problem with Paris," Pepper commented, as we looked for vacant chairs. "Too much money, and no Pater to control him. Our father ruled by fear, and Paris always toed the line. He wasn't a rebel until Pater died. Then my brother went crazy, doing all the things that would have scandalized Pater." She paused. "Of course, I'm not perfect, either. Pater was *so* upset when I got pregnant." Pepper shook her head. "What a crazy family I was born into, Liz, but I love them anyway. They're my kin."

"It's fun to know you, Pepper."

She smiled. "You, too."

At a sunny table we sat down next to a mother and her kids; when a ladybug landed on our table, the eldest girl said, "Now we'll all have good luck."

That superstition was new to me, and I thanked the girl for it. "We need some luck," I said, thinking of Tiffany. "I'll be watching for more ladybugs."

Pepper looked into the distance. "Wow," she murmured. "Who is this?"

Turning, I saw William walking toward our table. He was tall and so blond in the sunshine, and people noticed him. Seeing me, William's face broke into a beautiful smile.

"Liz, you're here. And you're safe."

"Sure, I'm fine," I replied, and introduced Pepper. "Why are you surprised?"

"I heard something happened at the cemetery," William said. "Is it true?"

"Yes, but how'd you find out?"

For a moment, William looked confused. "It was . . . well, from someone I know."

"Someone in the police?"

William shook his head. "No. You see—"

The ringing of my cell phone interrupted William. When I answered, I heard Tiffany's voice. "Liz," she exclaimed, "it was horrible."

Walking away from Pepper and William, I covered my ear against the noisy crowd. "Tiff, what's wrong?"

"I told Daddy I couldn't marry Paris, and he got so upset. Liz, he was crying. In the Empress, in front of everyone. People were staring."

"But . . ."

"It was just a mess, Liz. I can't hurt Daddy's feelings, ever again. I'm going ahead with the wedding."

"Tiff, where are you? I'll come to you—we'll talk."

"Not now. Daddy's so upset, he needs me. I'll stay a while with him, okay? Then I'll go home to Thirteen Oaks. I'll see you there."

"Sure, but—"

"Liz, I gotta go. Talk to you later."

The call upset me greatly, but I said nothing to William or Pepper. Leaving the FolkFest, we walked together to a transit stop where Pepper caught a bus. She was heading home to Thirteen Oaks, to see her darling Amanda. We waved goodbye, then William turned to me. "There's something I've wanted to mention. You see . . ."

Silently, I waited for him to continue.

Then William shook his head. "Maybe later, Liz." He paused, thinking. "There's a special event tonight at Carr House, which is the birthplace of Emily Carr. They're holding a Victorian salon, with refreshments and singing around the piano. Care to go with me?"

"Certainly."

William and I lingered at the Inner Harbour until evening came to the city. He seemed worried, but said nothing about his thoughts. He was very quiet as we strolled south on Government Street.

Carr House reminded me of an old-fashioned doll-house with its little windows and gingerbread decorations. In the garden, small signs carried passages from Emily Carr's writings. Reading them, William cheered up. "Emily Carr was also a prolific author," he told me. "Ever read her *Book of Small*? It describes her childhood here. When Emily was a girl, she'd come outside and sing to the family cow!"

I laughed. "It's nice to see you smile again," I told William.

At the side door we were welcomed by Jan, the cheerful woman in charge of Carr House. She knew William well because of his interest in the famous artist; after the introductions, she beamed at William. "It's about time you found someone special."

He grinned and shrugged and shuffled his feet, while Jan and I exchanged a smile.

Inside the house I met Jan's friendly daughters. She explained that the "marbled" wallpaper was hand-painted, and the elaborate outfits hanging on pegs were similar to the clothes worn by Emily and other members of the Carr family.

"People come to Victoria from all over the world," Jan told me, "just to visit the scenes of Emily Carr's life. Many are like pilgrims—they can relate to her struggles. She was an artist ahead of her time, and quite misunderstood. Much of the fame happened after her death. Do you know, only 50 people attended her funeral. Sad, eh?"

"Personally," William said, "I love this place. Imagine, Emily Carr's spirit may still linger here, within these very walls."

The parlour was exquisitely furnished in the Victorian manner. Above the fireplace was a large oval mirror supported by two fish carved from wood; I also noticed a framed portrait of the famous monkey, Woo, wearing a dress with a big yellow bow. "When Emily Carr lay dying," Jan told us, "that portrait of Woo was near her bed. She really must have loved her little friend."

Several seniors sat on velvet chairs, singing along as a lady made enthusiastic music at the piano. We joined in for "A Bicycle Built for Two," our voices loud. Then I glanced out the window. Into this perfect scene came a white horse pulling a white carriage, its big wheels slowly turning. A couple sat in the carriage, enjoying an outing through the yesteryear streets of the James Bay heritage neighbourhood.

But I got a surprise. The man in the carriage was Tiffany's father, Major Wright. Who was the woman?

* * *

Outside Carr House, William and I speculated about the woman's identity. Then I lowered my head, feeling shy. "I've got an idea."

"What's that?"

"Feel like going to the Ross Bay Cemetery?"

"Sure, but why?"

Now it was my turn to shuffle my feet. "You see, in the cemetery there's a stone angel. She's said to cry during a full moon. Maybe it's true."

William glanced up at the quarter moon. "But . . ."

"I don't really care about the angel, William. I just thought it would be a nice quiet place . . ." My voice trailed off. To be truthful, being with William had made me forget about the attack, but now I wasn't too sure about going back there.

But before I could say anything more, William nodded. "Next stop, Ross Bay Cemetery."

We walked east along Dallas Road. Above the ocean the sky glowed with stars and moonlight; we saw a ship passing by, its lights shining in the night. The tree-shaded streets of the city were quiet as people settled in; I saw a man walking two Scottie pups, but otherwise nothing stirred.

At the cemetery I paused, feeling nervous. I remembered the attack, but I overcame my fear. "Let's keep moving," I said to William. All around were the dim outlines of really old monuments to people who had once lived and loved in the homes of Victoria. Now they slumbered here; I somehow felt that their spirits accepted our presence on this beautiful night.

William looked at me. "Liz . . ."

My heart was beating in triple time. What would happen next? "William . . ."

I saw a movement in the dark trees. "Someone's there."

William laughed nervously. "You're joking, right?"

I shook my head. "I saw something."

"What are you saying—a ghost?"

"I doubt it." I looked at William. "I'm going to investigate."

"I'll go with you."

"Thanks," I said gratefully.

Out on the ocean a seabird cried, breaking the silence. Cautiously we moved through the cemetery, then finally took shelter behind a large tombstone. Close by was a monument, very wide and very tall. Carved into the marble were names and dates; at the top was a cross, and the name *deMornay*. A single red rose lay on the monument.

Standing nearby was Cambridge, the butler from Thirteen Oaks.

As we approached, Cambridge turned in surprise. "Miss Austen?" he said, wiping tears from his eyes. "Why are you here?"

"We're, um . . . out for a walk. Are you okay, sir? I mean, you've been crying."

"It's just the blues, Miss Austen. Occasionally I come here with a rose for Lady deMornay. She's the person who hired me to work at Thirteen Oaks. She was a fine, fine woman."

I nodded. "Hart and Pepper both miss her a lot. I'm not so sure how Paris feels."

Cambridge shook his head. "Master Paris just sold her painting at auction. Can you imagine? His own mother, and he sells her portrait for money."

Suddenly I slapped my forehead. "Listen, I'm being so rude. Please, let me introduce my friend."

To my pleasure, Cambridge knew William's name. "I follow the local art scene," he explained, "and people call you a rising star."

"Wow." William looked astonished. "That is so amazing."

"Your work is influenced by Emily Carr, I understand. In time you'll find your own, unique voice, but for now she's an excellent role model."

"That is just so nice," William enthused, shaking Cambridge's hand. "Thank you very much!"

I smiled, happy for William.

10

Early the next morning I talked to Tiffany, who was feeling slightly better. "It'll be a good marriage," she promised me. "Besides, I simply can't upset Daddy. What if his heart fails? Our family doctor warned me that Daddy has high blood pressure."

Tiffany left in the Jeep, heading for downtown and breakfast with her father at the Empress. I was in the sunroom reading Danda Humphreys' history of Victoria street names when Hart appeared. He was wearing a white shirt and black trousers.

"Hey, Liz—remember saying you'd like to get aboard a cruise ship? Well, close that book, because your chance has come."

"Excellent."

We hurried outside. "Cruise ships dock at Ogden

Point," Hart explained. "We're invited aboard the *Crystal Paradise*."

At the estate's 10-car garage, Cambridge waited beside the Daimler. "Normally I'd ride my bicycle to Ogden Point," Hart said, as we settled back on the limo's luxurious leather seats, "but we're running very late. I slept in. It was a busy night."

"For me, too," I responded.

"Quickly, please," Hart said to Cambridge, who was at the wheel. "We're late."

Hart turned to me. "I belong to a service club called Victoria A.M. We promote local tourism—for example, by welcoming cruise ship passengers to Victoria."

"Why belong to a service club, when you're so wealthy?"

"It's important to give back to the community, Liz. Besides, I've got my own ecotourism business. I like talking shop with other members of Vic A.M."

"Pepper mentioned something about you greeting the cruise ships. Exactly what happens?"

"We give each lady a flower and each gentleman a handshake as they leave the ship."

"That sounds like fun."

"I've got permission for you to join us. I just made arrangements with Rachel and Bob, who organize our Meet and Greet Program. They've been married for 57 years. Mary Helmcken also may be there. Her family goes back to Sir James Douglas, the first governor of British Columbia."

"Cool—I'd love to meet her."

"You ladies will wear splendid dresses from the Edwardian period, and the gentlemen will be in top

hats and evening suits. We'll get photographed a lot—
wait and see."

"Has Tiffany ever done this? I bet she'd look gorgeous in one of those dresses."

"I've thought about inviting Tiff," Hart replied.
"But she's engaged to Paris. It wouldn't be proper."

"I'll tell you something, Hart. I don't think Paris is
right for Tiffany."

He turned to me, startled. "Really? Why's that?"

"Where do I begin? There are a million reasons.
Haven't you noticed?"

"Sure, but . . ." A blush spread slowly across Hart's
face. "But what would happen to Tiff? If she didn't
marry Paris? What would she do? Where would she
go?"

I smiled. "She'd think of something, I'm sure."

When the Daimler reached the Dallas Road cliffs, I
looked for the *Outlaw,* but without success. Then I was
distracted by the sight of the cruise ship docked at
Ogden Point. Even from this distance it looked massive,
looming over the dock and the red double-decker buses
parked alongside many taxis and limousines for hire.

"Cruise ships stay in port all day," Hart explained,
"so most passengers come ashore to sightsee."

At a small building near the wharf we changed into
our costumes. The members of "Vic A.M." were a
cheerful lot; I chatted with Rachel and Mary while
their friend Flo helped adjust my elaborate hat and
gown of crimson satin.

Hart and the other men walked with us to the ship;
each of the ladies carried a basket of brightly
coloured flowers. The cruise ship's bow shimmered

with sunlight that reflected from the ocean waters, an impressive backdrop as we took photos of each other.

Cruise passengers waved to us from the many decks above. One of Victoria's famous hanging flower baskets was placed beside the gangplank for photo opportunities, and then the passengers descended.

At first I was timid, but the people were very friendly. "You look real English," said a man with a southern twang to his voice. "How about letting me get a photograph of you?"

I was impressed, listening to Flo speak in French to people from Québec and Europe. The others also kept busy, giving advice on what Victoria attractions to visit, plus constantly posing for photographs.

Then it was time to board the cruise ship!

We climbed the gangplank behind Tommy Mayne, a retired high school teacher who'd been energetically clanging a brass bell in his role as Victoria's town crier. Our identification was checked by a crew member at the top of the gangplank, and then we entered the ship's central atrium.

I looked up, surprised at the open and airy spaces above. In this large gathering place, passengers strolled or chatted with crew members; along one side, glass-enclosed elevators rose to the many upper decks. Bright waters streamed down a wall, framing a statue of a dancing couple. Nearby was a crystal piano—an amazing sight.

We began handing out flowers while answering questions from people curious about our outfits. The passengers came from many countries—and everyone said they'd like to live in Victoria. After posing for more pictures, we ascended a grand staircase that swept up to a collection of shops displaying expensive gowns, jewellery and perfumes.

Flo's husband, Eric, smiled at me. "Did you bring your platinum credit cards, Liz?"

"Unfortunately not," I laughed.

We chanced upon the ship's movie theatre, where a man slumbered alone amidst the empty seats. Flo took a picture and the flash woke the man, who looked around blearily. Giggling together, we scurried away.

The others were waiting for an elevator. When it arrived, we crowded inside. We adjusted our hats in front of the mirrors, while the elevator swiftly rose an amazing 11 stories to the Lido Deck.

Through a glass door I could see some people lounging beside a large swimming pool. We entered a restaurant where others were enjoying breakfast; when Tommy clanged the brass bell, they all jumped. Then everyone relaxed and smiled as we rushed around dispensing the last of our flowers. "Welcome to Canada's best bloomin' city," I kept saying—an expression I'd heard the others using.

Our duties complete, we received our treat—a late breakfast, courtesy of the cruise ship. The selection of delicacies was mind-boggling; we were offered 10 different juices, omelettes loaded with smoked salmon, fruit, link sausages, bacon—you name it.

Carrying trays laden with food, we went outside to the open deck. I took Flo and Eric's photograph beside a statue of a mermaid, then joined Hart, Les Chan, and Tommy at a round table. The others sat close by.

Munching our delicious breakfast, we enjoyed

Rachel's description of the deer she'd seen in her yard that morning. "Their coats were as sleek as this table-top," she said. "We even had a mom and two little spotted babies—they were so cute. I put out carrot peelings for them."

"We've had deer in our garden, too," Tommy said, "eating the tender leaves of the hydrangeas."

After finishing my meal I strolled to the railing, where I looked at the blue waters far below. A number of small boats had assembled, their occupants staring up at our mighty vessel.

Then my cell phone rang. It was William, sounding agitated.

"Liz," he exclaimed. "Can you meet me? I've made a decision—we must talk."

"Of course," I replied.

"Be outside the Royal B.C. Museum in one hour. I've got something really important to tell you."

* * *

Forty minutes later, Cambridge stopped the Daimler outside the museum, which was located near the Inner Harbour. "What a mob scene," I said, surprised at the number of people gathered on the large lawns outside the Legislative Buildings. They sat on rugs and alu-minum chairs facing the water, where a barge had been anchored. "What's going on?"

"Later tonight," Hart explained, "the Victoria Sym-phony Orchestra will be on that barge, playing classical tunes. It's an annual event called the Symphony Splash. These people have arrived early, to get the best spots."

"I wouldn't mind attending," I said wistfully.

"Didn't anyone tell you? Major Wright has invited us all to watch the Splash from his suite at the Empress. We'll have a choice view."

"Excellent!"

After waving goodbye to Hart and watching the Daimler drive off, I studied the museum. It was a large, handsome building of white stone. Through big windows I saw ancient totem poles that had been gathered long ago, perhaps from the very villages that Emily Carr captured in her books and paintings.

Then my heart lurched.

At the Inner Harbour I saw William—with someone else.

The two of them strolled arm in arm along Belleville; she looked pert and summery in a yellow dress and sun hat. Then, to my horror, I saw William hug the girl. As she hurried away, she turned to blow him a kiss.

I watched William walk toward the museum. I was horrified—frozen by indecision. I thought, *maybe she was in those photos that William scooped into hiding in his studio*. Pain stabbed me. I remembered seeing Hart with that pretty Lorna, who turned out to be family. Maybe this had the same explanation? Not likely, I thought bitterly.

William saw me and smiled. In the distance beyond him, I could still see that girl in her yellow dress. I really wished I'd never seen them together—I felt so down about it. I wanted to run, to escape the jealousy. It hurt so much.

As William approached, I produced a totally phony

smile. He looked surprised, but I didn't care. Bad vibrations ruled my heart.

"What's wrong?" William asked, looking at me with those wonderful eyes.

I refused to melt. "Nothing," I replied, giving him another frosty smile.

"Something's bothering you, Liz. Please, tell me what's wrong."

"Hey," I said, looking for a diversion, "this museum could be interesting. Let's take a look, okay?"

"Sure, but what's wrong?"

"Nothing much."

"Liz, there's something I need to tell you. That's why I asked to meet."

"Later, maybe," I replied. I was so sulky.

I felt terrible, especially when William fell into silence. I was quiet, too, lost in misery. We stepped onto an escalator; at the top, William turned to me. "Let's go see the woolly mammoth. It's my favourite exhibit."

"You go, William." I looked at my map of the museum. "I'm going to check out the First Peoples Gallery. It interests me more." I was lying—what I really needed was time alone, time to think. I'd never felt this way before. It was horrible.

"Okay," William said. "I'll meet you in the gallery. Wait for me, okay? I know you're angry, Liz, but don't walk out."

I watched William disappear around a corner. Instantly I felt alone, and awful. What monster of jealousy had seized my heart? I felt so guilty, and I badly needed to apologize.

Hurry back, William, I whispered anxiously.

I entered the First Peoples Gallery, where the lighting was dim. I was in a room designed to resemble a longhouse from the days when Native villages dominated the B.C. coast. I looked at the four totem poles supporting a wooden roof, trying to picture Emily Carr visiting a longhouse like this.

The gallery continued into a second large room containing many huge totems. Indirect lighting glowed discreetly, as did a red *Exit* sign over an emergency door. I studied a replica of a seaside village, complete with miniature canoes on a beach. The village looked perfect in every detail.

Then I saw William, reflected in the glass of the display case. He'd just entered the room.

William looked grim, but I wasn't surprised. I'd been really spiteful, and I couldn't wait to apologize. What to say? I stared at the miniature village, trying to find the right words. Then a loud buzzing distracted me, and a door slammed shut. Turning from the display, I looked for William.

But he wasn't there.

I searched the gallery, then walked quickly to the outside corridor. Tourists passed by, chattering happily. I couldn't see William—what was going on? Now I felt really bad about my sulky mood.

After rushing back inside the First Peoples Gallery, I hurried to the Modern History Gallery. I searched the face of every tall boy, unable to believe this was happening. I felt as if I'd entered a dream state, and I wanted to cry.

Entering a town from the Old West, I tried to decide

my next move. Happy people surrounded me, laughing and exclaiming as they wandered past the Grand Hotel and an old railway station and other exhibits.

At last I made a decision. After looking for William at the woolly mammoth, I left the museum. As enthused people hurried past, I took out my cell phone and called Laura Singlehurst.

"Please be home," I whispered, as her line rang and rang. "Don't let a machine answer."

Then Laura was there, her voice breathless. "I was outside, talking to the moving van guys. I ran to catch the phone—I thought it could be important."

"It is important," I cried, as tears rolled from my eyes. "Oh, Laura, please come get me. I'm at the Royal B.C. Museum, and I'm so frightened. Please drive me home, so I can talk to you."

"I'll be right there."

True to her word, Laura soon pulled up in a bright red Cadillac. "This is a rental," she explained, opening the door for me. "I've sold the BMW."

I told Laura everything. "I was so sulky," I moaned. "What if I never see William again? I was horrible to him!"

Laura patted my hand sympathetically. "There must be a simple explanation. What about the emergency exit at the gallery? You heard the door slam shut."

"You mean, William left that way?"

"He could have," Laura replied. "I think maybe his feelings are hurt, but he'll come back. Wait and see."

"I should contact the police."

"Not yet," Laura said. "Wait at least 24 hours, in case William shows up."

Soon Thirteen Oaks appeared ahead. At the front door of the mansion, I quickly thanked Laura, then ran inside. I was longing for a message from William.

But there was nothing. Alone in my room, I broke down and cried and cried.

* * *

Two hours later, Tiff returned home. In her room, I confessed my foolishness.

She listened sympathetically.

"What are your instincts saying?" she asked.

"To trust William."

"There's your answer. He'll return, don't you worry." Tiffany sighed. "I'm getting married tomorrow," she moaned, "and meanwhile Paris insists that we attend the Symphony Splash this evening after the rehearsal. But I just don't want to."

"Then, don't go, Tiffany."

"Paris doesn't want to upset my father. Daddy has invited us to his suite at the Empress overlooking the Splash activities. Everyone has to attend."

"I'm not going," I declared. "I'm too upset about William."

"Maybe he'll be at the Splash," Tiffany suggested.

"That's a thought. But what if he's with that girl?"

"Then the truth will set you free."

"I don't want freedom," I murmured sadly. "I want William."

Late in the day we attended the wedding rehearsal at the castle. The Major kept checking his watch, probably feeling impatient about the 24 hours still remaining until his daughter became Lady deMornay.

After the rehearsal Pepper returned home with her baby, who was fussy and maybe coming down with something. Major Wright left early in a taxi for the Empress Hotel. When the rehearsal ended, the rest of us crowded into the Daimler. I was squeezed in beside Kate Partridge, maid of honour to Tiffany. Kate lived in Victoria, and told some funny stories about the city as we drove downtown. The classic limousine attracted a lot of stares. Crowds of people were on the sidewalks, carrying lawn chairs and blankets toward the Inner Harbour.

"They'll never find a place to sit," Cambridge predicted from the wheel. "Forty thousand are expected for the Symphony Splash. According to CBC Radio, people started arriving at dawn to pick a good location."

We stepped from the limousine on Douglas Street. "Please, wait for me," Tiffany said to Cambridge. "I'll be back in a few minutes, and I'd appreciate a ride home."

Cambridge touched his chauffeur's cap. "Very good, miss."

Hart looked disappointed. "What's wrong, Tiffany?"

"Too many things to do," she replied. "Hey, tomorrow night I'm getting married."

Paris smiled at her. "Your father's going to be upset. I bet he'll have other guests, all anxious to chat with his perfect daughter."

"Well," Tiff replied, "that's just too bad."

A security guard checked our identification, then admitted us to the Victoria Convention Centre, which adjoins the Empress Hotel. We hurried past a magnificent indoor totem pole and climbed a few stairs to the hotel, where the reception would be held after the wedding.

I looked at Tiffany. "You're missing the Splash? Won't your father mind?"

"Maybe," Tiffany replied. She looked scared; she was breathing deeply as we entered an elevator and rode up. We stepped out into a hallway—it was very wide, with portraits of British royalty on the walls. Major Wright waited at the door of his suite; at his side was a woman I recognized. She'd been on the carriage ride with the Major.

"This is Marjorie," the Major said. "We met last week—we were both taking tea in the lobby. Marjorie's in Victoria on holiday from Texas." He beamed at Tiffany. "Marjorie's my date for this century's most romantic event."

"I enjoy high-society weddings," Marjorie told me. Stepping closer, she lowered her voice. "The deMornay family is, of course, *very* high society."

Tiffany looked at her father. "Daddy, I'm not staying for the Splash. I'm going home."

"Nonsense," the Major replied. "Come into the suite."

"But, Daddy, I'm getting married tomorrow."

"Please, honey. This is important to me."

"Daddy, I'm sorry. I can't stay."

Tiff quickly told me and Kate goodbye, then rushed toward the elevators. The Major took a step in her direction, then stopped. Glancing at Marjorie, he faked a jolly grin. "Kids these days."

Paris looked at him. "It's just pre-wedding jitters, Major Wright. Nothing to worry about."

"Let's hope so," the Major replied.

His large suite overlooked the Inner Harbour. Laura was there, along with several of the Major's Winnipeg friends, in town for the wedding. We exchanged handshakes and small talk, then I finally rushed into the adjoining room. I'd brought binoculars from Thirteen Oaks and was anxious to scan the crowd for William. With forty thousand in attendance my chances were slim, but I had to try.

From the window I saw an enchanting scene—the evening sun was a golden sphere that reflected from the blue waters of the harbour and threw long shadows behind the people who crowded the lawns below.

Laura joined me, carrying a platter of food. "The crab sandwiches are delicious," she said. "Or try the *paté de foie gras*. The taste is heavenly."

"Thanks, Laura, but I'm not hungry."

"No news about William?"

I shook my head mournfully. "Nothing."

"I'm so sorry, Liz."

The harbour was dominated by the barge where the symphony would play. On the water, music lovers had assembled to listen in canoes and motorboats, kayaks and cruisers. The shore was dense with people, and they covered every available spot as far as the distant steps of the Legislative Buildings.

"This is hopeless," I said, training the binoculars on the crowd. "William could be anywhere."

In the distance a helicopter lifted off from Ogden Point and moved slowly toward the Inner Harbour, sunlight glinting from its whirling blades. "Sight-seers," Laura said. "They've paid a lot of money for a bird's-eye view of this scene. A friend of Hart's owns that helicopter company."

On the barge, the members of the Victoria Symphony Orchestra warmed up their instruments. Then these sounds stopped, and we heard the opening notes of "O Canada." Immediately the spectators stood up, on the lawns and the streets and out on the bigger boats, to sing the national anthem.

The concert began with a rousing selection that received a huge cheer from the enthusiastic crowd. Then people nodded along to Bizet's "Carmen Suite" and Gershwin's "Fascinating Rhythm." But the big hit was a solo performance of a Mozart piano concerto by Victoria's 12-year-old Samuel Seong, who exhibited great self-confidence.

During the intermission we watched the Canadian Scottish Regiment march proudly past to the rattle of drums and the skirl of bagpipes. Glow ropes had appeared in the crowd, their neon colours beautiful in the gathering darkness; I saw a young Splash volunteer and another boy having a mock sword fight with lime green glow ropes.

With the binoculars I scanned the crowd, hoping, always hoping. Laura returned from the other room, auburn hair swinging. "There'll be some great music after the intermission," she said, "followed by the grand finale. It's the '1812 Overture,' Tchaikovsky's celebration of a famous Russian military victory over Napoleon's armies. It was written to be performed outside, with the loud ringing of church bells and the sound of cannons adding to the victorious music. The music went immediately to number one on the classical charts, and it's been popular ever since. It's rousing, cheerful stuff." She smiled at me. "We'll hear bells and cannons tonight, followed by fireworks."

"It sounds wonderful, Laura. I just wish William was here."

"Don't worry about that other girl, Liz."

"Thanks, Laura. I'll try not to."

Laura went to visit with Kate and Marjorie, the Major's friend from the United States, and I scanned the crowd with the binoculars. Hart joined me for a talk, and then Paris appeared. He dropped into a nearby chair and flipped through the pages of a magazine.

I tried the crowd again with the binoculars. "Oh, my goodness, there he is!"

11

Hart leaned close to the window. "William?"

"No, that kid Jason. The one from the *Outlaw*. He's beside the statue of Captain Cook—I'd know him anywhere."

I handed the binoculars to Hart. "I'm going down there. First that guy took a shot at us. After that, he firebombed the *Amor*, then he stole the painting and returned it. I want to know what's going on."

"Let me go with you."

I shook my head. "No thanks, Hart. I've got my cell phone, and I'll be perfectly safe in that big crowd. I work best on my own."

"How can I reach you?"

I gave Hart my cell number, then thanked Major Wright for his hospitality. After explaining my mission to Laura, I hurried to the elevator, took it down, and left the Empress. Jason was across the crowded street, holding a cell phone against his ear; suddenly he snapped it shut, and surveyed the crowd with suspicious eyes.

Then he was gone, down the stone stairs beside Cook's statue. Shouting for him to stop, I hurried forward through the crowd.

At the statue I groaned in dismay. On the causeway below was a solid wall of humanity; using brute strength, Jason was forcing a path through the crowd. People shook their fists after him, as parents comforted wailing toddlers and others expressed disgust in loud voices, but Jason just kept moving. Only once did he pause, when he turned to wave up at someone in the Empress.

All around were the rich sounds of powerful music. Without my noticing, the concert had resumed. I looked up at the hotel, searching for the Major's suite. All vehicles had been banned from the immediate vicinity, so the wide expanse of Government Street was filled with strolling people, many speaking foreign languages.

I walked south through the throng, envying people their happiness. Seeing the Royal B.C. Museum, I remembered my last moments with William. He'd have loved this scene—the night air was festive and the musicians on the brightly lit barge looked so spectacular, all of them wearing white.

People were clapping in time, while others bopped around to a Sousa march, a favourite of my dad's. I smiled sadly, wishing my family were here. I could have used my brother's help with this investigation, but he was on summer holidays with his pal, the odious Dietmar Oban.

My cell phone went *ta-ta-tring-tring*. It was Hart calling. "Are you okay, Liz?"

"Yes."

"That's good. Any sign of Jason?"

"I lost him in the crowd."

"Too bad. Listen," Hart continued, abruptly changing the subject, "I've got news you'll like. A friend just called, offering you a free seat on tonight's final helicopter tour. Cambridge is waiting with the Daimler outside the Crystal Garden. He'll take you there, but hurry."

Immediately I took off running toward the corner of Douglas and Belleville. "What's with the chopper?" I asked Hart as I ran with my phone.

"My friend owns it. Someone cancelled their trip, and he offered me seats."

"I hope you're coming along," I shouted into the phone, running hard toward the Daimler. I saw Cambridge waiting, the door already open.

"No thanks," Hart replied. "There isn't enough time."

"Thanks for the opportunity!"

The drive didn't take long. The helicopter waited near the wharf where we'd visited the cruise ship; it resembled a large insect with its giant blades and large windows. For a moment I imagined spotting William from the chopper, but even with binoculars he'd be impossible to see from up that high.

To my surprise, Cambridge asked for permission to join the trip. "Sure thing," the pilot replied. "There's enough space."

When the helicopter lifted off, I was unexpectedly reminded of what happened when I was a hostage at Disneyland. Closing my eyes, I pictured hot-tempered Serena Hernandez, and how she behaved. It was a horrible memory.

When I opened my eyes a few moments later, I saw people below in their yards and on apartment balconies, watching the sky for the coming fireworks. I sat in the best seat, beside the pilot. She smiled at me.

"We'll reach the Empress exactly as the '1812 Overture' concludes. Watch for the cannons to fire."

Far below we saw the fairy lights that decorated the Legislative Buildings, and the streets twinkling all the way to the ocean at Oak Bay. On the water, the orchestra's bandshell shone brightly.

Beside the Inner Harbour, orange flames exploded from cannons. "Those guns are fired by sailors from HMCS *Quadra*," the pilot told us. "They're antique cannons, brought to Victoria each summer for the Symphony Splash. They're firing blanks, of course."

A sudden explosion burst in the sky, scattering colours. "The fireworks," the pilot exclaimed, looking at the bright jewels exploding in the night. "Oh, aren't they beautiful!" It was thrilling to watch the eruptions of fire and light from here, and I kept wishing William could see this incredible scene.

Then, too soon, it was over, and numerous headlights sprang to life all around the Inner Harbour.

"There'll be a traffic jam tonight," Cambridge predicted gloomily. "Just the thing to set off Master Paris's bad temper."

Our helicopter headed south over the slumbering

trees of Beacon Hill Park. In the distance I saw the outline of the Olympic Mountains; close by, the Dallas Road cliffs overlooked the shoreline.

"Wait a minute," I said, sitting up straight. "Look at that boat—it could be the *Outlaw*. Can we get closer?"

The pilot glanced at her watch. "There's time, if—"

"No," Cambridge said sharply. "We must return immediately to Ogden Point."

"But," I pleaded, "surely . . ."

"My name is not Shirley," Cambridge replied crossly, "and I haven't got time to waste on a wild-goose chase. Master Paris will expect the limousine back at the Empress Hotel. He'll be furious if we're late."

It was hopeless to argue, and I watched sadly as the boat disappeared in the direction of Oak Bay. It could have been the *Outlaw*, but how would I ever know?

* * *

The next day was terrible.

I tried and tried to reach William by phone, without success. As for Tiffany, she sat at her window, gazing out to sea. I couldn't get her to talk, and she looked a misery.

At seven p.m., the wedding party gathered in the drawing room at Craigdarroch Castle. A marriage commissioner was there to perform the ceremony. Paris deMornay looked so smug; he wore a white tuxedo, and so did Hart, who was best man. They stood with us in front of the white fireplace, awaiting the arrival of the bride. A couple of dozen guests sat in chairs, glancing expectantly toward the door. When would Tiffany arrive?

From outside the panelled oak doors, we heard an organ play the opening bars of "Here Comes the Bride." Laura and the other guests stood up. The bride appeared, and my heart just about stood still; her downcast eyes were puffy from tears.

Beside Tiffany was the Major. Wearing an expensive suit and shiny shoes, he bristled with nervous energy. His eyebrows twitched as his blue eyes flicked from face to face. Father and daughter walked slowly forward, with Tiffany's eyes still on the floor.

I glanced at Paris; he grinned in satisfaction, his white teeth gleaming. Hart looked extremely unhappy, but he was a gentleman and would never dream of stopping the ceremony.

For a wild moment I thought I should do something—maybe yell, *Tiffany, don't,* and just see what happened. But I remained silent as the commissioner asked, "Who gives this woman?" and the Major presented Tiffany as a gift to Paris.

The ceremony commenced. Blood drummed in my ears throughout the long and terrible time; at moments I feared I'd fall on the floor in a dead faint. Paris promised his bride he'd love, honour, and respect (what a lie), and then the commissioner turned to Tiffany for her pledge.

Taking a deep breath, my friend looked at Paris. "I can't do this," she said quietly.

He frowned. "What?"

Tiffany swallowed. "I always loved you, Paris. But I can't go down this road with you."

Paris continued to frown but said nothing.

"You're doing stuff that is so damaging. Money is your god—and before, it never was." Now Tiffany's voice was clear; everyone could hear the words. "You're being so reckless, Paris, taking such chances."

"I doubt it," Paris said, but his voice lacked conviction.

"You know what's the worst thing, Paris? Other people get hurt by your shady deals, and you don't care. In fact, you don't even notice. Even when it's family like Hart and Pepper, and me."

"Okay, Tiffany, okay. Message received. Now let's get married, eh? The commissioner's waiting, and so's everyone else."

Paris took Tiffany by the arm, but she pulled free. "It's not going to happen, Paris. Wedding bells aren't ringing for us."

Fear crept into his eyes. "Tiffany, please." Paris pleadingly reached out a hand. "We both need this marriage."

Major Wright was staring at Tiffany from his seat in the front row. "What's going on?" he demanded. His friend Marjorie patted the Major's arm, trying to keep him calm, but he ignored her. "What's going on?" he repeated.

"Daddy, I can't. I don't love Paris anymore."

The Major stood up. He looked broken-hearted. "Tiffany, honey, what's the matter? Of course you're going to marry Paris. He's a great guy. Now listen, you're just having an attack of nerves. Don't worry, just—"

Tiffany put her roses into my hands. "I was going to throw you this bouquet, Liz, so you'd be the next one married. Now I can't."

I felt radiant with joy. Hugging Tiffany close, I whispered, "I'm so proud of you, Tiff. Now get out of here—before you change your mind!"

Paris grabbed Tiffany's arm. "Please," he begged, "don't leave me. I'm sorry for the times I hurt you. It'll never happen again, Tiffany. Don't leave—I love you."

"You liar." Tiffany shook off his hand. She looked wonderful—so defiant and proud. "You love money, Paris. You won't get mine now."

Then my friend was gone, out the door to freedom. Major Wright's jaw hung open, and Paris looked totally astonished, but the room hummed with excitement. The guests hadn't expected this!

Pepper rushed to me. "Wasn't Tiffany *wonderful*? That took such bravery—my brother is a first-class power tripper."

"I'm so glad she found the courage," I said.

Pepper beamed with happiness. "Hey, what about the cruise? What'll happen now?"

"You're right," I said. "I'd completely forgotten."

Major Wright had booked a luxury suite on a cruise ship to Alaska. That was his wedding gift—Paris and Tiffany were supposed to sail tonight at midnight. Now the Major was stuck with the suite—but I figured he could afford it.

* * *

Outside the castle, the wedding guests were still murmuring excitedly. I watched Major Wright speaking urgently to Paris as they climbed into the Daimler.

Hart and Marjorie joined them, and the limo zoomed away.

"They've forgotten us," I said to Pepper.

"Too much on their minds."

After talking a while with the other guests, we took a taxi together to Thirteen Oaks. Pepper went in search of Amanda, and I changed out of my bridesmaid's dress. Then I looked for Tiffany.

I found her in a chair, looking out at the sea. "Hey," I said, "I bet you're the talk of Victoria."

"I'm worried about Daddy," Tiff replied. "The wedding meant so much to him."

"He'll get over it," I said, sitting down beside her. "Why'd you change your mind?"

"Laura told me to ask my angels to give me direction. So I spent today thinking about Paris. He's been clinging to me like a weight, hoping I'd solve his problems. I need an equal partner to help raise a family, not some guy who acts like he's drowning. He's an okay guy, Liz, but the wrong guy for me." Tiffany sighed. "Paris slipped into some bad habits after losing his dad. I tried to help—it's my nature, I guess. But I felt like his mother or something, getting him through crisis after crisis."

"You put more money into his gambling?"

Tiffany nodded. "Paris used up all his financial resources trying to maintain his reputation as a party-on dude. He borrowed big-time from all his friends. Then he turned to gambling to fix things. Now everything's dried up, and Paris will hit the wall."

"He'll survive," I predicted. "You wait and see."

* * *

Later that night, Tiffany was summoned by her father to the cruise ship. She asked me to go along for support, and we drove downtown in the Daimler, with Cambridge at the wheel.

The cruise ship looked beautiful, its sleek white lines dominating the busy night at Ogden Point. Taxis and limos and tour buses were delivering passengers for the midnight sailing of the *Romance of the Seas*. From the many decks above, faces looked down at the bustling scene.

After the Daimler pulled away, we climbed the gangplank. I felt worried about Tiffany, wondering if she'd still cave in. The Major was skilled at using emotional power to control his daughter.

"What's going on?" I asked Tiffany, as our identification was checked at the top of the gangplank. "Why has your dad summoned you here?"

She shook her blonde curls. "I don't know, Liz."

A young ship's officer was waiting for us with a personal welcome, and escorted us into a glass-enclosed elevator. We rose rapidly, looking down at clusters of passengers below. From the elevator we entered the Royal Deck, where the corridor was wide and deep purple carpeting pampered our feet. Each cabin had a name; at one called Suite of Dreams, the officer knocked discreetly.

"Major Wright," he called. "Your daughter has arrived."

The door opened. The Major's blue eyes stared at us, then he turned to the officer. "Thank you."

The officer saluted.

"Come inside," the Major snapped. "Marjorie's here. She's going to be a witness."

"To what?" Tiffany asked.

The Major didn't reply. I goggled at the size and luxury of the suite; there was even a large outdoor balcony with a panoramic view of the ocean and mountains. Marjorie sat on a luxurious sofa; in her hand was a fizzy drink.

"Good evening, girls," she said brightly, nervous eyes on Major Wright.

Hands on hips, he stared at Tiffany. She held his gaze without flinching. "Well, young lady?" the Major demanded. "Where is your apology?"

"Daddy, I—"

"Because," the Major continued, "tonight I am the laughing stock of Victoria society, and it is your fault, young lady."

"No, Daddy. If you hadn't—"

Again the Major interrupted his daughter. "Never mind," he barked. "There will be no further discussion."

Opening his cell phone, the Major punched some numbers. "What's your ETA?" he said into the phone. "Remember—this ship sails at midnight." Snapping shut the phone, the Major gestured at Tiffany. "Go sit with Marjorie and have a chat."

My friend did as ordered. I stepped out on the balcony and sniffed the salty air. Far below, the scene was active; I watched the scurrying ant-like figures, then saw a taxi pull to a stop.

Paris stepped out and hurried toward the ship; with him was Hart deMornay—and the marriage commissioner.

12

Quickly I returned inside. The deMornay brothers entered
the suite, and Paris soon stood waiting to resume the marriage ceremony. The Major turned to Tiffany. "Sweetie,
please, do this for your dear old pop. Call me a sentimental old fool, but just think what this marriage means."

"Daddy, I—"

Major Wright stopped her with a gesture. "I have
this wonderful vision of my little girl marrying into the
aristocracy. Surely that's not asking too much."

Tiffany smiled fondly at her father. "I know, Daddy,
but face up to it. I will not marry Paris. That's my decision, and I won't change it."

Paris walked slowly toward Tiffany. I saw tears in
his eyes. "Sweetheart, is there no way we can work
this out?"

Tiffany shook her head. "No, Paris. My mind's made up."

"But . . ."

Tiffany turned to me. "Come on, Liz, let's get going."

Outside in the corridor, we walked rapidly toward the elevators. From behind, Paris called Tiff's name. "I'll take this cruise to Alaska alone," he threatened.

"I guess that's up to Daddy," Tiffany replied.

"I'll meet someone better than you."

"Good luck to her," Tiffany muttered, jabbing at the elevator button. "As for me, I'm out of here."

The elevator door opened, and I saw a young guy wearing a FedEx messenger's uniform. In his hands was a large metal tube. As we entered the elevator, I saw the messenger knock on the door of a suite.

* * *

Back at the estate we found Pepper in the library reading R.S.S. Wilson's *Undercover for the RCMP*. The baby was asleep upstairs. When Pepper heard about the events on board the cruise ship, her eyes glowed.

"You're something else, Tiff."

"Thanks, Pepper."

Looking exhausted, Tiffany left for bed. I stood at the library window, staring out at the ocean. Then, feeling weary and starting to cry, I dropped down on the sofa beside Pepper. "I'm so tired," I said, wiping away my tears. "Everything's just so horrible."

"What's wrong, Liz? What's happened?"

I was surprised. "You haven't heard?"

"About what?"

"I can't believe no one has told you, Pepper. I just assumed . . ."

"Told me what?" Pepper demanded impatiently.

"That my friend William has disappeared."

"*What?*"

Pepper was terribly upset by the news. She stared at me in horror as I described everything, starting from when I spotted William and the girl outside the museum.

Then Pepper leaned toward me. "Liz, I may know where William is."

"What do you mean?"

Pepper looked out the window. "William could be on Hidden Island."

"But why?"

Jumping up from the sofa, Pepper paced the library. There were tears in her eyes. "Liz, you've been so kind. Most people see a kid with a baby and turn up their noses. You and Tiff—that's not your style. You're good people."

"Thanks, Pepper, but what's this all about?"

She took a deep breath. "I helped steal the painting, Liz. I was the inside person. I gave the code to Jason."

"But, Pepper!"

"Liz, I had no idea that William was missing. It was strange to see him with Jason, but I didn't think anything more about it."

"What are you talking about?"

She stared at me with solemn eyes. "Jason's been hiding out in an abandoned boathouse on Hidden Island. Yesterday I saw his boat heading there—William was with him. You know my story about the unexploded bombs? It's not true—I made that up. I wanted to keep people off the island. That way, it's my private property."

"But, Pepper, why'd you give the code to Jason?"

"I was promised enough money to start my recording studio, so I agreed to help."

"Jason was going to pay you?"

Pepper shook her head. "No. We're both working for someone else."

"Who?"

"I can't tell you, Liz."

"But why steal the *Klee Wyck* and then return it?"

Pepper looked at the painting over the fireplace. The colours were so pleasing, the Laughing One so happy. "Because that's not the real *Klee Wyck*," she replied at last. "That's a forgery, a fake."

I was astonished. "But it looks so real!"

"You see, Liz, I told Jason the security code, and unlocked an outside door for him to get into the house. Jason escaped with the *Klee Wyck*. Then some forger made an expert copy, which you were lured into finding at Butchart Gardens. That was so everyone would relax, thinking the painting was safe."

I shook my head. "Why make a copy?"

"So the original can be sold, for major money."

"But where's the original?"

"Until tonight," Pepper replied, "it's been right here at Thirteen Oaks. After you found the forged copy at Butchart Gardens, Jason gave the original to me. I've kept it hidden here until now."

"So you think William's on that island? Then we must go there immediately."

"No problem," Pepper said. "There's an underground

tunnel from the library to Hidden Island. Nobody knows about the tunnel, including Jason. I didn't want him getting into our house."

"You didn't mind him stealing the *Klee Wyck*?"

Pepper shrugged. "Who cares, it's just some old painting. Besides, no one noticed the forgery. Paris, Hart—everyone was fooled. Remember the family meeting with Laura? Major Wright and the others— they all said how beautiful it looked." She shook her head, looking amused. "They were all fooled, every one."

"Including me," I said ruefully. "But that painting was so special to your father, Tiff. Didn't that bother you?"

Pepper snapped her fingers disdainfully. "Not even this much," she declared. "You know, when my father crashed the car and killed my wonderful mother, he was driving drunk. I'll never forgive him." Pepper gazed defiantly at me with those beautiful deMornay eyes. "No, Liz, I don't have any trouble about the painting being forged."

"You've been paid for helping?"

Pepper shook her head. "Not until the original is sold."

"Who's paying you, Pepper? Who's your boss?"

She shook her head. "I can't tell you, Liz. Please, don't ask."

I thought of another question. This one made me feel sick, but I had to ask. "What's William got to do with Jason?"

"I have no idea, Liz."

I decided not to press the issue. I had to find

William, and this was the closest I'd come so far. "Okay, then," I said. "How can we reach that tunnel?"

Moments later Pepper opened the library's secret panel; I smelled wetness and dirt. We stepped into a tunnel. As the false bookcase closed behind us, Pepper switched on a flashlight. "This tunnel's where I hid the painting," she said, "inside a metal tube. Then tonight a FedEx driver collected the tube from me. I was glad to see it go."

I remembered seeing the FedEx messenger delivering a metal tube. "Did he take it to the *Romance of the Seas*?"

"Yes."

"Pepper, tell me something. Tiff and I were reading a book in the library, then the book disappeared. Did you take it?"

She nodded. Her flashlight beam crawled through the black air to land on the book called *History of Thirteen Oaks*. "It describes this tunnel," Pepper explained, "and how to open the secret panel. I didn't want you discovering the tunnel, Liz. You're a detective—things could've gone wrong. I heard you and Tiff from the hallway, talking about the book. I tricked you out of the library, with a fib about Jason phoning."

I nodded.

"Remember when I made lemonade?" Pepper asked. "Before I did, I raced to the library, opened the secret panel, and hid the book inside the tunnel."

"I thought maybe Jason had stolen the book, while I waited for his call at the office." I paused, thinking. "I remember at FolkFest you asked if I had any suspects."

"I was so glad you hadn't figured it out."

Our voices echoed in the shadowy darkness. I put a finger to my lips, warning Pepper against speaking; I was worried that Jason might hear. My heart thumped noisily and blood rushed inside my ears, but I refused to stop—I was determined to find William.

The tunnel was scary. Enclosed by wet and dripping stone, we stumbled over loose rocks, hearing the noise magnified a thousand times. I kept thinking we'd step on a rat, and I was so thankful when our underground journey finally ended.

I could smell the ocean as we exited the tunnel, stepping onto a grassy slope. "I disguised the tunnel mouth," Pepper told me proudly.

"You did a good job," I commented. "No one would ever figure there's a tunnel here."

In the moonlight I saw the boathouse below; it was overgrown with weeds, and part of the roof had collapsed. "What's in that shack?" I asked Pepper. "The one beside the boathouse."

"Junk. Abandoned outboard motors and oars, that kind of stuff."

"Switch off the flashlight," I cautioned, "in case Jason's around."

Cautiously we descended the slope toward the boathouse. Nothing moved except the waves, thumping against the island's rocky shoreline. A bird cried a warning over the ocean, then the night fell silent.

At the boathouse we peered through a filthy window. The big double doors were open to the sea: the *Outlaw* wasn't there. "I've watched Jason's boat from my room," Pepper said. "He usually goes out around this time, for about an hour. He painted out the name, but I know it's the *Outlaw*. I figure Jason gets bored and goes for a ride."

At the shack we found the lock wedged shut with a chunk of wood. Carefully I worked it loose, then reached for the handle. As the door squealed open on rusty hinges, moonlight flowed into the shack.

William lay on the floor, his arms and legs bound with rope.

I rushed to him, very worried. His eyes were open, but he seemed weak and confused; I cradled him gently in my arms, as Pepper released the ropes.

William tried to stand—he seemed very shaky. "Liz," he whispered, "it's so good to see you. But how did you find me?"

"It's not important right now," I replied. "Let's get you out of here."

"Wait. I've got a confession to make. I'm so ashamed."

"What do you mean?"

"Remember I asked you to meet me at the museum? When I had something to tell you?"

"Of course I remember. I behaved so badly."

"Well," William said, his voice only a whisper. "I . . . I'm a forger. I copied the *Klee Wyck*."

* * *

I was shocked. Since Pepper had broken the news, I'd never considered who the forger might be. I guess I was too intent on finding William. "You were partners with Jason?" I asked, dreading the answer. Had I been so wrong about William?

"Nothing like that," he replied, shaking his head. He was slowly coming around. "I was paid for doing a job. Jason offered good money for an Emily Carr forgery, no questions asked. When I copied the original *Klee Wyck,* I had no idea who owned it. I only learned the truth after Jason kidnapped me."

"At the Dallas Road seawall, someone in a low-rider truck gave you money. Was that Jason?"

William nodded.

"How'd you get hooked up with him?"

"He'd been hired by some local who wanted to steal an Emily Carr and get it forged by me. Jason offered a lot of cash. I figured, why not? I desperately needed the money."

I turned to Pepper. "Did you know any of this?"

"No, and I can't believe it," she responded. "I had no idea William made the forgery."

"But the fake note at Butchart Gardens was signed with a W, as in William." I looked closely at Pepper. "Did you write the note?"

She shook her head. "My boss did. My job was to get the note delivered to you at Butchart Gardens. But I might have mentioned William to my boss. I honestly can't remember."

I was getting worried that Jason might show up, but I needed more answers.

I turned back to William. "Jason paid up?"

He nodded. "After the original was stolen, I received my first payment. Jason later delivered the *Klee Wyck* to my studio so I could produce the forgery. When he collected the finished product, I got the remaining money."

"Why'd you need it, William? To finance getting your mom to Arizona?"

William nodded. "But she turned me down. When I told Mom about the forgery, she called it dirty money. So I phoned Jason. I said I planned to go to the police. He laughed and said I was a criminal myself, a forger. I hesitated about the police, for just a moment too long. Jason grabbed me."

"Jason phoned when Tiff and I visited your studio?"

William nodded.

"What were those—" I stopped myself. "No, forget it. I don't want to even think about it."

"You know," William said, "it was so horrible when Jason said he'd attacked you in the cemetery. He—"

"Jason?" I exclaimed. "He's the guy who attacked me?"

William nodded. "I'm just so glad you didn't get hurt. Jason told me later about the attack—he was trying to scare you off, stop your investigation."

"Did you know where Jason hid out? Did you know Pepper was involved?"

"No to both," William replied. "I didn't even know why the forgery." Lifting his head, William looked shyly at me. "Liz, will you forgive me?"

There was no question. William wasn't a criminal, out for personal gain. He'd exercised bad judgement, but anyone might. "Of course I understand, William. Besides, you should forgive me! I was such a shrew. I was jealous because I saw you hugging someone."

"At the Inner Harbour? Before I met you at the museum?"

I nodded.

"That was my sister, Lucille. We'd had a visit, and she was going to work. Lucille was late, or I'd have introduced you."

"I'm sorry," I said glumly. "What a jerk I was."

I turned to Pepper. "Let's get William back to the house, then call for an ambulance and the police."

We left the shack, and William moved slowly up the slope. When we reached the tunnel, I looked at Pepper. "Help William to the mansion, okay? I'll join you there."

"But—" William protested.

"No arguments," I said, gently kissing him. "I'll be okay."

The moment they disappeared into the tunnel, I hurried to the boathouse. After the *Outlaw* returned, I planned to sabotage the engine so Jason couldn't escape from the island.

Inside the boathouse I smelled engine fuel. A sleeping bag lay on the small wharf; nearby was a jumbled heap of clothes and junk food wrappers. Empty cans of pop and beer were scattered around.

Raising my head, I listened to the night. Was that an engine I heard? I looked out the open doors of the boathouse, wondering if Jason was returning. Moonlight lay across the waters, where nothing moved but sea birds on the wing.

Then I saw the lights of a boat, heading my way.

I slipped into hiding behind a big oil drum; the wharf was slippery, the wood stained by oil from the drum. Safely concealed, I watched the boat approach. Jason was at the controls at the open stern, guiding the boat's passage toward the boathouse.

Jason secured the *Outlaw* and hurried from the boathouse. He carried food, perhaps for William. My time was short. Scuttling out of hiding, I climbed down a wooden ladder to the deck of the *Outlaw*. For a moment I watched the door, fearing Jason's return, and then I hurried inside the deckhouse. Looking around, I saw a table, a small galley with basic cooking supplies, and steps leading down to the engine. Fortunately it wasn't covered, making my task that much easier.

As I reached for the engine's distributor cap, though, my luck ran out. I felt a gun in my back and heard Jason's chuckle. "Turn around slowly, you little fool."

* * *

Jason's nose seemed once to have been broken, and his tiny eyes glittered. He licked his lips. "Yum, yum. You're cute up close."

"You're not," I declared defiantly. "William has escaped, and you're finished. The cops are on their way."

"Then, let's be gone. Go out on deck. William was my hostage, but you'll do as a replacement."

I did as ordered. Keeping his nickel-plated revolver pointed at me, Jason released the mooring lines and started the boat's engine. I looked for a way to escape, but it was hopeless; I figured Jason wouldn't hesitate to use the gun on me. Now I wished I'd returned to the house with Pepper and William instead of playing the hero—but it was too late for regrets.

"I know all about the forgery," I said, hoping to rattle Jason. "I even know where the original is."

"So do I—it's on board the *Romance of the Seas*.

My boss plans to take it to some crooked collector in Alaska. The collector's ready to pay top dollar for Emily Carr's unknown masterpiece."

The *Outlaw* rumbled out of the boathouse, turned into the wind, and picked up speed. Above the shoreline I saw the Thirteen Oaks mansion; I prayed that William and Pepper had reached safety.

"My boss made me hang around," Jason said, "waiting for my payoff. Then I figured, why not get all the money, not just my payment but every single penny. That painting's got to be worth at least a million bucks."

"You're not only dangerous," I said. "You're greedy, too."

Jason laughed. He stood at the outdoor wheel; I sat on a wooden bench, huddled in my jacket against the cold wind. "The *Romance of the Seas* left port at midnight," Jason said. "We're going to board it and grab that painting. I'll take it to Alaska and get the money myself."

"Are you some kind of hired gun?"

"That's right," Jason replied proudly.

He cranked up the RPMs, and the shoreline rapidly grew smaller. I could no longer see the mansion at Thirteen Oaks. Shivering, I hugged myself tightly.

"I was hired," Jason said, "to get the *Klee Wyck* forged. Your friend William did a great job, then he developed cold feet. He wanted to return the money. I got to thinking, what if he went to the cops?"

Jason looked at me. "I saw you once with William. You took a bus home to the Uplands, and I followed in my truck. Then I kept an eye on Thirteen Oaks, waiting my chance. I figured I'd hurt you, as a warning to William."

"I notice you're limping," I commented.

"Yeah, thanks to you," Jason muttered. "I decided to kidnap William, in case I needed a hostage. I followed him into the First Peoples Gallery at the museum, and said a bomb was strapped around my waist. I threatened to blow up the place unless he left with me." Jason's laugh was unpleasant. "William figured I was crazy enough to be a suicide bomber, so he obeyed. We stepped through the emergency exit, escaped from the museum, and went straight to the *Outlaw* at the Inner Harbour. William came along quiet and peaceful, because he was afraid people would get hurt."

Jason sighed. "It was boring at Hidden Island, so I went to the Splash for something to do. That's when you spotted me, but I got a warning from my boss and escaped in time."

"Just exactly who is this boss of yours?"

"Fat chance I'd tell you that."

"I bet your boss called you at the marina, when Tiff and I were searching for the *Outlaw*."

Jason nodded. "I thought the marina was a secure hiding place, until you came along. So I moved the *Outlaw* into hiding on Hidden Island and painted out the name. I probably should have done that earlier, right after I firebombed the *Amor de Cosmos*."

"How'd you know there was an abandoned boat-house on the island?" I asked.

"Pepper told me."

"And where'd you keep your truck?"

"On different side streets in Oak Bay."

"You never got your money, eh? What a shame."

Jason ignored my sarcasm. "My boss kept saying, *Wait, wait, wait*. Well, I'm sick of waiting." He looked across the water. I could see the pilot boat approaching the beautifully illuminated *Romance of the Seas*.

"Tonight," Jason said, "we're boarding that ship. I'll waste my boss and take control of the painting. I'll be the one who sells it for big money."

Jason looked at me. There was evil in his eyes. "And when I don't need a hostage anymore, you'll die, too."

13

At low throttle, the *Outlaw* wallowed in the ocean swells. We watched the pilot boat slide alongside the cruise ship, then the pilot jumped onto the cruise ship through the open door in its side. Immediately the boat turned away and began its journey home to port.

Jason cranked up the throttle; with a throaty roar, our boat closed quickly on the cruise ship. "When we reach that door," Jason yelled, "you jump in first. I'll be right behind. If you try to escape, I'll start killing people."

The *Romance of the Seas* loomed over us, so huge. I could hear its engines, and the slap of waves against the luxury vessel's massive steel hull. As the big door came closer, I got ready to jump. I was so tense I could hardly breathe.

"Don't betray me," Jason warned, "or everyone dies."

Suddenly we were beside the open door, and I leapt across. Landing safely, I turned to see Jason jump. The empty *Outlaw* began drifting away and was quickly lost in the night.

Nearby were some crewmen, their backs to us. They were shouting advice and encouragement at a television screen, where two teams chased a soccer ball across a green field. Jason gestured at a nearby corridor. "Let's get moving, before they see us."

We hurried through the sleeping ship; Jason's gun was hidden inside his black jacket. I could hear the muffled vibration of the engines—a constant thrumming somewhere far below. "You saw Paris here earlier?" Jason abruptly asked.

I nodded.

"Where?"

"On the Royal Deck, in the Suite of Dreams."

"You think he's on board now?"

"Maybe," I replied. "He was talking that way."

"Take me to the suite."

Quite a few people wandered the ship at this late hour. In the Grand Atrium four seniors were enjoying a game of cards, while a couple waltzed dreamily on a corner dance floor. No one paid the slightest attention as I boarded a glass-enclosed elevator with Jason and pushed the button for the Royal Deck.

"Why do you want Paris?" I demanded. "Is he your boss?"

"Shut up."

After a quick journey to the heights of the vessel,

the elevator doors hissed open. I saw the deep purple carpeting, the wide corridor, and the creamy doors of the suites with elaborate names. One door stood slightly open, and I looked inside. Room service was delivering a late-night snack. It was going to the suite where I'd seen the metal tube being delivered.

The waiter walked quickly to the elevator. Watching him go, I said nothing and didn't cry for help. I was afraid I'd get the waiter shot, because Jason had sneaked his gun out of hiding.

We continued walking along the corridor in the direction of the Suite of Dreams. As we did, I struggled to deal with a new shock—I had recognized the person who received the room service delivery.

* * *

From behind, I heard a sound. I turned to look, so did Jason—gripped in his hand was the shiny revolver. Something was tossed from a suite onto the carpet, and landed with a soft *thump*. I saw the Laughing One, her village and its totems.

"Hey," Jason said. "That's the painting!"

Hurrying forward, he picked it up. "Yes, this is *Klee Wyck*. But how . . ."

At that moment, someone stepped swiftly from the suite. Someone in a floppy hat and sunglasses, someone in an expensive blouse and designer jeans. The metal tube was raised high.

It came down hard across Jason's hand.

With a cry of pain, he dropped the revolver. I leapt for it, but the other person was quicker than me. Seizing the gun from the floor, she levelled the scary weapon at Jason, who was rubbing away the pain in his hand.

"Don't move," the woman warned. Turning to me, she gestured at the painting. "Roll it up, Liz. Put it inside the tube."

As I rolled up the painting, tears were streaming down my face. I felt so betrayed, because I had been tricked by someone I trusted.

The woman removed the sunglasses, and I saw her large, dark eyes. Then she tossed away the hat. Auburn hair tumbled down her back. I was looking at Laura Singlehurst.

* * *

"Pick up the mailing tube," Laura ordered me.

"Laura, how could you? I respected you, and—"

"*No talking.*"

Laura turned quickly to Jason. He stood beside the wall, still rubbing his hand. "Jason," she demanded, "what are you, crazy?"

"I do all your dirty work, boss, then you skip town with the painting."

"You'd have got your money, once I sold *Klee Wyck*."

"I doubt it," Jason scoffed. He stared daggers at Laura. "I was hoping I'd find you through Paris, but this was better. Why'd you come out of hiding?"

"Liz saw me. I figured she'd tell you, and I'd be trapped. I saw your gun and decided to get it. That's why I threw the painting into the corridor—to distract you."

"Are Paris and the Major on board now?" I asked.

"No. I saw them leave the ship before it departed from Victoria."

Jason took a step toward Laura, but her finger tightened on the trigger. He paused, looking apprehensive. "Take it easy, Laura. That thing is dangerous."

Laura pointed at the outside door. "We're going on deck. You two go first, I'll follow behind. If I need to, I'll use this gun."

"Laura," I said, "don't be foolish. Give yourself up, please."

"I already qualify for hard time in prison, Liz. That's not for me—I'll find a way to escape. Now pick up that tube, and let's get moving."

Outside on deck, the night was beautiful. Millions of stars were radiant over the sea, where I saw the lights of other vessels. From far below I heard waves rushing away from the hull.

"We're going to the bridge," Laura said. "Get moving."

I tried to think of a plan. Could I somehow use the metal tube against Laura? How would Jason react? Would Laura start shooting?

"Laura," I said, stalling for time, "why did you do it?"

"I needed money to start a new life. A new identity, a new country. No more maxed-out credit cards, no more unpleasant guys pounding on my door demanding I repay their loans. I was frightened, Liz, I was desperate. Stealing *Klee Wyck* was a great idea."

"You didn't earn plenty as a lawyer?"

"There's never enough money."

"When I first met you, Laura, you said someone had

called your cell phone, and a ransom was being demanded. I should have wondered how the criminal knew your cell number—I guess it was Jason who called."

"That's right."

"You set me up to recover the forged painting at Butchart Gardens?"

"Yes," Laura replied.

"Come to think of it, you almost gave yourself away. The note at Butchart Gardens was written in emerald ink. When I first met you, I noticed the ink in your pen was the colour of your green car." I shook my head, disappointed with myself. "I bet Fossilized Pete told you about taking Tiff and me to West Bay Marina. You must have called Jason and warned him to escape."

"That's right."

I looked closely at her. "Did you know Jason attacked me in the cemetery?"

Laura was shocked. "I had no idea." She turned to him. "You fool!"

Jason laughed angrily. "You're the fool, Laura. If you'd paid me, I'd be home in Seattle right now and you'd be sailing happily to Alaska with the Emily Carr masterpiece. Instead we're in bad shape."

"I agree *you're* in bad shape," Laura retorted. "But I'll get out of this—just watch me. I'm very resourceful."

"Laura," I said, "why'd you keep the original *Klee Wyck* in hiding at Thirteen Oaks, instead of somewhere else?"

"If the forgery was ever detected and a search started for the original, Thirteen Oaks was the perfect hiding place. Who'd ever look there?"

"You had the original—why didn't you skip town immediately?"

"The collector in Alaska made that a condition. He wanted the *Klee Wyck* replaced with a forgery, so there'd be no uproar about the theft. He told me to stay in Victoria, to see if anyone noticed the forgery. I decided to wait until after the wedding, then leave town."

"You're planning to start a new life in Alaska?"

Laura shook her head. "No, I'm heading for Hawaii. I love those glorious flowers down there. I'll get my money from that collector, then fly south pronto."

Central command for the *Romance of the Seas* was the bridge, the place where the officers and pilot safely guided the massive ship. A sign warned *No Passengers Allowed*, but it didn't stop us. The door was unlocked; Laura opened it and we entered the bridge, to the surprise of the people inside. An officer in a white uniform turned to us, saying, "What the . . ." Someone else shouted, "She's got a gun."

Stepping swiftly behind me, Laura pinned my neck with her arm. With her other hand, she pointed the revolver at my head. "No false moves," she warned, "or this girl dies."

The officer looked at Laura. "What do you want?" she asked in a calm voice.

"Contact the Coast Guard and order a medical evacuation. Tell them to send a helicopter immediately."

The officer picked up a radio microphone. "*Romance of the Seas* calling Canadian Forces, 19-Wing Comox. Come in, please. We are requesting evacuation of a heart attack victim."

"No fake messages," Laura warned her. "Don't get smart."

"Stay calm," the officer replied. "Think about surrendering that gun to me. It's the smart thing to do."

"Forget it," Laura snapped. "I'm not going to prison."

Laura released my neck, but held me close with a firm grip. She looked at the officer. "This ship has a prison cell?"

"A brig? Yes."

Laura pointed at Jason with the revolver. "Put this kid under arrest. Police in Victoria want him for numerous crimes."

"Including abduction," I said, "and sinking the *Amor de Cosmos*."

The officer gave an order, and Jason was quickly hustled away. He gave me a dirty look, but went silently. I breathed a sigh of relief, even though the situation remained volatile.

I looked at the pilot, who hadn't spoken since we entered the bridge. "Why did the pilot boat take you to the cruise ship?" I asked. "You could have walked on board."

"My wife is in hospital, so I was delayed. The ship sailed without me, knowing I could board from the pilot boat."

"Is your wife okay?"

"You bet," he replied. "We have a little girl, Mary." He smiled briefly.

Long minutes passed while we awaited the helicopter. Various screens and radars glowed inside the dimly lit bridge; through the big windows I saw the first traces of dawn's light, bringing the promise of a beautiful day. As pale colours slowly came to the eastern skies, the jagged outline of a mountain range appeared.

"Here they come," said the officer. Through binoculars, she studied the approaching helicopter, which was large. "They'll drop a stretcher down for the victim, then winch it back up."

"I'll be in the stretcher," Laura said, "with the gun and the *Klee Wyck*. When I reach the helicopter I'll take control. They can fly me to land, and I'll escape with the painting."

"Give up," I pleaded. "You'll never reach safety, Laura. Someone could get hurt on that helicopter—maybe you."

"No more chatter, Liz. Bring the metal tube with you, and keep quiet."

Laura looked around at the others. "All of you, listen up. I'm going outside with this girl and the officer. If you radio a warning to the helicopter, they will both die. Then I'll shoot myself—I'd rather be dead than in prison."

Outside, Laura turned to the officer. "Where will the stretcher be lowered?"

"Aft, at the tennis courts."

Hovering over the *Romance of the Seas*, the rescue helicopter made an enormous racket, its rotors pounding against the air. A door opened in the belly, then someone waved to the officer. A stretcher appeared and dropped swiftly down.

"It's not too late," the officer told Laura. "Give yourself up."

"Laura," I suddenly exclaimed. "The tube is empty—the painting is gone."

She turned to me, confused. "What?"

I held out the tube. "Look inside—the *Klee Wyck* is missing!"

As Laura leaned toward the mailing tube, I snapped it sideways, catching Laura's wrist a solid blow. The revolver flew up high; leaping forward, the officer grabbed the gun in midair. Quickly she turned and faced Laura with the revolver.

"It's all over now," she said quietly. "You're under arrest."

Laura burst into tears.

14

One year later, I attended Tiffany's wedding to Hart deMornay. She had requested a spiritual service, so Hart arranged for a ceremony at Victoria's Christ Church Cathedral, one of the largest churches in the nation.

Paris did not attend the ceremony. An audit of the deMornay trust had revealed crooked dealings by Paris, who had secretly drained a lot of money from the trust to finance his shameful ways. Paris left Victoria in disgrace, and now lived in Britain on a small remittance provided by his brother and sister.

Hart had quickly declared his devotion to Tiffany. She shared his feelings, but was determined to be certain of their love. Consequently they had spent much of the year hanging out and getting to know each other, making sure they would be equals in their relationship. They did all kinds of neat things—windsurfing, hiking the West Coast Trail, and even exploring the crystal-clear ocean depths at Powell River in matching scuba outfits.

As for me, I'd stayed in close touch with William. We'd exchanged e-mails and letters, and talked on the phone. At Christmas, William flew to Winnipeg for a wonderful reunion. When I arrived for Tiff and Hart's wedding, I was thrilled to see him waiting at the Victoria airport with pink roses for me.

Tiff's mother had come from Grand Cayman Island for the ceremony and was seated inside the cathedral in a place of honour close to the Major. The vaulted ceiling rose overhead, and the stained-glass windows glowed with the glory of love. The blues were so blue, the greens so green, the reds so pure and rich.

Now, at 18, I was the maid of honour. Kate Partridge had graciously allowed me the privilege. She was now Tiff's principal attendant, and stood with the other attendants to the left of the bride. To the right of the groom were the best man and the ushers. One was William, looking so handsome in a beautifully tailored tuxedo.

William caught me staring, and we exchanged a smile. Then I returned my focus to the service, which was moving and splendid. When Tiffany and Hart exchanged their first married kiss, everyone cheered and the bishop grinned. We all knew this marriage was made in heaven.

Flower girls scattered rose petals down the aisle for the newlyweds, and the cathedral bells pealed in celebration as we gathered outside in the sunshine. As I talked to William, a ladybug landed on my arm, a lucky sign of more happiness to come. There were hugs and kisses and photo opportunities, and waves from passing tourists, then the wedding party piled into white stretch limousines and we took off through Victoria, yelling from the open windows. It was such a relief that the wedding had gone perfectly!

The reception was held at the Crystal Garden, just behind the Empress Hotel. Long ago this had been a famous swimming pool; now it contained tropical vegetation and was home to flamingoes, lemurs, and even the Golden Lion Tamarin monkey (looking at its bright eyes, I was reminded of Emily Carr's Woo).

At the south end of the Crystal Garden was a hardwood dance floor and many large tables; here everyone gathered for delicious food followed by dancing. The Major had brought in two bands for the occasion. One was Victoria's own Big Band Trio, which played great rock, and the other treat was Gator Beat, with authentic Cajun music from deep in the American southlands. Everyone was into it, from kids to grandparents, dancing and singing. What a celebration.

I danced mostly with William. He'd given evidence against Jason, who was in prison. So, sadly, was Laura. William had been sentenced to community service for his misdeeds, and was conducting art classes for seniors.

"They're wonderful students," William said, as we danced together. He was so handsome. "Now I'm hoping to combine my art with teaching."

"William, there's something I've been wanting to ask. For a year, actually."

His eyebrows rose. "What's that?"

"Remember at your studio, you swept some photos into a desk drawer and locked it?"

"Sure."

"Well, I've been wondering . . . Well . . ."

"Go ahead, Liz. You can ask me."

"Were they pictures of some girl?"

William roared with laughter. "Not a chance. I took those Polaroids for reference, as I worked on the forgery of *Klee Wyck*."

"That's all they were?" I said, greatly relieved.

"You're the only girl for me, Liz."

What good news! Now I felt quite chatty. "It's so nice your mom's health is better," I commented brightly. William had sold a painting for a large amount of money and used it to finance getting his mother to Arizona.

"Yes," William said. "Things are going well for my mom."

Things were also good for Tiffany's dad, who was with Marjorie. She'd introduced him to high society in Austin, Texas, where they now lived. "I'm very happy," the Major told me later, as we waltzed together. "You know, I almost sacrificed Tiffany to my romantic imagination. I honestly thought she'd be happy married to Paris. All that stuff about gambling really shocked me. Liz, what a fool I was."

"Tiffany's certainly happy now," I tactfully replied.

"I just hope Paris learned something, and is happy in Britain." A whimsical smile crossed the Major's face. "I remember Paris as a boy—he was such a nice kid."

"I guess people can change," I said. "Tiff was smart enough to recognize that."

"You're a good friend to Tiffany, Liz. I apologize for my sarcasm about your hyperactive imagination. That was rude of me."

"No problem," I said lightly. "I've been called worse."

"What about you, Liz? Any wedding bells in the future? Can I hope to attend another wedding soon?"

"William and I are taking it easy on that one, Major Wright." Then my face split into a big smile. "But so far, so good!"

"Wonderful," the Major exclaimed. "You deserve nothing but the best."

Next I danced with the happy groom. "Guess what," Hart said. "Tiff and I have given the estate a new name—Two Oaks." He smiled. "When our first baby arrives, the estate will become Three Oaks."

"I like it. The old name never appealed to me, perhaps because of my slightly superstitious nature."

"We've recovered the portrait of my mother, and it's back on display at the mansion. Pepper decided to live on Hidden Island with Amanda so we built them a nice cottage. Tiff and I have also invested some money in Pepper's dream to have her own recording studio."

"That's wonderful," I said.

After the dance, we joined Tiffany. She was so happy. I hugged her, then Hart. "Why aren't you Lord deMornay? You're the right type—kinda regal, you know?"

"The title belongs to Paris as the oldest child, but I don't care." Hart brushed Tiff's forehead with a kiss. "What matters is that I found my Lady, and we'll always be together."

I wished Tiff and Hart great happiness (later, she threw me her bouquet of trumpet-shaped calla lilies) and then I joined Pepper at a mouth-watering display of desserts.

"I was so worried," she told me, "about facing criminal charges for helping Jason steal the painting. But instead I got community service. I've been helping street people."

Pepper's eyes travelled to a table where her little girl sat with Caleb, the best man. Amanda was laughing happily as Caleb performed a trick of magic. "Amanda's the light of my life," she said, smiling fondly at her daughter.

"How's the music business?"

"I've signed my first artist. We saw her at Beacon Hill Park, giving a concert for the trees."

"I remember. Her songs were so good."

"Liz, thanks for all the e-mails. You've been a pal."

We joined William at a table. He was talking to his teacher—the noted Victoria artist Robert Amos, who was a great friend of Hart deMornay. Robert, of course, hadn't known about William's actions, but had some interesting insights about the technical aspects of his forgery.

"Emily Carr painted on both canvas and paper," Robert explained. "William used acrylic paint, which dries immediately and is very flexible if a canvas is rolled up—but William was smart enough to make it look like oil. With scientific instruments, the forgery could have been detected, but to the people at Thirteen Oaks it looked exactly like the original."

"Two Oaks," I corrected him, laughing. "And hopefully by next summer it'll be Three Oaks."

One last surprise remained, the perfect ending to a perfect wedding. Glancing at his watch, William jumped up from the table. "Liz, we must hurry."

Together we rushed outside—the night was warm. People wandered along Douglas Street; some were window-shopping, while others gazed at a beautiful horse and carriage waiting outside the Crystal Garden. The driver wore a top hat and tuxedo.

"Please step inside our carriage," William said, smiling at me. "We're leaving for a mystery destination."

"Really? Wow."

What a luxury it was, riding through downtown Victoria in that splendid carriage. In my beautiful dress I felt like a character in a fairy tale, especially when we passed the Inner Harbour and I looked up at the towers of the Empress Hotel. Enjoying the slow *clip clop* of our horse's hooves, I sighed at the sight of the exquisite lights outlining the Legislative Buildings.

Passing Carr House, with its gingerbread decorations, I thought of Emily Carr as a young girl and wondered if she could have anticipated the many twists and turns of a life that would bring such fame. Her genius and determination had inspired William to become an artist, and I felt certain that great success also awaited him.

"Happy?" William asked.

"Mmm," I whispered, cuddling close. "We're living a dream."

Along Dallas Road we followed the cliffs, watching lights on the distant shoreline. In the sky was a quarter moon—such a romantic sight. The minutes passed quickly, and finally we arrived at Ross Bay Cemetery, where our carriage stopped.

As we stepped from the carriage, I looked at the cemetery, feeling confused but trusting William. Above us, the silhouettes of trees moved gently in a light wind. Holding hands, we walked into the cemetery and soon reached our destination.

"We're at Emily Carr's grave," I said.

William nodded. "This is a special place, Liz. That's why I wanted to visit here tonight. I'm praying that Emily Carr will bless us both."

I hugged William and kissed him. "William," I whispered, "I think she already has."

Websites to Visit

Tourism Victoria:	tourismvictoria.com
Maritime Museum:	mmbc.bc.ca
Art Gallery of Greater Victoria:	aggv.bc.ca
Craigdarroch Castle:	craigdarrochcastle.com
Butchart Gardens:	butchartgardens.com
Carr House:	emilycarr.com
Victoria A.M.:	victoriaam.com
Royal B.C. Museum:	rbcm1.rbcm.gov.bc.ca
Crystal Gardens:	bcpcc.com/crystal
Hospice Society:	victoriahospice.com
TerrifVic Jazz Party:	terrifvic.com
Robert Amos:	robertamos.com
Eric Wilson:	ericwilson.com

About the Author

Flo and Eric Wilson in Victoria

For many summers, Flo and Eric have enjoyed welcoming cruise ship passengers to Victoria, where they met and still live. Together they researched the attractions featured in *The Emily Carr Mystery*.

Eric's roots are deep in the city he describes in these pages. His mother was born in Victoria; along with her sisters, she grew up there in the days of Emily Carr.

If you visit *www.ericwilson.com* you can read the exciting opening chapters of all the Eric Wilson mysteries.

THE ICE DIAMOND QUEST

A Tom and Liz Austen Mystery

ERIC WILSON

The yacht, driven by its power, was closing in fast. Ahead, the sea roared against a low reef, throwing white water into the dark night.

Why is a mysterious yacht flashing a signal off the coast of Newfoundland on a cold November evening? Tom and Liz Austen, with their cousins, Sarah and Duncan Joy, follow a difficult trail toward the truth. As they search, someone called the Hawk and people known as the Renegades cause major problems, but the cousins press on. In the darkness of an abandoned mine and later on stormy seas, they face together the greatest dangers ever.

"I read *The Ice Diamond Quest* and now I'm hooked on books."

—Tamara K., Lachine, Québec

ESCAPE FROM BIG MUDDY

A Liz Austen Mystery

ERIC WILSON

The air was blasted by thundering engines as the gang raced past us, escaping the scene.

I turned to my aunt: "Holy Hannah! I can't believe what just happened!"

Former Death Machine biker Billy Bones grabs Liz Austen's arm and whispers: "The password . . . is . . . NOEL. Remember it!"

Remember it? How could she forget?? That one word launchs an unforgettable road trip across Saskatchewan aboard the *Mañana Banana* and plunges Liz and her Métis friend, Marie, into a deadly world of kidnapping, international smuggling, and biker gangs with murder on their minds. The question is: will the girls elude the bikers' clutches and escape the dangers of Big Muddy?

"This book rocks!"
— *Chelsea D., Black Creek, British Columbia*

THE CASE OF THE GOLDEN BOY

A Tom Austen Mystery

ERIC WILSON

Headlights shone in the distance: a police car, moving fast. It swerved to a stop by the curb, then Officer Larson leapt out and ran swiftly inside. What was going on?

An investigation into the kidnapping of his schoolmate leads young Tom Austen to the seedy Golden Boy Café and an unexpected encounter with a desperate criminal. After getting one step too close to the kidnappers, Tom is taken prisoner and needs all his wits to survive.

The adventures of Tom and Liz Austen are followed by fans of all ages across Canada and abroad in countries like Spain and Japan. Voted 1992 Author of the Year by the Canadian Booksellers Association "for introducing children to the different regions of Canada," Eric Wilson has shown many young people the delights of reading.

"It was fantastic, wonderful, breathtaking, stupendous, amazing, and very, very hard to put down. I liked it so much I skipped breakfast to finish it off."

—*Seth R., Massey, Ontario*